D0398544

THE RECIPE FOR REVOLUTION

Also by Carolyn Chute

The Beans of Egypt, Maine

Letourneau's Used Auto Parts

Merry Men

Snow Man

The School on Heart's Content Road

Treat Us Like Dogs and We Will Become Wolves

THE RECIPE FOR REVOLUTION

A NOVEL

CAROLYN CHUTE

Grove Press
New York

Published simultaneously in Canada
Printed in the United States of America

This title was typeset in 12-pt. Granjon LT with Bernhard Modern by Alpha Design and Composition of Pittsfield, NH.

First Grove Atlantic hardcover edition: February 2020

FIRST EDITION

ISBN 978-0-8021-2951-2
eISBN 978-0-8021-2952-9

Library of Congress cataloging-in-publication-data is available for this title.

Grove Press
an imprint of Grove Atlantic
154 West 14th Street
New York, NY 10011

Distributed by Publishers Group West

groveatlantic.com

20 21 22 23 10 9 8 7 6 5 4 3 2 1

Author's Note

The Recipe for Revolution is one of several novels that make up the *School on Heart's Content Road* "four-ojilly," a series of overlapping or parallel books that focus on different characters and their place in the story's key events. Characters who play major roles in one or more of the books may be only walk-ons in others. Each book stands alone. No need to read them in a certain order.

Welcome

to

The

Recipe for

Revolution

. . . as told by many witnesses: friends, family, spies, agents, demons, critical thinkers, and other beings, testimonies verifying and conflicting, some voices very large, others somewhat tiny.

Author's Note 2

There is a character list at the very back of this book to help with identifying important and semi-important characters. *Don't twist your head trying to keep every character straight. Continually referring to the list is not necessary. As you read along, eventually characters who are meant to matter a lot will become obvious. Others are walk-ons, walk-bys, faces in the crowd. I, myself, love character lists because I like to refresh myself on how characters look and how they might be related and associated. Maybe you do, too.*

List of Icons

Home (the St. Onge Settlement)

Neighbors

Claire and Bonnie Loo and other women who run things at the Settlement, usually speaking to us from the future

Others speaking from the future

Voice of Pirate Radio interrupts

The voice of Mammon

Out in the world

The Bureau

The screen insists, scolds, grins, cajoles

The Apparatus speaks

Secret Agent Jane Meserve speaks

Voices of the Crude and Raw speak

*History as it Happens**/ History (the past) and critical thinkers

The deepest voice speaks

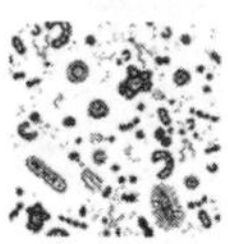

Microorganisms speak

Deep State

Bruce Hummer speaks

Dear Reader

Cyberspace

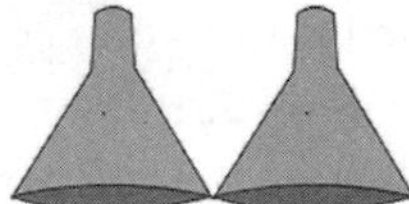

Think tanks and tin hat conspiracy theorists

**History as it Happens* are settlement-made books of "news" and illustrations.

Contents

Some say it was 1999.
Some say it was 2000.
One thing for sure,
the years, they do blur.
In those years,
big things
happened in America.
But you never
heard about some of
them. They were erased.

Here's
the
Story

BOOK ONE:
My Good Behavior

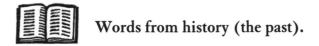

Words from history (the past).

"If I repent of anything it is very likely to be my good behavior."

Henry David Thoreau

SEPTEMBER

The voice of Mammon speaks.

For the preservation of this edifice that holds high what is fine and fair, there can be no being too hard on the threat.

The Apparatus speaks.

O masters! O lords and ladies of national and transnational finance, State Department, Pentagon, big media, and other vast grasps. You, the majestics of boardrooms, deeper rooms, private jets, mists, seashores, and "lost" memos; lords of strategic worth; gods of this universe! I am your whip, your bulwark, your sword, your Weedwhacker. Proud to serve you.

Duotron Lindsey International's CEO Bruce Hummer slitting mail open at his desk, tugs out a grayish newsprint article from Maine, sent by an acquaintance who knows of his summer property up there on the coast.

He leans back, reads. It's a full three-page, dated feature including photos. Written about wacky people. Very strange. He reads every word. And he stares at and into a face staring back into his brains from a blur of moving and monsterific merry-go-round "horses." It's the face of Gordon St. Onge.

From a future time, Claire St. Onge speaks.

This story is a noisy one, my own voice a merest chirp in the roar. But I can say without the vulgarity of pride that though many voices will wrench this story of him into a confusing and grainy spectacle, I am more than any of them your true tour guide.

Delivered.

He is alone down at the old farmplace by the tar road called Heart's Content Road, as picturesque as its name implies, especially fifteen years ago, when it was still Swett's Pond Road, picturesque with a capital P.

It is the house and 920 acres where he grew up, an only child, overly adored, and this land, never worked in those years, no tilling, no grazing, just croquet, while the fields were kept mowed by his papa and a neighbor's borrowed tractor. No barn. That burned long ago. But there are still the old shedways. There is still the ell kitchen, the porch with lathed columns that stand out white in the night from the morose hair-thin glow of the quarter moon. Inside there is still that old dry smell, a house of generations of solemn ghosts.

Yes, it is dark outside now. And inside, too, but for the anemic, yes, thin, single fluorescent old tube light over one of his desks in the officey part of the cluttered kitchen made by taking out the old pantry shed wall. Such thrifty light gives his hands and the opened Fedco catalog the same cold color. He is almost forty and uses old-man reading glasses. He doesn't flip through this catalog but stares into its depths, *Frostbite*, *Wolf River*, *Yellow Bellflower*, *Zestar*. He positions the words *Monroe Sweet* centrally within his entire being, the apple of memory, nearly unbelieved, his Tante Ida's "pink pies." Panoramic with longing this great big memory is because he was allowed by his mother Marian to visit Tante Ida and other of his father's people only ONCE.

He supposes this Aroostook apple will thrive here in Oxford County, but if he invites a couple of these trees into the Settlement orchards, to thrust the solidity of the pink-flesh apple itself into the present, to give it life again in the now, would it not transform the fruit to unremarkability? Death to the spell of memory, deeper in the grave Tante Ida! Her eyes, as black and starry as his papa Guillaume's, would finally close.

So lifting from the page to the next, his eyes behind the reading glasses readjust. Eyes pale green in a stewed cabbage way, and dark lashes. Not eyes of bird-of-prey-yellowy-pale nor wolf pale. Just a mixed ancestry pale, where there was maybe some jumping of the fence, those silent hearts and peckers that never speak in the records of town halls or in letters in a trunk . . . this dissonance of history's beds and tall-grass fucking have filled the warm ponds of his eyes with a green of forbearance. And a Tourette's-like flinch.

He spreads his hand upon the English morello cherry, a huge hand because he is a giant guy as seen by the average. Six-foot-five he is said to be. Seems he is feeling the heartbeat of the page, the heat of this tree where cherries will be hurled into Bonnie Loo's pies, Bonnie Loo the star cook of the Settlement, Bonnie Loo of the present moment, not twinkling with the magic of death and boyhood memory, Bonnie Loo who can cut you down with her orange-brown eyes and the long considering way she lets out lungs full of cigarette smoke. He sees her clearly the last time she looked at him, three hours ago. His neck muscles tighten, a certain kind of fear.

There are headlights on the wall. He leaves the catalog open flat in the weary light and pushes back the wheeled office chair, pockets the reading glasses, stretches.

Going out onto the old piazza he sees that it is a van and no one is getting out yet. Engine running. Headlights still blazing upon the ell of the house, blazing at him.

As he steps outside he buttons the top button of his shirt and trudges straight into the light, digging into the graying chin of his short dark beard.

Van door opens. "Gordie . . . hey . . . I'm sorry."

The voice sounds familiar in a way that makes his head break apart and swarm, searching for which decade it hurtles at him from. Not as far back as Tante Ida's pink pies.

The van is patchy-looking and has a sorry-sounding skip to the engine. The guy still has a ponytail, though he's looking a bit thin on top. Long skinny jaw. Professional-class teeth. No beard. A laugh like hiccups, like Goofy, the big cartoon dog.

Jack Holmes. Gordon embraces him. Jack laughs. "We got lost and rode all over hell or I'd have been here earlier. Then for a second, I thought no one was here. I thought maybe you sold this place and moved up back with the others. With your . . . uh . . . harem." He laughs.

Jack Holmes, yes. One of those guys who started out in law school, headed for "success," then descended into social work and educational newsletter stuff, sporadically funded statehouse lobbying for ridiculous things like support for prisoners' rights, which don't exist, and the rights of all races of ex-cons, minimum wagers of all races, welfare recipients of all races, animals, trees, clean water, and breathable air. So Jack Holmes pitched "success" overboard. And yes, the descent has continued, Gordon suspects, eyeing the mottled van.

Gordon stands now with his hands in his pockets, smiling funnyish. "Well, it's good to see you. You're looking good for an old warrior on the losing side. Howzit goin'? I mean *personally*."

"Gordie, I don't have a personal life," Jack says with his little hiccupy laugh. Then he grinds his fists into his sides. "*Cold*. Feels like a frost. Shit, you'd think this was the Alps. The difference in the weather here is mighty noticeable."

"Come in then."

The guy turns back to the van, kind of hops over to the door, which is still hanging open, wiggles a finger for Gordon to come. Then stops, turns with his back to the van, and says, "We need to talk. I want you to meet these people. You can't get the picture unless you . . . see the picture, okay? These are neighbors of mine. You remember Aaron Rosenthal?"

"Yep."

"Well, I heard somethin' . . . from the grapevine . . . that you . . . well, tell me if it's not true . . . but I heard you took in a kid . . . an orphan of the drug war. The newsworthy dangerous-as-the-day-is-long Lisa Meserve, her little girl?"

Gordon stares into his eyes, says nothing, but wiggles both eyebrows.

"Okay, I thought so. Well, Aaron, he—it's bad news. You probably heard he went to federal prison."

Gordon lowers his eyes.

"In fact, Aaron doesn't exist anymore. He, ah, killed himself in prison . . . down in Georgia. He uh . . . beat himself to death." He laughs his burbly laugh.

Gordon looks back into Jack's face. He says without expression, "Pretty funny." Then the Tourette's flinch.

"Real funny. And neat. I mean, it would take a certain gift, wouldn't you say?"

Gordon nods.

Jack hugs himself now, gets a shiver. "Jesus, it feels like snow." He looks up. "Well, anyway, Aaron had that place over in Norridgewock . . . nice chunk of land . . . it was actually his great-aunt's . . . she left it to him . . . but just this little bungalow . . . I mean a big dog couldn't turn around in it, but, man, there was land. Seventy acres. Pretty spot. You know, something somebody would want to grab from a person too poor to finance a team of lawyers. Well, Aaron's wife dies, Michele. You didn't know her. She was after *the days*. She died of breast cancer, age of thirtysomething. And guess what. There's two kids . . ."

Gordon's eyes leave Jack's face and slide over to the van. Then back to Jack's eyes.

". . . then he marries Sarah,* who adopts his kids legal smeagle. You know Aaron, attuned to details. He might have had too many interests but you can't deny his clearheaded perfectionism. I mean, he was a complex man. And life goes on. Sarah started a little kennel. Raised Dobies. And, well, you know Aaron had a . . . green thumb . . . just enjoyed organic farming and . . . and . . . marijuana retailing. You know Aaron . . . wouldn't hurt a soul . . . no stealing, no drunk driving, a million friends, a million customers . . . and one enemy . . . that's all it takes is one enemy . . . a spy or somebody mad at you and their finger dialing the drug war hotline . . . *one call*. In this case, it was a spy." He lowers his voice. Jerks his thumb toward the darkness beyond the open van door. "These guys have seen action, Gordie." Shakes his head. No laugh this time. "They broke *her* arm. Blinded and loosened one eye." Points at the van. "Had the kids in foster

* Don't forget the character list at the back of the book.

homes . . . two different ones, for two years." Jack jerks his thumb toward the van again.

"And the narcs grabbed their house and land," says Gordon, folding his arms across his chest.

Jack snorts. "You psychic?" He snorts again. "Yeah, the usual. A great tradition. Like the cavalry and the surveyors behind them riding in to save the day . . . from those goddamn hostiles . . . yep, very American tradition. Oily as clockworks." He opens his palm on the van roof. "Come look here and see what's been made homeless, roaming from one relative's place to another. No one wants them. Though of course the DHS would steal the kids again if she hadn't lost their hounds in the dust. It's one of the DHS rules . . . you can't move a lot."

Gordon steps closer, looks inside. A woman about forty with straight white-blond hair and dark roots, haggard face, her gray eyes on him. Neither eye looks very "loose" but she has an expression like a dog that wants to rip out his throat, like a dog that's been poked and poked and kicked and kicked and kicked again. Her face is the color of ice. Her shoulders are small. She's bunched up in a big sweater but she still looks cold, even with the heater blasting away and the engine running.

Two preteen or early teen kids. Painfully beautiful faces. Thick blond brushy haircuts, deep Jewish eyes, both sitting up perfectly straight like two bright mushrooms that have appeared under a dark damp porch. He remembers Aaron so well now, ever alert. Aaron, always joking. The kind of jokes that *tried* to be funny but his sense of irony was usually poorly timed. But you laughed because Aaron was sometimes a little too sad. You wanted to stand between him and that blue-tinged zone. Maybe he *did* beat himself to death.

"Hey," Gordon says to the woman.

She stares at him, looks him over. Her mouth opens as if to snarl. She's missing a tooth. She says, "Hey."

Jack whispers, "You want them, don't you?"

Gordon looks again into the fierce weary eyes of the woman and then backs out of the van doorway, then nudges a finger along down one side of his mustache. "For how long?"

"Forever, I guess."

Benedicta is delivered. Two nights later, a lilac-color dusk and the songbugs creaking thunderously in the tall grasses and mountainy miles of foliage.

Gordon steps off the porch of the old gray farmplace with intentions of heading up to the Settlement along the woodsy path, a shortcut with a little bridge and large, sort of fantasy trees leaning in. Tonight is his night with Misty in her cottage with her cats who all despise him, his body usually occupying the best of Misty's sunporch chairs as he and she gab about their day. And then he of course always takes up most of the bed. For the cats he doesn't even make an effort. No invitations to his lap. No stroking them to set off purrs. Also he groans in his sleep and sleepwalks corpselike, which causes all the tails to flick in disdain.

Now, just as he takes a deep breath of the evening, he sees someone standing by the monster ash tree in the sandy lot next to the road, a small elderly person with a two-fisted grip on a leatherlike pocketbook bigger than a bread box. He veers in her direction. There is no parked car and he only vaguely recalls a vehicle slowing down a half hour ago, maybe stopping on the tar road, maybe a thump that would be a slammed door, but he was upstairs washing up.

He can see that the old person is smiling up at him and that she wears no glasses. Her eyes are possibly blue, hard to tell in the flagging light. In his deep big-guy voice, he asks, "You looking for me?"

Her hair isn't white but an ashy light brown with a neglected perm, the hair jaw-length and listless, but thick and combed with a nice part on the side. She wears a dark button-up sweater, jeans, sneakers. Her nose isn't small, snoutlike, or curt. Maybe once she was quite handsome. She has been nodding her head to his question, her eyes wide and seeming to show some sense of humor about the moment.

He has a sinking feeling, knowing someone has dumped her off. The way people sometimes dump off boxes of baby rabbits or, once in a while, a pup.

"Well," says he. "Let's go up where all the hot corn muffins are and get the world by the tail."

Once they start up the wooded shortcut, he fumbles for the small flashlight hooked to his belt along with his batch of keys. She isn't talking. She must be fuzzy of mind. He reaches for her hand as they come upon the rooty part of the trail. He thinks about the aspirin bottle he keeps at all times in a pocket but just keeps on swishing the light through the overbearing purple dusk inside the crackling-underfoot tunnel of old trees.

On a different evening. Alone with fifteen-year-old Seavey Road neighbor girl Brianna Vandermast who visits *a lot.*

She stands so erect and easy by the scarred dark table in the farmhouse dining room, the old blue-with-white-polka-dots wallpaper Gordon's mother herself pasted up once upon a time. How musty-cool this room is but the cherry-pink ceramic cherub in the corner hutch cabinet looks overheated.

Bree spreads her ringless hand on the thick, stapled document lying amid three empty coffee mugs on the long leafed table. She asks, "What is this?"

He is just now entering the room with two more mugs, these with maple milk in them, one for her, one for him. His eyes widen. "Oh *that*. Well, in this world there's *your* Recipe. Then there's *their* Recipe."

Her voice has always had a smoky edge. "*Project Megiddo,* it says. It's the FBI. But what are *you* doing with it?" She giggles.

He positions the two brimming mugs on the table. He glances at her face, which is purposely hidden by squiggles and twists of shining young-girl hair, perfectly orange hair, her face deformed by whatever it was that went wrong when she was the size of a thumb . . . or earlier . . . maybe when she was a mere idea . . . though who could imagine Bree, her honey-color eyes set apart like a funhouse mirror image and her mind that to him once seemed shy, nervous, or something . . . but, no, he is beginning to understand that she is not nervous of anything. He bets that the coil of her brain is radiating far more redly than her hair.

He explains, "*Everybody* has a copy of that thing. It's not top secret. It was issued to fire departments, cops, EMTs. Rex* . . . you know . . . he's with the volunteer fire crowd."

---

* Don't forget the character list at the back of the book.

"I figured. Cuz of the red light on the dash in his pickup," she says in a warm way.

He grunts. "Richard York. He's just like you. He loves to share. He's probably churned out half a million copies of that report."

She giggles.

"Drink some of your ambrosia, Athena," he chuckles, pushes her mug easy-careful across the table toward her hand, which is, yes, ringless, but speckled and dashed with three shades of musclcy purple, one shade of red, one splotch of yellow ocher.

She reads aloud: "The attached analysis, entitled Project Megiddo, is an FBI strategic assessment of the potential for domestic terrorism in the United States undertaken in anticipation of or response to the arrival of the new millennium." She doesn't look into his face square-on. She never does. But her eyes drift toward his shoulder, his work shirt, and his Sherpa-lined vest. "Have you read this . . . all of it?" She flips through, pausing, blinking.

Gordon speaks in a cartoony play-voice, "If we is to hassle Mr. York about reading our stuff, it's only fair we reads his."

She tsks. "Looks like the FBI wants to scare everybody, huh?"

He says nothing. The expression across his dark-lashed eyes is smirky. His cowlicked hair adds greatly to his appearance of *What? Me worry?* though "weary" is a more accurate word.

But her voice becomes almost academic and there, see her touch her chin with a musing finger. "I mean . . . their language is . . . well, you know, Poeish. You can hear funereal music in the background. I mean . . . it's funny . . . but *not* funny. Cuzzz they are trying to make the militia movement guys into something . . . *terrorists*." She giggles. "I mean it's *not funny* . . . but they sound so . . . like . . . bad actors in . . . well, like Joe Friday!" She hiccups with laughter.

He pulls out a chair and sits with a tired groan.

"America needs to be divided," she says. "Divided we fall. That's it in a nutshell. We . . . the little guys. Meanwhile, these . . . these cops or whatever they are . . . they get *paid* for being dangerous and . . . and silly." She flips the top page, lets it drop. "I hate to see people be such suckers. There's got to be a way to outsmart a bunch of funny cops." She snorts.

"So," says he, "I saw where the print shop did up about two hundred more of your Abominable Hairy Patriot flyers. What are you going to do with those?"

She giggles. Guiltily. She's aware of the ethic of thrift Gordon stands firmly on, so she might be feeling she has wronged him? "Oh . . . like, we've been passing them out, around. Bulletin board at the town office and IGA. Telephone poles. Windshield wipers."

"You and your wicked comrades from the Socrates group, right?"

She hesitates, then says lushly, "Sure. Comrades. Which reminds me . . ." She steps around one of his towers of books, a plastic crate of oak tag files, and a couple of satchels of yet-to-be-answered "fan mail" to the nearest darkening window. She keeps her back presented to him. Always her back (and perfect bottom). Always her profile (within the veil of her long hair). Never, never square on. She will face everybody but him, even though he and she have been together so much this summer, perfecting the three versions of *The Recipe for Revolution*. Is he wronging her to feel suspicious . . . of . . . something? That she is scheming things that she is too young to realize are too hot to handle?

Some here call her gifted, her art, her welter of calligraphy, her way of leading the other girls around by the nose. But she is not sixteen yet. She still believes that monsters can be tamed by princesses, that the world beyond the Settlement gate can be fixed.

She tells him, "I reached the people I told you about . . . the . . . leftists. The ones with the folk school project, the ones who printed that great brochure on democracy versus corporate power."

He is suddenly and deeply silent.

"They said it would be their pleasure to come," she adds.

All at once he slurps and sucks and splutters and slobbers away at the edge of his mug of maple milk, the syrup settled languidly at the bottom, then with a red bandanna from his pants pocket, cleans his heavy dark mustache like a cat, defiantly and precisely. And still he offers no words. Runs his tongue over his teeth, getting more mileage out of the maple.

She steps back and turns toward the corner hutch.

One of his eyes tends to widen when he's overawed by life, the other eye narrowing and flinching. This is happening now. "You send them our Recipe? I mean *your* Recipe. *You* are its mastermind," says he.

"All three versions, yes, which include the one-page flyer." She giggles. She is reaching to touch one of the pink cherub's wings. Now his eyes swipe down over the whole of her. Logger girl. Yes, she really does work in the woods with her father and brothers. Often she has turned up at the Settlement for the East Parlor Socrates nights covered in sawdust, smeared with bar and chain oil and the sour grease of the machinery.

He has seen artwork by her, on her passions: woods, sky, work. Her brush refuses to sit, stay, lie down, and happily throws 8.5-magnitude seismographic cracks in all that's revered.

Yes, the wide slow sway of her hips makes her, in spite of her face, a sexy girl. And yes, she is only fifteen. And he is more tired by the minute and also curious about her stopping in tonight, almost always another hint for him to save the world, always the romanticized plunge into the chasm, like Malcolm X or Emiliano Zapata or Big Bill Haywood. Oh, to be fifteen and foolish, thinking every landing to be so dreamy, so soft, so green!

"Well," says he. "Keep me posted on when these new friends of yours plan to ride into town."

She strokes the cherub's other wing. She's a tall girl. Almost six feet. He's a tall man. Six-five. He realizes how at times when he's near her, she and he seem of a species apart from most Settlementers . . . except his oldest sons and daughters and then his wife Bonnie Loo, who by virtue of the Bean family legacy, is of rugged and towering stature, too.

He is grateful to be sitting down. He's been up since four. His headache is there right where it always is and basketball-sized. He leans back in the old dining room chair. He watches Bree carefully.

She speaks in a most dreamy way, "What kind of mind believed in wings?" She has, obviously, no interest in her portion of the maple milk.

Gordon says huskily, "Millions still believe in angels. And pregnant virgins. And kings visiting Bethlehem on camels that must be turbo camels to make such good time from North Africa . . . uh . . . . hours after the babe hit the hay. According to Christmas cards."

She is a bit more in profile to him now, no response to his camel wisecrack, and withdraws her hand from the rigid pink wing, though her fingers are still in the cherub's personal space. "I guess you'd need wings to flap up to heaven." She touches without hesitation the cherub's bright penis, then declares with a release of held breath, "Heaven is on earth."

The last gooey swig of what's in Gordon's mug goes down. He reaches for her full cup, draws it to himself.

Speaking from the future, Claire St. Onge remembers some things.

It changed so much about our lives at the Settlement. That *Record Sun* feature. And all the "wire" pieces and talk-show fervor that came on its heels. We could never hide anything again and we had plenty to hide, all that which made up Gordon's humanity. He was stood on a stage now. He was cut into "bytes," a collage for the titillation of America. All of us at the Settlement were part of that collage, like some sort of jokey frat-boy art.

But our gardens wagged in the rains, simmered in the sun, and our children continued to be vivacious. And our elderly elders wore their invisible crowns, chin up. At times we could pretend nothing had changed.

When I get a minute, I'll tell you a little about the reporter who was the first to crash into our lives . . . the lovely and fox-cunning Ivy Morelli of the *Record Sun*. Bonnie Loo hissed that she was a bitch and a cunt, but to me she seemed just another vulnerable sticky soul snagged by our towering king of the Settlement hearth.

The voice of Mammon considers.

This glowing growing of free exchange, these acquisitions, accumulations, these deserved accretions, the flow, as unencumbered as the sea, is the rock of civilization. It is immoral not to defend it!

The Apparatus speaks.

Overlords and overladies of the free world! You rang? I bend. Gladly.

There is no weight to your trillions, once the currency of evergreen and gold, now just the sheen of the scrolling screen, your gains mounting taller than the twin towers, those dispensable giraffes that soon will go down in the hot dust free fall of our ingenious brew of delicacies. You rang? At your service! Proud to serve! *Kabooooom!*

No need to concern yourselves with that which walks on billions of legs, the restless, enraged, suspicious, unpacific folk of the homeland and beyond, such flesh the weight of rubble. At your service! I will stun them, freeze them solid, with precision, the inexhaustible constant constant constant televised flutter of that hot dust and fire and live bodies dropping like apples from a cloud-tall tree. But also I will arrange smaller terrors, these "lone" gunmen and bomb men of and on the busy streets, schools, movie houses, even church! Mosques! Whatever!

Proud to serve you, gods and goddesses of the global exchanges, I give you the full and juicy terror of this nation and more, oh, to keep that terror in high red, a crescendo like Ravel's *Bolero*, like a thumping bed, yet one more mass shooting by a dog-toothed depressed non-man "loner," another *bang! bang!*, another sprawled child and choking-on-her-tears mother, today and tomorrow, *bang! pop! boom!* You rang? Oh, yes, I am proud to serve.

But for now, for this warm-up before the truly BIG DAY of box-cutter magic, O lords, O ladies, in my ever-resolute service, I am soon ready to give you this lunatic, armed and dangerous, weird-for-blood spectral signifier of what all good Americans abhor, that god of a little dot on the map of Maine: Guillaume St. Onge. Take him from my palm.

A Brief Flashback to June

From a future time, Claire St. Onge remembers way back to the June morning when the reporter Ivy Morelli first turned up at the Settlement, uninvited.

So this, of course, was before her *Record Sun* feature changed everything. It was the morning of the solstice march and one of the biggest breakfasts of the year, where we'd be joined by good-sport neighbors and friends out there on our big screened porches, after the sun rose—the sun, the god of all life, according to many peoples of this world. And to us, *significant.*

The mountains that cradled us were blue-green that day, and wobbly due to the steam being so full and lustrous.

Beth St. Onge* remembering that June day of Ivy Morelli's sneak attack.

Gordon got shit-faced drunk on cider, then drunker and drunker, then you'd know a big stupid gorilla when you see one. He made a bad impression on the reporter. *We* weren't feeling proud, either. He would only once in a while fall off the wagon like that but why'd he always pick the awfullest times to do it?

---

* See character list at back of book.

The reporter, whose hair was tinted purple and who wore a yellow dress, very short, and striped socks with black, buttoned-up shoes like out of a junk store . . . and tattoos of pink and turquoise kissing fish going around her thin upper arm, you couldn't miss them . . . she seemed about to call out the marines when Gordon got to teasing little Michel Soucier, holding him down and letting out a dangly hot icicle of drool over the kid's face, Michel screaming, then Gordon sucked the spit back in, a rare talent.

Penny St. Onge remembering.

Ivy Morelli had told Gordon the night before that she had decided against doing a piece for the paper. She said to him, "I'm your friend." But some people use that word loosely.

Steph St. Onge's recollections.

Before she left, Ivy Morelli agreed to come back another day, when we'd have a tour crew ready and the Brazilian heat would be gone and normal Maine weather back. But when she returned in a fresh dress of moons and stars it was almost a hundred degrees, according to the first piazza's six thermometers which usually all read different.

Bonnie Loo (Bonnie Lucretia) St. Onge remembers the tour day.

My cigarette tasted like insecticide. My stomach shot to my ears. Me in the shade of the trees in the Quad, saw them herding her along through the suns of hell, between Quonset huts and mills, Ms. Media, who I knew would fuck with us. Her cute little artsy outfits and tropical fish tattoos circling her little upper arm. Her laugh was a foghorn, which was tricky because you'd assume here's a person who is just one of us, not the smooth snooty type, but then you see the permafrost blue eyes.

I scraped the ash off my cig on the underside of the picnic table. I rose. I was going to cut her off at the pass.

From a future time Claire tells us how it went.

I look back with shame. For here was mass media's great ruthless blue eye inside the very heartbeat of our home and I was being some show-time master of ceremonies, throwing out an arm and an open hand, oh, view this fortress of cookstoves and kettles and bubbling stuff!!

Admire the canning crew and supper crew, svelte teens in shorts and aprons, soft shoulders. And the tykes on stools, half naked, burned and nicked and bruised. Feeling the food with grubby appendages, wagging their heads like inchworms, watching, mimicking, feeling their futures in their palms. Many with that nose, those cheekbones, the likeness, a species particular to this location, this altitude, cradled by these certain surly hills and the arms of too many mothers.

Geraldine St. Onge, one of Claire's cousins from the Passamaquoddy Reservation.

We worked nearly a dozen hardwood-topped tables in that summer kitchen. Acres of glinting still-hot canning jars, the quart kind, the sixty-four-ounce kind, and the widemouthed, twelve-ounce kind, bulging with deep green leafy, or seedy red. June's harvest.

The reporter curled a small hand around the handle of one of the tall green hand pumps at the end of one of the slate sinks. When she looked up her mouth was smiling. Her cold-blistering eyes studied everything.

From a future time, Lee Lynn St. Onge confides in us.

Gordon has always fussed over the danger of the media. So of course, some of us here asked, "Why did he invite her here?" For he *had* agreed to an interview alone with her at the farmhouse, but then he panicked and talked in riddles and . . . well, none of that matters. The question is: Why did he say yes in the first place? Was it the sound of her hearty wiseacre-yet-letdown voice on the phone?

Had his spine of resolve, usually thick like one of the monster tree supports of our summer kitchen, buckled under the weight of something so nimble and invasive as yet another fertile female?

Back in the Cook's Kitchen. (There are three kitchens.)

Ivy Morelli turns away from some chitchat with a small doleful little boy named Rhett. She stares in resplendent wide-eyed discomfort at the hulkingly too close voluptuous Bonnie Loo.

Ivy's small clover-pink mouth flattens against her teeth, an attempted but fizzled smile.

Bonnie Loo smells like cigarette smoke. And that queasy weedy ointmenty smell of all the Settlement candles and soaps and salves that Ivy's tour has highlighted, the vats and kettles of witchy Lee Lynn St. Onge's corner of one Quonset hut, and kids too little to stir scalding stuff stirring away. But the smell is especially now wafting from Bonnie Loo's two-toned whorish-looking hair and body.

Okay, her eyebrows are comely. One has just arched. Like a question. How gleamy the eyes, contact lenses for certain, and out of those eyes seems to come the mile-wide gusty voice, speaking to Ivy Morelli, "Thirsty from your tour?" No waiting for a reply, just leans over one of the steel sinks, braless, the damp, filled-out green T-shirt a quickening exhibit of obscenity as if it were part of the tour, somewhat literary, somewhat theological, somewhat instructive, like *Never look this floozyish or you will be eternally damned*. But there's no stopping Bonnie Loo, the wagging Atlas breasts, if Atlas were a woman, she cuffs at a bulky tin cup that leaps to her other hand. Now dips water from a speckled kettle. That black and harshly orange topknot of hair tosses around from left to right shoulder. She straightens up, cup in hand. This, too, is a demonstration, this one on how to operate the Settlement plumbing? Yes? The cup is held such 'n' such a way.

The little reporter asserts, "I'm okay. I had plenty of beverage at lunch."

But Bonnie Loo now throws her shoulders back as humans do who are not expecting blows to the gut from the enemy, but showcasing her vulnerable parts because the enemy izzzz *weak*.

Again Bonnie Loo's hot orangey eyes are driven into Ivy's.

Ivy *almost* lowers hers, just the merest flicker.

Ah hah! Bonnie Loo the victor!

But I am your friend, Ivy's inner voice pleads. Well, I am Gordon's friend. Cringing friend, shuddering friend, I-vow-not-to-write-a-single-word-on-you-guys friend.

But Bonnie Loo stands back reproachfully, some grudge grander than the victim-seeking-mass-media betrayal on the horizon, the seconds ticking away, her upper-body dimensions unclouded by the T-shirt fabric, as thin as paint.

Nobody in the whole crowded room makes a helpful wisecrack or cheerfully scolds in order to end the tension. Everything weird about this flow of seconds is unweird to the onlookers.

Ivy keeps her eyes on the big enamel cup as Bonnie Loo dashes the water from it into the flared opening on top of the tall dark green pump, raising the pump's impressively long arm and clenching the fingers of her broad hand around it, works it hard. And Bonnie Loo's own arm, yellowy dark from her Maine mix of bloods, heritage that whispers of peoples stirred and shuffled, blurred and ruffled up together because of ships, because of snowy trails between lodges, jammed ice in big rivers, then jammed logs, the blur of big woods greener than the heart can stand, gray waters, green waters, human heat, and myriad hungers. Then Bonnie Lucretia Bean was someone's foxy-orange-eyed black-haired infant, chubby little doll arms, but now grown, now a towering brute, now holding not the pump-priming cup but a pretty little ceramic one, maybe nearby is a matching saucer, the Colonial America carriages, ladies and gents, preening blue and mauve.

The cup is ever so suddenly overfull, drizzling. But the great pump's arm proceeds. The little dainty cup gasps. The lake under earth rises to swallow Bonnie Loo's golden hand and slim silver wedding ring in a blur. Up, down, water pound-punches, making a cold breeze on Ivy Morelli. The cup, the unending overflow, that terrible abundance from so deep under the Settlement's granite footings, how can it not be polar?

Now there! The dripping cup is thrust into the mass media's hand.

"Here. Drink up," Bonnie Loo commands.

And Ivy Morelli herself overflows with her deepest "HAW! HAW!" but doesn't draw the cup to her face for she is locked in a pause like the solstice.

Bonnie Loo, now with her hands on the hips of her long skirt, one with intricately embroidered flora and elfin faces around the hem, says low and moltenly, "Good God, it ain't poison."

Claire remembering.

By August, the yearnings of the *Record Sun* enterprise were grander, less complex, and with more grasp than that friendship notion of little Ivy Morelli. And so her hand was forced. The big-spread feature came with no warning, just *pow!* It was not hostile. In fact, it was becoming to us. But as my crow says . . . my crow, you know, the one who is different from all the others, the one who comes to my cottage's sunroom window for cracked corn . . . someone's abandoned pet, he ducks under the open window or flaps in ahead of me as I open the back door. He has a good view from the Norfolk pine in its tub near my chair and midday coffee, or flaps into my bedroom where the tall bedposts are, ripples his feathers tightly to give his whole self a gloss, checks out my stuff. He loves *stuff*, a true American. So I had my copy of the *Record Sun* open in my sunroom on my little carved toadstool table, holding my head, he was there, cocking *his* head as if to join me in considering the photo of blurred Settlement-made merry-go-round critters surrounding Gordon's face and upper body. How Gordon could look both benevolent and dangerous was not a trick of the photo but it sure was an opportunistic photo.

Crow's voice, resembling a tinny cheesy-made boom box, pealed from his seesawing black beak . . . "DING DONG DING DONG. Oh, God. Get the door. DING DONG. Oh, God. Get the door. Oh, God. DING DONG."

***History as it Happens* (as recorded by Montana Bethany St. Onge. Age nine. With no help).**

I personally know and truly experience how Gordie's telephone rings all the time now since the newspaper thing. Lots of people calling about the way you can get your own very nice windmill with help from our crews that teach stuff. And homemade solar buggies. Or CSA* farm ideas. Some call to make fart noises or groans. My mother Beth says not to encourage these meatballs, just hang up. But I am very smart in dealing with meatballs and I tell them I am so smart I can find out technologically right where they are and cops are already on the way. This is an exaggeration, of course. Not a lie. Once I kept a meatball talking for a half hour at least about how he knows a million cops and is not worried. I said there aren't a million cops in Maine.

In case you are reading this a hundred years from now, the phone is in Gordie's house. No other phones. Settlement is up in the mountain. No phone there.

So one of our mothers who had come down to use the phone says, "Who is that, Montana?"

"A friend," I said. For you guys reading this installment, I did not lie. It was just an exaggeration.

Also the mail is now like an explosion. Doesn't all fit in Gordie's mailbox. That's the only mailbox. It stands on an old post by the driveway at Gordie's gray wicked old farmhouse. No mailboxes up in the mountain where I live with everybody at the Settlement.

I sign up for the mail crew now, the part where we sort and deliver to the cubbies in the Cook's Kitchen and Winter Kitchen. I am, of course, very good at it.

Also nowadays some of the guys like Oz and C.C. (whose name is really Christian Crocker in case you read this a million years from now) and Dane go to the post office in East Egypt riding horseback. Oz never walks on his two only legs. He's a lost cause. Someday he'll marry a horse, says Ellen, one of my father's wives.

Also people drive up the long dirt road to the Settlement these days just to look at us and take pictures. Some use binoculars to make like a doorknob or a button on your shirt look big. My mother calls them assholes, tourists, and rude fuckers. I'm absolutely forbidden to go out to these cars to have my picture taken or to show them how much stuff I'm good at which happens if you get educated here in this supreme best and now totally famous place.

---

* Community Supported Agriculture.

Edward "Butch" Martin, Settlement twenty-year-old, tells of what he remembers about fame.

Um . . . well, the newspaper did us in late August and after that bunches of nose-trouble types drove up the Settlement road to study us . . . from the parking area and edge of that nearest hayfield . . . well . . . um . . . some came over to the shops or Quonset bays to ask questions about our projects. Gordo was okay about that, building the cooperatives was his, you know, glory.

But man, we got mostly, you know, sightseers . . . like maybe they went to drive by a murder scene or house fire, then they come look at us. With binoculars!

Okay, only one with binoculars. But several cameras and camcorders. And they backed their cars and SUVs over one of our hayfields, squashing it.

So down where the gravel ends at the tar road, Heart's Content, we put up a gate. Well, not a real gate. A horizontal pole. It was temporary, right? Little dangling sign said to KEEP OUT. And nice and handy, a message box. Neighbors and CSA volunteers and customers for our stuff could just lift the pole, right? It wasn't anything but self-defense. Not even violent as there's so much twitter about these days. So what's the crime?

Seems like it was a matter of seconds the *Record Sun* has a big motherfucking picture of our little pole and KEEP OUT sign. Beside the picture they had a runty little story, not like the Ivy person's. This one called us "separatists" and went on about Gordo being "their leader" and that he "seems more nervous."

The Ivy article on us had been wicked warm . . . um . . . you know, because like she . . . *liked* us. This new "news" had an edge like something had changed.

Penny St. Onge remembering.

And then it went AP. All except what Ivy, dear dear Ivy did not include, though she by then knew . . . Gordon's polygamy . . . and how many children here were his. She left that part a blank. But you could tell, the great slobbering questing baying mass media was circling.

They used photos that Ivy had taken but didn't select for her piece, ones that showed shadows and hints. Gordon's pale dark-lashed eyes boring into the lens, the short gray-chinned dark devil beard and the merry-go-round of kid-made mounts blurry with motion. Not horses, but monsters, born of cruel minds? And the kids themselves in certain shots, grubby and drizzling and Third World. The ominous KEEP OUT sign.

My only child, Whitney, blond jouncy ponytail, Gordon's lopsided smile but not the full cheek-twitch, she our bright-shining-star fifteen-year-old, his oldest. She had gotten awfully quiet as a few of us stood in the Settlement library with the latest dozen AP clippings spread across the big table in gray lusterless rainy-day light. I hugged her to me.

"Well," said she.

"Well," said me.

Critical thinker of the past.

The law locks up the man or woman
Who steals the goose from off the Common.
But lets the greater villain loose
Who steals the Common from the goose

Anonymous

Meanwhile Secret Agent Jane Meserve, age six, almost seven, visits her mother. She speaks.

The only way I can get here today is that Montana's mum drives me. Montana's mum is named Beth. She has hair sort of the color of my mum's but in long wiggles. Mum's is straight. Mum's hair is actually brown but she has always used Light 'n' Streak, which is so pretty. I don't know Beth's real color, but the beauty crew works on her a lot. She says, "Hands playing with my head have a calming effect."

Mum always says my hair is a good color without doozying it up. She calls my hair "wash and wear," which is so funny.

Sadly, Mum has the orange outfit again but we don't talk about it cuz she gets tears in her eyes. We have to sit at the table and no touching. Mum looks at me a lot and she always says she loves my secret agent heart-shaped sunglasses, then winks because it's our secret together, about me being a spy. These glasses are white on the outside edges, pink where you see through so everything looks pink. While Mum looks at me, Beth talks all her wisecracks.

I want to give Mum a hug bad but they have a way of making sure you never hug. It's a cop-guard in his brown outfit and gun who has a chair but hardly fits cuz he's about five hundred pounds with a stomach that bulges front and sides and back. If you squint, it looks like he's wearing an inner tube thing for floating in the lake. He's taller than Gordie but his hair is shaved, not a real fade but more like a little hat and also what Beth calls a Kung Fu mustache. This she whispers so loud, then says in her voice, which is deep and crunchy, "He's the one they probably handcuff people to when they take 'em up to court, right, Lisa?"

Mum flashes her eyes over at the guy who is now looking at Beth and then he looks away.

Mum says she misses me so much. Today she has lost her tan even more. Definitely no sunshine here. Mum always has to work on her tan. She says my father, Damon Gorely, is the best color. I saw his picture once. But she actually met him when he was at his concert and very famous in rap and hip-hop. Mum says I am golden like a Gypsy queen and she would give anything to be me. But today we don't talk about our usual stuff, tans or hair or outfits or *me*. We mostly listen to Beth, who is telling all her jail jokes and then says, "Oh, fuck. I have to pee."

If I get a word in the edgewise of Beth I'll report to Mum about the food they want to make me eat at the Settlement and at Gordie's house, where my guest room actually is. I will never eat fish with skin in ten million years. And they have big rules about sugar. When Mum and I and our Scottie dog Cherish lived our regular life in Lewiston there were no rules. We had TV. We had sugar. Now there are jail rules and Settlement rules and I'm so sick of it.

I am getting tears in my eyes but I don't make a single noise.

Mum gets tears in her eyes and no noise from her, either.

We almost touch.

Forward Again to September

Egypt town hall parking lot. In a small metallic blue-gray car waits a fellow wearing a short-sleeve golf-style shirt.

An old dark-green-and-white Chevy pickup pulls in and the giant, a bit slope-shouldered Gordon St. Onge steps out, a tax bill or some such in his huge hand, a harmlessly overcast expression on his bearded face. Three little boys are on the truck's bench seat raising hell. A perfectly nice apple with no bites sails out the open passenger window and bounces toward the groomed town hall shrubberies. No seat belts but gun racks, yes, with one gun. No, actually it's a large carpentry level. For newspaperly photo purposes, guns are better, but the golf-shirt guy flies out of his car anyway and seems to be blocking Gordon St. Onge's next step.

Gordon nods, eyes scanning the guy, now his Tourette's-like cheek and eye flinch as he registers the camera that is snapping several "frames" of him about three feet from his face and so his expression hardens. And this malevolent burning look, the Mertie's Hardware billed cap and old bloodred chamois shirt, all a testament to his class, which of itself sustains the accusation of wrongs, a generalized inexhaustible infamy, are frozen forever in digital format.

History as it Happens (as recorded by Montana Bethany St. Onge. Age nine. With no help).

Today the mail was worse than ever, like a "goddamn ton of bricks" my mother Beth screamed when Oz and C.C. and Jaime dragged all the feed sacks with letters and stuff into the kitchens.

Also we got more meatballs on the phone down to Gordie's house. I handled three of them all at once and got them to confess they were calling from the Maine Mall. I am very good at this, better than Jane Meserve who believes she's a secret agent, which is ridiculous. She is not even seven yet and cannot spell. Actually with spelling I am better than the *Record Sun* which made *four* typos in the article about us.

Gordie was depressed or something because another newspaper guy nailed him with a picture that went onto a front page in Massachusetts ←(notice my perfect spelling).

They always take lots of pictures of him and pick the scariest ones and call him "the Prophet" or "with militia connections." All our windmills and gardens and conservation projects that Ivy liked aren't mentioned now. They say Gordie is "a charismatic leader." My mother, Beth, says if this keeps up, the FBI will be in here with tanks and CS gas . . . which she heard is explosive in close quarters. She says the government loves to explode things because Americans like to watch explosions. It's all very exciting but when I said tanks were funny she squeezed my arm HARD. "Shut up" . . . her actual words. And she looked afraid. Not her usual self, which Gordie calls an "unflappable smart-ass wench."

On talk radio they talk about how Gordie has *twenty-five* wives. That is a bit of an exaggeration.

Claire's cottage.

He trudges up the flagstone-and-vinca path to her yard, the velvet-skinned white birches yeowling in the wind. He notes there is a ceramic cup left on the little stone bench from where you can, on a less misty day, see for miles, including the reedy narrow end of Promise Lake with all its wee islands, some too small to build on, a few barely the size of trash-can covers.

Claire's friend Catherine and her child Robert have been staying with Claire, a tight fit, and he has heard that this Catherine fancies the little stone bench, the view, the peace. But too windy and yeowly today for peace.

And besides, Catherine has been gone for several days, being straight-out busy at the university, Professor Catherine Court Downey, the interim "chairperson" (Gordon's word) of the art department, she who is under Gordon's skin in ways contradictory to skin.

He has carried here, for Claire to see, yet another newspaper that has been squeezing out more sensational mileage from the Settlement "situation." Yes, his home is now being referred to as "a situation." And this is a fearsome turn in the road and Claire and her tiny steeply roofed cottage of colored-glass panes, reservation baskets of sweet grass and ash, and lusty hanging plants, and that carved dark-stained furniture, made by him, are the cave of comfort he crawls into when most stung by fears, most uneasy. He sees her in his mind's eye, standing in her open door, those twenty years all layered, twenty layers of soft transmutations, all the Claires, starting with that age-thirty Claire, his first bride, her strutting little figure, the sway of her hair, more hair than figure, a mane of mirror-shine black. No glasses in those days. Just eyes. Black eyes. Unexcitable eyes. And yet, they were thunder eyes, speaking eyes, eyes that often could rivet him to the wall. Or the bed, as the case may be.

It wasn't until he had betrayed her that she began to put on weight. But before that, oh, how she used to swing those hips. Nearly ten years older than he, an "older" student (if you aren't fresh out of high school), USM history major, history and archaeology, the stirring finds of recent digs all over the mean curve of the planet, oh, she, Claire, was both ancient and ripe.

It is through his especially developed feelers of the heart that he knows he has missed her, her after-the-noon-meal "quiet time" when she reads over her university students' compositions, these from her adjunct position in the same building as the "chairperson's" office. So he can surmise Claire has had an interruption other than himself.

But here is *the* crow, not the usual bunch who scream jocularly over the cracked corn on the two windowsill shelves. But *the* crow, the one who recently breezed in to win Claire's heart, perched today on the lumpy man-sized kid-made "sculpture" near the front door. Part of a beech tree, this sculpture; looks like a fellow with too many arms. Mossy flappy logging boots are fitted to the locations of the feet, if there had been feet.

"Art by kids is sicko," his wife Beth loves to observe. Though this sculpture is hardly as disturbing as the kid-made merry-go-round mounts that the *Record Sun*'s Ivy Morelli photographed, and all of America now gasps over, those eyeless leering monsters of molten colors that blur around Gordon in his most famous media image.

The wind now brays awfully.

The crow's feathers flicker just as Gordon's dark brown hair flicks and flops. The bird cocks his head. Gordon is not charmed by this crow's moxie. He just stands stiffly, his eyes on the other's eyes.

There are no shadows today. Everything is sluggishly and hysterically straightforward. The bawling wind rises up and once again tests crow and man. Inside the cottage a door wind-slams.

Gordon's eyes narrow, his fingers tightening the rolled-up paper.

Crow shakes himself, which means he has something to say, gets a more secure perch on the beech sculpture's square head, and out comes his scratchy advisory voice, "It's Bob. Don't answer the door. It's Bob. It's Bob. Oh, God, it's Bob. Don't answer the door."

The other crows are in the pines many yards west of Claire's yard. Across the wraithy white-mauve sky darker clouds go scudding along helplessly. Gordon aims the paper like a revolver at the sassy crow. Crow hops, turns to one side, says quite clearly, "Salad. Yuck. I ain't no friggin' rabbit. Yuck. I ain't no friggin' rabbit."

Gordon again pictures Claire in the doorway, this time just her round most recent self, the way she would look today, her hair beginning to gray, the spectacles and the vast bustline in a rough-knit sweater. Oh, that for once this afternoon his plans would dead-bolt silkenly into place. She would offer him tea in the cloudy-today sunroom. She would rub the sleeve of his shirt over and over and over.

Crow expands his wings as if to rise, settles again smugly in the same place, then imparts, "Thou art the thing itself: Unaccommodated man is no more than such a poor, bare, forked animal as thou art."

Gordon knows this bird has not really spoken this last bit. It's just absurdity and stark loneliness merging in the frontal lobes of his,

Gordon's, brain. It can happen to anyone, of course. It's absolutely *not* a form of insanity.

From a future time in her secluded Cape Elizabeth home, Janet Weymouth remembers her own transformation and Gordon St. Onge.

The right thing and the wrong thing are like two wrestlers you are trying to pull apart, their legs and arms entwined.

My dream for years was that all the children of the world would someday be born into a life of significance and choice and the delights and profundity of great art and great music, and they would be spared of toil, would know only meaningful endeavors, that if America brought its rare luminescence to all the remote and bitter and sad foreign places of this world, to educate . . . yes, educate!!! . . . this dream would unfold. *Educate!* The secret, I presumed, was education. Show them the better way, bring them technology, medicine, clean habits, birth control, equality, and opportunities for expanding business and trade, and they will rise above their situations.

But my friend, that roaring creature with the raised fist you would eventually see on your television and in so many papers, his face being painted by the shadows of low helicopters, this in the coming months, *he* who has sat many times in this very room, growled, "You're bringing them the ruthless US empire and war."

Oh, sometimes he was energized and hopeful, and then *poof!* . . . something I would say? . . . or some malignant vision that would cross his ever-so-pale, dark-lashed eyes . . . he was not a movie-star-handsome man but he would draw your eye, and there he'd stand in this room, a raw compelling profile, yes, compelling, a man with no faith but in devils.

No, in those moments he saw no buoyant days ahead with humanity streaming together in peace and educated choices. He saw no safety. No "rare luminescence" on the horizon. He said that nothing in history has ever played out that way, that I'd have to change human nature and nature itself first.

And yet whenever he came calling, he was my friend, as his mother, dear heart Marian Depaolo St. Onge, was my friend.

This morning at 7:30 or so, I sit by the corner windows of the front study, with the newspaper folded on my lap and with a tiny pot of tea, which I have instead of breakfast . . . this major newspaper, not the *Record Sun* but one from the larger national chain, which my family owns, and yet on any subject of its fresh-smelling pages I do not believe a word of it!

I turn the paper facedown on my knee. And I hear both the sea, which makes the floor tremble, and the humming of my heart's disappointment. And the sea, smashing on the rocks like many tons of broken glass, tells me it already has no memory of us. I have finally come to see there is no grand flourish I have to offer to save the world, even as I have for so many years been able to force the fates, to exact favors, to MAKE things happen, to FIX certain minutiae that need to be righted if I am to have my way.

No, I did not give him money. And no, we were not lovers. I am nearly twenty-five years older than him, he was but thirty-nine years old then. Though I have touched him, felt the dragonlike mass of his body in mutual embrace, for I always squeeze and squash what I prize most and it will always be said that he did the same.

The sea pounds. Its power is in its lack of wishes and of dreams.

Mickey Gammon, fifteen-year-old member of the Border Mountain Militia, and militia captain Rex York off on an errand.

Mickey considers how the dark pounces earlier and earlier in the usual September way, but the weather is fucked up. Most of the guys in Rex's militia say that global warming is just a lie made up by the environmentalists. But at the last meeting, Rex told how his friends in Alaska have been writing for a few years saying the permafrost is melting. And it's so bad now that one town has to move because the houses are tipping over and seals, which are usually born on ice, are being born in water due to all the flooding caused by the melting, which is picking up . . . the melting . . . it's really going fast. So the seals are drowning as they are born. Thousands of them. And then there's Greenland. Coasties Rex knows say, "Kiss Greenland good-bye."

Doc, who has combed-special dark hair and small, mean-looking ears and a "Western Mass" accent (which makes words like docks and rocks sound like dahcks and rahcks to Mickey), had said, "Alaska is pretty close to Russia." He said this with significance.

And Art who is round and smiley had said, "Yeah," with significance.

And Doc had said, "Commies and environmentalists have the same roots. Most likely Alaska is crawling with some of each. And those types *all* lie."

Phil, one of the guys who had been sitting deep in Rex's old leather couch, was looking from Doc to Rex and back and forth as he said, "So Rex's buddies are Russians? What kinda names they got, Rex? Any—"

Doc interrupts with a wave of disgust, his wedding ring giving off a dull glow. "I'm not talking about them. I'm talking about the Alaskan general public. Their environmentalists lie to *them*. Their environmentalists *caused* the weather change so they could get some sort of federal subsidies."

"HAARP's* up there," Art reminds them. "So that could be used on themselves to change the weather."

Rex just stared at these guys and their words going back and forth.

George Durling, who is very sick from something he got in 'Nam, he's a red-haired skeleton actually, he says softly that Planet X is approaching. "The earth's core is heating up due to that."

This starts them all on the subject of Planet X but Rex has no comment on their news that most of the world's telescopes are shut down and that there's been a lot of fishy goings-on involving the Vatican and governments concerning information on the "tenth planet's" approach.

At most meetings Rex is quiet. Sometimes he is totally quiet, just staring at them all as they get out their maps and survival goodies. Rex's steely silence and cold eyes are a comfort to Mickey. Predictable. Like his own steely silence.

So Rex didn't argue about global warming at that meeting.

But tonight as he and Mickey go along in the truck, windows down, T-shirt sleeves flapping in the weird hot watery night, Rex says, "Once

* High Frequency Active Auroral Research Program.

the caps are gone, we'll heat up fast. You know how it is in the spring around here once the snow is off Mount Washington."

Mickey nods, his eyes on the red-but-not-presently-flashing volunteer firefighter light on the dash. Mickey feels spooked. Rex's grave voice speaking so out of the blue on the subject, and yuh, the weird not very Septemberish heat, and the creaking night bugs that sound like old souls, old souls that have special foresight to *know* they are about to be cooked into crispy end-time questions marks. And then there's Mickey's knowledge that he and Rex are headed up to the Lancasters. Willie Lancaster. One of the guys in Rex's militia.

Soon they'll be there.

Mickey almost sighs audibly, but instead releases a huge breath very slowly. And silently. And privately.

Willie Lancaster.

He breathes again. In very slowly. Out. Very slowly.

Rex is driving with one hand, feeling his sprawling-along-the-jaws dark mustache with the other, the glow of the new-truck gauges on his face.

Rex has been getting nervous lately about his computer. He says Echelon is for international spying and Carnivore is for spying on patriots and Earth First! types and Indians and Black Panthers . . . "basically anybody who, in the political sense, is out of diapers." Mickey's ears perked up on this as the words "Earth First! types" sounds like environmentalists to him and he knows this is where Doc would leap in to say his thing about hanging "Earth First! types" or "boiling them in oil" if he were here now. Rex seems more worried about the US government than anything else in the world. He uses the words "aggressive spy agency" three times.

Mickey knows Rex hates to be watched. Everybody has their thing. With Mickey's mother, it's spiders. She's quiet all the time until a spider gets on her sweater or pant leg and then she is not quiet. Willie Lancaster hates to be "caged" (and this spring he got to be in the Cumberland County Jail for a few hours). Mickey hates to be surprised. Not even little surprises. Big surprises sort of paralyze him. So of course he hates being around Willie Lancaster who is out-of-control-in-your-face-all-over-the-place. But tonight Rex has a message for Willie.

The message is about the Virginia militia guys coming up to Maine for the Preparedness Expo in Bangor. Rex wants this message to go to Willie in the in-person style. Not that he's carrying big secret plots or anything. He just does not want "ears" and "eyes" that have not been invited. Rex calls spying on citizens "un-American."

According to Rex, the mail is okay as far as getting through unsearched but not dependable (in the way of diced and chopped and swallowed by the post office mangling machines). "It's like taking your letter or package and throwing it in the road." Everybody has a few P.O.-mangled-their-mail stories.

They pass Gordon St. Onge's farmplace, which is dimly lighted like some spacecraft. Or the gauges in an old model car. Aways after that, up the hill, they pass the dirt road, which, if they turned in there, goes through some swampy woods, then up through the open fields of the St. Onge Settlement, totally unseen from this road. And somewhere beyond the fields, beyond the Settlement itself, up behind the Quonset huts and pens and sheds, is Mickey's secret tree house.

All the guys of the Border Mountain Militia think everything for Mickey and his brother is all lovey-dovey and hunky-dory. But Mickey's secret reality is the tree house, and the spiders that have moved in there with him. And the near frost of certain nights.

Another piece of a mile on this tar road, which nowadays is called Heart's Content Road, though it *was* Swett's Pond Road for years, is the Lancaster place.

Mickey breathes slowly in, slowly out.

The smell of Rex tonight is not just fabric softener but a minty gum smell, and now and then Rex's jaws work, then for awhile he just holds the gum somewhere in there.

Mickey has his usual unwashed smell. And his ponytail is so yellowy streaky dirty it has the look and texture of a big worm. Tree house accommodations are limited. Not that Mickey had ever been like Rex, who is clean in every way. Clean food. Clean body. Clean ideas. Wedding ring but no wife. Rex's wife is bad, ran off with some other guy, got a divorce. Rex is good, Rex stays faithful FOREVER.

Rex was in 'Nam. Rex does not talk about 'Nam. Rex doesn't talk about the wife. Rex is about fifty, Mickey guesses, close to it. Though there's never been a mention of age by Rex, no birthday cakes with fifty candles or jokey cards around Rex's house, no "over the hill" black balloons.

Now in the road, standing broadside and staring at the oncoming grille and twilight-time parking lights of Rex's truck, is a smallish short-haired mostly white rangy mash-faced curl-tailed long-legs-in-back short-legs-in-front no-collar free-as-a-fruit-fly dog on his way back to the Lancasters from another mission of beg-borrow-and-steal at the Settlement.

Rex goes for the brake until the dog steps aside. Rex's face with the heavy outlaw mustache and pale eyes is as unchanging as a cement wall. And no cusses. Rex never reacts to anything. Almost never. Well, Mickey has seen quivers ghost-thin along Rex's jaw concerning Willie Lancaster and another militiaman being in the *Record Sun*, reportage on Willie's detainment after a disturbance in a bar, no drink involved, "just idiocy," although Rex has confided at other times to Mickey that Willie is smart. "He's smart. And he's a problem."

And then Rex's other Willie-related jaw quivering, the bright bird-chirping day when Willie left the militia meeting in Rex's kitchen to climb up onto Rex's glassed-in front porch to lie in wait, flat on his belly, for the carload of Jehovah's Witnesses working their way through that part of town. He landed squarely midships of their little group with a ghoulish shriek.

No one was hurt.

This is a standard Willie Lancaster stunt, often while he is bare naked. But what irked Rex the most in the barroom scene and the leaping among the Bible ladies scene was that Willie was in full Border Mountain Militia uniform, the BDU* camo jacket with mountain lion patch, the pistol belt and pistol, the works.

Mickey remembers most clearly of all how none of the JW ladies in their dressy shoes and mid-shin skirts and churchy sweaters screamed. They just launched smilingly into their thing and pressed a *Watch-tower* into Willie's hand and everybody else's, all the other guys who had burst out from Rex's kitchen upon hearing Willie's wounded animal shriek.

* Battle dress uniform.

But Jehovah's Witnesses are probably experienced in surprises. One of them especially had that look-you-in-the-eye warmth without a flinch in her posture, though her eyelids batted on each word of her questions as if to make it clear you had nothing to fear, that she was not going to hurt you, heaven forbid. She even reached to touch Willie's hand once, to maybe steady him as she spoke of the coming times.

Now at the top of a grade, there's an opening on the left, a treelessness, and there's a lot of pink light on the garage side of a modern-type house. This is the neighbor across the road from the Lancasters. A retired schoolteacher and her son who pretty regularly call the sheriff on the Lancasters to try to make the Lancasters be quieter, to have less barbecue smoke, less music, less roaring idling engines, less Willie.

There on the Lancaster side of the road are trunks of pine trees, really huge and rising way up into the night. A few of these trees are as big around as small rooms. Looks like just trees at first if you weren't accustomed. As Rex slows his pickup and eases to a stop behind an old rug-covered snowmobile, the dim purply-green light of a TV flutters over the closed drapes of the Lancasters' mobile home deep in the trees.

Usually a few more of the short-haired small mongrel pug-faced white-with-spots dogs can be seen hurrying outside through the dog door located at the bottom of the larger human door of this mobile home, three or four of them, dogs with earnest ways. But it's too dark out there now to tell what is moving around.

Rex steps out, presses the truck door shut.

Mickey gets a cigarette ready in his mouth before he reaches for the truck's door handle. *He's smart and he's a problem.* Mickey feels those words are skimpy compared with the can't-be-measured lightning bolt fact of Willie Lancaster.

Rex starts ahead.

Mickey knows that there is a lot more to the Lancaster residence than you can see here at night. More vehicles. More buildings. More stuff.

Rex moves slowly along the path, his military boots scrunching twigs.

Willie's shop is totally dark. The five-story pink rocket-shaped house a few feet beyond there is where Willie's daughter Dee Dee and her husband Lou-EE St. Onge live. That place is pitch dark, too. And there's another mobile home that is "connected" to the lighted one by a little trellis thing. This smaller trailer serves as bedrooms for some of the Lancaster teenagers. Meanwhile, a few small bands of light from the neighbor's house make it through the Lancasters' mighty pines.

Mickey sees the recent memory of Willie's face in his mind's eye. Willie with his gray eyes, not steely and gray like Rex's, but *sly* and gray. And there is Willie's brown Jack the Ripper beard and his teeth, which are sort of bucked.

Right in front of Mickey now is the vague shape of a portable chipper and a flatbed truck, which Mickey knows has these words on the doors: WILLIAM D. LANCASTER & SON/LANDSCAPING AND TREE WORK. Another determined slash of pinkish light from the neighbors causes part of one fender to glow.

Something touches Mickey's pants leg. He gasps . . . audibly. He can sort of make out a white dog down there. Now he hears it panting. And sniffing.

Rex is there on the low step of the dimly lighted trailer. Rex is saying a soft, "Hey, boy" to another dog.

Now he is knocking on the trailer door. Two authoritative, hard-but-brisk thwomps.

Mickey pulls relief from his cigarette, his lungs translating the smoky message of tobacco to his soul.

Rex knocks again.

Yes, sometimes Willie answers the door buck naked. Especially if it's hot and there is a bunch of guests he can torment with his naked antics. There is often a crowd of guests at the Lancasters'. Though the Lancasters *themselves* are a crowd. Sundays especially are chaos.

This is not Sunday.

"There's *someone* here," Rex says in a low, patient way.

Mickey smokes and waits.

Rex knocks harder. Mickey can hear Rex's jaws working the gum in a calm businesslike rhythm.

FLUMP! There it is perfectly in front of Mickey, that is, between Rex and Mickey. A face that floats. A grinning head hanging by a string from the sky.

Mickey has grabbed for his cigarette in his own mouth, for some reason . . . but "Urmph!" the hot red cigarette eye burns the top of his hand.

He can tell Rex has turned. But he can't see Rex's face. Burned hand hurts, but now Mickey's heartbeats hurt, too.

Mickey puts the fuzzy features of the floating head together. It's Willie, of course. Willie who had plummeted from one of the majestic pines, Willie in a dark work shirt that had been mated with the dark yard. Even now the face seems extra-dimensional, the big frozen somewhat bucktoothed grin, the Jack the Ripper beard, the eyes that love fun.

Mickey's T-shirt is sunshine yellow with *Q-City Engineering Conference 1992* on the loose flapping chest. *Always* his T-shirts are oversized.

No one says anything. Rex reacts to this FUN with accelerating grimness.

Willie moves in closer to Mickey.

Willie's hand is pushing an object into Mickey's hand. Mickey starts to recoil, just as he had that first time he met Willie and later when, as a gift, Willie had held out the service pistol which is now Mickey's treasure.

Oh, yes, Willie must know he terrifies Mickey. You can just tell, Willie LOVES Mickey's fear.

Now Rex speaks matter-of-factly, "You hear anything from Davis?"

Mickey rolls the object in his hand. It's a big plastic bottle. He realizes what it is now. Last meeting at Rex's place, Willie had said he was ordering something for Mickey from a vitamin company. He is always rattling on about the deals he gets on health stuff, especially colloidal silver which he says is good for everything except killing crabs. Then he always laughs diabolically. He called the stuff he was ordering for Mickey "Saint something . . . something wart." He claimed it was "good for depression." He said, "Losing your little brother would make you weird . . . which probably explains why you're weird." Then he was cackling again, his buck teeth jutting out.

Mickey had corrected him. "It's my nephew."

"Whatever," Willie had snorted. "It's war, George." (Willie always calls Mickey names like George.) "You know? A war is on us. And you got shell shock." He squinted at Mickey as if to size him up. "The medic will deliver!"

And he had said if it worked for Mickey, made Mickey sleep better, he'd order him more. How did Willie know Mickey couldn't sleep?

Mostly no sleep since his brother Donnie kicked him out. It wasn't Jesse's death that cut into his nights so bad. Once Jesse was dead, there was no anguish for Jesse. Dying, done, all gone. It was before Jesse died and Mickey still lived with the family and would wake in the night to the little guy's shrieks or Donnie and Erika fighting over Jesse's dying . . . or those silent nights when Jesse was drugged up and quiet.

Donnie, Mickey's brother. Donnie, shithead. The echo of saying, "Go away" over and over and over, a hundred million times all night, no sleep in the tree house, squeaking tree, silent spiders, a feeling of heaviness, of rottenness, of the brother-voice saying, "Go away."

Mickey gone but alive.

So Willie Lancaster does this nice thing, orders the stuff and here it is in Mickey's hand. But why can't Willie do this nice thing like everybody else? Why does he have to scare the shit out of you first?

The voice of Mammon as it watches Duotron Lindsey International's chief executive officer, Bruce Hummer, standing before the network mikes as he announces another 55,000 layoffs at the Guston, Wisconsin, plant.

See the stocks! Rise. Rise. Rise. Rise. Rise. Rise.

Bruce Hummer, CEO of Duotron Lindsey International, in the night, awake and thinking about growth.

You hear it everywhere now. They say the CEO of a corporation needs to be socially responsible. How?

Dear people, put your ear against the wide sky and listen. Hear *THE G-WORD.** Feel the hard G of that word. Talk to it. Ask its conscience.

My compensation package is just one small (relatively speaking) fragrant flower of the corporate universe.

Who am I? Just one CEO. Just a cocky-looking but shy strategist with styled hair who obeys the laws of this sky-sized entity. He who

---

* Growth.

does not obey this tidal wave dear soulless master will be placed outside the wall. And waiting in line to replace him, a thousand thousand more. And behind them, a thousand thousand thousand more, spiffy and speedy and harder in the bones. And behind them an endless river of more, evolved into a butter-blur of no hesitation.

Duotron Lindsey International's CEO Bruce Hummer, on yet another corporate jet circling yet another significant city, in plenty of time for a significant meeting, now reading a paper from his last hotel. His eyes widen at the headline of an incidental AP piece with the dateline: Egypt, Maine. He looks around a moment, then looks back at the article, reads every word.

And now on his face, a smile like residue.

One day in the Settlement's mail, routed from several feedbagsful to Gordon's desk.

My dear Gordon,

Come. I need your help. Might you indulge this old woman in a little coup de main? Remember that essay you tongue-in-cheek sent me a couple of years ago about Maine: Terra Onde de Mala Gent!? We need to talk, dear friend. Call me tonight if you can.

Love, Janet

PS:

I read yours and Bree's Recipe with great interest. Who is Bree? Tell me all about this heavenly person.

History (the past) 900 BC. Ancient Mammoneers speak.

Here they come, envious low men and their familiars. They intend to climb our walls. See it in their eyes, envy and cunning. Softness won't stop them. They are not as human. They are the sons of goats.

From a future time, Cory St. Onge remembers.

I was just fifteen years old back then, almost as tall as he was . . . yeah, I mean my father, Guillaume St. Onge. And I was getting the build. So we were two of those who were the muscle on the road crew . . . along with two pairs of red Durhams . . . heh heh.

Okay, and so we usually worked the haying crews, too. He was at the mills more than I was . . . rough, planing, and shingle.

Also keep in mind that the wind turbines and power lines and boosters needed a lot of human touch, so there we were, Johnny-on-the-spot. Gordon's cousin Lou-EE was our best climber, though he had what some guys here called "the slow disease." I mean, he just really was a slow guy. Same age as Butch Martin. But slowww, like a geezer.

In winter we all had a hand at shoveling and plowing snow but Butch Martin was an ace ox driver so in the warm weather he was doing a lot of plowing and harrowing fields, and we had an ox-pulled baler, so Butch was the one who worked the gore for the hours when it wasn't too hot for oxen. If it was too hot for those ol' boys, we put the tractor to work.

Butch, he was twenty. He wasn't a brother to me by blood, more of a distant cousin, but we were planted in the same Settlement forest, so we were fitted the way saplings do, heh heh . . . and eventually had arrived at full size. He and I often went together to deliver furniture to the co-op building in Gray and we both did meat cutting and Christmas trees. Sometimes I helped him work on the Settlement vehicles, that's how we kept the old monsters stickered though I can't say they passed Gordo's standards for gas mileage. But life isn't perfect.

If you were working with Gordo on any project, he'd talk you to death. Working with Butch Martin . . . he was the silent type, but for his trusty kazoo, always in his pocket. It was how he explained himself, little tunes . . . from moody to broody to cynical humor.

Well, the big project this day was roofing the cottage for the new family . . . the Rosenthal people* . . . so there's *the roof* and it's a devil

* Don't forget the character list at the back of book. ☺

of a job where you need a tender . . . you know, to get the shingles *up*. And Eddie says, "Where's Kirk?"

Kirk, who is Butch Martin's younger brother, never signed up for dirty-work crews, but Eddie, their father, will say, "A soft body is as bad as smallpox or polio."

So Kirk gets dragged into some of these jobs and either he's huffy and grumpy about it or he's singing chain-gang songs that he makes up because he's got a mind of exceptional wit. He's an inventor, a philosopher, a scribbler, and a comedian. So where I'm going with this is it's just after breakfast and unfolding before us is a big day on the new cottage's roof. Where's Kirk? He's not signed up for *any* crews. So Eddie Martin says to me and Butch, "A soft body is as bad as leprosy. Go get Kirky and save his life."

From a future time, Butch Martin remembers.

So, um, it was after breakfast. Gordo and John and Oh-RELL and my father, Eddie, were setting up the staging at Silverbell Rosenthal's cottage . . . Silverbell, that's what her name was . . . I hadn't even seen her. She was *mysterious*. She *sort* of didn't exist. But her kids . . . Eden and Bard . . . *they* existed. They were twins, about twelve, both quiet but not afraid to meet your eyes. Small permanent smiles. Like cats.

Cory and I were on a big search for my brother Kirk. There's Evan and there's Kirk and there's me who sprung from our parents . . . that's my father's word, sprung . . . "sprung from the loins" he says . . . whatever.

My mother is cousin to Gordon so there's a little relation to Cory . . . but you'd swear Cory came direct from Princeton, the part of the reservation where his Ma Leona sprung from, and Geraldine and Claire . . . all cousins. And Cory had this thing at that point with his hair, parted in the middle, tied back. And he was going to wear out his BDU camo jacket with the blue-and-gold shoulder patch that featured a fir tree with the words in a crescent: HOSTILE INDIAN. The camo jackets were for special occasions, meetings, and such . . . I had one, too (no HOSTILE INDIAN patch), but I didn't wear it to the furniture co-op, Bean's Variety, and the town dump . . . nor to do a roofing job. Cory was like Gordo in that he was one to draw your eye even without efforts. But he wouldn't leave anything to chance. Anyways, Cory, being only fifteen, saw no danger in "the extra mile" it took to step dead center of *the big eye*.

Some kids said they'd seen Kirk helping with the compost bucket brigade crew. This is taking the buckets out of the bathrooms . . . buckets of shit, piss, sawdust, and peat . . . and they get dumped into the bins you layer with chopped-up old leaves or straw and it turns to soil. Good soil. We've had it tested a bunch of times. Moisture and the oxygen that lies between the carbon of the straw and the nitrogen of *the stuff* . . . it makes heat. And the microorganisms feel like they are at the beach . . . ha ha! . . . no, actually, they go to war and they compete . . . *just like humans* . . . and that makes the whole thing work. And I guarantee you, my brother Kirk was *not* helping *that* crew.

Then Bonnie Loo said he had mentioned going up to the windmills with the battery crew. I wiggled my eyebrows at Cory. He wiggled his back.

One of the old guys on the first piazza, all of them playing poker with actual money, said Kirk was splitting wood with the firewood crew up near the mills. Was this some joke?

Whitney St. Onge, from a future time, remembering.

Uh-oh. We were caught. I didn't glance at my coconspirators but I'm hazarding a guess that Rachel looked abashed. There we were all clumped around one of the typewriters in the print shop doing THE DASTARDLY DEED. And there in the doorway were Butch and Cory looking big and brutal, eyes on Kirk who stood beside me, pen in hand. Kirk always had a way of standing so straight his back was arched. In those days he wore a tiny fashionable, though out of fashion, pigtail in his otherwise trimmed brown hair. So, okay, he was out of fashion but that was Kirk, a true nonconformist . . . you couldn't even call him *that*, because nonconfirmists always conform to the *new* difference. Kirk was nobody's mirror image, just that maybe he inherited your basic weird character genes from his dad, Eddie Martin.

Meanwhile, Butch was your standard hunky redneck guy to look at him, walnut-color eyes, dark hair that was not long, not short. He was dusky-skinned from working in weather and from Lorraine, his mum, who was of a dark look and yet an unremarkable look. Also for Butch no weird bejeweled doozied-up belts like his father's or flashy print bow ties and blinding orange or pink dress-up shirts as his brother Kirk often wore. And the middle son, Evan, just a plain guy but not as hunky-brawny as Butch. Evan possessed more gawk. He had a rough time with acne and scarring, almost a burned look across his long face. But Evan was not in the print shop that day, and not in the doorway closing in on Kirk.

"Well," says Oceanna, kind of sidling nearer to me to block the view of what was in the typewriter though everyone knows Butch is dyslexic . . . quite so . . . and doesn't read. But she obviously feared Cory's dark ranging-about eyes because obviously he and Butch, too, were picking up on our vibes.

Meanwhile, Bree was standing over by the old monster printing press's alcove because she was in love with the thing and took every chance to fondle its curves so she *seemed* not to be central to us and THE DEED.

Well, they got their man and bullied him away to the roof job and the rest of us all let our breath out simultaneously because THE DEED was still perfectly on course.

By the sea.

Janet Weymouth, of old money, enounces her words in the accent of old money. Married to more money, she is a patron for all, assuring them of their heart's content, and so she would be as visible as the full moon in the black night of this room, *if* it were night.

Not quite sixty-five, slimly tall and straight, yes, a book would balance on her head. Always speaking hushed, taking you by the wrist. Her eyes float toward you as a destination on a vast plain when you are speeding toward it as a helpless passenger. So circumscribing those blue eyes, the eyes of a kindly spider, one who quickly wraps you in favor.

Short hair. Dark blond, not a flicker of gray. Gray has been banished. Breath neither mist nor cloud, more like peppy child-ghosts. And there is a fragrance from her body you'd never sniff on anyone else. Something priceless. Like tall heated grasses and wild roses by the cold sea. Oh, yes, of course, she lives by the sea. Or is she *of* the sea? Her occupation of any sort of space lacks foot scuffs, heavy rustlings, thumps, and clomps.

And see for this occasion today she is wearing a dress of Mother Earth blue. She has many other blues, such as sugar blue, clarion blue, tropical blue, blue of realization, temple blue, blue of frolic, blue of beneficence, blue with the merest flutter of silver, blue of contrition, trick-the-eye green-blue, blue of the last waltz and the peacock and the dragonfly and permafrost and blue moons and bluebells, whole blue, horizon blue, ever-blue, steep blue, Eden blue, jay blue, breezy blue and hurtling blue and blue sprite. And all of those blues match her eyes perfectly!!

Yes, now Mother Earth blue for Janet Weymouth who is mother of this day. Although she is not one of the organizers. She just appeared at one of the final planning meetings and all who were present bowed down.

So what is this day about?

Republican governors have come to Maine for a huddle about block grants and thus more than thirty governors' wives are being entertained by "the committee," which includes, among others, members of the Maine Historical Society and Maine Arts Commission, the Chamber of Commerce (of course), and some significant representatives of education, media, and Maine's Republican Party (of course).

When Janet Weymouth had warmly suggested to the committee that her friend be invited to speak to these thirty-two governors' wives, she said only: "My friend is the many. He is the tableau vivant of all hope and possibility." And yet there was even more mystery in her lack of additional remarks on the speaker's qualifications. But her wishes being always their gladly obeyed commands, they consented.

So much is at stake for some of them here, thus there are a few cramps of unease behind some of the perfectly constructed smiles.

A bus carries the governors' wives from their hotel to this reclusive site, the Dumond House, a stone mansion, sometimes open to the public, a museum by the sea, high on a rocky point, a lot of floor-to-ceiling small-paned windows and stone paths winding through the gardens of tiny sylphlike flowers.

Janet Weymouth's own home is less than a mile from here, similarly situated on rock and pulverized sand and bobbing, almost giggling, with wee late-summer flowers.

A solid step is placed beneath the open door of the bus. Security men in black funereal suits swarm. Down step the wives, high heels or nearly high heels on every little or large pair of feet. They are dressed in tans, grays, summer pastels, one daring red. Although their faces are varied, heart-shaped, round, long and bony, middle-aged and young, dark and light, and their souls like all souls are gaseous, free, and frisky, they deploy identical gestures and smile the same smile, perfectionists of professionalism, prisoners of their own ascendancy.

Now they are herded preciously into the main parlor and settled in with their coffees and teas and gay hors d'oeuvres. And there is a lot of small talk. *Profoundly* small.

Eventually, someone whispers of the arrival of the speaker. But who *is* the speaker? The name has been omitted from the program.

Now being ushered in by hosts is a rangy group of people which is NOTICED by everyone here. Mostly kids, some three-if-they-are-a-day having to be pulled along by their chubby hands by women and adolescents, and lots of kids of the wiggly five to eleven ages marching along with purpose.

Most of the kids carry voluminous satchels and they are a confusion of races, pink, golden, and brown like a politically correct advertisement for RVs or unlimited long-distance telephone service.

Look closer, see that long-legged golden-brown child covertly studying the seated governors' wives, her eyes behind two pink heart-shaped lenses with white plastic frames. Her dazzling yellow sundress is too short, the heels of her clogs are too high as she weaves and wags along with one hand spread at her hip. You'd be reminded of a fashion model on the runway or an MTV star but she couldn't be more than seven.

Another youngster, this one teen-sized though it's hard to determine the sex with such thin patchy hair, a lot of scalp, the face and arms and hands mottled with sores. Well, he seems to be a boy. Something about his ambling gait. Bushy pants have stylish tucks. The shirt an old-timey French workingman's smock in a coarse brown fabric.

But even more unfortunate is one of the adolescent girls whose greenishly-gold eyes have an unnatural feline distance between them.

She is nearly six feet tall. She wears a handsome emerald green dress. Her hair is long tortuous crayon-orange curls and ripples. She hefts three pregnant-looking satchels. On her feet are tall lace-up logging boots and tall thick brown socks.*

Now here comes another almost six-foot gal, large-framed, late twenties (thereabouts), carrying a threeyearold (thereabouts), both woman and child having fountainlike topknots of dark hair, the woman's streaked with brassy blond-orange. Eyebrows shapely, eyes too glittery, obviously contacts. But the dress! A black T-shirt material and no bra. Breasts like two heads. Nipples like two noses, though not as big as her actual nose, which is significant. And what are those things dangling from her ears? Spray-painted acorns. Only slightly less tasteless than bottle caps.†

The child she totes stares with suspicion at the garage-door-sized stone fireplace with decorative birch "logs" stacked in its center.

Several teen girls in long skirts of the same coarse brown fabric as the afflicted boy's shirt cluster around the redhead, swinging more fat satchels. Embroidered kerchiefs keep their hair back. No jewelry. All wear moccasins and socks.

Something about this group. Almost biblical. Like thieves and lepers and whores and shepherdesses. *Fascinating*.

Now along comes a short, rotund woman, her dress professorial, gray, and tasteful. Like many of the tykes, she has the dark Passamaquoddy eyes (the governors' wives would say "indigenous"), encircled in the woman's case by the steel-rimmed lenses of old-timey spectacles. Her hair, slightly graying, is in a braided bun. She wears a plain silver wedding band. Her taking account of the dozens of VIP faces does not waver. To her they might be nothing but print on the pages of a history too far back to hurt anyone now . . . maybe the Cleopatra years. Or the Stonehenge days. She herself is about fifty, her eyes, yes, as black as the future into which this castle-weighty event is already wobbling on into eventual myth.‡

* This is Gordon's neighbor Brianna Vandermast.

† This is Bonnie Loo St. Onge.

‡ This is Claire St. Onge.

Shuffling past the security men in black are more tykes laden with lumpy satchels. More teens. The eyes of the security folk seem enchanted by the satchels.

Last but not least, a six-foot-five-ish, age fortyish man with a tigerish and yet oxlike heavy way of carrying himself, the tallest man in the room. Wears a spotless bleached chambray work shirt under a lopsidedly knitted black sleeveless cable-knit sweater. Dark green work pants. Worn work boots. Lots of keys like a janitor. No wristwatch. Beard trimmed, lightly grayed on the chin, but a dark heavy mustache. Noticeably pale eyes with dark lashes. One eyebrow raised. Like a misgiving. As if he is in the wrong place. He, too, eyes the overloaded satchels toted by the kids. He must not be privy to the meaning of the satchels. For sure, he himself is not schlepping one.

Now Janet Weymouth of the old money and blue dress and cloud-sweet breath steps from another table and instead of her usual wrist-grip, places her long arms all the way around this man and, close to his ear, whispers.

And he grunts like an animal.

She releases him. She is now flushed. She spins around and introduces him to the people at her table, all the while gripping his wrist.

There is, among the thirty-two governors' wives and their bodyguards and twice as many hosts, a subtle disturbance, nothing visible yet, much as a field of tall weeds ripples when a short-legged browsing critter moves through it. You can't see the animal. You see just the grasses and flowers being bothered.

The invisible blood pressure gauge in the air is rising, members of "the committee" are still smiling, though, and a man with a high cheery voice takes a few moments to play with the mike at the lectern, then welcomes the prestigious visitors (the governors' wives), generously thanking certain groups for their hard work, tells a harmless joke, and after a whispery moment with Janet Weymouth, introduces the speaker, "Gordon St. Onge, historian, educator, and theologian," which causes the tall speaker in his work shirt and sweater vest to turn questioning eyes on Janet Weymouth, now three tables away. And she smiles a sly smile, winks. And then after a little more introduction, there's a lot of nice applause as the speaker steps up to the lectern and yanks on the mike to bring it up to his level, though he still has to lean down some, which gives him a sensual crouching intimacy with the little lectern.

Two men of "the committee" are murmuring with the black-suited men near the door. "Yep, it's him. The right-wing separatist with all the guns and wives."

The speaker thanks the introducer, awkwardly and off-mike, then picks from a pants pocket a folded-up speech and then from his chest pocket under his sweater a pair of cheap-looking reading glasses.

Now he lays the folded reading glasses on the lectern and spreads and smoothes the speech with his work-thickened hands. Absorbed in this task a few moments, he finds a full water glass in the cubby under the lectern, then looks around the room . . . happily. He looks, it seems, at each and every face, his sort of weird dark-lashed, pale eyes widening, then softening, blinking with humility like some faithful, elderly, perhaps forgetful servant. The room is deathly still.

And then the lecturer speaks into the mike: "A brief history of my *home*," the word *home* drawn out in a low warning growl.

This is met by more silence. One of the governors' wives in the second cluster of tables leans forward as if to sip from her coffee but instead whispers, "Charming" to the others at her table. Her tone *could* be sincere.

Then, without looking up, the speaker says quietly into the mike, "Welcome to Maine. Terra Onde di Mala Gente." He is not smiling. Therefore, not joking. So no one chuckles. The silence has thickened into a perfect ice.

As the speaker fumbles his old-mannish-looking glasses onto his face, he murmurs into the mike, "My home is a town called Egypt, Maine. In the mountains." Now he stands there silently, just staring at his written speech squinting as if he's lost his place. The audience has allowed itself to shift a little, clear a throat or two, swallow chewed-up coffee cake, and breathe, while the speaker's youthful companions paw through satchels and pockets, zippers going *zip zip*.

The speaker sighs a sigh magnified by the sound system into an enormous sad thing. You see, he had asked one of his teenage daughters to retype his speech, but what he is now looking at is nothing he has ever seen before. He reads to himself now, not moving his whiskery mouth, moving just his dark-lashed hornworm-green eyes and a finger digging into his bearded chin absently. This is what he sees:

Brothers and sisters, sisters mostly, I am here before you, a mere redneck man. But I'm of the same species really truly as you, brothers and sisters. With a glance anyone can tell you are proud of yourselves.

You are all stinking apes but you are proud nevertheless. Your DNA is less than one percent different from a chimp's but you still hold your chins high because, as anyone can tell at a glance, somewhere you have assets and accounts obscenely bulging and all these men in black here are bulging with guns, encircling you to draw the line between yourselves and—

The lecturer stands back from the mike and, tugging off his glasses, looks through the great arched window of many small panes at the sea that is pushing sluggishly in around a deep cleavage of rocks. He does not look at the audience, just replaces his glasses and goes back to looking at his written speech, which he has yet to read from or vocally refer to in any way. He does not notice, even though there is that scratchy rustling zipping sound behind him, that the youngest kids are opening their huge satchels and anchoring onto their heads larger heads. Papier-mâché likenesses of chimps or monkeys. Obviously kids made these raw works of art. Perhaps to go with the speech? All that conspiring behind his back!

And so now the audience is laughing. There's release and relief.

The speaker is smiling broadly. Shows his crowded bottom teeth. His pale eyes watch them all as they are laughing, the governors' wives and various agency hosts. Their laughter is nice. Human and nice. He nods, although stubbornly he doesn't look behind him to see what's so funny. One of his weird pale eyes shows a spark-flash of foreboding.

Now he slips his reading glasses back on and looks at his paper where he left off and again reads to himself, then closes his eyes. Tightly. Like pain.

Detour.

Now the monkey-headed children begin to step away from their tables, barefoot. Like monkeys. Some now have armloads of three-foot-long awfully yellow papier-mâché bananas. Some are turning real steering wheels as they rush around erratically between tables and in the open space by the grand fireplace, their primate feet slapping. Signs pinned on their clothing read: American MOTORIST. There's tailgating, there's passing, *"Honk! Honk!"* One gives another the finger. Now there are crashes. Victims lie dying, moaning, some perfectly still, a stiff head rolling away under a table among VIP legs and feet.

Now with an unpleasant growl and a sign, HAMMERHEAD FELLERBUNCHER OPERATOR, a monkey steps through the bodies to the fireplace and kicks the decorative birch logs apart. Here comes another monkey with a sign: TANK OPERATOR. Another: FIGHTER JET PILOT. Lots of growling and shoving each other about. Here, dragging a length of hose, is a CHEMICAL BROADCASTING TECHNICIAN. Must be only about two years old, rear end fattened by a diaper.

Coming along next is a CARBON EMISSIONS MISINFORMATION PUBLIC RELATIONS EXPERT. Also in a diaper, he/she holds with two pudgy hands a cardboard TV with aluminum-foil-covered antennas. On the "screen" is a face with a leering smile.

It takes five medium-sized monkeys to heft a cardboard box that reads: THE WALL STREET ECONOMY, while a baby, the youngest yet, no monkey head, smilingly carries a mashed-looking *tiny* box that kitchen matches come in, on which, if you are close enough, you'd read: MAIN STREET ECONOMY.

Here comes another larger box: FRAGILE RESOURCES.

Another: FOREIGN POLICY . . . FULL SPECTRUM DOMINANCE.

HOTLINE TO THE BOMBS arrives on the scene, bread-box-sized, painted red, the letters banana yellow.

The monkeys now go into high gear, goofing around, reckless and full of brinkmanship, leaping, poking, shoving, kicking, a punch that looks real, the boxes dropping to the floor, a monkey with a sign saying ELECTED OFFICIAL and another APPOINTED OFFICIAL and many REVOLVING DOOR ADVISERs crowd around the fallen boxes to fight, poking papier-mâché eyes. The crumpled matchbox gets stomped to a more complete flatness. The bomb box and foreign policy box go skidding and careening. Bombs away!

A tall teen-sized monkey strolls into the center of the riot and holds out a fake mike into which all the brawling monkeys do muffled cooing sounds. On the figure holding the mike, a sign clearly reads: BIG CORPORATE TITAN CONTROLLED MEDIA.

Now more bananas are unpacked.

There's a serious brawl over the red BOMB BUTTON box, one monkey biting another in the arm. The box now pinwheels across the floor in a jolly way.

An ELECTED OFFICIAL monkey grabs for it. Another two tackle him/her and all land in a pile squashing this box of many thousands of nukes.

The lecturer, Gordon St. Onge, keeps his weird Macbethian eyes on the audience. They have stopped laughing, not that the security men and organizers were ever laughing. But the governors' wives had at first been entertained, though uneasily. Now they might be asking themselves, *Where is this gang going with this? Momentarily the speaker will say something that will add a positive twist to this . . . Maybe this is really a well-known theater group and Mr. St. Onge a local playwright of comedy stage productions*.

But now he just stands there fondling his temples with the spread fingers of one hand, head bowed.

Someone at Janet Weymouth's table leans over to whisper to her and she winks both eyes and pats this person's hands.

There is other whispering by those who recognize Gordon St. Onge from all the recent newspaper photos.

The security men who stand (yes, bulging with guns) at the doors watch everything that breathes and makes a shadow.

The monkeys are now in further chaos mode. One even jumps off a chair.

Gordon St. Onge has begun pawing through the pockets of his sweater vest and work pants, searching for something. He says huskily, "I was asked to do a speech about my home. This—" He now has his stapled papers in hand again, gives them a little shake. "—is not my speech. Where is my speech? There was a switch. Someone is giving my speech right now in Tanzania. Or Lone Creek, Mississippi."

Laughter explodes and one of the governors' wives waves her hands at the others . . . She is obviously this crowd's Mississippian VIP.

The speaker again slips on his old-mannish-looking specs and frowns at the stapled speech. Lifts a couple of pages, squinting, shrugs his thick sloping shoulders. Again the specs come off. He smiles beguilingly at the wives. "This is *not* my speech. Mine's somewhere."

Now lots of monkeys wearing signs that say POOR OF THE WORLD charge the pile of bananas just as Gordon St. Onge finally turns toward the fireplace area to behold the spectacle.

The FOREIGN POLICY . . . FULL SPECTRUM DOMINANCE teen-sized monkey whips out a toy rocket launcher truck and hollers, "POW! POW! POW!" as he blows away all the monkeys wearing POOR OF THE WORLD signs and RESISTER OF OLIGO OPPRESSION. Then, like a trophy hunter, he stands with one bare foot on a heap of bananas.

Gordon St. Onge eyes the men in black by the door.

A committeeman at a table near one of the doors whispers huskily to another, "This is definitely inappropriate for this audience."

The other nods.

Several committeemen farther into the big room begin to whisper, "Who the hell is this St. Onge guy? Find out."

A committeewoman overhears and whispers, "Phil says he's been in the papers . . . a radical right-wing type. Really scary."

"Right wing?" One of the committeemen forgets himself and speaks aloud. He looks across the room at Janet Weymouth. His expression of astonishment is Chaplinesque. And a small man in a brown suit, carrying a pen and rolled-up paper, walks to the table of whispering committeemen and bends to speak with them and they all nod gloomily and gesture toward Janet Weymouth's table. And the woman at the next table, who has pulled her chair closer, whispers, "Mrs. Weymouth says she's known him since he was a child . . . he has some connection with the Depaolo family."

"The Depaolos?" the brown-suited man's voice cracks teenagerishly on the name. Now he's striding briskly away toward another table.

FOREIGN POLICY . . . FULL SPECTRUM DOMINANCE kicks a very hungry-looking monkey who is crawling along on all fours and whose sign reads REFUGEE. The FULL SPECTRUM DOMINANCE champ-chimp adds more bananas to his stash as four small monkeys in sundresses, dressy shoes, silky scarves, and wigs, carrying purses, prance toward the thickest cluster of governors' wives. All but one find empty chairs and sit, crossing legs. A helpful committeeperson unfolds a chair for the extra who, once she is seated, positions a hand with a little snooty finger up, miming the holding of a fine china teacup. Some of the real governors' wives humor these imitators with smiles and friendly whispers.

Meanwhile, the brown-suited man is working his way around the outside tables of the room, visiting various members of the committee. The name Depaolo is murmured, followed by wide eyes, then shrugs, while "right-wing extremist" is hissed.

"But the message of the children borders on Marxism, wouldn't you agree?" insists a committeewoman in a suit so white it vibrates.

Gordon St. Onge abandons the rogue speech, stuffing it and his glasses into the lectern cubby with the water glass, and steps away. No need for the mike, because he is getting close, sidling closer and closer to these VIP gals. The nearest one has dark eyes and gray-streaked hair of a cut that may have cost more than brain surgery. He looks down at her hand curled on the table. Her other hand rests in her lap. Her nails are not polished but are long and shapely. He and she are now eyes into eyes as the racket of the monkeys plays out near the fireplace. And beyond them are the tall arched windows framing the sea and its deepening pulsing tide and brutal rocks.

Gordon St. Onge rubs his eyes then spreads his left hand over the chest of his black sweater vest, over his heart.

Janet Weymouth's expression is serene, her eyes are fixed on the speaker's profile. A few people have approached her with urgent queries. She has given them little pats. Little consoling pats. Then glances back at the speaker to catch his eye and when she does, she winks.

Now, as one of the monkeys drops the already staved-in red hotline box to the 7,100 nuke warheads making another discomfiting *clomp*, one of the agency hosts remarks gruffly to another, "It is said he molests little girls. His twenty or so wives aren't enough."

The subject of this matter, the tallest guy in the room, locks the fingers of his right hand around his belt near the buckle, an open, darkly aged steel square. His eyes slide from one set of VIP eyes to another, and settle on one face in the second row of clustered tables. She has nice warm eyes. Short chestnut hair.

The men in black (FBI? state police?), standing with legs a little apart in all doorways now and behind the outside rows of tables along the walls, have a tight-thighed look, a ready look. Their eyes are riveted on the speaker and his accomplices, while he, Gordon St. Onge, steps back to the lectern and stands there hanging his head. When his sadness becomes ever so ballooned in his big neck, he swallows and the mike near his face amplifies the swallow to cannon booms. He draws the palm of one hand down over his face. He jerks from the cubby the stapled speech that his kids wrote and reads out loud from the last page, "My home is in those hands." Jerks a thumb back toward the action, another cardboard box bouncing recklessly across the floor.

On he reads: "Clever species, we Homo sapiens are. How inventive! How sophisticated and complex!" He rubs the mike now with a huge palm. Spanks it. Speakers against the ceiling thump and scrape. And on he reads. Gravely. "But sagacity does not make humans *not* dangerous dumb-ass *stupid* primates. Am I right?" He gulps from the water glass that was in the lectern cubby. The whole thing. Then he laughs, one snort. His eyes smile.

Now he stands back, wiping his mustache and beard with both wrists, eyes on the audience.

"This is embarrassing," complains one committeeman to a committeewoman, both from the Department of Education.

"The world in those hands," Gordon reads. He's not smiling.

"This is quite negative," another woman says quietly.

A man in a light-blue suit sighs, looks across heads at Janet Weymouth's elegant profile.

A person at the next table says, "Think. Think about that face. Look familiar?"

Another committeeman leans in. "He's our own homegrown David Koresh." He tee-hees, then looks over toward the table where Janet Weymouth is sitting. "Funny woman, she is." Tee-hees again. Folds his arms, looking happily entertained. "She's gone *way* beyond her shareholder activism."

At the table of adults who came with the speaker, the beachball-round Passamaquoddy woman picks a stray banana off the floor and finds room for it under her table.

The tall, scary, and, yes, *infamous* Gordon St. Onge just sort of roams around. Distractedly. Stops, raises one eyebrow flirtatiously at a governor's wife who has wonderfully floofy longish gray curls. She flushes and looks down at her hands with a small smile.

Then the scary speaker walks toward other tables of upturned faces, rubbing his hands together, smiling sheepishly at three women all dressed in varying shades of rose. He does something boyish and playful with his shoulders, setting off that Tinker Bell tinkle that is his bunch of keys. A trickle of sweat looking more like a small jewel makes its secret path down under the ear of one of the governors' wives. This, even though the room is cool.

One of the committee hosts near the doorway, talking partly to himself, partly to the fellow beside him, says, "Well, well, well . . . this is certainly a mess."

"As if we needed this today," says the other.

Gordon St. Onge steps to a table, presses his knee and thigh against it as he gazes into the eyes of the governor's wife who wears the red dress, which burns like fire in the center of this room of dark woodwork and stone, window light and soft lamps, coffee, and pastel cakes. The woman might be afraid of being made to look silly by this lower-class creature and then she feels it on her shoulder. His audacious hand. She still doesn't raise her eyes to his whiskery face but looking across the great parlor space filled with faces, she smiles a good-sport smile.

The speaker leans low, almost grazing the woman's face with his dark graying beard . . . he's *that* close . . . and whispers, "You got an aspirin you can spare?"

The words "No, I don't," flutter out of her mouth with a laugh. She *seems* apologetic.

He straightens to his full towering self, squinting from the brightness of the great arched windows, and turns to another table. Here a coffee-color dress and its dignified wearer, a round-faced graying blonde in her late fifties, pearls, brown eyes, her hand beside her pretty teacup . . . saucer . . . little squeezed tea bag there. The speaker touches her shoulder because he, Gordon St. Onge, is a toucher. No one is out of bounds. A camera flash goes off from near the entrance and the speaker turns abruptly away, lowering one side of his face against his shoulder, as upper-class criminals being led (rarely) from court in handcuffs usually do. And then he makes a sudden move, which causes the security people (probably, yes, FBI) to visibly jerk a foot or elbow.

But Gordon is almost merged with the lectern, and the stapled speech crackles in his hand as he strains to see its words without his reading glasses. "My home. *Our* home. Our treasured round planetary rock. Our existence. In the hands of monkeys. I ask you to hearken to and fear this." Done.

Then he is pushing his way through the men in black and the scrambling photographers, camera light bursting behind him, and, yes, there is applause, not a standing ovation but a nice trickle, a *reflexive* civilized little clapping.

Now he is out into the late-day sun, and that gray-green vertiginous smell of high tide, down down down his boots go along the stony winding path, past the parked bus, past some wild rose dangly with hips, stops to paw through his shirt pocket up under his sweater vest, his pants pockets . . . sort of frantic . . . then you see he is crunching hard on aspirin straight from a bottle, like a drink of cheap wine, because the pain of caring too much is a beastly thing.

The Weymouths at home.

It is the home of rich people. A place so serene, so old, stone and shingles and arched windows, leaping tides and high rock with pools and periwinkles, beaches, reeds, fields, and there along the lane, trees huge enough to have scowls and to touch lofty sylvan fingertips from one side of the lane to the other. Not a lot different from the Dumond House, where the governors' wives were entertained earlier today.

Feet don't make much racket. People here turn doorknobs in ways that cause doors to seem ghostishly mechanized. With some rich people, it isn't just the stuff they own but also that uncanny silky lack of sound to their rooms and halls, to their infinite elbow room, their invisibility when they so desire, that which makes their daily lives particular to them. Where is the clatter? Where are the squeaks? Where are the bumped knees? None of that. Just an airy escape dream, one of those where having open arms is all it takes to fly.

A pony-sized but light-stepping French poodle is pleased to meet Jane Meserve, who is still wearing her heart-shaped secret agent glasses in case there is some deception needing special and high-powered vision in shades of pink. Meanwhile, the dog apparently has known the seven-year-old twins Katy and Karma St. Onge in past visits. He sits before each one and offers a gracious but quickie high five.

With all the papier-mâché heads and bananas and cardboard signs back in their satchels, tucked into car trunks and truck beds, the two dozen tykes and teens milling about in the Weymouth rooms are just ordinary-seeming American youngsters, except for, perhaps, that weedy, fruity, algae smell of Settlement soaps and salves. Among the startled haut monde at the Dumond House today there is the impression that all of these kids have been sired by Gordon St. Onge. This is not true. And yet this is not the only *uh-oh* and gasp and freighted falsehood that will follow him to his grave.

Janet explains the poodle's name. Argot. "In old France, it was the language of thieves. And the land of thieves. Their part of town."

Argot, maybe not really as big as a pony, but big as a collie, stands among all the visitors, his humanlike eyes moving from one face to another as each one speaks. All over him, his tremolite-gray puffs, so often and lovingly brushed, a dog so clean and airy it is as though you only imagine him.

Chris Butler, the teenager with the skin affliction, has open sores today, even on his lips. A lifelong torment. But also Chris is a pianist with the gentlest touch upon the keys so that the melodies flow skinless, bodiless in a majesty larger than the one thin sore patchy-haired teenager who straddles that piano stool. He is *Beauty is, as beauty does*, as they say. He is not a child of Gordon's *but is*. Because Gordon St. Onge possesses all who come to him for the sanctuary of his granite-cored hills, and his many halls and rooms, which are *never* hushy.

Chris smiles quirkily and wonders, "Does Argot steal?"

Janet laughs her velvet laugh but doesn't take Chris's wrist, though she does lean quite close and her breath is a shimmer of mint. "He did when he was a boy."

Claire snorts over this.

"Please, all sit, if you'd like, and have something." Janet names wines that sound no different from the language of thieves.

The twin girls, Katy who looks most like Leona, and Karma who has inherited the intensity of Gordon's eyes, tell of a desire to go out on the beach, and so Argot accompanies them, as well as a young woman named Eva who is in the Weymouths' employ and very, very reticent but smiley.

Of course, at least eight other youngsters troop after, Argot glancing back over his shoulder to graciously acknowledge them with two precise wags of his stick-shift, ball-ended, four-on-the-floor sort of tail.

Gordon doesn't sit. He's restless. He gazes out the broad windows. At the ocean. As if he had just today discovered it and is bewitched. He stands there close to the glass with the solid peachy-blue light of the Atlantic's high tide and the sky cast over his face and sweater vest and shirtsleeves and on his fingers that wrap around the stem of the glass that is filled with something dark red and virile-looking.

A woman who resembles Janet but is no relation quietly wheels Janet's husband in. Morse Weymouth. A man who once would, with his gray, sometimes baleful eyes, look into your eyes in a direct way. His questions were direct. That short, broad-chested, fierce man. Gone! His nonprofit environmental lobbying organization, he was its father and its stoutest funder. The project has had only small victories but Weymouth money, money so old it may have once been backed by the king of England's corporations, will never run out and so the little organization is still alive even as the man is dying.

Morse Weymouth. Since his stroke, his mouth hangs open and he breathes noisily. He leans to one side. Or is it that he *sags*? Or is it more like *sinking*? A once formidable warship in full sail, heavy with cannon, swollen with righteous wrath, coming at you over the glitter of sunny seas, now just squeaking, bubbling, groaning, down, down, down till the bowsprit is spookily unnamable, easing down through the depths, shorter, shorter, till you can see *nothing* there.

And so he does not speak and he refuses to look at anything above table legs or knees.

This is the first time Gordon has seen Morse this way. He steps from the window. He doesn't push a brotherly hand-and-wrist-grip on either of Morse's limp hands. He doesn't fake a cheery, "Howzit going, Morse?" He just goes and sits on the little footstool close to Morse's feet as if he were a big loyal dog. He aligns his wineglass bottom with a fuzzy coaster on the nearest low table and sighs terribly.

Janet makes no comment, just turns and smiles sorrowfully at Claire and Bree and Beth and Geraldine. Claire's eyes inside her steel-rimmed specs are always without twinkles, now truly just two black starless nights.

And Bree? Brianna Vandermast? Neighbor of the Settlement but she is also *of* the Settlement, fifteen years old, almost six feet tall, august among the other teens that she usually hangs out with, her admirers. Strident ripples of red-orange hair and, oh, those eyes, each honey-gold-green eye lovely but for the strained and awful distance between. That face startles persons beholding her for the first time. She is watching Gordon as he sits so helplessly near the once powerful Morse Weymouth. Yes, Morse is now just a sort of likeness of roadkill and wouldn't such cruelty cause Gordon's reason to be to accelerate? But the buttons and switches that usually set him into obsessive and thunderous motion over the sight of suffering seem to all be busted.

Through the open French doors to a sunroom, the sea can be heard best, its mighty FLOMP! and broken-glass-like hiss.

Now Bree answers Janet's many probing and heartfelt questions.

Janet asks, "Don't I know you? From *The Recipe*?" This is a reference to that lyrical political outpouring of calligraphy from this girl's pen, which once photocopied, with a dandy orange top page, Gordon had mailed to many. And maybe Janet was one of the only ones who read it.

The girl answers huskily, "Yes, *The Recipe for Revolution*. We wrote it together." Her cursed eyes again slide onto Gordon, still motionless on the footstool, then back to Janet's face, that face, how it emanates both kindness and mischief shamelessly synchronized.

Gordon's hands rest now, one on each of his knees, till he finally reaches for his wine.

Morse Weymouth's hair is thickly gray on the sides, thin on top. His orange-sherbet-colored button-up camp shirt. Big square pockets on the chest. Nothing in the pockets. No glasses on his face. He always wore glasses. Never contacts. No laserings. No vanity with him. But seems now there's nothing he wants to see. He shows absolutely no reaction to Gordon's nearness. Makes no sound but his bestial breathing. That in and out wide-awake snore.

Gordon glances at Claire and then to Bree who is now carefully listening to Janet tell about how when she was about Bree's age, she was so shy she passed up the chance of getting to know Tommy Dorsey* when he visited her father in Connecticut. Dorsey and some band members "stayed THREE DAYS at my family's home and I managed not to run into him the whole time, except at dinner, where I made not a peep. Normally if there was just our family, I *talked* and . . . oh, I had such a giggle . . . quite strident . . . and when that happened, my mother would have to discreetly pat my hand, which meant *Shut up*." Her voice softens as secrets must be ever soft, "There were half-hour stretches where I hid behind shrubs and trees outside, rather than meet Mr. Dorsey on the paths or the lawn. I'd see him and his friends out in the garden . . . was there a tulip tall enough to hide behind?" Janet giggles. "Not for someone as shy as me."

And the girl Bree with the devilish red hair and far-apart eyes giggles. Bree doesn't know who Tommy Dorsey is or was, but giggles among gigglers are hazardously infectious.

The waves beyond the windows *flomp!* and *hiss*. And the scent of the sea is a kind of whammy on the souls of the mountain-loving Settlementers.

Eventually Bree goes outside to smoke. How boyish her smoking mannerisms are, due to her years of working in the woods with her father's logging crew. Tanned, trim-waisted, with ripped-short fingernails, no jewelry or floral hair doodads. Tomboy. But the sly fire in some of her sidelong gazes always gives her away as "boy crazy."

Gordon can hear through the sunporch doors and screens Bree chattering with his daughter Whitney, also age fifteen, who doesn't smoke; and Bonnie Loo, his wife, who does. Bree is talking *a blue streak*! Small talk and jokey anecdotes, all that easy human back-and-forth spilling from Bree's lips as with Bonnie Loo's, between their sharp poofs of smoke out there on the flagstones beyond the sunporch. Bree has never talked like this with Gordon St. Onge. Not in that careless chiming way. To him she has related her radical ideas cautiously . . . and *The Recipe* . . . low and rimey . . . yes, cold . . . yes,

* Big-band leader of the 1930s–1950s, along with his brother Jimmy.

withholding. But with Whitney and Bonnie Loo and Janet, with everybody but Gordon, Bree izzzzz *warm*. Deep, deep, deep, deep down he knows why it is so.

Minutes pass.

Bonnie Loo, in her black dress and her brassy blond-orange-streaked dark hair scrambling around fountainlike from its tortoiseshell clip, is returning from another set of rooms with Janet and says, "He's not a theologian. He just—"

Janet's laugh, like thick carpet, like silent doorknobs, like sea-struck light through clean glass, rushes to each person's hearing. "My mother always advised, "'Lie all you want as long as it's not for yourself.'"

And then from his stool at Morse's feet Gordon hears Claire telling Janet, "I rode from Egypt with Gordon in his truck . . . and Chris was with us. The others were all in the other cars. We had no idea there was a hijacking of Gordon's speech in the works. I'm not sure how I feel about it."

Janet says, "The talk I expected him to do was more of an essay, sweet and earnest, lightly edifying. So maybe . . . the children know Gordon's heart better than he does. And better than I do."

Claire says nothing.

Janet adds, "Anthropocentrism is dangerous and needs some second thought."

Claire says flatly, "It seemed to be a subject over the heads of the audience."

Janet whispers, "Well, you see, it *was* about theology. A theological critique. Christianity, which has so shaped the West, is anthropocentric. It's very large . . . this . . . thing the children did. Seems to be the very thing Gordon has concerned himself with in many a discussion at our dinner table here. I don't believe *anything* was hijacked today. It was . . . scintillating . . . and right out of Gordon's soul."

Claire says nothing.

More drinks.

And then the kids come roaring in from outside with sherbet containers filled with wet jarringly pungent shells.

More drinks are offered to Gordon, Claire, Bonnie Loo, Penny St. Onge, and the other St. Onge wives on hand. And Aurel.* And even Bree and Butch and Whitney and other teens. Laughingly refused by all.

A late dinner. Two of Janet's closest friends join them. Both introduced as artists. The Settlementers have met one of them before. The food appears on the table in a stealthy way. Gordon's loud eating sounds catch a few looks. Morse Weymouth is not at this meal. Janet explains that Morse doesn't want anyone, even her, to see him *being fed*.

The chatter along the great table is, of course, of the afternoon and Gordon's "lecture" and how it was received.

"It was received enthusiastically!" Janet almost crows.

Gordon's smile is just a tired scrawl, one darkly bearded cheek bulging with marinated squab. He hasn't swallowed yet as he asks, "Was I there?"

His daughter Whitney, fifteen (not as pretty as her mother, Penny, it is often remarked, too much of Gordon's bungled expressions minus just the Tourette's-esque eye-cheek flinch), divulges, "Yes, we messed with your speech . . . but we knew you wouldn't read what we wrote aloud . . . like 'you are all stinking apes' . . . " Her freshly brushed (in the Weymouths' bathroom) blond ponytail whips left and right as she nods both ways at all the giggles and snorts up and down the silver-crystal-china-cluttered table.

"Hey," Chris Butler pipes up. "Where were the husbands of the girl governors?"

Janet covers her mouth lest she spit out oozy roll on a graceless, fully liberated laugh.

"Prowling Wall Street," one of her friends offers, this artsy friend with almost a crew cut, a long feminine neck, and earrings that must weigh as much as tire irons.

"Wall Street," a large but not very old Settlement kid, pistachio-color eyes in a Passamaquoddy face, giggle-gags, "*That's* like Ceiling Street!"

"No ceiling," murmurs Janet's other friend, she a large-boned broad-shouldered Mae West look-alike in a toned-down gray pantsuit, sitting near the boy. She leans toward his ear, "The sky is the limit."

---

* Pronounced Oh-RELL.

The nearest row of little kids along the table all nicker and snicker sagely, though they understand nothing of this joke . . . not the *depths* of it. Among these kids is a girl, eight or thereabouts, of Passamaquoddy looks but for, again, the green eyes; she has a fat lip, looking fatter by the minute. Yes, pain goes with the job of being a monkey MOTORIST.

More food, whole platters of baby birds.

More bread.

More wine.

And a light dessert of wee cookies and pineapple ice.

At last the table talk zeroes in on shareholder activism, both Janet's and Morse's passion in the last few years. "Have you read Bob Monks's latest book, Gordon? I didn't send it to you yet, did I?"

Gordon says, "You did and I read every word. Test me."

This gets a laugh.

"Bob is a man of courageous integrity," Janet almost whispers.

Gordon nods. He is pondering the stocks his mother signed over to him, the whole portfolio being only a bony malnourished wormy shadow of its former self due to his "wasting" (his mother Marian's word) his minor wealth on Settlement life and on the hundred or more denizens there. "Losers" his mother calls them, all except Claire, the only wife she acknowledges. (And his many children? Nonexistent in her bristling gray eyes, so there's nothing to discuss there.)

He glances up at Claire not far down along the other side of the table, her grave dark eyes behind those old-timey specs watching him steadily. She knows like no one else how far belowground Gordon's depressions can go. Here she is dressed in her university adjunct history/archaeology teacher clothes looking quite distinguished and spiffy even as she grows more obese every minute, it seems. But most of all, to unknowing eyes (for instance new university students'), she always looks a little scary.

After the meal, Gordon and teenage Bree are alone a few moments, poking at books in a small parlor off the dining room, books with no jackets, just the naked brawn of brown, tan, blue, green, and black fabrics; you'd expect a first edition of *Wealth of Nations* to start shivering in order to catch your eye. Books of an age so old that some have a lot of spouting on eugenics, disguised as philosophy, though nothing of the sort has ever slunk from Weymouth lips. It's just that Morse and Janet have always gotten all melty over striking book spines, unintermittent as bricks.

Bree glances through a book, *flip flip*. Mostly she inhales books. No, Bree is not yet a true Settlement resident, still a neighbor's daughter. Her roiling long red hair hides her wrongly formed face from him. She has some sort of magical *gifts* and, it is this that makes Gordon St. Onge nervous, magic *tricks*, the only way to define her effect on him, and worst of all, her influence over most of the Settlement's girl teens. How she often presses him to be a revolutionary leader, *as if anyone* could put smoke under the asses of Americans, all so schooled and TVed into blushingly low quotients on bullshit detection and high quotients on self-virtue. Or do Americans, including himself, ever so perfectly and beyond utterance or action, realize that they are in the deepest pocket of the hot gut of the oligo-spider's intransmutably web-wrapped global edifice, too total for any of us living beings to crawl free of?

And besides his being ill-suited for the ill-fated idea of being a leader to save the day, for a world on fire as we speak, if there's an ounce of leadership on the scene here, it is hers!! Isn't Bree's calligraphical and poetic *The Recipe* the reason he wound up here today via the Dumond House? Somewhere in this home Janet may have the stunning, stapled-together document propped under a soft rosy lamp.

Now Bree and Gordon stand side by side studying paintings, one a *real van Gogh*! Small. Vincent van Gogh painted in such a frenzy that probably there's enough of his stuff for everyone on the planet to have at least one. But of course, you see them only in museums or in homes such as this.

And Bree? Genius painter in her own right? Perhaps now somewhere on her person . . . knuckle crease or behind an ear . . . is a smidgen-stain of cadmium red or titanium white. His eyes graze over her nearest hand, up the wrist, sleeve, then at the blazing wilderness of her hair, which she uses, yes, *always* to hide her face from him, only him.

And so Gordon touches Bree. Spread fingers push through the hair to her ear. This, which is his nature, with everyone, friend, family, or stranger. Even governors' wives. Touch is speech. And he is a yakkety man. But Bree pulls away. Well, she giggles, then pulls away. Turns her face from him, leaves the room.

He stands alone, listening to the happy furor of his children and to Janet's lively crew-cut long-necked artist friend, teasing Janet's Mae West friend, who replies with some low sour-voiced remark that cracks up all those old enough to get it. And he hears tattling hoots over Argot tiptoeing by in the hallway with a box of waxed paper.

Gordon hears his wife Penny's voice, "Usually dogs steal *food*."

Janet's voice, "Actually he isn't stealing. He's tidying up."

All their banter soothes him. He roams into the hallway and over to the large parlor and sees the sky to the east looking stormy, the sea blackening, while across the room the west pours light of promising pink over the rugs and circle of good-natured couches and high-backed chairs.

A woman comes into the room. A woman he's never seen before. Gray-haired. Wears a sweater and skirt. She tells Gordon that Morse would like it very much if he would come down to his room and read to him. "The Bible," she says and smiles. "Now that you're a theologian."

Gordon knows this joke is coming from the Morse he always knew, the before-the-stroke Morse.

So he *can* communicate. When he wants to. And this is one of his little jokes.

But when Gordon arrives in the huge, well-lighted, yellow-walled bedroom where Morse waits in a hospital bed with a rosette-pattern comforter spread over him, there really is a Bible, a white one lying on top of the comforter, and Morse wordlessly indicates the cloth bookmarks.

Gordon doesn't sit. He paces and reads in a booming preacherly voice from the marked pages, uncommonly favored passages of war and deceit and terror and servitude, where no one is redeemed.

Back to the small parlor.

Again Gordon stands alone, communing with van Gogh. And those other paintings, some by people he's met here before. Probably somewhere in another room there's one by Vaida with the crew cut and long neck and tire iron earrings who is here tonight. But for sure, none in this room are lighthouses, sailboats, rockbound Maine coast, no stacked lobster traps or shed walls of bright trap markers, those that so many seaside homes often have in great supply.

Janet comes to him and stands, head cocked, studying him so quietly that it is only the star of blue catching one corner of his eye that makes him turn toward her. His smile is a banner, a big forced smile showing even his twisted bottom teeth.

She says gently, "I'm worried about you."

His smile tightens, now no visible teeth, sheepish.

"Something is going to come of this . . . what you did today, my friend."

He shrugs. "I didn't do my speech. Brats prevailed." Then he laughs.

And *she* laughs. "At dinner, you said they should all have their bottom ends warmed. An idle threat, I'm sure."

"Rumors are that at the Settlement they die of hard labor," he says deeply.

"Your children scare you."

He rubs his eyes. Both hands.

She says, "Your presence at the Dumond House was stunning and important and thought-provoking. It really still *was* on the theme of home as your essay would have been . . . only this was home versus nihility."

"It all worked pretty slick, didn't it?" He sighs. "Even the bananas." He rubs one eye now with a palm, eyes burning, teeth visible again, framed in dark-and-gray beard, a third kind of smile, not easily identifiable. He has so many kinds of smiles. "I still don't know who the mastermind was. That's the one who needs to be locked in the stocks."

"Your new friend Bree. I heard them talking. She's a natural stage director."

His face drains of color as if he were surprised. As if.

Janet giggles. Almost a Bree-giggle, then breathes, "Something will come of it. Really. Some breakthrough in the conservative camp . . . through the wives!"

He enfolds her in his arms and kisses her noisily twice, once on each ear.

She croaks, "I'll be deaf for a week, you brute."

Leaving.

It is dark. A tangle of ocean smells, both stinky and fragrant. Lots of windows down to catch the last of it, windows of all the Settlement vehicles that are revving up in the Weymouths' circular drive of little stones, pressed deep as cobble. It's hard not to notice how there is no one standing in the limp spread of Gordon's truck's low beams.

Gordon has a melancholy flash of the visit some of his family had here this past early summer. They'd arrived in only one van. For Morse's birthday. More adults than kids that time.

Morse was still Morse. Before sunset that time he and Gordon walked along the private beach, the twins, Katy and Karma; and the poodle, Argot, so many yards ahead they were just small guttering squeaks above the big *bloooooompshshsh* of the waves. The kids and dog reached a wild field and merged with its shadows. The two men got into the revisionist histories of American Colonial pirates. And the not-so-becoming empire building of Abraham Lincoln and McKinley and Teddy Roosevelt. And now the United States' 1990s covert tiptoeing to complement its overt bullying and bombs. So involved in their talk, Gordon was startled to see Argot walking by his side, eavesdropping. When finally they reached the field, the girls were eager to show them a milkweed caterpillar in his fine birthday-party stripes.

Karma introduced him (or her?) as Noof, a kiddie name that made no sense. But hurrah! A name!

Back at the Weymouth house, one of the quiet kitchen helpers had found a roomy jar for the caterpillar to ride home to Egypt in. The dark eyes of the twins were plashed with the baby pink and baby blue colors of the sunset that shot through the kitchen mullions as they watched Noof moving along on his milkweed leaf and they knew, with no explanation, that Noof had turned a page for them. In the coming days it would all be known.

And so when they were leaving that early summer night, Karma had run toward the open van door with the big jar against her heart.

And Morse stood smiling one of his almost Tyrannosaurus rex smiles, with a million teeth, and he arched his back, as if under stage lights, as the Settlement van's headlights swept off to the left and away. And that was that.

This time all that was worthy to carry home from the beach and fields in jars was shells and one nice black cricket, for the munching yumming-it-up stage is over for future monarchs and the party stripes are gone.

History as it Happens (as recorded by Montana St. Onge with no help. Age nine).

The people who lived at the ocean, Janet Weymouth and her friends from somewhere, were very impressed with everything I said. They also said I did an excellent job as the monkey flying the fighter jet.

The whole time Jane Meserve did not take off those stupid sunglasses with pink heart-shaped lenses and white frames. She thinks she is very sexy and gorgeous but she never *conversed*. She just kept clinging to Gordie and saying, "When are we going?"

My mother says Mata Hari* was never that clingy.

Several papers report the Dumond House event.

The *Record Sun*'s headline is:
CONTROVERSIAL SPEAKER ST. ONGE RANTS,
THROWS 33† GOVERNORS' WIVES FOR A LOOP

A color photo shows Gordon in profile standing next to a table. Two seated women are looking up at him. They look stunned. He looks vicious. And big. BIG and VICIOUS.

The screen squawks.

Oh my gawd see this urgent don't-miss-it newsy moment!! Guillaume "Gordon" St. Onge, known by many as "the Prophet," *terrorizes* a roomful of upstanding persons including the wives of governors from

---

* Spy.

† Yes, typical newspaper error.

thirty-six states. Here's a mini clip of dozens of immaculately dressed and coiffed persons in an alcove all springing aside as the glowering giant plunges through to the exit. Hear his warty marshy bullfrog-deep voice as it croaks something to someone who didn't skip out of the way fast enough. Fear in St. Onge's wake is palpable. Danger is in the air.

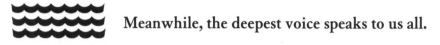

Meanwhile, the deepest voice speaks to us all.

How I'm taken for granted is a sign of my godliness, that my pull and exhalations are your true universe, heartbeat of a planet. I am the sea. All is fed because of me. All comes and goes into and out of my sweetly lathered chemistry, my pH, my open soul, my cup, my deeps.

But you, the conduit for rude change, risen on hind legs and with curious fingers, you are the dumb gear of your vaster oneness, you have crucified this rangy source in me. And so this universe of jumbo monsters and velvety clouds of the wee has already begun to blink out, one finned wriggling hungry star at a time. There will be no judgment but there will remain no sustenance. No barnacle. No snail. No fillet. No feast.

Concerning the aforementioned tip-off—

The screen is blank.

Also on the morning following the "governors' wives" affair and the Weymouth visit.

It is cool, a mistake to have set up breakfast out on the piazzas. Everyone is a little or a lot hunched in sweaters and jackets. Some shiver. The old ones in rockers and wheelchairs complain the most. Right now some are being escorted away to the Cook's Kitchen to be close to the woodstoves. The Elder Assistance crew is, as ever, directed by young Vancy St. Onge, boxy faced, wilty-haired at times, other times with tight law-and-order spit curls. Today it's the spit curls. Small languid piggy eyes with nearly no lashes. Prominent bottom lip. Square boxy body with stout arms and legs, and those double chins, all being even before she was pregnant. White blouse swaying and poofing in the currents of motion, like a sail. Always starting out the day fresh, white. But not after feeding eager-wide or clenched mouths various breakfast stir-abouts. And there is one fellow known for slugging and spitting who has two teenage bodyguards who call him Rocky and keep his quick bony fists in line but they are useless in keeping brightly colored or white or gray spits from the bull's-eye of Vancy's broad white-shirted belly. Therefore Vancy looks like an artist's palette, today specifically one used in the rendering of a battle scene.

And have we mentioned already that Vancy is a skilled midwife?

Everywhere at once! Yes, the white sail. A fleet of them, it seems, so utterly revolving are her locations in parlors, kitchens, the shops, and broad piazzas, the cottages hither and yon. All those stout brown-haired Vancys! Each one with the slim silver ring of Gordon St. Onge.

There is, this morning, the distant staccato of acorns letting go up on the side of the mountain, striking the metal roof of one of the shady cottages. There are candles here on the tables because it is not full daylight. Settlement-made candles in their Settlement-made stained-glass lamps. The smell from them is greasy-sweet. On platters and in tin pans there are loose towers of steaming second-batch cornmeal pancakes and rolls made in experimental fashion, herbed to distraction by Bonnie Loo, the mad-scientist cook.

See Bonnie Loo now in the doorway to the kitchens, a robust twenty-seven-year-old of that streaked orange-blond-black fountain of hair knotted with a piece of scrap quilting cotton. She has had to tape one of the bows of her glasses, eyebrows shapely and dark and forbidding. Her unraveling dark green sweater has loaded pockets.

Gordon likes to sit at the head of the long connected tables, though he doesn't always do this, intensely sensitive to possible resentments of other men here, old traditions felt deeply, as the eye feels a piece of grit and thinks it's a stone. This morning Gordon has taken this end-of-table seat in a heavy slow-motion way that seems full of portent. He is square-shouldered in a fresh but old navy blue work shirt, no jacket. Hair combed with a careful part. Is that a little frozen breath you see coming from his nose? He stares off at something as Settlementer Paul Lessard murmurs to him some urgent matters of their lives . . . doing the monthly water-level check on all the batteries, trouble renewing a certain permit, and over off outer Pleasant Street in North Egypt, Bob Leighton's dug well is dry. May need to put up a sign-up sheet for a tile-making, tile-setting crew and, of course, diggers. With shovels, coffee cans, and pails. Neighbors in need? Settlement helpers are on the way.

Paul Lessard is a pointy-faced, clean-shaven man with eyes of a sometimes reproachful-seeming brown and a long straight nose, a Frenchie nose, with frozen breath squirming out from it. He is stuffing a hunk of warm buttered yeast roll into his mouth. He wears a black corduroy jacket with tiny checkered flags, the race-car kind, crossed on one chest pocket.

At Gordon's right hand is Stuart Congdon of the wild red hair, sky-blue eyes, and squat broad-chested troll physique. Only about five feet tall, if that. He has just arrived, his shoes wet from crossing the field, the soggy soles had chirped like a nest of tiny robins. This chirping had made everyone turn and look at his feet. Now that he is settled, he says nothing to Gordon and Paul but starts up a quiet chat with the teenage girl next to him, one of those who will be on that plane with him to Texas soon. The Death Row Friendship Committee. This girl has a big-necked soft-knit top that shows the strap of an undershirt but she is hugging herself, her nose red, her eyes full of tears caused by the cold.

Over by the brightly lit Cook's Kitchen doorway* are two men with coffees. These are two drivers down from Belfast, one of the Maine Community-Made Furniture Cooperative exchanges, here early to pick up a tractor-trailer load of pine tables, chairs, beds, cribs, bureaus, hutches, and cabinets.

There by the door of one of the shops, a group of kids are gathered around the visiting shoemaker. They ask pointed questions about everything but shoes. Where is your car? Which cottage are you staying at? Do you know my mother? How come you hate butter? Were you fat once? Do you know peak oil? Climate change?

There by the low stage, a group of teens are setting up a few props for a quick breakfast-time skit and there are Rachel Soucier and Jaime

---

* The vast building of kitchens, shops, and parlors is horseshoe-shaped with nearly all doors opening directly onto a continuous screened horseshoe porch and all of this wraps around a quadrangle of trees and grass.

(son of a Settlementer "single dad" named Rick) with their guitars, hoping to engage everyone in a happy start-the-day sing-along.

On Gordon's plate, nothing. Not yet. He has waved away various offerings. His hands are in a pile on the table. He sees Lee Lynn arriving, hand in hand with her beautiful bright-faced toddler, Hazel. His wife, his child. His pale eyes again spring onto Bonnie Loo, her brassy, dark hair in that purple raggedy piece of cotton, that cable-stitch sweater of forest green giving her handsome olive complexion and amber eyes an autumnal magic even if her expression is as sour as a lake of lemons. It's the first morning she's cooked breakfast in a while. Her pregnancy doesn't show yet, except by sound . . . the sound of occasional retching. This will be her third baby by him. He sees up ahead a crisis coming between himself and Bonnie Lucretia Bean Sanborn St. Onge. There will be no shock. But all of life's severings do bleed.

And stepping from the kitchen are Aurel's wife Josee Soucier and six-year-old Jane, both carrying pitchers of fresh tomato juice. Jane looks regal. Dressed in head-to-foot black.

Gordon's eyes move quickly from one face to another. So many faces here to account for. And he accounts for them all. If you are not at a meal and were expected to be, he, before anyone else, will notice. The sights and sounds of the Settlement men and women and children; and the round fuzzy nearer mountain rising up blackly against the pale orange east, where the sunrise will need to claw and slog its way up through those few jam-colored clouds; and the shorn fields still in deep shadow, a deep gloamy blue; and the shorn ewes, more nappy now than a month ago; and the lambs, looking more like sheep than two months ago, all in anxious clusters near the gates and Quonset huts; and that funny little hum of two electric buggies crossing the Quad, all this a one-piece tapestry under the loving and, yes, panicked scrutiny of Gordon St. Onge's zigzagging eyes.

He leans forward now with his elbows on the table and bites at a broken nail. He hears his oldest son, Cory, pulling a nearby wooden chair out from this table, making a celebratory sound from his throat up through his teeth . . . something like reveille. All over this boy's left hand and wrist words and numbers in pen. Reminders. Which is a little bit like Lorraine Martin, who hurries past now with big notes clothespinned to her sweater. Almost nobody here at the Settlement is naked of responsibilities.

Gordon's eyes swing over toward the throaty belchy laugh of Suzie, who is married to Andy. Both Suzie and Andy have the puckery eyes of Down syndrome, but their love is as lustrous as any other couple's when they are squirming warmly beneath the weight of each other's bodies or holding hands across the breakfast table. What is there about Suzie and Andy's perfectly focused quiet fire that makes Gordon St. Onge more whole?

Now he watches with rigor and chilled soul the arrival of Jordan Langzatel from Portland. He is the nineteen-year-old from the university whom Gordon's oldest daughter, Whitney, soon to be sixteen, calls "my sweetheart," and he has come to take her rock climbing in New Hampshire today. But Whitney must tote along her chaperones: Bray, one of the Settlement twenty-year-olds; and C.C., a Settlement neighbor. This is a Settlement rule so ancient, so rusty, too utterly and totally politically incorrect, and yet Jordan Langzatel takes it and lots of other Settlement customs in stride. So far. And the Settlement notoriety? The radio talk-show hysterics? The sensational photos and TV clips *meant* to scare? And now this morning the new tidal wave of terrors over what some talk-show hosts are describing as "Gordon St. Onge getting past security to threaten nearly forty governors' wives and the governors themselves." It's the "Dumond House incident" or the "Cape Elizabeth episode."

But Whitney's sweetheart seems unfazed. Where he stands now among a group of young Settlement mothers, there's lots of giggling. Gordon studies the scene. The boy is blond. A tall, broad-shouldered critter like himself, often clowning but in the eye a dirk-like stab of seeing the largeness of the world, of the life, of the predicament. Something familiar there. Except for Gordon's darker hair and time spent on this "mortal coil," it seems Whitney's got herself a man cast from the same mold. But of course.

Jordan's hiking boots aren't new. The collar of his wool shirt is turned up. A freshman at USM. Ready to declare his major in chemistry. His home state is Nebraska. "Like being at sea only no waves and more solid," he has said with a smile. His accent to a Mainer's ear is a spider that paralyzes o's and a's. Or is it that he reverses them? This causes the eyes of Mainers to squint.

Will Gordon's cherishling Whitney St. Onge leave the Settlement someday?

Leave town?

Leave Maine?

Whitney, blond bouncy ponytail, brighter than sun through a crystal; remarkable eyes, almost Hollywoodish; and classic nose like her mother Penny's but goofy in the smiles passed on from his seed. The searching mind? His. But like Penny, love is calm, all is calm, enthusiastic but not confused. Girl at ease.

And what is she to the whole Settlement? Heavenly gift.

Here it is. The possibility. Tentacles reaching in. And restless youth makes its expeditions out. In, out. Closer, farther.

A little girl with white hair and white eyelashes takes hold of Gordon by the leg and calls up to him, "Gorgi!" and holds up her arms. This is not his child. And he is not her father. But when you are a little stubby thing whose life is measured in months and you are of a solid tribe, DNA has no dazzle for you; what has dazzle is only such matters as stout arms that raise you up cathedral-high.

Once the child is up in Gordon's lap, she stands, one foot on each of his thighs, and grips his head, gazes around his head at those who hunch miserably in rockers there in the growing freezy daylight along the shingled wall of the building inside this porch, and she has an expression a little bit like that of George Washington crossing the Delaware (the artist's version) as though Gordon were a vessel that could withstand the blackest, meanest, coldest waters.

But this is not so. Gordon St. Onge is not indefatigable, not even a minor hero, not even a mildly self-assured man. He is, as we know, filled with terrors and self-doubt. The grip of his massive arm around the little one's hips feels right to her. But he is weaving inside. Burning in shame. Feeling somehow still suspended in a certain blunderish nudity before the eyes of thirty-two governors' wives and their protectors. What was he to them but a cheap thrill, an interesting attraction, an experience they can add to their lists of trips, adventures, conquests, and purchases?

The tiger came to our brunch. He had big paws. Big teeth. He had a large litter of cubs bouncing about. He flirted with us. On his hind legs. And he had been trained to talk. He made no sense but it was amazing all the same. We'd like to have seen him dance, too, in a little circle. And to bow low. Dance, tiger, dance!

History as it Happens (as recorded by Gabe Sanborn age six and a fourth years old, edited somewhat in a hurry by Oz St. Onge age thirteen with disturbances by Draygon St. Onge age four).

Today we started an investagishon of the secret lifes of bacterias, the ones in the humanur compost bin. A bunch of us. It was wicked funny. We all died laffing exep Kirky. He had done resirch and sayd the microorganism are our anchint relitives and we are still 80% bacteria right in our sells. Called Simby Oh Siss.

When you dump the piss shit peet buckit stuff with layrs of shredded and chopt leaves and straw and othr carbns the micro guys make heat. So the big piles in the bins get condishons for fung-eyes and then the fung-eyes fix it so erth worms move in and enjoy Delishis lome.

Gordie and Oh-RELL have a place they go to for tests for path oh gins and so far so good.

Kirky says the micro guys make there heet from ~~compition~~ competition and war.

Beth sayd to notiss they doant do any musick or art or good deeds.

Bard sayd maybe tiny musick.

Kirky says the book only minshins war and COMPETITION.

The voice of Mammon.

Teachers, mommies, daddies, may I ask you a question? Is not competition at all costs the thing *you* made? Teacher, teacher, weren't "Success" and "Excellence" and "Performance" the name of every game? Higher and higher scores. Isn't winning how you taught us to define life? The gold! The gold! Wasn't I your golden child?

Claire remembering her ghost child.

We were married when I was twenty-nine and he was only *twenty*. Just a boy. But, of course, his six feet and five inches towered over my five. What quickened my blood besides our lust was that all around him wavered that edgy harassing phantasm of light, the light of a thinker, a ponderer. He was unsusceptible to suggestion. His mind was not like others, not a receptacle. It was an auger. No TV for him! He always had a serious book going slow but sure. And journals. Acres of those. And all this would fire him up into a tizzy. My darling boy chatterbox. I thought this was good.

We had a rented place in Mechanic Falls that had once been a variety store so the front yard was tarred. We had no unmet needs moneywise, if you compare it with reservation life or if you put it next to most people's lives. His mother's people were the Depaolos of Depaolo Bros. Construction, which was painted in brawny letters on the doors of the brand-new pickup Gordon had use of, all dusty from a site. Yes, the Depaolos. The ones who always had and still have substantial connections at the statehouse . . . the House, the Senate, the departments, the governor, the media, and the heavens. Get it? Endless closed-door "bids."

Gordon and I both had a thing for history, me leaning toward archaeology, all that life and death at a safe terra-cotta-and-rust distance, while he was swept away by something else, something dangerous to one's spirit.

Not to say he couldn't frolic. Before that vast and noisy Gleason and Depaolo holiday assemblage, cousins and uncles and so forth, he was a legendary clown and at job sites a legendary hard worker. Oh, boy. In that manner, familial love prevailed. Both ways. Loyalty reigned.

But when we were alone he said to me in a raspy ugly croak that I should never let myself get pregnant. He said *soon* this world would not embrace life, *soon* there would be no ice, swollen seas would swallow shores. War! No corner of the world cozy enough to be unruptured by all that is "fair in war." *Soon* much more mind control and sky control (his word for surveillance), *soon* automation of nearly every job description. *Soon* refugees would scale like hot magma every parallel and fence of the globe. No bedtime stories there.

Who would bring a little person down to *that* from the lofty sweetness of nothingness?

He was lean and had that dusky Italian-French-Indian-black-Irish skin and no gray yet in his beard. And I was golden! And I was silken! I could flash my long hair so guys would blow their horns and call "Hey, honey!!" I was *not* like what I am now. I was not fat and fifty. I was plush and high voltage. I didn't need glasses. I didn't have insomnia or leg cramps or reflux. And we were, like all young things, *very* frequently joined. Yeah, like a stirring green deep in its clay vernal pool and an immense thirsty oak root.

I used birth control. But it failed me.

These were days when Rex York visited a lot, hadn't met his Marsha yet. He was such a gentleman but this was the tail end of a couple of hard-drinking years he and Gordon had had and some wild antics I'd rather not dwell on.

Gordon always called him "my brother." Or "my blood brother."

Rex came home unwounded from the Vietnam War and its horrors and shames and from the clamor of many brothers, came home to bleed on the beaches of Maine, as the tale goes. Bikers from a planet of giants taller than Gordon in a phantasmagoria of fists, brass knuckles, nunchucks, and at least one knife were the lullaby that put Gordon and Rex to "sleep" in the Old Orchard Beach sand and seaweed and incoming tide in the late summer dark. The story ends with Gordon dragging Rex, sometimes conveying him bride-style, to the truck, a pint or so of blood left in a long razzle-dazzle trail all the way up East Grande Avenue and on and on, fuzzy on where they had left the truck.

After Marsha and that white lace and white cake, and then the baby, Glory, Rex's dignified wooden-faced self wasn't at our kitchen table so regularly, not till we moved to Egypt, where it was just a skip and a jump between us.

But that night in Mechanic Falls when I told Gordon I was pregnant, nobody else was there. It was winter. The tarred front yard was plowed wide open. The air was cold and stinging with the exhaust of passing cars. He was gripping an armful of groceries. I said I was pregnant before he pressed the truck door shut.

I couldn't see his face, just his shape in his heavy work jacket. As he shifted the bag it crinkled, some glass jars clonked. He didn't say anything. Another two or three cars passed on the busy road, headlights cold and the smell of exhaust like devil breath billowing around us.

Claire and endings.

We drove through snowstorms to both the preappointment and the thing itself. I had cried myself empty already so on these journeys I was as composed as a marine. After all, this abortion was an act of "mercy" . . . his word.

Okay, you get blood. You get hot cramps. And you get hollow. And then I knew that if I was to stay with Gordon till the end of time, I would need to get my tubes tied. Forget vasectomy. Redneck men do not do that. Not to themselves, nor to their male dogs and cats! I am sure, as I tell you this, that you will see Gordon with different eyes and your heart will be turned against him solidly now.

I, too, hate him for this. But I also hate me. It was *together* that we committed our grueling mercy.

Claire remembering how the Settlement was born.

Gordon's mother Marian? Well, her parents were from Portland. Her father's people, her Italian half . . . Munjoy Hill. Her Irish-descent mother's people were all wedged into the West End: Libbytown and Gilman Street, Valley Street, and Saint John, near the trains. But as her family's construction business grew muscles the brothers edged their way up the coast, in oceanfront properties with stone lions and wrought-iron gates.

But Marian married a power-shovel operator, Guillaume St. Onge. From "the County." He almost wept, "T'a ocean smells like a gutterrrr." He always used a lot of extra r's.

Marian countered, "The County is too far from America." Thus, the compromise! Oxford County. *Lower* Oxford County, "near America." Marian never uses extra r's. But lots of little corrosive bites were needed in the reshaping of her beloved on this and other issues involving a "respectable life."

When Gordon's papa died, Marian gave the farmhouse and 920 acres in Egypt (Oxford County) to Gordon (their only child) and to me. Marian was always warm to me and bragged me up on how I got my master's degree, saying I'd "go far in a career." She never said in that special withering tone, not even a slip of the tongue, no lapsus linguae for her, anything racist.

My family had more to say on race, Gordon's race, not in words but in the narrowing of eyes and the making of clown faces. One of my uncles always said, "All white people have new trucks. They've got no idea how it feels to keep an old shit-box duck-taped together."

And sure enough, Gordon and I would show up to visit in the Depaolo Bros. rig and my uncle Ray just sucked through his teeth and looked ever so smug in his wisdom.

When once I said, "Ray, it's *not* Gordon's truck. Gordon doesn't own a vehicle now," Ray slid his eyes over that rustless prince of a vessel and said, "Who *does* that truck belong to? Some rich Indian?"

I covered my eyes with a hand, could hear clearly his happy snivels at his quick wit.

"No," said me. "Bunch of Eye-Talians." I used the pronunciation I'd heard so often from various Maine corners. I loved teasing Unkie Ray.

Shortly after the gift of the farmhouse and land, Marian signed over half her shares in the Depaolo business, including several restaurants and all her investments in other businesses through her broker. It was scary to me. I had always imagined winning the Megabucks, for instance, to be a seat on cloud nine. But no. This treasure chest posed grand possibilities for fuckups. Not to mention *shame*, when I recall my uncle's sniff of pride in his hint that there was no such thing as a rich Indian. So what was I!!! No longer Indian??? Was I now some bubbling corpse with no heat? No handsome blood tie to my handsome (even with his several missing teeth) straight-shouldered thick-waisted Unkie Ray???

Was I now a wraith, invisible to my most dear ones except for scorn and jest? A profligate? A reckless waste, a hoarding demon?

So then Marian was up in Wiscasset (with the stink of the sea . . . ha ha!) and we were in Egypt on Heart's Content Road, which, when Gordon was a big little boy and for some time after that, was still called

Swett's Pond Road. It took only two trips with that one pickup truck to move all our stuff from Mechanic Falls.

Gordon's cousins came to live with us . . . cousins on his father's side . . . from the County, the valley, Maine's proud crown, people of that icebound river, Fort Kent, Wallagrass, St. John, St. Francis, Allagash, St. Agatha, Frenchville, Daigle in New Canada, Eagle Lake, Soldier Pond, heights and lowlands, potatoes and rocks, steep-roofed houses, priests and family and nowhere to go but the in-betweens wide open to miles and miles and miles of road like over rolling sea, not many roads, just three roads, 11, 161, and 1 of the leaning blue-green and dark deeps and full-boil blowing snow in the in-betweens . . . wind is *everywhere* there, no droopy flags, no laundry that just hangs, no rigid hairdos. There were all these cousins who spoke the patois or some of it. All these who we'd been driving up to see quite regularly, six to eight hours away depending on how fast you drive and whether or not you stop to pee.

Well, now they were here in Egypt scheming in their tight-family all-jokey way, Souciers, Lessards, Pinettes, Eddie and Lorraine Martin, and of course blood brother Rex, hovering over journals and blueprints, no room for food on the dining-room table, and whenever Gordon breathed words like "windmill" or "solar" or "the main building with quadrangle and porches" or "the Quonset huts" or "the sawmills," it was as if he were beholding a precious child, our newborn, the cutest, the smartest, the biggest, the best.

I no longer heard him rave and nearly sob against the global system of endless-to-the-end growth and its frantic hungers and machinating spooks and proxies of terror and war.

I'm not a gooey smiler, but inside I felt the sun was rising on my name: Claire St. Onge. Life could now begin. My dear one was no longer clawing the stony dungeon walls of his fears. He and I were plotting with steady down-to-earth people to raise up this bright thing, this settlement not far from Gordon's father's grave, which, by Guillaume Sr.'s request, was up up up past the vernal pool, up up up into the reverie of trees at his little bitty hunting camp almost a mile from the farmhouse. In all directions from the flagged markers at the building site of the Settlement's soon-to-be main building were such humpy little mountains where the sun would startle us most mornings by bounding like a big yellow dog through the tip-top trees, and the moon from that same cleavage was a fairy-tale spectacle, white or honey with sugar and salt stars stirring and beating about in both calm and fury.

So then here came more of Gordon's Aroostook County cousins and mine from the reservation and folks from around Egypt and Brownfield whom Gordon had grown up with or knew of. And some of these brought their aunts, unks, and grammies. And kids.

I remember our first feast on the big porch outside the kitchens, my cousins Leona and Geraldine and Carol all younger than me, Tambrah still young enough to have an excuse for being "overactive" or "hyper" as you might say, her older brother Macky telling her to "shut the fuck up" . . . well, we were all raising our hands to pledge to make a dignified life for ourselves, that we would *be a people*, that we would teach the kids, who were watching us closely from their seats at various tables, how to be a true community, because *out there* was, yes, a growing fearsome irresistible high-tech *system* with a life of its own. A life that was pathological and unstoppable, with oligarchs with no different turn of mind from those who nailed small-time thieves and other human beings to crosses to curb the annoyance of "bottom feeding" or uprisings of the same. But we were safe here!!

I watched my husband's face. He was all teeth, a big triumphant grin. He was no longer cornered by *it*. He was no longer a boy, that boy I married, practically pissing himself with despair. No, he was past that. He gave a little writhing of the shoulders, a sort of standing-in-place swagger.

Everyone hollered, "I pledge!!!"—a roar (with squeaks) of commitment, better than even our wedding vows, I thought at the time.

Then we all did a laughy screaming encore and I howled it loudest of all, "I pledge!!!"

Claire remembers more.

After six years we had a network of solar-wind-agriculture communities, mostly in Maine. Up to Aroostook, "the County," there in the St. John Valley, where, yes, wind has that constant voice, we focused on our off-Settlement projects; oh, we were on the road there mighty often. And also to Washington County where my brother Stevie and his wife organized a bunch to raise one starter windmill.

My uncle Ray gave a quirky smile when Gordon and I and Leona showed up in our old Ford with the skip in the motor and rusted cab mounts. Gordon, as you may have guessed, wasn't a Depaolo Bros. employee anymore. I was never to ride in a satiny new truck again, not as Guillaume St. Onge's wife.

Also we had people in New Hampshire we consorted with, some of them experimenting with the making of inverters. Nobody being especially efficient. A lot of breakdowns happened. But when we reminded ourselves that we were *a people* now, we saw *in*efficiency in a new way. It's not always the *done* but often the *doing*.

Meanwhile, crews were banging away on yet another and yet another cottage, now having settled a good part of open field and new cleared areas, pushing up into those shady lanes of the steep rocky woods. There would be a little private cottage for each of the families and for others. So much time spent out and about, night was a solace requirement for some and for others it meant other things. We were not striving for sacrifice for the sake of sacrifice. We wanted our cake and to eat it, too.

Gordon and I still kept nighttime residence down at the farmplace, where the only phone was. And the lights were still running off the CMP* meter that Gordon triumphed over by keeping the rooms vivaciously dark. And Marian's two cats who decided not to move to Wiscasset still lounged about in baskets of socks and boxes of newsletters or in cupboards where they were just sets of eyes.

We left the kitchen and porch doors unlocked so anyone who needed the phone could get in. On one of Gordon's desks next to the *plain black dial wall phone* was a coffee can loaded with change and I-owe-yous for toll calls. And a standing tall spike driven into a board, its sharp point up, always loaded with scrap-paper phone messages, some scribbled by small kids. Example: *gt wan bod*.

But you'd not see me there in the light of day. I was always on the fly. When not up at the horseshoe main building of kitchens

* Central Maine Power.

and Shops with crews and committees or at USM being unfruitfully employed as an adjunct, good chance I'd be up at the solar cottages, the one shared by my cousins Leona and Geraldine, or at Penny's . . . Penny was a nineteen-year-old sweetie from town whom everyone loved but she tended to be alone too much, married to old Russian novels. At that time she was trying to learn Russian phonetically and would practice on us. And we'd say some phrases or words back. Penny said in a former life she had lived near the Taiga. She remembers stone bridges, too, and some small modest blue onion-dome buildings. "I'm not a spirity person. It's just something that flashes into my noggin from time to time." Then, "Tee-men-ya-nee-ravyisya!!" Or "Mirr EE Druzhba!" And then we'd all shout it back. With Russian we felt you had to shout it. It's a deep-heart full-lung language.

Those solar cottages were out there on the sloping field, near the apiaries, clear of the woods but not far from a line of courtly old field trees. You could watch the grazing sheep and cows and two black mules from the doorsteps. You could see the irrigation ponds ruffle in breezes. And, oh, those red-orange and eerie green sunrises and sunsets that would so ceremoniously and enrapturingly scald your soul. How did we get so blessed?

Claire recalling surprise.

Our CSA project took off like a bat out of heaven, you know, where people from town could invest money or work time in the veggie crop in return for shares of the harvest. We had about fifty people sign up early on, including a group of professional-class ladies wearing cute sun hats and special gardening gloves. Many CSA folk introduced themselves on first meeting by putting out a hand to shake, as if it was a business deal, which, yeah, I guess it was. Made some of us realize how outside upper-caste America we were, that we hadn't comprehended things the way of the utility eyes-into-eyes handshake, that as rednecks we were always in a liturgy of work, side by side, a different sort of utility.

We also did farmers' markets and supplied some of the IGA's produce. Gordon got interested in town politics for a while, him and our

John Lungren who, freshly divorced, joined the Settlement in our second year. Egypt embraced us.

Gordon was, as he'd been for his uncles, the Depaolo Bros., in those big construction projects, an up 'n' at 'em worker. He hurtled into the beer and cider overly much at times and had his moods but still managed somehow to be in six places at once, hauling, hammering, digging, and wiring, all while gabbing away about the latest project, the raising of another Quonset hut (if you call mortar and cinder block "raising"), or milling out shiplap for the new sap house. Then the furniture-making co-op meetings. Or purchase of four Jersey cows. Or driving Paul Lessard's father to a doc appointment, a chance for Gordon to keep his patois polished up, since that's the only language old Reggie spoke or understood. And Gordon loved teasing kids, though he was warned that tickling could cause nightmares and saying brown cows give chocolate milk could create distrust.

Another favorite practice of his was to smooch old ladies. Or to sneak a plastic rat or worm into their apron pocket . . . even though he was warned such a thing could stop a rickety elder's heart. He was an ear feeler, a shoulder or wrist squeezer-stroker. Well, he was an obsessive fondler.

Okay, so I guess it was inevitable what I missed at first. He had, in his private firmament of sparkly nights, tall yellow grasses, and soft rooms of rugs and hand-stitched quilts, merged body and soul with my cousins Geraldine and Leona and Carol. And Tambrah who was seventeen. Also with Penny, with Steph, with Gail, with Lee Lynn, with Beth, with Glennice, with Ellen, with Maryelle, with Vancy, and, later, more. They would never see him as I had, the sometimes sheepish boy with the dusty new pickup truck and big construction outfit lettering on the door. His bewilderment. His overt terror. He would always be to them the sun in the center of the Settlement galaxy, a man of miracles, their rescue from the frigid, calculating, nothing-is-sacred handshakes and move-over-buddy outside world.

Claire tells us of the detour.

When I caught on to his betrayal of me I said to him in a voice as calm as burned toast, "Don't ever touch me again."

I fetched me a lawyer. Divorce time. "I don't want any of the St. Onge land or investments," I sniffed. "Just a big fat clean divorce."

Gordon made a few scenes but when I threw a dining-room chair at him and his chin deep in the dark forest of his short beard squirted blood down his shirtfront, he stopped looking into my eyes. He saw, I suppose, time unwinding backward.

Still in the future time Claire dredging up the memories.

After the divorce I lived with Sonny Estes in East Egypt Village. Two years. Sonny was a good man, steady, sturdy. He gave me little presents. He liked buying things for me. He'd blush as he'd lower the little box or bag into my keeping. He worked for the state. Road crew. Union man. He knew and understood the dark history of a pre-unionized past. He wasn't "gullablized," as he called it with a shake of his head, by all that deep steep pro-corporate bullshit that had bubbled all around him since his boyhood in good old Republican Maine. I was proud when he murmured some nugget of organized people's triumphs that he managed to locate and took so to heart. In this way Sonny was a flag-loving patriot . . . yes, flag on an aluminum pole in his dooryard going *clang!clang!clang!* in the wind.

In Sonny's hands being drawn down the pole and folded up preciously each night, the damn star-spangled thing didn't seem to me to be so ugly.

Sonny wasn't rich but not on the edge of poverty-terror, either. But he was generous by nature. And his family sprinkled around the area, parents, two grandmothers, sisters, cousins, and such, were mostly pretty sweet people. Gentle.

Meanwhile, back at the Settlement, all those women now knew about each other and there had been some brawls. Tambrah went after Lee Lynn with a fist, bruised her enough so that even Lee Lynn's most potent witchy remedies couldn't stop her own tears and little gasps that went on for days after the onlookers hauled Tambrah off the crouching victim. Tambrah drove Maryelle away with just the look on her face, Maryelle never to be heard from again.

Then, back in East Egypt Village, Sonny, though soft-spoken, could get raw and growly when overtired. So the lid would open in his sweet-ruffled-brown-haired head so you'd hear what he was really thinking. He said, "You're getting fat," and I was, yes, getting pretty chunky. I went inside myself into an awfully chafed place. And besides, as I was getting fat in *his* eyes, he was getting to look tiny in mine. A real TV man, his expression glazed and dazed by his network shows and rented videos *every* night, *every* weekend. While I was tied up at the kitchen table with student essays, the tinny cheap otherworldly shouts and sound tracks of the TV and *nothing else* began to chew on my soul. Gosh, after all those months in Mechanic Falls where I begged Gordon to be a little more fond of television! To Sonny, who never drank, never smoked tobacco or weed, TV was his dope.

I was raring to go live on my own, maybe close to the university. I made several calls while at the adjunct office and was waiting to hear back about two fairly okay apartments within walking distance of the campus.

So I was on my way home from the university to Sonny's place after classes late one afternoon, pulled into the IGA in Egypt, came to stand staring at the plastic see-through cartons of cheese tortellini, which I knew had enough calories for a family of brontosauruses. It was a tight mass of scarlet in the corner of one eye that made me turn and look up. Gordon. There alone. Red chamois shirt all tucked nice into his belt and jeans, old work boots, no cap, just his cowlicky hair and dark lost-at-sea-for-days scruff of beard and great thick drive-me-crazy Zapata mustache and an expression that could mean anything. He did not move a muscle. He was like a deer in the headlights. His one "crazy" eye didn't flinch or widen or squint Tourette's-ishly.

I wasn't needing to wear specs yet in those days. Just my own wide eyes. See, it was as if I were looking at a skyscraper against blazing sun.

And Claire recalls this.

So I came to live in my own small dear cottage. He himself directed the crew that set the cement and framed up the roof, walls, and floors. He himself wired my lights. No photovoltaic panels, commercially made, nor the beer-and-soda-can ones so many other cottages had for just collecting heat, because this cottage was on the shady lane up a long rocky ledgy steeper hill. We had semi-to-barely-dependable electricity from the windmills. Then he used the table saw to groove the pine wall boards, the way I like, made me a big bed of pine, all that lathing and dark brooding stain. He painted around the many-paned windows of the tiny "sunroom" and hand-carved a tiny table in the shape of a toadstool, just enough flatness on top for a book and a cup of coffee. In one of the kitchenette windows he set colored glass, the kind you can see through, a blue world, a red world, a yellow world, a green world, pale purple, brown. Worlds of my birches and my violets outside and slopy field below.

He himself made my bookcases and built-in drawers and a cedar chest with carved bears loping across the front. The older women here whose hands could not rest, who were always tugging on a stitching needle or running a thickness of fabric under a presser foot, gave me quilts in classic patterns and stirring colors. One in all browns. And then came rugs.

At first, once I moved in, the agreement was that he would stay away from my cottage. I'd see plenty enough of him at meals and through the day when I wasn't going to the university. But then one damp and weedy, peppery-sweet, early spring evening in the big sandy Settlement parking area, me coming home from somewhere and he coming home from somewhere, our vehicles parked end to end, we stepped out and I touched him casually on the forearm of his nice thick flannel shirt. And just like that other time at the IGA, he froze. It was a raptor's grasp the way I closed my fingers tighter around that forearm, as far as my short fingers could reach, maybe digging in some.

And that was that.

Now I am one of *them*.

Bonnie Loo Bean Sanborn St. Onge speaks of the past, her pre-Settlement life.

My mother has always been into God, Jesus, and church doin's. But I have always been more of a thinker, more of a Big Questions person. More of an explorer. Maybe even a sort of scientist. And tough. No matter what happens, I don't worship or whimper much. What I do is bitch. That is waaay different from worship and whimper. And with me, so much has happened that would make a grown man cry, as they say, but not ol' Bonnie Loo. Until that day in the IGA parking lot about six years ago. I had the Volvo. A seventeen-year-old Volvo yuppie car. A kind of strained-baby-food-peas green. Seats torn up, funny brakes, but still chugging. But you know, they are very expensive to get fixed. I had Gabriel with me in his car seat. He was still nearly brand-new to this world but old enough to have a human expression on his face like he recognizes you and kinda likes you. And when you weren't expecting it, that big grin that showed the pointy tip of his tongue. He had a nice big face, chubby arms, nice and solid, my side of the family. Well, the Bean side. Pomerleaus are shrimps. Yuh, my mum. A funny, chain-smoking, churchy little shrimp.

Anyway, Gabe was with me and I was coming back from Bridgton. Probably the dentist up there. I refused to do commerce with the rotten moneygrubbing bastard here in Egypt. Kill me first!

Anyway, I'm tootling along, speed limit, which my stepfather Reuben reminds me all the time makes cops think you're drinking. You're supposed to speed like a lunatic so they'll think you're sober. "Wake me up when things make sense," I always tell him. Anyway, I was almost home but I turned into the IGA here in East Egypt and right behind me are the blue lights. Double Bubble, as we used to say as kids.

I stopped the Volvo between two parked cars and the cop comes over to my window and he is NOT FRIENDLY. He has a face like a photograph of a face. Hair like a boot camp marine. Smokey hat. And a voice like a computer. "License and registration and insurance," this computer voice says and he looks at my sticker on the windshield, which is expired because of the exhaust and the rocker panels and a bunch of other shit.

I get out the license and registration with shaking hands. And then the insurance card.

In the back seat Gabe is smiling tongue and all at the cop and swinging one of his legs, thumping his little sneaker on the car seat. But the cop was NOT smiling back. Cop was a machine.

Cop says he's going to have to write me up for the sticker. Not even a warning, which is what they usually give. And maybe it was the cold way he said it. Maybe I just couldn't take one more cold voice out there in the world. I burst into tears.

This made the cop mad. His hand passing back my license and registration and insurance card and ticket made real thrusts, like anger, pissed-off anger. Like I made him sick. This made me cry even harder. I thought I'd choke. I did everything to stop but I was being swept away in horrid gags and gasps. My face was probably this great big red mess.

Little Gabe is by now crying, too, back there in his car seat.

I remember I was wearing my regular glasses all the time in those days and they dropped, first somewhere in my lap, then wound up on the floor. I could hardly see.

Cop keeps standing there. I thought he was going to hit me. I grabbed my sweater off the seat and held it to my face and then I was just really screaming bloodcurdlingly into the sweater and Gabriel was screaming and twisting in his car seat and I could hear his little sneakers driving into the plastic footrest of his seat, trying to push himself free.

"You all right?" the cop asks me. It wasn't the same voice, not the cold voice, but almost an edge of feeling to it and I noticed, something I hadn't at first, that his accent was the accent of these hills, that he sounded like me, my dead husband, my brothers, my little half sister, my mum, everybody I love. And this made me scream even harder, the soft edge to his voice and the accent of love.

I blubbered through my big square crying mouth, "My husband is dead! I loved him!!!!" The sweater I was holding flopped to the floor. Gabriel gasped, breathless. "They took my house! I can't win! I can't win! I can't keep up! I can't pay for everything! I can't do it! I can't just paaaaay for the friggin' exhaust . . . just like whip out the friggin' money like I just carry a big wad around with me!!!" I open my eyes and see him backing away and he turns in one kind of tough, arrogant, get-out-of-my-life motion and as he walks away, I scream, "PIG!!! YOU FUCKING PIG!!! YOU PIGS KILLED MY FATHER!!! And probably my HUSBAND, too, if he hadn't died first! You PIGS threw me out of my house, which was MY house!!! Threw out this little BABY!!! YOU PIGS ARE PIGS!!!!!" I wanted to get Gabriel out of his seat and hold him but I couldn't think of how to get to the back seat and undo the car seat . . . I couldn't *think*. I couldn't do anything but scream and I hung my head and gripped the wheel and yanked on the wheel and punched my head against the horn and it beeped a little and I screamed screamed screamed, "Jesus!" Of all things, "Jesus! Jesus help me!! Help me Jesus!" And the snot was running out of my nose and my tears were mixing with the snot and drool was coming from my mouth, everything mixed and running down my chin.

I think I screamed like this for about ten minutes. Who knows what neighbors mighta seen me as they walked by from their cars to the IGA too terrified to help, seeing the cop, seeing my Volvo, knowing it was me, figured I had DONE SOMETHING BAD. Then I see the cop is still sitting there in his cruiser behind me, all this time, a good ten minutes. Just sitting there without his big Smokey hat on his head.

I lean forward again and hang my head and grip my head . . . yes, now I was gripping my head or my ears or something. I was really losing it. And Gabriel was still screeching and fighting his car seat.

Cop's voice at my window again, "Are you sure you're all right?"

"You know what it's like to work two jobs . . . two AWFUL jobs?!!!!" I screamed at him. "You know what it's like to work twice as much to make half of what you need to live on? I don't drink!!! I don't do drugs! Not even grass! Okay, cigs. I fuckin' smoke cigs! I drink coffeeee!! But I don't have pretty clothes—" I grip the chest of my T-shirt and stretch it out at him. He's wearing his shaded cop glasses but I can see his eyes get big and worried and he backs up again. "You do NOT know what it's like!!!!" I howl.

And you know what the fucker says? He says nothing. He just goes away again. This time for good. In less than a minute, I see his cruiser slide away and I manage to get Gabriel out of his seat and I hug the hell out of him and I kiss his face and I laugh and kiss kiss kiss that little fat face and, oh, how I love that face and his husky little laugh . . . and that laugh finally comes after a while. And I wonder what am I going to do? Nobody can help me. My family, Ma and Reuben and them, are struggling enough . . . and Reuben sick with the soon-to-be-in-the-graveyard disease . . . and my cousins and their families aren't making it, and my uncles, my aunts, no one. I can't live with any of them squashed into their space, sleeping on their couches and all we do is fight . . . cooped up like that. I *hate* to fight with my people. It is the worst thing to fight with your people. Ma says once families could help each other. No matter what else went wrong, you had a place to go. And usually some land so you could set up a little house next door or a trailer and have a little space around you, but close enough to share stuff and protect each other and be there for children and emergencies. But now a trailer costs as much as ten big fucking fancy houses with two garages apiece and mink-lined septic systems. And then there's all these fucking snoopy hard-assed grand selectmen sneaking around trying to catch you breaking a code and there's codes AGAINST everything you do these days down to how thick your walls are and how many doors!

Nobody has land. It's all chopped up, owned by outer space aliens or New York people. Or companies! And also *if* you add *anything*, a room! a shack! A *tepee*! to your existing place, *up* go the taxes! Fine if you're rich but if you're not rich, taxes are paid from a pound of flesh from the cardiopulmonary region of your bod. Where can I turn? I am so so so scared. Jesus, am I scared.

Anyway, that was then. Like I say, the day the cop gave me that ticket was about six years ago. Now, I live at the Settlement. Home at last. Gabriel is so happy here. And now my two younger ones. We have this cute little house that I designed. It's painted a pale pink, like cotton candy, with dark green trim and a wooden, old-timey door—like something the woodchopper probably lived in, the guy that saved Little Red Riding Hood, wonderful little fairy-tale house with tiny bedrooms and homey rugs and chair covers embroidered purple and yellow. And you would not believe the handmade quilts Lucienne and Jacquie have given me. Those things take nearly a year to make! Yuh, this is home with a capital H.

I don't have one of the full-photovoltaic houses. And I'm not hooked up to the wind-power line. I'm too far up in the woods, where some of us prefer to be. There are some of us whose souls would die without trees and mossy rocks and ferns and trilliums bunched right up to our doors. So I get some of the charged windmill batteries brought to me, which is *not* economical because batteries wear out fast but I conserve and I have a few real nice kerosene lamps to use on rare occasions, celebratory occasions. I grew up with kerosene lamps. I know how to clean and trim them. I can do it with my eyes shut.

I have a green enameled woodstove. And guess what! Wood magically appears in my woodshed. And snow magically disappears from the path. And there's the Window Washing Crew that makes the rounds. And there's always some older kid out there in my yard doing his duty for the old. Ha ha! I'm almost twenty-seven. Just a matter of days. Anyway, most of us don't need to have a lot of electricity in our houses. We spend so much time down at the Shops and Quonset huts or in the gardens or out on errands down in North Egypt . . . or other things in other places, one thing or another.

When you live here, you are not alone. Not alone in the "abandoned" sense of the word. Not destitute, not scared shitless. You will not wind up waiting on a public housing list for a cement cubicle in a treeless, stinking, cement city. You will not eat from a trash bin. And nobody can get you—no cops, especially no cops. You don't see any cops here unless they come as friends of Gordon. He says, "They're just working men and women like ourselves." But I say shit, Gordon would make friends with a poisonous snake. But you know Gordon, he just says, "It's not the police, it's the policy." Okay, like it's not the snake, it's the swamp.

History as it Happens (as written and edited by Montana St. Onge, age nine, with no help!).

In case you are all reading this a hundred years from now, what do you think? Jane Meserve came from nowhere to live down to Gordie's house last spring. Poof!

She says to me her father is a rap star that her mother *met him once. Met once!* Is this believable?!!! Maybe Jane only met her mother once. I hardly can tell if her mother exists. Oh, she was in the newspaper as a big drug criminal. Some of the mothers here say do not believe corporate-controlled media or the police. Whatever. Jane's mother is in what my mother calls the slammer. My mother is Beth St. Onge in case you are reading this a hundred years from now.

Different people here take Jane to visit the criminal. She is in the Androscoggin County slammer, which uses a lot of gas to get there to see just one criminal.

Jane is kind of brown like most rap stars but she only has talent in how to have wicked tantrums and fits.

Nan Waters, who is seventy-nine years old and has bad feet and gas, said Jane Meserve needs her rear end warmed till it peels. I happen very personally to know that is an idle threat. Violence is rare here. But (to kids especially) you can *threaten* mass murder, human sacrifice, being hanged by a big toe, cooked in a stew.

History (the past), an old-world Mammoneer of the 1700s (a king's thoughts).

Uh-oh. What is all this "liberty" stuff going on? The Enlightenment rageth in crazed minds, especially in Paris, and this Thomas Jefferson character who some call the "most dangerous radical in the world" is just one of many. *Liberty!* they shout. Obviously, its time has come.

Blame it on the printing press! Page numbering. And coal, the hot hard heart of progress. Blame it on time.

As a peculiar scum forms on some deep waters, so the talk of "liberty for common men" now squeaks all over Europe! Beware new leaders! Prepare! Be watchful for when the heads of monarchs and bishops lie in their baskets, for the job then for you is to pose the common man's "earned wage" slavery as "liberty" and let him *believe* that his flag and his constitution are his liberty. The crystal clear and literal liberty must never be his.

And capital?

In this fashion, I dare say, the aristocratic men of new nations will someday be not men but systems. Yes, a montage of many machines and magicians. This is profound. Surely in this fashion *nobody* will be free! Every human head will BE a basket. Every human heart will pop in confusion, indecency, and fear; restlessness and stupors; structures and hollows; and continuous tiny civil wars. No conscience will rule. Even the cruelest monarch has had a moment of conscience, a powder flash of integrity! But not so with a god-sized system.

History as it Happens (as written and edited by Oceanna St. Onge).

We have agreed on no censorship but I have to express my pure and colossal disgust over Montana's last *History as it Happens* installment about Jane and state as fact that it is nothing to be proud of.

Jane Meserve through Bonnie Loo's eyes. Bonnie Loo speaks.

Bev and Barbara, two ladies who *practically* live here, have done a lot with Jane, even though I know it's been a big inconvenience for them because of their living in town in that wicked modern yellow house with all the glass and grass. They are a couple of saints as far as I'm concerned. They've been the same way with a boy here who has a bad heart and with cantankerous old Marge. I don't know when Bev and Barbara sleep, let alone the fact that you drive by their house and *the grass* is always cut and almost blue-green, no weeds, not even one proud-of-itself dandelion, and everything is kept spanking clean. And they keep a *swimming pool*. Mostly for Barbara. And a swimming pool doesn't take care of itself. They have to treat it every day and vacuum the damn thing.

Some of us have helped a little with Jane, to take the burden off Bev and Barbara and Gordon. Old Lucienne has spent a few nights at Gordon's place where Jane won't budge from but rarely. And Lee Lynn brings little Hazel down some afternoons. Vic's wife Ruth came once, the night of the solstice march. We are hoping Jane will settle in and feel more at ease and then eventually spend daytimes with the kids at the Shops, and get outdoors more, *in the air*. And then eventually take a liking to one of the families, a family who will take her in as their own. It would be nice for Jane to have brothers and sisters, to be included. *Feel* included. Because her mother Lisa is never going to get out of prison as long as this country is run by the esteemed and lofty in *suits* and *robes*.

Today I've encouraged Bev and Barbara to take a break, swim, rest. But they'll use it to work on painting their garage. This is the way they are. God luv 'em.

This morning, I made up a satchel of stuff from the East Parlor. Some games, even that Cathedrals of Paris game Whitney made a few months ago. It has really cute little buildings of papier-mâché, modeled after real-life old cathedrals. Whitney is a real architecture nut when she's not talking physics and the "big picture" or *boys*.

My two oldest kids, Gabe and Jetta, have "business" at the Shops, so it's just me and Zack and the bag of games and books. Zack and the stuff rolled along quite nicely in the little wagon, as long as I stayed on the paths. Zack is almost two. They say "terrible twos," but I like two-year-olds. I'm not crazy about new babies. They can't talk. I like a kid to talk. I like it when they say cute things. Zack really comes up with some doozies. What a little monkey. What a doll.

Well, here we are in the kitchen of Gordon's family's old farmplace and I am trying to get Jane interested in going outside to play, maybe up to the old merry-go-round. It's a deep-crackling-blue-sky day, room temp, not one of the abnormally thick and oveny sweatbath days we get nowadays for "normal." I want to get out and feel real September's arms around me.

But Jane just stands there by the table with her arms folded and stares at the phone. She says, "My mother is going to call me today."

Well, I don't know what to say about that. Bev didn't mention her mother calling. And at the jail you don't just pick up the bedside princess phone and poke buttons at your leisure. But I don't want Jane to think I don't trust her, so I say, "Well, let's just see what's in the satchel." I get out one of the games. Candyland. It's good for kids Jane's age. The cathedrals game might be a little too sophisticated. Sometimes I'm not sure *I* follow it. "Want to play Candyland?"

Jane says, "Okay." Her eyes are very, very dark. The irises are as black as the pupils. And they shine. Really beautiful eyes. But sulky. In fact, right now you might say her eyes show contempt. She hates me and Zack. It's plain to see. She keeps her arms folded across the chest of her satiny shirt. It's a bright orange top, almost like a halter, the side and back cut low. A kind of Saturday night top. Her skin is gorgeous. Darker than mine even, a really velvety dark gold. And her hair! Jesus. Thick ringlets, dark brown, really long if it were straight. She wears it up in a beaded squeegee. She is a gorgeous girl. I guess that's what you get when you combine liony Africa with shamrocky

Ireland, an almost mythical little goddess, at least in looks. But everyone says *inside* Jane is plain fear. Wellll, there's where I draw the line. There is nothing plain inside that kid.

Okay, so I explain to Zack about the Candyland game, though I know all he'll want to do is carry the draw cards and plastic men around and grab our pieces off the board and chirp things like "He wee goooo!" So I can see there is going to be work here for ol' Bonnie Loo. It's okay. I'm just glad the humidity has let up. If the mosquitoes from the marsh would leave us be, the day would be perfect. I'm even going to say I'm having less nausea today, knock on wood. Just one little wave when I first woke up.

Jane's cold steamy black eyes watch my hands gathering up the little piles of draw cards. "Come help me do this," I suggest pleasantly. She slowly turns her head from side to side, her eyes on my face. I try another approach. "Which one of these stacks of draw cards would you like to shuffle?"

"Neither one," she replies.

I look up at her face. You can see the African ancestry across her eyes and nose, mixed in with Indian or something, but her mouth is a small curved "white" mouth. Her tongue, it's one of those things you inherit from your folks . . . a tongue that you can roll like a tube and also you can point it. It's an inherited thing. Jane is presently using the point of her tongue to stroke her top lip in a gesture of bored sensuousness.

If I get nervous, I talk too much. Why am I nervous? Why is it important to me what this nearly-seven-year-old brat thinks of me? I am talking away and when I look up, she is not listening, just looking at the phone or out the window or at the refrigerator or at one of Gordon's heaped desks.

When I say, "Ready to start? Which of these men you want? This green guy or the yellow?" she says, "I'm not playing." Her eyes sweep all over me.

The phone rings. Black. On the wall. Still has a dial. Jane hurries long-leggedly and grabs it. She tells the caller in her husky confident voice, "He's not here. Would you like to leave a message?" And then she listens. Shrugs. Sighs. Holds the phone out to me with two fingers, like a dirty diaper. As I take the caller's message, Jane storms out of the kitchen with a rattle and slam and *errk* of swollen old doors that lead into the other rooms.

After the call, I get Zack out of the biscuit wood cupboard, where he has found a cat, and the cat is scratching Zack on the face just as I am jerking the little door open and the cat zooms out, a very black Halloween-looking cat . . . and Zack wails . . . and bleeds.

I lead him by one hand to the doorway that goes to the attic stairs. "Jane!" I call.

No answer.

I find some tissue in my bag to dab Zack's blood with. I know lips are dirty and swarm with germs, but lips also heal. Lips are superior to science. I kiss Zack's scratch and his sobs let up some.

I go back and pick up the game. Phone rings. Another call for Gordon, this about saw logs. "He's with some of the crews up on the mountain fixing something that broke with one of the turbines," I tell this caller. "You ever want something to fill up your time, get you some windmills."

The caller chuckles. Caller is an older feller I've known all my life, some relation to my father and to my stepfather, Rcuben. George Lampron. Not much of a talker in person. But on the phone, you can get him to make a few noises. On the phone, a person can't just stare. So George explains what he wants to tell Gordon and I write it all down, all eleven words, and when I hang up, Jane is standing there. Her black eyes cut right through me. "I'm bored," she says. As she speaks the word *bored*, her eyelids lower, and her chin raises ever so subtly, a gesture for the most spoiled of the rich.

I say, "Help me get Zack's cat scratch to heal. You know, like distract him."

She just keeps looking at my face.

I say, "You know who I mean, Jane? Zack . . . my little kid over there." I nod at Zack, who is in the open doorway to the piazza staring sadly after the cat. He loves cats. But his chubby squeezy little hands do not appeal to cats. He looks so cute in those pants. What a set of clothes my kids each got! I'm not into sewin' that much unless it's art like the man-sized Godzilla that sits in a rocker in the West Parlor, which was designed and manufactured by yours truly. But some of them here just love to sew, *just to sew*. What they aren't making for my kids, it's other stuff being passed down, all stuff in good shape. Clothes come at us like a big high tide. Right now, he's in these sailboat-print bibbed shorts, yellow and red. The chubby dimpled look of his legs just about melts me.

I say, "Zack, come here, sweetie. Jane and I have some more love for your scratch to heal. Dr. Jane and Dr. Mumma will help!" I say this joyously and run and grab Zack, whose face is still tear-streaked but who now explodes into husky manly laughter, wonderful rolling laughs, and I carry him to Jane. He is heavy. He is big for only two. A big solid beautiful child with kinda dark chestnutty hair and gray eyes and a significant nose that will someday be striking with those gray eyes. You gotta admit that the ways you give your children generosity, gentleness, resistance to lies and crap are no longer important to most people. They say these are things that could keep your son or daughter from *success*. But good looks, a good-looking huggable gray-eyed man in funny pants, will always be in fashion, will always be a hot item.

I am so pleased that Jane lowers her face, her long dark ringlets flopping, and kisses Zack on the top of his head. A really sweet kiss. She smiles at him and she says rather firmly, with a professional distance, "Get well now." And Zack smiles at her and laughs but then frowns and points toward the door. "Kitty scraffit roing-in . . . he wid hurt you."

Jane says to me, "What else you got?" She goes over to the satchel and pulls out a book, a Settlement-made book by Faye Sears when she used to hang out here daytimes.

Phone rings. I answer it. A girl. Early twenties. Maybe younger. Asks for Gordon. I tell her about the turbine problem. She asks me who I am. I hesitate. I say, "Who is *this*?"

"Hannah Sturgeon."

"Are you a CSA?" I ask. "No," she replies. Just a plain simple no.

"If you leave a message, Gordon will get back to you." I guess I sound rude. But I can hear Gordon's voice reminding us all, "Social workers, media . . . do not talk to them." And then there's the deeper thing. The shadow with bodiless hands that chokes my throat. The exhaustion of waking up each day infinitely betrayed. By *him*.

"Is it my mum?" Jane is asking behind me. I lower myself down into Gordon's desk chair and slide my hand down Jane's neck to her back and hold her to me and when she lets me do this, I hug harder and very motheringly as Hannah Sturgeon explains she is looking for her husband, who left this morning to bring a compressor to the Settlement. "Oh," I say. "That's probably where he is. Up at the Settlement. This is Gordon's house on Heart's Content Road." And she asks what the phone number is up there and I explain there is no phone up there and so we get that all straight and hang up in a friendly way.

Jane now pulls away as I stand up and return the phone to its cradle and Zack is pulling books from the satchel and little papier-mâché French 1400s cathedrals and Jane is standing again with her arms crossed, her black eyes hard on my face, chin raised. "I'm *bored*."

I try all the games. Jane gives a really tired indulgent "Yes" to each one, refuses to help set up, then once it's all set up, she says casually, "Guess I don't want to play that one, either. What else do you have in here?" and drives a hand roughly through the satchel, pitching books and little cathedrals onto the floor. "That's stupid." "That's stupid." "That's stupid," she is saying matter-of-factly as each thing goes matter-of-factly to the floor.

I suggest we play cards. When I suggest War, she agrees eagerly. She says she has played that before. She even kind of chuckles to herself, remembering something, as I am shuffling and counting out all the cards into two equal piles.

Four plays into the game, she has won the first three plays, but then *I* win one, so she tosses her cards so they skid across the table, some dropping into my lap. She holds her forehead. "This is the worst day of my life," she says. "So boring." She sighs. Keeping her head down. Then she raises her face slowly, calculatingly, her very long golden fingers flick out at me as if to summon a bark from a trained seal. "Do you have a car, whatever-your-name-is?"

"My name is Bonnie Loo. And I often have use of a car, but not today."

"Let's go to McDonald's. I'm *so* hungry."

"I have a snack planned for nine o'clock and then a pretty snazzy lunch. Gabe is coming down with a basket at noon."

She wrinkles her nose. "Yuh, I can imagine."

"It's really nice thick soup. Chicken noodle."

Jane rolls her eyes. "Sure. With chickens in it."

I say, "Chicken soup has chicken in it. Always has."

"Never mind," she says, standing up. "I don't want any. I *want* to go to McDonald's. That's all there is to it."

I look across the table, up at her. She isn't looking at me, she's just kind of picking her fingernails, which are short, chewed, kid-looking fingernails, but you can imagine them to be long and painted coral. I am speechless.

"Well?" she says.

I say, "Gabe and his friends will bring the basket at noon. But at nine, some of the girls will come down with a snack. Some apples. It's only eight-thirty right now, Jane. Gotta give them time to pick the damn things. Imagine. Fresh apples. Still crispy from the trees. Can't get any better than that."

She sneers. "Gross."

"You've been getting too much sugar. Today will be sugar-free."

"No!" she shouts and this makes Zack jump and he looks from Jane's face to mine to see if this means something ugly.

"Fresh apples are good," I insist. "Unless you'd rather have bananas. Barbara brought a mess of bananas over this weekend, nice and firm. She brought enough of them for a hundred monkeys." I say this, hoping to make her laugh.

She sweeps away. Long arms floating around. "This is stupid," she snarls.

I suggest she and Zack and I sit out on the piazza, seeing that Zack has already disappeared around the corner there. "Ever played I-Spy-With-My-Little-Eye?" I ask Jane as I stand. "It's a game we don't need to set up."

She follows behind me, her head hung to one side, miming a person who is weak with the agony of boredom.

I find my favorite wicker rocker and sink into it. It crackles all around me like a nest. Zack has taken an interest in the wooden trucks Gordon keeps around. A logging truck and a lumber truck and a box truck that holds two wooden oxen. All Settlement-made.

Jane stands near my chair. I am on her right, but she whispers as if to a person standing to her left, "I am starved." A whisper filled with sorrow, on the edge of tears.

I will not ask DIDN'T YOU HAVE ANY BREAKFAST? I will not ask it. I know about the food problem they are having with Jane. I know breakfast this morning was probably offered twenty ways, all ways refused. Bev is always saying, "Poor tyke, it's the only way she can take control over her life right now with this terrible thing that has happened to her and her mother, this Dracula-like bloodsucking evil thing, this separation of the living from the living. Two living deaths, mother and child."

But Gordon tells us that Jane's grandpa, Pete, "says the food thing isn't new. The FOOD THING is as old as Jane is. Pete says Jane has controlled the tides and the rise of the moon and stars since her birth. Her first howl brought everyone to their knees. She was born with an IRON WILL. Jane WANTS. Jane GETS."

I've never met Pete. But I believe him.

I look into Jane's eyes now. I feel fear. I know she will grow up. She will probably grow up here at the Settlement. She will share in all of our lives. In *my* life. We will love her. But now as I look away from her powerful, unflinching, boiling, dark eyes, I feel afraid.

And now her voice, "Why do you do that stupid thing with your hair?"

"What do you mean?" Actually, my hair is fixed a little like hers. I have it up in a squeegee, a red squeegee. And my hair tumbles thickly over the back of my head and some loose squiggles on the sides. This is what my brother Dale calls "Cavewoman Hair." Mine isn't ringlets like Jane's. Mine is just wavy, thick, and ripply and a little bit stringy at times. For some time now, I've kept it streaked blond through the dark, dark being my natural color. Yeah, the blond is actually kinda orange. Some like it. Some don't. It's me. It feels right. I have my contact lenses in today, so I'm the best I can look. I'm no Meryl Streep or Michelle Pfeiffer, but I'm not ugly. The five fake teeth I have on the bottom don't really show. And I've learned to take good care of the teeth I have left.

Zack's father, my present husband, Gordon, yes *the* Gordon, he will hold my face with both hands and whisper stuff that makes me embarrassed . . . stuff kinda like poetry . . . only he makes it up. And his kisses and sex are urgent and deep. VERY DEEP.

So why is it that now that I look into Jane's eyes and see her revulsion at me that I BELIEVE she is right?

She won't sit down. She crosses her arms like a floor manager or a teacher in a classroom and she smiles and shakes her head. "And you ought to do something with your face," she says. "An operation. You ever hear of those operations?" And now her voice seems so sincere and truly helpful. "My mum says some people get to be really oldish but you can't tell because they get the doctor to stretch right here." She steps over to me and places the tips of her fingers on my jaws. Her fingers are warm and firm and instructive.

"Jane, I'm only twenty-seven years old!"

She jerks her hands back, folds her arms again, but with one hand free to gracefully gesture, "I know *you* aren't that old. But the wrong shape."

I sigh.

"You can get a whole new face and *ribs* removed," she adds.

I laugh. "That's showbiz people."

She looks at me pityingly. Then an endearing warm expression, a motherly expression. Now she flutters her eyes and she flutters the fingers of her gesturing hand. "You know, I'm just trying to help you find guys."

"I *have* a husband. A gorgeous husband." I take a deep breath. I realize with horror that Zack is too quiet. But there he is, arranging some dirty coffee mugs in his logging truck. One actually has some coffee in it. Zack is meticulous and adept. His thick chestnutty hair in the silvery dappled light is one of the triumphs of my life. I ask Jane, "So have you ever played I-Spy-With-My-Little-Eye? It's fun."

She looks interested. She stands one foot on top of the other and stumbles a little, like a regular six- or seven-year-old getting the squirmies.

"What we do is this. One of us picks out an object, but without the other knowing what it is. Keep it a secret. The other person has—"

"I'm bored," she says, laughing gently, as if to try to soften her words. As if she means no harm. She is just stating a fact. Like the fact that when it rains, you must pick up your picnic.

Bonnie Loo continues.

After lunch, Jane isn't interested in a nap. And I gotta admit, *I* am bored now. While Zack naps on a pillow-covered porch swing, I doze off on the soft old mildewy sofa with the black cat curled on my ankles. I wake with a start and realize a good hour must've passed. And there is Jane standing there, arms folded, now wearing her sunglasses, which have white frames shaped like two hearts. She is staring at me. She had been watching me sleep. Seems I am more interesting asleep than awake.

I smile at her. And rub my eyes.

She doesn't move. Neither her face nor her body moves. She just keeps standing mannequin-still and staring at me with those adorable (I must admit) funny white-framed glasses, as if through them she can see all my secret sins, my rages, my murderous side.

I smile again and get up.

She uses one finger to give her special glasses a micro adjustment.

Duotron Lindsey International's CEO, Bruce Hummer, strides briskly toward the elevator with the numbers rippling along overhead conveniently toward "23," his floor.

Thirty-one cents an hour. What is the expression on his face as the warmly-dickered new figure of thirteen cents an hour appears so crisply in his mind? This, the special-deal-to-America minimum wage in the People's Republic of China coming closer each day, negotiations rat-tat-tat in his night dreams in accents of Chinese businessmen.

Look into Bruce Hummer's eyes if you are standing nearby. What do you see? Cauldrons of greed? Ice and stone? Fact is, they are a warm golden-green brown.

Out in the world.

The multinational corporation Duotron Lindsey (cluster bombs, artillery shells, napalm, high-hoopin' missiles, and various dainty war widgets, bioweapons, and lawn sprays) with annual profits totaling $20 billion last year, has laid off eleven thousand more people in the Midwest and seventeen thousand in California in its plan to restructure the two locations, primarily to part-time no-benefits positions, and at other levels, "contracting out" (or "outsourcing"), as well as the relocation of a section of the Chester plant to the women's prison in Pontooki. Minnesota.

Also fourteen thousand to sixteen thousand people will be replaced by computerized voices and robotic hands. All this in order to fulfill a projected $27 billion for next year, and, *of course*, an even more ample and sexy figure for the year after that and after that MOOOOORRRE in order to continue tantalizing investors, who, like small children with TV remote controls, are so grimly playful.

THE END OF THE WORLD IS NIGH!

Well, the end of *some* worlds.

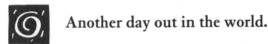

Another day out in the world.

Among the thousands laid off by Duotron Lindsey, a man in sales named Doug Russell, silver-haired, broad-shouldered, fine bearing, with a funny, crooked, coaxing, "adorable" Felix-the-Cat smile, and a big kind of arm-wrestle-type handshake, who has given all his life to the company and was never home, *never home*, was never a father to his daughters, husband to his wife, never could be, just married to the job, as nuns are married to God. This man, Doug Russell, after hearing the news of his layoff, is missing. Missing for a few days. Missing. Nobody knows where he is.

Now on Tuesday, shortly after 9:30 a.m., he has turned up at the Duotron Lindsey regional corporate offices, his hair oddly messy, no suit jacket. Wedding ring gone, tie gone, funny crooked smile gone. No, he isn't drunk. He is *alert*. He carries two coffee cans that slosh with liquid.

People are looking at him. Even those who don't know him sense *something*. And they see him unhesitatingly, with shuddering depths of resolution none of us will ever understand, pour the watery contents of the coffee cans over his hair and face, chest and back, feet and shins and thighs, and then flick a match, which, with a great orange crackling weirdly soft whomping roar, covers his entire shape with fire and fills the lobby with horrified pandemonium.

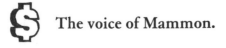

The voice of Mammon.

Growth! Growth! Growth!

Out there.

Today another American factory closed. Another dozen family farms withered . . . "Get big or get out!" Another factory restructured, downsized. Another many thousand people temped and temperamental. Another forty factories and six hundred family farms evaporate. Another seventy factories, two thousand local "micro" businesses, and seven thousand family farms lift off into the clouds.

Concerning the aforementioned complexities, the screen remains—

Blank and dumbstruck.

So what *does* the screen show us tonight?

Here we have interviews with welfare mothers. Look close. Here's one in Boston, sitting on the stoop with a buncha kids. How many kids? Fifteen! That's a lotta kids. And we just *know* they're all her kids, with fifteen different fathers. Hear her talk. Bad English. A really ignorant stupid type. (Not like us.) A real pig. And she's black. "We" have nothing against black, of course. But . . . you know . . . this one is *not* a black to be proud of. Not a nice Harvard black or We-Shall-and-Did-Overcome black. This one is a grungy black. Grungy ultimate. Poor. Lazy. Soaking the taxpayer. But sexy. See her hair! Rippling and fixed to attract. Look at the sexy way she smokes. Cigarettes IN FRONT OF THE KIDS! Cigarettes paid for by YOUR tax dollars. And here's a white one. Gawd! She has twins! And nice clothes! Probably a shiny car hidden off-screen. She is telling us something. What is it? Something about "busted pipes." She is whining. Thinks the world owes her! But also, she is laughing. Hear that giggle. What's that she's saying now? Sweet little-girl voice, eyes all aflutter. "I love men." Did she say that? Most likely that is what she said.

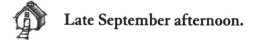

Late September afternoon.

In the valley of the St. Onge Settlement robust acorns let go . . . *thwack!thwack!thwack!* upon Quonset hut roofs and orderly stacks of old rusty-edged metal roofing and *clonk!* on an inverted plastic pail, the iron, the steel, the aluminum, the slate, all in array around the sawmills and furniture-making Quonset hut guarded by helpful oak giants. A rhythm band of the queerest sort is playing a march.

The figure in brown flannel check and green wool crossing the Quad and sandy lot with a basket like Little Red Riding Hood is the Settlement's chief cook, Bonnie Lucretia Bean Sanborn St. Onge, who we all know well. She has managerial and caustic traits at times, and mythical traits of violence. She has a hale stride.

She passes through the nearest Quonset hut's wide-open bay as through a sieve, leaving light and rhythmic *thwonks!* and silent grasses behind.

Up the dim stairs to the attic.

She knows which room, though this is her first time bringing a meal. *Ground control to Silverbell Rosenthal! Ground control to Silverbell Rosenthal!* some of the other basket deliverers had sadly joked when returning to the kitchens.

Bonnie Loo shifts the basket. Her broad knuckles, used once or twice to pummel other wives here, it has been falsely rumored among newer residents, now punch the pine door, jolly punches, *shave-and-a-haircut-two-bits!*

She knows there are no windows in the room beyond this door but before the door inches open, she expects lamplight. But there is only dark, from which the sharp immobile-featured white face and white *Common Ground Fair 1990* T-shirt of Silverbell Rosenthal* emerge.

Behind Bonnie Loo the four-watt baby-pink night-light bulb in the wide, tool-cluttered hall broadcasts what it was intended for, a

* Yes, this is the woman with two kids delivered by Gordon's old friend, the barely-making-ends-meet socially responsible lawyer, on that chilly night in the farmhouse dooryard.

sleepy nighty-night dimness. Bonnie Loo wags the basket. "Brought your dinner."

From the dark, looking out.

Silverbell renamed herself in college. She *was* Sarah Bowen. That was before she married Aaron, then the Bowen part also went the way of the winds of change. She wasn't a feminist in how you'd want you and your man to be on separate ships through life's journey.

So why Sarah to Silverbell?

To erase her given name, her mother's and father's gift, wasn't there something wrenching in her soul even before the storm, the SWAT storm, faceless men in black first shooting her Doberman pinscher in the kitchen, *pow!pow!pow!pow!pow!pow! pow!pow!pow!* taking nine shots to down the screaming dog. Then a black mirror-shine boot stomped the newborn puppies! It is said this is to provoke you into attacking a police officer.

So maybe she did that . . . raised her hand to the shooter or the stomper . . . it isn't clear. But they broke her arm and stomped her head. Same boot that solved the squealing puppies problem? Well, today you can see something about the intensity of one of her eyes.

Then it must have been her husband, unprovoked, who raised a hand to the red and noisy panoramic scene before him because they thumped him around for a while, although his crime of growing the plant was heinous enough to earn him all those rib and kidney and hip and belly kicks and, well, it all happened so fast and there were so many of them, memory is more about sound than seeing. It was, after all, the middle of the night and both husband and wife, and then the wailing kids, were tipsy with the surprise of it.

But of course it would be hard to see anyway, with her eye bulging like a baby's head coming out into the world. Oh, boy, blood izzz hot. And there was a lot of her blood gliding down from not just her eye, but nose, one ear, and mouth.

Somewhere beyond the haze of surgery and morphine drip everybody was missing. Aaron gone to a cage. His children (she had adopted them, so let's say *their* children) carried off to a secret undisclosed location. Did *their* heads get stomped, too?

No, as it turns out. But when she looked for them she found that DHS is another sort of SWAT operation . . . total and unflinching dominance. They strip you for the crucifixion, parade you through the courts bare and friendless . . . DHS does *not* allow friends. Family? Forget it. Mum, Dad, aunts, brothers? Reports get made up with descriptions of people you don't recognize . . . everyone is a child molester, everyone is a drug addict, a sadist, dishes left in the sink, listless, no ambition, never gainfully employed, angry, poor students, thus poor in purse, no car, no license, they move too often, unfit as grandparents or aunties. They shout a lot.

She never thought of her family that way. Something is left out! Something is stretched thick, something is stretched thin.

But of course since the police seized all the land and the house and Aaron's truck . . . listless, oh, yes, that's herself. And the report states that she is dysfunctional due to constant trembling, jumping at the least sound, she screams in her sleep. Is antisocial. Like a stag beetle in the ground.

And the biggie? That she stood by without calling authorities while her husband, Aaron Alan Rosenthal, grew the plants and *sold* the dried product.

You.will.never.see.Burd.and.Eden.again.ever.

But Aaron's and Gordon's old friend, Jack Holmes, the lawyer, made calls, worked lawyerly magic. And so the children came "home."

However, Silverbell thinks the DHS is right. She is not fit. She is not fit *now*.

And her eye? The one that was loose and burning, bulging from her face, blind for weeks but somehow, in all the rumpus, that eye did not stay blind but sees right through the silly joys of ordinary life and out the other side. And what she sees this moment is the dark ominous all-powerful bearlike creature they call Bonnie Loo standing in full black silhouette in the unendurable roar of baby-pink light.

What remains.

Silverbell's voice more wooden than the door, "Okay." She makes room for Bonnie Loo to pass, she who smells kitcheny and fresh-airy, but also there's a brittle odor of cigarettes.

"Were you resting?" wonders the guest as she tries to look into the darkness for a surface to place the basket upon.

"Not exactly."

"I just didn't want to disturb you if you were. But if I left this out in the hall, mice would beat you to it."

"Mickey and Minnie," Silverbell wisecracks. Her hair is blond, growing out darker, shoulder length, straight as water off an eave. Maybe silky when it was clean. And brushed. But it is not cared for today, or yesterday, either, or before that. On her feet bedroom slippers with golden plastic-by-product semi-sheen bows, the from-the-big-box-store-into-the-trash-can-in-six-months model. She shuffles along. She snaps on a Settlement-lathed pine floor lamp, a paper shade of dancing black-masked raccoons, the store-bought-in-1940s kind, and then returns to ease the door shut with a hand that seems at first glance injured. But no, it is trembling.

Three beds. Two are for Bard and Eden, almost thirteen, both kids seeming undamaged after the drug warriors and DHS wrung so much of life's juice out of them. Even after the court ordered them returned to Silverbell, it was six more months when each did not see the other's face. Yeah, even the brother and sister, these twins, were, as Silverbell was, allowed only guarded visits, which were canceled with no explanation, always at the last minute. Power has no master.

Now Bard and Eden have Settlement friends, maybe at this moment they're riding horses together, maybe helping with the casting or costuming or last-minute research for a history skit, maybe leading a Simon Says game for a bunch of squirmy tykes, or picking pumpkins. Or peeling pumpkins. Or scrubbing floors. Or sorting mail. Or with a crew off to the planetarium in Portland via two or three old patched mumbly Settlement sedans.

Bonnie Loo positions the basket on the bare breakfast table, lifts the basket's cloth. "Tomato soup herbed to perfection; real smoked deer jerky; warm bread and cold butter; tea of the mint variety; three cheeses, goat, cow, and reindeer . . ." She winks.

Silverbell sort of smiles, one eyebrow frowning. She enjoys the joke.

Bonnie Loo keeps going. "Salad with my special green Popeye dressing. And apple pie with some Cortlands, some sheep's noses."

Silverbell does not blink.

Bonnie Loo says, "Sheep-nose apples are shaped . . . kind of like a beet. I put any apple in a pie. I like a mix. And that's it. I meant to bring you an extra hand-wiping rag but nothing's really greasy here."

"I like all the stuff you brought."

"I know. I know everything." She chuckles. "The Settlement has many mouths."

Silverbell's eyes narrow. Maybe a headache?

A long silence.

"Oops. I'm such a bubble brain. Forgot to introduce myself. I'm Bonnie Loo. Usually I'm cooking. Or canning. Lately a *lot* of canning."

Silverbell's gray eyes gleam briefly. These are gray eyes with a darker gray outer ring. Gives her gaze an intensity beyond the vigilant eyes of a survivor. Her voice is not silvery or bell-like but clucky, henlike, but also her voice is direct. An arrow. "I know who you are."

Bonnie Loo runs her large hands down her sides, fingering the hem of her dark green sweater. She had expected this room to be hot. Or cold. Air trapped from another day or night or year. But it is comfortable and the beds have Settlement quilts and in the center of the floor is a warm braided rug of maroons and blues, capering pinks and martial grays. Wooden drawers, the kind you can stack like those roomy cardboard file boxes in office storerooms. Some novels on the night table. Some pottery holding wild blue asters, which will soon fade to fuzz.

This bouquet is probably a "healing" gift from Lee Lynn St. Onge. And that smell like balsam but also peppery . . . a Settlement-made candle or one of Lee Lynn's witchy salves. Lee Lynn, the witch of salves, teas, and tincture; Lee Lynn, young but with some early gray, like dark and gray straw, like, yes, a witch. Gordon's wife Tambrah once punched her in the face, circling her, while Lee Lynn's police siren voice, always so irritating, inflamed to a full scream, broadcast the emergency to the skies, north, south, east, and west. Lee Lynn was so hunkered down in one of her gauzy hippie dresses, her long arms wrapped eel-like around and around and around herself to shield against Tambrah's dancing, skin-rippling, grunting, biting, hair-pulling, sucker-punching, eye-purpling frenzy. There were many ways to make a stand over possession of Gordon in those days. Tambrah's was in two parts, where in a few weeks, she, like Claire, would leave. Back to the reservation in Tambrah's case, while legends of her ferocity stayed behind to cast warning of polygamy's hazards.

"Are you sometimes called Silvie? For short?" Bonnie Loo asks with a smile.

"No." A blunt sound, not as airy as a word. The young woman's eyes had sprung onto Bonnie Loo's broad dusky face.

Bonnie Loo clears her throat. "They've started your cottage. It's all framed."

"I know."

"Then you'll have windows." Bonnie Loo is privy to how Silverbell has been pressed to join the family at meals or to sign up for a crew, always to a blank stare and no-show. As with the girl Jane Meserve, some blame it on trauma, some pronounce her an "introvert." Settlement mouths bark and Settlement hearts are sticky and Settlement hands will make tidy. But it's no accident that the sucker-punching Tambrah's legends have become braided with Bonnie Loo's, for Bonnie Loo's posture and sometimes pissed-off tremble of the lip show possibilities one might not want to test. She says, "Well, I ought to hustle. Big load of shell beans to fuck with. And my wash has been on the lines for four days. There's been a crow getting in my cottage when the kids leave the door open. He tells me there's an eighty percent chance of showers and a sale on drill bits at Mertie's Hardware." She chortles. "He—"

"I heard about you."

Bonnie Loo turns to face her directly. She grins. "Oh, I'm sure."

"You don't have to worry. I'm not interested in him."

"Who?" Bonnie Loo pictures the wheedling crow. She sees him cocking his head and fluffing himself up to twice his size before pooping or his reedy voice the last time he spoke, *Sign up now! Don't miss this chance! Diamond-like brooch for every occasion!*

"Your husband." Is Silverbell smirking? *Your* husband. *Your your your . . .*

Bonnie Loo fingers the cuffs of the deep pockets of her sweater, a sweater roomy enough for when the baby, *his* baby, begins to really show.

Yes, actually she has lost it and attacked Settlement women. It was Beth, smart-ass Beth, only last winter. Well, it was a pushing and shoving fight, Beth laughing the whole time, but Bonnie Loo got in some squeezes, one around the throat that Beth pretends to forget. But oh, so many witnesses!! It is on record. It is in the *History as it Happens* books in the amazed "voices" of kids.

Bonnie Loo says, "Okaaaay."

Silverbell squints. "I don't want to get my sources in trouble. But they warned me that you . . . are . . . violent. I can't say who told me."

Bonnie Loo bows her head, blinking. She slapped Ellen. She threw a baked potato at Geraldine. "Lee Lynn has been up here a lot, but—"

"No, not her . . . *she* didn't tell me."

"Well," Bonnie Loo sighs. "Actually one of Lee Lynn's best traits is that she is not a gossip. Not a *mean* gossip. She sees herself as a healer. Just don't get me mixed up with Tambrah. Tambrah is gone. You'll never meet her. And . . . the *History as it Happens* books . . . kids stretch everything. Maybe your kids've been digging into Settlement history." One hiccup of a laugh.

Silverbell tucks some of her stringy hair behind an ear. "It was Gordon who told me." The hand at her ear now has a real elderly shakiness.

Bonnie Loo takes note.

"Well, that . . . whatever I *did* do, it's history. This is now. You are safe here and . . . at home. Believe me." And yet in this very moment Bonnie Loo is straightening to a fuller more bearlike height and bulk, as if to rise up beyond belief to swipe Silverbell Rosenthal away. *Away*.

Silverbell almost moans, "I don't think this is the place for me to live." And yes, her hands are shaking mightily. And this causes Bonnie Loo to have a flash, the body memory they call it, of her own hell, her father once younger than she is now, falling from the sky through police floodlights, the squirting black red meat of him bursting through his shirt, and from his head, face . . . *crack! crack! crack!* . . . every shot fired by them emptied more of him into the weeds around the loaded logging truck.

"Is there anything really really really special I can make you for supper tonight?"

A sharp "*No!*" Silverbell holds her hands against the front of her white T-shirt, her trim stomach, hands steadied. "This you brought will last for the rest of my life." She snort-laughs.

"You'll . . . love your cottage. It has a view of the sheep. And there is a smaller cottage going up near you. Benedicta's. You've not met her yet. She's a cute elderly lady."

"I might be gone soon."

"Don't leave the Settlement cause of *me*. *I* might be gone soon."

"I didn't mean on account of you."

Bonnie Loo sees how unrumpled all the beds are, a pair of rocking chairs with seat cushions of the same fabric as used in many dresses, skirts, and kids' sunsuits here . . . obviously Silverbell has been sitting in the dark in one of these rockers. Or standing? For hours of every day? "Did you tell anyone else you aren't staying? They're hammering away up there making you a place."

"He's scary."

"Who?"

"They say he can hypnotize people, brainwash them."

"Who? You mean Gordon?! That's horseshit from talk radio."

"I don't listen to talk radio."

"Who said it?"

Silverbell backs up to one of the rockers, sits very carefully.

"Before I came here. Everybody was saying it."

"But now you can see he's not that way."

Silverbell doesn't reply.

Bonnie Loo steps closer to the rocker with Silverbell in it. "If you leave, where would you like to go? We know people all over the state. Someone could help you find a job and a rent. What kind of work do you do? Besides raising dogs."

Silverbell says nothing. Her eyes flood.

Acorns smash upon the roof. Seems like hundreds.

Bonnie Loo swallows. That empathetic stone in the throat. "There's no rush, for God's sake. It's not like you're on the side of the road. You can take your time to figure things out. Everyone says Eden and Bard are doing okay."

Then Silverbell says through clenched teeth, "He touches me."

Bonnie Loo's eyes widen. "He?"

"Gordon, yes."

"*Touches* you?"

Silverbell glares at Bonnie Loo and waves a hand with spread fingers. "Yes."

"Where the fuck does he touch you?" Bonnie Loo hisses.

"My ears."

Bonnie Loo explodes. Fiendish laughter. Wide open jaws. Ugly almost cruel guffaws.

But wait, Silverbell Rosenthal's long hollow face is opening with a smile. Now laughing, too, a fearsome crowing, a hee-haw, a screech. Both persons teary and heaving and breathless, wiping their eyes.

Duotron Lindsey International's CEO, Bruce Hummer, on yet another corporate jet circling yet another significant city in plenty of time for yet another significant meeting, now reading yet another headline.

Yes, yet another AP offering. Dateline: *Cape Elizabeth, Maine*. Shows a figure not blurry but motion-stirred, backing away from the camera as he pulls himself into the open door of a pickup truck. Eyes, one narrowed with white redneck HATE, the other raised open wide with LUNACY. Or so it would seem. Phrases in the one-column piece leap out. "Militia connections," "wives of 40 governors" and "terrorized."

Bruce Hummer separates the page from the rest of the paper and folds it preciously, as you would save news of a friend.

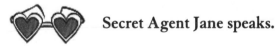

Secret Agent Jane speaks.

It is night, but I woke up. Nothing to do.

Today I saw a picture of Jeffrey, who we are going to visit in Texas. He is on the wall in the East Parlor. He is not a kid, but grown up. Age nineteen, I think. He is very quiet-looking in the picture. He is the color brown like my father, Damon, who I saw his picture, too, only a million times. This Jeffrey person is wearing a white outfit like in a hospital.

It would make you cry about Jeffrey. The government is going to KILLLL him in his jail. They will hold him and kill him. Gordie says the government guys are like hyeeenas with bad breath and big pink asses and that this shows the human race is *not above*. When Gordie gets upset about the human race he blows up with noise. Beth calls it *rants*.

I am just on my bed now, drawing Jeffrey like his real picture, only better. Pictures you make are good because you can make him get away. He can fly. And maybe get invisible while sneaking. I make yellow rays shoot out from him. And a smile. And in each hand he has presents with bows. And by his feet is presents with bows. And one present has a red heart. That one is from me.

***History as it Happens* as recorded by (Termite, Max, Weetalo, and Benjamin).**

Last spring when we did the OCEAN was when it all starts the Monarch terrarium we built in the empty shop. Call it the royal chamber. Next we went to a house of Claire's friend of college. She does Monarch WAtch. It's called MASS TAGGIng. Hundreds of people do it. This is how the way they do it seeing the Monarchs go thousands of miles like birds.

We sent off for books mapS PosTErs and pam-flits. It tells how THE South they call the Monarch King Billie which is a King whose colors were blAck and OrangE. He was in England and WANTED to OWN IriSH people Misty says. But the butterfLiEs were hERE. And some IRisH people went hEre.

We did skits on The Metim morfiss of MonaRcHS afTER eating taSTY Milk Weeds. Katy and Karma called the first one Noof. So Noof goes to Mexico and some humans here go to TEXAS to see JEFrey who the govinment is Going to murdEr.

A lady on the kitchen radio who says shE has a spy who knows THAT Place she means Settlement said you can't call this stuff edUcation going to visiT death row and skits and Work. She said time to send in the ATHOR itties and police. Misty called this friteninG.

I wonder if when the friendship comitee is flying in the jet they might sEe ouT the winDowS Noof and other thousands of buTTerfies flapping Along on their WAy.

We will soon know this.

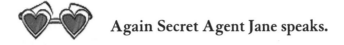

Again Secret Agent Jane speaks.

It is almost Texas. Our trip. They don't really want me to go. I heard this: "Jane has enough prison visits in store with her mother, and this Death Row thing could get pretty heavy." This is what the mothers said behind the door. With my secret agent hearts shapes glasses I can hear everything.

So then Bree, who is one of the grown-up girls and is very tall with red hair and a horror face that you get used to, let me be on the Death Row Friendship Committee and I told her how bad I wanted to meet Jeffrey. Bree said, "Sure." But then the mothers all said, "No." But Bree whispers to me very whisperishly, "Jane, *never* take no for an answer." And me, I said back to her, "Exactly."

Out in the real world.

Jeffrey is almost twenty years old. He has been on Death Row in Huntsville, Texas, for five years, waiting.

He has had appeals, he thinks, though he never sees a lawyer. A few times he got mail but he never sees articles, memos, or reports by the many Texas "state" lawyers who are in a panic about how they can't deal with so many habeas corpus cases.

And so Jeffrey waits. He waits for whatever comes.

Today something is coming. Today. They are flying all the way here from Maine to see him and put their hands against the wire of his visiting cage. Fourteen children and seven adults. The rules are only two at a time and only an hour total. So he is interested in how this will work.

He keeps all their letters. Their letters are funny. He likes the jokes they send. Kind of twisted jokes. Gary Larson. Bugs who talk. Laboratory guys who invent things like a monster that has a lot of heads, the heads of the Brady Bunch. Yeah, that one, he gets it one hundred percent. And then the one where this hospital night watchman is doing secret experiments in static electricity by sticking all these really fat newborn babies on the ceiling. And then there are the homemade cartoons and jokes. Some ain't bad. You have to believe the well-meantedness of some people for you to trust their sick humor.

These people from Maine are all coming to Texas JUST TO VISIT HIM. They are white kids, he's pretty sure. His sometimes buddy Jeddy, a Panther, a Muslim, suspects they are Buddhists. Or Catholic Workers. Then Jeddy added with a snort, "Maybe they're missionaries. They got a thing for the soul inside the dark face. You seen what they did to Queen Liliuokalani. First they save you, then they jail you." He did his special laugh that sounds like haunted wind in eaves. "But you already here!!!" More haunted wind laugh.

Jeddy who is about forty is educated. He reads all the stuff about peoples of the world getting the shaft and others kicking the ass of the oppressor, which is inspiring. Jeddy doesn't hoard his education. He's like one of those who helps you cheat on a test by giving you the answers. Only there's no test.

Meanwhile, Jeffrey likes to imagine his visitors won't be anything like the ones who stole Hawaii or moved the Cherokees or firebombed the MOVE guys in Philly. His new friends will turn out to have stepped out of one of the *Far Side* cartoons: man-sized cockroaches or woman-sized flies pushing baby buggies with maggots in them, cows who walk on their hind legs and drink martinis until a car comes by, space aliens who rob chicken houses, puffy poodles who get engaged to junkyard dogs, lionesses who spit out tofudebeests, and sharks showing vacation slides of human legs dangling from inner tubes. What the hell, today he smiles.

Portland jetport.

At six a.m. Gate five, long before the sun spurts over bunchy many-roofed but flat South Portland beyond the runway, the Settlement Committee (or gang, depending on your view) boards the plane. The flight attendants warn against running and swinging their satchels. The Settlement adults are somber, life's accumulated political realities weighing down the corners of their mouths.

Buckled in, the kids look out the windows and point. They wait. They watch other passengers snapping the overhead compartment doors shut. They giggle about the air vents and pamphlet pictures of people sliding out of the jet's doors on slides into the sea.

Then, in due time, the plane lifts off, up, up, and up.

The flight attendants do a bit more scolding when they roll along the wagons of beverages and nuts. Settlement kids are too perky. The fourteen *zhoop-zhoop*ing kazoos are definitely not a hit.

Secret Agent Jane wears her heart-shaped glasses and her chin held high. Today for the first time she feels herself to be one of the Settlement. You know, life. Us versus them. It's always been so.

Press conference.

See all the mikes! Hear all the networks and see the press corps leaning inward . . . their important rustling . . . their rapid-fire clear voices asking yet another question of Duotron Lindsey International's infamous CEO Bruce Hummer, who, yet again, has laid off more thousands, is headed out of this country in search of the cheap, the "willing tos." See Bruce Hummer's infamous face tilting slightly as if to chew a piece off the largest mike. See his hard jaw working into knots as he listens to another question. Hear his answers fall over the miles of a nation, like velvet. The face grows. Fills the screen.

The voice of Mammon explains.

Growth! Growth! Growth! Growth!

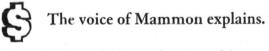

Academics despair. Here's Zygmunt Bauman, excerpts from one of his books, which nobody reads, *In Search of Politics.*

The global quantity of available work is shrinking—this being a structural problem related directly to the passing of control over crucial economic factors from the representative institutions of government to the free play of market forces . . . Hans Peter Martin and Harald Schumann, economic experts of Der Speigel, *calculate that if the present trend continues unabated, 20 percent of the global (potential) workforce will* *suffice "to keep the economy going" (whatever that means), which will leave the other 80 percent of the able-bodied population of the world* economically *redundant.**

Meanwhile, concerning the aforementioned subject.

The screen seems to be blank.

Cory St. Onge, age fifteen, speaks.

So yesterday off they went, them who were going to Livingston, Texas. Not me. Gordie and I and Rick went over to Rex's place. John Lungren followed in the lumber truck so he could do a delivery afterward. We ate Rex's ma's cookies out on their porch, which is glass instead of screens. Rain was smashing down on the flagstones leading to the porch and it sounded like a bunch of guys stomping on the porch roof. And even though we hadn't gotten wicked wet coming in, we all smelled like rain.

One of Rex's most devoted "men," some kid about fourteen or fifteen, was lurking around in the shadows of the kitchen that was lit only by a wall lamp over the sink.

The rest of us out on the little porch were talking about the militia movement . . . our favorite subject, *heh-heh*.

This stuff really boils my blood . . . the farm crisis. Somewhat mostly in the 1980s, in which the government and banks manipulated the force of gravity. Now it is no longer called a crisis, just a commonplace occurrence of farm auctions, the equipment, the land, the life and suicides made to not look like suicides. Politicians call it natural selection. You know how migratory birds smash into the guy wires of tall towers. Smart birds would fly around them, so the maggot-assed politicians say of both birds and men.

So John Lungren who is always packin', he is gazing out at the rain that's driving down on the other side of the glass. He's going back and forth in one of Rex's glider chairs. He says, "It's like McDonald's brags

---

* And this was before almost total Artificial Intelligence and robotization was the Market God's command.

of the 200-billionth gray burger being sold, these agribiz lobbyists and their puppets, they see a farmer's life as just another gray burger." And somehow his revolver is magically in his hand, his thumb on the action, aimed out into that silver sheet of hard drizzle, and I'm like feeling it in my arm, wrist, my clenched teeth . . . the burning . . . and maybe the hottest part of my rage is how so many millions of two-leggeds in this nation of delusions thinks such a feeling is not normal. Hell, it's normal. It is love for your fellow man, and I don't call the oligos men.

John slips the firearm back in his shirt and I'm wondering a lot of things.

Bruce Hummer confides in us.

Can I tell you a little something about myself?

In this drawer of my desk are three hundred Nembutals. You see, when you have a magic wand, when you are almighty, you can get anything you desire. Merchandise-wise.

Sometimes I line the nameless bottles up and they look cheerful. Helpful friends in amber plastic. I twist one of the caps off. I sniff the contents. Once I ran a big glass of water to prepare.

The only thing that stops me is that I would be found with wet pants and a goofy look on my face. But that is coming not to matter anymore.

Okay, I have told you about myself. More than I intended. Fortunately, you can't hear me. No one can. This office is the ultimate desolate place.

Concerning the aforementioned complexities—

The screen remains blank and dumbstruck.

BOOK TWO:

Pleased to Meet You

Portland International jetport. Settlement people waiting for Death Row Friendship Committee's return flight from Texas.

Foggy. Flights out of Boston can't get off the ground. And none are lifting off from here. Paul and Jacquie Lessard and Rick Crosman trudge off to the airport food vendor by the escalator to buy frozen yogurts. Nathan Knapp has gone to find a men's room. Gordon St. Onge stands at the big plate-glass window looking out into the dark fog. Arms folded over the chest of his short black-and-red wool Sherpa-lined vest. Plastic billed cap (*Bean's Logging and Pulp*) low over his eyes. The graying chin of his short beard looks more electric than the overhead fluorescents. A lot of people have been staring at him. They actually stop in their tracks and gaze, the way some would read graffiti on a turnpike overpass.

A moment ago, someone actually asked, "Are you Gordon St. Onge?" Some whisper and stare. But all in all, they let him be.

He hunches deeper into his vest and layers of shirts. It's hot as hell in here. Dry heat. He is dripping under his clothes but can't get the nerve up to take off his wool vest and outer shirt. He feels big and stupid and bare enough. He does not feel like a "prophet" or a "leader," as some have called him. He feels weird in these kinds of places.

A man steps up beside him at the plate glass, looking out. The man is of average height. A confident man. Ultra confident. Gordon reads this right away. A man, Gordon thinks, who might gauge your value by your financial portfolio, not by the weight of your soul. This guy is not dressed like a politician or an attorney on the go but he does, indeed, move like one. He wears an olive-colored camp shirt with patch pockets and faded and worn but not witheringly ragged jeans. Gordon sees a sport jacket on the plastic seat the man has just been sitting in. No valise. No computer, such as so many carry now. Not even an overnight bag. If you leave your carry-on unattended these days, it will be considered a bomb by airport authorities, and confiscated. Then your valise or satchel will be somewhat detonated. And maybe you will be mercilessly grilled.* Gordon looks into the guy's face. He is nearly a Rex York look-alike. Maybe it is not an attorney's bearing, maybe military. But what is the difference?

The guy looks at his watch. It has a breathless little hairlike gold second hand, sweeping away the moments, unlike Rex's watch face, which is black and complicated and manly and cluttered with life-saving outdoorsy data.

Gordon looks back out at the fog.

The man speaks. "Gordon St. Onge, we met once. Mutual friends . . . Morse and Janet Weymouth, at their home . . . a few years ago."

Gordon seriously studies his face, Rex's face. Rex's age. Late forties, early fifties. But the mustache is trimmer, doesn't crawl down along the jaws. And the eyes are not pale and steely like Rex's but a boggy brown-green. And rather warm. And the voice has a touch of Deep South so that the word "at" is pronounced "ay-hat" and "friends" is "frey-yends," single syllables made sensuous and sludgy, though Gordon has heard southern accents less diluted than this. This guy's words are wrenched by so much world travel and so many crowds but still his subtle drawl has its beguilement.

Someone passing by is now staring just as hard at this man as others have been staring at Gordon.

Now he puts his hand out and Gordon puts his hand out and both hands lock hard. "Bruce Hummer," the man says.

Gordon nods. "I . . . ah—"

---

* Remember this is pre-9/11. Now they'd probably taser you.

"It was a long time ago," the guy says with a chuckle. "Neither of us was infamous then."

Gordon squints, blinks. He thinks the guy does seem familiar, but not from any of Janet and Morse's dinner parties. It's the name, *Bruce Hummer*.

The guy offers no more priming of Gordon's memory, just says, "Fog's going to keep a lot of people stranded for the day. I'm thinking of renting a car and driving down to beautiful fog-free New York."

Not just his accent but the disciplined march of his phrases is mesmerizing.

Gordon is starting to really feel the weight of the airport's overheatedness.

For a couple of minutes they discuss the fog. And they agree that airport architecture does not fall into any category of art. Bruce snickers, "Even a pipe organ booming away on Bach, lighted candles in crystal chandeliers, lovely gals in rustling skirts, gents in capes bowing or clip-clopping by on white stallions couldn't beef up the ambience in one of these vinyl caverns." They both chortle grimly.

Bruce Hummer asks Gordon questions. Gordon, not likely to ask a stranger questions, just dutifully answers the questions asked of him. "Family coming back from Texas," and "I saw her earlier this month." Then a wink, "She looks great in blue." He swallows. "But Morse. Not great. Not good."

Bruce presses his hands to the plate glass, palms flat, fingers spread, a heaviness creeping into his soft drawl. "Morse is mortal, it turns out."

Gordon runs some fingers preeningly down one side of his own mustache, thinking he needs to be drunk.

The stranger smiles as he also seems to have come three steps closer. "Janet said your kids are all sharp as tacks."

Gordon groans with the Dumond House memory fluttering and flickering panoramically.

Bruce is now telling of a piece of property he owns up on the coast, near Bar Harbor, oceanfront. His eyes flick down over Gordon's red-and-black plaid wool vest then back to his face, that kind of peacocky dark and gray beard with the intense, uncertain pale eyes in dark lashes. Not Hollywood handsome nor would Manhattan give the time of day to such a visage. But in a mountain hollow, Bruce doesn't doubt, this Guillaume St. Onge is the sun, the moon, and the stars to those many and several hearts that rumor has it, and media has it, are all his.

Bruce confides, "Lina and I had a small place built there but we never used it. I mean *never*. Not together. I just came from there now. It's my self-inflicted solitary confinement. Just me and the chipmunks. And acorns coming down." His closed-mouth smile is a long-lasting scribbled line of sorrow. He squeezes his eyes shut. "*Lotta* acorns." Opens his eyes in a goggly way. "Why so many?"

Gordon says, "Well, it's—"

Bruce interrupts, "I am proud to be in the midst of a divorce that lacks vengeance. Rare, mind you. Divorces in my world are not usually so." He is close enough now that he grasps Gordon's upper arm. "*My* world, sir . . . is . . . afire with opportunities." Pause for effect. "And vengeance. Even between dearly beloveds. *Your* world, my sources tell me, is in an enviable limbo. An enviable failure. Opportunities for you all are just . . . what? . . . bales of hay and buckets of milk?"

Gordon's Tourette's-like eye-flinch is getting up some velocity.

"I can tell, Gordon, that you don't stay abreast of certain kinds of minutiae . . . for instance, the *Wall Street Journal*, with its little sketched cameo portraits . . . or even television, yes . . . the sound bytes, the artful press conferences starring individuals who . . . have . . . well . . . hey! Hear this. One of my dreams a few nights ago was about *you*." In a silky one-piece motion the guy draws a pen from his chest pocket, a ballpoint, slim, silver. He smiles yet again. His smile, like his motions, like his voice, like the costly pen, is his suit of armor, hushy and recondite, made differently than for horseback jousting, made for this grand epoch where killers and the killed seldom meet.

He says to Gordon, "You were on a bridge but it was also inside a room. That's all. The rest is fuzzy. But hey . . . what a coincidence." Now a business card materializes. He writes on the back, presses it into Gordon's hand. The print of the card informs Gordon that Bruce Hummer is Chief Executive Officer of Duotron Lindsey International. What Bruce handwrote on the other side is: *Janet's and Morse's friend.*

Gordon seizes in the dead center of his mind's eye the word *friend* exactly written in that silky black ink. He is mulling over how much hope Morse Weymouth had placed in shareholder activism. Morse called it democracy, sickeningly true since pencils and US election ballots are as fairy dust in a four-year-old's storybook. Gordon holds his breath. The new knowledge that Morse has been chummy with the CEO of Duotron Lindsey, the war weapons manufacturing giant, who no doubt has received those personal phone calls of Janet's, her hushy wrist-grasping voice calling "Bruce" by name and this man's velvet-throated devilishly seductive accent answering, sickens Gordon. He has known the Weymouths *forever*. His mother Marian approves of them, of course, in her lifetime endeavor to wear status like a warm coat against ice and snow. But Gordon has . . . yes . . . has loved the Weymouths . . . as human beings . . . as very special human persons. And now what? Is it that all those in the upper classes just suffer too much from politeness? Or do they see each other across a crowded room and fly to each other's arms . . . figuratively speaking . . . in order to eat well, drink well, and at times satiate themselves in meaningful pretend combat? For they are all winners in the *big* picture . . . like lions dining on the bleeding spoils, they cuff one another, but their only *true* enemy is the great mass of human antelopes that is alive only to lie still while being chewed on. In reality this balance of humanity is kept alive only *to serve*.

He thinks of Morse's legislative battles. Tinkering at the edges of the edifice but never raising his voice to the ideology of masters over slaves, never sounding off with too much of the belly and the balls. Okay, not *always* well-mannered, okay, but not one word *ever* about even a fleeting wish to end slavery. Oh, they say slavery ended. Horseshit. The world writhes in slavery. And of course it's the nature of the human species . . . it *will always be so*. In one shape or another it will go on and on and on.

If only Morse had wept for the slave, keened wetly, held the slave in daily awe, even just spoken aloud of the slave.

Maybe Morse never gave a fuck about slaves. Only the "environment" mattered.

And Janet? Does she privately grieve for those chained to debt, cursed by meekness, swept from their homelands, flash-frozen (figuratively speaking), and packed into computer work cubicles, phone marketing cubicles, fellerbunchers, assembly lines, and cell blocks?

He shivers to see the Weymouths in this new dark light. He swallows hard, hotter and hotter in his wool.

Bruce is right there. His expression is odd, like that of someone who sees a ghost or maybe a flying saucer but knows better than to let on. He, Bruce, holds up a hand, a traffic cop's *Stop!* and says, "So, no TV or Internet at your compound?"

Gordon stands soldier-straight and grunts, "If I found a TV on the property, I'd order it to go before the firing squad."

Bruce laughs, withdrawing his hand, looks down the rows of plastic chairs to the X-ray-equipped entrance of this bright waiting area. He turns to Gordon again. He sucks in his breath, tightens his stomach, a fit-looking man, like Rex, but, yes, different from Rex. "I know you, Gordon . . . your politics, your . . . habits. I've been following you in the papers . . . and the Internet has more on you than on George Washington. Oh, these sources screw up but certain essences remain. You've moved the masses." He stares straight as the path of light into Gordon's eyes. "That's a dangerous gift."

Gordon's eyes don't flinch Tourette's-ishly but his dark mustache flickers. He hears the airport announcements, which are staticky. He sees discouraged faces of those fogged-in passengers, sitting, standing, milling. He believes somebody has turned the heat up in the demon furnaces under this temple of sacrifice where people are ferried to and from the skies, to and from other realms, nearer and nearer to civilization's implosion. His mind bounces. He says to his new friend, "They say it's another two hours before any planes in Boston will get off the ground. That's where my people's connection is. And no flights *from* here. I've got cider in my truck. Let's go out there and sit awhile in the pretty parking garage and shoot the shit and get shit-faced."

Bruce, with a grin, snatches up his jacket and follows Gordon on a search to find the other Settlement people so they can be told of this plan, minus the cider part. No introductions are made with these quiet frozen-yogurt–eating people.

The gray area.

Bruce twists around and hangs his sport jacket on the gun rack that is against the cab window behind his head, then, with a hand spread on each thigh of his washed-out jeans, watches Gordon pouring the clear-as-vodka cider from a plastic milk jug into two Settlement-made pottery mugs. Bruce's mug has pink painted hearts and someone's initials scratched into the pottery. Gordon's mug has what might be squid and octopuses, or might be girls with flowing hair. And initials. Very homey. Very well-equipped truck, ha ha. But also the cab smells of the damp day and of greasy tools in tin boxes on the floorboards under his, Bruce's, feet. And there's a goaty stink, maybe the striped blanket spread across the whole bench seat, or something under the seat, or maybe it's Gordon's plaid vest, which lies now between them. There's the gray hollow smell of the parking garage floating in at the open windows.

And maybe there is a smell to risk, such as defying the law against riding with an open container of alcohol while you're not a good pal of the state's attorney general, for instance. Although Bruce wouldn't venture many bets on that one, the whole Depaolo clan being pretty well dug in. But there are hazards Guillaume "Gordon" St. Onge is known to mess with; are they worth the consequences, where both roads of the fork lead to ruin? To being roasted?!! And yet some say he is an ultracautious man, stiff with fears and guttering courage, other than his in extremis philosophies. And isn't there a kind of yellow-gray stink to the end of the universe, where you look at the diagram on the last door and it says, "You are here."

Risk interests Bruce more these days. Veritable risk. Accelerating personal risk. In his world his job is to stack those sandbags against the storm. Have his people be shoulder to shoulder with the writers of bills, to spurn regulations. Jeopardy of any stripe, even competition of any species, must be muscled to the ground, fairly or unfairly. Media friends must be whispered to. Handcuff them with treasure. Protesters must be cordoned off into back alleys or shackled and toted away from the awful scene. One can steer one's perfect corporate ship only under sweet skies and smiling waters.

Yes, the ship is unassailable. But Bruce himself? He has decided that the pills are too girlie a way to go. Now on his shopping list is nylon rope. He is getting closer to the YOU ARE HERE door. This little party with St. Onge is only a hiccup in the velocity, no worse than the fog on the runways and in New England skies. He sighs full-chested deep.

Gordon, meanwhile, has been seeing with glances that Bruce's hair has started thinning at the temples in the same way Rex York's hair has. Rex, his "brother." The same dark brown with very little gray. And the mustache, which erases boyishness from any face, giving canniness and tenor to the eyes.

Sneak-peeks at Bruce's hands show slim straight fingers, the nails fussed over, trimmed, and pearlescent. Nothing like Rex's hands, which have wired hundreds of homes, raised and killed and cut up and paper-wrapped dozens of steers, disassembled and reassembled countless guns, smeared on gun oil, grasped and knocked back, squeezed at and flipped over and thrust in lever action, bolt action, rolling block, thirty-shot clips, and then dealt with bad carburetors, spark plugs, radiators, transmissions, and wrastled into position that prized wind turbine, the one that crowns the Settlement's bald-topped mountain, which Rex's crushed finger surely remembers on certain rainy days.

Gordon wills himself not to let his eyes keep drifting back to his guest's hands, as he would try not to stare at deformities of burn victims and people with nose rings, tongue rings, shaved and tattooed heads.

And Bruce is doing the same. Trying to resist the awe.

The truck faces out to the angled cement ramp so people on foot, toting luggage, trudge past, some eyes looking in at Gordon and Bruce fleetingly. Exiting cars flash by.

After the first drink, Gordon observes the horrible truth that there is no men's room in the parking garage and points to a hole in the floorboards of the truck. "On a dark night on the Maine Turnpike, with somebody else driving, I have used that hole." Both he and Bruce cackle over this and Gordon buries his head a moment in his arms folded over the wheel, then surfaces to burp.

Bruce glances around the cab of the truck, pokes at the plastic Godzilla dangling from the rearview. Smiles a little. He says something more about the weather. He absently fingers the truck's slack and rattly door handle. Says a little bit about airline ticketing and flight patterns. Once, turning to glance out the back cab window, he fingers the empty gun rack prong above his jacket, as plastic as the Godzilla. Red cheesy plastic. In his eyes, a warm faraway look, his mouth set, teeth gritted.

Gordon remembers reading about an expensive matchmaking service . . . an article someone had sent him . . . was it in the *Wall Street Journal*? . . . it was a service where a CEO can get a compatible and trustable friend. Gordon has never been this close to this kind of guy, high-powered, mind like a cat's, a lotta carcasses in his wake. No, never *this* close. Morse and Janet, old-money people, like people born from the ash of volcanoes, he would not associate them with the sleazy sociopathic maneuvers people like Bruce Hummer have committed, grasping and stabbing his way to the blood-slippery tip-top accumulation of those take-your-breath-away gadgets of war.

But this is nothing like what Gordon would have expected. Bruce Hummer feels too familiar.

More cider? Sure, sure. More cement smell. Plenty of exhaust from vehicles mumbling past.

Bruce is describing two nearly grown sons by his first wife, a two-year-old by his second wife. "A while back, I brought Kelsie with me to Maine for a couple of weeks. Kelsie was fourteen months then. She was sick to her stomach the whole time and kept asking for Jill. Jill is her au pair. She never once asked for her mother and it was clear she didn't feel she could trust me. I was essentially a stranger to her. Trust is no longer a thing of this world, brother."

Gordon's eyes widen at this word, *brother*. Rex, he calls brother. Many others, too, in those moments of waxing fraternity over shared large or tiny griefs.

Another refill with the pale burning smooth cider, which Gordon explains was made in old bourbon kegs, and using Red Delicious apples. A Settlement recipe, top secret.

Gordon, in a low register of the voice, confesses some of the parts of Settlement life one might call *strife*. It just dribbles right out of him. Is Bruce craftily manipulating him to let down his guard? Wouldn't someone who 24/7 plots dominion over swaths of humanity and natural "resources" turn this moment of buddying into a bit of sport? Like the legend of the scorpion and the frog, isn't it his nature?

But Bruce now looks away, staring into the cement, at worlds within and beyond. He says, "I hated my teens. I was not—" He laughs, a braying sort of laugh. "—sociable."

Gordon makes an exaggerated face. Call it shock.

Bruce says, "I'm more of a sniper than a haggler or a hugger. But you train yourself to do what you need to do."

Gordon wags his empty mug back and forth. "I sympathize."

Bruce laughs. "Maybe."

Gordon says, "Well, I do. I'm not . . . *social*."

Bruce says, "I'm from Alabama." He laughs. "Well, I'm still *from* Alabama."

"Yeah?"

"I can't go back."

"That's common," Gordon says with a sigh.

"I can only step out of the space capsule. Can you imagine floating like that? All the . . . all that is unfeasible, unworkable, insuperable, insurmountable, and ludicrous, falling away like chunks of dried mud . . . and off you go."

Gordon squints. "But you like your job, your life?"

"I love my job . . . the job. The job. But they don't call it a *job*. They call it working hard." He raises an eyebrow endearingly.

Gordon pretends to toast him with his empty mug.

Bruce wags his head. "Alabama is gone gone gone gone gone."

Gordon rests a hand on Bruce's shoulder. "Man, you okay?"

"No."

Gordon grabs the wheel of the truck. "Today we are in our space capsule, way up over the fucking fog. We don't give a flying fuck about fog . . . or fucking anything."

Bruce titters.

Gordon's hand reaches back for Bruce's shoulder, the hand that can never get enough touch. With children and women, it's their ears. With men, shoulder-and-forearm grips, bear hugs. His cousin Aurel (Oh-RELL) tells Gordon, "Mon dieu! You *do* paw!"

Bruce swigs from his cider. Three noisy swallows.

Gordon says, "Morse. *Our friend*. If only the stroke had killed him outright. Why this dragging on?"

Bruce agrees it is painful to see Morse this way. Obviously, Bruce has been a recent visitor at Cape Elizabeth, not just relying on the phone calls, e-mails, whatever.

Then Bruce presses Gordon to elaborate on his politics. On that subject Gordon can be explosive and some would be loath to press that button. But following Bruce's question and the echo of silence after the question, Gordon just noisily sucks on his mug, forgetting it's empty. He sees that even Bruce Hummer's profile is Rex's, the straight nose, the short indignant chin.

And so Gordon sets his empty mug on the dash, places both huge callused work-thickened hands along the bottom of the steering wheel.

Is Bruce waiting for Gordon to reply? To spill all his "political" guts?? Bruce's listening silence is spiderish. He tips the pink hearts mug to swallow the last of what's in it. A predator is always keen to weakness and so he can't miss Gordon's fatal innocence. But also he sees a simple thing, the powerful mass of the neck, shoulders, fingers, wrists spreading in its desire, its passion, multiplied by myriad future followers . . . it spills over. How does that go? His cup runneth over . . . while, uh . . . you the magnifico will lie down in the valley of the shadow of death. You will fear no evil. *But you will fear the innocents*!! The cup dribbling, drizzling with refugees, unemployed, underemployed, overemployed, and enraged and enraptured. There is nothing about the St. Onge phenomenon lost on Bruce Hummer.

He snorts. A big grin now, and tells a really bad joke about martians . . . maybe once it was a good joke, but his timing is all off.

Gordon understands that as they drink more, they become more alike. Two sloppy confounded goofballs. Ah, the beauteousness of drunkenness.

Gordon refills Bruce's mug, then his own. Both men's eyes are getting red-gray and liquidy, the eyelids thickening.

Gordon is now back to explaining about the bourbon barrels and Red Delicious apples, repeating himself.

Bruce chortles softly, raises his mug. "To our posterity!"

Gordon's mug is meant to touch Bruce's gently but clonks it. "Oops!" A good bit sloshes out onto both of their laps like lukewarm piss. Then Gordon says gruffly, "To our future world's beautiful people!" Takes a long swilling gulp-gulp-gulp from his mug.

Bruce copies him.

"Where's the john in this godforsaken place anyway?" Gordon snarls.

Bruce points at the hole in the floorboard.

They both laugh like hell.

Bruce's magnificent wristwatch churns away the moments, the unexcitable tiny hands more exacting than human breathing, human heart, and the march of lymph and blood. Never once in this cab has he glanced at this exquisite instrument.

Gordon again begins to ramble about the apples, the barrels, slurring slightly. "Rrred Delicious. *Not* delicious to eat 'em. Like a tennis ball and a pear that had a . . . baby. But fermented, they—" Kisses the bunched fingertips of his own right hand.

Bruce burps between his teeth, not softly.

Gordon groans. "I'mmm going to accommodate yourrr request, brother."

"My request," repeats Bruce, his eyes searching his inner fog to locate this puzzling phrase.

"My politics," Gordon reminds him with a sniff. "I neverrrr vote."

Bruce marvels, "You don't say."

"Well . . . I vote for referendums and road commissioner . . . selectmen . . . ah . . . clerk."

Bruce nods and waves his cup so that the contents dance out onto his hand and somehow splatter the windshield. "Oh'm fuck," he declares.

Because he's squinting with laborious effort at a thought, Gordon doesn't notice Bruce's bumble. He says, "Last time . . . to vote . . . I waz bee-trayyyed."

"You don't say."

"I voted . . . I wrote him in . . . a write-in, see? He sounded so good. You ever hear of him? Vermin Supreme."*

Bruce's pupils flare as if darkness has fallen.

Gordon touches Bruce's upper arm with two fingers. "He *promised* that if he were elected—" Burps largely. "—he'd see to it that everyone got a pony."

"You don't say."

"Well, he didn't get elected . . . but . . . rrreliable sources said that there are not enough—" BURP! "—ponies."

Bruce runs a hand through his hair as if to tidy up but somehow this causes his hair to look like two brown horns.

Gordon cocks his head listening to the yakking *inside* his own head because outside his head nobody is talking.

---

* Vermin Supreme is a real candidate in *New Hampshire* elections. He's yet to run in Maine.

Gordon says in a balloony squashy murmur as if another burp were moving into position, "All the people . . . all identities . . . all derms . . . all the issues people . . . all of them who clobber each other . . . it's a civil war on low heat . . . you know full well what I mean . . . if we all instead looked up in the friggin' sky at you corporate supremacist guys, you'd all be dead!"

Bruce sits up straight, turns his head to face Gordon's face full on, and grins ear to ear, "You don't say."

Gordon's pale intense eyes waver, then he seems to find something gorgeous about the dashboard.

His passenger speaks in his tensile drawl, "I know you have a firearm in this truck, Mr. Militia . . . somewhere. Behind the seat maybe?"

Gordon says nothing.

Bruce says, "There is nothing, Mr. Militia, that will stop this high-tech most profoundly complex global grid of power except when someday it hits the big wall. Love will not cure it. Not even your . . . your *Recipe*."

Ah, so Janet showed him fifteen-year-old Bree's "document" flyers. How tender a picture this makes! Those two crowned heads, Janet's and Duotron Lindsey's, together over the earnest oh-so-hopeful thrashes and swirls of calligraphy of that one-of-a-kind child.

"No," Bruce goes on in his hot velvet fashion. "Nothing can stop this matrix. The toothpaste is out of the tube. The mule is out of the barn. The hornets are out of the hive. Our species spreads, blooms, the protons deliver. But just for the beauty of it, the fine art of it, the black and blue of it, you might earn some awfully sweet satisfaction if you're willing to . . . to one at a time, in rapid succession, supposing you inspire a chain reaction, blast the brains out of every man and woman of the pyramid's high-water mark, and every one of them who dares replace them, doing it purely for the ripe raw red chef d'oeuvre of it, because it will just regenerate a dozen new heads for every one that rolls . . . but, oh! For the pageantry! That for a little day or two the muzhiks would be kings. Oh, you can do it! And you can start with me." He places his thumb between his own eyes matter-of-factly. "Right here."

Gordon snorts, one syllable of light laughter. Because this is funny. Now a real laugh crashing harshly into Bruce's silence.

"You chicken?" Bruce wonders. His green-brown eyes, which one could describe as tender, press Gordon all over.

Bruce feels into one of his rear pockets, one haunch raised awkwardly, the storm of alcohol inside him giving him no grace. A large brass key appears in his fingers. He pitches it onto the nearer thigh of Gordon's work pants. "Find a man who has the guts to do it. My seaside cottage. Real swank, but no security. It's 17 Island Rock Road. I'll be there every weekend over the next four weeks. After that, I can't say. In and out. Take your chances." With his slim ballpoint pen, he scribbles something on the back of another of his beige-colored business cards, pushes the card into Gordon's hand. "I'm serious," he presses on. "Be smart now. Don't miss this once-in-a-lifetime opportunity."

Gordon frowns down at the key. Then closes his eyes. This izzzz symbolic, right?

And now silence between them, and anything but innocence. The key remains on Gordon's thigh. A boasting, entirely terrestrial, bigger than the space it occupies. Once, when Gordon glances up to scan the face of his passenger, he sees nothing but the brisk perfection of the man's one visible ear. Yes, perfect. Those stiff swirls and the mysterious dark canal, uniform with all other human ears and yet, from individual to individual sui generis. The mystery of the-one-and-only will never be known.

Then Bruce says, mildly, his eyes more bloodshot than they were the moment before his last spoken word, "A toast."

Both men now have hair that is at the same time cowlicked and somehow windswept.

Gordon says, "Wait." He struggles with the cider jug cover, which came off so easily before. Refills Bruce's mug, overfills his own, splattering his left knee, shin, work boot, clutch pedal.

Bruce laughs, sags against the passenger door. The mugs then come together.

Gordon croaks, "To our future world's beautiful people."

Bruce sort of shouts, "To whatever happens!"

Again the mugs come together, *crack!* And cider shoots everywhere in a loopy silver rain.

Gordon takes a swig, then pushes his mug through the air toward Bruce, who isn't there but is pissing on the cement wall behind the truck, the celebratory hole in the truck floor forgotten.

"To my brother," Gordon murmurs deeply to the vacant seat.

Bruce returns, needs to slam the truck door four times to get it shut.

Gordon now visits the cement wall, the broad brass key in one of his chest pockets, its meaning confounding.

Then the talk peters out, their brains furry with alcohol bliss. Three chins-up suited men pass with computer valises gently swinging.

Both Gordon and Bruce burst out into weepy laughter at the sight. Bruce quotes from Carl Sandburg, "The fog comes on little cat feet. It sits looking over the harbor and city on silent haunches and then—"

"Hey! You've got a literary bent."

"I'm good at everything," Bruce jokes.

"Can you cook?"

"Damn right. I can do, among others, Korean, Persian, Cajun, and I'm a genius at packing lightly for the trail."

Gordon stares at him. "That's impressive. *Trails*?" Then he snickers in cider-awash happiness.

"Up down and all around!" Bruce says in singsong.

Both are taken by ragged guffaws and Bruce slides down in his seat knees up, jerking his head from side to side. And the next hour revolves carousel-like around this silliness, burps, and trips to the cement wall.

Finally there is a sudden silvery brightness at the narrow porticoes of the nearest downward ramp. It is the thinning fog. And they hear a jet arriving. The roads and ramps and sky are swollen with fumes and thunder and hurry.

Big Delta flomps down onto the black wet glassy-looking runway and the Settlement's Death Row Friendship Committee emerges in straggly single file from the open door marked Gate 6.

The Lessards and Rick Crosman (the Settlement's finest fiddle maker) and Nathan Knapp (the Settlement's "Peace Man") lonnng done with their frozen yogurt stand together with Gordon watching these beloved faces become tangible out of the bleary milky stir-about of stranger faces, metallic walls, carry-on luggage swinging to and fro. The sacredness of THE FACE, the familiar gait. All else is a wash of background gray. Jacquie Lessard opens her arms to crush Margo St. Onge and her own Alyson together, all three talking at once, hopped-up and squeally.

Erin Pinette, dragging a heavy satchel, gives everyone quiet, world-weary hugs.

More and more Settlement kids file out from the Gate 6 door. Here comes Secret Agent Jane, gorgeous and stately, no heart-shaped glasses on her face today, her eyes blacker and more sizzly than ever.

Gordon isn't smiling. He does not *look* drunk but, rather, looks nobly exhausted. The only way you'd guess he was sloshed was if you inhaled the air around him. He stands with his hands behind his back in a sort of military fashion, breathing slowly, as in hibernation, eyes on the door even as the Settlement faces have ceased to appear.

Of barely more stature than the kids, five-foot-tall troll-doll-look-alike Stuart Congdon, with great orange flames of hair and beard and a bulge of belly that often shows boldly and baldly and belly-buttonishly between his belt and T-shirt hem (today a vest sweater of feathery mauve and a plaid shirt fit him well), hefts his carry-on backpack and someone else's satchel of a print of sunflowers, trudges straight past Gordon without a glance, but growls, "Looks like *I'm* driving."

On a small private jet out of Portland.

He holds his head cocked sideways, staring with strictured unease at nothing but the weave of the upholstered seat in front of him.

***History as it Happens* (as recorded by Liddy Soucier).**

Everyone says to include my age in the report. Okay, I will be sixteen in two weeks. Rachel says it's for when people read these books a hundred years from now and FACTS WILL MATTER. Okay, this reminds me. Remember the jillion forms we had to fill out to visit the prison. We all were to be in a form. Each and every one of us had *eight* forms.

You would think we were the criminals, all the digging into our pasts we had to agree to. Lorraine Martin said don't take it personal. Del and Stuart laughed and said most of these Death Row Friendship Committeepersons don't have pasts long enough to dig into.

Then when we got there to Livingston, we had to go through a bazillion doors and archway beeping things and have people frisk us. After they'd already snooped all through our pasts, now you are checked in your pockets, hair, ribs, *feet*!

Believe it or not this is my first report for *History as it Happens*. Writing for the record is not my forte. I write mostly poems.

So it was not allowed for more than two people to visit Jeffrey so before we went we had already divided up the list of inmates the pen pal organization sent us.

There was Marco, Jian, Chris, DeMonte, Ben, Michael, Rayvon, Sonya, Jake, Steven, Kristina, Jon, LeDante, Ernesto, and Jeffrey.

Lorraine and I got Ben. When he came into the little wire and glass room he was in handcuffs with a guard.

Visitors don't have to wear handcuffs. Seems like we would. But for some reason they let it go.

The guard was short, or *seemed* like it next to Ben, who was like Gordie, very giant, like what Beth always calls Mr. America. But Ben looked African, not African-*American* but real true African like he had no Indian or Irish ancestors or any of that fooling around and pot melting that goes on here in America. His eyes were like the eyes of God floating in the night.

Side note: Later, Lorraine said Ben had an old face, not old like a great-grandpa but like old people who went way back and had a geography that wasn't shifting so much but was like a humongous tree with roots going below the earth's crust and then opened wide and nobody ever had to ask, "Who am I?" and "Where's my inner child?" Time was a very straight bold line. At least until the 1600s.

I had to laugh at that because I was remembering how when Ben talked to us, he talked wicked soft but it was in a Very Big City, USA accent. So *he is us*, just plain unromantic USA.

Anyway, so when Ben and the guard guy came in, the *little* guard guy, he's taking off Ben's handcuffs and neither one of them were happy-looking people. It was as if they were all set to murder Ben *today* and everybody was all braced for it.

We had been sitting there, smiling, before the door opened, me and Lorraine, but then we weren't.

History as it Happens (as dictated by Jane Meserve, almost age seven, with painstaking assistance by Alyson Lessard, age fourteen).

Before we went to the jet, I said I really really really do not want to see ANYBODY but JEFFREY . . . get it!!! He's the *one*. I want ONLY JEFFREY and that's that.

So Stuart and I went to see Jeffrey. It's different than visiting Mum. Texas has more cement and stuff and cop guards feel your organs like doctors do.

It was glass between us because Jeffrey is a dangerous killer. I heard that news tells it that Mum is a dangerous drug dealer, which is different than killer . . . even though *really* Mum is a dental assistant. So maybe Jeffrey is messed up by the news. He is really tall and really skinny for a killer.

We put our hands together on the glass. Me and Jeffrey. And Stuart and Jeffrey. Through the phone that they make you use Jeffrey had a jokey voice and he laughs nervous at everything. Then he asked me if we were Bootists or cathlic workers. I explained to him that where I am staying everybody works till they drop. But not me. I'm just a guest. My Mum is in jail for the drug war, a war *in* America.

Jeffrey said he knew about the drug war. And he said DEFINITLY there is war IN America.

I told him everyone at the Settlement eats and slurps on horridable foods like fish with SKIN and if you suggest very nicely to go to McDonald's it is a mortal sin.

Stuart rolled his eyes. He told Jeffrey that I am a drama queen.

Jeffrey laughed.

I said I am a queen in certain ways.

Jeffrey laughed again.

History as it Happens (more by Liddy).

My mother (Josee, for the record) says Gordon's mother (Marian, for the record), you never see her, she doesn't like the Settlement or us, she gave Gordon hell because on the radio a caller said how us kids go to visit prisons, that we will pick up uncivilized evil loser low-life ways.

Gordon says you can't pick up uncivilized evil loser low-life ways in an hour and forty-five minutes.

My father (Aurel, for the record) said Gordon's mum Marian St. Onge, for the record, is always already calling us all losers. So where is there to go from there?

My Tante Jacquie says kids shouldn't know about the death penalty till they grow up. It could give them heartache and confusion.

Gordon said maybe that's true.

Bev and Barbara said there is no recipe in stone for growing up.

Penny says one must always fill up with opportunities for thought even if it provokes moral indignation. One needs to be amazed at how a DOCTOR is hired to poison TO DEATH a RESTRAINED human person and it isn't called murder by politicians. She said one needs to realize that the whole thing is not a cartoon, not a movie with actors or a video game or a game of checkers.

Claire said Abraham Lincoln hanged dozens of Indian chiefs because they wouldn't crawl on their hands and knees while Lincoln and other hotshots built their empire. She said the older she gets the uglier American history and American history-making get, that maybe it *was* wrong to immerse the younger kids in the full truth.

Gordon said, "Baloney. The kids are handling it better than himself."

Beth said, "Hey, remember when Gordon got so upset about them killing the retarded guy in South Carolina that he, Gordon, threatened to wet himself and he was raving and pulling his hair and those people visiting, the soprano singer and the other one said Gordon ought to see a psychiatrist."

Leona said, "Oh, well, the kids are back. It's done. Let's move on."

History as it Happens (as dictated by Jane Meserve, almost age seven with assistance by Bree Vandermast, age fifteen).

So I forgot this. Jeffrey said he got the pictures I sent him that I drew. He said they made his day. He asked what kind of church I go to. I said, "Church? You mean the white things?"

He laughed. Then he asked Stuart if he knew Jesus.

Stuart said in a very nice way he guessed he wasn't ready for that.

Then Jeffrey asked me if I knew Jesus.

I said, "Is he here? Is he a dangerous killer?"

Jeffrey laughed the most over that. He said, "He's here."

I said, "Does he *work* here or is he . . . stuck here?"

Jeffrey laughed so hard and I saw all his missed teeth. I will remember forever him laughing and his sad eyes all drippy with happy laughing tears.

BOOK THREE:

Dangerous Gift

The voice of Mammon explains.

I am utter power. I am violence that finds no limit, no finish, no regret. Even on an ordinary day in ordinary America, with everyone on the scene smiling and crowing, "Nice day, isn't it?!" you all are, in the private canyons of your skulls, aware of what noncompliance will get you.

On the ballot of the managed flow, optimism is the one box for you to check. Helplessness is joy. Hopelessness is joy. There is no box for fighting back. You dream of it, maybe brag of its sweet imagined reckoning, but no fellow slave will stand with you. There is only utter terror in the face of utter power. There is only strange strange joy, strange strange frozen obelisks of joy, strange strange howls of joy.

One evening at the old farmplace on Heart's Content Road.

Gordon alone but for Secret Agent Jane asleep upstairs.

No, he is not the charismatic prophet talk radio has described him as, or the terrorist cult leader the newspapers *hint hint hint* at. Nor is he the prize of strength many Settlementers would swear to his being, with whom so many here have aligned their hearts.

The smiling old woman's appearance one night after Jack Holmes drove into this yard with Silverbell and her kids has left Gordon shaken. It's not as if she and they were the first. He suspects that in time, dozens of cars and trucks will show up outside, doors slamming, engines churning away leaving figure after figure under his big ash tree, refugees of the wheel of progress, faster, faster, faster the wheel rips up lives, spits them out at this address.

Oh, and of course each one is that hot cinder of sorrowing humanity, part of the watching eye of the whole of creation to whom you can never say, "No occupancy" or you shall be damned. And isn't it this that is pitching so many lives overboard, the very thing he feared back in Mechanic Falls with Claire? So all along *it was true!* The reason for this tiny Settlement nation carved out from the blackest depths of his fright is given warrant. *We killed our child because it was so.*

But then he was deceived, raised by his own cleverness out of the chatter of truth to sire a city of innocents who now must face the *ha ha!* "free world" and its plastic dagger to the heart.

He carries a mug of maple milk into the old parlor, which is even more heaped with books and files and unanswered mail than the dining room and kitchen. And photo albums Marian left behind. He sinks onto the divan that doesn't squeal but screams, yes, the same one Marian left behind, amid other furnishings Claire left behind. He flips to the last pages of *Project Megiddo* from the Bureau's busy hand and reads on from where he left off days ago.

Tock. Tock. Tock. The nice clock that was Marian's. Its sound trickles over his skin. It's not about time. It's about hypnosis. *Tock. Tock. Tock.* His eyes close. *This report is not us.* Not Rex his brother, not himself. Not any of the militia movement guys he has heard out (between gusts of his own ranting). His future is being shaped by the hands of strangers in some unknown way. *Tock. Tock. Tock.* Here comes the past. No nasty surprises. Nasty, yes. But all is known. Thus the past is cold comfort.

Rex York. His "brother." Yeah, back then Rex drank. Now you can't even get him to eat a cookie, it's just a regimen of push-ups and laying out plans for outdoor bivouacs. *Winter* bivouacs. How to live by eating frozen moss and bark. How to hide. And back home in his attic, he is always at it, collecting "patriot" gossip on the World Wide Web. A fussy, fit, fifty-year-old "captain" of the Border Mountain Militia, one kind of response to the oligarchy's very cold thin smile, that is, when it's not grinning steamily and reminding you to "Vote!"

He, Rex, can show you computer communiqués of dates for martial law, though the event never comes to pass, not in the way he imagines it. Meanwhile, acres of so-called antiterror bills in the pipeline, just needing another OK City bombing patsy, therefore more public consent for total surveillance of us all, no, not public *consent*, the public will *beg* for it. Speaking thus, Rex seems more military now than when he was still fresh home from Vietnam, so they say. Gordon and Rex became brothers a bit later. Gordon had to reach eighteen before catching Rex's cautious attention, while Rex's reputation as a combat vet was always right between your eyes if he was near you, even though he never spoke of it. Never.

Gordon can't forget that rolling twinkle of good humor in Rex's eyes after a six-pack and two whiskies. No loud talk. No gooey grins. No irritability or caustic remarks to fire up barroom brawls. Just the eyes, those two wide-open windows of drunkenness giving you that sudden peek into his usually oh-so-private carefully managed self. See his shell-less self, his squishy clam self, like the one we all have but steely people like Rex keep covert.

Oh, how Gordon looked up to Richard York! Gordon eighteen and then nineteen, Rex pushing thirty. Drinking on the iced-over lake; drinking at card games in kitchens or at Letourneau's Used Auto Parts; drinking at the Cold Spot, so called in summer, Hot Spot in winter . . . they actually change the sign each season . . . though way back then it was still the Lakeview Lounge, though there were no windows then to view anything through, just maybe the trash cans out back through the wee square window in that particular door.

And then on to that special seething summer, parties ripe and raw, hither and yon, and all the fairs, especially the chilly end-season Fryeburg Fair. A Harrison reefer dealer thought Rex and Gordon looked alike, the dark-lashed pale eyes, of course.

Yes, oh, yes, back then Rex and Gordon did reefer. They did it all.

And the crowning episode, in that late 1970s summer, an episode that is legendary and repeated locally as often as Paul Revere's ride is in Boston, in this case on a night at Old Orchard when even the sea breeze was hot, Gordon and Rex and Big Lucien Letourneau rolling into town, parking on the hill near the OOB Fire Department just as the big trucks swung out in a scream of red lights and horns.

Cop cars shrilled. Someone threw a firecracker from a car window . . . *bang!* . . . too close to Big Lucien's head.

Unmanned Harleys, some full-dress, others not, all with slanted front wheel in park mode and glittering, with only inches between, shoulder to chrome shoulder, nudged up to the curbs on both sides of the street as far as the eye could see.

Cops were at every corner. Bouncers at all the club doors. Bikers elbow to leathery elbow on sidewalks just arriving, black-gloved, rippling with menace. Pounding music from each doorway, amalgamating sickeningly with the music from near and beyond. Smoke, the legal deadly kind and the illegal munchies-craving kind. Live strippers with what looked like taxidermy eyes. Broken glass. Fights. A knife wound with no visible knife and no Sherlock Holmes to solve the absurdity. A lake of blood. Blood looked more conscious than the guy who was stretched out loosely next to it.

Gordon and Rex and Big Lucien somehow made it out of there alive and somberly found the somewhat dark beach, all three of them toddling with baby legs from whiskey and vodka, bleeding onion rings from every pore.

The beach was like a visit to the dark new moon after what was behind them. Such peace! The sky sputtering with hazy stars, some alive and whipping about, others wobbling. Sand too soft. Gordon couldn't make his ankles work right. Seaweed crackling and mussel shells and periwinkle shells and some unidentifiable squashy stuff that expelled a dead froggish stench like what dogs love to roll in.

But as precious as all this seemed at the moment, a not-so-good thing was hunchedly moving toward them. Big shapes in the dark. Bikers without bikes. Bikers each with a dozen fists pounded the shit out of Gordon and Rex, although Big Lucien, who, as we may or may not recall, is little, ran like the wind and made it all the way to East Grande Avenue without stopping. He told them this weeks later without shame, at a poker game at "the yard" (the yard being Letourneau's Used Auto Parts, Big Lucien proprietor . . . when he's not out drinking and womanizing or in jail or running for his life).

Meanwhile, back at the beach, Gordon lay in what felt like a litter of warm puppies but which really was his bleeding into sand and parts of him that were swollen in uncomely ways. But also cold lips kissing his shirt and kissing his numb-stinging fingers. Cold kisses portend what?

The incoming tide!

Gordon grunted and moaned and mewled his way to his feet. "Rex," he croaked, his throat like a Salisbury steak from the many punches and hard objects. Nunchucks? A hammer? A cement block? Was Rex underwater? Was Rex even there?

Gordon has such a furry soupy memory of dragging Rex from the passions of the tide, his own four broken fingers and sort-of-popped-out, sealed-shut, crispy eyes, nothing compared with Rex's transformed identity . . . a man-shaped sculpture made of red-pepper sausage. Oh, yes, all was meat that night.

Gordon dragged Rex and then carried him bridelike back to their truck.

Gordon was painted perfectly with Rex's blood, the heat of Rex's livingness, burning down through the weave of his own T-shirt front and down his legs to his work boots and then, alas, inside the truck saw Rex's fists were worn down nearly to just bare naked bones. How savagely Rex had fought for his own life, how now in this blend of blood they would always be brothers. There would be trust between them even if "America" *was* plotting to rip the ground out from under them. Oh, yes, *especially* if it was.

Okay, so with Rex's militia, though the two men argue to exhaustion over all the specifics, or Gordon raves and Rex becomes coated in frost, Gordon sees what no one else sees, sees that what is past is always bleeding without cease. And like Claire's abortion, the bad rap militias, those not propelled by the infiltration of G-men but simply of Rex's sort, prepared, prepared, prepared, in their queer-seeming nervousness, shall be vindicated.

Shutting off the small kitchen lamp, Rex York heads for the attic stairs to bed.

The living room's front drapes, shimmering and whirling with headlights, make his heart jump at this hour. He freezes.

The brilliance intensifies around the mutter of an engine, the deep boast of eight cylinders.

He moves lightly back through the kitchen to the glassed-in porch without putting on any lights and he just stands there, listening to the slams of the truck doors. He can make out Gordon St. Onge's silhouette next to the dark bulk of the old Settlement truck and another man behind him. And a swingy-hipped tall female.

Without a word, Rex pushes open the glassy storm door and allows the three visitors to enter. Now in the kitchen, lit only by lamplight from the living-room doorway, Gordon doesn't swipe off his billed cap, just sits down at the shadowy table and spreads before him a thickness of papers.

Rex tugs the chain of the ship-in-a-bottle lamp on top of the old cluttered dresser by the cellar door, noting that the room has instantly been swollen full of the weird warm grassy swampy smell of Settlement-made soaps and salves. But also the stink of cigarettes.

Gordon says with a whine, "I want a cookie."

It's true, Rex himself doesn't touch sugar. Even without sucking in, he's awfully muscular in the middle for fifty. Dark blue Dickies shirt and pants. Never short of wiring jobs large and small, his van out in the dooryard reads *York Electric* and shows a smiling lightbulb on the go. Little work cap on the lightbulb's head, pliers in one hand. Rex himself never wears a cap when on the job. But always the black military boots with the pants cuffs down over. Unlike the lightbulb, Rex is not a smiler. Because of the clipped, brown down-to-the-jaws mustache and his grainy silences, his eyes have the power to bore into you. Your skin sort of rustles all over under his stare.

Meanwhile, you might notice that the hair at his temples is thinning but his wedding ring is as thick as it ever was even though his wife Marsha is remarried, and living in Massachusetts. Gone. Gone. Gone.

Rex isn't short but seems so when next to the giant Gordon and Gordon's giant fifteen-year-old son. And the girl, also taller than Rex, these two youngsters still standing.

In the center of the top page of the stapled papers next to Gordon's hand, Rex sees the FBI seal, like a wide-open but crusty eye.

Cory St. Onge. Mostly Passamaquoddy in the face like his mother Leona but there's that Frenchie sparkle to his eyes you'd know instantly was Gordon's father's if you'd been around that far back. And yes, Rex was. Meanwhile, Cory doesn't ask for a cookie.

Rex remembers this kid back when he was Leona St. Onge's bushy-haired long-armed infant being passed around to be cooed over and bounced, one of the two oldest, whom Gordon managed to plant in two women in what seems like the same moment.

Noticeable is the fact that Cory has started to let his last haircut grow out enough to have it tied back with rawhide. Does *not* look like a hippie. Looks like a pissed-off Indian warrior, which Rex would never say impresses him because he is not the praise-and-compliments type, but *he.izzz.impressed*. Mainly because Cory is on his side against that which wants to roast the common man.

Rex "is loath against" the FBI but also academia and TV-radio-print talking heads always blathering to divide the common man by occupation, by "privilege," by skin, by past horrors, to paralyze the common man's defenses, to shrink 'em and, yes, divide 'em. But here in this kitchen the common man is a titan, the enemies of the common man are specks.

And the girl. A recent development. Not a stranger though. She was here, for instance, when Gordon brought a bunch of kids around for the CPR tourniquet-and-fire-safety-tips meeting. Several men from the Border Mountain Militia were on hand, and as tough as they think they are, they all looked weirded out by the girl's grotesque face. No introduction has ever been made to explain her connection to the St. Onge family. And he's never heard her name. In true redneck fashion, identities of new visitors will eventually tumble down in bits and dribbles as natural as sunlight and starlight. But one thing is for certain, though she's not an actual leper, she could, if these were the Jesus of Nazareth days, use upon her face the "laying on of hands" by the son of God. Or by today's methods, about fourteen surgeons.

Rex also can't miss that the girl appears to be memorizing everything in his old farmhouse kitchen. He doesn't trust her. Not that she's an operative and not that he, Richard York, is overly paranoid. It's more of a tripled-full-alert cognizance in the back of his brain like when one of his Winchesters is stacked in the back of the attic stairs with a chambered shell and so it is too alive to forget.

Rex reaches amid some plastic and glass clutter next to the linoleum-covered drainboard and long sink, then places a foil-covered pan on the table by Gordon's hands and the stapled papers. And he pulls out a kitchen chair for the girl. Rex, first and foremost a "gentleman."

Gordon sighs. "Well, the Patriot Movement citizen militias, excitable Christians, and various white types of the anger and violence class, with crazed minds and racist objectives are expected to blow everything up on January 1, 2000, in this coming year of our Lord, A.D."

Rex's eyes grow warm with about five rogue twinkles for about five quick seconds. Still he has nothing to say. Nothing yet is necessary to say and, besides, Gordon always does such a stellar job of filling in any silence with vast blobs of unnecessary yak.

Cory now straddles a chair at the table.

The girl is also, at this point, sitting, watching Gordon's shirtfront from the corners of her wide-span eyes.

Gordon sniffs indignantly. "Well, we citizens' militias of whatever stripe shouldn't feel too select. I read where climate-change-worried scientists, tree sitters, and animal cruelty objectors are considered terrorist enemies of America, too. And high school kids who pass out useful facts about the military, *their* booth too close to the booths of the military recruiters set up *in their school* . . . these kids are listed as, get this one, a *credible threat*. Union organizing today in the age of corporate conglomerating . . . watch out! You are an enemy of America! Pissed about poverty? Watch out! Feeding the homeless in parks? That's against the law. Off in a paddy wagon you go, you un-American scary guy. Terror terror terror. The list is long. The United States bombs away in Panama, Yugoslavia, and Iraq, just to name a few, this is spreading goodness. If you call it spreading vile expansionist shit, if you call it criminal, you're an enemy of the American people. So, as I say, militia movement folk just gotta stop feeling the specialness of the spotlight."

Cory murmurs, "I read this Megiddo thing, too," and stares down at the wonder of the text before his father, stapled and restapled, copied and recopied, worn by the hands of so many Settlement readers . . . including some of the mothers who use it as the reason above all reasons to avoid Rex. So the thing is rubbed, picked, and chafed to softness. Carried about preciously.

Now foil rattles and scrunches as Gordon's hand finds a cookie. Then he pushes the pan toward Cory. Cory takes a cookie but seems he just wanted it for something to look at while his father yaks on for a good five minutes in his usual circular way.

The girl's eyes continue to slide around the kitchen of this home Rex and his mother and his daughter share, his daughter Glory whose hair like this guest's is also red and long and ripply, no, not red . . . Glory's is dark auburn. And Glory is beautiful, disastrously so.

Standing against the sink, Rex, when he gets a chance, speaks solemnly, "It's not the intention of any patriot group I've been in communication with or read or heard of to attack the US government for religious purposes or otherwise. Except for the common-law guys, the word is 'stockpile.' And 'Be prepared.' To be prepared for when or if the government makes a move on *us* . . . to disarm us. Or any illegal force makes such a move on the American people . . . or, as I mentioned other times, martial law for whatever bogus reason. There've been rumors—" He pauses significantly. "—that martial law would be declared on January first, following a government-initiated emergency."

Gordon jumps in. "You know I don't buy this martial law fretting because of the FBI's and Pentagon's and CIA's place in *the permanent state of exception* within the American state. We have *always* a suspension of the juridical order. It's part of the whole shebang!" He makes a funny face, which Rex refuses to acknowledge, then rattles on. "There are all those folks who think they need a new computer so when the three zeros blink into place on January 1, 2000, the end of the computer-dependent world won't happen . . . a tale probably initiated by the big computer companies whose sales have stabilized and whose growth is subsiding."

Cory laughs.

The girl's eyes, not entirely veiled by her loose and blazing hair, seem to regard Gordon's hand with obvious (to Rex) worship. So what else is new, Rex thinks to himself.

Cory laughs again. "Gordo, *that* is just crackpot conspiracy theory. You see scheming behind every closed door." He winks a long dramatic wink at the girl, his tongue in his cheek.

She laughs like a grown-up.

Rex says nothing.

Cory is now smiling with satisfaction at the bottom side of his cookie.

The girl's hands are red and yellow and orange in the seams of the knuckles and around her nails. Her smiling mouth is actually pretty, like a pink bow.

Gordon munches and grins at the same time, speaks now with a mouthful, "Well, *certainly* I am paranoid. FBI *said* citizens' militias are paranoid. And I'm not one to question their expertise." He places his right hand, open-fingered, on the Megiddo report before him. "Actually, all I've witnessed face-to-face and via snail mail on the citizens' militia scene is a preponderance of . . . of normal Republican bullshit."

Rex directs a refrigerated glare at Gordon's profile, then raises his chin and looks away toward the door to the glassed-in front porch.

Gordon swallows chewed cookie. "But not as right-wing as what comes out of the big think tanks and certain foundations. And all that Intel spooky shit on the Internet. In fact, those are no doubt the Adams and Eves origin of all right-wing thought."

Rex does not want to argue tonight. He lets the bait vaporize into the infinite galaxy of Gordon's opinions, which Rex has always considered to be as red as Mother Russia. He notices the girl has a pack of cigarettes in one pocket of her work shirt as the great bursting jumble of her hair swishes somewhat to the side. In this break in Gordon's blathering, Rex speaks gravely, "If you were not familiar with the Patriot Movement, and you read that report, you'd be worried about people in the movement. But the FBI is not worried about people in the movement. They are not expecting any bombs—"

"Because," Cory marvels in his rumbly, cracking fifteen-year-old voice, "*they know everything*. If something's in the works, they're part of it, egging someone on, like McVeigh with OK City."

Rex tries to continue where he left off. "They are not worried, not expecting—"

Gordon interrupts him. "Think about it. They want to—" and off he goes with a rather up-and-down, over-and-under philosophical speech. Then fetches another cookie, stuffs it into his cheek, and finishes up his rambling with *muffing* and *sluffing*, which nobody can understand.

Rex speaks stiffly: "The report is going out to all low-level law enforcement agencies, city, town, county, state . . . and the media and various organizations set up to save the world from the right wing, so they claim. But it is inadvisable to forget that these professional fund-raisers with their broad-brushstroke lists . . . and all the surveillance agencies and politicians know how to make people sweat. I would not be surprised if the fund-raiser outfits helped write this report. No question in my mind that this was written to drum up terror *in* ordinary Americans *of* ordinary Americans . . . and that creates terror in general . . . a generalized fear . . . a panic. Public mass hysteria is useful to all those birds."

Gordon garbles words around another huge cheekful of cookie, "An old frick," which, translated into English, probably was meant to be *An old trick*.

Cory laughs. "When they blew up the OK City building, the media announced for several hours that it was right-wing militias or Arabs. One said right-wing militias *and* Arabs. Midwest farmers and Arab rebels shoulder to shoulder! Call me sentimental but I love it."

Rex again gets a simmering whiff of cigarettes. Must be the girl smokes no less than a pack a day. All her clothes and that hysterical mane of hair are saturated in the toxic stench.

Gordon pats the report affectionately. "FBI said that the citizens' militias are paranoid about the UN's plan to disarm the citizens of the world but they didn't exactly deny the UN stuff. It was worded as if the UN *did* want to disarm us . . . but that . . . to be worried about it made us paranoid. They stated that the Gun Owners of America president, what's-his-name, shouldn't talk or write about this fact, that it would make people even *more* paranoid."

Cory still hasn't bitten into his cookie, just rocks it on the table. "Gun Owners of America is a newsletter for Democrats with guns, isn't it? And I've got some Earth First! friends who are pro–Second Amendment. One has a shotgun for woodchucks in their collective's garden. Another an AK for target shooting and so forth."

Rex's eyes have narrowed. His arms are now folded across his chest. As usual, this St. Onge bunch has taken the talk into territory where the air seems to have no oxygen and is crowded with distant shadowy characters he does not trust.

Cory chortles. "G-man logic is that to be informed and armed at the same time is to be paranoid." His chortle turns into a giggle.

Gordon stares into his son's dark eyes which are wet with giggle-tears.

The girl is staring through the plate of cookies out through the other side.

Suddenly, a harsh *ca-chunk!* Gordon turns. "What's *that*?'

"Refrigerator," says Rex.

"Sounds like it's in pain."

"It still works."

"I never heard one do that."

Rex steps to the table, pulls out a chair, finally settles in.

Gordon says, almost in a jolly way, "Law enforcement agencies can get a better position at the congressional trough when they have people shivering in terror."

Rex senses that "the Prophet" and his "followers" do not really care about building the militia network. They just get high by wallowing in the idea of it. Rex can't fathom this but does not confront or accuse.

Gordon is still (happily, it seems to Rex) going on: "And there are so-called antiterror . . . ahem, police-state bills lined up waiting for the public to cheerlead them into becoming law. Everybody gets a little something."

Cory distractedly taps his own nose with his cookie. "That's where another government-executed act of terror will come in. Like the declassified Operation Northwoods back under Eisenhower, tabled as Kennedy came in . . . where they planned to shoot a plane of college kids down and blame it on Cuba . . . or shoot some people walking around in Miami and blame it on Cuba. But CIA operatives later on really did shoot a plane down somewhere . . . I forget where . . . but it's common knowledge. And one did a car bomb in New York. Blamed Castro. The US government loves *certain kinds of right-wing stuff*. As long as it's a roadblock to socialists, the Red Sandwich, and all that."

Gordon grins broadly and his wild eye opens so wide that it seems the eyeball would plop out. Rex doesn't dwell on the whys and wherefores of this almost holiday pleasure in their voices but he has a flash, a three-second accounting, that the real and felt sting of what an enemy can do to you is owned by only one person in this room, Richard York, who was *there*, with real rockets, real roars and shrieks and crumbling walls, and pounding pounding pounding guns behind and in front of barely human whines, dripping jungle, land mines, and ingenious traps, *Kabooom*! a slack-mouthed head rolls along in front of you and the solid watery stewing heat and heartbroken feet, fireblazing sticks and bones, chemical wilt of vine and bough, all the many stinks scrambling down your throat. Dying sounds: brays, mewls, moos, sobs, baas, one-syllable cussings, bellers, silences between the *Booms!* and you are with the weight of another man on your back, your pack, running, hunching, crawling, yeah *crawling*.

Rex rubs his face, looks at the plate of cookies, "sees" the head and shoulders of his mother, Ruth, pressing each cookie with the cutter, giving shapes to their sweetness just hours ago. Ruth York, not a granny-looking older lady. She's only sixteen years his elder, her still-black hair held back by a silver clasp, T-shirt snow white with a rearing palomino stallion, a cactus, a prairie dog, and a rattlesnake in striking pose. Heavy medallion of bronze on a chain. It's a wolf's head staring out from an aureole of sun. Her usual bracelet, turquoise. She has not one iota of American Indian blood in her veins but she, with his father just before he died and their American Legion friends, flew to the Southwest as a tourist and left her heart there. Well, one of them. She has a *lot* of hearts. And in some ways she is his best friend due to their mutual rocklike dependability and their mutual silences.

Rex refocuses on the softly lit room as it is now. He does not want to feel riled at Gordon or the boy. They are not the enemy.

But their hands move in the periphery of his sight, churning with their words. His own black-faced compass watch looks readier than ever to do service, ticking away the moments, pointing north, while his hands are folded in a mannerly fashion on the table.

Gordon's deep wandering voice says, "The guys I'm hearing from via the US mail, patriot groups and so-called Christians, seem only to get launched into action when some rich rancher can't anoint himself king. And one real estate critter in Massachusetts they were all hopped up to go and *defend*. The irony is that militia groups being in service to the rich rancher and real estate mogul is probably okay with the Bureau and whatnot. They do it themselves every day!"

Cory says huskily, "At least the Panthers used to arrange free breakfasts for kids. They had something like justice in mind. You know, love and outrage." Cory's cookie breaks in half seemingly by itself, a half to each hand. "FBI put the bullets to the Panthers, sent in spies, and did plenty of framing, like of Mumia on death row and the one girl who escaped to *Cuba*, Assata Shakur. You are not supposed to rise up. The proof is everywhere. So if I think the government wants to control all us little people, then—"

"You bear watching." Rex states the ominous fact.

"Hey," says Gordon softly in his run-out-of-steam mode. "Speaking of rising up, my brother, have you finally read *The Recipe for Revolution*, the short version at least, the one that has the cartoon Abominable Hairy Patriot?"

The girl makes some sound. An abrupt intake of kitchen-sweet air.

Rex's eyes spring to her face, then to Gordon's face, which is now struggling with that Tourette's-like eye thing again.

So this girl is the one, the mastermind of the booklet with the orange cover and of the other writings Gordon has been so proud of. The big one, *The Recipe for Revolution*, kind of lost him. Not to the point enough. Not that Rex is stupid. It's just that some minds are fueled by the gorgeousness of life while other minds are more straight on and wound tight like trigger springs.

"I gave them to Todd. I let him borrow them." Rex feels caught. But it's true. Todd, one of two teenage members of his group, seemed charmed by the stuff.

Gordon sits up straighter.

Rex adds, "But I skimmed it first. It was pretty good . . . like poetry."

The girl tips her head in a little thank-you nod.

Cory says, "She's a swashbuckler. Watch out."

The girl giggles.

Rex nods at that face that looks like a fantasy movie's special-effects human-lioness and her sort-of-gold-sort-of-green eyes are on him.

Cory remembering. He speaks.

One night after supper, a bunch of us were sprawled in rockers on the long porch next to the Settlement kitchen doors. I especially remember Rick Crosman and his son Jaime, and John Lungren and Lou-EE St. Onge and Paul Lessard and Jeremy Davis and Butch Martin. And me, of course, heh-heh.

John Lungren was a quiet guy but when he spoke, it was in a measured way and something you'd need to hear. John was a finish carpenter and had that climbing-all-over-everything build, gray hair, steel-rimmed glasses with large lenses just slightly out of fashion . . . heh-heh. He was leaning back in a deep wicker rocker, knees high, but looked full of portent, not foolish.

He said that as we speak hundreds more small factories are grinding to a stop and big ones up up and away, not his exact words. He groaned and said not that labor unions have lost their needfulness but they were losing their stoutness. We knew all this, but it's like a chant and warriors' drums. You repeat. You repeat. It empowers the blood. And he was going somewhere with this. "More farms, thousands more, are being auctioned to agribiz." He said a guy he knew from "home," Millinocket, a guy named Tiny Tim, told of a guy he's been in touch with, Steve. Steve and Jeannie, who farm in one of those black dirt states, Michigan maybe. Steve, the farmer, was all set to blow his brains out all over the cab of one of his trucks but just as he was sorting through his ammo boxes his neighbor stopped by, another ruined farmer. The neighbor talked militia. Some of the common-law stuff, which we were all suspicious of, bit of a dead end. Whatever. John said Steve, the depressed farmer, was alive and wearing a thin pissed-off *undepressed* grin the next morning because he was fervid to see the militia network *grow*.

Butch Martin remembering back then. He speaks.

Rex York's militia . . . um . . . it was at first about fifteen guys, not always at once. When a bunch of us from the Settlement got interested the Border Mountain Militia attendance about doubled in size. He had another bunch of . . . um . . . *names*, who were just *names* to me. I never saw them.

But I was getting antsy and so was Cory, because even with the winter bivouacs, the Border Mountain Militia was . . . um . . . well, it was like we were all just floating in an oarless rowboat.

All the talk of a national network sounded pretty limp . . . um . . . you know . . . like *fantasies*. Some of us guys, the under-twenty-fivers, had started spending deep and meaningful time with the anarchists tenting up on Horne Hill at Jaxon Cross's father's place. But still something kept us going back to Rex's kitchen and Rex's glassed-in porch.

I personally watched how it was, how the more helpless some of Rex's founding members, older guys, would seem, so helpless-feeling in the face of the total power and limitless violence and LIES of Washington and its satellites, the more they needed to *pretend* they were not taking it lying down. We were . . . in the way of nature's way, um . . . you know, like Sitting Bull said about the difference between individual fingers versus a fist . . . um, small scale, yeah . . . but maybe, like Cory says, evolution hasn't kept up with global dominion over us all, that our brains still get twitterpated over an eensie army of brothers.

So, um, another thought was how these guys twisted their heads to call themselves patriots. Patriots of any country are proud to . . . um . . . you know, be led by a ring in the nose. So for that little while, they weren't what they thought they were.

Things were becoming more obvious, all this war on the world stuff by scheming advisers, State Department, CIA, Pentagon, Oval Office . . . it was *not* a nation's self-defense . . . but most of Rex's non-Settlement guys were not ready to let go of the glow behind the pledge of allegiance to the flag that they had recited a hundred billion mornings in school, hand over heart, and the belief in the American virtue of saving the world from black hats. You could not get too logical with these guys. But that didn't make me . . . um . . . want to dismiss them. These guys were scared and Rex's cookie-smelling kitchen was a safe place to talk big, talk tough, talk mean, talk personal family-sized self-defense, talk a little bit crazy, and to PRETEND you were a man.

So, why did some of us young guys who were pretty snuggly with the anarchists on Horne Hill still turn up dutifully for the Border Mountain Militia meetings? Why? Why? Why? Well, man, think about it; it's *all* pretend anyway, isn't it? Name one single thing you can do to stop the red-white-and-blue boulder from rolling and bouncing toward us all with its intentions of *full spectrum dominance*. The big rock is on us here in the United States as well as out there, right? "Full spectrum dominance," the government's own words, means all little people on this planet look the same to the big cocks on top of the global human pile.

So man, oh, man, I couldn't let Rex down. *That kitchen was* the *only America*, the one that the big cocks thought they had but totally didn't.

Seavey Road. The flower-shaped night-light breathes *out* its soulful glow. The open octagon window breathes *in* the almost lurid sweet night air, overly warm for September.

Bree, the neighbor girl, fifteen, sits on her narrow bed, fully dressed, having just arrived from being out. Her posture is a ready *march-forth!* square-shoulderedness. Her wide-set honey-green eyes flick in her head in grave study of her innermost strategic maps.

As always, an old green work shirt and jeans. Tall scuffed logging boots, steel-toed, these that she wears while working the woodlots with her father and brothers. The kind of boots so many Settlement girls have turned in their Settlement-made moccasins for, in their delirious admiration of her, she whom they call "our logger girl," she whom they never knew at all till this summer, now the center of everything.

Yes, tonight, she had again "borrowed" her sleeping brother Poon's truck, leaving him the usual note on the kitchen table: *Be back real soon*.

Poon is one of those people that you can easily push around. He holds his heart and his opinions deep as dud depth charges and so his objections to his fifteen-year-old sister with no driver's license running off with his pickup are always just the slight reshaping of his eyes, a perfect sorrow.

Bree's room seems so spacious these days since all her "art stuff" is over at the Settlement in the Quonset hut attic "studio" she shares with Claire's very dear and totally pretty university friend, Professor Catherine Court Downey, who says she is staying at the Settlement "only for a while." Catherine calls it "some healing time," which refers to her getting off a bunch of pills and onto a "perfect diet." Not that she has weight to lose. Just something more impenetrable than flesh.

Her four-year-old Robert is not gregarious but rides easy on the wave of Settlement humanity of various ages. He does his part. His father is Vietnamese-American and is only a figment in most ways. You never see him, not at the Settlement. Does he even know that's where the professor and Robert are off to? "A businessman on the go," Catherine has bragged or complained; Bree's not sure which, for at the oddest times Catherine sings her sentences.

Catherine never works on her watercolor painting in her half of the canvas-tarp-divided studio. On her studio cot, she often rests from her teaching, meetings, and paperwork, her interim-chairmanning. And shopping. She shops *a lot*, the browsing kind, but also the back-seat-and-trunk-heaped-with-bags kind.

Meanwhile, this little bedroom at the home of the Vandermasts no longer stews with the vapors of turpentine and linseed oil. Its revised purpose (besides a bed to sleep in), its consequence to "a world needing rescue" has been delivered in fabrics of blue and gold.

Take note that in one corner of this room is a roughly carved eagle perching on a hop hornbeam pole and, tautly rolled around it, a flag. *And yes, this is top secret.* A creation made right there at the Settlement under Gordon St. Onge's nose, so to speak. Well, really only on evenings when he was off making shingle or lumber deliveries, this urgent mission was accomplished deep in the bowels of the horseshoe of porches, kitchens, and shops, the Clothesmaking Shop to be exact. Over a dozen teen and preteen girls had designed and/or cut and/or stitched this full-sized state of Maine flag look-alike, the sailor, the farmer, the moose, the Christmas tree, the star with rays. And DIRIGO (*I lead*). Then across the top, applied in tall blocky letters of roadside warning sign yellow-gold, a new declaration: THE TRUE MAINE MILITIA. Oh, yes, all ready to go for when the time is right. Plans are in the works, plans that make Rex York's militia seem like a bunch of old bulls hunched under a tree watching rain clouds bounce along in a swollen sky of red-white-and-blue hopelessness.

Now the true revolution begins!

The shame of night.

Rex York isn't whimpering yet but his whole big bed trembles. He sees corpses, all alike, wooden as old baby dolls, arranged quite neatly on cheap orange wall-to-wall shag carpeting, or so it seems. Everything turns washy, then back to stark. The corpses are not death gray but orange, as though their wooden visages have a very bad maple stain.

And the corpses' heads are fanned with decoration like relics of ancient Egyptians. The corpses breathe. Bellies and chests expand, lips flutter, noses hiss. Hissssss.

Rex notices that one corpse is now standing, not threateningly. In fact, the face isn't clear to Rex so it may not be looking at him. Nevertheless, Rex begins to spook.

He wants to get away but he's lying on the cheap orange carpet and can move only his jaws. His jaws have vigor. "Arrhhh-huh-hh-eeeee-ooooo!"

This is the same sound he always wakes to, the girlie ghosty wail. It shames him that he can't even scream like a man.

He doesn't have recurring dreams like those some people tell of. No, *his* war dreams never repeat. Hundreds of horrors. No repeats.

Ah, life! Ah, New York!

He is crossing Lexington with a crowd of high-school-aged kids, a woman wearing white nurse-like stockings, a woman who looks like a Russian peasant from fifty years ago, and a few homeless mumblers. Mostly his eyes are on the little smoke shop over there, with the newspapers in the racks so fresh they look cold. Cold print, like fresh fruit. Sweet. It has always moved him that way.

He sees the face of Gordon St. Onge. It is the thousandth time—sometimes in this city, sometimes in other cities . . . even Tokyo! . . . the big guy's face or form, moving toward him menacingly, in that way he would have his hand in his shirt or jacket on the handle of a gun. And in the night, EVERY NIGHT, he hears that tiny click of doorknobs turning, all the doorknobs at once. His apartment like his summer house is full of doors and sharp-edged waiting.

The key. When will it be returned? Oh, this. His fantasy! Like two boys playing in a tree. Does St. Onge, on the other end of this daydream, imagine his role of stalking? This game, not globe-sized but one-on-one, life or death, the ultimate challenge.

A few times a day, every day, Bruce relives that two hours he spent with St. Onge . . . every word, the gray light, the rank coolness of that truck cab, cider and goat and greasy tools and the oddness of his host's eyes.

He arrives at the racks of fresh newspapers and magazines and looks back over his shoulder at the rush of faces and their rolled-up umbrellas tucked under elbows, sacks, and valises. He can almost hear a larger-than-New-York rustle of voices, St. Onge passing on the word to minimum-wagers, temps, ex-cons, and those millions all over the country and beyond who are sick to death of debt, who steam at yet another lordly lie. And all the little doggie ones who never questioned before now squashed into dinkier and dinkier and colder and colder apartments with three grown kids whose only chance for success is retailing street drugs or dealing in stolen goods, especially handguns, where urban America's stiff gun control laws have given black-marketing a rainbow with a pot of gold at both ends. And then there are all those in the hemispheres of East and South, their confusing yet simple hell of the West's Darth Vader foreign policy . . . oh, say can you see, by the dawn's early light, the beauty of Duotron Lindsey subsidiaries' cluster bombs and hellfire missiles? And playful "drones," still in the secretive conspiracy stage.

Oh, yes, they're speaking the name Bruce Hummer as Gordon St. Onge murmurs to them, "Brothers," all snapping and clacking the warm action of their large magazine rifles. Like the Vietcong, they could pop up *anywhere* now. *Bruce, Bruce, Bruce*, they croon.

Midafternoon of another day, Gordon alone up across the field from the old farmplace.

He settles down tiredly on the edge of the motionless merry-go-round platform, the bright animal figures above him, frozen in frenzy, raised paw, hoof, wide jaws, sludgy eyes. All are monsters made with tools and paint in the hands of kids. And with the assistance of one gasoline generator, these disturbing beasts can come to life, churning in their monsterific colors.

A cat has followed him, a stringy young kitteny cat, solid charcoal gray. Not a hunter. Just a follower. She glides around on the platform, touching things disdainfully with her nose the way cats do.

Then she shoves herself against Gordon's side, snakelike.

A single-engine plane drones along smartly through the vague-looking insincere sort of clouds, clouds as thin as thoughts, sky being almost the very best blue. Burned-looking goldenrod leans. Viny stuff creeps around. Except for the plane, everything is so quiet. And quite frank. Nothing lies.

Gordon takes something from the pocket of his jacket. A large, almost square brass key.

Now a beige card. He looks at the card awhile, not reading the words and numbers, just staring *into* it, and then his fingers and a thumb press and prod the card as he stares downhill awhile at the tarred Heart's Content Road.

Then he holds the key with the slender jagged part upright. And he looks into its sheen.

Cat paw reaches out and gives the key a serious ambush cuff.

"Yeah," Gordon tells the cat. "That's the idea."

From a future time, in her oceanfront home in Cape Elizabeth, Janet Weymouth remembers.

Did I contribute in any small way to the direction he took?

I relive every conversation, reread every letter, hearing my own words, assuring myself that I am in no way to blame, then, a few days later, I find myself anxious again. I see clear as ever his brooding profile one of the last times he stood in our front room, barely hearing anything anyone said to him, something inside him that could not see the positive aspects of that day . . . yesss, more than thirty riveted governors' wives and such a perfect little coup de théâtre by his exuberant progeny. I wanted to see triumph on his face. But he recoiled.

Maybe there was tension between him and Claire. Or him and the redheaded girl. Age fifteen. They said she was a neighbor. I repeat: age fifteen.

Brianna Vandermast. "Bree." Writer of *The Recipe for Revolution*, which he had mailed to me a couple of weeks earlier, two drafts and a flyer version. I repeat: she was age fifteen. It was said he had twenty wives. I wondered if she were one. Is this what decent people do?

Gordon, the child of elegant and proper and sturdy-of-heart Marian St. Onge who, as part of the influencial Depaolo family, often appeared with one of her engaging brothers or uncles at functions, the small private kind and those scintillating fund-raisers in Augusta or Bangor or Portland.

I cannot count the times she honored my invitation to have lunch here, just the two of us in the garden or on the beach, laughing like girls. Or we met at restaurants. Such a tall rawboned young woman with the liquid grace of the sveltest among us, meticulously dressed, her dark hair never curled though curls were the rage in those days. She had what you might call a bob.

She had an unusual marriage. She'd married a heavy-equipment operator from one of her uncle's crews. When she spoke of him, though it was rarely, her cheeks flushed. I heard from others that her marriage was as deep and meaningful as her friendships were, her friendships always being of the more prominent classes than whence came her darling "Gary," Guillaume St. Onge Sr., who, it was said, was a head shorter than her and of a slim wiry build.

This is what I'm trying to tell you, this pain for me of the hairpin turn I was about to make away from Gordie, whom I had known since he was a quiet but droll ten-year-old, yes, quiet *and* watchful *and* droll. And even from Marian, as virtuous as earth and sky, I would soon consider cutting ties.

No, it was *not* on account of the red-haired teenager or the wives uncountable. It was a daydream I had begun to have . . . a day-*mare* . . . where the Roman centurion asks, "Are you associated with this thief?"

Present time, before her hairpin turn, a letter arrives at the Settlement.

He can feel her excitement and breathiness, even in her handwriting.

She tells him that eight of the governors' wives have contacted the committee about HIM. And of course his talented children. Their various women's clubs and civic groups desire "the honor" of his presence. "You know, tea and crumpets and tall ceilings."

As kind of an afterthought, Janet explains that one of the "governors' wives' husbands" (her little joke) "has invited you to join him and a few others for a semiformal dinner at the governor's mansion. We are talking South Dakota. Some people from the Commission on Indian Affairs will be there and one of their state senators, Wally Dodge, who is a closet environment man from way back. Wally was told you're a "tree hugger" but you can straighten that all out when you get there in a way that nobody but you can do. As you once remarked to my friend Marcia that you are not a tree hugger . . . you are a tree. And she hugged you!"

Her PS reads: *Gordon, they need to hear your lively message. Fac-to-face. It has power, believe me. Call me if you can. When I call you I only reach three-year olds.*

Gordon writes back.

Dear Janet,

Again I want to thank you for being so welcoming to my family. And all that delicious food.

And it meant a lot to me to hang out with Morse awhile. It's upsetting to see how fucked up he got by the stroke. I can't believe the way time evaporates. It's been six years since the McNelty hearings. I've got gray in my beard and yet I know there will always be that Morse-worship in me. He is THE ROCK. There is a forever bond between Egypt and Cape Elizabeth. Whatever happens tomorrow, that will not change. To both of you I pledge my love.

I still keep that 5 × 7 and the clipping of Morse and J.J. and Bob at that first shareholder activism symposium. Here in the kitchen by my desks it is framed. That he can still convince people to press those vital changes in culture on resistant people of the investment class through his past writings, which never lose their voice, including that foot and a half of shelf space here in my hallway, means his voice will always be, as ever, cannon thunder.

About the gracious invitation from his governorship and the eight gals, I must respectfully decline. Will explain later.

Keep in touch. As ever, I invite you and Morse to visit. There are quiet places here where we can be alone but I so wish for you to smell the late summer fields and woods and to lay eyes on these foothills. Our tallest, our "mountain," has the windmills and when the sun is right they reflect like pure gold so you can see them from the comfort of the East Parlor windows.

Are you tired of me nagging you guys to come visit?

Love, Gordon

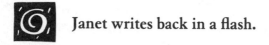

Janet writes back in a flash.

My dear old friend. Are you irked at me? I know you really want to get your ideas out THERE. But I'm not surprised by your letter. I knew all the while you were here that something was wrong. You weren't yourself! Please, let's talk about that.

Love, Janet

And love from Morse. He can still speak your name.

He reaches her by phone.

He says deeply, "More than anything, I wish you'd come see us here. I want to show you the shops and that view of the mountain. We'll fill you with country food and good stories. And you can see for yourself where Noof the caterpillar has led the kids."

"Yes! Yes!" she cries out. Where did her usual soft feathery reserve fall away to?

"I've visited your place dozens of times over the years," says he. "But you've never been to Egypt even when you and my mother were so tight. She didn't do much entertaining here other than croquet with my kid cousins. But today this is a regular convention center!! Why—"

"I know it. I know it. Per—"

"Why don't you come Sunday? I'll have a crew down by the road just to open our little gate for you. Just for you. And Morse. I owe you. It would mean a lot to me, and to the others here."

She sniffles happily. Sighs. Says she would like that very much.

But on Sunday, though the crew of young teens waits by the gate for nearly two hours, letting neighbors pass, the Weymouth car never shows up.

Late evening on one of the big porches, the one off the kitchens, see the flutter of Settlement-made candles in stained-glass holders of blue and lavender and rose.

From a circle of rockers Gordon's tired voice suggests a strange thing, strange in the timing (no recent incidents of troublesome strangers).

He asks some of the men and teenagers what they think of building a roomy guardhouse down by that horizontal hornbeam pole that serves as their gate. And then setting up a real gate. "We can paint it black to suggest doom beyond that point."

Couple of chuckles.

Others shake their heads.

Some squint at him wonderingly through the blue and purplish waverings of candlelight.

Nobody but a pack of restless preteen boys thinks a guardhouse and a real gate are necessary.

Gordon lets it go.

The late summer songbugs creak and chirr all over the near mountain and downhill toward the unseen dirt road below and the tar road beyond where his farmhouse faintheartedly casts its dull fluorescent light from kitchen windows. No gate at all *there*. Just wide open yard, parking area of dirt with the many-limbed ash tree, old torpid sentry.

And the night is blacker now than a month before. The air not as puddingish. In the coming weeks the blacker skies will be crunchy with stars.

Rocking chairs on these Settlement piazzas creak. Murmurs. Sweaters. Warm teas. Some elders are over there outbragging each other over a game of cards at one table, little mounds of pennies, pennies still good for *something*. Tall candle lamps give off a helpful yellow upon these elders' hands.

Gordon pushes up from his rocker with the carved bear heads on its back. Cup of hard cider in his right hand. If you watch closely you will maybe see something in him begin to accelerate.

Next night. Sawlogs and strangers.

In the hurtful scream of the sawteeth, in the formidable chugging roar of the diesel engine, under the light that is brighter than any of the other electric lights here in the Settlement, a log opens like butter, eager to please. Product and sawdust and bark edgings separate from the life force just as cleanly as from bone and bruise, as when the creaturely spirit flies away under the butcher's knife. The iron wheels stroll along the track. The carriage aches, burdened.

For the crew every shirt button is buttoned. Nothing to catch and draw one in. You see, the saw is blind.

The crew here does not converse. It is as though each man's head is a planet in deep space, inside a great rolling star's gaseous thunder.

It was after supper that they had started up again, finishing an order to be ready for the next, which is also tonight. Two mills running, rough mill and finish mill, both orders split in half between the two.

Gordon and Eddie Martin work with heavy peaveys on the brow, a log, barrel-round, bound for the carriage, it would be glad to crush you. Unlike the saw that would *unwittingly* open you up, the log *knows* you, the log *hates* you.

Up the long grade from the tar road below, the load of "off-Settlement" fir logs for the next order comes chugging halfheartedly, early. Beyond the crew's earplugs and plastic earmuffs, sounds merge pleasantly, like distant highway traffic, so that behind their backs, the tractor trailer truck just peacefully glides into view through the twilight, a profligacy of chrome, amber cab lights, fog lights, and running lights, a building-sized black wall of dizzying lights, hissing and braking now beside the cabless trailer into which the sawdust from the present operation is being blown.

Paul Lessard, Lou-EE St. Onge, and Jay Harmon, working that end of the mill, notice the young driver dropping down from the high cab, trotting through the clunking, murmuring world of sound outside their ear protectors, piece of paper in his hand. Now entering the open-sided mill, he finds the head sawyer, troll-doll-like Stuart Congdon, and presses the order into his hand.

Now there is another set of lights out there, a car stopping behind the loaded, idling truck. Headlights go dark. A minute passes and no one gets out of that car.

Jay points to it. Truck driver shrugs, shakes his head. Seems the car isn't with the truck.

The work goes on, the load of rough pine of the first order topping off nicely. No hitches. Chuff-chuff. Screech! Zinnnng! Wham! Clang! Sounds detected more in the face and chest than in the covered ears.

Still no one gets out of that mystery car.

After five more minutes, Paul steps out across the weedy yard, pulling down his ear protectors, looks down into the car at the vague spot of a face. Window glass slides down.

"Need somet'ing?" Paul asks a bit brusquely.

"Looking for Gordon St. Onge," speaks another vague spot of a face, this one in the back seat behind the driver, hands grasping the headrest. Not a familiar voice. Not a neighborish accent. Paul snaps a match under a cigarette.

He imagines these people lifting aside the pole that is "the gate" with the sign at one side that reads: KEEP OUT, which would mean either they've been invited here by somebody in the Settlement. Or? Or what? "You reporters?" He draws the harsh smoke from the cigarette, lets it back out grudgingly through his teeth.

"Please no!" A woman's voice laughs. "We're friends."

Paul looks around, back toward the screaming saw and rolling carriage and the whine of the loader as another log is eased onto the brow and there are Gordon and Eddie digging in with peaveys, Gordon back-to, green work shirt across his huge back, orange work gloves, and then stepping back, now bending or squatting for something, out of sight beyond the half wall, standing again, mind on the job.

Paul says, "He iss busy . . . not to be rude, I mean, he iss . . . we are . . . behind." A chimera of smoke hangs around his face from the glowing cigarette in his fingers. He turns again and looks back to the operation, then back to the gray spots of faces. "T'iss an emergency?"

The driver's voice. "No. We don't mind waiting. We've come a long way. Well, we happen to be in the area."

Paul makes a little tsk of a laugh. "Ah . . . well . . . we'll be running till two, maybe three, maybe four in the morning as it looks now. *Some* breaks, but t'ey're short."

The spot of a face on the passenger's side in the front leans over to say, with a friendly laugh, "That's okay. We're night types." The other strangers chuckle.

Paul is having a real relationship with his cigarette, another passionate pull. Blows smoke out. The idling tractor trailer and the racket of the two mills running at full throttle is a strain on conversation. Even now, the driverless tractor trailer in front of them lets out a sudden dragon-like hiss. Paul shouts, "Back to work!" and sidles away, glancing at the rear plate of the car. *Massachusetts.*

Once inside, he stands at the bench and scribbles off a note, which he puts in Gordon's gloved hand, and Gordon reads: *You have company. MASS. I told them you were busy. They are not in a hurry. If you leave us with this tonight you are on my personal shit list FOREVER.*

Gordon goes out to the car and talks for exactly one minute, sends his guests to the shops with a riskily unsealed note from himself to Claire and Suzelle and Lee Lynn, who he knows are around up there with one of their committees.

Note reads:

I'll be up as soon as humanly possible.
Make these guests comfortable. Coffee or
something. They've driven a long way. They
smell of brick and ivy. Or something.

And at 2:10 a.m., after the first mill shuts down, Gordon slumps into a deep chair in the West Parlor with coffees and muffins constellation-like within the spool table's soft light, a ticking antique clock, and four wide-awake left-wing political organizers.

They introduce themselves as friends of David Luce, whom Gordon has known well for over twenty years. Luce is an old labor organizer and civil rights activist, close to some of the Catonsville Nine, all those Vietnam War–era struggles, the civil rights movement before that, then later he was an antinuker, a been-in-jail-many-times-for-the-cause type guy, a guy whom Gordon has always admired as you would admire a fire-eater or rodeo rider, a guy Gordon can only *imagine* being like. With shame, Gordon never forgets how he himself couldn't even manage being town selectman for more than a few weeks, and how, with his tail between his legs, he crawled home to hide in his own black choking depression and drink. And this is the appeal of the militia movement. To just sit around and bitch. All that chest puffing done close to kitchens and pickup trucks in diner parking lots. He marvels at that difference as he rubs his bleary eyes with the heels of both huge hands, then glances at the old but not faded American flag spread out on the wall behind two of the Massachusetts folks' heads.

He finds his faithful bottle of aspirin, tosses three into his mouth, then while chomping on them as though they were yummy, snatches a muffin from the bright bowl on that old power-company-spool table. Muffins, coffee cups, hands, and countenances are all flushed by the nearly carnival light of four tall rose-and-cream-colored stained-glass candleholders, Settlement-made. The room is thunderously sweet with the odor of the cedar ceilings.

He faces the four organizers now with a really stupid little sheepish smile. They're all in their late forties, early fifties, dressed in bulky sweaters and jeans and nice sneakers, except the woman, whose shoes are suede. Gordon is suddenly struck with how much their expressions resemble the right-wing militia guys', fierce and serious. He sits up straighter. He LOVES these people! He loves, yes, all these bucking, rearing, kicking various way-out-there-on-the-fringes folk, outnumbered by the great castrated majority. He wants to hug these guys, to wrestle, to smooch 'em, to play. But he just looks down at his mug of coffee and the zucchini muffin, large and tender as a newborn puppy, in his hand. And he shifts his feet, his old work boots fondling what lies under them, the dozens and dozens of Settlement-made small-medium rugs, hooked, rag, and braided. Layers upon layers. Gives the floor a squishy uneven outdoorsy feel. An arduous test to footdraggers.

One of the guests is talking, explaining how impressed they are with how Gordon and his family have snagged the media. This is the woman, a pixie-sized, straight-backed, narrow-shouldered little thing with steel-rimmed glasses on a sturdy limb of a nose, a yellow sweater that gives her skin a buttercup hue despite the pink lamplight. Short, dark-blond hair in knucklelike curls. She has boyish mannerisms. Uses her hands a lot and she also uses big words, ones that Gordon usually sees in print not bailing out of people's mouths.

He looks over a time or two at a guy named Olan who is an intent listener. Small black bright eyes that are too wide open, as if he's about to scream *Help*! He is bald with a graying fringe and small red ears. Clean shaven, though sorta shadowy at this hour. His sweater has pockets that he keeps his hands inside, as though he's cold. Maybe he is cold. Gordon can't tell yet how the room feels, he's still warm from his work. He should ask about their comfort but quickly the thought is jerked away by the words tumbling around him.

Another guy is Frank. Tall when he was standing. Panoramic shoulders. The room is bulging with his shoulders, and Gordon's shoulders are broad but at this hour of a long day they're in deflate mode. The stranger's shoulders are more chub than muscle but, due to his alpha-male bulk of spirit, are the number one shoulders tonight. And his hair has wisdomy gray at the temples. Sweater does not have pockets. Hand in his lap snaps a ballpoint pen over and over. Slowly. You couldn't call it nervous. More like a coded message. Or a slogging rhythm to victory. Jaw like a trestle. Black-rimmed heavy-looking glasses. He does not talk. Engrossed by what's on the walls and in the corners of the room. Kids' drawings of the human anatomy, organs pasted on in layers. One figure wears its brain on top of its head. A human-sized rag-doll Godzilla relaxes in a chair by the dark windows, reading a book on birds. Stacks of *History as it Happens* books on their shelves of honor.

The third guy looks as if he's been crying but he explains it's really allergies and the damp weedy late September night. He also looks cold.

Gordon pushes out of his chair and steps over to the solar hot-air wall grates under the bookshelves, gives the latches to two of them a nudge with the toe of his boot. A little eager warmth dribbles from each grate. He turns and smiles in a sorrowful way at the allergy guy and says, "Maybe you're allergic to the cedar ceilings. Some people are."

"I'm allergic to everything," the guy says with a miserable smile. He has a short beard, long neck, long fingers. Wedding ring. Gray snoopy darting eyes.

Now Gordon starts a fire in the woodstove and the wide-eyed Olan offers to help. "You allergic to wood fires?" the woman asks the allergy guy, whose name is Billy.

"I am. But I'm also allergic to water and sky."

They tell Gordon how they've been traveling the country seven years now, doing facilitated discussions, a sort of folk school project, to get people to rethink how "corporations have seized the everyman's democracy." They give him details on how in Illinois, Wisconsin, California, Texas, "Mass," and Maine, Ohio, too, they have held quite a few of these seminars and the response has been "invariably enthusiastic, usually generating at least two more seminars in their respective regions."

"You never hear about them," Olan explains. "Not in the mainstream media. But for those who care about democracy, it's an underground wildfire, so to speak." They proceed to explain to Gordon how quiet it all seemed until recently . . . now all these big protest demonstrations against IMF, World Bank, WTO. "Bang! The cork has popped off. Again, the corporate-controlled media ignores this stuff or calls the big protests a small group of disgruntled troublemakers."

The long-necked short-bearded sniffling Billy speaks in a husky, almost emotional way. "Word of mouth, Internet, newsletters, independent presses . . . all the alternative media . . . and networking groups like ours got the whole thing off the ground! But without commercial media we can't reach the greater population. The big media are propaganda, omissions, psyops, created needs, distractions and —"

"Fibs," Gordon interrupts.

"Misinformation for sure," Olan says helpfully.

Gordon laughs. "Liar, liar, pants on fire."

"So mainly at this point, whether it be educational seminars or protest demonstrations, those who get involved are professional people . . . artists, college kids, and chronic activists," the woman, Jip, explains, placing her coffee cup on the table, leaning back in a snuggly way into her big chair. "This is where you come in, Gordon."

Gordon nods and nods and stares into his coffee as the visitors, particularly the woman, Jip, launch into the matter at hand, reeling off words like *ingress, disband, separative, recumbent, enmity, insurrection, toxic tort cases, habitat, apportionment, discord, usurp, bon mot, syntax, impresario, hegemony, disseminate, incapacitate, sequestration, pro forma, trajectory, praxis, critical juncture,* and *judiciary,* as well as *malfeasance* and *purloin.* Gordon gets a weird little smile on his face, as though there's a prank about to be pulled.

Jip explains that she's an old friend of Morse and Janet Weymouth's daughter, Selene. "We were classmates at Princeton."

"Small world," says Gordon, trying to keep his one-eyebrow-raised-madman look off his face.

"And I'll tell you now what a bright young woman Bree Vandermast is . . . "

Gordon closes his eyes. Really mashes them shut. *Bree. Bree. Bree.* Yes, of course, she had *told* him of inviting these people and they now, like rabbits, are pulled from her sleeve. Stupidly he had underestimated her.

" . . . We've had a wonderful correspondence with her for several months now," Jip goes on. "I was hoping to meet her tonight. I thought for some reason that she lived here. Something she made a reference to. She hasn't e-mailed me in a week or so."

E-mail? Well, yes, the Vandermast household would have a computer.

Billy sighs. "When she first requested that we bring a seminar here we were booked up and shorthanded and . . ." He looks over at Olan. "Olan had a bunch of Labor Party obligations jump out at him, so . . ." He trails off.

Jip explains, "Bree has been sending us some tantalizing packets. Copies of old unpublished essays of yours that *should* be published . . . and maybe we can help you with that . . . and she sent clippings of some of your old letters to editors and some of her poetry. *And,* especially impressive, *The Recipe for Revolution*, both versions and a related flyer, which she informs us was a collaboration between you and her. And then other flyers she and other young people made." Jip waggles her eyebrows. "The stuff of insurrection," she says with a measured smile, then, "And there was the *Record Sun* feature and its infamous offspring around the country. Then we found a bit of press coverage of you presiding over an event in Cape Elizabeth, Maine . . . uh . . . thirty-three Republican governors' wives . . . what was that really about?"

"Thirty-*two*. Newspaper error. And . . . well . . ." Gordon swallows coffee. "Much ado about nothing."

Jip chortles. "Well, the ripples will matter."

"Many people in America do not take to me," Gordon says. "I come off as a goofball to them. I *am* a goofball, actually. Then there're those who think I fuck two-year-olds and ride in a tank. Which is bullshit . . . and the funniest thing is how I'm now known as the Prophet." His flinchy eye flinches, so pale in its rim of dark lashes, the other eye widening. Sawdust all over his old outer shirt and work pants. Looks like a worker bee loaded down with pollen, a strange,

strange, strange-looking guy who would be off-putting not lovable, right? Gordon shrugs. "I'm nothing."

Olan pipes up, "Exactly! Send a real flesh-and-blood working-class person from the backwoods of Maine into the very heart of the American empire where the average Jane and Joe are feeling bled out and your message can hit home and—"

Frank snorts like a trumpety fart. Stops Olan cold.

Gordon squinches his eyes. Tired but roused. He considers. There are no backwoods in Maine anymore. Every hill and hillock with a leafy sucker poking out of a stump or four-inch sapling left on it is accessible by some sort of road. No old growth left. No old-fashioned "thrifty Yankee" people. But plenty of machines that chatter and thunder and spew. *Zinng! Zinng!* Bunch and slash. Mountains of debt. Every shack, trailer, ranch house, and split foyer mortgaged till the end of time and a great fat satellite dish on the front lawn. But the professionals from "away" cannot let go of "backwoods," "ramshackle," "grinding poverty," "illiterate," and "incestuous." From their cement and brick and tooting horns vantage point, or in sailboats and on beaches, they struggle to describe what they see here. They have no true reference point. But he feels these particular guys are well-meaning. And for this he lowers his head, a little respectful half bow.

Olan goes on, "Gordon, as Jip has said, the people *you* can help us mobilize are rural and small-town family folk. The protest scene is crawling with college kids, professorial types, dyed-in-the-wool radicals, and feminists, which is not a complete picture. The poor blacks and black working class are nervous, for good reason, such as brutal racist cops. But the white working class and poor aren't there because they've been . . . *ignored* by organizers. *Totally.* A bad mistake."

Jip says, "Studies now show that most of the nation's population is small town, white, working cla—"

"And igNORED," Olan stresses. "By progressives."

Gordon is thinking *ignored* is the wrong word; *scorned* and *ridiculed* are the words.

The allergy-wrecked Billy clears his throat. "I noticed in the clippings there were some legislative hearings on education you testified at eight years ago . . . I checked the date . . . that was coincidentally the same day I was up there with some people to attend a hearing on that big egg farm obscenity, when social workers were first complaining that they were being run off the road going in there with Spanish interpreters and OSHA was just starting to murmur, 'EGREGIOUS!' so we may have passed in the halls."

"Small world," Gordon says, again with a smile, thumping his right boot a time or two, then looking over at the big guy, Frank, who is staring at Jip, while Jip is staring back at him. They look mad at each other. Or should it be: their eyes are filled with pique, umbrage, acerbity, ebullition, and acrimony.

Jip looks away from Frank's stare, back at Gordon, who smiles, and then she smiles, and Gordon looks back at Olan, who nods, and a cricket begins to chirp magnificently from behind a stuffed chair.

Gordon speaks cautiously: "So . . . you like the *Recipe*, huh?"

"Genius," Jip says quickly.

He nods, his eyes moving away from her. An unexplainable wretched feeling moves through the room toward him, old and earthy, like the smell of the cedar.

Olan says, "Gordon, we were hoping you might like to set us up for a few seminars around this area . . . with various groups . . . like churches or clubs . . . if you'd be interested in that . . . to start with."

Gordon nods, a suggestion of a nod, his blanched green eyes slipping away from their faces, down to the sawdusted knees of his work pants. "Well, it sounds neat. I'd like to do that . . . if I can find people to hold still long enough. You're all certainly welcome to have one here at the Settlement. So that gives you *one* anyway."

"You're a charismatic person. People are drawn to you," Billy explains, leaning forward, hands together, prayer-like, between his knees.

Frank's eyes move from a corner of the room directly to Billy's profile. Frank sighs disgustedly and the mile-wide shoulders heave.

Billy explains, "Frank doesn't want leaders, charismatic or otherwise."

"Well, Frank's right that democracy shouldn't be about leaders," says Olan, "but—"

Frank's voice, a big, patient, not-at-all-angry-sounding voice. "Democracy is *not* about leaders. That is correct."

Gordon watches this and then says quietly, "I'm not a leader. And *not* charismatic. I'm an introvert." Then he grins.

Jip laughs, scratching her fingers into her stiff, dark-yellow lamb curls as if this statement is so absurd that it's made her itchy. "*You*? An introvert?"

"That's right," says Gordon. "I'm not an organizer. I'm . . . nothing like you people. You're all great. You are . . . uh . . . absolute paragons of insurrection." He sniffs proudly at his choice of words. "But I can never be anything like that."

Jip says motherishly, "Whatever you are is fine," then switches back to a lawyerly or professorial tone . . . definitely a pushy bitch . . . but *nice*. "The point is that you know tyranny when you see it and you can draw people, mainstream, if you will. Okay, so you're no organizer. We are. We'll do the organizing. You're not a leader, you're a nice juicy carrot. You're not a leader . . . so Frank can cool off about that . . . he can chilllll." She leans forward and speaks into Frank's eyes. "Frank gets edgy when people rejoice over an MLK postage stamp or Martin Luther King Jr. *Day* or—"

Frank snorts. "That was a movement made up of thousands of civil rights activists, little church groups, thousands of sacrifices that are not applauded because—"

"Maybe there's only room for one guy on a postage stamp," Gordon jokes.

Frank says, "There would be nothing wrong with a *Civil Rights Day*, except that Americans might be reminded that it took organized insurgency to bring civil rights about. Right now they believe King did it."

"And it's interesting that Malcolm X has been deleted from the mainstream heroes list," Gordon says. "Panthers were scaring the white rooster, I guess."

"King was scary, too," Jip says. "He, too, was all-encompassing . . . he too spoke for all the poor of the world and was drumming up some heat over the Vietnam War. Leaders who are like him and Malcolm X . . . they inspire. They *educate*. So the empire assassinates them. That's a sign that they *were* a threat to the empire." She flicks her eyes at Frank, then away. "But Frank's point is not lost."

Gordon smiles sheepishly. "I love ol' Nelson Mandela. Militia leader *and* charm."

All the guests shift a bit. No comment.

Gordon swigs more coffee.

A long group silence if you call all the sipping, chewing, stove's crackle-pop, and cricket-creaks silence.

"A little charisma isn't going to hurt anything," Olan now insists. He turns to Gordon. "Frank is just playing devil's advocate. He's already agreed that getting you involved would at least get us a few well-attended seminars in Maine, and maybe a rally or two."

Olan's teeth are tall. Gold caps show on both sides behind the eyeteeth.

Frank has tsk-tsked, dropped his big beefy left leg from his right knee, recrossing his legs, then sinking deeper into the couch. Now he presses a finger to the nosepiece of his black-framed glasses.

"Frank's not playing devil's advocate," Billy teases. "He's just pining to get back to Newburyport and meet with Neal Sealy* about that grant."

"Fuck you," says Frank with a shadow of a grin and pretends to throw his coffee cup (empty) at Billy, who, gigglingly, covers his head. Then Frank's shadow of a grin passes and he looks stern again.

Gordon watches Frank hard.

Olan says, "When I was a little kid, I was so bored in school, I think my jaw hinges were permanently damaged from yawning. If only the teachers had been more . . . more theatrical, more wacky, more charismatic. If only they stood on their desks."

Frank rolls his eyes.

Jip jumps in. "EXACTLY! We're forced to compete for the average American's attention with the dazzling television stars, with ludicrous ads and noisy news, all the best noisy flashy diversions and lures into consumerism and passivity and corporation-worship and vast omissions that vaster sums of money can buy."

"I love ads," Frank says with a grave expression. "My favorite is where the nuclear power industry father figure voice tells us that THE SYSTEM IS WORKING."

---

* An organizer who will not show up in this book. ☺

"That's an investment ad," says Billy, sniffing into a white handkerchief.

"Doesn't matter," says Frank patiently. "Whoever he is, I love him, I want to give my life to nukes."

"Investments."

"Whatever."

Gordon is *really* staring at Frank now.

Frank shifts his legs again. Looks around the room. Yawns.

But now Billy is raising a hand to get Gordon's attention and he speaks in a soft apologetic voice. "One thing we see as a problem is . . . your association with the armed militias . . . you know, it draws a tiny few . . . but mostly it turns people off."

Gordon raises an eyebrow. "What people?"

"Most people. You said it yourself . . . about the tank."

Gordon's right boot jiggles a bit. He looks from face to face. "Talking down the corporations . . . and capitalism . . . that turns people off, too."

"That's right," says Olan, his small dark eyes wider than ever. "So we have enough going against us. The militia association would be double trouble, worse than double. It would erase us from the playing field."

Jip says, "The sensibilities of—"

Gordon interrupts, "Mammon is the only consequential sin."

The organizers all look at Gordon carefully with the *uh-oh* exchange of glances. Sin? Like in the *Bible*? But for the moment they're not touching *that* one.

"This has to be a peaceful movement," says Frank with narrowed eyes.

Billy sneezes five times in a row.

The cricket now behind the seated Godzilla chirps cheerily, but with portent.

"It must be nonviolent," Frank insists. "Not a bunch of crazies with guns and racism and paranoia-à-la-grande stockpiling *stuff*. That's what you'll draw when you say the word *militia*."

"The militia people aren't crazy," says Gordon. "Just one of the ways people *deal*." He sighs. "Except those that the FBI primes and entraps to give themselves a heroic image. And to scare, yes, scare. They could make *you* guys scary, too."

Frank scowls. "It's been done."

Jip pats Gordon's knee. "I'm sure you know some who are earnest. But nevertheless . . . our commitment is to nonviolence. And to educate as many as possible about corporate myths. To draw, not repel. Guns turn most people off."

Gordon stands up. "More coffee?"

They all agree to more coffee.

Gordon asks if they'd like to spend the night. "There's plenty of room."

"No, we've got to get back," says Jip, standing now, looking around the candlelit room once more, at all the books and murals and posters, the soft chairs. "But thank you!" She gives an old-fashioned bow. A *real* bow . . . like Broadway.

But they drink more coffee out in the quiet Winter Kitchen, which is still hot from supper, and they talk some more. They suggest November as a time to meet again and set up the seminar calendars, and possibly a little road trip for Gordon and some of the kids.

"We'll figure out some little skits for the kids pertaining to corporations usurping the power of flesh-and-blood people," Billy offers cheerfully.

Gordon's eyes almost cross. "I doubt there exists a way to channel their theatrics into a . . . uh . . . straight line." He tugs out his red bandanna and slathers it over his coffee-soaked mustache. "They lead themselves."

Olan suggests, "Well, maybe, Gordon, you could have a little talk with them before we meet in November."

Jip says, "Bree told us about your homeschool here, how it encourages—"

"Anarchy?" Gordon says while rubbing one temple.

All the organizers chuckle, even Frank.

Gordon likes these people, the little vapors of win-win that wriggle off their skin, their ease with each other, their crackling minds, their joshin', and a sparkle of hope he sees reflected in his coffee, which he is staring down into. Yes, they have seduced him.

And yet—

And yet—

And yet—

It's still September. Late morning on a Sunday. A nice normal cool flutter of leaf-light. Normal is much appreciated.

The after-breakfast kitchen crew is still swarming the Cook's Kitchen, wiping, splashing, thunk-rattling the hand pumps, stacking pottery plates, and there's the *clank!* and *clonk!* of the big kettles and long pans being shoved back into their bins.

Next door, through a short ramplike hall, is the Canning Kitchen, also called the Summer Kitchen, and you can glimpse them out there with all the harvest colors under the knife or being stirred or in the tall finished jars lining the long worktables. From that direction, in jeans and a floppy chambray shirt, short-legged, round as a good potato, Claire St. Onge steps into the Cook's Kitchen and sees what first seems like a kitchen-invasion of the US Marines. Camo-battle-dress uniform shirts and tight pistol belts, some with black leather holsters showing off the handles of sidearms. Identical olive-and-black patch on each left upper arm, the mountain lion and distinctive lettering: BORDER MOUNTAIN MILITIA.

And, well, this army isn't invading but milling about. Claire's stern dark eyes, however, remain stern.

At another doorway, the one to and from the big horseshoe of porches that line the quadrangle side of the horseshoe building, fourteen-year-old shy Alyson Lessard hovers, her pet black-and-brown sex-link hen in her arms. Pooky the hen is extroverted and loves a crowd. With cocked head and golden eyes she watches all that moves.

Alyson believes the sign tacked up on one wall by Bonnie Loo this summer is there just for her. It reads: *No live chickens allowed in any of our kitchens.*

So Alyson, in her shin-length autumn-brown skirt, baggy autumn-brown socks, moccasins, fuzzy old sweater, and coyly short brown hair, keeps her eyes lowered as she strokes Pooky's stiffly feathered back . . . oh, to never meet Bonnie Loo's mean queen eyes!!

Claire has come to deliver two russets that have arms and legs, and another that resembles the head of Mickey Mouse. At the edge of one worktable she lines them up. Bonnie Loo studies them, then nods, speaks in a flat oh-so-weighty way into Claire's bespectacled eyes. "God's art."

Claire nods.

Bonnie Loo frowns. "Well, the Big Guy made the earth and the firmament first. *Then* he made Mickey Mouse."

Okay, Bonnie Loo is wisecracking but now a true God-fearing soul steps in from the Canning Kitchen hallway, Glennice St. Onge. She gives a little wave to Rex and "his men" and then hugs Bonnie Loo. "How are you feeling this morning?"

Bonnie Loo snarls, "I didn't need to ask my throw-up pail to accompany me so I guess that's an improvement. I just got here, though."

Glennice tenderly advises, "Be easy on yourself."

The sunlight of this, one of the best days this year, flicks breezily in starbursts, spinning orbs, and diamonds through the tall, many-paned windows onto the floors of tiny handmade, discordantly colored, painted tiles and on the backs and sides of several rocking chairs. But the windows face southwest and so only suppertime is when this west wing of the horseshoe can fully celebrate the sun.

Kitchen crew bobs about. Mostly teenagers, but not all. And see there, Vancy St. Onge of the square face and loose white shirt is still feeding old, old, old Millie Lungren, John Lungren's mother. Millie eats like a tropical fish, little nibbles from the baby spoon and Vancy's coaxing.

John Lungren himself is gray-haired but hard in the arms and clear in the eye, those warm gray eyes situated there in his sixty-ish-year-old face, for he is one to consider *your* words rather than rattle on. In this way he'd put you to mind of Rex, just a lot less frosty. And he's one to shave everything off his face. Steel-framed eyeglasses and ordinary white-gold-color stretchy-band wristwatch, dark green pocket T-shirt and jeans, work boots rather new. Bonnie Loo has just handed him the funny-shaped potatoes and tells him, "Pass these on. Conversation pieces."

Bonnie Loo is wrestling with the nicotine devil for her fetus who is still smaller than a cigarette. At the *moment* she's winning. Though in the early a.m. it was easy not to smoke due to the lurch of nausea. But now the hunger for both food and the poison begins to flex.

In a rocker near one wall of cubbies is Gordon, who has one arm around six-almost-seven-year-old Jane Meserve who we can now officially call Secret Agent Jane due to not just her special all-seeing heart-shaped rose-tinted sunglasses but to the little black book in her smock pocket. She has books stuffed with everything you'd want to know about the wrongs of Settlement life if you can read her drawings, almost no printed words because those take sooooooo long.

Her outfit is Settlement-made, greens and yellows, much embroidery around the neck and cuffs. Her curly dark brown geyser of hair is reined in by a yellow squeegie that has a large yellow cloth flower made by a Settlement mother. Gordon fondles one of her ears and she sighs.

She is ever so self-conscious and aching for invisibility today. She leans more and more into Gordon, her secret-agent glasses trained on Rex, who she has met before and suspects is lawless. And yet he has such coplike ways and she has come to tremble at times in the vicinity of cop guards and the like.

Rex has his sunglasses on, too. No hearts for him. His are cop-style metal rims. And Claire, too, is now studying Rex. Claire and Gordon have had some little rows over the idea of "encouraging Rex" in what many mothers here call "his strange hobby," especially when Gordon insisted some fairly young kids attend one of the Border Mountain Militia meetings!!! Gordon persuaded (persuaded is not the right word but we'll use it for now) all the mothers that kids' immersing themselves in the militia experience was crucial to education and neighborliness. "We've already," said he, "established that the Settlement isn't about mainstream, standardized, rote, pablumized education."

"Next he'll be taking them to a whorehouse," Beth St. Onge had growled.

Thus, Claire is in some kind of whirlpool of feeling right now.

Several teenagers of the cleanup crew exit through the door to the screened porches.

Beth St. Onge, of the heart-shaped sort of English-Irish aspect and blond squiggly hair and trundling gait, though she's not heavy, squeezes two wet dishrags, one in each hand, over one of the long shallow sinks, and asks, "How much you guys collected so far?"

Montana, Beth's precious nine-year-old, stands nearby, unusually quiet but with a managerial posture and matching expression on her chubby face, fists on her hips. Her blond braids are thicker than hangman's nooses but not as thick as a ship's winching cables, though she is, as everyone who lives here knows, a ship unto all in her wake.

A stocky guy named Art, wearing the camo BDU shirt and patch and with a sea captain's white beard and twinkly blue eyes, replies, "Over three hundred, just from ourselves. You people are the first place where we've come to beg." Then he guffaws.

Two more teens and two women of the kitchen cleanup crew vanish.

Standing by the windows are a couple of sleepy-looking gray-haired militiamen with soft olive army caps in their hands and regular uncoplike eyeglasses on their faces.

And there is Willie Lancaster, neighbor from up Heart's Content Road, the one who brought fame to the Border Mountain Militia this past spring by being arrested, in uniform, with another member (not present here) in a barroom in Portland. Arrested, yes, for also wearing a holster and an unloaded service pistol (as he is doing here now) and flashing a Bible. He was detained, photographed, then released as no law was broken, but maybe the police thought Willie Lancaster smiled too much. He is smiling now, a little bit bucktoothed, a cat-that-ate-the-canary smile. Not quite forty years old, no gray in his brown Jack the Ripper beard. Yes, he is presently quiet but exploding with quietness. And he paces a little. And yes, he was smiling this way in his recent jail picture, his "book him" picture, unlike most people's jail pictures ,which show them looking disoriented.

Another wearer of the Border Mountain Militia BDU shirt and patch, pistol belt, and gun, is a member about age fifteen but small for fifteen. Streaky blond hair with a ponytail the size of a pinkie finger. His eyes are gray with a wild, woodsy critter aspect. This boy is Mickey Gammon, who lives secretly in a tree house on St. Onge land, furnished with his Bible, an extra shirt in a damp brown bag, some snack foods, and his new sleeping bag bought with bucks he has earned from jobs the militia guys put him in touch with, like mowing grass, babysitting, crawling under a lake camp to fetch out a dead skunk. He does not smell like a skunk but smells robustly of zero bathing.

He hasn't forged all the way into the room but hangs back near Alyson and Pooky the hen still framed in that door from the big screened porches. His eyes keep flicking toward Willie Lancaster as you would keep your eye on a sky of cloud-to-ground lightning moving in from the west.

Pushing up the sleeves of her dark old store-bought jersey, Beth slyly asks, "So you guys do this a lot? Run around and raise money for causes?"

The chatty Art says, "We raised six hundred for some Indian people who got flooded. And a scholarship for Brent Ham to go to USM . . . about nine hundred."

Beth pushes up her sleeves again and a bunch of pretty nice teeth appear in her face suddenly, she looks like a curly yellow dog picking a fight. But she is now shrieking happily, "The Lions Club with guns!!!"

Nobody can see Rex's eyes because of his sunglasses but he turns his head to face Beth square on, with not even a faint smile of appreciation for her great wit, but most of his militia is chortling good-naturedly.

Gordon rocks back hard almost pulling Secret Agent Jane off her feet and says deeply, "Pretty soon you'll be giving poor kids free breakfasts."

Rex shifts to face the nearest archway opening in the wall of cubbies, beyond which is the grange-sized room full of long tables for cool-weather meals, and says tonelessly, "That job appears to already be covered by yourself."

Beth narrows her eyes, "I don't get your joke."

Bonnie Loo has gone and come back from the Canning Kitchen with a jar of apple jelly and some sort of preserves that look nearly black. Probably both are still warm. Bonnie Loo's wearing her glasses today, the ones with tape on one of the bows.

Beth's daughter Montana has marched to the archway that Rex was looking through. She's quite close to Gordon with his massive arm around Secret Agent Jane while Jane's heart-shaped sunglasses are directed at the jars Bonnie Loo is setting out on the workbench closest to the visitors.

Gordon says, "Not to repeat this too much but the intent of the Black Panthers was for justice and a decent life for all, which you guys know was in the pledge of allegiance they used to foist on kids in public schools. Sounded good. But was meaningless. Also the Panthers—"

"Wait a minute! Wait a minute!" Beth interrupts lamentishly. "Gordon, are you going to go on and on? We've *heard* this."

Her daughter, Montana, still with fists on her squishy hips, doubles —no, *triples*—her corrective frown on Gordon's quirky smile.

He says, "Hush up, woman. My point is that there are similarities . . . like this community stuff. Although the Panthers dodged . . . and *took* . . . a lot more bullets from those sworn to protect the overlords of the free world. We should be standing shoulder to shoulder with the Panthers . . . those in prison, especially, because of—"

"Wait a minute!" Beth again cuts in, her stance now identical to her daughter's, fists on hips. She's cracking up, trying to say more but sputtering and gasping and gagging. "So . . . *you* guys . . . are . . . *gasp! gag! gasp!* the *Pink* Panthers!!! *sputter! gasp! gasp!*" And from there she is lost in cackles and now pulls down her long dark jersey sleeves in order to sop up her tears of laughter on one arm.

Others join her in her hilarity, maybe only because it's catchy, but Rex is like a cement sculpture of himself.

Bonnie Loo is back-to. She's sawing up slices of her white bread on a worktable. No one can see her restrained snickers; just an almost undetectable vibration in her shoulders is visible.

A freckled skeletal redheaded militiaman is making no sound but shaking all over with his mirth, eyes on Rex, as if it's Rex's possible aggravation that delights him more than the wiseacre Beth St. Onge.

Dee Dee Lancaster St. Onge (married to Gordon's nineteen-year-old cousin Lou-EE), herself eighteen and waddlingly pregnant, charges in from the porches, brushing between Mickey Gammon and Alyson. "What. is. so. funny?!!" she demands, her gray eyes laughing along before she has the answer. On her heels a humorless black Scottie dog who never turns her head, just moves her eyes and eyebrows. The dog's name is Cannonball.

Dee Dee freezes when she sees Willie Lancaster. She punches him in the arm. "I heard there was a big cockroach infestation here this morning. And here it is. One big cockroach."

Willie's self-satisfied smile widens. He muckles onto* her arm in its red-and-black-plaid sleeve and pins her to himself. "Apologize or I'll lock you in the closet, brat!"

Meanwhile, Montana, with undulating braids, steps closer to the rocker that Gordon is sprawled in like a merry well-fed king, his arm still protecting Secret Agent Jane from the Settlement whirlwinds, and Jane is nuzzling his shirt.

Montana speaks in a lecturing voice: "He's *not* your father."

Jane doesn't regard Montana, just says, while looking off toward the sun-dappled windows, "He's not your father, either."

Montana, fluffing to a larger version of her large self, steps closer. "Gordie. You're my father, aren't you?"

Gordon's pale green eyes in dark lashes slide over Jane's shoulder to Montana's pale green eyes in dark lashes. "You two need to bury the tomahawk."

Jane sneers at Montana. "My father is brown."

Montana's fists are more sturdily on her hips. "Where is he then?"

Jane says saucily, "He's busy."

Montana jeers, "Biz-zeeee."

The secret agent raises her chin. "He's famous in rap."

Gordon and Rex, both in grave, flat voices, are now discussing the fire and the burned-out family that needs the money the militia is collecting. Jane grips hard some of Gordon's untucked blue plaid shirt, her eyes black as beginnings and endings, handsome nose, long movie-star neck, her arms move like symphony music but for a twinge of six-seven-year-old clumsiness.

Montana looks too much like Gordon, the nose that on a man seems noble on a little girl seems storklike, one wild eye, the other squint and flinch, the goofy grin that is goofy on her father but on her, with her ruthless sense of superiority, poses as bared fangs.

Glennice St. Onge keeps up a come-and-go to the Canning Kitchen. Her specialty is the outdoors part of food production, lugging seedlings, digging, hoeing, taking the tractor out in some cases, picking beans, chopping squashes, digging potatoes, all that sun and mist

---

* "Muckles onto" is a term commonly used in Maine.

and all those biting bugs. But she and her harvest crews are not in a separate universe from the kitchens.

"You guys are collecting money for the Haydens?" Dee Dee asks the guests as she continues to slowly and softly punch her father Willie Lancaster's arm. (Note that if she is married to Gordon's second cousin Lou-EE, that makes Willie family to Gordon, right?)

Several nods reply to Dee Dee's question.

She trudges pregnantly over to the wall of cubbies and paws around for an envelope, then tugs out a dollar. "Who is the Border Mountain treasurer here?"

Art, with the sea captain's white beard, accepts the dollar. "They're my neighbors. They'll appreciate it."

Dee Dee frowns. "I wish I had more. I heard they lost everything."

Says Art, "They got their old cat out. Sometimes you hear everyone got out but they don't count pets. They ought to count them."

Dee Dee frowns again. "They didn't even use to count people . . . like in burning factories . . . before unions were organized, that is."

Art gives her a stiff, wincing smile. Obviously, she's pressed up against one of the boulders of disagreement that most patriot movement enthusiasts have placed at the entrances of their caves and castles of reasoning, while Dee Dee always dances around them and punches their arms.

Now arriving from the sun-slanted screened piazzas (porches), an old woman smiling at each and every face. She doesn't miss even one. Her blue eyes crackle with stars, clear as skies because she has no need for glasses. Her hair has only tweaks of gray, no perm, no "cut" either, though it is somewhat short. Just two tortoiseshell barrettes keep it niced up.

The skeletal freckle-faced red-haired militiaman who looks for sure to have something impendingly terminal, shouts, "Mrs. Nichols! What are *you* doing here?!!"

Claire pulls a kettle from an iron spider on one of the wood cookstoves. "Benedicta, you want tea, don't you?"

The old woman nods and her smile has staying power. The stars in her eyes inside the crinkles and puckers of age cast their steady alertness about the great kitchen.

"Call her Dick. Everyone calls her Dick," says Art.

Gordon's whole face, not just the usual parts, flinches. "Dick?"

Claire says, "What about our guests? You people want coffee? Tea? Tomato juice? Berry juice? Carrot juice?"

There are several "I guess I will, thank you" for coffee, one for berry juice, and two "No, thank you, ma'am. I'm all set."

Nobody but John Lungren notices as Vancy St. Onge helps teetering Millie Lungren to her feet and out the door.

Militiaman Art says in a low gossipy murmur, "Steve Marden's mother-in-law. He *said* she *moved out* but he's planning on keeping her *checks*. Social Security . . . *that* is a federal crime."

Gordon's eyes slide to the old woman who is standing by the sinks, dressed in a new blouse of the same green-and-yellow fabric as Secret Agent Jane's outfit but with jeans and sneakers, blinding lime green lacings, a more sporty image than Jane's.

Gordon ruffle-fondles Jane's hair, messing it.

She says irritably, "*Don't*, Gordie."

He says to Art, "I can't feel right calling her Dick."

"Benedicta's a mouthful," Art points out. "But keep in mind that's what's written on those checks . . . Benedicta Nichols. And the deed, too. It's her house and land they're in, them and their kids, the whole pack. And Steve's job is a joke . . . he needs to move up from that. And Debbie don't work at all except yard sales with Sue Mason. And if you watch closely you'll notice they're always returning cans. Soda. Beer. And I known them to buy *steaks*."

Gordon nods.

Art lowers his voice even more. "So she *moved* here?"

Gordon has been watching Benedicta, who is cautiously and turtle-slow selecting a fern-print cup from rows of Settlement-fashioned cups, mugs, and tumblers still draining after the cleanup crew's steamy bustle.

"So *you guys* get the checks?"

Gordon looks at Art. Shrugs almost imperceptibly, a headshake so slight it could be one of the Tourette's-like flinches.

"So Steve gets the checks," states Art momentously.

Again, Gordon seems to be leaning into the winds of another one of those head-slamming beat-you-with-a-baseball-bat paradoxes. It always affects him like a muscle disease. Then, "She landed here.

She's staying with the Pinettes till her cottage is built. We're decking it this week. But she and the Pinettes . . . they love having her. She loves them. It's a love fest." He smiles warmly. "Maybe she'll wind up just staying there."

"Marden. He shouldn't be getting away with it . . . keeping her checks. That's taxpayer money," Art grumbles.

Gordon gives a sly smile. "Actually your federal income taxes don't go anywhere. They're erased. It's a whole different operation from the money Congress spends. The money Congress spends, those *trillions*, the Federal Reserve issues through the books . . . computers today . . . endlessly. States and towns and counties have to raise money for expenses. But not your America." His pale eyes are glowing with the fires of another heating-up harangue.

Jane groans. "Gorrr-die."

Gordon's tone might be a bit too teacherly for Art's comfort.

And Rex shows impatience by staring at Gordon with a slight widening of his eyes behind his dark glasses, so there's more sparkle there. A signaling. Signals come from every direction of the kitchen.

Beth moans, "Oh, Jesus."

Gordon is like a loaded dump truck that has crested a hill, words coming faster. "Modern Monetary Theory it's called. It was their way of regulating currency and the circulation. But definitely it's for regulating the economy. And Social Security is not what we've been told. It's not perfectly contained. *They* can steal from it, the archdemon motherfuckers. But the program was designed to look circular, not paid for out of any other taxes except the Social Security tax. Our kids here study this. Ask any one of them about it. Federal income tax is *not* for expenditures."

Montana, already close and still with arms akimbo, leans in, "Modern Monetary Theory is easy to understand."

Yes, Gordon has been bullshitting Art in that he leaves out the word *debt*. He would dearly love to slather around the wonders of the idea for a possible new progressive global tax on capital to pay that towering debt. But he (and we, too) can figure quite correctly that Art's heart never slackens from its wish to protect the nobility.

Art's posture has gone straighter, his sea-captain-bearded chin is raised. "But Marden shouldn't get away with that no matter."

Secret Agent Jane reaches to cover Gordon's mouth with her long-fingered golden-brown hand.

He pulls one of her earlobes and she giggles. He looks up at Art. "When you consider what the State Department, spooks, and Pentagon are getting away with, scoffing at international laws made after Nazi Germany was behaving so badly . . . so now who's the criminal, doing war crimes and all that? But jeepers, the stakes are high, lots more than a little Social Security check, more than just the cheating it takes to feed the kids, steak, whatever . . . and pay for heat. More than silly dinky little shit like that! For the overlords the stakes are to rule the world!!" Gordon bats his eyes as a ruler proud to rule might.

Montana edges closer, places her hand on the front edge of the chair arm in front of Jane, and Gordon's eyes fall on her. He pats his lap, spreads his knees, and she lunges into that treasured space the secret agent shall not *totally* claim as her own!

Gordon grunts as the wind gets knocked out of him by his hefty daughter, then just rattles on, for Art's edification. "And they plan to roll all us little fuckers up in virtual chains and real barred dungeons, whatever nationality . . . the people under the bombs are nobody to them and you and I are nobody to them. Now *that* is a piece of meat! *That* is steak! *That* is what we need to be keen to, I believe. Though I would not say it's unnatural, but it *is* unnatural not to feel the sting, not to know what direction the sting is coming from! I'm not telling you what to think, my brother, but there's something to mull over in all this . . . how they get away with setting us up to despise our neighbors. In *that* there's something to steam over! And to fear!"

Rex actually audibly sighs, heard above the chatter of others in the room and above Gordon's rumbles. He, Rex, turns around and faces the view of part-shade part-sun goldenrod and stout maples beyond the floor-to-ceiling windows that he clearly remembers as rough openings and studs, sawhorses, cardboard boxes of nails, nails, and sawdust on the floor. Meanwhile, Gordon's voice moves into and out of Rex York's skull . . . "We need to fix in our minds for now and evermore that those with the desire for total power *do indeed conspire. Majestically.*"

Art blinks. Lips stiff with irritability and maybe shame. "I knew that."

Claire moves close to Rex, asks, "So, in addition to money, the Haydens need what? Do they need help cleaning up? Rebuilding? Where are they staying?"

Rex looks at her and the light from the windows shows plainly his eyes behind his dark glasses. "In Brownfield. Her people. But that can't work for long. Two bedroom Cape. Ten people." He looks down at the Scottie dog who has decided to sit next to his boots, facing the same way he is standing.

Claire says, "Watch out . . . don't pat her. She bites."

He studies the large head, the eyebrows like some fantasy troll's, the small but tanklike body. He makes no comment.

Overhearing their talk, one of the gray-haired militiamen says, "Yeah, I bet they'd like help. Maybe you guys could interest them in a turbine. Their land is, as you know, out in the wide open on Horne Hill."

"There you go. Just your cup of tea," Art says with a cackle, his cheeks still pink from the unease over Gordon's monetary zigzags and what felt like a scolding. Maybe not everyone in the Border Mountain Militia is a fan of Gordon's. "Or you could take the Haydens in if Dick here doesn't want the cottage you've started on."

Benedicta has situated herself in a rocker near the little table where her teacup and saucer have been placed. Her spoon swerves and tinkles, making little tea waves. She asks Claire, "Whose side are you on?"

Claire cocks her head at this.

Bonnie Loo warns Rex that the "damn dog bites," then commands all the guests to pull up a rocker and have some warm buttered bread or squash muffin with their coffee.

And so they all sit.

The Scottie dog follows Rex to his chosen chair and sits again by his boots.

Dee Dee says to Rex, "She won't bite *you*. She likes you."

Rex says nothing. He now makes a point, it seems, of not noticing the dog who makes people nervous. The dark dark piercing eyes keep track of Rex's hands. Her hackles are not raised but her tail doesn't wag. She's very still, like her cast-iron name, Cannonball.

John Lungren, having considered the talk of a windmill for the burned-out family, carries one-handedly a folding chair from the Winter Kitchen and tells about a turbine for sale on the Moody's store bulletin wall. "No home is complete without one," he says with smiling eyes.

Nobody notices as Rex slips the Scottie dog a chunk of his buttered bread, which she snags into her vast pink maw with her tall yellowy teeth.

Talk of checking out the wind turbine on Moody's bulletin wall gets serious.

Talk of bringing the Haydens to the Settlement also escalates.

Gordon tells Art he'll come by tomorrow with some cash for their collection.

Art salutes Gordon hand-to-forehead.

Gordon salutes Art.

Montana, cuddled close to Gordon, has a soft contented expression, her cheek squished against his shirt under which is located his huge pumping heart.

Cannonball is now drinking from someone's creamy coffee that has been set on the floor. "Stop that!" Dee Dee scolds and hauls the dog backward with a two-handed grip and warns, "Caffeine will make her think she's Napoleon."

Willie Lancaster rocks his chair with some vigor. His black military service pistol holster is silken with buffings and grease. The angled sun skates on and off his left shoulder and gives life to his olive-and-black mountain lion patch. Each of his gray eyes shows the possibility for ruckus. He's not out to intentionally bother lawmen or the guardians of the mores. Or Rex. It just happens. He is in most ways an ordinary man with modest desires.

After a few minutes he's finished his black coffee, and both his and Cannonball's eyes burn like worlds afire.

The voice of Mammon speaks on foreign policy.

It is said that a weasel will wring, rip, and kill clean everybody in sight before settling down to feast on *one* corpse.

In some ways Mr. Weasel has it wrong. In some ways he has it right.

Critical thinker of the past.

Mammon led them on,
Mammon, the least erected spirit
That fell
From heav'n;
—Milton, *Paradise Lost, I*

Bruce Hummer, Chief Executive Officer for the war-widget-bioweapons-energy-lawn-poison-and-other-stuff giant Duotron Lindsey International, announces in his clarion voice another major layoff.

This time only nine thousand workers in the Michigan and New Jersey plants, some mid-level management and some low-level management included. He explains there will be new projects—development and restructuring in Mexico and Indonesia in the upcoming months—and pending the admittance of China into the WTO, plans for "good things" there as well. He reveals that what remains in the United States now is mostly warehousing and distribution and other services, and computer programming, natch, all of which will require a much smaller work-force on the home front. A *lot* of robots. He adds almost melodiously that the labor unions in the United States are the reason for all this pain.

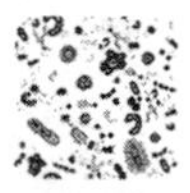

The voices of microorganisms speak.

We are your ancient relations, for you have risen from our dark tumid loamy underneaths, our wet tuneful heat, our twiggy competition and pungent wars.

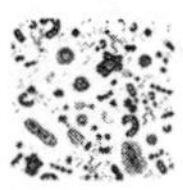

Microorganisms have more to say.

The naked truth, the unvarnished, sorry to relate, sorry to expose your twaddle, but there has been *no rise*. You are nailed in place by the webbed mother of life; she has no honor students, no progress, no supremes.

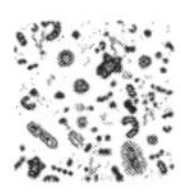 **Voices of microorganisms loud and clear.**

We watch you and you watch us as we waltz, unable to pull away. Forever, we are your sturdy sires, your founders, your mix and match, your middle eye.

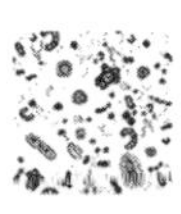 **You can't shut them up.**

You with your heat, competition, and war, bigger in noise and tonnage, yet we share the deeps, snout to snout and cell on cell, welcoming embraces in the grave.

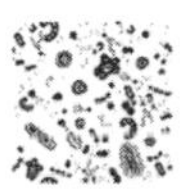 **The voices of microorganisms and the Beatles.**

We are you and you are we and we are all together. ♫

 **From a future time, Claire St. Onge tells us about her friend, Professor Catherine Court Downey.**

I can still see her! That late summer and fall she was forty-four. She had all the mannerisms of a person accomplished in her career from a long line of career people; questing people; people who are herders of others, keeping them correct, moving them along. But she was an artist with an eye that looks both outward and inward.

Her watercolors with feminist themes were ensconced in many local galleries and I saw impressive catalogs of her work at shows in Boston and Hartford and New York. She was interim chair of the USM art department for a few weeks that fall. Careerwise, she had a lot on her shoulders.

She could be sharp with you, confrontational, unlike the blurry indecision of so much of her work, though some might prefer to interpret her paintings as reflective.

She had Frida Kahlo eyebrows. Eyes that changed color with the mood of the sky or room, muddy-green to amber or blue-brown infused with spite. Frizzy black hair in a hard nut of a knot that left all of her beautiful face relevant. It would *seem* she did not hide any of herself.

I often found her barefoot in her office. She was both erect and dissipated, her favorite sweater, loose, shruggy, pale pink, and creeping toward the outer edge of one shoulder. Pale pink is no coincidence because above all she was heartfelt.

Gail St. Onge.

You call someone like her "Ms." She was stately. Very pretty and stately.

Bonnie Loo remembering the professor.

Bitch. You only need that one word. No need to go on about it.

Carlotta "Lolly" St. Onge.

She was kind to me. I was one of those who saved a place for her at the table. There were many besides me here who couldn't get enough of her. When she was feeling off about something, you know, nervous, she'd trill, "Isn't this wonderful!" You know. She'd sing it. She's like, "Oh, how blessed we are!" *Trill trill.* This pertaining to a platter of fried moose heart and onions. We all watched and listened closely because this added tension. All people who live in a *potential* paradise *love* tension, an *impending* fight. Like for instance, her and Gordon. Oh, boy.

Claire remembering more of what brought Catherine to the Settlement.

Late that summer before the semester was sprung on us, there was one of those orientation luncheons with pleasant chitchat on the back lawn of Luther Bonney Hall. Catherine somehow wound up out in her car, windows up, sweltering in the big parking lot heat, disoriented, laughing in a fainting-away fashion that spooked me.

By the time the first week of classes was ready to dig in, she was not making sense . . . mostly I suppose because it's hard to be straight-out honest about addiction, even with a good friend. That was the first time I met her four-year-old, Robert. I suggested they come live with me and my family for a little while, for Catherine to have some healing time. It was in Robert's dark eyes I saw no other way.

I only once met Catherine's husband Phan, a Vietnamese-American businessman. He wasn't in-your-face captivating but he was easy to like. A gentleman. No sharp edges at all. Little businessman jokes told in his zingy-zongy accent, which I had to listen close to, to be ready for the punch lines.

Robert was a smaller version of Phan. Gentleman. No sharp edges. Easy to like. Then easy to love.

As Catherine was falling apart, Phan was on the other side of the world on a six-week business trip and I couldn't bear to abandon these two to their empty house.

The problem was, I, too, had been hiding part of me. I hadn't confessed to Catherine about Gordon . . . about our *odd* situation. I had just always been calling him my ex. But now that she was here we set up a cozy pallet of rugs and quilts and a camp mattress for her and Robert next to my big bed in my cottage's only bedroom, where she slept and read for many days and I told her the truth. She seemed to take it all with a grain of salt.

Her only major complaint at first was that one warm late morning while Robert and I were busy at the shops, she heard the stretch-screen rattle in the bedroom window, then flop to the floor. She had swept aside her pretty purply privacy tapestry between the beds to see what the commotion was. "A horrible bird! A raven!" had filled the room with spanking wingspan and was "crouching villainously" on one post of my bed. He cocked his head, fluffed himself, and sermonized eloquently, "It's five o'clock! Get your ass up! It's five o'clock! Get your ass up! It's fi—"

She threw her sneaker at him.

He ducked it. "Zucchini patties again! I ain't no friggin' rabbit! Zucchini patties again! I ain't no friggin' rabbit!"

Catherine had screeched at him, then sobbed. The preposterous actuality of the Settlement had become fully manifest.

When I got home, the crow was outside on the front yard sculpture fixing his feathers. He eyed me as I pushed open my door but said nothing.

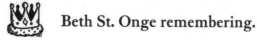

Penny St. Onge remembering Catherine Court Downey.

She was kind to Brianna Vandermast, who was still "the neighbor girl." Yes, our Bree, who had been for years painting in oils at home where she lived with her father and brothers. I can't begin to describe how gifted Bree was with pastels and oils . . . using mostly rag paper and beaverboard. After a crew made a large Quonset hut attic space into a studio for Catherine and Bree, a rounded dormer with a fan to suck out fumes, a Homasote partition down the middle for privacy, Catherine showed Bree how to stretch canvases and they chattered away and became great buddies.

Bree began off and on wearing her hair clipped back from her face, like Catherine's. So Catherine had impressed her like a spark to the soul.

But then once Catherine got free of the pills (some prescribed but most off the street), she wasn't around much. Robert was swept up into many crews and activities but also the terrible woodsy boy gangs that cussed, hunted for Bigfoot with "swords," and heaped up grass huts in the fields for experiments with war and matches. Court-martial after the field fire and the First Aid Shop, not in that order. Then, too, he was riding in the big trucks with the men to deliver lumber waaay past bedtime. His nickname became Mr. Buddy.

Catherine, meanwhile, was absorbed in teaching, shopping, and divorcing Phan and lots and lots of trips moving little things from Portland to her Settlement studio space where she never painted, while on the other side of the Homasote partition Bree wielded her brush with wicked abandon, *without* propriety, and doesn't propriety include the feminist "bridle"? (Bonnie Loo's word.) Catherine would call that bridle freedom, equality, and correctness. But for certain, Brianna Vandermast would mule-kick *any* sort of stall.

Beth St. Onge remembering.

Meanwhile, Claire's friend Catherine thought some of the Settlement rules were too crazy to believe. For instance, the "no TV" rule. She told several people here she would bring her TV anyway. *Secretly.*

She'd invite a secret select group to the grand opening up there in her studio . . . aka TV room. She'd serve wine, cheese, and crackers. She said, "We need to bring a little class to this . . . this *farm*."

I suggested she fetch some X-rated stuff. Women being fucked by donkeys maybe. She gave me a look like I was covered in pus, which was the exact same look she always gave me. I know she didn't like me.

I found this TV development *very* interesting. No, I found it *fun*.

It wasn't going to be a donkey that was going to crash in on her party. More like a great big steam-snorting bull.

Catherine Court Downey speaks.

Three women settled around me at the breakfast table with their cups and muffins, one with a long-legged toddler on her hip.

And there came a teenage boy, one of my favorites. (He wore curve-toed elf shoes!) He stood an unusually tall high chair, wooden and solid, painted cherry pink, next to us so the toddler could oversee us all like a small king.

Swirling around us were smocks and skirts with densely embroidered flowers and birds. You thought skirts went out with hat pins, girdles, and the red letter A? Once these women, mostly mothers, barely twenty, were all seated, there was Lee Lynn standing there. Flying around graying-brown hair, although she was only about thirty or thirty-five.

You could easily get confused about which ones of these hundred beings were *his* wives. But you'd not forget Lee Lynn, ill-favoredly memorable with her fire truck siren voice, the Halloween hair, and gauzy dresses. And she wore bells. She wore bells, yes. Large rusty sleigh bells. Little shiny jinglebells. *And* a clanking metal cuff around one ankle, like a slave. She thought this was attractive? She herself a wraith. It was impossible for me to fathom what that massive pile of muscle that *he* was would find to excite him in Lee Lynn. But there to prove it was his overly thrifty thin silver ring, as all the wives had, and her round-faced stout little daughter Hazel, who stumbled along behind her with *his* eyes, with *his* dark hair, and *his* several kinds of smiles.

This was called the Winter Kitchen, the size of a public school classroom; no, it was larger than that. "Can I get you a little three-grain toast, Catherine?" Lee Lynn mewled with her slave-like little bow.

For the brief time Robert and I stayed with these people the ghastly realization came to me that Lee Lynn and the others thought she and I were *alike*! That we'd fall into a robust friendship! Both of us were aware of healthful thought and practice, so they would say. But draw the line there, please!

Had they sicced her onto me well-meaningly . . . she often shadowed me, it seemed. Everywhere I roamed, the rooms of the Shops, porches, brick paths, grassy Quadrangle, she'd spring up and plead with me, *Oh, Catherine, is there anything you need*?

"I'm fine," I told her and held her silvery eyes with my own because I was *not* afraid of her even though I sometimes imagined her long arms and fingers as deep ocean tentacles that could tear me out of my chair.

She stroked my shoulder and then I glanced to see her retreating back, her bright dress, gory orange, toiling around her. Her child Hazel remained, smiling with almost neon pleasure at the other toddler up there on his pink throne.

Yes, I was there. And Claire, my only true Settlement friend, was *not* there. She'd left for the university early. Another dark candle-flickering morning where I find myself at the opposite end of this jumbo Settlement kitchen from the man who, if you are lucky, you will never know one like.

I held my eyes on him directly across the rose-color candle lamp in front of my plate and the long lane between doubles of candle lamps down the center of the fifteen-foot table. He scribbled something on a receipt-sized paper then handed it to the boy nicknamed Oz, who was about thirteen. Oz St. Onge, one of his sons by a Passamaquoddy mother, not Claire. Yes, as you watch the churn of children with Gordon's face amalgamated with everybody else's face, you are confounded.

"Did you hear the coyotes last night, Catherine?" someone asked.

I winced. "Yes, and I heard guns." I plucked bottles from my basket of essential minerals.

"Well, Aurel's crew does that to scare them," she told me with a sparkly little smile.

"Coyotes are opportunists," complained another.

"Is that so?" I didn't want to talk about their guns. I was wondering where my Robert was. He loved to lose himself in this crowd. It was worrisome enough that he'd been among those who set each other's grass forts on fire. I rolled a few capsules in my hand.

"Dub meee! Dub meee!" shouted the toddler in his skyscraper chair and Hazel leaned against the table and I saw with amusement that she in her mother's fashion had one Christmassy jinglebell on braided yarn around her wrist.

My tea was lukewarm now, the way I like it. I began to take the first of my herb capsules.

Astrid. Well-dressed, even to be here at this . . . this farm . . . thick brown hair with a professional cut which could *not* have been brought into this world by the eight-year-olds and twelve-year-olds of the beauty crew here. On her wedding ring finger was *his* cheap thin silver gesture.

She leaned in and hugged me. Did not smell like hot hay bales and frogs as most of them did, their foul soaps and salves concocted and brewed and stewed by Lee Lynn. Astrid smelled like Ivory. A bit of justified rebellion? She murmured, "You look wonderful. See? All you needed was to slow down. The world is too fast, even for the best of us." She touched my tiny bun of hair with just a fingertip, a butterfly pressure.

Then she was on her way, dissolving into the munching crowd, *zhip-zhipp*ing kazoos, bouncing halos of candle-lamp colors.

Brianna Vandermast was never there for breakfast, rarely for other meals. She was heavy on my mind.

No, Bree was never around because she lived with her redneck father and brothers, none to be trusted as far as I could see . . . well, Bree was being sold for sex by them and sexually abused by Gordon, too. You see, her paintings spoke for her. Art does not lie. It leaps from the innermost recesses of the self and screams for help.

A square of warm corn bread was set before me by a gentle hand, *another* wife, Misty.

Again my eyes turn to watch *him*. What in the world is wrong with me that I let my four-year-old son linger with this man *out of my sight*!

Always Robert gaping up at Gordon as if the giant were supernatural. As if he were benign!

Again I peer across the many heads and shoulders, lifted forks, raised cups, laughing, choking, bursts of song, baby wails, to watch the unnatural creature stand up to receive on one palm something steel or iron, some machine part . . . his giant Passamaquoddy-looking son Cory's outstretched hand, their fingers touch. Oh, Gordon, long-armed supple chimerical thrill, no category on this planet, you steal another day from almost a hundred people who could be living normal lives. Even my son's! And you *steal, steal, steal* from me, even now, into this future, you steal from me my center, my balance.

I have, yes, seen his true essence in Bree's paintings. Under the trembling brush, she had torn open his violent sorcery. His many nude likenesses, great and flushing, goose-bumped in snow, part man, part hooved titan, while from rock fissures poured his fat babies, no, pouring not from women, but from rock!!!!

Therefore, I was compelled to act.

Lolly St. Onge remembers the invasion.

The whole group of us whom Catherine had rounded up to break in on Bree's private studio space kind of shuffled in shame under the big lights. It was hard to look at the tall sort-of-window-sized paintings of Gordon and hard *not* to look.

Misty St. Onge remembering.

So then Catherine shouted that Bree had to "come to terms" with being sexually abused by this almost forty-year-old man, that the big paintings were evidence. Gordon was Bree's nasty demon that she needed to cleanse herself of . . . well, something like that.

Then Catherine, still shouting, said that Bree's big book of X-rated drawings, which she had shared with all the Settlement girls, resembled her father and brothers and this proved they were selling her for sex. I saw those drawings and oh, boy, they actually did resemble those guys. Sort of.

Claire.

Yes, I was among them in Bree's bright paint-and-turpentine-scented studio space with all those fantasy Gordons in suspiciously accurate nudity, seraphs, Minotaur, Satan in blue fire. I, *of course*, suspected Gordon of *the deed*. At least *at first*. What my heart despairs of most was watching as Bree drove out of the Settlement parking lot, *betrayed*, her private very special studio space penetrated, you could say, *raped*. Her brother Poon's truck, her at the wheel, really threw out the dust.

One morning at breakfast.

Winter Kitchen. Windows closed. Wood cookstoves purring and popping, too much heat. The hours for breakfast are almost over but Catherine knows there will be plenty of stuff left. She carries her little basket of herbal treatments to the table at which Gordon sits near the little stage where teenage Eric, who calls himself Ricardo, still plays his morning music on a guitar, tender music and a melodramatically tender expression to match.

Catherine tugs off her gray jacket and slips it over the back of her chosen chair. On her walk down here along the brick path, the sky showed signs of brightening but the sun was tangled in hemlock trees up on one of the farther mountain's shoulders.

Now in this west-facing interior, it's only the tall green and yellow stained-glass candle lamps for light.

Gordon is drinking beer. Yes, beer for breakfast! His buttered toast is untouched. He does not presently seem roused by alcohol. He just looks at Catherine warmly and says he heard she enjoyed seeing pigs, sows, goats, and whatnot last evening.

"Yes!" Catherine trills as if *she* were the beered-up person. "They were wonderful . . . *all* the creatures. I asked Aurel to show them to me. He's such a nice man. The animals are well-treated."

"Yes." And he smiles again. Warmly.

She loses the restraint that she usually keeps around him, so embraced by the warmth of the moment, the heat of the rooms, bready buttery frying smells, preening almost creaturely guitar riffs, and Gordon's one flinching eye, one widening eye that now seem boyishly endearing, the gray on the chin of his dark beard almost unbearably trustworthy. She speaks in a voice not her own. "After classes today I'm going to my house for more belongings. I have a small television I can use in my studio. I have videos. And DVDs. Educational. You have such clever kids here. I bet one could install an antenna strong enough to pull in the analog. We should stay abreast of the news . . . of what's happening *out there*. In the *real* world."

He has shifted his huge frame tigerishly to face her fully. The guitar music stops, voices and clanking dish sounds all over the room die down as if in deference to him. "We have a rule here. No TV. It's an important rule."

In a future time, when she remembers this moment, she will remember not the softeningly clanky, mumbly sounds of solace and smoky smells of the three-times-daily feast, nor the tremulous light of the glass candle lamps, but that widening pale yellow-green eye on her and how in the tingling bore of her spine, in the cold perfection of her always crackling intelligence that has gotten her three degrees, she made the dear, dear promise to herself that by the end of the week she'd be watching an elegantly done French art film in her studio. Because what was between her and that face, that thick neck, those shoulders, and all the rest of what he was that could inspire the paintings in Bree's studio by Bree's innocent hand, paintings, yes, of Gordon. Shocking! Pornographic! Zoolike! . . . all that remained between such a creature and herself, Catherine, was war.

She is no longer the crippled, breathless, exhausted, stuttering drugged thing Claire invited here.

On the bridge. East Egypt Village. Bree remembers that gold-and-blue late September day. She speaks.

I saw his old Chevy truck turn down into the parking lot of the shut-down woolen mill just as I was arriving at the dentist. You'd know it was Gordon even if it wasn't that green-and-white rig of his because he drives like a ninety-nine-year-old great-gramp. I had been at my

Aunt June's for a few days. The invasion of my studio had been like a hellfire missile to my heart. But the damn dentist appointment. You can't run away from your calendar!

I could hardly believe it when I saw that green-and-white truck poking along.

I crossed the road and up onto the narrow walkway of the bridge and I watched as he and some guy raised the hood on a car near the old loading docks and bays with pink "No Trespassing" signs. And all around the tar was broken and weeds were strutting their stuff and panting out their seeds on schedule. There was a very special moon in the works, too fat and bulgy and high-powered to be unfelt even in the daytime by all us species meant to propagate.

Eventually he looked up and saw me and he read me, heard that gravelly crunchy sound of my inner moon.

I took one hand from the pocket of my new dress and waved to him and after a time, when they were done down there, he came up on the bridge after me.

Left Dad's truck at the dentist and followed Gordon down across the crumbling tar to his truck, which I'd never sat inside of before.

He drove S. L. O. W. L. Y in his usual way, narrow back roads that knot together, and though we talked about ordinary things, there was to me a clear understanding of where we were going, maybe for him something more full of jeopardy but clear, too.

As we talked, I smoked, with cig out the window in my tough "logger girl" manner. We rode for hours in a sort of circle.

He stopped the truck by some woods in Harrison. He crawled up on top of me and his eyeballs were almost inside my eyeballs. I could see rogue red and black hairs in the dark brown of his beard. His eyes were squinting, out of focus. Old eyes. Yes, almost forty. I am an artist. When you are an artist, you see galaxies in the eyes of friend or foe. Your own eyes take full account. It's all about the eyes. When it isn't about moons.

He said I was beautiful, discount dress and all, and that's when my days-long sad shame was cast away like stars across the sky in glory.

Then we went into the woods. Then we went deeper into the woods. I remember how a bee came along and she liked my hair. I remember he and I were standing there rocking, holding and rocking. I remember thinking all my romantic teenage thoughts but also a paralysis of wonder.

And I saw in my stupid teenage way how all the evil in the world would lay itself aside as he, Gordon, would call all the poor, meek, dishonored, deformed, disheartened, and displaced to himself and lead them home. He, the teacher! He the steadfast ram.

I look back now on this notion with mortification because surely, by this naive pursuit, I had a part in his ruin.

From a future time, Catherine Court Downey remembers her shock by candlelight a few days later.

Our evening meal was served on the big porches though there was shivering at some tables and also complaints that the inside kitchen tables should have been set up instead.

I had just hurried in from the parking lot, easing the screen door shut behind me, and my son Robert called shrilly, "Hi, Mommy!" from several tables away. It hadn't taken him long, only a few weeks among this rowdy gang, to lose his civil ways. He was immersed in Settlement industry and daily celebrations and I was becoming a fringe person to him. It was like a new part of his character, this trilling lust for fraternity and turmoil. I had mixed feelings, of course.

I never signed up for any of their work crews and activities, salons, committees, or trips because at the university I was in a marathon of classes, student conferences, faculty meetings, and was, during that brief time, interim chair of my department, the art department. Not to mention the long zigzagging drive between Portland and Egypt. Gordon called me "the chairperson." Only once did I sense he was speaking fondly, that look he gets only in the eyes . . . not his flinching eye lunatic look . . . but a flirty teasy twinkle. All the other times he called me that because of his unabashed (no surprise) sexism.

That night he was absent from the meal.

As people all around me were munching bread and spooning soup, talking with full mouths, a baby clanking its cup with a big knife, which a not gentle male hand snatched away, setting the child off into a wail; into this racket I overheard in whispers and hisses the name of Reverend Andy Emery. The person's name meant nothing to me. But in the speakers' throats were constrictions of uneasiness and fear and they were all deliberate in keeping me out.

The porch eaves still dripped from the long rain of the day, moths pounded themselves to death on the screens. Some squat, some tall blue and purple and red stained-glass candle lamps gave all the whispering faces a vile flush as though they plotted acts unspeakable.

I leaned closer.

They ceased to speak.

Were they gossiping about *me*? Or my son, maybe?

But then at the table behind me I heard Claire's pretty cousin Geraldine St. Onge moan, "This is so dangerous."

When I turned and asked her, "What's wrong?" she covered her face with both hands. Sitting with her was Penny St. Onge, a blonde with that long-necked film-star comeliness, usually warm with smiles and warm of voice. She just raised her eyes to me, eyes that were welling with tears of terror.

Before the meal ended I would learn the consequentiality of that name, Reverend Andy Emery, a man who needed a cane to stand, whose voice was a series of coughs and creaks, no longer a preacherly boom, whose blue-and-black dully repainted Pontiac was the same big sagging boat of a car he'd had for thirty years, the car that had been parked under the ash tree at Gordon's old farmplace for an hour a couple of days earlier, which as everyone here but me knew, meant Gordon was about to "marry" yet another woman. The visit to Gordon's house was actually laughably, hysterically funny, a little counseling session such as most clergy do a few weeks prior to a *normal* ceremony in legal, honest, normal marriages. So dumbfounding! This minister playing along with Gordon St. Onge's self-proclaimed power to make the laws of our government and foundations of our civilization bend to his hungers.

Secret Agent Jane's special all-seeing glasses reveal all truths.

Bev is washing a dish in Gordie's kitchen so she doesn't see anything. I am hiding. It's the best window in Gordie's freezing living room that you can see from if you want to see him and Bree in the yard.

Wicked rainy day but with these glasses I can see perfectly. I can even see Gordie's dress-up jacket which is only for "events" . . . like pipe organ where you sit in hard red chairs and when Gordie eats chocolate moose in Portland. Bree is smoking a cigarette, nothing new. Her dress is very pretty and her yellow hair flowers, except for her whole awful face, are wicked beautiful.

I'm *trying* to draw her perfectly in my spy book but real life has more rain wiggles and more eye stars. Something happens. He kisses her fingers! Too funny.

The ride.

Two riders. One elderly horse the color of adhesive tape. Officially he's a pinto, some black markings, mostly on his face.

The rain dazzles all eyes, even those eyes under the riders' logging hats' narrow brims, some would call these hats crushers, one green wetted to black, one stoplight red wetted to blood-crust maroon. Their long legs dangle. Their soggy wedding clothes weigh heavier and squirm colder as the horse stays perfectly to the up, up, and up little mountain trail even with the reins tied together to droop at the base of his mane. No saddle but some plow harness and some Caribbean-looking baskets, woven and old and stuffed to bulging, and a cinched saddle blanket of heavy gold and brown stripes.

Arkie, the horse, sniffs the rich dank woodsy sometimes dangerous (he thinks) air, his tall ears standing forward, his glassy, blackly filled cauldron eyes having skull-like, yes, black patterns around them to scare or amuse. His hooves squish through the dark moss and muck. Arkie, though mirthless, seems not to mind anything that is asked of him and he is appreciated for panicking at nothing, no "rearing in hand," no believing a fully-in-bloom moosewood bush is a tiger, though in his heart he knows monsters exist.

Gordon is not a skilled rider, therefore always picks Arkie. And it seems that Arkie, ripping grass out on Settlement hillsides among the other horses, always picks Gordon, moseying toward the gate with his eyes on Gordon's eyes.

And now here on the mountain, Bree, the "bride," infused with shivers, has no complaints. Gordon envelopes her with both arms, his chin on her hatted head. Much of her wet red hair serpent-slides around his sleeves, binding him to her as Arkie steps ladylike around a fountain-shaped thickness of yellowing fern. Bree is age fifteen. The groom is thirty-nine. Some Settlement women often tell how researchers have proved that neurologically, those under twenty-four have a brain lacking full development so their judgment isn't good enough to choose to enlist in the military, to choose the right ways to operate a motor vehicle, to choose to drink or do drugs, to choose a lifelong career, to choose a spouse . . . and so on. "Before age twenty-five you are just a pollywog!" Lorraine Martin has been heard to say many, many, many times.

To Bree, her choice looks like a panoramic movie, or an epic novel, with generations flash-lived, eras swimming past, and scenery in volcanic colors and music of thunder and flutes. And faces all interlocked by story.

And what at this hour does Gordon St. Onge feel?

Wet.

Also his head aches in a rusty way. In one of his pockets a bottle of aspirin is tucked. When they reach the old hunting camp, it will be dry and will stink deliciously of eighty-five years of woodsmoke fires, bacon, and beans. The mice will have triumphantly shredded anything shreddable, sprinkled the table and shelves with a million mini turds. The windows will be palpitant with green rainy light. To him this day is no movie, just syrupy and prickly non-absolutes. Nevertheless, Bree with the deformed face and full-fire mind is treasure. Is there something hazardous about her willpower that he has forgotten? He fondles her left hand, the silver ring he made her, identical to those of his other wives. And therefore just?

From a future time, Bree speaks of that day at the camp.

I have forgotten none of this!! The rain softened, then stopped. Our plan was to sit out on the little open porch eating our squash pudding and boiled eggs and maple milk, his idea for our wedding feast. This was while Arkie, who was a great wall of white because he stood so close to the porch, munched on his wedding feast grain and three "drops" apples.

Beyond Gordon's rocker was a bear the size of a five-year-old human kid, nose up, a proud bear, the work of a chain saw sculptor who had a feather touch. On this tiny porch I kept scooting around Gordon's knees and feet to go feel the little bear's wooden fur. I'd blow my cigarette smoke away from both bear and man.

This bear had been one of Gordon's father's cherished possessions, his father whose name was Guillaume though Gordon's mother had renamed him Gary! Like you rename a dog! But also, as you know, Gordon isn't really Gordon. Gordon told me with an amused snort that at his birth his mother, in naming her baby Guillaume, must have been having one of her tornadoes of tenderness for her man. But as the weeks passed she was back to her cool obsession with social image. Image and status, the great revolving flashes of her guiding light. And *her* real name was Mary Grace but she had changed it to Marian. The more he told me about his mother, the less I could picture her being *his* mother. I could better picture my own mother being mine and I don't remember her at all, her having died from the grille of another car that was passing a line of cars and trucks on a hill. It came at my mother like a freight train, mashing the life instantly out of her skull, her milk-filled breasts, her lullabies.

Through all our talk and slurping down of our feast, Gordon and I fought mosquitoes.

Gordon said, "I can't remember where he said he got it." He was referring to his father and the bear.

I told him I loved how it was the same color as the old porch, seemed to be growing right out of it. "That sort of thing gives me a nice sort of creeps. Like coming upon ancient ruins in the woods . . . like the galleon in *A Hundred Years of Solitude*."

"You've seen ancient ruins . . . *actual* ancient ruins?"

I giggled, "Noooo. But there's something in us all, isn't there, that is awed by places swallowed by trees and unseen by human eyes for centuries, that then reappear as if we were falling through time backward?"

"Claire says things like that. Are you part Passamaquoddy?"

"Claire has a degree in history," I said a bit chirpily, "and a minor in archaeology."

"Right," said he.

I sighed. Claire, older than Gordon by eleven years, the only wife who'd been married to him by Maine law, now an ex by Maine law but wife by Settlement law, the fragile law of a silver ring. I don't think she ever let go of her special powers over Gordon. How were she and *Marian* alike? Maybe in some deeply buried way, like with a good archaeological find.

"My papa . . . he came up here a lot," Gordon said, clanking his spoon against the bowl now empty of yummy spiced squash pudding.

To get away from your mother, I thought to myself, but I guess I thought wrongly because it turns out Guillaume Sr. aka "Gary" was a laid-back cheery sort, fondly amused by all his wife's rules for maintenance of her "aristocracy."

The deerflies were swinging around and pouncing on poor Arkie, who would shake his head, his black-streaked white tail flashing.

Then more mosquitoes.

We rinsed our camp dishes very fast in the very slow stream where deerflies got some serious hits on our damp faces and ears, necks and arms before we were able to get back to the little cabin, tumble into the deep of it, and slam the door.

The green wicker rocker near the long sideboard-workbench crackled as I sank, me feeling rotten and guilty for us to be inside and Arkie alone outside in torment. But soon the floppy saggy cool-sweaty lime-color daylight became dusk and the deerflies evaporated.

But now it seemed all the mosquitoes were *inside* the camp, even some large almost celery-color species we'd never in our lives known.

Next, midges. Like spirits, they penetrate wall, windows, closed doors. Each a measly dot, each an awe-inspiring bonfire to skin.

The camp smelled of epic dampness.

Iron bed. Iron springs. Shortly, we would unroll the quilts and blankets we'd brought.

Little cupboard doors hung open, glass canisters of toilet paper, sugar, coffee, a 1960s B&M bean can of pens. A curtain of spiderweb swayed across each of the small windows. The plank floor pitched into a funhouse warp, lower on the side where the bed was.

In the dimness I watched my tall a-bit-slope-shouldered husband paw through drawers for candles and a fat jar of matches. He never cussed at the bugs chewing and sucking and augering him. But his free hand, like Arkie's tail, was constant and reflexive in defending himself while his mind was elsewhere.

I considered how Gordon was, with every gesture, with the meal, the candles, the quilts, unfurling a ritual. Yes, to *him* it was a ritual. I counted the times, nineteen. I've heard them say there have been no honeymoons to, for instance, Paris, France. Too much fossil fuel? Or his sense of fairness like the nineteen identical silver rings.

I in that moment imagined it to be Paris, the wood blurred into grainy stone, the low ceiling soared to a magnificent height. Thousands of candles were being lighted by thousands of hands, each one mini-torched as a signifier of perfect love that stays perfect in spite of death or bodily ruin. Or deformity. Thousands!! A barrage of sacramental flutterings.

Of course I was only fifteen, and as I told you before, romantic, oh, so *very* romantic, and entirely made of the properties of boiling sugar water.

I gave the wicker rocking chair a playful shove forward and back. *Scrape-snap*! I looked quickly to see the flame of the match in his hand and then he held it to the first candlewick. *Hisssssst*. A bloom. It made the grayed "cathedral" walls breathe like bellies. He looked into my eyes, not smiling. Because for him this day was something more consequential than happiness.

From a future time, Catherine Court Downey speaks.

The evening was chill enough that the meal was laid out in the Winter Kitchen with a wounded red setting sun licking the grange-hall-sized room's walls through the tall low-to-the-floor many-paned windows. Only two of the candle lamps were in use, both blue. Such muscular combinations of light ennobled these otherwise common people's faces. They were *all* beautiful!

My child Robert was on the tiny corner stage with four other small boys grouped around the chubby blond pigtailed girl they called Montana. A kazoo band she had organized, a very grown-up eight-year-old, I must say, whose speech was enunciated, almost genteel. Their concert trailed off soon enough and I watched Robert's shining black hair bob along as he rushed to claim a chair among his buddies.

The wood cookstoves in the infernolike Cook's Kitchen were crackling. Two archways stood in the great wall of cubbies that divided the two kitchens, a roomy cubby for every person to receive mail in or in which to keep such articles as gloves or sweaters or flashlights during the day. Also coat hooks were nicely spaced on a boarded area painted creamy light orange. Corkboard areas were smothered in sign-up sheets for the crews, committees, shop activities, field trips, also a steady stream of announcements, notices for selling or trade, and a preponderance of Gary Larson *Far Side* cartoons for some reason.

Thus there were two doorways through which blooms of heat and blazing electric light would egress from the all-utility Cook's Kitchen into the Winter Kitchen with its red-blue almost medieval dream shadows.

The tables were loaded. Trough-sized platters. Bucket-sized serving bowls. Glass pitchers. Carried to and from primarily by women, of course. Women who favored embroidery and long dresses and aprons with many tucks and flourishes made mostly in their sewing shop, sometimes by kids, so there were many earnestly worn lopsided clownish shirts and vests. And no matter how cold, you'd see some bare feet!

Someone had come to touch a match to the candles at my table. These candles made of beeswax and hot fat or something, smelled like a slimy bog except for the ones that smelled like a thirsty lawn.

The red devil sun slid down the wall behind Brady and Sadie, who sat across from me, our table one of the smaller ones. Their heads were in the darker bluer light while their chests and hands were on fire. They were new here like me. Even more recent. They were now, as they were every day and night since they arrived, stunned into silence. Brother and sister. Still tow-headed. Brady, secretly to most people here, was dying. AIDS. Yes, it was Gordon who had invited them to live here, but for the rest of my life I will question his motives because I do not see Gordon St. Onge as a good man in any shape, form, or manner.

Lorraine Martin was to my right scribbling down some reminders, which she always wore stuck to her clothes with clothespins. She was a tidy dark-haired efficient woman, married to a fellow named Eddie. They had three grown and nearly grown sons. She was much too ordinary and normal and sane to have lived for so many years in this backward, sexist, almost cartoon life created by a crazy man.

To my left was Beth, one of the wives. White trash through and through. Her mouth was like a toilet: f*!^ this and sh!# that. Police officers were pigs, degreed people were f*!^ing goddamn yuppies. I doubted she could read. Some of the kids were hers by *him* but I hadn't figured out yet which ones. Her hair was shoulder-length blond curlicues, always damp on hot days because she would be raving, "I'm hotter than a witches cun*!" and run to stick her head under one of the Cook's Kitchen hand pumps right over a sink of dirty dishes and crank the handle up and down with the arm of a stevedore . . . I mean her *arms* were not big but she was so full of herself.

This night she reached across the table for some of the steaming "chipmunk" meat, that's what she called it. I myself could not always recognize what tame or wild creature they had roasted or fried. That night not really some chipmunks, I hope. She flashed one eye at me so I knew she was trying to upset me. Then she jabbed Sadie's elegant hand of pewter rings and snorted in a jolly way, "Have some. It's wicked," with her sweater cuff dragging across the platter of biscuits, then pushed the meat platter up against Sadie's dish with a rough *clunk!*

"Wicked" is a word that can mean anything *but* wicked when coming from a trashy Maine person's mouth. It will always be a mystery to me, those "wives" of his, how different they all were from one another. What *was* the common denominator? It bothered me because Claire was my friend and I had respect for her. She was nothing like Beth. How could Claire be intimate with *him* knowing he'd also been intimate with Beth? Oh, what am I saying!!! He'd been with . . . or as Beth would say, he had "poked it to" eighteen others.

I was uncapping one of the bottles from my little basket of essential herbs and essential elements when, in one of the bright archways in the cubby wall, a figure appeared. The red sundown blazed along his whole left side. Gordon. Who I hadn't seen for a few days due to his very private "wedding" and "honeymoon."

Hard not to notice that at least half the room fell silent. He fixed his weird pale dark-lashed eyes on me. Yes, me! One eye flinched in that Tourette's-like manner, his shoulders braced to show triumph? He smirked, a plain ugly smirk, the tips of his teeth in the red light and dark beard, yes, smirking in that way one might while drawing a sword from the torso of a mortal enemy, all the while goring me with his eyes. But he called to Beth and Lorraine, not me. He said huskily, "Tell the chairperson that what wasn't true before about Brianna getting messed with by the monster *is* now true."

Brianna? So his new "bride" was Bree?!!

And, yes, I had tried to protect her. So he was publicly declaring his perp status and at the same time declaring *me* his foe. The beauty of the evening switched immediately to ash and sorrow. How could this ever be my and Robert's home?

From a future time, Penny St. Onge speaks.

The public is always looking for someone to lynch or send through official channels to the gallows. Conservative or liberal, there is a lust to see an agreed-upon villain of the other team put in the hot seat. It's the chicken-pecking-a-fellow-chicken-to-death thing. It's fearsome.

Remembering that summer, Misty St. Onge speaks.

From the distance of the public eye Gordon would be seen as a predator once that eye knew about Bree. And Gordon knew that. I have come to appreciate Bree's and his special little pocket of trust in this wobbling world, but the risk in his flaunting himself to Catherine was suicide. Because Catherine was not safe ground.

Gordon wasn't stupid, so what was this about? And he was never suicidal. Dark and vexed, but not this leap into the teeth of the abysm. It was beyond understanding. I will *never* understand it.

Lee Lynn St. Onge thinking back.

All I would see was police in my dreams. All day my face was numb. I couldn't swallow.

Josee Soucier speaks.

Poor Bree.

Lorraine Martin.

As I had stated before, under the age of twenty-five you're still a polliwog. It was wrong of him to exploit that biological fact for his own biological facts.

From a future time, Cory St. Onge recalls.

I was only fifteen myself at the time and vague on what the danger was. But it didn't take me long to think it through. To clarify. The prisons are crammed with people like Gordo who for a day or two forget who is in charge, they who can crush you like a paper cup.

The crime in this case? Child molestation.

So you picture a groping drooling creep grabbing a ten-year-old in the night. A four-year-old maybe? To the lawmen and court, politicians and prison keepers, the details of Bree's and Gordon's situation wouldn't matter. The way America is run its like a factory, all gears and grease. Workers have to do three shifts a day feeding its maw with captives.

Let's get one thing straight, Bree was a rock. If she was ever down, she was up in a twinkle, up and swinging. Get it? *Some people feared Bree*. She was one shrewd woman. She was a chieftain. She had impressed Settlement girls older than she was to be her groupies.

I liked Bree a lot. I didn't spend much time feeling pity for her. We always had too much work in late summer and fall. That's where my head was at and, you know, my anarcho-militia ruminations. At all the fuss and whispers and whines about the "new wife" at meals, I just rolled my eyes.

Whitney St. Onge, Gordon's oldest daughter, then age fifteen, speaks from a future time.

Bree was family now. At one of our many secret woodsy meetings, we fit and ready soldiers of the True Maine Militia all cheered and wolf-howled joyfully at the details of the wedding and did a wicked group hug, Mrs. Bree in the middle, squished and smooched by all of us.

Also here's Bonnie Loo remembering.

I was reaching a point. Between a rock and a hard place, as my stepfather Reuben liked to say. That's where I was.

Portland, Maine.

Outside the Department of Human Services office there stand just three very quiet hooded men. Terrifying in their quietness, their spaced feet, their crossed arms, the eyeholes cut in the black fabric just above the swells where their noses are, eyeholes that seem to see more than ordinary eyes see, and feel less than ordinary eyes feel. These five figures abreast on the sidewalk face the double glass doors with the department lettering. They wait.

Pewter girl.

Midafternoon of yet another day where Bonnie Loo's somewhat acne-scarred face is as piping hot as the bread loaves now on the "Hoosier cabinet" racks. Baking and early-day canning done but the big woodstoves of the Summer Kitchen still cheep and tick and snap. Late September on the many kid-made calendars plastered everywhere, but mid-July on the skin. Okay, so the Greenland ice sheet is melting and Egypt, Maine, foothills are hunkering uneasily about so much dread promise, but Bonnie Lucretia Bean Sanborn St. Onge revels in the usual pain of the stature of head cook within the iron fortress of the many hot stoves, slate and enameled sinks, and tall hand pumps. And besides that, today she has something very tiny on her mind.

She turns away, up along the single ramplike step into the inside kitchen, rakes her hands, more buttery than floury, over her embroidered apron and the hips of her jeans, yeah, Settlement-made, no logo. As she hurries along, eyes on the floor, she uses a bandanna to clean her glasses of steam and mop her dripping face and neck. Stuffs the bandanna back into the kangaroo pocket of her red apron. She is grieving for her pewter girl. Pewter boy is still safe in her kangaroo pocket but pewter girl is not safe.

She studies the painted floors of the first piazza as she treks along past that regiment of rockers and wheelchairs where many elders keep watch on the Quad. And also Benedicta, the new old woman, who isn't sitting but standing between two rockers and a little behind them. There is her small crescent smile, eyes leaping with fun today. One hand on the back of each occupied rocker, she gives a little jerk to both to be sure she has their attention and speaks in her scratchy way to one of Willie Lancaster's small free-spirit white dogs who is near, "Get her! Sic her. Bite her!"

The dog just keeps lapping his privates but Bonnie Loo has looked up to see several old persons silently chuckling.

"We're a tough bunch," Benedicta says into the eyes of old Arthur Martell.

Maybe Arthur is a little impressed with Benedicta, life of the party? And maybe also Laurent Roy is feeling warmed by her hand on his shoulder. Her other hand on Arthur's shoulder now. Her fun goes on, her small smile not at all changed, a smile suitable for sweetness and for cruelty. She sings out, "Who's on our siiiide?"

More chuckles as Bonnie Loo has now reached the library door. She does not look back though she feels something has followed her. Nothing has but the whole place purrs louder and louder with damnation.

Now she picks up speed past six shop doors, two of them closed. Voices. Work. Study. Play.

And damnation.

Meanwhile, from this point on the wiped-clean unoccupied tables, all the empty rockers and old couches, dangling mobiles and toys, and see there the sun is oozing away, taking the polka dots of the Quad's leafy light, leaving hot blue shade. Out beyond the screen, Lorraine Martin is, as usual, plastered over pockets and hems with clothespinned reminder notes. Other than this quirk, Lorraine, brown of eye and hair, is a medium sort of person, focused and needed. "Clerk of the House," some here call her.

Bonnie Loo leans toward the screen and sees that one of the girls who are visiting this week from the reservation is poking with a tape measure along the outside of the porch, reading out loud numbers that Lorraine scribbles onto a scrap.

Both girl guests are about thirteen.

Bonnie Loo calls, "You guys see an earring? Pewter? Dutch girl?"

No, they have not but Lorraine promises, "We'll keep our eyes peeled."

It is the First Aid Shop in which Bonnie Loo recalls last feeling her left earlobe, and pewter girl had still been dancing then. The door is ajar. As she nudges it open, her heartbeat skitters, not because she sees pewter girl on the floor because pewter girl is not on the floor. She has just begun lately to fear going from one room to another, the door that opens to a different light, corners that resound with a queer silence. But see, the First Aid Shop is not in use. There is nothing here to startle. One of the blood pressure cuffs has been abandoned there on the clean pine counter. Sometimes there is a mess from kids cutting up gauze or there are puddles against the mop boards where one of Willie Lancaster's ever-roaming little white push-faced dogs has dribbled his name. Or tipped over the trash. Or just gotten left behind the closed door.

First Aid Shop cupboard doors, walls, windows are all afloat in September afternoon orange, that slant of it that always stirs her. The floor tiles here are all a skim-milk white in order to reveal what shouldn't be there, in this case pewter girl. Not there.

Bonnie Loo backs away. Soon she is crossing the grassy Quad still retracing her steps of the day, eyes down. No gleam in the grass. Now no gleam in the sand of the parking areas. Just the sand and gravel that glint and sparkle in the new-angled sun to match in eerie pleasure the creak and whir of tall-grass bugs in late summer symphony. Pleasure? Not today. Maybe it's been a while since Bonnie Loo felt any delight.

She asks all those working inside the furniture-making Quonset hut if they've found an earring. "Nope" and "No, I haven't" and headshakes. She appreciates the cooler air here. And the piney scent. But the racket of saws and lathes drives her back to the bright small side bay and the alley made by the other large Quonset hut.

But now she shudders to hear big hearts, a lot of big cantaloupe-sized hearts plomping on the ground, somewhat synchronized in their tachycardia. She turns toward the open sun and gravel lot. Horses, big, yes, especially being so suddenly there and up-close in a choppy trot.

And now the deep grumble of one board-sided farm truck, with the cooperatively purchased wind plant chained on back, ready for the trip to Lincoln. Gordon and two young boys in the cab. Gordon with dark glasses and massive forearm along the window, fingers on the side mirror. The truck brakes easy without the squeal it had the other day. The Settlement repair shop guys are the ones to thank for that. All is in full boil in preparation for the trip.

Were the horses racing the truck in this heat? Bonnie Loo cannot tell what is going on. She just keeps feeling spooked by the thumping of the hooves and the deep glittering eyes of the riders, the wobbly, choppy look of them all moving through the dangerous unnatural heat.

Silverbell Rosenthal's twelve-year-old Eden rides like a soldier, like a *general*, like George Washington, her expression chiseled, but she wears shorts and a pink T-shirt, her blond dandelion hair pinned down, some tied in two tiny tails. Her horse is a tall pinto, pale vanilla spots on white. The hooves *thump! thump! thump!* cutting up the sand.

Rachel Soucier, small for seventeen, new short yellow hair (made short and yellow by the beauty crew) flying in a sweat-wet flip-flop. Her mount is a dark bay with a star. The hooves keep that beat, *thump! thump! thump!*

Gordon is out of the truck as the third rider, Geraldine, who is Claire's cousin and Gordon's wife, reins her slippery-looking dark mare, no star, no blaze, no stockings, toward him. Maybe it's Geraldine tonight on his calendar. There are ways to find out if you are one to stand it. Bonnie Loo thinks the hooves that don't cease thumping are going to give her a heart attack.

See there, shapely, zesty Geraldine. Keeps her cool-to-the-touch-looking black hair cut short, *trusting* the beauty crew. Sometimes it comes out well, other times not, but how does it matter? Nothing can defile that face, that posture, that glow. She had been one of those behind-Claire's-back early wives. And all this time, no pregnancy. She's too well organized for that, brags about the efficacy of *the pill*. She never slouches, never wearies. No fits of wrath though her nit-picking can, in others, start flash fires. Nipping at everyone's heels. No surprise that she loves to overpower and steer about the youngest scariest horses.

The mare she now straddles is not exactly black or brown. She has a bronze-color ghost breathing muscularly throughout her tight dark summer coat. Such small sharp hooves chopping away at the packed gravel. Big rolling eyes, turning with strategy. Tender mouth closed around the bit and bite-you-to-death tall teeth, breathing hard through spiraling nostrils, head slanted to better home in on her job of circling, almost hugging, the wind-plant-loaded truck. *Thump! thump! thump!* As Gordon, untidy due to so many hours of work, oil-splattered sportsy-gray T-shirt, rag-thin red bandanna tied dog-collar-style around his neck, dungarees worn and torn, Geraldine's most challenging beast, steps away from the truck, the horse is cutting hard between the truck door left hanging open and one of Gordon's elbows. There now his hand is reaching to press the metal nosepiece of his sunglasses. He is forced to jump to the side. He laughs.

Kids inside the truck laugh.

The other riders turning around in their saddles laugh.

Geraldine's face, contented chin, turquoise-and-white-striped sailor collar top, deeply sleeveless . . . bare brown arms soft yet tight with her unquenchable strength, her bronze horse cuts a sharp left, jangling and pounding, circles Gordon again.

Geraldine's black eyes are terrible in their mischief and his secret eyes behind his dark glasses are easy to picture, his all-encompassing appreciation and laid-back good temper for what is done to him in the name of brotherhood, of fellow feeling, of love. This is just that. This is not suck-biting hickey-making kisses or wrenching around in locked coupling in tall grass or bed. And this is not reeling in another new wife. This is nothing at all. Nothing!

Gordon trudges up the stone path to Bonnie Loo's pink Snow White–and-seven-dwarfs cottage.

All the little houses around have their lights out, but the light of her bedroom window is blazing. She is not expecting him. It is a rule unspoken but distinctly realized, a rule evolved, made by practicality, made by *them*, these women, that his nights with them be preplanned. A wife would expect his soft knock on the outside door . . . or maybe no knock, just his heavy step.

But tonight he is surprising Bonnie Loo. He hears hammering inside. He steps in. Living room and bitty kitchen dark. Two closed doors off the kitchen. Then the one off the little hallway, which is closed, yes, but with a brilliance along the bottom.

He stops at the first door. Gabe's door. Gabriel, who is Bonnie Loo's eight-year-old by her deceased husband, Danny Sanborn. Gordon spreads his hand on the door. As if to feel a pulse or an overly warm forehead.

The second door has postcards taped on it. This is the door of the two little ones, his own kids by blood, Jetta and Zack. He touches his fingers to this door, cocks his head, listens, moves on. Toward the door with the light behind it. The hammering has stopped. "Gordon?" Bonnie Loo's voice.

He finds her pushing herself up from a kneel, hammer in hand. It's the rats again. Rat home improvements on her Rat Palace.

He doesn't care for rats. Even those docile white lab rats of Bonnie Loo's. But here he is in a room full of waddling fat two-year-old rats and skidding, scuttling agile younger rats. Bonnie likes to let them out to play, though they are also very good at escape, in spite of all her desperate "escape-proofing" on this rat skyscraper and two large four-story wings.

About twenty rats, give or take a rat. All males. Graduates of USM's psych department, where Bonnie Loo has sat in on classes on and off over the last few years. At the end of each semester, she rescues all the students' about-to-be-chloroformed rats who have each been trained by food deprivation and food reward to put a marble through a hole in a tuna fish can. Names like Knee-Jerk and Diogenes. Pink-eyed, whiskery, twitch-nosed, and friendly. On one exterior wall of the Rat Palace is the enlarged black-and-white glossy of Donald the Rat wearing a little blue hat. Donald was also the name of one of the university's psych teachers, a man who paced a lot and never looked you in the eye. His eyes weren't pink. He couldn't wiggle his ears. But nevertheless.

Bonnie Loo seems happy to see Gordon.

The rats seem happy to see Gordon. They stare at him a moment, some swaying their heads ever so slightly from side to side, then back to the business of checking out Bonnie Loo's desk supplies, bureau drawers, trash basket, and windowsill of pretty blue and green bottles.

Bonnie Loo's pregnancy is somewhat noticeable against her short cotton gown. She is looking at Gordon, swinging the hammer to and fro across one thigh.

He observes, "I see you're expanding their east wing. More of this room is disappearing to the prosperity of rats, less room for Bonnie Lucretia. And where, pray tell, will I put my boots when I'm in that bed?"

She cocks her head. She's wearing her regular glasses, which make light now streak across her foxy-orange eyes. Her ripply brassy orange-blond-and-black hair is down, flopped around her face and shoulders in such a way that makes you know she's not thinking much about appearance tonight. Her smile, it's always a little crooked, trying to hide her four false teeth, which she believes are hugely noticeable.

"They get along better when they have space, and are busy. I just put some more objects in there for them to explore."

Gordon's eyes sweep over the floor, all the floors of this house and many of the others being Settlement-made hand-painted tiles that are warmed by copper pipes under them, which are made hot by passive solar in the leafless cold weather. The tiles are a storm of colors. He doesn't want to step on any rats. He walks carefully to the cage, uh, *palace*. He sees, added to their toys, a piece of white conduit and a battered old tin sugar canister, made in the days before plastic ruled the world. The canister has a sentimental-looking decal of purple lilacs.

His eyes move back to Bonnie Loo's face. "But why aren't they in *there* exploring?"

A decorative and very old blue glass Vick's Vapo-Rub jar falls from the windowsill into the trash can. The rat on the windowsill hangs his head down, trying to make out the location of that leaping bottle just as three rats leap out from the trash can.

Bonnie Loo laughs. "Watch this, Gordon." She lays the hammer on the bureau. She sinks to the bed and arranges herself spread-eagle, her head and tangly hair on her pillow. She is a tall, long-armed filled-out young woman. Even without pregnancy, she really covers the bed. She forces her voice up high and bubbly. "Help! Help! Help! Help!" Countless rats leap to the bed all at once, a genius and disquieting choreography, rats in midair, rats landing, rats in one rippling white wave, swarming over and around Bonnie Loo.

Gordon lets out his breath. His face is plastered all over with his most *wild* wild-man look, one eye wide, the other squinty.

"HELP! HELP! HELP! RATS! I'VE GOT RATS! HELP!" Bonnie Loo squeals happily.

The rats freeze, their ears fluttering like wee pink flower petals, then they scramble around faster and faster and faster, a lumpy white tidal wave, four and five or six at a time over Bonnie Loo's arms, legs, pregnant belly, and thinly covered swelling breasts. Two rats there on her pillow, digging through her thick hair. One leaps over her forehead, his stiff tail carried along behind him in that most accomplished ratlike style.

Gordon applauds. "Smart rats. How'd they train you to do that, Bonnie Lucretia?"

She chortles over this. Sits up carefully, trying not to hurt any rats. "The little bastards got out last night and I was so tired, I didn't round them up. They got under the covers with me and chewed fifty fucking holes in my favorite apple blossom sheets."

Meanwhile, one rat, who is not much of a group person, still hanging out on the sill of another window, lightly steps along over a row of tiny ceramic unicorns. His magnificent tail works to deftly balance him, while his enormous hard-looking testicles give his rear end the ungainly look of an old Rambler station wagon.

Bonnie Loo carries the rats one by one to their skyscraper, which is made of "chewable" pine but has a cage-wire front and nine stories with trapdoors in the floors to climb up through, all floors built like open-faced drawers. Now the rats all head for the same place, the top story, where the view is best.

Bonnie Loo goes out to her mini-kitchen to fill up their water bottles.

Under the glaring two-hundred-watt bulb, which Bonnie Loo has hung for all her rat projects, Gordon pulls his shirt from his belt, starts to unbutton, settles on the bed (carefully, in case of an escapee under the covers), and starts pulling off his boots. He also scans the bed for rat turds, sees none. Cleaner, at least, than a college fraternity party, these boys are.

Bonnie Loo comes back with a glass of water for herself, sets it on the floor on the side of the bed. She picks the Vicks Vapo-Rub bottle from the trash. She fetches the hammer from her little desk which is stacked with science books and recipe books. Over the desk, papier-mâché planets hang motionless from the fine string around a papier-mâché sun. She tromps across the room and carefully places the hammer back in her box of tools. "Tidy tidy," she coos. She turns back and Gordon has gotten off the bed and is standing right there, real close, right in her face, still dressed but barefoot, shirt out over his belt. Takes her face into both hands and says quietly, "Bonnie."

"What?"

"I'm so sorry."

"About what?" She asks the question. But she is choking up. Tearing up, one tear already hurrying down her cheek. It's the thing she can't speak of, the way Rex can't speak of his year in Vietnam. This, her dark, dark deep jealousy that is slowly killing her.

She wants to say, *Don't hassle me. I'm being good. I haven't hurt anybody lately. Just me*. But she just makes a kind of funny face.

He says, "I'm sorry that I can't be a real husband to you."

She makes another funny face. Looks toward her Rat Palace, where twenty pairs of pink eyes peer down at this interesting business of humans embracing. They are particularly enthralled by the way Gordon's hands are doing something rough and good-feeling to Bonnie Loo's neck and shoulders. And he says, "You need a husband who every goddamn night can do this for you, especially when you're pregnant. You give me children. You give me *everything*. And what do I give you? One friggin' night a month?"

"It's okay."

"No. It's not okay."

"It's okay."

"No, Bonnie, it's not okay." He stands back, and sees, visible through the nightie fabric, her great dark areolate breasts, larger than the last time he visited, readying for the needs of a late-winter baby. He says, "For some people, it's okay. But you are . . . a . . . a beautiful big hungry soul. And I can see that the circumstances that force you to be here—"

"It's not just circumstances."

"But you're not happy!"

She tells him quietly, "I'm okay."

He takes her shoulders. Little rubs. Her skin the same temperature as his hands. Bonnie Loo lets her head loll from side to side, head hanging, eyes closed, ripply brassy black hair swaying. And now she stops. And now she just *screams*.

His hands tighten.

She cries out, "You're right!" And then she shrieks as if fighting off a killer. And she pushes at Gordon, pushes him away but then grabs his shirt and falls against him but then shoves him again, now just starts strangling herself with both hands. And all the rats up there on the top floor of their palace twist and hop violently, ears flattening.

Now the little cottage thumps and bangs as the children hurry from their beds, eight-year-old Gabe in the lead, bursting through the door. The kids surround their mother and Gordon.

"Mumma!"

And "Stop!"

And sweet-natured dark-haired Jetta, in her footed sleeper, gives one of Gordon's hands a vicious clawing and Bonnie Loo keeps shrieking and thrashing around while Gordon tries to hug her to him and not-much-more-than-a-baby Zack is beating his father's hip with a pillow.

Bonnie Loo starts to pull her own hair, wailing.

Gordon snarls, "Quit the shit!"

She screams, "Kill me! Kill this big stupid fat-assed bitch!"

"Bonnie Lucretia . . . baby, baby, baby . . . no more."

Now a voice from the kitchen. Gail St. Onge's voice. Gail from next door. (Yes, another St. Onge wife.) "You all right, Bonnie?"

Gail steps in, Gail with flowers tattooed around her neck, cigarettes-and-sun-and-age seaming her face. Gordon insists, "She's okay. She's just upset."

By now, Bonnie Loo is sobbing redly and wetly.

Gordon and Bonnie Loo rock from side to side, her arms around him, his arms around her.

And Gail says a soft, "Okay," and backs out and Jetta runs after her with, "Mumma squeezed herself!" And then there are a few whispers before Gail makes her polite escape.

And Gordon feels into a shirt pocket, now holds a hand up and on his palm is Bonnie Loo's lost pewter girl earring.

She looks up at his face. His worried face. She is everything to him. *Each . . . Wife . . . Is . . . Everything*. Each wife a lifeline. Adored. Absorbed. Chewed and digested. But never eliminated. He is the absolute freak, the twisting and turning force of his heart, getting bigger and bigger to accommodate more. Terrible heart. She pictures it livid and turkey-neck blue with its engorged million tiny veins as with every species of swaggering male, a mind of its own, hot and ticking, opening again and again, whipping the air with its sticky tongue to take in more. MORRRRE!

Bonnie Loo's face whitens. With horror. With adulation. Worse than jealousy this confusion, his unbearable difference.

Five-year-old Jetta speaks between two solemn sighs, "I hate tonight."

Now little Zack, under the truth-telling bare two-hundred-watt bulb, hugs one leg of each parent and commands, "Okay now. Okay now."

While eight-year-old Gabe sits on the edge of the bed, watching with squinted eyes. He makes his voice as deep and dismissive as possible. "Stupid."

And now her little important-sounding sniff, a decision? Or just a reflex? Bonnie Loo's head and jaws readjust. FSSPTT!! Gordon's eyes scrunch shut as—

She spits in his face.

Claire remembering that September with a big sigh.

Things had started to simmer down, the mail was coming in smaller billows, the phone's jangles mostly just friends, family, neighbors, and our established cooperative folks on the other end. The media was getting bored with us. Hurrah!

Beth wisecracked, "We're just getting used to being Public Domain." She always said it like a name, either on purpose or as one of her grammatical car wrecks, or maybe that Bethesque poetic license. Sometimes when Oz and his pony express mail crew came back from town, the horses stupendously laden, Beth would snarl, "Public Domain says she's going to use that friggin' shit for woodstove kindlin'."

But really each day was sinking sweetly more toward normal. Until—

Op-ed appearing in the *Record Sun*'s thick-as-a-wrist Sunday paper.

It begins:

> *Some of you may have the idea you are in danger. Let us be more specific. Some of you can clearly imagine that in the not-too-far-off future, "they" will come and put you and your family out of your home. All you have grown up and worked for is threatened by some large conspiring force.*

And the oracle op-ed voice goes on with many bloodcurdling details, then in bold booming print:

> *YES, OH, YES . . . SOMEBODY IS GETTING READY TO TAKE EVERYTHING AWAY FROM YOU. EVERYTHING.*
>
> *We are members of the True Maine Militia, not to be confused with the "plain" Maine Militia or the Border Mountain Militia or the Southern Maine Militia or the White Mountain Militia. But with those militias, we do have a bit in common.*
>
> *Like them, we are not ostriches.*
>
> *We are angry.*
>
> *And we know the government sucks.*
>
> *It is not a government of We, the People, but one of Organized Money, of Big Faceless Transnational Financiers ruling through their shrewd tool, the corporation, the lobbyists, the foundations, the prohibitions, the military, the spooks, the media. And money laundering and fraud and other creepy stuff.*
>
> *Welcome! We welcome EVERYBODY! We are not a right-wing militia. We are not left wing, either. We are NO WING. We are everybody's militia!*

Now there is a small cartoonish humanish footprint. It has claws. Then the article gets going again.

We have always thought of ourselves as warmhearted, nice people. NO MORE! We are ready to cut the corporate jugular! Corporations out of our lobbies! Corporations out of our campaigns! Corporations out of our courts! Death to the corporation that can't behave itself and SERVE US, the flesh people!!! And the EARTH. You say, Oh, poor rich faceless financiers will start to lose some of their money if they can't control us. Tough, lettem eat cake!

Now there is an elaborate cartoon of Bree's Abominable Hairy Patriot as he has appeared in some versions of her *Recipe* and flyers, lovable but stern-looking Bigfoot with hands on hips standing on a mountaintop. He wears here a tricorn hat, camo vest, and army boots. Usually he is barefoot, to show his big hairy feet. And usually he does not wear clothes. Behind him now waves the American flag.

The op-ed finishes with:

The True Maine Militia already has a lot of members, but not enough. Our goal is a million, for starters. Because we are planning the Million-Man-Woman-Kid-Dog March on Augusta (for starters) and we will all be armed. With brooms. We will arrive at the doors, all the statehouse doors, and begin to very very gently sweep the great floors of this, which is our house . . . yes, The People's House. We will sweep out every corporate lobbyist. Corporations OUT! We the People in!

And if this doesn't work, we'll be back next time with plungers!

If you are interested in joining up, it is totally FREE. No dues. Just promise you will be angry and you will be nice. Get in touch with us today at militia headquarters, RR2, Heart's Content Road, Egypt, Maine, 04047, or call 625-8693 or find us the old-fashioned way. Sundays are best. We'll open the gate for you! We love you! We are your neighbors. Keep your powder dry and your ear to the ground! Let's save the Republic together!

The article is signed.

Militia Secretary, Bree St. Onge
Recruiting officers, Samantha Butler and Margo St. Onge
Other officers, Whitney St. Onge, Michelle St. Onge, Dee Dee St. Onge, Oceanna St. Onge, Carmel St. Onge, Kirk Martin, Tabitha St. Onge, Liddy

Soucier, Desiree Haskell, Scotty St. Onge, Heather Martin, Erin Pinette, Rusty Soucier, Chris Butler, Lorrie Pytko, Jaime Crosman, Shanna St. Onge, Alyson Lessard, Rachel Soucier, Christian Crocker, Buzzy Shaw, Theoden Darby, Josh Fogg.

It then continues with another dozen names, all girls.

And just in case readers need help making connections, the *Record Sun* editors have, oh, so helpfully, set a box at one side with a summarized rehash of the Homeschool-Settlement-Border-Mountain-Militia relationship as well as a mention of the thirty-eight terrorized governors' wives. And then the two eye-popping photos. One the already used and reused and used again by the fourth estate from here to Miami, LA to Seattle, and all that's in between, the blur of resplendently creepy merry-go-round creatures with Guillaume "Gordon" St. Onge in the middle of the muddle, his face of contrasted light, one eye so pale it seems to be a ball of marble in the socket above a black bear pelt beard.

Second photo frames the Settlement "gate" arched by a green blush of boughs. And there's the KEEP OUT sign. This boxed area reads: GATES OF ST. ONGE SETTLEMENT WILL COME DOWN IN A BIG WAY.

An oddly warm late September dusk on the Settlement Quad before Gordon's eyes see the op-ed.

Tyrannosaurus rex is two stories tall. His mega-huge box-shaped wooden feet are spaced fifteen feet apart, his toes made of log ends, his "little" two-by-four pine arms and dowel fingers reach out in the air ahead so that you can picture him grasping cow-sized prey. His big smile is made of wooden slats painted white. He is scary by day. Scarier by night. But, you see, he is a loyal friend to little kids who are sometimes too rough with him, climbing onto his stiffly ruffled tail, racing up his interior stairs to the little room in his head. And yeah, he also serves as a hangout for adults who smoke.

Tonight is going to be very dark. Slabs of clouds slide into position.

Five Settlement men are having a smoke, not that all are smoking but they are all together in that encircling wreath of poison. Gordon is not a smoker. His cousin Paul Lessard goes through phases of being "cured of cured tobacco." Tonight he's cured of it, using both hands to wave around and gesture as he explains some concerns about their "Lincoln project."

Against one huge foot and ankle of the goodly green beast, Gordon leans back, his arms folded over his chest, one booted foot out before the other.

From the nearest screened porches of the big horseshoe of buildings that frame three sides of the Quadrangle, there are voices of a small group of people leaving. Most will be walking uphill to their houses and cottages in the fields and woods by the way of bricked paths in the cases of those with walkers or wheelchairs or baby buggies or solar buggies. A few screen doors slam almost all at the same time. Meanwhile, certain shops and the library and kitchens remain lighted, as well as one of the piazzas, which flits and glowers with candles in colored glass holders.

Yes, the crank calls on the Settlement phone, the mail, and radio chatter *had* begun to trail off a bit. But at this moment the phone down at Gordon's house is flying off the wall. Gordon doesn't know this.

Two of the men of the T. rex group are turning away, one headed toward the parking lot, the other heading for his woodsy cottage. He's still smoking as he disappears into the night.

"Everything is ready but the bastardly flatbed," says the remaining smoker, Rick Crosman, Settlement fiddle maker, orchard man, windmill builder, and welder, as well as one of those who work in the thick of things during sugaring season in the spring of the year. And he's always on hand for haying, butchering, roadwork. And general carpentry.

"Ray making a search for d' clush ball, him. I promise he waste hiss precious day farrtinng arounn' wit' dose Martells." This is Gordon's cousin Aurel speaking, and through the dim light his dark eyes blaze and quest each face for an agreeable nod.

Gordon says, "Well, we either get that right . . . with the part from Martell's. Or we put new leafs on the back of the Dodge and load the plant onto that. We had to do the brakes on the Ford anyway. It wasn't wasted time. This trip just gave us the boot in the ass we need."

Rick sighs in exasperation. "Still, this clutch ball business sucks. Time is tight."

"Better here than while on the road," Gordon says with a laugh.

Rick frowns. "Even so."

"D'options are not dat plentiful," Aurel insists, pulling off his Vietnam War bush hat for the manyth time and smoothing his hair.

"We'll make it," says Gordon huskily, consolingly.

Rick starts rolling another cigarette, darkness be damned. He can do the whole thing by feel. Probably smoked since he was two.

Rules here at the Settlement include, as we've heard, "No TV." Then there's the one where babies must never be taught to say "Mommy" or "Mom." Gordon says greeting card companies invented Mommy. And yet tobacco smoking is never questioned. Except no smoking indoors or in vehicles. But outdoors, cigarette smoke dangles everywhere, thicker than soup.

Aurel lifts a hand to wave to passing figures, one person headed toward the parking lot but she has now stopped over there near a picnic table between two big high-limbed oaks.

Gordon peers around past both the dinosaur's shins and sees that it is Bree, his bride. The "Parlor meetings" of teenagers have been running late these days, and running intensely. Sometimes West Parlor, sometimes East Parlor. Other times they gather in the Library. Or even the woods, unbeknownst to most two-leggeds over the age of twenty. These are not the educational gatherings organized by Settlement parents and such. These are more special. While they are in session, doors are kept closed and a guard is posted.

Yes, this is, as you might suspect, the True Maine Militia in its covert beginnings. Though rumor bleeds through the Settlement that this is nothing to snort at, many of the men here at the Settlement have snorted in delight. So girlie, so cute.

But Gordon is edgy. Gordon does not think girl militias are harmless.

"Hey," Gordon calls to Bree softly as her course has veered toward him, her hip-swinging limber walk, her silhouette against the dim light of the East Parlor porch squiggly and shuddering from so much thick hair, hair to her waist, hair the red of all his worst recurring hell dreams. And yet, only days ago, he had felt nothing but tenderness as he slipped the silver ring onto her finger and Reverend Andy Emery had said the words about forever love.

Gordon resumes his at-ease position, back pressed against the wooden foot of the "sculpture," arms crossed, turned toward the men and away from Bree now as she steps in closer to his side.

Talk of the Lincoln project is petering out. Aurel and Rick greet Bree and she strikes a match in a manly way, which she has, of course, learned from her brothers and from other guys with whom she has worked in the woods logging during her formative years. You can tell she is at home with a bunch of smoking guys, older guys especially. She inhales and exhales from the cigarette pleasurably and tosses her hair.

In a few minutes, Rick and Aurel are both done with fretting over the Lincoln situation and both depart.

Gordon sighs good-naturedly.

Bree giggles. "I was on my way home." She means her father's house a few miles away. She has not rushed to move to the Settlement since her marriage.

"I thought that's what you were up to." He sighs again. Good-naturedly.

Silence, except for the murmurs and twitters and chuckles coming from that nearest big candlelit porch.

Gordon looks straight up at the dinosaur's arms and hands and then on to the big grinning head way up there among the high oak limbs. He looks back down square into the birth-defect-stretched face of his bride. She is staring at him. A burning gaze. A week ago she was shy! Something has changed in her since they said their vows. No more nervous giggles coming from Bree. No more hiding behind her hair. See how fully she beholds him. Her far-apart yellow honey-color eyes move over him in a sticky way.

"So, how are you, Brianna?"

She giggles. So okay, she *still* giggles. But these are no way, no how, the same giggles.

He draws a hand over his short beard, gives the heavy and darker mustache a quick two-fingered taming. Sighs. There are tall-grass bugs creaking and whirring far and near. No airplanes. No distant car engines. Just the way the earth and sky and present time all beat together like blood through a heart.

"How are *you*?" Bree asks, a happy echo of his words.

He chuckles deeply. "We're both doin' good."

She giggles again but the giggle splutters off into a smoky deep velvety womanly laugh. "We're mixed, remember?"

"Ayup." His arms are again crossed over his chest, not self-protectively but in the way of a lot of tall big-boned guys who don't know what else to do with those long arms, especially now as he moves from side to side, scratching his back on T. rex's huge foot.

She says, "It's all illusion. Time. Space. All this tomorrow and yesterday stuff. All this separateness of bodies stuff."

"You sound like you're on LSD."

She laughs heartily.

"Your militia, Brianna . . . all that sweet nice love stuff. The big boys in DC will worry. Love conquers. A known fact, baby."

She seems to be glancing toward the porches, then whispers, "I want to put my eyeballs against your eyeballs again so we can mix some more."

He almost chokes, his laugh too sudden. "Jesus."

She laughs. "I mean it. I want more of your soul. I just got a little, little eensie pretty sweet piece before, that perfect warm little part of you that didn't hurry fast enough to make it back in when you closed your eyes too soon, the little doors of your soul. Remember?"

He says with playful seriousness, "It was a mistake. My intention was to completely jump out of my body and bury myself in there with *your* happy sweet *dangerous* soul, which is still captive inside you, warm with life, and believes the world can be saved."

She whispers, "My husband, I am so happy."

Voices on the near porches are fading in and out, passing through shop doors, thrusting to and fro in rocking chairs, stooping to lift things, yawning, maybe swallowing a last-of-the-day coffee or some hot milk.

She says, "Well, I guess I have to get home. Dad has to move equipment tomorrow to Fryeburg. No sleeping late."

"Logger girl by day, philosopher and militia officer by night."

She wiggles the fingers of one raised hand and turns herself from side to side. "Adjustable and adaptable."

"Sophia," he says, stepping away from the wooden support, now very close to her, Sophia in reference to a calligraphy letter she wrote him BEFORE they met.

"I am not your Witch of Wisdom, sir. I am your Witch of Duty, *remember*! The world needs *you*."

"You ride my neck."

"Yesssss!"

These references and remembrances, made up of only the two months since they met, fall between them like many many of those ultra-pink plaster cherubim Bree is so fascinated with. But all of them armed with souped-up crossbows, he notes.

He sighs worriedly. "Brianna, forget that duty stuff."

"Nag nag nag nag nag." Again she wiggles her fingers at him. "I will nag you very well."

The porches seem too suddenly quiet. No doubt some of these occupiers of that big busy porch are other St. Onge wives. They wouldn't be able to see Bree and Gordon clearly out there under the looming Tyrannosaurus rex but for sure a certain extrasensory detection is at work, beaming in on Gordon at all times to catch him breaking his own self-imposed rule: Never fondle a wife in front of others. *NEVER*.

"Well," says Bree, now hugging herself.

"Keep your powder dry," says he. (This means gunpowder. A little militia joke.)

Before Bree reaches the parking lot.

She is overtaken and overwhelmed by a large pack of mouth-breathing cartwheeling tykes and preteens, a rolling tidal wave of brats and cuties with his face, his broad frame, his dark hair, who sweetly bully her toward "a wonderful surprise" and away from her brother's truck up there in the open lot.

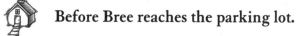

Moments later.

There is an ominous pale shape in Claire's hand. Her voice in the dusk says, "Gordon."

And Geraldine's voice also speaks in a tight way, "I guess you've already seen this."

And Gordon, who was on his way to the hay barns, now turns in the gravel lot, the sole of one work boot setting a small stone to rolling, says ever so carefully and ever so deeply, "Seen what?"

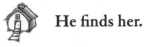

He finds her.

Yes, there she is with her ton of coiled tumbling hair. It's the attic of the furniture-making Quonset hut, a room where twelve-year-old Kirk Martin, creator and mayor of the amazing, magic, glowing, and twinkling solar-powered electronic table town, has been demonstrating for Bree all things that moo and flutter, croak and choo choo and buzz. And also squashed elbow-to-elbow in this leaning-in huddle around the table are all the small and medium children, their faces so barely dusted with light they appear to be planets and moons in the table town's sky.

And yes, there in the doorway is Gordon with a section of the *Record Sun* in one hand. "Everybody but Bree clear out." This means even Kirky himself!

And so there are whines from these subordinates and calling Gordon a "jerk" and other squeaky fuss. Montana of the thick blond braids and strenuous dignity runs her tongue out at him as they all stomp out.

Bree hears all the doors slamming at the foot of the stairs and beyond while the high-pitched protests fade. She smiles at Gordon as she remarks, "We could have gone someplace else to talk."

Gordon just says, "Brianna." He's not the same man that he was out on the Quad a half hour or so ago when he looked so amused and tender and, Bree likes to imagine, horny. He . . . is . . . someone . . . else. She knows now not to smile anymore.

He steps close and sort of slow-motion shoves the newspaper into her hands.

Bree says, "I thought you'd be proud of what we did. Kind of a little birthday present to you."

"No, Brianna. You did not think that."

"Oh, okay, yuh, I knew you would be worried . . . but that *duty* would speak to you." She sees-hears now an even more grayed, granite, and now dangerous mountain-avalanche thunder in his eyes.

And he sees the honeyed, sly, sneaky serpent-in-Eden dangerous look in *her* far-apart eyes and slight twist of sass to her perfect bowlike fifteen-year-old mouth.

He pivots away. Because when his tears of frustration and fear come, nobody in this world should see them. But also unseen by this werewolf bride is his blush. Shame?

There is no sound to his tears. There is no sound to the rent and rip. But he and Bree can never go back. *As if* with a fifteen year-old you could ever be, in the words he still hears in her smoky voice from almost an hour before, "eyeball to eyeball."

Now in her room with the little octagon window.

She hugs herself hard. Is she pretending he is in her arms? Or maybe she in his? After all, she's only fifteen, and this is what fifteen-year-old girls do. Her wrongly spaced eyes are closed. What does she see against her eyelids, which glow with the light of the little octagon window? The man? The children of the man? Those children she will "carry" and "bear" and then *share* with all the Settlement nurturers? No. She is sworn off childbearing. Overpopulation sucks.

She whispers, "Gordon and Bree." Not just with a fuck and a ring, but with a mission. Yeah, duty. He is only pretending not to understand, right? This marriage. It isn't just man and woman. It's a marriage between the Settlement and the future! Save the future from—

Well, she doesn't have a word for it now. Something even vaster than corporate folks and their charters waddling around beyond Bree's steamy little world. Something about evil she has no definition for. Yet.

Duotron Lindsey International's CEO, Bruce Hummer, slits open mail at his desk. It is a folded newspaper article.

He taps the desktop as he reads. It's almost two pages of op-ed, including illustrations. Photos, too. It holds his interest to the very end.

Janet Weymouth arrives at Ocean in a Shell to meet two friends for their usual coffees and one muffin cut into wedges to share.

She is the first to arrive. She looks tired in violet. She glimpses a newspaper spread on the table of the next booth, dishes and cups not yet cleared by the waitress. This place is small and slow and she is okay with that. She is starting to revere *slow*, to realize how deeply you can snuggle into *slow* while *fast* is so attenuated. So cruel. So cold. So fraught with force. Thin on promise.

There is something on that open page. She steps close, plucks it from the eggs-and-jelly-drizzled mess, spirits it away to her corner booth.

It is *them*. A gutsy op-ed is a happy echo of the invasion of monkeys in tanks and fellerbunchers. Dropping the cardboard bomb button! What vinegar! What moxie! She has feared their pizzazz would be wasted all locked up behind gates in those hills.

She intends to share this with someone. Yes, yes, the two friends soon to arrive. But also with her daughter. And yes, her son. No, not with Morse, who is more dead since three days ago and was more three days ago than he was three weeks before. Well, she can read it to him. Maybe he hears her. But maybe he doesn't. Soon there will be certainty. Dr. Grossman said she could probably count the hours. She tried to reach Gordon to have him join the sad stream of family and Morse's closest friends in saying good-bye. But she got only a busy signal. Now she knows why.

She recognizes the Bigfoot creature from red-haired Bree's *Recipe*. The mystery girl.

Her two friends are stepping in, bells ajangling on the café's door. How funny! *Both* are wearing shades of purple! Good coincidences are made in heaven.

Bruce Hummer, if he could speak to you, heart-to-heart.

Yes, this edifice is my master. This prowling upright *thing* with a thousand times a thousand times a thousand heads nodding and considering on its own accord, a million times a million times a million fingers counting, a billion times a billion times a billion feet of thunder, the planet's awfullest crucible. The mother of earth, both the creator and the prey, she is shrinking, trembling; the hands that rip her tenderest and toughest parts are hands she herself birthed. A fatal masturbation, you might say.

There is no measurement for progress because there is no honest definition of it.

But, folks, I stand before you all, one hundred and sixty-nine pounds. Nothing could be clearer to your eye. Smash me if you think it'll make you feel better. But don't look! Your world is unraveling. *I* know. I am keeper of some of its most fearsome secrets.

Another dangerous secret.

Rain makes plastic slippery. But it's not a large TV. Rain makes what looks like hiccups on the roof and hood of Professor Catherine Court Downey's little mint-green car. Now the hatchback slaps quietly back down as two young Settlement mothers who have promised, oh, so hushily, to keep THE SECRET are ahead of her on the gravel, taking turns lugging the set and opening doors and guiding the way up the dimly lit stairway to Catherine's half of the Quonset hut attic studio. And so now the Settlement has one TV.

As the rain lets up, the stout maple in Rex's yard runs with tears and trickles, the roofs of the old farmplace plish-plash water onto stone steps, and an inverted plastic pail at one corner of the porch plunks.

Gordon pulls in snug behind Rex's already parked gray work van, with the smiling lightbulb on the go. YORK ELECTRIC.

It's Saturday. No sign of Rex's truck.

Now a newish silver truck edges in alongside Gordon, big square-jawed shaved face behind the glass and slowly swishing wipers.

Tall guy of the broad-shoulders-big-neck build, like Gordon himself, but dressed in head-to-foot camo and visored boxy camo army hat, Border Mountain Militia patch on his sleeve; he steps out. Big

John. Ever since Gordon has known him, this neighbor has wallowed in camo, in army, in the play of it. A Vietnam-era vet like Rex, only different. Maybe not as much real-life war actually came his way during the conflict. Neither Rex nor this guy rattles off combat stories, so there's not much to sort out there. But Big John holds the present more as a friend than Rex does.

Big John ambles manfully around the front of his truck. He carries today not one of his modern military black plastic or camo plastic Bushmasters, the ARs he's so fond of, but an old Winchester, wood worn dark, iron worn dark. In his other hand a newspaper.

Gordon gets out of his saggy baggy sinking-cab-mounts old Chevy and presses the guy's shoulder. Big John is Rex's hotshot second in command. "Watcha been up to ol' buddy?" Gordon asks almost tenderly.

Big John shrugs. "Nothing to write home about."

"Richard says your new job takes you to Timbuktu."

Big John laughs. His big square clean-shaved jaw is almost Hollywood. But also forgettable. Rememberable is that laugh of a gentle giant. "Well, next thing to it. But I've got five days home to sort out the dust from the dead house plants. You heard I'm single now?"

Gordon nods. "Something to that effect. I missed out on the juicy details."

"Juicy I wish." John holds out both the newspaper and the rifle for Gordon to check out. Gordon knows even before he sees his own face in photo ink what the article is about, groans, "Oh, yes." Abandons the paper on the wet dark green hood of his truck. But the Winchester. His eyes light up. And he has two hands now to fondle it. "Where'd you get this? Not in a public place."

Big John chuckles. "You wouldn't be holding it now if I did. Collectors are like fisher cats. They can jump seventy feet."

Gordon jerks the lever to check the breech.

Big John says, "A guy over in the Northern Kingdom. His friend died. Left his property to his daughter. She all but gave it to Chris. He's not into Winchesters. He didn't *give* it to me." He chortles with the jolly despair of parting with a slab of cash. "But—"

Gordon interrupts, "Well, yeah, you don't see many of these floating around in the here and now. Eighty-six?"

"Uh huh. Original. Made in eighty-seven. Second year production. So what happened to your thumb? You're still dripping, ol' boy."

Gordon's thumb is wrapped thickly in gauze with a big consummately round red polka dot dead center, and, yes, it might be dripping. He wipes his sleeve along the rifle's forearm and receiver just in case. "My wife bit me."

Big John raises his square chin, eyes stippled with stars of good humor. The pail by the house is still plunking but the plunks are farther apart. The air smells like wet fields. And warm truck engines. "Your wife? Or did all of them bite you at once?"

Gordon smiles and flushes. Tall-grass songbugs are doing their thing, always the same marching rhythm of creaks, enviable solidarity or a vortex of competition?

Rex's newish red pickup swerves into the yard, easy does it, squeezes in between Big John's rig and the stacked firewood.

The sky to the north has darkened like a movie introducing peril.

Gordon aims the rifle at the bank across the road, then lowers it, eyeing the open sights. "My eyes are so bad."

Rex's truck door slams.

Now a little white car pulls in. Looks like a sneaker, that latest style of little shit-box car. Music quite loud. At the same time, Rex is coming around from his truck, too dark a day for sunglasses. His steely eyes zigzag over the faces of the two men, the rifle, the bloody bandage.

Big John remarks, "His wife bit him."

Rex nods. Raises the soft brim of his army cap, his silent hello. It's not a canvas bush hat. He has made no souvenirs of his overseas experience.

John, who is nearly eye-to-eye in height with Gordon, is smiling big and quirky. "Exactly which woman did this? Any I've met? I met Claire. And her sister, Leona."

"Cousin. Leona and Geraldine and Lolly are cousins."

"Yeah?"

"This one's Bree."

Rex's steely eyes zero in and widen between Gordon's eyes.

The car door slams.

Gordon hands the rifle to Rex. "Looks babied, aye?"

"Yeah, babied," Big John says. "*And original.* Imagine. It's been around for over a hundred years. I have my brother's replica made fifteen years ago and it's dinged up. This one has only one minuscule scuff under the forearm."

Rex handles the rifle admiringly. Says, "I just heard back from Brad Evans, Virginia militia. Three of his men and himself will be up for the expo."

Mailman in a flashing-lights station wagon whines to a halt by the York mailbox. Slaps open mailbox. In goes one lonely but glossy and shrill advertisement. Horn beeps.

Rex turns, gives the mailman a nod.

Gordon and John nod also as the car pulls slowly back onto the road.

Gordon says, "I don't see much of Dave lately cuz the mail is so ridiculous, we have to fetch it at the post office. No kidding, it would fill a truck bed."

Big John says, "Your kids went by with horses. And a real mule. I go, *What're you guys carrying around? Looks like body bags.*" He chortles. "They said they were the pony express."

Gordon rolls his eyes. "Well, they're having fun. But it's nothing to envy."

"Oh, I don't envy it," Big John laughs harshly. Then turns to Rex. "I'll be in the Midwest that weekend of the expo, I'm sorry to say. Give my regards to the Virginians."

The music that has been playing in the white car parked beyond Rex's truck goes off and a door can be heard creaking open. Appearing now in a long-sleeved T-shirt of peacock blue and jeans, neck choking with a dozen silvery and gold-color lockets and necklaces, then on the ears earrings that spin, hair like Bree's in its resemblance to a thousand snakes, those painstakingly brushed curls, but Bree's snakes are red, this girl's are deep, deep auburn. Glory York. Rex's one and only child, almost twenty. Employee of the month at her job. Looks like Rex across the eyes. As she passes, she studies the faces of the two visitors. Gordon hasn't seen her in months. She's different. Older, yes. But something else, the way she tries to hold Gordon's eyes, but though he nods to be friendly, he looks back at Rex very fast, maybe because he already knows Rex's eyes are repeating that hard widening look that happened when he heard Gordon say the name *Bree*. *Wife*.

Gordon gets it. He feels a snowy warning tornado of wind lift him a foot or two (in spirit) and slam him against the near grille of his truck. He speaks in a half swallow, "Like I said before, Richard. If you need extra room to put those Virginians up, we have plenty of places to have them. Bed, food, the works."

Rex nods, does something odd with his tongue, like doing an inventory of his teeth.

Big John wonders, "So, what's that in the paper, Gordo? That bunch of people named St. Onge. True Maine Militia and all that."

Glory is inside the porch now, letting the storm door close against her hand as she's still giving Gordon the look. This never-before look. Is this what fame does? But he's known Glory since she was born! One thing he is *not* is some sort of Uncle Creepy. And he hears a sort of whine in his mind's ear, his voice speaking to Rex, if Rex could hear his thoughts, *I promise you, my brother. I'll never touch that little girl.*

Rex fondles the old Winchester, this babied old treasure, its old silken action, its old satin skin. He lines up the buckhorn and front sight on the same bank that Gordon had. Today Rex is dressed in weekend garb, no Dickies. It's dungarees, brown T shirt with chambray over that, and that soft olive-drab army cap. And yet he still does not have that comfortable slobby look most people rush home to from jobs. He is forever on duty.

Now Glory is gone. Somewhere inside with her grandmother, Rex's ma, Ruth. Very nice people. Very ordinary people. Even the divorced-and-gone Marsha . . . all very normal. Why do they all feel so dangerous today?

Gordon is fooling with the tricky childproof cap of his aspirin bottle, extra hard to get open with mangled-thumb-wife-war-wound.

"So," says Big John. "It was just kids that did that op-ed?"

How to answer that?

Gordon crunches aspirin between his molars.

Rex lowers the rifle, tips his cap back a bit, and raises the gun again on a giddy yellow splutter of goldenrod along the top of the bank, then down below to the waves of three-seeded mercury thriving in roadside sand. The gray day makes no contrasts. Pupils of eyes embrace color supremely. Smooth-gray, pink-granite, yellow-white stones framed and blotted precisely, one at a time, in the sights.

Gordon murmurs, “Well, it’s hard to explain but that op-ed has direct correlation to this.” Raises his wounded hand, the stunning scarlet polka dot now shaped like a scarlet oval, still spreading sunsetishly on the snow-white gauze.

“So,” says Big John with a grin. “It was a *wife* that did that article and you were beating her and she bit you in self-defense.”

Gordon grins, big big, his eyes to one side remembering the scene earlier today at Bree’s family’s place where she attacked him for his stupid joke about that very thing, her “need” of a “good licking.” *A joke. A joke, okay?* He was not freaking out as he had been at Kirk Martin’s table town room. He had calmed. He had gotten hold of himself. But out of his big mouth the joke sprang into her ears through the loud distortions of rain, into which also his jokey eye-twinkles were obscured and then the sky of their little newborn marriage fell. She had muckled onto his shirt and almost broke his neck pushing and pulling . . . but he did not fight back. Then she bit him. Then she dropped to a squat and sobbed. Then he left. *Because he was afraid of her.*

“Well,” says Gordon.

Rex turns with rifle lowered, facing Gordon and Big John. Rex says to Gordon, “Cat got your tongue?”

Gordon blinks, grins.

Rex says stiffly, “The other day with Art you weren’t lost for words . . . all that about the Modern Monetary Theory. Sounded like one of your good-buddy attacks that you launch into with me all the time. Which to me is just all that little-boy socialist crap you’ve been slinging since you were wet behind the ears back in the day. So I ignore it. But sounded to me like you wanted to make an enemy of Art. I think you came close. He’s good people. Remember when you asked to come to our meetings, you were promising not to be a gorilla.”

Gordon’s eyes flinch and widen. “So you’ve been steaming over that for days?”

A motion in Gordon’s periphery sight. Glory back again, behind the glass storm door, holding a perfect polished store-bought apple. And she’s watching the three of them with laughing eyes as if maybe they’re about to do a clown act. Gordon’s eyes have only briefly slid over her sassy gorgeous young alabaster white face and dark-lashed gray eyes, and even though her aspect is now as solemn as Rex's, she waves. He gives her an almost kiddie wave back, then swings fully back to face Rex, "So this is like the real military. No discussion. Just take orders."

Rex sighs. "Just don't fight with people, okay?"

Gordon squints.

Rex says, "About Mrs. Nichols's checks, Art's not calling up on any hotlines to report people. This isn't Russia."

Gordon frowns. "There are plenty of hotlines in the United States. You know that as well as I do. Remem—"

Rex puts up a hand, the *stop* gesture.

Glory vanishes.

John says, "So, Gordo, you going to the Preparedness Expo with the captain here and the rebs from Dixie? Going to check out the preparedness goodies?"

Gordon grunts. "Buncha capitalists exploiting the common man's justified fears."

Big John laughs deeply.

Rex says to Gordon, "If more than four wind up coming from down South, it might require more space, unless they're bivouacking . . . plenty of outdoors here. But that's not been discussed yet. I'll keep you posted. Myself or some of the others'll stop by up there. I know your gate isn't meant for us."

Gordon says warmly, "It's not meant to keep out friends."

Rex scowls, a slight dipping of the eyebrows. "Someday you may need some serious security. Maybe surveillance. Something high-tech."

Gordon makes a noise on the verge of a giggle.

Rex studies him darkly.

Big John says, "I can see it now. You people up there . . . one phone . . . no microwave ovens, no TV . . . but a hundred surveillance cameras. *Heh heh heh heh*."

But Rex and Gordon are in a showdown stare. Rex is winning. Then he says to Gordon, "You think this is funny."

"It's just that . . . like John here is saying . . . some things are ironic. You know like—"

Rex puts up a hand. "Don't."

Gordon notices around Rex's eyes more age than last week, more tiredness than ten minutes ago. And he thinks, *Okay, there is danger outside. We need not argue that point except the feathery fumy details. But you see, there is something fearsome inside.*

Another day passes. Six o'clock news gives details of the newsworthy reappearance of three hooded men outside a Department of Human Services office, this one in Augusta.

Not much for details. They harassed four women who were leaving the offices. They did their terrorizing all within a ten-minute framework and were out of there.

None of the men could be identified.

One woman was taken to the "emergency" for trauma, as she was threatened with hanging, and saw a noose in one man's hands. Another man clasped a Bible.

One man was agile. Incredibly agile. Some suspect he might be a professional boxer or karate expert.

At the end of this item, a few people are interviewed to find out how they feel about this.

Midday. Wiscasset, Maine. Marian St. Onge brings her guests to the backyard.

Guests are Gordon, his thirteen-year-old son Oz, and also his baby son Gus, who is on a long rope. Gordon doesn't look as if he planned on driving over here today. Something's come up. Looks as though he's come home from a construction site, which in the Depaolo family olden days was okay. But it's not how you looked on a visit. This is a visit.

Baby Gus with his thick Beatles haircut, identical to his mother Lolly's, reaches the end of the rope and pulls. Like a small but sturdy dog. His overalls are fat in the rear end. Old-time cotton diaper and rubber pants? Marion tsks to herself. She won't look either grandchild in the face. She might normally snarl elegantly over Gordon's orange-sherbet-color T-shirt and shredded dungarees and hayseed and hay tassels in his seams and hair. But in a mini moment of unconditional love, she seems not to notice this crime. She's just so pleased and electrified in her pale Irishy eyes to see him.

There's no view of the ocean from here in her backyard but you can smell it. The nuclear power plant doesn't put off a smell. Just other stuff. And the ironworks, no distinctive smell or noise of its traffic reaches this green and flowery niche. But there's the crackle of the white wicker chairs as you settle there and cicadas enjoy ecstatic digestion in the hot boughs overhead. Dappled sunlight strafes your knees. Broad strokes of open sun are in easy predictable motion over the iron and wood sculptures of horses and deer and cherubim and replicas of famous athletic-build nude Greeks being eaten by dogs and vultures. Or they are staring up into the sky in deep thought, inwardly giddy about philosophy and the arts and ships setting out to take over more of the world to bring foreigners a better way in trade for everything they possess.

Also some glass-topped tables. A swing under the stout oak. Narrow flagstone paths with violets and vinca snaking through fruit trees and hydrangeas. A small goldfish pond reflecting the white bunny clouds and hard blue sky.

Gordon flops a small yellow pullover sweater on the nearest table and a lumpy green moon print handmade diaper bag.

Oz peers into the goldfish pond with blazing interest as if it were home to barracudas. He is as chatty a guy as his older brother Cory but is deathly quiet whenever he comes here, which is almost never. He's more likely to see his other grandmother, Leona's mother, who has a serious, almost mournful face but says things to crack you up. *Constantly*. By herself or as straight man to Granpa Paul who mugs Curly, Larry, and Moe's* *yuk-yuks* and *woo woo woos* and *see the clouds*. Leona has a billowing fondness for her dad but he's not the central character of many good stories. She has about twenty stories of her mother smashing things in fits of temper over the years, pitching stuff at her husband, her kids, the neighbors, the dog. Footstools, telephone, cuckoo clock, plate of noodles. Stuff you can see and hear coming, too bulky or slippery to pick up much speed. No hospital-type injuries. Just ducking. Just mopping.

---

* Hollywood's Three Stooges.

The idea of Mim smashing and making stuff go sailing makes Oz laugh. It's part of her stage presence . . . her fiery love . . . her immortality. While Marian St. Onge makes him feel as though he has gotten somehow wedged into the hollow ground crevice of an enormous tarantula. She meets his eyes sideways, never cracks jokes, never laughs at his.

Oz, with his faint horse smell, dark T-shirt, baggy camo shorts, skinny legs, and black hair of French-Italian-Passamaquoddy sheen, roams over to the oak tree swing and gets comfortable.

He gets the swing seat to spin around lazily. He's looking forward to himself and Gordon and Gus leaving this chore behind and driving a little way north to see a guy about starting a solar cooperative there, a guy who *loved* the *Record Sun* feature last month, the one Ivy Morelli the bouncy little reporter wrote. Then the guy was jostled extra much when this latest, the True Maine Militia's op-ed, jumped out of his mailbox.

True Maine Militia "officer" Samantha Butler had smirked, "Ha! Ha! Mr. King Shit owes us a thank-you on bended knee for all this new co-op interest!"

Back over by the glass tables and wicker chairs Marian now has a pinched look. "Gordon, what happened to your hand?"

Gordon's fresh bandage has no blood showing. And yet it bulges significantly. He says lazily, "Oh, you know. The work of holding everything together back home."

She sniffs with a blend of restrained scorn and true worry.

He notes that today her eyes glint with her contact lenses. Tiny shell earrings are almost the same wraithy pink as the stones in her tasteful right-hand ring.

Gordon says, "Well, about Morse. She called you, too, Janet did, right?"

Marian scowls. "Yes, he's bad off. A bad time for them." She's walking away from him, pressing her open hand across her midriff as if she expects a karate kick there. "Stay where you are. I'll get our coffees."

He walks around following Gus, who is of an age still measured in months but can walk fast and likes to mess around with danger. The little guy is surveying the distant fishpond, his cousin-brother on the swing, the bobbing turning-blue hydrangeas full of droning women bees, stingers on hair trigger. "Hi-go!" he commands. Gordon does not loosen his grip on the rope. The harness made of the same fat cotton rope as the leash is still well-knotted.

When Gordon sees Marian returning with the tray, he pulls Gus along in her direction and Gus hurls himself down and wails. Gordon drags him over the grass. This catches Marian's eye but she says nothing, just sets Gordon's cup out. And hers. She has changed her sweater vest to a darker blue one with tiny buttons. Gordon is touched by her efforts to put on the dog even for him who would love and fear her even if she were wearing a barrel.

The baby is screaming and pulling grass to pitch at his father. "He acts Italian, doesn't he, Mum?" he says. "Irish, too. Like both your halves." He chuckles.

Marian squinches her eyes shut and shakes her head, slight sad little shakes.

"Don't tell me you've never heard such a racket before." He laughs huskily.

She looks at Gordon levelly. "Once you told me his grandmother at the reservation smashed all the windows out of a car with a tire iron. Or stove poker. Or something."

"No. Not *his* grandmother. His mother isn't Leona. You've not met Lolly."

"Guess I'm confused," she enounces clearly.

"So." Gordon sits, hauling Gus in like a bluefish, letting him tire, then tugging the rope a bit more. Gus's howls shiver the air and now some grass splats into the lap of Gordon's dungarees.

"Wow!" Gordon praises. "Good aim!"

"You will have him attacking you with real objects in time," Marian warns.

She picks open a box of ginger cookies. She holds one up, her gray eyes on Gus's face, which is overly indulgent for her to be with his children, but it seems she is trying to make a point about proper rewards and distractions.

The air pressed tight with the sound waves of shriekings for miles is suddenly empty and pure. Even the cicadas above and songbugs below have stopped. Gus, sniveling and gulping, pushes himself up and walks in a manly way toward the treat. Takes it. And says politely, "Tank-way." The child looks long into her soul with his teary brown eyes.

Gordon says, "That's Passamaquoddy for *I'm in gratitude to you, O gracious lovely grandmother*."

She says, "Tell the other one to help himself."

Gordon's eyes slide to his beloved Oz, legally Jason, treasure of the Settlement, expert horseman since the age of seven and now foreman of the mail crew, bewitched by all animals, even rescues mice, among other virtues. Keeps a personal scrapbook of favorite postcards and magazine photos, animals and laughing people, Gary Larson *Far Side* jokes, and his own childly scrawled poems, some funny, some deep. Presently he is ambling toward one of Marian's elegant sculptures, a horse in repose. No chain saw artists represented here.

Gordon says softly, "We came as a delegation of love. To make sure you will be going to the Weymouths'. It's his last hours. Janet and Selene and Richard* want you there."

"We aren't that close anymore. I'm *not* immediate family."

Gordon's eyes flinch and flare. Rope in one hand, coffee in the other, he tells her, "They seem a little perplexed by that."

"I'll go to the funeral."

He stares at her, trying to figure something. "Do you want me to drive you? *Before* he's gone from us?"

She makes a face. "I have my own vehicle."

"Yes, I know. But . . . as a family. You and me. Claire is ready to leave now."

She glances at Oz, who is moving away from the sculpture, his head turned, dark eyes skittering on her as if he were a criminal leaving the scene.

She croons with sarcasm, "No mile-long caravans of your vehicles wending their way to Cape Elizabeth?"

"No."

She is sitting down now, knees together, stirring a packet of some substance into her coffee.

Says he, "Well, I thought I'd try. You certainly don't *have* to go. But I wanted to come see you anyway."

Her attractively short clipped hair is streaked gray through the dark, so becoming with the pale eyes. Her posture is that of a woman

* The Weymouths' grown kids.

tied to a stake for burning. She says blisteringly, "Janet would be scheming with you just to get us together, you and me and your . . . the residents of your property."

He sees on the tray an object rolled up in tissue paper. "Well, that's nothing I'm in on. I just think she misses you." He considers asking Marian if she saw the op-ed. Decides not to go there. She *has* had one or two flashes of the awful thing but stiffens at the thought of mentioning it. It would only beckon on board an instant dispute.

Gus opens a hand toward the cookie box. "Mo."

"That's Passamaquoddy for *please*."

Marian tsks. "You remind me of your father. Never a serious moment." She digs into the cookie box and in a voice both instructive and ruffly, a voice that is almost grandmotherly, says, "Pleeeeze" into the baby's now penetrating gaze. Then to Gordon, "His name is—"

"Gus. Short for Miles."

Marian squints. "Miles is only one syllable, Gordon."

"Well, right. I think he named himself Gus. You know how those things stick for life. And hey, Guillaume and Gordon are each two syllables."

She ignores this.

He begs, "Please, Mum, go see the Weymouths. We can plan it so we aren't there at the same time if that's how you want it."

Her gray eyes, their lids and underneaths softening downward with the years, slightly tear up. "I just want them to forget me."

He squints. He knows what's coming.

She lifts her chin with weary pride. "I'm embarrassed. I've lost so many friends due to your ridiculous lifestyle."

"You didn't lose them. You pitched them overboard." He offers Gus a cookie. "Last one for today." Then stuffs the box behind himself.

Marian scrutinizes this. Then she watches Oz dissolving through and into her fruit trees along one of the pretty stone paths. She says curtly, "That boy won't relieve himself in my garden, will he?"

Gordon shrugs. "Maybe. He's nervous of you. Asking to use your house . . . would take the courage of someone who . . . who thought you liked him."

She shivers. She has touched her coffee cup with only her fidgeting fingertips, not yet with her lips.

Her fine old home with its worn-to-oceany-gray plain shingles and dark green trim, low-roofed arches of the long back entryway, swanky-windowed add-ons including the barn-sized sunroom, then those small Englishy dormers in a row, all original on the third floor of the main building. All those complex roofs, tiled with slate impressively mossy. Ivy climbing everywhere. How silent it all is in its weighty beauty and its broad unwelcoming invisible moat.

Gus holds his chubby hand out, palm up, first to Gordon, then to Marian. He may have the Beatles haircut and his mother Lolly's shining Passamaquoddy hair but for a ghostly overlay of his mother's small face, he looks like Gordon, especially like Marian's father's family. He could almost pass as a Depaolo and hurtle into the laughing, scolding, booming Italian fray.

He, Gus, *PLOMB!s* the glass table with the flat of his hand. Marian's coffee sloshes over.

"No more sugar," Gordon says. "Keep your teeth."

"Bish!" shouts the scowling Gus, eyeing both Marian and Gordon.

Marian's eyes widen. "He's talking dirty."

Gordon says, "He's had enough sugar for today."

"I see I've done wrong."

"Absolutely not. All grammies give cookies." He stands up suddenly and grabs Gus a bit too roughly and Gus, startled, howls.

"I came prepared!" Gordon hollers over the yowls of the baby. He flops Gus over his thighs as he settles back into the wicker chair, tugs from a dungarees pocket a child's toothbrush, and begins to dig around in Gus's wide-open screaming mouth.

He can hear Marian calling out between and over the blasts of Gus's distress.

"You shouldn't be so rough with a child that young!" Then, "I should have known better than to offer one of . . . of those people's kids something not made of tofu!"

Gordon looks up. Grinning. "Tofu? You mean that hippie stuff?"

"I'm sorry. Cookies are wrong with you people."

He lowers harnessed Gus and his long trailing rope to the grass, pockets the toothbrush, and says, "Mum, I *saaaiid* you've done nothing wrong! We have desserts all the time!! Mountains of sugar!! But Lolly said *brush his teeth* so I *brush his teeth*!! You used to harp on it all the time yourself!!! *Brush your teeth!!! Brush your teeth!!!* But now it's hippie weirdo hocus-pocus!!! You just *love* to be sad!!!"

It's harder to be heard now because Gus has ramped up his wailing, one finger in his mouth to soothe himself after the brutally crisp brushing. Gordon, still hanging on to his end of the rope, steps to Marian's chair, dragging Gus, and he pulls at Marian's wrist.

"Don't," she snaps. "Do not paw me!"

But when he tugs, she rises. He wraps his free arm around her and teases, "Oh, best and finest mumzy squeezy squeezy kissy kissy!" Gus, now down on his side, is kicking at Gordon's ankles. Gordon says, "Mumzy, your ol' squash brain son is so sorry! We are in dire misunderstanding . . . oh, oops! . . . watch out . . . don't step on him."

Gus is between their feet and ankles biting the rope and kicking indiscriminately. And he is crying. And Marian is crying.

Gordon drops his arm from his mother and looks around. "Mum, what's in the tissue paper on the table?"

Marian is dabbing her nose and each eye. *Snivel-snivel.* "It is a gift for Claire." *Snivel-snivel.*

Gus is up now, hurrying for the cookie box.

Gordon leaps and snatches it.

Gus screams, "BISH!!!"

Marian places the tissue-wrapped object in Gordon's free hand. She tells him, "It's my grandmother's, before she was married. It will fit Claire, I think. When you two were planning your wedding, I couldn't find it for the life of me. Please see that she gets it now."

He digs around in the delicate paper. Emerges with a wide ornate silver ring chunky with many bitty pearls and little sand-sized bits of mother-of-pearl. And maroon things, probably garnets. The initials "M.P." are etched inside.

Yes, Maria Profenno. Ah the Maria stories he has overheard, not from Marian . . . no way Jose! But from the Depaolo unks and cousins. Legendary brawls with her daughters-in-law. Threatened one with a gun down on the waterfront before Portland's Commercial Street and all that area were gentrified. Ripe air. As though the low clouds were made of fish guts. The nights were dark as night, not lighted for dressy shoes.

Yes, Maria Profenno smashed her way, no sneaking for her, through the glass of her son's third-floor apartment . . . having rockingly, side-to-side (she was a fatty) soared up along the fire escape . . . *smash! tinkle! crackle! sizzle! crunch!* . . . pulled Lo Lo (her son's wife) out of bed by the hair. Maria, yes, round and very short, in a grinding-churning-bulldozer-tracks sort of way always won her battles. The sweetly pink but ostentatious ring was Maria's before she became fully Maria . . . before guns and busted glass . . . but those tiny pearls will always feel hot to the touch.

Suddenly he realizes Gus has stopped his racket. He looks down and sees he is . . . uh . . . brushing his teeth! The brush must have flipped out of Gordon's pocket.

Gordon speaks into the clear silence. "This ring means more to me than you can imagine. I accept it with all my love, Mum. And I know Claire will love it. Looks like it'll fit her."

Marian is now watching Oz reappear. She says, "If it doesn't fit, she can just keep it in a special drawer. I want her to know that I, and the family, still think of her. Always."

"Yes," says Gordon with an ugly oily but megavolt bolt of something like depression slamming through the center of him. He sees Oz approaching, the boy's hands limp at his sides, the boy who easily masters great blood-rich god-muscled beasts, seated loose in the saddle and yet in this place he is, to the woman of his own flesh, a blank spot across the green grass except for the fear that he might piss on a tree.

Gus, however, is now standing squarely in front of Marian like a waterfront gunslinger, a midnight window-smasher. He still has his toothbrush in his mouth but turned with the handle in, bristles out. He is smiling seductively. Charm. Yes. Another Italian trait.

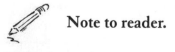

Note to reader.

Don't forget this. It is *Claire* who is supposed to get this ring.

Another delegation of love.

The Weymouth circular driveway is a stilled vortex of parked cars clean and gleaming as new dishware. The late day is sultry, foliage on the overhead boughs hanging like tongues of the dead. Not the sea breeze you'd expect.

An old boxy ass-dragging Settlement car mutters into an opening in the shady bushes.

Argot, the pony-sized gray poodle with human eyes, is not smiling but his panting in the awful heat makes him look as though he is. However, his whole self is flowing with gladness and his life's calling, which is not spelled out in his head in English or the language of thieves. Nor is it praised. But this calling has no hesitation or apology. Here goes . . . he pisses on all four tires of the Settlement car, with his high-raised leg, just as he has marked all the other visitors' cars, including Senator Mary's politically correct economical-on-gas pipsqueak little silvery hatchback with her leathery laptop case on the floor of the front seat.

Once inside the Weymouths' home the air is less hot and floppy. The high ceilings are like cool skies. The Weymouths' newly teenage granddaughter Gretel gives them all her welcoming hugs, even almost-teenage Bard Rosenthal, whom she has never met, but she is captivated by his deep dark eyes burning with his private misgivings and delight due to his privileged place as Gordon's right-hand man today.

Gordon squeezes Gretel's head with just one Mr. Maine-sized arm, which forces out of her tender middle a raw shriek. She gasps to see his heavily bandaged thumb. "Whatever happened!?"

He whimpers. "I was bit by a mountain shark. It attacked me with no provocation. Fortunately, I've already had my rabies shot."

"Oh, Gordon," she swoons. "Your life is turbulent!"

From a future time Claire recalls that day.

We had just gathered ourselves inside that broad entryway when there is Senator Mary, her tight little cap of dark hair almost reflecting the open squares of windows. Her dressy shoes were on the move, *clack! clack!* and there was something of a lightweight suit but it was conservative and made her blend with memory so well there is nothing but her head, feet, and hands I can remember to describe to you.

She moaned that she didn't even have the spare seconds needed for coffee. She had already completed a ten-and-a-half minute press of one of Morse's cool hands in his cheerily yellow walled-off inner sanctum, but Mary was skittering across the clock.

She was now distributing those rubber-stamp cheek pecks to all of us Settlementers and asking after Marian. She said she hadn't seen Marian in a sequoia's age. Gordon said Marian had a new car, sporty, red. She liked to zoom around in it leaving cops and teenagers in the dust. Her brothers and cousins were always stopping in. No one need ever worry about her being bored or lonely.

A few weeks before, we had caught Senator Mary in less of a rush. Gordon and I and a big bunch of Settlementers, Ivy Morelli of the *Record Sun*, and another state senator, Joe Savigneau; we had all run into each other at Portland City Hall following a stirring phantasmal Kotzchmar pipe organ concert.

We found a restaurant that was a good sport about our loud lively kazooing troops. Then out of nowhere, so it seemed, the floor opened and in brimstone and sulfuric flames stepped a hotshot corporate lobbyist who recognized the two senators and who sat with us awhile and pitched friendly jabs at the senators and especially at Gordon. Well, maybe his jabs at Gordon were more prickle than compeer. But every ticking second of that evening in Portland, the music, the politics, from starting gun to finish line, could be considered educational, right? Our shining kids, learning and yearning to learn more! Forget the talk-radio callers who say our kids are cheated. What *is* the definition of the word "education" anyway? The word is a whammy. And here we are today . . . *more! more! more!*

Now Senator Mary was putting into each youngster's hands sky-blue-and-gold flyers for the fall art festival she sits on the board of. "Call that second number . . . or call me. Your gifted family needs to have some entries in this event. Please do it. I've sent you one of these already but . . . as I understand it your mail is suffocating . . . my flyer is somewhere at the bottom." She made a funny face.

We all smiled painful smiles.

But Mary was hiding something. She didn't reveal to us oldsters her top secret collaboration with the soon-to-be up 'n' at 'em True Maine Militia. Yeah, her lips were sealed.

 **And then.**

Gordon gives Claire a look as the kids are carrying the boxes and satchels of Settlement largesse in like a spring runoff brook dividing around him and her, jugs of maple syrup, maple candies shaped like leaves and pursed-lip suns. His look says he is awfully glad she wore that short-sleeved blush-pink summer dress with the embroidered hem and her heavy graying black hair in a single braid down her back. And she runs her eyes over him to drum out a similar mushy love song.

A basket of nicely grimy white potatoes is lugged past. Basket of berry preserves, basket of weedy sneezy soaps, beeswax and animal fat candles big as oatmeal cartons, balsam-needle pillows and pie-sized cloud-white goat cheeses in a cooler.

And now Selene Weymouth's voice, the words only brisk rustles to Gordon, for she has Claire by the arm, and between cartons of green beans and baby pumpkins, Claire evaporates. Into the depths of the Weymouths' majestic ocean house, Claire is being steered by the elbow to Morse.

Meanwhile, back in the front hall, Janet appears. Relieved to see Gordon. Gives him a rocking-side-to-side hard hug. "Oh, your hand! What happened?"

Gordon tells of the rare type of giant mountain quahogs that roam in gangs and rip you with stolen chain saws.

And of course Janet plays along.

Dane and Alyson and Bard, joined by Gretel, make a last trip out into the heat to the big ol' beastie car for the *big* pumpkin still veiled in delicate veins of unripened green. "It can orange up on your doorstep," fourteen-year-old Alyson Lessard advises.

Gretel takes Alyson's elbow as her aunt Selene had taken Claire's. Alyson has left her beloved pet chicken Pooky at home though Pooky would have loved a day out. Alyson herself is flushy-warm-faced, brown-eyed, brown-haired. Her short dark cotton tunic has an embroidered neckline and is worn loose over her long skirt. Moccasins on the feet. Old-world in dress and manners. She bows a lot, not a curtsy, just the head and shoulders, but the effect on people is often remarkable, a kind of sadness, considering how some things time throws away even though they're better muckled onto.

Dane, Gordon's twelve-year-old son (tall as a twenty-year-old), born to Gordon's wife Astrid, has an easy arm swing to his gait, did not inherit the blabbermouth gene, always seems "calm as a cookie." And, though he never bows, he says "Ma'am" and "Sir," almost like a southern boy. He hefts the television-sized pumpkin while everyone else carries the jars of applesauce, one apple pie, and a Settlement-made copper cow.

And Bard? He's got the pie. Yes, he's one of Silverbell Rosenthal's narrow-faced twins. He looks tired. But also hyperaware, like someone who has just climbed out of a manhole after being lost for years in black mazy miles of ancient sewer or subways.

Next morning in the yellow room.

Gordon now sits in a cushioned chair beside Morse's bed in the sunny room with all the yellow-and-white paper, porcelain, wood, and cottony surfaces. The bag of Morse's urine is pretty well hidden under the cumulus-white spread's long hem.

Gordon stands and paces.

He sits on the edge of the bed.

Then he's up again. Gordon does what he does best when feeling tortured. Talk.

He tells jokes. He remembers the OLD DAYS. He is full-throttle yak-yak.

He looks good today, no tired rings around the eyes. No headachy squint. His shirt is faded chambray. His hair and beard are damp from one of the Weymouths' several shower spigots in one of the several modern bathrooms off one of the eight guest rooms, the one he and Claire spent last night in. But maybe he looks awfully troubled because Morse Weymouth's brown eyes, now deep and bulgy, show so little. The eyebrows stand bushier on the ridge of his skull, which presents itself as more skull-like even since yesterday when Gordon saw him first thing, before the meal.

Yesterday, when Gordon had walked into that yellow-and-white room with Sharon, the nurse on duty, Morse had made a distinct "ung" sound. His eyes had moved toward Gordon a time or two, but as if the eyes were heavy boulders.

Today's nurse, Deb, has gone out of the room. It's just Gordon and the dark boulder eyes there on the pillow.

Gordon chatters away to the gravity-flattened bedridden form. "What worries me most is if you're in pure misery *beyond* your misery, but added misery due to being trapped with my blathering. But I have no way to tell. So forgive me if you can't stand this. I'm going to go find somebody who can help me find that Bible you wanted me to read out of last time we were here. So when we do this, just pretend you're listening to the Bible station on the radio, one of the kind that heals with love. Hold on. I'll be right back pronto."

A face in the hall.

Turns out to be Bard in the kitchen doorway. He's listening to Gretel Weymouth, who is telling him about friendly porpoises. She puts a light touch on his upper arm, just as Janet would do in order to rivet you with her soft breathy words and soft breathy eyes. Bard's small blond head turns toward Gordon, who has a white object in his hand.

Gordon gestures to Bard.

Gretel chirps, "Oh, he wants you, Bard."

Bard treads after the door-sized shoulders that slip easy-careful into the sanctified bright room facing east. There's the boom-swishhhh of the sea on the mean-looking rocks outside the open window. There is the sound of nothingness from the rich old guy.

Morse meets God.

So Gordon has the Bible, the one with the white leather cover and the verses still marked as before. And there is Bard.

Morse's eyes don't turn toward the boy or lower to the Bible, but just stay vaguely on the source of noise, Gordon's whiskery mouth.

One of the embroidered markers is at the Revelation.

Gordon is thinking how Morse has always been a sort of socially liberal capitalist, gradually becoming outraged at certain warts on the capitalist critter's face, and angry at certain players. He wasn't into basic system change like what Gordon pines for. Whatever *that* is. Gordon can't imagine one yet. "You've got a Cinderella faith in the humans," Gordon once told Morse. And Morse agreed. But whatever it was that made Morse who he was, he was not Mr. Fire and Brimstone Fundamentalist Bible believer. He never mentioned God or Bible verses even lightly.

But Gordon . . . well, he never uses the God words much, either . . . but there is the Power that haunts him, argues with him when he is alone. And there are times when Gordon, alone, thumbs through the Bible, and in his hands, it's electric! stinging his palms, one of the oldest records of the human heart and head, the human storm and all its terrors, from on high that wrath of clouds, and from within, as it was. As it izzzz. As it forever shall be.

Here and now, with his dying friend, his childhood hero, Gordon reads the old English translation's rhythms of the never-ending threat of humans versus humans.

Now and then he acts out very funny commercials from "Radio Churchland." No reaction from Morse, no smile. The quieter Morse gets, the wilder Gordon gets. But how can Morse get any quieter? There's no guarantee that Morse hears any of this performance. But Bard, whose name does not signify quietness, is listening. How to navigate his life hereon? Can you learn anything from Gordon's outrageous nerved-up well-meant antics?

Bard eyes Gordon tugging a pastel lavender sheet from the white louvered linen closet to wear like a God robe, the hooded kind, one hand held aloft with the open Bible, the chambray cuff of his work shirt showing and his big bandaged thumb pressed against the word *Holy* on the clean white leathery book's cover. In slow loud enormous booms of his always deep big-guy voice, Gordon says, "GOD SPEAKETH!"

No reaction from Morse.

Bard now stares at his own foot.

Gordon steps closer to the bed, lays the book on the chair. He leans in, places both hands over Morse's heart. It is beating beautifully.

Gordon now speaks in his plain ordinary voice, "My old friend. Everything you have ever done pleases me . . . uh, I mean God. You made the polluters mad. You made Ms. Forest Products almost wet herself once, and those fuckers with LD#34 blah blah. They were shits. Fuck 'em. God loved how you kicked their asses. Trees love you. Water loves you. Air loves you. Bugs love you. Moose love you. Soil loves you. The sea loves you. These *are* the face of God."

Gordon stands, straightening his back. He squints toward the window with the great big yellow triangle of sunlight on the rug in front of it. He glances at Bard. Bard just stares down at his feet.

Gordon turns back to look into Morse's unshining eyes. He says, "One of the first times I remember you was in those days when I used to go up to Augusta with Uncle Tommy . . . long before the term limits. Every time his term was up, he'd get out all his old signs and reuse 'em. I remember they were orange and blue. Light orange cuz they were faded. Then the term limits got voted in. For a while he'd switch back and forth. House. Senate. House. Senate. Two complete sets of signs. Same three suits. And way back there even before *that* I remember all that about saving Bigelow Mountain, making it a preserve. Tommy against. Governor was against. And you were *for*. And as it turned out, the Maine people were *for*. I remember you as the guy with all the teeth. I remember you smiling at Tommy like a cartoon cat. I thought you were kind of scary. Maybe Senator Tommy Depaolo thought you were scary, too . . . that smile. I'd give the world to see that smile now. Shit."

Bard feels the sea beating and shivering in the wall behind his back. He smells the ruthless cold slosh of life through the open windows.

Gordon rearranges his God costume so that now just his short dark beard pokes out of it. He again places his hands on Morse's chest, the thin flannel fabric, the warm chest. Bard's eyes are now riveted on this, the soft silly give of the chest. And Bard, who knows devils, who has been descended upon by devils and their heat and their privileged law, their black Kevlar and handcuffs, their black midnights, their breaking of a woman's bones, the cancellation of her screaming eye, the screaming dogs, the punching of bullets, this Bard, this broken-in-the-middle young boy who is going to be "all right," they say, tries to wrap his searching mind around *wealth*. Because at the moment *wealth*'s preciousness, its shield, even in its own domain, doesn't exist.

Soon the spectral guest arrives.

Now the streaky-blond-haired and hush-voiced Janet Weymouth suggests, to the gray-haired almost silent woman Margaret, wine for herself and Gordon. Claire and Selene Weymouth are treading the purring beach in the hot evening dusk with too many leering and closing-in clouds.

Gretel tells Alyson and Dane and Bard that she won a computer that "does too much" and she wants to give it to the Settlement as it would be just right for them. "Mimi says the Settlement isn't online yet." ("Mimi" is Janet.)

Alyson glances at Gordon, who is testing on Janet one of his big philosophical (way out there) ideas about why humans seem to be *un*able to have more than 100 or 150 people in their circle of relationships and responsibility.

Janet says, "It's called relational ratio." She reaches for Gordon's big wounded right hand and asks, "Why, dear friend, do you suppose humans are so prone to war? How easy war is to declare when outside a hundred people, it's just concept, not the urgency of the heart? Perhaps this is why humans will never evolve beyond beastly governments and war. Relational ratio is not flexible. It's in the design. As the brain is on top, the stomach is in the middle, the feet are below. Nose above the mouth. Ears on the sides." Janet has definitely begun to lose her exalting faith in the humans to dig themselves out of the proverbial "hole." Once this was not so. For instance, a few weeks ago.

Argot crosses the carpet ever so lightly and sits next to Dane but stares at Janet, as though waiting for stage directions in this most uneventful theater piece. However, quite suddenly, the floor rumbles. And the walls, too.

Who is the fearsome guest who will soon be on the doorstep?

Bard's eyes widen. Like those of a war vet with PTSD. He is, as we know, a drug war vet. "Uh-oh," says Gretel.

Gretel and Alyson are the same age or thereabouts. Gretel is a small person with an aristocratic bearing, while Alyson is a bit taller, soft-shouldered with a balmy expression and callused hands from hauling shit buckets, tossing hay bales, milking goats. Gretel says not to worry, that if the power goes off, the backup system will kick in. "We have relied on the backup six times this summer. Before this summer, I don't think it was ever necessary . . . just for the ice storm. And now fall! There seems to be no relief in sight! All that climate change business." She shivers prettily and yet not without the crisp authority natural to the denizens of her class.

Janet stands up, eyes twinkling. Argot's eyes stare twinkling into Janet's eyes. Maybe Janet and Argot have a plan. Two lovably villainous characters in this theater piece that is getting more interesting. Janet switches off two lamps and then the wall switch (the dimmer kind) for the small chandelier. "There!"

Everyone laughs. Even Bard, a low chortle.

"Oh, Mimi!" the granddaughter scolds breathlessly. She whispers to Margo, "Mimi's schemes bring only the illusion of continuous danger. Really we're safe."

Doors softly *thwomp* shut as Selene and Claire are back, hurrying to another room, the library it sounds like. Selene is talking to a third person. Must be her cell phone?

Then.

Another deep-earth deep-sky rumble and three dining-room windows dance with light.

It is decided that Janet's group will go to the next room, the one with the eighteen big windows, and watch the "show." Janet goes ahead to snap off lamps there, too. She's wearing a pale short-sleeved summery dress which makes her look ghosty. When the others reach the big room, they find her standing there in the dark. She is the singular pale blue eddy of light.

Argot, so very light-footed for so large a dog, enters the room behind all the others; he is a spirit, too, but quite a nice huggable gray.

The thunder and lightning are getting bigger and closer too fast.

The ocean is distressed. Wind rattles even this grand house, makes it seem cardboardy.

"How small we are," Janet observes. She keeps standing there with her hands folded, still looking mischievous when the lightning accentuates her face, but maybe it's only really creaturely fear.

Gretel Weymouth slips from a small adjacent room just as a spooky Bach fugue begins to trumpet and tremble from hidden speakers in the walls.

Dane St. Onge makes four kazoos appear, holds one out to Gretel.

She laughs. Gretel, like Janet, is dressed in a pastel summery sort of thing and her hair is light of color, yes, ghost-color, and so it is as if she brings more supernaturalness into this room, more angel luck.

"Kazoos will change the atmosphere!" worries Gretel. "Kazoos are too . . . too good-natured. Too lovable." She laughs. "We want scareeeeee." She laughs. She laughs. She laughs. "Kazoos are—"

"A challenge." Janet finishes the sentence. "You have to work harder for the proper effect."

Alyson says happily, "I have always thought kazoos sound like bee people."

As a kazoo is pushed into Bard's fingers, his sentinel dark eyes smirk. He watches Alyson and Dane raise the instruments to their lips. He does as they do.

The walls and windows flash and shake with the brute light and the taut intermissions of blackness. Inside and outside, the contrasts test the eyes of all persons, human and dog. The kazoos buzz. They swarm.

Gordon is deathly quiet, staring not at the windows but at each of the shadowy faces around him. The weird light-and-dark distorts and makes his beard grayer, his eyes deeper and closer together, nose bigger. The pipe organist in the walls pumps and pounds and presses out Bach's highest and most earnest intentions and beliefs and certainties while the kazoos caper.

Now with the storm right on top of them, the tide wrapped around them, around the house, everything glistens blackly *out there*. The many windows don't lie.

Bach ends.

Gretel Weymouth steps into the other room to start something else. Ravel of course.

Margaret brings the wine but Gordon says, "Thank you, but—" and shakes his head.

Janet hugs him a long while. Gordon hugs back. It's as though they're dancing but caught in stillness, like humid trees.

Argot sits. He stands. He sits.

"We should be lying on the floor," advises Dane. "Lightning comes from earth and meets with conditions in the sky . . . ionized . . . uh . . . or something. The electromagnet thing . . . or something."

Alyson adds, "Yeah, conditions invite the electricity, which is always below."

Bard is thinking, *Lightning loves hollow trees, pine, popple*. But he is, as we know, not outgoing in groups so this wisdom goes unshared, just stays filed a couple of inches behind his yellow bangs.

"We have lightning rods," Janet soothes them, her voice nearly a whisper against Gordon's shoulder, and now Gretel steps close, too, and so Janet's arms go around both figures, a very full embrace, while she suspends her glass of wine at her fingertips and hides her tears.

Another crackle of sound and light and Gordon sinks to the floor, arranges himself spread-eagle.

Alyson laughs and joins him, stretching out alongside him as best she can against the X of his spread-eagle body.

Argot steps lightly to them and sits with his rear against Alyson's feet, his eyes still on Janet.

Gretel stretches out alongside Alyson.

Now Dane.

Janet laughs silkily. "Better safe than sorry. Come on, Bard, our new friend. Be not a temptation to the gods of levin." She swallows his left wrist with her left hand. He drops to the carpet.

Janet places her glass of wine on the nearest windowsill and then joins everyone. At first she sits next to Gordon, knees up, arms around her shins.

Music by Lewis Spratlan now lumbers out of the walls. Big music. "How grand we are!" Gretel exclaims, then sighs.

"How small I am," Janet says breathlessly. She is now on her back, arms at her sides, corpselike.

On the windowsill, the glass of wine suddenly lights up. It shivers deep red. It's the only color of livingness against the black and white of the immeasurable abyss beyond it.

Janet says in a sudden way, sneaking up on her subject, "Gordon, I still hear from Donna Frazier. I think she has the hots for you."

"Mimi!" a delicate but reverberating shriek from Gretel. "Some people are relaxed by wine. Not my Mimi. She becomes controversial."

"Gretelmunk, I have had only *one* swallow. But maybe it was the coffee cake."

Gretel tsks happily.

Crash! CRACKLE! BOOOOOM! Seems as though this house is about to be flung off from its wet lonesome Cape Elizabeth rock. The Settlement people are speechless, not used to the benefit of lightning rods.

Argot stares unwaveringly at his mirror image of prankish grace, Janet.

"Donna Frazier would probably send a private plane here right now to get our Gordon for herself while the Honorable Governor husband was off on some overnight Montana hunting trip."

Gretel groans. "Mimi, somebody needs to subdue you."

Gordon says nothing.

"Who's Donna Frazier?" Dane asks in a somewhat low uncracking voice.

"One of thirty-two governors' wives whom Gordon and company stunned with the truth earlier this month. They had their deepmost intuitions confirmed. Their bubbles were popped, summarily pierced."

"Meeeeemeeeee!" Gretel pretends to fume.

"I am speaking of the bubbles of illusion in which they live."

Bard has no idea what this talking is about. They're just words in a dry pile on the expensive rug between them. Although he has heard around the Settlement recently about the monkey presentation to a bunch of governors' wives, he just can't picture it.

"Gordon hates lightning," says Alyson with tenderness.

Gordon doesn't dispute this.

"Gordon is a chicken," she teases and reaches to tug at his shirt where it lies upon his tensed ribs.

"Rooster," Janet corrects her.

"Mimi!" Gretel exhales full-lung-sized indignation.

Janet insists, "Gretelmunk, I'm just trying to steer this conversation back to his presentation at the Dumond House, how a little follow-up would—"

"It's just co-optation," says Gordon.

"You've changed your argument!" Janet scolds him. "You *were* saying that they were just treating you as a trained animal . . . dancing bear, you said. I think co-optation may be more like what it is. Morse would definitely agree. Though I do not rule out that some were drawn to you as a charismatic individual. Don't worry, my dear beautiful friend, I will never pester you to go to Montana and make Donna happy."

"The Dumond House is excessive," says Gretel. "It looks like an auction warehouse. Meghan's recital was there. There was no room for the humans with all the antiques and *junk*."

"Yes," says Janet. "It's a special place."

Gordon is silent, braced for more lightning and more references to his "talk" and the governors' wives.

Dane says, "Gordo, there were FBI guys there, right?"

"Just the routine sort," Janet offers cautiously.

"Routine as dish soap," Gordon says grumpily.

Bard has right along suspected that there were weird depths to the monkey skit day but due to the flow of this conversation his blood feels sort of jazzy as if he suspects he's part of some giant conspiracy. His fingers tighten possessively around the solidly made wooden kazoo. From here to Montana, governors are having urgent meetings to deflect the power of the Weymouths and the St. Onges and maybe the lady senator that was here, the one with all the kisses. Yes, this is BIG and he is part of it, Gordon's right-hand man.

Whatever it was that Janet was about to say, she swallows it as there goes: *CRACKLE! CRINKLE! HISS-BOOOOOOM!!!!* Everything in the room is whitened while the room's living occupants flare like dog-shaped and human-shaped flashcubes. Big murderous sound of electricity splitting raggedly up through the atmosphere but nobody even mildly screams. Janet has folded her hands comfortably (or funereally) over her middle and speaks as warmly as ever. "Did I tell you that Pam Anderson asked if I would send her a tape of your talk? And all the commotion of the darling monkeys in the background."

Gordon's eyebrows go up, unseen in the uneasy darkness. "You have a *tape* of it?"

"An audiotape, oh, yes. I'll have Jerry Arnold send you one. He has the master. I'm sorry, it slipped my mind."

"Well—"

Gretel interrupts, or rather begins talking at the same time as Gordon has said *Well*, "What was your talk about, Gordon?"

"I never *gave* my talk," says he.

Janet whispers, "The talk he planned to give starts with the first Maine people mooning the French explorers."

In the dark, Gretel tsks. "*Mimi* would remember."

"And there are Trojan horses, pink lights, Beaver Cleaver, and a bushy-tailed fox," Janet adds.

BOOOOOOOM! Crackle! This with a live-sounding tearing shriek and something huge and metal being crinkled up in a giant hand.

"Jeeeeepers!" cries Alyson. "*That* was close."

"Lightning rods! Lightning rods! Oh, thank you, lightning rods!" Gretel sings.

Bard finally opens up. "Lightning tends to pass through conduits, wells, chimneys, and hollow parts of trees."

Gretel agrees. "It blew my uncle's pine tree into splinters. It was like two-by-sixes all over his yard."

"Poor baby woodpeckers," says Alyson softly.

Janet says, "Thunderstorms remind me of the pre-pre-*preeeee* Pleistocene Epoch."

"You remember prehistory, my old Mimi?" Gretel teases.

"Oh, yes. It was a lovely era. Ice, air, and disorder."

"Mimi, you're beautiful," sighs Gretel.

"Thank you, G.W."

Gretel sits up. "Where is the tape of Gordon trying to give a speech with monkeys taking the upper hand? I'll play it now while we're all in danger."

Gordon clears his throat. "Let's not."

Janet reaches and pats Gordon's hand. "Gordon says no. Let's obey his wishes."

Gordon says, "Gretel, let's hear you play that kazoo again."

She giggles. "Next time you're here. I need to practice. I want to get *I Wonder as I Wander* down perfectly for Christmas. I'll dedicate it to you, Gordon."

"I'm honored."

Janet pats Gordon's hand again. "You *will* come back at Christmas. I'll ease off on my references to the Dumond House talk. I would die if you stopped being my friend because I didn't know when I had crossed some line. And after all, it's not lost on me that you're sensitive about that day, but more importantly, that you're sensitive to the predicament of this world . . . Gordon, you're too awesome for this world."

Gretel says, "Mimi, awesome is a kid word."

"Before it became a kid word," Janet tells them all, "it was a word pertaining to things larger than life, and deeper than life."

"A Moses word," observes Gordon with a snort of pleasure.

Alyson pats Gordon's shoulder.

The next *crackle-BOOOOOoooooooommmmm!* of heart-quickening sound and fluttering light is so close to the windows they trill and rattle chinkily. And within the edges of what seems a universe-sized wall of sheet metal being shaken at the exact moment as that blast of TOTAL light is framed between the blind black impendingness of the next awful whiteness, there standing in the doorway, in chittery light-show fantasia, is the face and form of Bruce Hummer.

The storm finally stomps away.

Under two stained-glass light fixtures, the Weymouths' two bustling kitchen people are setting out napkins and plates and silverware in the next room in susurrant readiness for the pageant that the Weymouths have always called food. *Snack* is not in their vocabulary. Here we have on the long table crabmeat salad to go with chewy bread. Funny cheeses, funny cheese sauces. Tureens of lobster bisque. Trays of roasted vegetables of every color under the sun. Smoked mussels, smoked bluefish, smoked turkey, funny little toasts and crackers. Fruits cut to look like blossoms. Large but slender slices of melt-in-the-mouth orange cake. Wines with names only Argot can pronounce and mixed drinks if you so desire.

Claire sits across from Gordon and Bruce, her round old-timey glasses reflecting the milk-and-honey and sun-yellow squares of the stained-glass lamps above. But nothing can obscure the black black penetration of her eyes, especially if you're not forthcoming.

Bruce asks Janet questions about Morse's condition.

Gordon eats noisily.

Claire has wound her braid into a lumpy gleaming bun before coming to the table.

Bruce has turned toward her and puts on the charm. She replies to his questions and smiles at his jokes but she's struck dumb in her guts by the fact of him.

Selene Weymouth's husband and son have arrived in time to find places at the table and dig in. The traffic between Boston, Massachusetts, and Cape Elizabeth, Maine, was like a heavy miles-long soldered-together art installation made of found objects, Selene's husband reports.

After the meal there are hushed one-at-a-time and two-at-a-time pilgrimages to Morse's yellow room.

Henry, about fifteen but broader-shouldered and shorter in the legs than Bard, says he has memorized "all the secret passageways of this castle." For instance, the little back hall and door to the perfectly shabby room with the TV and box of video games. He leads the way.

Well, the video player seems out of order.

They poke through the shelves of board games and books. Henry locates a teakwood treasure chest. "Wait till you see this," he whispers mysteriously and lugs it to the antique table that's draped with a paper map of the arctic and scattered with penciled lists. Henry lowers the treasure chest to a stool. Inside are foot-tall chess pieces and a board with green-blue and teal-blue tile squares as large as pieces of sandwich meat. Unfolded, the board covers almost the whole table.

"You have to stand and heave hove every time you make a move," Henry says with a laugh and a sigh of irritated reverence. "It's ridiculous."

Bard's eyes are wide on the tallest piece.

"Neptune," Henry tells him.

The king, a god really, grips his trusty signature trident. Beard like Niagara Falls but not enough to curtain the roiling muscles of his naked self. His crown is spiked with six short harpoons.

The queen gets Niagara Falls–like hair for the head, which does not quite accomplish giving her naked self much modesty, but she's a mermaid so she has less to cover. Both king and queen have seaweed necklaces. The queen holds a trident, too, not to be outgunned by Mr. N. She sits erect of spine on a pope's-hat-shaped rock, undiminished by the weight of the sea. Bishops are octopuses. Knights are mermen wrapped snakelike around and upon giant sea horses. Rooks are lighthouses. Pawns are everybody else: lobster, crab, squid, a tuna, a shark, a porpoise, seal, baby whale, clam, and so forth, all small.

Each piece is crafted of some sort of glass that looks like mother-of-pearl, stirring with those oily colors as each hefty figure is handled. Half are heavy on deep blues, the other half more pastels, like peach and pink and polite sort of you-go first sea-mist greens. The weighty bases of all the pieces are ringed in pearls. For real? Doubtful. Not in a kids' den room.

Bard fondles a lighthouse. "I've played chess before . . . but it was a long time ago."

Henry tips his head with a kindly and maybe a little bit kingly twinkle in his eye. "A refresher course is in order. We shall refresh!"

They pull up chairs.

Meanwhile.

Out in the kitchen Tasha and Jessica, both in the Weymouths' employ, wash and wipe all platters and utensils, kettles and saucepans and work areas dearly as if blessing it all.

Gordon has offered to take Argot out on the beach if he can find his right-hand man. He stands under the blazing kitchen lights riffling through the big drawer where Janet assured him there was a stash of flashlight batteries. He and the two young women are teasing back and forth about which is worse, summer or winter.

Turns out grandson Henry Weymouth Austin is missing, too, so Gordon does the math and gives up on Bard as a dog-walking companion.

Bruce now returns out of the hallway from Morse's room, sees Gordon, and joins him with a lament in his muddy green-brown eyes. He picks up a greasy butcher knife, holds it pointed up. "Hey, Gordon. You see another one of these around?"

Gordon studies the hand, the knife, Bruce's face with the brown Rex-like mustache around a mouth that is braced bitterly against his teeth.

"Find one, Gordon. Let's go in there and put our friend out of his misery."

The two young women look at each other, then appear to forget what they've just heard.

Gordon rubs his beard, thinking how it is to watch a fellow creature crushed in the middle of the road. He has wondered since he first got here yesterday why not an extra blast of morphine? He's sure the Weymouth family members have pondered all their options. *They* would have options. *They* would not be shackled by the law as most of us would be. He guesses they have decided to just go with nature's flow, trusting that nature is not the cruel mother Gordon believes her to be. He sighs. "With a good knife sharpened to a hair's width and an applied stroke to the carotids and jugular while the creature is distracted, it's so fast and painless, some see it as a sacred act." He sighs again. "But this, as you know, brother, isn't in our hands tonight."

Bruce lowers the knife. One of the young women has her eye on him. "You know I was joshin'. Sort of. But . . . a thing like that is maddening to see. Mercy. It's like a fire truck heading out to do the right thing, lights, bells, horns, sirens . . . then you just crash into a big ol' brick wall."

The gift.

Bruce offers to go along to the dark beach below the massive outcropping of rocks upon which the Weymouth house is enthroned. Argot is the first to reach the sand while Bruce remarks, "I wasn't expecting to see you tonight. Janet never mentioned that you all would be here. I consider it a meaningful coincidence." He laughs. "Not that I'm superstitious. But there's a continuum . . . to our . . . conversation that is heavier than rain and other scientifically proved principles."

Gordon says, "I've known Janet since I was born. I would consider this one of her schemes. She's a fun sort of girl."

Bruce laughs again, inhales lustily of the oceany air.

Argot is illuminated in the swish of both flashlight beams, his tall gray poofed hat and trimmed ears and his humanlike eyes full of more devilry and goofiness than when he's being host within the Weymouths' tawny and sepia and staunch gray interiors. He playfully varooms away out of the stage lights' clarifying range.

Bruce's flashlight is the new LED type. Stings your eyes. Cuts into your brain. But nice and light to carry. Suddenly he halts. "I have something for you, Mr. Militia." He frisks his pockets, dress shirt, and dress pants, the pants a lukewarm but costly gray, the shirt with stripes of a more wraithy gray, when you could see them back under significant Weymouth lights. Here on the beach, no moon, three stars. All is a metallic blue-black with spritely flashes and wan mirages.

Like a haiku writer, Gordon is thinking in a tired choppy way. All excess is swept away tonight. Even Weymouth formalities are blasted to smithereens by the queer suffusion of death's threshold.

Gordon hears keys. Bruce's space-alien blue LED beam is working to identify something. Now the slipping off of one key from a small ring. He says drolly, "You've got the key to my summer place but I forgot this one. It's my place in New York."

Gordon says, "Right."

"Just in case you guys get serious . . . you need access. I'll tell the doorman to expect you all." He steps forward and presses the key, smaller than that broad golden one Gordon already has, into his palm. "You see, Mr. Militia, things are ramping up with all us war merchants and State Department ghouls . . . and especially the spooks God bless 'em, and all sorts of hapless assistants, mafia, and funnymen. You need to make your move fast, *all* of you on the side of righteousness."

Gordon says stiffly, "Thanks a million, old friend."

Bruce's flashlight goes off.

They walk on through the metallic sheen with only Gordon's old-timey big golden polka dot of light chafing along on the sand.

Gordon chills with a present-feeling flashback of how when bikers come out of the dark and begin to crumple the freshness and innocence out of you . . . and then you get lapped and smooched by the sea, you realize what your true weight in this world is, how gravity and contention will always stalk you.

But now, though there is danger, there is nothing solid he can run from. As in a third-rate movie, the evil is a withered mummy, dust, and writhing bandages. Nothing is really there!! And besides, he is too contaminated to separate himself from the mummy's reach.

So they walk. In a sort of elderly way. The packed wet sand feels good underfoot, against Gordon's work boot soles and Bruce's dress shoes, there where the tide has punched and thundered upon the whole coastline, then pulled disdainfully away from all the human-made desecration. From the night sky looking down if you were up there, there are so many lights in America it looks like pink jelly. The Weymouths' wee share of coastline is just a black blink, an erasure. The heat of two men and one giant poodle is even less than nothing.

This is different from when they partied in the truck cab at the airport and got cidered up. Now, in this clearer state Gordon is even less certain of what it is that Bruce Hummer is doing to him and what his own defensive moves should be. If it is anything, it is Bruce making fun of him, mocking the common man's small efforts to stay off his knees. If . . . It . . . Is . . . Anything. Okay then, for now he just swings his arms and strides along, counting four more stars that have crawled out from the unbundling clouds.

After a bit Argot reappears, exactly as a full-moon-sized nauseating smell slaps the faces of the two men.

Both flashlights strike out at the source.

It's a dead seagull, cooking in its own juices, dripping and percolating with helpful carrion beetles around both sides of Argot's jaws.

"Stay off!!! You bozo!" Gordon hoots, pushing out with his boot into Argot's chest.

Bruce is giggling ghoulishly.

The dog circles them, then tries again to present his gift.

With more of his Alabama drawl than anyone lately has heard from him, Bruce says, "Take it away, sir. No more fermented seaside-themed gourmet dishes tonight! We are right full. Take it back to the cooks, my good man!"

Next day on the road going home, Gordon driving, Bard in the front seat with him, Dane and Alyson and Claire in the back seat.

Silence of the humans. The old sedan speaks, creaks, chirps, and growls. An echo in Bard Rosenthal's head. Of his chess game with Henry Weymouth Austin and easy talk, but especially of the lady, Janet, in the storm, sort of whispering, "How small we are."

End of another day.

Oh, but there is no end to a hay day. Two crews are still stacking bales, the bales heavy, the scent transportive, hayseed creaturely. Another crew is due on board after dusk to finish the remaining truckloads and ox wagons that are lined up between the barns all the way into the first curve of tractor path in the two near fields. Last crop of the year. All is right with the world.

Gordon is with his damp rowdy crew heading toward the Quad. Chubby scent-pillows roll along with them, not the scent of the fury and hurl of the sea but that of the Settlement's humbly managed bounty. The crew's approach to the big screened piazzas is hungry and hurried because supper, too, is in the air. There is no air today that lacks smell or flavor or memory.

Gordon's bunch of keys on his belt loop sings.

Among these singing keys is the one Bruce Hummer had pressed into his hand on that dark night. Small, tarnished. This Gordon could see once he had a moment near the lamp by the bed of the Weymouths' guest room he and Claire shared. And no, it is not a key to Bruce Hummer's snazzy Manhattan apartment. It's an old post office key.

Claire remembering.

Before we left for home, we were all out there by our old jalopy, older and more forlorn than the cars and trucks of the Weymouths' gardeners, kitchen people, and nurse, which were gathered in the lot beyond the trees.

Janet, powdery and all swan-grace, and yet mischievous as always in the eyes and almost rebellious-looking in her sweater and jeans, was hugging and rocking our Dane and telling him, "You'll win lots of hearts. Be merciful."

I know I caught her off guard with, "Janet, how did you and Morse become friends with Bruce Hummer? Isn't he one of those dragons in the middle of the path of shareholder activists' most earnest knights in shining armor? He's . . . you know . . ." I sort of chuckled. ". . . Not . . . not . . ." I couldn't think of a word that wasn't belligerent.

She stood back from Dane but still held his wrist. The pupils of her eyes were square on mine. There was no shame in her gaze. "He and Richard* were friends at Bowdoin. He was a boy once, you see. A complicated young person . . . maybe lacerated on the inside . . . by *difference*. A difference I still today can't describe. It can be easily confused with *in*difference. But we got terribly attached to him and as you know, such a thing is often a two-way lane. He is our . . ." Now she seems stuck.

"Secret?" Gordon fills in for her.

She closes her eyes. And nods.

See the mutinous hand arranging gourmet sneaker-smelling cheeses and peppercorn crackers, two bottles of wine, both red. Not hard cider in a grubby plastic jug. Not "giraffe piss," which is what she, Professor Catherine Court Downey, has overheard Gordon calling cheap-brand store-bought beer.

This is the night. She knows in her heart what a worthy educational tool television can be. A blazonry of knowledge will arch across this broad valley prison so that as changelings these shackled redneck women and various others will rise from the lead weight of Gordon St. Onge's hand and flutter to the skies.

* Her and Morse's son.

The videotape she now turns in her hands is about AIDS and HIV. So much misinformation to undo. She samples a cracker and waits.

There they are now, climbing the stairs almost on tiptoe, her secret little flock.

They seat themselves in the two little rows of folding chairs. A teenage boy, Jaime Crosman, is designated lights operator . . . off go the lights!!!!

The screen bursts to life under Catherine's liquidly graceful hand on the remote panel.

And yes there is other sneakiness. From a future time then fifteen-year-old Samantha Butler recollects.

In true covert militia fashion, for this particular set of actions we decided to meet in the shadows. We gathered in the nighttime woods just beyond the sap house. We had three significant items on the agenda.

Item number one. What to do about our Mrs. Bree, who had gone AWOL on us since Gordon's tantrum up at Kirky's table town room. According to our star witness, Cory, it was intense.

Item number two. Go over the whole list of contacts we'd made for the big Lincoln surprise. Lincoln would be the True Maine Militia's grand opening. Cut the ribbon please!

Item number three was to maintain communication with Senator Mary for the statehouse siege. Or "Operation Corporate Sluts."

You can see we were not like Rexy-poo's militia. What we were about was to educate and organize America! To save the WORLD!!! This needs to be done through the Honey Principle, one of Bree's terms. And what famous person was it who said *Revolution should be irresistible?* So bring out the feasting, singing, and bunny-hop. Bring out theatrics!!

From a future time Oceanna St. Onge looks back on that night.

Both the Rosenthal twins, Bard and Eden, were in attendance. They were two of the best True Maine Militia members, full of cunning and ardor. And they could keep a straight face even while being tortured, having had their basic training by the crinkling disfiguring horrors of Drugwarlandia. Because, see, they were still smooth and cute on the outside. Actually, the solar buggy lights put all of us in a rather attractive and silky profile. And the primacy of our mission added that little shiver of the *beatific.*

Dee Dee, our wise-ass dear uphill Lancaster neighbor, was on her throne of quilts, more pregnant by the minute, less her bouncy self by the minute, resembling more one of our recent Blue Seal grain bags of fan mail. Her hub, Gordon's third cousin Lou-EE St. Onge, our honorable artillery officer, was still with one of the hay crews jamming bales into those last deep spaces of the ridge field barn, floodlit in and out as bright as the beach by wind-power magic. So he was not on hand to stand around and be his nothing-to-say statuesque self. But he would be our majestic man during our major EVENT that would take place after the statehouse action.

There were fifteen of us present in this particular muster, counting Cannonball, the gleamy-eyed stoic Scottie dog sharing the quilt throne with Dee Dee.

Dog okay, but no little humans. Not one exception. For intense strategy meetings the risk was that when tykes leave they immediately tell everything. And as the old saying goes, Loose lips sink ships.

Whitney was in mid-word, reporting the good news about WERU's *sweet* cooperation on the Lincoln action, when suddenly *Kerpow! Kerpow! Kerpow! Kerpow! Kerpow!*

Alyson Lessard looking back.

Gunfire. It seemed to be coming from the direction of that sandy bank behind the Quonset huts. Oz and Termite both at the same time killed their solar buggy headlights.

From out of the future Whitney St. Onge tells us.

The headlights that illuminated our all-important meeting snapped off. And then we saw it. You can never imagine it if you have not been in the woods at that precise *time* of year, that precise hour of the clock, maybe even that precise *year*, the moon's noon pouring down in a solid but oh-so-feathery God-pillar of silver, pure smoldering sorcery. We were stunned to a more august silence.

Alyson again.

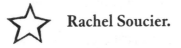

Across the little lane and rocky opening stood the sap house, its steel roof glowing weirdly.

No wind. No stir. Not like a photo but like something compelled to hold its breath.

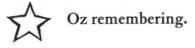

Rachel Soucier.

Smaller pillars were here and there and little rills of Tinker Bells. But mostly it was bottomless blackness, fright but not *evil* fright, more a jumbo-sized reverence, that way you fathom your precious luck, by which you know you were chosen *to be there*. You could have missed it! You could have been in an open field, on an open highway, a city street, a suburban patio with just the big flat papery moon pasted to the ordinary sky and the vast open earth as smooth as cement.

Or you could have been too early! Or too late! It's true, twenty minutes would change everything.

A single tree toad peeped wobbly, rubbery, as crazed by the sight as we were.

The echoes of gunfire were long sucked into the earth. There was only the electrifying calm.

Oz remembering.

Eventually, our secret meeting recommenced.

From a future time Professor Catherine Court Downey testifies.

It certainly was fear that made the Settlement people unable to keep secrets from that creature. So *he* found out.

The AIDS documentary was nearly to the credits when we heard him storming up the stairs and all his keys jangling . . . like a team of sleigh horses. He didn't knock, just poured his whole avalanche-sized self in and ordered two of *my* boy guests to lug *my* television outdoors and shoot it!! With a bandaged hand he gave over to the boys the key to a drawer of ammunition!! Teenage boys!! Imagine the recklessness of allowing teenage boys such access!!

The next day I walked alone to where I was told the television set was. There it sat. Just a frame and shards and all those toxic electronic components dangling or scattered. Can you imagine that sort of lunacy!! Can you imagine such resistance to knowledge. Barefoot, pregnant, and of flat-earth beliefs; that was the rule he'd imposed on not just his wives, but everybody. And with all those guns and bullets in his personal keeping, who would question his authority?

There by the ruined TV in the gray hush of a humid dark dangerous-feeling day, I began to tremble. Till that very moment I felt I had been free to leave, to move back to Portland anytime, my son and myself. But as I stood there, head bowed, I knew that I, too, was being held hostage, that violence surrounded me like the rotation of an immense sea storm. One step back toward Portland and he would know it. All eyes were his.

Beth St. Onge looking back on that summer.

So then along came the phone bill. The professor had made calls on Gordon's phone all over the whole friggin' globe, mostly to her soon-to-be-ex-husband whose business was, yes, everywhere. She was not placing change or bills or even I-owe-yous in the toll call can on Gordon's desk.

To the Winter Kitchen wall up here at the Settlement, Gordon nailed the bill with its long dangling opened-out pages, *seven* of them, and a note:

Anybody who puts their hands on the Settlement phone again to make a bill that looks like this will have their hands hacked off with an ax.

And so, finally, Ms. Court Downey took her kid and left and I was one of them who witnessed with my own peepers her driving away. You see a face like that and those two hands high and square on the wheel, the sand kicking up under the little politically correct tires, and you aren't friggin' blind, you see and you comprehend about fifty square miles wide around her, that bloom of revenge.

Clair sorrows over her friend's departure.

Catherine was gone. And her darling four-year-old Robert whom we all loved, especially Gordon. Yes, Catherine gone, Robert gone. Gordon had been far more patient with doubly difficult persons so it was still an unsolved mystery to me why he couldn't have some tenderness for Catherine, who, more than at any other time in her life *needed* us all and *needed* the arms of these foothills, the rooty paths with mossy ridges stippled by light and shadow, and by trees so old they had faces, while suckers waggled on stumps and always there the waist-high fern, little bridges over sassy brooks and dry spring-runoff beds, rock and stone, ledge and cairn, the flowered singing fields, the gardens, especially the kids' gardens with, in some cases, more merry scarecrows than plants, and praise be, the big clean air . . . because Catherine was above all else a loner, a meditator.

Oh, dear Catherine, skinned alive eternally, crucified by feelings . . . her long walks here were her balm.

It was *not* that Gordon was impatient with addicts. It was *not* exactly that Catherine was a swatch of the ethically insolvent goofy consumer culture fabric of the new millennium life that he so justifiably despised. It was *not* about his authority defied, because we all backed Gordon in his repulsing of corporate-controlled mainstream television's intrusion. It was *not* Catherine's quirks of personality, no more a pain in the ass than anyone else's. It was *not* anything!

Oh, but he wanted to hurt her, no? Yes?

Something sadistic? Something about Gordon that was not Gordon? Some flinty-gray gargoyle in its square egg trying to hatch behind the forehead bone between his eyes, his pale dear eyes?

Denise's Diner.

Quarter to one, in the afternoon. At the lunch counter is Rex York in his work Dickies, no cap or sunglasses but always the black military boots, cuffs over. His chicken salad sandwich is half gone. Pickle gone. No milk or sugar in the coffee.

Stool on his left is taken by Ray Finn, whose head looks smaller these days. Or bigger. Big ears bigger. Or something. Papery maybe. Baby chick featherlike yellowish-white hair. So much chemotherapy. Makes you into a new species. Ray has been gabbing with Ernest Bean to his left about the news and about what the newscasters or news "personalities" have said and sound bytes from elected representatives. Rex, who usually has no facial expressions, no clues for you to figure what his brain is working and playing with, gets, at this moment, a quick-flash grumpy look.

He hears in his mind's ear Gordon blaming everything on "the founders," always grousing about the "rich slave-owning founders" and "their damn constitution, our country's first NAFTA," unless he's blaming capitalism or Columbus or God. Rex admires the founders, reveres the constitution, and is under God's thumb; you do *not* point a finger at God. Though he gets it that Gordon is using the word *God* a little too loosely, really meaning *the nature of life*, it still chafes him. He thinks how weird Gordon is and how the men on the stools to his left are so ordinary, so silkily predictable . . . and safe. The men talking of "voting-in the right person," of "making America number one again," in all their rote and rapture, do not give Rex chills. Gordon does. Especially lately. More so every time they get together.

Gordon would say the "elected officials are just there on the television and top-of-the-fold-paper photos to fill up the space so well with their large faces that you can't see behind them the transnational-supranational neofascist neofeudal oligarchal kleptocratic globe-sized high-tech *bombs-away!* media-weird-psyops corporate supremacist power network. Faces with too much transplanted hair in "grand thick pompadour temple-domes on top and too many state-of-the-art teeth inside." All the women with the "same hairdo talking in mean-assed ways to be as *good* as the men." Faces like the screens as large as skies. Manipulated and narrowed-down domestic *issues* "tumble from the many teeth, economic justice hidden in one cheek, the cement-stiff fixed foreign policy stuffed deep in the other cheek, and what to do about the wrecking of climate, forest, soil, and sea they hide in a hole somewhere . . . like giant killer chipmunks!!"

And: "All this talk by THE FACES sets into motion the little and large civil wars here at home. Conservative lynchers, liberal lynchers, all single file or abreast. There are plenty of problem people that the big FACES can point out to you that are *dangerous* to you or *disgusting* to you and their very being, their very existence must be OUTLAWED!"

And overly often Gordon ping-pongs this term around: *deep state*.

Not that Rex is a rote and rapture man like most Americans. But for Rex, this, Gordon's (and often joined by his yakky kids') insistence on the deeper and the darker forces, the complex and intertwined, in their very plausibility, makes it sometimes hard to swallow food.

He tunes out Ray Finn's voice and hears the guy to his right who used to be the road commissioner's son. *Used to be* meaning there has been turmoil and bile. There was money stolen. A hundred bucks. This son, Jeff, dark-eyed, scruffy three-day logger beard, sweatshirt over plaid collars, is still pretty young and his new wife has deformed hands, they say, like fins. Whatever the past, Rex feels it is none of his business about the hundred dollars because Rex puts small stock in gossip and besides family feuds have two or more sides and if you hear and *believe* only ONE side, you are a fool.

And besides, he rather likes Jeff Johnson, who forsook California, they say, who forsook an art career, who is telling all who will listen about the people who bought the Fitzgerald place. "This guy from Massachusetts, standing by the road by his new mailbox, sees Brendan Carver coming up the road." Jeff snorts in wonder at what happens next. "Brendan was walking along there, Mushy Meadows Road, right? So it's June, this past June, right? He had a Savage. He had drilled the sights on for Rick Day . . . that's only the next house after this Mass guy's place and so Brendan just figured he'd mosey up there and after all he wasn't exposing himself or dragging his wife by the hair or spreading jet exhaust from here to Paris, France, in order to experience the world. He was just lugging an old gun through the sunshine and if yuppies can jog in those funny plastic suits and helmets and goggles and whatnot, then Mainers ought to be able to stretch their legs, too, right?"

All through this telling the whole counter has been muttering and chuckling with little splotches of intent silence.

Jeff goes on. "But the Mass guy demands to see Brendan's hunting license."

The whole counter groans in sync.

"Brendan ignores the arrogant yuppie fucker but you know Brendan's always got that little smile. So he's going along nodding and smiling. The guy starts yelling, 'Where are you going with that gun?!!"

All around Rex are headshakings. Rex stares at the three-pot coffee warmer along the wall.

Bang! A bird hits the window nearest the door and people at the tables are despairing; some guys at the counter swivel to look as a woman in a pink-and-white-striped sweater hurries out.

"I thought they only smashed into *clean* windows," chuckles Ray Finn.

And now Rex hears the rustle of someone coming to stand behind him.

Meanwhile, Jeff Johnson is saying, "The yuppie guy keeps yelling at Brendan. 'Where are you going with that gun?!!' And Brendan just smiling away in his, you know, his way, he says in a plain nice-guy voice, 'Goin' fishin'."

The big laughter, lots of cackles, tee-hees, and howls of merriment seem to make ruffles on the water, coffee, and tea in glasses and cups.

But Rex does not even flash his straight-line almost-smile because this kind of thing is a fearsome thing, not a *ha ha!* thing. He stops chewing, closes his eyes. This is one of the things Gordon so often rattles on about . . . that who and what you are shall be outlawed. The laughter all around Rex's body and head and plate and coffee and stool is like an electric current to his central nervous system. He can imagine himself smashing plates, punching a laughing mouth. He wouldn't holler. He has nothing to say. He would just fight his way out of the web of moronic *ha ha's* into the free currents of inexpressable grief.

Now the person standing behind him shifts rustlingly and shifts again, then addresses him, "Mr. York."

Rex swivels his counter stool slowly and looks up into a smiling face.

"Gary Larch," says the stranger, thrusting out his large hand.

Rex, always the gentleman, shakes the hand, though in accordance with his shale-like manner.

Their wristwatches match. Both black and complicated with important explore-the-wilds data and the oozing away of time and its fantastic crucibles.

The guy's tiger-stripe BDU shirt, its sleeves ripped off, is worn over an ironed-looking peach-color short-sleeve dress shirt. A bit tall, this guy, with the very local *MERTIE'S HARDWARE* spelled out on his billed cap, but he himself is not a local. In a town of less than a thousand, counting dogs and cats, if you're from "other lands," it takes more than a handshake for your scent to lose its size and velocity and heat. Rex catalogs the guy's tallness, his large-boned wrists, the way his bottom lip juts out due to his overbite, his square clean-shaved jaw. The eyes direct, recording Rex's summed parts in equal measure. But the guy's laugh is disarmingly like the lovable cowardly lion's in the old *Wizard of Oz* movie. This makes the dangerous calculating eyes different from the first impression. Unless you're Rex, who does not easily give up reading all unknowns as land mines, booby traps, or the feathery glint of the front sight of an enemy sniper in the awful green and sun-eddies and slop-muck of tall rice.

Rex has, yes, shaken the hand, but he does not stand.

"I keep hearing so much about you," Gary Larch burbles lionishly.

Jeff Johnson is now telling about another out-of-state party who bought a great hunk of the Diamond International land and the huge Mitchell orchard property, which was nabbed by the town for taxes. "The new owners blocked off the old town road . . . the Crosman Road, right? It's legally supposed to be open. But there are boulders in front of it now and even Lloyd can't get in to do the Stackpole graves. Selectman said to him, 'Just walk in with your mowers.' That's four miles!! Selectman said, 'We're on the side of business.' What business are these guys in? Buying woods, stripping them, reselling them in lots, is what I first thought. But a third of that is swamp, vernal pool, shit like that. I just know that if you're a prince, the selectmen are gonna lap your ass. All the rest of us are crap. Business, my ass!! You ever see those selectmen be nice to Bertie at the Kool Kone?"

The sounds from the counter and beyond in response to this are more laughter, gusts and capers of *hee hee's* and *huh huh's* and little *meows* . . . as if you could diminish the foe with fun instead of flaming arrows or rockets. Gary Larch speaks quietly into Rex's eyes, the laughter all around swallows his vowels but Rex still manages to sort out what the lion says, which is, "I thought I'd stop by sometime. At your place. You around tonight?"

Rex asks, "You looking for someone to do some wiring?"

The cowardly lion laugh burbles. "More important things than that. I'm concerned with the direction our country is taking. Like you folks here were just saying, bullies want to grab. Government bullies are behind this. Feds for sure. The socialist strongmen are ready to make their move. Probably setting the stage for some busloads of illegals . . . just waiting for more socialist support . . . and before you know it, you'll have no work. A hundred Mexicans or Somalis will be riding around in vans with cute lightbulb cartoons on the sides given to them free of charge by the state, undercutting you so you'll have to work for *them* to feed your mother and daughter."

Rex's eyes widen slightly at these specific mentions of his family in this stranger's mouth.

The guy again laughs lionishly. "In Montana, we took it personally, the government setting us up for roasting. Yeah, we took it personal."

Rex makes no comment, swivels back a few notches toward his plate, fetches the last of his sandwich.

The sun is dousing the tables by the farther windows, shoulders, hands, plates, balled-up paper napkins. And it halos the bleached hair of Liz the waitress, a cousin to Gordon's Bonnie Loo, rawboned, bosomy, acne-scarred, and as you'd expect, calls everyone "Hon." And somehow she is related to Jeff Johnson's first wife. This, one of the ways the fort wall is built around Egypt, is the way a character like Gary Larch will be vetted.

"I'm working in Lewiston six days a week, Mallory Foods. Today I'm at large." The laugh. The purring storybook laugh that changes the eyes.

Door opens and the pink-and-white-striped sweater gal strides back in with a big smile. "He flew off after I held him for a bit and rubbed his temples."

"D'ja give him an aspirin?" Floyd Perkins calls from the counter.

The expected chuckles bounce along the length of the diner.

Rex swivels back and again takes the measure of the guy, his eyebrows, pores, buttons, fingernails not bashed or chipped, the very special black watch.

"Lotta people got skewered in the Midwest," says the stranger. "Farmers forced to play musical chairs. It's all government shenanigans; you know that . . . elsewhere fishing and the loggers and farming, too, all government standing on people's guts. Crushing business. I guess you've probably noticed Maine getting targeted. It's the environmentalists in bed with Mr. G. All these takeovers. The nationalizing . . . big grabs for the big woods. Communists. Environmentalists. They make it so loggers can't make a living, then the vast acreage is a sitting duck for—"

Rex says, "I guess you got it all figured out."

"Oh, indeed. *Somebody's* gotta watch these people. And they need to be lassoed. You folks in Maine . . . I heard you and your . . . uh . . . friends are about to head up to the Preparedness Expo in Bangor. There'll be some worthy goodies for your perusal. Preparedness is next to godliness." The lion laughs.

Rex swallows some sandwich barely chewed. "You're eager on that, it looks like."

"You guys plan to stay up there over the weekend?"

Rex shrugs, looks at his own black compass watch, nearly one-thirty. And for the record, he is facing southwest. Mr. Larch is facing south.

"Well, Rex, if you're available tonight, I have some incredible equipment to show you that I'm planning on demonstrating with Bob Vincent . . . he has a booth at this show. He's had displays at shows all up the east coast. You know Bob, don't you?"

"No."

"You need to be introduced. He's the real thing . . . puts his labors where his mouth is." Lowers his voice. "No one can call *him* a kitchen militia. He's able to raise capital to support his work. By that, I mean impressive sums. And those guys are weapons experts, not Billy Joe Bob and a squirrel rifle. There's been some documentaries going around about him and his people. Maybe I can get you a copy. He was in 'Nam. Knows his stuff. You guys could use a lot of tips to give you credibility. I mean, Rex, these guys are the *real thing*. Beyond even Oath Keepers. They take patriotism to the spirits of the founders and the buck stops there. The founders were *not* environmentalists . . . nor did they interfere in any way with business, nor did they dole out to the poor. Or get on their knees for gays. No taxes! These guys like Bob are the very ghosts of 1776!"

"I wish them all the luck in the world." Rex presses his folded paper napkin to his mustache. He makes a Herculean effort to have his mouth smiling when the napkin draws away.

"You know Steve Seavey?"

"No."

Slaps Rex on the shoulder. "Hey, you've got a lot to look forward to. This state is loaded with knowledgeable men . . . the real thing. We need to get together. I could stop in on one of your meetings and bring my goodies. I've often been able to let a few things go cheaper than what they are tagged at the expos. I'll lose in the bargain but you Mainers need to catch up a little . . . getting laughed at hurts sometimes. I'll fetch a copy of the documentary on Bob's people. I know your guys would be interested. I've run into a couple of them around."

The pupils of Rex's eyes broaden like an owl's.

Gary Larch goes on. "Your guys seem restless. Probably would appreciate contact with some patriots of the more organized variety beyond this little turf."

"You okay, Larry? God, you okay?!!!" someone yelps, leaping to his feet across the table from a choking man.

Other people rise, two rushing at the bent-forward gasping man who fills his booth bench amply with a body as perfectly round as a small planet. His cap has fallen into his plate but he has stopped choking.

Relief swells up and down the length of the diner.

"Jesus, Larry, *never* laugh at Stevie's dumb jokes while you eat!" calls a gravelly voice at the far end.

Larry, getting color back in his drained face, laughs a lusty "*Ho ho ho!*"

Rex slips a few bills under his plate and nods at Liz, who's laying out a place setting three stools past Jeff Johnson who is wolfing down a slab of lemon pie and listening to the customer on his right murmur some gossip involving young-sounding first names, which mean zero to Rex.

Gary Larch leans toward the counter and scratches his phone number on a plain slip of paper, holds it out to Rex who closes his hand around it, nods civilly, slips his metal-frame sunglasses over his pale unremitting eyes, and heads for the cash register.

Evening. Operative Marty Lees (aka Gary Larch) at "home" in a rented trailer behind the old Wilson farmplace within sneezing distance of both the York residence and the St. Onge Settlement. If he could speak to us, here are his words.

If only there weren't always others fucking up. When I was a member of the Rapid City SWAT team there was the incident I got blamed for . . . I didn't do it . . . I wasn't there till it was all over. So, see, I was their fall guy. So then I wound up in with the plastic fork boys at Marion doing surveillance on turd mold for America, which got me sprung early . . . due to my excellence in that line of work. When it comes to protecting my country from turd mold I make my moves without a flinch.

Okay, so then I went on and cleaned up a few bad boys in Texas, moving along to Montana, then Colorado, both Carolinas, most of the Midwest . . . part of the job is to tape and report, sometimes to testify, always to eventually vaporize myself and scoot on to where the enemy is festering virulently elsewhere.

Well, this Maine situation is, in most ways, the same old thing, like product on an assembly line. Dull as dirt. But better than in Marion, okay, so I'm thrilled. Hey, I'm saying thank you to the lamb of God or demons of generosity who love Marty enough to keep him out of Marion and the like and out in the fresh air.

Okay, but I bet you'd be queered by what I had to deal with today. York is fucking nursing home material or he's a noble psycho. I already introduced myself to him at the big Lewiston gun show in the lobby there by the snack vendors.* TWO *fucking weeks ago*! We talked for *an hour*! Well, *I* talked. York just stared at me like I was the plate-glass window onto the parking lot.

It's not like I'm a forgettable person. My own stepmother, before our estrangement, said I looked just like the governor of Nebraska if he didn't wear glasses.

---

* Timing is off. The Lewiston show is in March. Please honor our poetic license. ☺

Whatever. I need to get ensconced in the Border Mountain Militia and offer the baby jackasses new improved ideas on how to be *newsworthy*.

Oh, yes, William Daniel Lancaster and his pal wearing service pistols *un*concealed in a bar and being detained for forty minutes, that's semi-newsworthy. I have Lancaster down as one that if you get his trust you'd be able to twist his impressionable, suggestible action-figure self around your pinkie and in a couple of weeks you could have yourself another Tim McVeigh ready for when needed.

But my handler says York and St. Onge are more useful, more, *heh-heh*, dangerous. I've run into St. Onge. Yeah, he *looks* dangerous. But he has no record of throwing a banana peel on the sidewalk and the guy drives like a shaky hundred-and-twenty-year-old great-great-great-great-auntie. Although, yeah, he *is* newsworthy. So my job is to make him dangerous. Or help him stumble into a hole and become beholden to lawmen, to help America in its greatness and tallness, to learn that he, you, and me and we are nothing if not part of a truly supreme plan, none of this self-designed wild-animal homeboy-kids-and-old-folks shit.

I'm only a little man in all this business but I've SEEN and HEARD things to make you couch turnips call me a liar. Don't bother me a bit.

But here's a thing I've heard. The big brains never rest. They're always working on a new terror to set forth blowing in the breezes, but also newer and more gorgeous technology, that sheer and utter sky eye you can all hold in your hand while smiling like idiots.

I'm proud to say that in this still old-fashioned past I assist Americans in believing that there are *so many successful* LONE assassins, as many as ants, and also that there are so many people who are THERE when they aren't there. And bushes that aren't there that *were* there as in the MLK operation in Memphis. Americans are very proud to be hoodwinked and I'm proud to help them because Americans and AMERICA are. *not.* the. same. thing.

America is a mountain trail to the stars. America is God's will. America is a golden law written across the sky with a never-to-be-counted number of smart missiles and bing! bing! bing! trade agreements pointed precisely at every square inch of the planet. America is an immortal punishing power. And I am America!!!!

Emerging.

Once up inside the first piazza, Silverbell Rosenthal finds what she has suspected. Does it help that Gordon has a "safe" grip on her arm? The young men, elbows beside their plates along the tables, look overly alert like cats caught in the act of stealing, so calculating, watching her. Certain women, like the commanders of ships, giving advice fore and aft, giving orders above- and belowdecks, some with hands on hips in doorways or near that small, slightly elevated stage where her kids Bard and Eden have had roles in skits and the kazoo chamber music orchestra. Bard and Eden nowhere in sight now. They have floated away from her as if all along they'd been just pink sunsets, just as they had floated and flowed *to* her, already made, when she married Aaron.

"Well, there you are! There she is, everybody!! We thought you were cuckoo! But you look fine! Nothing wrong with her, is there?!!!" This is a little lady there among the other old ones who are lined up in rockers or wheelchairs along the dark-brown shingled wall. But that one speaking is standing with one hand each on the backs of two chairs with two oldsters who are slicing with needles into piles of yarn. Pumpkin color, variegated blues, forest green, and scarlet. Some in the wheeled chairs are baggy-faced, some bony as forks, some look two hundred years old. Many pairs of spectacles. Many crisp hairdos. Slippers. Ballooning black orthopedic shoes. But the standing one who is loudly crowing, "She's not crazy!! She looks all right!!" has sporty sneakers with lime lacings, feet spaced like a prizefighter's, jeans, and a sweatshirt with "Red Sox" blazoned across her little self, no curly do, not much gray, no specs. Her falconlike blue eyes follow Silverbell all the way along to the next porch.

"See ya later hot tomata!!" the old gal calls, and a few of her comrades chuckle pleasantly. Silverbell and Gordon move on past doorways and other circles of chairs, tables end to end, dangling mobiles, shivering green and tawny tree light shafting through the vast yardage of screen.

Silverbell speaks in a seemingly chipper way, "That old lady your mother, Gordon? The one with the mouth?"

"No. That's Dick, leader of the pack."

Silverbell laughs. Insincerely. She can still feel the falcon eyes on her back. Kids are running all over the place with foody faces, leaving half-finished plates, asking dozens of squeaky questions. Kids like roaches pop into and out of things. Where *are* Bard and Eden? Well, being nearly teenage, they're no longer nuzzly. They no longer cling. Once they seemed like two shoulder bags, dangling from her, and she'd say, "I'll be glad when you guys grow legs."

Now, she and her escort work themselves deeper into the more shadowy end of the second porch and there are the rushing whispers of lots and lots of teens and near teens, all girls, all globbed together in their own nation. All stop their hushy talk when they see Gordon's head and shoulders slowly barging through the crowd.

Silverbell's heart is fast, her breathing slow. Gordon may have it in his head that she needed his little push. Well, she brushed her hair. That was her major effort. For *him*. Now he is leading her by the hand through a tunnel of sounds—forks and spoons against dishes, scrape of chair legs on the wooden floor, all ages of persons, murmurs and teasings and the steady voices of serious plans, and down along between two more tables she is led deeper into this busy humid center of his passion. His family. Yes, passion. It is clear that he is all about passion.

"This is Silverbell!" he announces to a smiling face. And, "Meet Silverbell!" A few faces look into hers with varying degrees of discomfort or strained nonchalance. But now, another smiling face. Now another edgy look. For you see, Silverbell Rosenthal is a ghost. Silverbell smells like dust. Not *dusty*. But dust itself.

Gordon kneads the shoulder of a part-Gordon-part-Leona preteen girl who buries her face in his shirt, which impels him to let go of Silverbell's hand. For a few moments, he embraces the girl, an embrace as total as a swallow.

And on and on, more faces. Each face opened to Silverbell, each face a welcome, even those with a cautiously whickered, "Hi, there."

Gordon notices that Silverbell is trembling. He stops and gathers both of her hands into his and rubs them, the extraterrestrial coolness, the elderly shaking break his heart. Her outgrown hair-blonding job parted brownly in the middle, her T-shirt black and baggy over her twiggy antlike shoulders and neck and arms, this body that suggests a nimble good-natured grit that defined her once, and Aaron Rosenthal, too, until their walls were crunched by America, yes, transgressed, yes, warred upon in the name of liberty and justice for all.

Gordon says, "Sarah," in the softest way, like milk, gets her to raise her eyes to him. "You're good. This is good."

There is never enough grit and good humor to face the unimaginable, to remain unchanged. And so grit is convulsed to dust.

But Silverbell is looking suddenly alert and slips her cold quaking hands from Gordon's. She says, "Hazel. I know Hazel." Lee Lynn's toddler, sunsuit and moccasins, thin scrawl of dark hair, big smile. Gordon's smile. Hazel holds a handmade corduroy starfish with both dimpled hands. The starfish has been embroidered masterfully. Seems like such a waste for a baby toy, and yet, in every direction you look around on these two piazzas, embroidered figures and symbols, gold and blue on a sash, red and orange on a vest or collar, mauves and lavenders and violets and an almost vibrating purple.

Silverbell squats and peers into baby Hazel's round flushy face and round gray eyes. Eyes into eyes. The embroidered starfish drops soundlessly. Hazel smiles. She is looking quite penetratingly into each of Silverbell's eyes and between Silverbell's eyes, then reaches to pat Silverbell's cheek tenderly. All the women in the nearest doorway make sounds of delight. Hazel draws her hand back suddenly in order to applaud herself, smacking her chubby hands together and now beaming up at the faces she has known since birth, from one to the other.

Way back in the Cook's Kitchen, a pan clatters to the floor.

A strong teenage voice with only a few cracks calls out that the "History Play" is about to begin and several kazoos buzz merrily, "I Wish I Was in Dixie."

And somewhere . . . from outside beyond the screens? . . . drifting along to nag you, like a hand on your shoulder, is the stink of a cigarette. And at the nearest screen, a fly buzzes. And another just-walking baby girl staggers past with half a dozen purple ribbons in her yellow hair. And a white pushed-face Lancaster dog jumps up onto a straight-back chair, snatches a crispy chicken leg from a heaped platter on the table. Gordon says to Silverbell, "Let's get you a place. Come sit with me." And she says, "Okay" in an agreeable voice.

Bonnie Loo has come back up onto the piazza from guiltily "enjoying" her cigarette. There's the boom of a drum and the "History Play" begins. Bonnie Loo watches the narrow back of Silverbell as she is led to a table of smiling nodding faces.

Gordon finds a place with a chair for Silverbell Rosenthal and one for himself beside it, but first excuses himself to go use the "gents' room." When he returns, she has vanished.

"Where'd she go?" he asks Misty St. Onge, who looks up from rocking her empty yellow flowered teacup, eyes on the little stage where the history skit is under way. To Gordon's huskily alarmed inquiry, Misty gently shrugs.

About Lee Lynn, witchy healer.

Well, she both heals and chafes. The tweety, whistly, whip-poor-will ambulance-wail heights of her voice could crash your ship on the rocks. Even when, as she approaches, she has not spoken yet, your skin squirms and your inner-ear hammers and anvils remember trouble. They associate her close-together round eyes, her long jaw, and her vocal cords with the splitting of atoms (*almost*). Not a classically pretty woman but the floaty fabrics that whip about and gather airily, oh, grace! Her gray crone-straight straw hair! Is she thirty-two (as records would show) or three hundred and thirty two,* back from the horrors of the witches burned at the stake, unkillable?

Today only one small brass cat bell shivering its warning tinkles from her leather collar. She is soooo skinny and soooo long, heaving, vertical, feeble, stout in the way of the heart but blind to reading your annoyances. But oh she is earnest. Even when she oftentimes presses all your wrong buttons, if you know Lee Lynn you know she means well. Ridiculous in all her mismatched elements, she is nevertheless a Settlement anthem.

Baby Hazel is not with her now, but left to the many-armed protective Settlement circumscription. Lee Lynn flounces and flutters to a rocker in Silverbell Rosenthal's "cave," you might call it. There

* More poetic license. The Salem-Danvers trials were actually 1692 and did not involve burning.

is only the four-watt baby-pink night-light frothing weakly inward from the hall. It raises up textures in the room so mirage-like, as if it were a crystal ball. Until Silverbell Rosenthal pulls the chain to the lamp with its paper shade of bears that illumes in its own homey and homely way. Then she closes the door. The fort is sealed.

She doesn't sing out, "Welcome!" But she might be happy to see Lee Lynn, the one who is said to have crouched and sobbed while Bonnie Loo St. Onge or Tambrah St. Onge (long since moved away), or *somebody* wicked, punched, pulled, kicked, and wrenched her, back in the days when Gordon's web of too many hearts was being found out.

Crouched.

Yes, that nugget of worst possible shame, which Silverbell Rosenthal had smelled within herself, just like, yeah, shitting herself as the SWAT team, black as hangmen, black headgear, black gloves, black plastic-stocked rifles, and black boots, a black chorus of commands, but mainly this: "*On your knees*!!" One figure had smashed the bedroom mirror with the plastic butt of a gun, this to prove that her face shall never know itself again.

Oh, but the dogs had stopped wailing; maybe it was Aaron who had clammed up. The dogs had also stopped moving but for one of the fat month-old puppies grunting and mewling for the raw barely breathing pile that was his mother, the rest of the little skulls crunched like "drops" apples by boot heels. Why did they, the SWATTERS, let one live? What was their pleasure?

But also maybe Silverbell is now ever so glad for Lee Lynn's weird savoir faire. Lee Lynn is the only one at this point who signs up to bring her the basket meals and always, too, lots more weedy tinctures, weedy teas, weedy salves, weedy soaps. The basket is there on the lap of Lee Lynn's see-through black dress, yes, the small but swollen-with-milk breasts, curve of a hip, knees, all like creamy faces in smoke.

"You've been sleeping?" Lee Lynn wonders.

"No."

"You sit in the dark."

Silverbell shrugs. Today's wrinkled gray-green T-shirt reads: *Celtics* and has a ring of shamrocks. Her jeans are oversized and rolled at the cuffs on top of her slippers. Hair snarled. Her eyes are bunchy as if she were just waking but for now we'll believe her claim.

She goes to a rocker but just stands beside it with a hand on its back.

Lee Lynn cocks her head of gray hay hair. "You didn't stay. At the meal. Gordon was disappointed. We all were." She is slowly stroking the cloth that covers the basket.

Silverbell replies in a gravelly way, "Well." Then, "Gordon is very nice to me. He . . . knew my husband years ago." She flutters her eyes mischievously. "It's too funny how . . . you know . . . he has to put up a schedule for when he spends a night with one of you. But there's onleeeee *one* Gorrrdonnnn," she croons.

Lee Lynn's little mouth in her long narrow chin and jaws wrenches. "He's a beautiful person."

Silverbell considers. Then says hushily and sincerely, "Well, I won't argue with one of his . . . dear ones."

"So after you disappeared from the piazzas you came back here to your nest," Lee Lynn suggests in her whistly cooing voice with its Chicago accent that no one could help noticing among all the Frenchie and other Maine-type speech on hand.

"No. I went with my son to make a call."

"Bard is a good soul."

"Yes. And he already knows where everything here is. He's an ant."

Lee Lynn laughs in her earnest way. "Gordon's kitchen. Communications Center."

"It's the only phone?"

"Yes. And cell phone reception doesn't exist up in this part of town. Thank goodness. Studies show they cause brain cancer. Not the studies that cell phone companies do or lobby for, of course."

Silverbell lowers herself into the rocker now, rubs her eyes. "I called my brother . . . to see if he has a dog for me. I knew he had some from the same dam as my Delila who . . . the police shot." Her voice doesn't quiver but there's a thick pudding quality to saying the name *Delila*. "There was a puppy. They didn't stomp *his* skull. But when they took us all away . . . he was there. I guess . . . he starved. Or something. He might have been wounded. He was screeching like he was wounded."

Lee Lynn shivers. Her breasts begin to leak. She grips the center of her dress. Her heart is pumping. She has a flash of what she knows of Jane Meserve's mother's summer-day drug war arrest, cops leaving the family's Scottie dog in the hot car with the windows up, dragging Lisa Meserve away in handcuffs. The dog was later found dead of the heat, having crawled under the seat, the dog, the Scottie, that breed so dignified and stoic, named Cherish.

Cherish. Is it safe in this world to cherish?

Silverbell says, "So my brother has Delila's sister . . . from a later litter. But still she's not a pup. She's four. She's been . . . *difficult*, he told me, and could use individualized attention. I can train her."

"A Doberman, right?"

"Yes."

Lee Lynn claps her hands together. Applauds. Then peals, "This is very good news!" She pats the basket, one foot taps happily, skimpy moccasins, bare ankles and legs though it is a cool day. As with the gauzy dress, it's clear she makes her own heat. She twitters, "And your cottage is coming along. Did you see it when you were out?"

"No. But Eden and Bard have been working with the crew. Eden is good at design. She has a picture in her head of the rooms, the way the windows will face. She's sketched out little blueprints for me so I can see how cabinets and furniture will be arranged. She's very good at that . . . at schemes." She laughs softly but with a lively edge. "I don't mean she's dishonest. She doesn't hide anything. She's quite . . . quite okay."

Lee Lynn rises from the rocker and shows off some of the contents of the supper basket. A candle, she holds it up to Silverbell's nose. "Clover," she says, then there's a tea made of sumac flowers. Red. "Tastes like lemon." She paws for the mason jar of soup. Still warm. And applesauce, still warm. Her full-of-milk breasts wag like those of the Doberman the cops shot. The filmy fabric of her dress seems more of an idea than something you'd call clothing. A velvety Dobie would be more clothed. "And here's your bread . . . and butter, butter, butter. You'd do better to drop that butter but at least our cows aren't on commercial hormones and antibiotics. And they enjoy the sun and exercise. Snow on the eyelashes. Fun in the pond. It's very pleasing to watch cows swim!"

Silverbell caresses the candle. Her hands have a little shake to them. And she has that ghosty smell. All that silence, all that slumber, all that dark.

Lee Lynn asks, "You think you'd like to try coming to a meal with the family again?"

Silverbell works her lips around, pokes one cheek with her tongue. "I prefer it right here."

Lee Lynn is quick-quick to say, "Well, whatever makes you comfortable. It's just so pretty out this time of year. I was hoping you'd sometime like to hike along with me and my wild-crafting crew."

Silverbell cocks her head. Her dirty hair doesn't make a silky tumble to her shoulder but holds its place as she puts a finger to a mason jar of weedy tea, tries to make out the tiny lettering on the hand-printed label.

Lee Lynn coos, "Sooo that is for if you're ever feeling a little nausea coming on. It's raspberry leaf. Start with this nice big jar to keep on your kitchen shelf in your new cottage! Make a quick tea, hot or warm, with or without honey, and your nausea will subside. Don't hesitate to ask for more. I need to see you always well. Your wellness is my reward." She sighs. Her round eyes sweep Silverbell's profile. With her hand she strokes Silverbell's wrinkled T-shirt sleeve.

Acorns let go above, meeting with the steel roof, so much like gunfire.

Silverbell wrenches from Lee Lynn's fingers. "Oh, sorry. I'm just . . . jumpy."

Lee Lynn sighs again, then she chirps, "There's no shortage of raspberry bushes here on the side of that hill, by the sawmills!"

Silverbell covers her face a moment. Both hands. As if her face aches. Draws her hands away to nod politely along with her guest's tweets of enthusiasm.

Silverbell says, "Well, that sounds good."

Lee Lynn notes for the manyth time that when the acorns strike the roof or when in some other part of the building there comes a *thump!* the dust-smelling weary elderly young woman, who has given herself a lovely fairy-tale name, flashes her eyes wildly to the door. Well, it's true, monsters really can come out from under people's beds in the night, or rather split-crack all the doors and all that was under your feet melts like candle wax and that night will keep on repeating and you'll never *ever* be done with it.

Now she, Lee Lynn, pushes the jar of maple candies aside there in the large dark beautifully shellacked basket, hunting for one more remedy.

From a future time Oceanna St. Onge tells us of how it went.

I was fourteen years old. I was tall. And rangy. Unlike my twin Margo who was and still is more medium in width and height, pinker in the cheeks, and has hair more like Mama's that, besides being her exact shade of brown, understands the words *lie down and shut up*. Mine was, and still is, like that of an alley cat bracing for a fight.

And Margo would never be caught wearing purple. She was a browns and greens kind of girl. Still is.

I was probably swimming in the most boom-bang purple, a fee fi fo fum purple, maybe a glow-in-the-dark purple, maybe a killer-shark's-open-mouth purple, that day my father and I went up to check on the person everyone called Silverbell. A princess name. A locked-in-a-tower-by-a-jealous-stepmother name. A really great name!

We (he and me) were tromping up the stairs in the largest Quonset hut that had a bunch of rooms in the attic, emergency space and all that, Bree's and Professor Catherine's divided art studio, Kirky Martin's table-town-and-his-other-inventions room, and the little apartment for Silverbell (and her kids though they preferred camping out). The stairs and hall of the Quonset attic were precariously dark. The four-watt pink night-light bulbs that ran constantly off the wind-power lines hardly shit a shadow on all the brooms and tools and ice augers and other booby traps. Gordon and I wore boots so our arrival was with plenty of clompy warning and so before we even reached the pine door with the little pink and yellow statice wreath on it (as in home sweet home), we heard a low growl. In the pink underwhelming dimness, our eyes met.

So Gordon raps with the heel of his bandaged hand and it was like a bunch of guys on the other side with knives and machetes and hatchets and harpoons busting up the door at the level of our faces. And along with that the bellowing of a beast like on the way to Mount Doom, quite Balrogish, and then silence between the rips and roars, a pregnant silence. And a thin, almost soundwave-thin scent of marijuana.

"Sarah," says Gordon with his whiskery chin close to the door. Sarah was her real name but she didn't want that name though the tender way he spoke it, you couldn't think he was harboring any disrespect.

And yet the murderous clawing and chopping and teeth-snapping snarls drove into higher gear.

"Maybe she's out," said I.

"No," said he. Then, "Sarah," he said again and *then* there was rolling thunder and a wobbling-CRACK! of thunder and then a blow-the-whole-of-creation-up thunder from the moist maw of the fantasy creature that seemed to now originate from a place much higher than Gordon's head.

Then, he, my father, said in a husky way, "Okay, Sarah."

Oh, and there on the floor, I forgot to mention it, snug to one side of the door, a large shellacked basket. The basket deliverer was obviously given, just as my father and I were given, the teeth-snapping declaration: *You shall never know Silverbell again face- to-face.*

Geraldine stands in the lighted open doorway of her cottage watching Gordon coming up the darkened path. She has been expecting him.

He steps in, sweeps a black-eyed Susan out from behind himself, and as Geraldine takes it from his hand, he bows deeply. Beneath his feet is a small hooked rug with a pinecone design in the center and braided loops around the edge. But not much else in this cottage is that old-fashioned, for Geraldine is of modern, even tacky tastes, a gray utility feel here, well-organized, officey, no slobby, no softy.

She plucks hay chaff from his dark T-shirt sleeve and with one eye narrowed, says, "I thought you guys were chopping squashes this afternoon."

"Everybody wanted us to mow the pond field Sunday. We just did some loose loads. It was the right thing. Weather's brewing."

"I would have signed up if I'd known. I want to work the mule with the rake."

"You'll have your chance if we do that little Merrill field next week. Their guy is getting out . . . but it's already gone two years. Not my kind of stuff."

She picks more seed from his chest. "You'll itch all night. I don't want that in my bed. I'm going to heat you some water."

"I'm sorry. We went until this very second. I didn't want you waiting around much more." He stands in his most slope-shouldered, too-tired-to-sit way as she begins to pump water into three speckled kettles. Her eyes stay fixed on the swirling water under the pump. No staring into the eyes of her loved one tonight. She takes him for granted. That is a good thing, not a bad thing. Even if it is illusion that he will always always always appear right there where he promises to be. Geraldine is one who never counts death in any of her mathematics. As she pumps the long iron handle, filling the last kettle to brimming, her arm not tiring, she hears the melody of the falling water, feels the pleasure of a day's worth of completed tasks. This, with her reverence for horses and this big hale man, means that they can move small mountains and make each day's end clean of doubt and blear. That she herself is capable in her own fashion. Unlike Marian St. Onge's accusation, Geraldine can't be tagged "loser."

With his still bandaged bitten right hand and also bandaged other hand (work-related mashed tendon) Gordon is unknotting a damp red bandanna from his neck, worn not cowboy-movie style but dog-collar style. This he claims is to keep the jaws of deerflies, horseflies, and moose flies from tasting his jugulars. But Geraldine thinks it is vanity. Or rather, *statement*, his chance (if you should ask) to expound on the real origin of the term "redneck," labor unions organizing there in the coalfields of the South, for instance. That blaze of scarlet cotton across the necks of marching thousands, yes, wearing *the red*, carrying that loaded rifle, up against the ruthless Pinkertons who had the power of the gods behind them, the United States government with its moneyed footing. Yes, he, her dearly beloved, lives to expound. But tonight he is dumb with exhaustion and she likes that version of him quite well.

They both hear it.

Something.

Gordon steps toward the ajar door sideways, reaches one hand to pull it wider.

A chesty growl up snug with the screen, eyes lighted green, long blade-like head, and that scribble of small clenched teeth between four towering fangs bared to the gums. It is standing like a human, one paw to each side of the door.

Floating behind and to the side of this pointy-eared weapon is ghosty Silverbell.

"What's up?" Gordon asks that pale no longer comprehensible face as he stuffs the bandanna into his pocket, his throat . . . his, uh . . . *jugulars* now bared above the dark T-shirt's neck. He steps closer to hear Silverbell's answer and to fill the door with his six-foot-five-inch self as barrier.

The dog begins to chomp through the screen . . . well, she *tries* to, she can't quite get her teeth around the flatness of it, then drops to a crouch, every hair bristling, mostly just the brown muzzle and eyebrows visible in the dark.

Silverbell's voice speaks lightly, matter-of-factly, pleasantly, "She's only warning you."

"Yeah?"

"She's communicating to you that she has the capability to rip you up but not yet, not till I give the command."

"Yeah?"

"I'm training her to attack on command. To leave nobody alive. Kill 'em all and let God sort 'em out, as they say." She laughs gently. "Just joking. It's just so nobody can frig with me. She's just . . . self-defense. I'm training her to warn first before she annihilates. In *some* cases a warning. In other cases there's no time for a warning. Or no warning deserved."

Gordon hears Geraldine moving close to him, a hand on the center of his back.

The dog hears, too, and its lungs fill with more deserved or undeserved warning air to be blasted through the ever-deeper voice box.

Gordon says, "For training, one would expect permission from the . . . uh . . . simulated victims . . . and don't they wear special padding, Sarah?"

Silverbell might have spoken but her voice is ground under the tracks of the dog's tanklike irregularly accelerated growl.

Gordon says, "Geraldine, stay back, would you? Go on back to the sink."

"What's going on?"

"Just stay back."

Geraldine backs away a little bit. "Who is it?"

Gordon tells Silverbell, "There's nothing to be afraid of in the Settlement."

Silverbell makes no sound of the mouth or throat, no clap of the hands. But her posture settling brittlely must be a signal to the dog, perhaps unintended, because a hideous wet gurgle is the dog's response. And an attack-crouch tightens along the shoulders and maybe the rear parts, which Gordon can't clearly see.

"Sarah, how much control do you have over this animal? And why are you *here* at this cottage?"

"She'll do whatever I tell her."

"And why are you *here*? Why is she being trained to attack *me*?"

"It's just practice." Silverbell gives a tight half-laugh. "I won't let her go all the way unless someone frigs with me."

"Sarah," Gordon speaks in a soft almost watery way. His inclination is to open his arms to her, compelled, too sticky in his ways, always set to push himself on the wounded. But what if what is soothing to the pale woman on the other side of the "weapon" is to be never touched again? To be never *among* the living again? The life's journey of her fingertips, shoulders, fist of heart, warm glands is done. Maybe only an empty distant planet would soothe her.

She turns away and the dog, black beast against black autumn night, sweeps into her turn.

But also another black sweep, the vapor of voice inside Gordon's skull blathering the fairy tale that began almost twenty years ago. *There is nothing to be afraid of in the Settlement. You are safe. You are safe in the Settlement . . . behind the hornbeam pole and dangling little pine sign that reads KEEP OUT. You are safe.*

History as it Happens (as recorded by Montana St. Onge, age nine, with totally no assistance).

The new kids here, Bard and Eden, are camping out in the cottage that isn't done yet. The building crews are hurrying but Bard and Eden can't wait. They have quilts for pallets and flashlights for night and they won't tell me where they do toilet. Their mother is named

Sarah for real but you are supposed to say Silverbell but my father mostly calls her Sarah.

Bard and Eden are twins, not from one zygote. They are almost thirteen years old each. They think that's like being able to vote or run the world. Baloney to that. And they don't scare me.

Today on my way for the breakfast crew, it is dark except for one skinny line of perfect red under a mile-tall wall of quiet cloud of grayish-bluish-blackish. I stop in to their cottage and just walk right in because they don't even have doors yet or windows. Just big door and window holes called rough openings. And also headers.

They wore sweaters and quilts over their heads.

I asked Eden if she remembers her real mother because Silverbell is not their actual mother in the way of insemination and neonatal and all those important terms. She said, "Yes." Bard said, "Yes" but I tested them and I can tell they were just faking it.

We were having this visit by flashlight and I sat on a sawhorse because I'm tall even for my age. I said, "I'm on the breakfast crew this morning."

Eden said, "I'm going to be on the haying crew when the weather clears. I'm doing windrows, also helping Geraldine with the mule. Anne is her name, a good mule name. Don't you love it they named her a nice name, not Stewball. After that field that's pretty small, another neighbor wants us to do a little piece. I love mules and horses, don't you?"

"It's not my thing. I'm more into literacy." Then I asked them both, "How come you're here, not with Saraaah and the mean dog?"

"We like camping," Bard said.

I said, "Aren't you really afraid of the big mean dog?"

They shrugged in total simultaneousness, which means yes but Eden said, "No."

Then Bard snorted in a macho way and said, "Vesuvius ripped my uncle's ear and his arms. Mom can handle her though. She's a dog trainer."

I said, "People here are against big mean dogs. What is Sara*aaaah* Rosenthal going to do about *that*?"

I could see even by only the flashlight spots on the walls their faces stuck with no answers to that.

Thick dank unstarry evening. Tall-grass bugs in vociferous song and the mutter of an old V-8 one-ton flatbed rolling in snug with the shingle mill.

Driver's-side door screels open and Butch Martin, age twenty, plucks from a pocket a thumb-sized flashlight. Dane St. Onge on the other side, age thirteen, tugs a wool shirt from one of the cab-mounted gun racks. One door closes easy. The other needs a show-it-who's-boss slam. *Blombk!*

Butch begins to head for the open lot with his distinctive lumbering walk.

That's when Dane feels the heat and goo of the man-sized creature's mouth on his throat and on the end of his chin . . . a thousand fast gargling pinches, fast as the speed of light . . . or at least as the speed of sound. The pencil-sized teeth are now occupied with his left sleeve but not his arm so nothing bleeds . . . oh, maybe just the claws that graze his hand, making sketches and scribbles.

The noteworthy details are Dane's stupid-sounding almost soprano wail of shock and the attacker's deep and garbled *gotcha*!

And though Butch says nothing, he has pretty fast done the magic of causing a tire iron from the truck floor to appear in a swinging arc close to the dog's skull just as she ducks and, with the grace of a soul leaving the body, flows toward a pale oval human face above a white T-shirt and bare arms and this face has no mouth, none showing the gray flicker of speech such as: *Bad dog* or *Good dog* or *Off!* or *Come!* or *Oh, I'm sorry, guys*. She and the brute just merge with each other and the black edge of the woods.

Heart banging like a war drum, Butch whispers slow and drawn out, "What . . . the . . . fuck?"

But Dane, leaning against the truck hood, is having difficulty asking such a philosophical inquiry of the night.

***History as it Happens* by Rusty Soucier (some editing help by Rachel Soucier).**

We were late doing our compost rounds and had to pay the price. That means dark is a yucky time to be dumping forty buckets of you know what. This was way after supper, more dark than ever. I had the solar buggy with the headlight that is tilty so I rode behind Evan and Ben and Faira and we were just by Gail's gate when one of the white dogs of the Lancaster people . . . his face is squashed and his legs are short and his fur is short and his tail is curled and his name is Toad and he visits Gail mostly when he isn't down on the piazzas or kitchens stealing perfectly good meat off the table or pissing on the walls . . . so he's going along in his usual marchy way and then we all saw it . . . the Doberman trained to kill flew out of nowhere. The worst was the little guy screaming because the Doberman shook him then dropped him. Toad was lying there making noises like a sink drain (not funny) and the Doberman just drive into space. Outside our headlights nothing was left but foggy nightness.

Meanwhile, on the path we all realized the little guy was a body with its head turned the wrong way and only one leg not paralyzed and he was still gurgling softly. And little whimpers. Evan screamed, "I'm not standing this!" and beat Toadie's head in with a rock. Made my stomach sick.

Later . . . today . . . at breakfast this morning, still dark, Butch was telling Gordie and them about how the dog had ripped Dane's shirt and slimed his neck. That on top of what we reported about Toad and other people getting their two cents in because they'd had scares, too, because the lady's dog was being trained to kill, Eddie Martin said. Eddie is Butch and Evan and Kirky's father in case you're reading this a hundred years from now.

Rick Crosman, Jaime's father, said the lady Silverbell was training the dog to protect her. "So maybe she's a lousy trainer."

"She's crazy as a coot. Let's face it," said Ray Pinette. "I'm beginning to wonder if she was nuts even before the narc raid."

"What are we going to do?" everyone said.

Gordo, he just sat there at the table with a bottle of aspirin in the middle of his plate instead of food and his finger tracing the glass colors of a glowy candle lamp. His mouth hung open a little like babies just born, like you see in the *Your Weekly Shopping Guide*.* He looked funny. I don't mean to be insulting.

---

* A real paper in the Oxford and York County areas of Maine.

In the following hours.

Darkness after supper, cold enough to quiet the ancient-ever whirs and creaks, that rumpus in tree and grass that makes late summer melodious, now as still as though it never were.

Here comes widower John Lungren, so ordinary a man you'd forget him in a minute after laying eyes on him. Gray hair in skimpy scriggles at the temples, always combed to obedience, while thick and horsey on top and back. Steel-frame glasses contemporary for his generation. Work clothes, work boots, gold-color stretch-band wristwatch with phosphorous dots on the twelve, three, six, and nine. Beside him his solid stout mother wears a light yellow cardigan sweater and dressy pants, her hair forced into a curly helmet by the beauty crew. Though she'd *never* use such a term as "eye candy," truly she was, in her day, in these fixins, mouthwateringly conformingly hot stuff. But now, she shuffles along, her hand upon her son's trustworthy arm.

This is the west side brick path that leads toward the solar cottage they share.

Gordon and his wife Glennice are on the edge of the same path, swishing their flashlights. Glennice and John talk over the top of John's mother's bobbing head, a few words about the turbine and truck underneath it, which are ready for the upcoming Lincoln trip. Glennice is eager to fraternize with the Lincoln Christians, not enough souls here at home as pumped up on God, the Son, and the Holy Ghost as Glennice is. There are dancing dots on the large plastic frames of her glasses, reflections of the handheld lights that sort of bless the path that brings Gordon to her cottage. She will read aloud from the Bible tonight and he always listens closely but makes no remarks (as a rule). But when she asks him to join her in prayer, he will, her soft earnest phrases, his like the rumble of a storm on the rock slope of some God mountain. She will always be convinced that he has been especially cast by the Lord for a purpose beyond most people's imaginings. And yes, beyond even her imaginings.

Someone is coming toward them on this path of brick. Only lately has a figure in the dark here made Settlementers edgy. And, sure enough, the reason for their worry unwinds like smoke and then formulates, a snow-white face and white T-shirt in the bouncing yellowy eyes of Glennice's and Gordon's two flashlight beams. This is the creature on two legs and then there are the brown-muzzle, black devil ears, and four legs of the other creature. Woman and dog had been stepping along in harmony, the dog off-leash, the dog looking not ahead into the bouncing lights and the back-and-forth of voices but at the whole of her master, watching for signals?

Okay, so it is not the dog who is the danger but the master, right?

They both stop on the path and tonight, the dog acts like a good ol' dog, no hackles up, no lunging.

But the record has already been set as far as John Lungren is concerned, John whose brain does not chase its tail as Gordon's does.

There is no alteration in this present picture of inoffensive woman and doggie dog and yet John plucks his mother's hand from his arm and draws from his open red-and-black plaid overshirt a revolver. He aims it at the silent weeds to one side of the brick way and click-clicks the action of the cylinder, saying, "That dog can't live here. That dog is a loaded gun. *This* is a loaded gun, too, but I have never terrorized kids or folks with it. Or killed a harmless little mutt with it. But I *will* kill a dog that is making life hell here."

Silverbell clasps her hands in front of her T-shirt but even the two hands together can't still the tremors.

Glennice shuts her eyes tight.

Gordon is thunderously silent. He seems about to speak but only sounds now as though he's grinding his teeth.

Silverbell's eyes have flicked to Gordon, all eyes put in frightful distortion now by the underglow of flashlights aimed down at brick. But Silverbell Sarah Rosenthal can see perfectly the yarn ball of Gordon's brain tugging his eyes away and downward in powerlessness. He has earned in this hero test a big fat F.

John's mother starts forward, as if to continue on her way, both her hearing and her vision made up of gray shushing dots and fuzz darkling into irrelevance.

John grabs her arm. She yelps in surprise. He hauls her back into his one-arm embrace at his side. His fear has transformed his humanity into a spear point of chipped flint. He is not surprised at Gordon's paralysis, that ol' boy with his head ever-dulled by his ever-hot heart. It nauseates John; he turns to one side and spits in the grass.

Therefore the moment is John's alone.

The darkness and several dim near and distant cottage lights, some in quirky colors, seem to hiccup, up, then down. It is as though the St. Onge lifeboat is sinking from too much rescue.

John aims the revolver at the Doberman's comely narrow-eyed long face in profile as her eyes are bound to Silverbell's fingers, which are still trembling. And now Silverbell's chin trembles. A lowing; yes, a cow sound comes from her widening mouth. Nothing like *Please don't*! Just anguish so majestic that, like the moon, the sun, or a mountain, it cannot lower itself to chitchat.

How softly Gordon speaks her name, "Sarah." He has never been able to account for much more than that with her, her lunacy like quicksand up to his cheekbones. It matters not that he has blamed lawmakers, then law enforcement. No, because the resulting garbage, the rot of their deed, is here. HERE.

John's voice now, rich and low, shed of its list of demurrings, "You know, Miss, it's like in the song that goes, *Give me three steps, mister, and you won't see me no more*. You know that song?"

Silverbell's trembling has switched to ripples. And no more lowing, just choking cries.

John, still grip-embracing his mother with one arm, quite smoothly and one-handedly works the cylinder of the revolver to its empty chamber, stuffs it back into the holster inside his outer shirt. He speaks crisply and clearly as though reading a courtroom sentence. "Instead of three steps, that animal has *thirty hours* . . . to be gone."

History as it Happens (as recorded by Montana St. Onge, age nine. No help by anybody).

Everybody has been talking about the dog John L. wanted to kill. Everybody was wondering if Bard and Eden's make-believe mother would make the thirty-hour deadline. Even though the mothers all say no roaming after dark till the dog's gone, I decided to go to the source and FIND OUT what's up. This was twenty-four hours later when I go visit Bard and Eden in the cottage with no doors and no windows, just holes. I had my flashlight and my brother Rhett along for the job. He is four years old in case you read this thousands of years from now. Rhett keeps losing flashlights. Sometimes down the compost toilet hole. So flashlight-wize he's on probation. I'm good at keeping him in line.

I said, "Knock! Knock!" in front of the big darkish empty space that is their door.

"Come in!" Eden's voice yells.

There were other visitors already there. Termite and Seth and Faira, who are all big kids age-wize. They are smug and weird when hanging out in this cottage as if they are all on serious drugs. I've been watching them and sniffing whenever I visit.

I hunt around for my usual seat, the sawhorse, which had been moved down the little hall. I move it back to my spot after I brush off the nails and sawdust with one hand, pointing my light with the other. All they have for light tonight is one fat candle, which is against the rules for kids.

The whole place always has that new wood smell. There is a ticking sound. They keep their alarm clock down between studs of one see-through unfinished bedroom wall.

Rhett is looking around with his mouth open.

"So," I say. "Has she got rid of the dog yet or will there be a firing squad on it like Catherine Court Downey's TV?"

Seth and Termite look like they are about to crack up but they just stay as silent as dumb chewing cows. I swish my light over their dumb Indian-style knees sitting and dumb empty hands.

Can't help observing Faira's hair is wrecked again by the beauty crew. Her hair is black from Passamaquoddy lineage but there it was now the colors of traffic lights. Some red. Some green. Some yellow. And it was all broomed out in tufts, some chopped so close to her skull you could see skin.

I would never let the beauty crew lay a finger on my beautiful blond braids that are like Heidi's in the book, which is an imported foreign story about eating bowls of goat milk.

Also on the subject of Faira, who EVERYBODY says is pretty and Evan Martin calls a "dish," she has a space between her front top teeth. When I once said that is quite a shame, Eddie Martin, who has an answer to everything, said the ancient Greeks believed if you had a space there you were sexy beyond words. I pointed out that we are in modern ages now, where science is more important than sex and what happened to Faira's teeth growing like that is a mistake in nature, a DEFECT.

So anyway, there in the cottage of two-by-four inside room walls and no doors I say, "So, what is Saraaaah going to do with her precious animal?"

Eden is a blonde with small dark sneaky-looking eyes like something that steals your chickens and a smile that isn't for friendship. She says between her many small teeth, "Problem solved."

"Yeah? How?"

"She traded Vesuvius in for a thousand-pound African crocodile." She and Bard laugh and Seth and Termite and Faira have these little bitty snitty laughs like they think I believe that rot.

I say, "The . . . dog . . . is . . . a . . . problem. And that's that. No jokes. She has to get rid of the dog. It *was* thirty hours." I glance at their alarm clock with my flashlight. "*Now* she has six hours left."

Bard says, "She decided not to do that."

"She has to," I say, folding my arms to show I'm tied in with the people of authority.

Rhett says in his usual mopey way, "What's that?" He points at a big cardboard box with a bedspread thing over it. Probably a bale of heroin.

Eden says, "Our stuff."

Rhett keeps looking around. He looks dumb but he has the eagle eye when something's not right, just like I've trained him. Now he's studying a weird trunk like pirates ran around with, but not real huge. He says, 'What's *that*?"

Bard says, "My friend gave that to me. It's a chess set all in big ocean figures."

I wrinkle my nose. Then I say impatiently, "Your mother-person is in trouble here. That dog is going to be dead meat."

Eden and Bard look at each other and make sneery faces.

Rhett says, "Hey. You ever hear of shiny windows?"

"Coming soon," says Eden and she gives Rhett a friendly pat on the head. "Rhett," she says. "You are very special to me."

He shrugs. He always looks worried and morose. But he's a fool for flattery. He has a weak will.

I say, "I'll have to report this to John Lungren that your mother-person *Saraaaah* isn't even trying."

Eden smiles. "*She and Vesuvius are gone* so cool your heels, vulture."

"Gone where?" I narrow my eyes to perfect slits.

Eden and Bard and Faira and Seth and Termite just look all snotty and green-candlelit with flickers and snotty mouths *not opening* and snotty eyes glowing in snotty rotten happiness of a rotten snotty conspiracy.

Claire recalls.

Silverbell and the the dog were nowhere crouching or cringing in any Settlement buildings we searched. Gordon called his old friend Jack Holmes, trying to locate names, addresses, and numbers for Silverbell's brother, her parents, her dead husband Aaron's parents. All Jack had was the brother's name and a town. Our phone crew did most of this research while young Lily Davis and Samantha Butler sang the praises of the "World Wide Web" . . . the "search engine" versus "yodeling from the mountain."

The brother had moved twice since last spring but we finally got his daughter's chirpy voice on the line. She said they hadn't heard from "Sarah" in a while. Oh, and how was the "Dobie" working out?

Augusta, capital of Maine. A rented conference center.

A pink-cheeked black-suited murmuring usher seats Gordon and Claire next to Marian, billows of their weedy weird Settlement smell convulsing high and low. Marian thinks the kind of swampy-cedary-ragweed smell especially pours out of Gordon's old and only dress jacket, a tweedy gone-out-of-style sport jacket that he wears without a tie. And the shirt!! A chambray work shirt!!! The trousers? *No* trousers, just dark blue Dickies!!! Though at least they look new. No stains. No battery acid portholes. No red bandanna around his neck to make his redneck labor union class-warfare statement. His hair and beard are trimmed. But why couldn't he leave his clump of janitoresque keys at home?!!

Claire, however, passes Marian's status test perfectly (but for the swampy cedary cloud), wearing one of her several USM adjunct outfits, a dignified gray, her shining hair up in a braided twisty severe black bun while the silver hair at her ears is looser. Claire's always glaring midnight dark eyes behind her wire-rimmed glasses certainly suit the moment, unlike Gordon's flinching pale devil eyes, which appear to be looking for trouble.

Marian smiles at the both of them, however. An angel on her shoulder whispers, *Yes, these two people could die tomorrow and you would grieve beyond all imagining. Death is striding among us with his terrible wand.*

Marian, already sitting as straight as possible, straightens further as if a lance were run down through her from noon to hell.

Gordon notices all of this, and the fact that her dress is the same gray as Claire's warms him.

He also can't fail to notice that the number of state dignitaries and other VIPs that are filing in is so great that the walls of this vast space seem to bulge outward. And by God these guys and gals are all wearing gray!

It seems to Gordon that the space is too modern, too unremarkable, too plastic and beige to honor Morse. He was told that according to Morse's wishes this memorial would be here in Augusta, which does not surprise him but . . . but . . . also Gordon is disappointed by hearing that inside the casket is a car-battery-sized box of ash and bone bits. How can that honor the largeness of MORSE?

Gordon would have suggested a closed casket with Morse's whole stocky self stretched out in there so that the pallbearers would experience, one last time, Morse's avalanche-like inclination to give pause.

As Gordon reaches for Marian's hand she lets him, though she doesn't lean into him, which he wishes for. She continues to be straight as, yes, a prepared corpse, a beautiful corpse.

With her head in profile to him, the gray-streaked dark hair, her nose, yes, that Italian profile like those statues of Caesar . . . if Caesar had been born a girl . . . and Gordon suspects Marian has secretly been under the scalpel of one of those docs who do little poofings of the face and mini paralyzings with squashed bees or milked bees or some such, the details escape him, but he just sits there loosely, fully marveling at how lovely, how striking she has *always been* and in old photos of his parents together or individually, how handsome his papa was, too . . . *short*, dark and handsome . . . the French, the Indian slamming together with Marian's Irish-Italian, two shockingly good-looking people, which as a kid he didn't notice or care about. They could have each had three eyes and noses like turnips as long as they loved him. But now, this moment, he sighs at the dead end of their comely genes, considering how he, their only kid, had turned out to be less of a looker, too much action in the face, especially the mouth, especially the eyes, *all of it*! A tornado of frowns and smiles and meaningless winces. And as he ponders this tragedy his whole face scrambles and one neck muscle jerks.

Now appearing in his peripheral sight is Janet, just arriving here with the family. She sidles (gracefully of course) along the empty row of seats in front of Gordon and sits sideways on a chair, her silky brown dress so butterflylike . . . well, *moth*like, being brown. She reaches for Marian's hand and Claire's hand and speaks ever-so-hushy to all three as Gordon has placed one hand on each thigh of his work pants.

Janet breathes, "He wanted Augusta. It was his wish." She blinks her eyes. Her eyes shine. Tears are welling.

Gordon nods.

Marian and Claire make small warm sounds.

Janet goes on, leaning in closer, "Don't pass this on *but* . . . his real wish wasn't quite like this. You know what a prankster he was."

Gordon's eyes twinkle. Marian's and Claire's stern expressions are sustained.

"There have been a few . . . minor alterations to his wishes on the part of the family." She always hangs on to people's hands or wrists too long and now is no different, the intimacy of it, the once shy girl having found the way to erase a crowded room, drawing just *you* in; on and on and on, you are her prisoner. And yet all these hands involved are cool and dry. Thanks to air-conditioning. No "sweaty clam rakes" as Gordon always calls hot kid hands in hot Settlement rooms.

Janet tightens her hold; her light, almost blue-smelling perfume closes in, too.

"For instance, he said *no memorial* with all sorts of speeches saying what a wonderful guy he was. He called it *critique*. He said even benevolent critique was a kind of power. All those people *grading* him . . . he said *grading*, yes . . . while he lay there helpless, unable to grade them back. Or defend himself. Or correct errors. Also, he said *in writing* that he wanted to have his ashes *pitched* . . . yes, his word in writing was *pitched* . . . around the front lawn of the capitol building, and the Blaine House and the park and the parking lots . . ." She snickers, then sniffs, then tears up again. "*Use only pinches of my ashes . . . pinches*, his exact word . . . *so there'd be plenty to go around*."

Gordon is watching her mouth hard for more of this treasure . . . Morse's humor, but sincerity, too . . . well, okay, Morse's *wrath*, his sound and well-warranted immortal wrath.

Janet's hands still keeping the huddle intact. She says, "And inside the statehouse . . . a pinch to each room and the elevators and the halls, the walking tunnel, then into the capitol building. All these people here today . . ." She's down to a whisper, a hiss. "He did *not* want them *here* standing shoulder to shoulder with their practiced smiles saying phony niceties about him. No, he wanted to haunt them one at a time, make them trip on rugs, lock them into the men's room, shut off the lights, freeze the elevators, moan in the stairwells, make Governor Baxter's bust growl, and Joshua Chamberlain's painted image break wind. He wanted them all to feel weak and worried or wearied. He said . . . or rather he *wrote* that he was a paralyzed puddle of flesh in a wheelchair but in ashes form he would rise up in a terrible cloud and choke them all to death." She lowers her chin, her whole face.

More VIPs shoulder their way between other VIPs, ushers looking worried, fearing quiet chaos and complaints. The seats on either side of Janet are now filling with gray suits.

Janet, whose handsome face also has known scalpel-and-squashed-bees-assistance as Marian's has, looks up, looks into Gordon's eyes with her teary ones as she feels for the dotted hankie in her pocket; it's too late, tears make shining paths down both cheeks. "We made a mistake, didn't we?"

Then, it's all over.

Gordon realizes he has not seen Bruce Hummer at this great betrayal of Morse's wishes. Ol' Bruce would be a real star to this herd. But perhaps not to *all* of them. Senator Mary, for instance, from one of those old Portland waterfront Italian families which never hit the jackpot like the Depaolos but just counted Sundays and holy days and grandchildren and great-grandchildren and great-great-grandchildren there on Munjoy Hill and outward. All of them counting on Senator Mary to remember them in the face of Augusta's bedeviling temptations.

But as far as Duotron Lindsey's chief exec is concerned, Gordon was not *really* expecting him. Bruce Hummer, the *secret friend*. One might suspect there is an ugly side to the Weymouths that cleaves to Bruce and he to them? But wait!! What is it that makes *Gordon* like Bruce? He, yeah, likes him, right? Oh, yeah, yeah, Gordon likes everybody. No hurdle there. Well, Claire would point out that he did *not like* Catherine Court Downey. Well, okay. But why does Bruce continue to hang around kooky somewhat dangerous rebels like the Weymouths? But Gordon doubts Bruce is off sulking, the uninvited brokenhearted outsider. Gordon can almost see Bruce in his private jet, out there over planet earth ingeniously and sniperishly fucking over peoples of the *whole planet*, for Duotron Lindsey and its front companies, largest stockholders' growth in the next quarter, yes, but also all the money laundering, manipulation, extraterrestrial lobbying, phantasmal trade agreements, DEEP STATE smoochy-smoochy, and full spectrum dominance with the military, State Department, and whatever. Yes, the majestic golden thing, the same size as our forsaken planet, floating and bobbing along above, held aloft by the force of no one hand but worshipped by billions of hearts: MAMMON, the very thing that rocks this room of dignitaries like a cradle.

Finally the days of the Lincoln windmill-solar-co-op trip are upon them.

Bonnie Loo's small pink cottage is at the end of a stony uphill path, situated squarely between four behemoth low-limbed lumpy-from-disease beech trees. Transoms over the windows and between the windows. Fairly normal windows. But in the three wee dormers, shaped sharply like inverted V's, star-shaped windows amaze the eye up there among the cloying beech limbs. Though Bonnie Lucretia has her dark side, it is plain to see she has taste for light. Fluttery freighted woodsy light.

You first pass by Gail's place, which is painted Easter chick yellow and has fewer windows. A rotary clothesline with a pair of beige-gray socks hanging. A big friendly *Hi, there!*–looking oak tree off to one side, the rest maple. Gail's cottage is set close enough to Bonnie Loo's that the yellow clashes with the pink.

We see a lone crow coming in for a landing on Bonnie Loo's dark-green fence; he folds his satin wings, cocks his head to perfectly eavesdrop on the voices chattering beyond the screen windows.

Penny St. Onge hurries up the path and as she pulls open the gate, the crow's sort of metallic voice says, "Shit! All out of tuna!"

The front door of the cottage is ajar. Penny steps in.

Bonnie Loo's other guests are all standing around the living room, obviously having also just arrived. Beth has one of the last-minute lists of what needs to go to Lincoln.

Penny smiles at them all. Yes, Penny who is magazine pretty, girlish blond ponytail, such a nose! Such eyes! Elegant neck and a mouth that smiles the same on both sides of her face. It is said by many that she is more attractive than her now sixteen-year-old daughter Whitney. Whitney is pretty in *some* photos, but has too many of Gordon's grimaces and expressions of sheer astonishment and kicked-around-hound-dog humility and perfect sorrow and what some on talk radio suggest to be sneers of derangement.

Penny speaks. "Claire, that crow that likes you . . . he's right out there." Points at the screened window.

"Everybody watch what you say," Claire chortles.

Gail says, "I like his weather reports. Like a-hundred-and-twenty-mile-an-hour winds on top of Mount Washington." Gail is among the early arrivals. Gail with the sun-and-cigarette-hardened face. She is standing close to the side window with a clump of hemlocks beyond, darker and deeper than the beeches. Her reflection there on the many panes shows her short brown braid behind her. She is a forties-close-to-fifty gal with flowers tattooed in a circle around her neck, down around the collarbone, which shows in the V of her work shirt. Sometimes she still wears leather but her Harley Davidson days are over. The booze, the drugs, the restlessness, the miles, the good friends and wrong friends, and the bad deals are, for her, not talked about. She's no storyteller, anyway. Her voice husky, quiet. She seems at times too urgently grateful to be here in this place and time.

And though Gail is a bit leathery in the face, her features, when you squint, are nice. Like so many here, she wears the plain silver ring of you know who.

Then there is Beth. Her stormy squiggles of longish blond hair flop as she touches her toes several times, then does some enthusiastic stretches that wind her a little. She says gaspingly, "That crow is getting too fat to fly, livin' off the dole."

Claire says, "He was raised by humans, obviously. He seems to have no crow friends."

"Somebody dumped him off." Ellen's flat voice matches her granite expressions. Ellen has a black eye of obscene red-purple from surgery this week to remove a raisin-sized growth. She was quick to stake a place on the couch.

Claire and Steph are still milling.

Yes, all these visitors are St. Onge wives.

Bonnie Loo is standing in the doorway to her tiny kitchen, hands deep in sweater pockets. Her glittering (due to contact lenses) eyes are the fox color that Gordon has fallen into forever while every few weeks Bonnie Loo carts a few more possessions back to her mother's and stepfather's place.

"So the pylon crew headed up to Lincoln yesterday afternoon," Claire is explaining. As two others settle on the couch on either side of Ellen, Claire remains standing, looking commanding in her steel-rimmed specs, small feet wide apart. She is wearing one of her professorial jacket outfits, not tweed but tweedy. This is one of her USM adjunct days. She is sort of on her way out.

Gabe, Bonnie Loo's oldest, almost seven, is here now lying on the rug with a towel over his face. Rehearsal for a play? First aid crew practice?

Steph says, "Lorraine can't go up in the caravan tomorrow. She has to come along later. They're going to be over in Baldwin doing that genetics thing. Critters hatching. Fruit flies . . . or something."

Penny goes directly to the oak rocker by the brightest window and sits, careful not to step on Gabe. She is only half listening to the chatter about the Lincoln trip. It is a big nice thing but nothing new. They've all done it before, all over the state and in New Hampshire. Up go the windmills. And the network of friendships builds around the making of electricity and heat and fuel of a kind that some call "clean," others dismiss as "hippie." Right now behind the Quonset huts the partially assembled sections to the steel tower are fastened to three flatbed trucks, the turbine on another. Ready to roll.

Bonnie Loo asks the assembled faces, "Any of you see one of the big green anchor buttons to my sweater? I lost it either from here to the Kitchens or from here to the parking lot."

Several noes.

A couple of sympathetic headshakes.

Beth squints. "Bonnie, you'd lose your head if it wasn't tied on."

Bonnie Loo sighs. "I'm going nuts." Then she speaks to Gabe, whose face is still covered. "Another reminder, Gabriel. No swearing in Lincoln."

Gabe seems dead. His fingers are opened flat on the green floral rug.

Bonnie Loo tells him, "And we'll probably have to say grace in Lincoln."

"When in Rome, do as the Romans do," warns Beth.

"These are devotedly Christian people." Bonnie Loo adds. The motionless Gabe moves not one muscle.

"Like Glennice and your Grandma Earlene," Steph reminds Gabe.

Gabe continues reply-less and responseless.

"Right," says Bonnie Loo. "A lot of believers . . . like left-handedness and pink eyes."

"And like that family in Center Ossippee we did the great solar sled race with that time . . . lest we forget," Penny adds with one of her gentle smiles.

"As many religions as there are mountains and lakes. It means a lot when we're respectful," Claire muses, sort of to Gabe, sort of to everyone. She turns now and sees that Bonnie Loo is tugging a bandanna from her pocket.

Brown-haired pink-cheeked Steph smiles in a sad-looking way but it's just subdued pride. "I'm not worried about Gabe or any of our bunch. Our kids are good kids. They have lived in love all their lives. They kind of shine, I think."

"Did it feel good to sleep late for a change, Bonnie?" This is Penny. She is giving the rocking chair arms little squeezes.

"Once I threw up and turned myself inside out I felt absolutely one-hundred-percent perfect." She blows her nose into the bandanna.

Ellen is puffing her cheeks in and out. This seems to somehow make her colorful swollen eye look thicker.

Now Claire is giving Bonnie Loo a one-armed love squeeze.

"It sucks," says Beth. "You'd think having a kid in you was the same as swallowing a basket of cobras."

"I'm not sure what the purpose of morning sickness is," Steph says softly. "There must be SOME purpose."

Bonnie Loo snorts. "It makes you drooly and ugly and smelly and keeps the man off you so the pregnancy can set well."

There are many clucks and giggles.

"Bev and I just came back from Bridgton," Penny explains with a sigh, "and there are more cars this morning by our gate. One was a reporter who wanted to talk with the True Maine Militia. Said he was from New York."

Beth giggle-snorts. "This must be how the Beatles felt."

"Gordon tried to get Evan and Jaime to go down and nail up another sign. *Anyone trespasses will be shot. Try it.*"

"So poetic."

Steph winces. "Gordon is getting more paranoid every day. A sign like that would be a bad mistake."

Then after a few more remarks around the room on that odious possibility, Steph softly breaks in, "Any news on Silverbell, where she went? And if she's okay?"

Sad headshakes all around.

A couple of sad noes.

"What has Gordon said to any of you guys about it . . . what happened when John said . . . his thing? I haven't heard his feeling on it yet," Penny wonders, her pretty mouth turned down.

Gail says, "He won't talk about it."

"Well, neither will John," Bonnie Loo adds.

"Glennice told us at breakfast prep or we'd not've known that it even happened," Gail tells the group.

Beth clears her throat. "Well, Montana said Eden and Bard know plenty but are clammed up, too."

"Somehow this spooks me," Claire murmurs.

"Me, too," Penny says.

Ellen is leaning forward now, rubbing her hands together. She is barelegged with old white sneakers and white socks, baggy shorts, and a *big* purple blouse, not as purple as her eye. Scruffy short light brown hair in two childly ponytails. She says huskily, "Well, I didn't come all the way up here to set around and talk about Gordon's mental problems. Or Silverbell's weirdness. I was . . ." She levels her eyes on Bonnie Loo. "Sent."

Ellen always has a momentous way of saying things. Everyone is leaving a polite silence for her to fill.

"Natty's birthing crew," Ellen states importantly.

Bonnie Loo does not smile with appreciation for St. Onge wife Natty who is heartily loved by everyone else.

"You heard she's starting pains?" Ellen's eyes sweep around the room.

Gabe remains unchanged. Towel doesn't even quiver with his breaths.

All the women except Bonnie Loo express variations of concern over Natty's labor.

Ellen says somberly and importantly, "Since they figure she'll deliver tonight, Gordon is probably going to be up with her all night . . . and . . ." Ellen can't miss the hard look coming into Bonnie Loo's eyes. "They wanted me to find someone to drive his truck to Lincoln in the morning . . . with him as passenger . . . since he'll probably sleep most of the way and—"

"I certainly won't," says Bonnie Loo, pulling her sweater tighter around her.

Ellen makes a distinctive popping sound with her cheeks.

"Well, fine. They *were* hoping you would. But no problem. How about the rest of you since you're all right here. Kill a buncha birds with one stone."

Before anyone can answer, Bonnie Loo says evenly, not looking away from Ellen's one pale unswollen eye in her long-jawed face, "Get Glennice to drive him. Glennice thinks Gordon is God, right? Speaking of believers."

"Gordon is God, right?!!! Gordon is God, right?!! Gordon is God, right?!!" This a thin but grandstanding voice outside the screened window.

Eyes flashing to the window, Beth snarls, "I'd say kill and dress that sucker but he'd not even fill one sandwich."

Crude and raw layers of the dead speak.

Compressed and sagging millenniums crush my green and twiggy bliss, steamy grave of goo, long forgotten. Then found. They drilled down for me, their drill rigs so humorously tiny to the eye of God.

The voice of Mammon speaks.

Growth! Growth! Growth!

Again crude and raw layers of the dead speak.

And upon this treasure, a civilization and vaster population were built on a promise of saving struggle, and truly I did work with ease what they would work with groans. But still there were groans. Never will they find happiness but they believe incessant happiness is their purpose and so to find it they lean forward faster.

The voice of Mammon speaks.

Growth! Growth! Growth!

Yet again. Crude and raw layers of the dead speak.

But all that waited at the end was that I would be sucked down, the last sweet best gigabarrels slipping thinly as through a stripy childly straw. What remains is asphalty clot and curd, tar and unsplit rock and the cellars of Atlantis. And war. Easy is gone. And hugging the sky my death-color rainbow bewilders you. My three centuries of service now a hot taunting wattle to sag so ill-favoredly upon you.

Lo, but remember your industry and populations require hot fuel! Your voracious capital requires growth!

The voice of Mammon speaks.

Growth! Growth! Growth!

Crude and raw layers of the dead don't give a rat's ass if you aren't listening.

Soon the frackers clang and split the homelands, I to be exported away! away! This way, thataway to make the old worlds new. Growth! Growth! Growth! the nexus commands, also simpering and puffing and orbiting the lords of other nations, hunting down the less delicious tarry drops and tailings ponds to mirror the burning birds. And so the new old feudal thing, the future owned by the few, as from the past I whisper the legends of my amazing feats and those infinite populations that even survivors can't fathom. They couldn't eat hot sky. Nor cyclone. Nor flood. They couldn't breathe hindsight. That will be part of the legend.

Butch Martin speaks.

So, um, you know, we have this, our co-ops and such. That morning, you could feel it in your chest, dumb as a dead bunny that you swallowed whole, this stupid blob of hope.

We were on our way.

Critical thinker of the past.

> "I have never had a vote, and I have raised hell all over this country. You don't need a vote to raise hell! You need convictions and a voice!
>
> —Mary "Mother" Jones

In a future time Whitney St. Onge tells how it went.

So! Lincoln or bust. I was driving the Ford we always called "the Vessel," but it was temporarily now our official True Maine Militia command car. At the pole at the end of our dirt road, Sammy leaped out to check the message barrel. As usual it was chockablock full of communiqués to the True Maine.

The Settlement caravan headed down Heart's Content Road. The dark sky was opening up in peach-color mists. The woods and stone walls were at their stations. One could almost believe they were permanent, that there was such a thing as permanence.

Samantha Butler remembering.

So, the officers of the True Maine Militia were squashed into that one car and we knew what no regular Settlement person knew, that there was a big surprise about to happen in Lincoln, the thing we engineered so deftly, so ABSOLUTELY. Radio people, TV crews, *Bangor Daily News*, and so on. Guillaume St. Onge, big and loud, wasn't going to be a roadblock to democracy in America!

Oceanna St. Onge recalls.

Keep in mind that Bree had no role in our Lincoln scheme till now. She was as innocent as a chickadee egg. She had been one-hundred-percent missing from the Settlement since she bit my father.

Whitney again.

I remember Bree was wearing something orange. A T-shirt, I think. No jacket for *her*! She just had a couple of wool shirts tied around her waist. Bree was *so* durable! Everybody admired her. And now she was married to my father. That put her up about ten thousand notches. Officially grown-up. Officially something even beyond that.

And so Bree's silhouette which was normal-looking in the semi-dark car, as I glanced across at her, was majestic.

She was quiet and distracted. This would be the first time she and Gordon would lay eyes on each other since she bit him and nearly broke his thumb. But we knew none of those details that day.

Gordon, like many of us, was always patched up with first aid crew gauze for work wounds. It wouldn't be until months later that the thumb story was Settlement legend, though quite overshadowed by the legendary *other thing* that happened later on in the month of October.

Rachel Soucier speaks.

I remember that Bree was wearing something orange. I think. Something bright. And Samantha, our Sammy, was militia-themed, red neckerchief, camo jacket, flashing white-blond hair with chocolate brown Comanche-style head rag. She was making all her noises as she was pawing through the stuff she'd hauled out of the message barrel, flashlight going from side to side as she read.

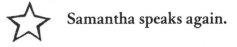

Samantha speaks again.

I remember Bree was in the front seat. She wore pink. Like a flower. I think it was pink. Maybe apricot. Whatever. I remember worrying that she'd get pregnant by the Hotshot King and not want to fool around with democracy anymore, that she'd turn Mama-ish and mushy and useless to America. Tsk. Not that prego Dee Dee had gotten mushy. I guess it was the whole part that Gordon played in Bree's situation that got on my nerves.

Rachel Soucier.

Well, that day anyway, nobody was going to stop us. We were the militia. We had brains in that car. We were revolutionaries!!!!

Samantha.

Okay, so our militia intended to declare war on faceless power, on the big boys, their damn system. No one was going to stop us. Not even

Gordon. A year before, I didn't even know what a *system* was . . . or Mammon . . . or the so-called "self-regulating market" (and its government subsidies, self-regulating ha ha . . .) or "externalizing costs" or the Ninth Amendment to the Bill of Rights. Or psyops. Or special ops. Or any history of the common people like all those great slave revolts and mutinies and stuff that regular school never revealed. All this urgent stuff that Gordon himself was the great loud encyclopedia of . . . then he turns around and gives a constant red light on our doing anything about it!!!

For me, it was really a declaration of war on . . . you guessed it . . . on Gordon. During that hour of my life he was as much the system as any other system was. In fact, in Settlement life he was the only system, right? Almost a solar system.

My mother, Cindy, said we should be grateful. "Because of him we have a secure home."

I shot back, "So the strings attached are that we get on our knees when he walks by?"

She really hee-hawed over that, then said, "Touch the ground with your forehead." Then she cuffed my shoulder.

Thank our lucky stars she wasn't one of his "wives." In her passive resistance to the harem idea she had said heck no to power, too!

Bree remembers.

And the sun rose tail first, thrashing in its orangey late September way through the woodsy points and spears on Egypt's tallest foothill. Then we turned northeast onto more open road, picking up a little speed, and then we were on our way.

Pregnant Dee Dee Lancaster St. Onge (married to Gordon's cousin Lou-EE) remembers that ride.

The sun rose into the pure sky, the sky wider there on the open road. But still there were woods, what was left of the woodsy woods of Maine. Seemed like those trees were full of spirits. Or were they full of reporters? Exactly what the True Maine Militia hoped for!!!

Whitney.

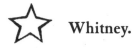

"*Who Rules the World*?" Samantha read this title aloud from a book in the message box pile. And, "*The Dawn of the Corporate Empire . . . Good-Bye Nation-States* . . . that's the underneath title."

"*Sub*title," Bree corrected her.

"Sub subby subeeeee," said Kendra B. to tease.

More rustling and lots of fluttering of the flashlight there in the back seat.

"There's a note inside that first book, see?" This was Margo's voice.

Samantha read it to us, "From your neighbor. Thank you. What you are doing is fantastic! But I can't give my name. I can't be associated with a militia."

Michelle sighed. "Mum says we made a mistake calling it a militia."

The flashlight went off suddenly just as the rising sun punched through the windshield.

"Maybe it makes us sound weird," said Kendra sadly.

"No way!" Sammy howled. "All the sissies can go fuck themselves!"

Our Sammy. She was hard.

But also she was right. If we did what 99 percent of Americans found tasteful and tidy we'd be calling the voting-for-preselected-and-presorted-politicians "democracy" and we'd believe the preselected and presorted TV news was real news. Well, that's if we *had* a TV, one without bullet holes.

Dee Dee Lancaster St. Onge speaks again.

I wriggled out of my three sweatshirts. Yes, here we were, all these trim women warriors and me. Yes, that was me in the roomy but filled purple sundress with green leaves and vines embroidered around the neckband and over the shoulder straps. I looked like a huge grape.

When the sun got to really pounding and stomping on the glass, we rolled the windows down.

Where did the cool morning go? And the deep blotless sky? Now all haze and yuck. This is late September *in Maine*, not Guatemala.

This with the climate and everything else, where is it all going? And there under my purple sundress my little guy was adding on his last pound of pudge.

What a stoooopid idea to have a kid in these times. But . . . no . . . it is *not* an *idea*. It is what we are, living beings driven always forward, a vicious hunger for going toward the light, a vicious hunger to bring forth more of your own species. A painful beautiful jangling overpowering indefensible vicious hunger.

Forgive me.

From a future time, we hear Gail St. Onge speak of the drive up to Lincoln, Maine.

I rode with six adults and one toddler in one of the station wagons. It seemed like just one of our usual good-neighbor projects, one that you would kind of semi-forget, all blurred with details of other projects we had done around the state. We had done so many. We could break records with the speed and ease of pitching our big and small tents.

The younger kids had packed their usual Settlement-made presents for our hosts, loaded with the tents in trunks of cars and under truck seats: wooden necklaces, Blueberry Homers, snowshoe harnesses made with roofing rubber, and whoopee cushions also made with roofing rubber. The little boys called the whoopee cushions "fart pillows." So you see. It was just the usual, right?

Settlementer Suzelle Pinette remembering.

T'e older boys and girls brought along a quart of homemade biodiesel fuel for a show-and-tell and t'e accompanying recipe. T'e trunks and back seats were spilling over with youthful generosity, some gifts for Lincoln adults, too. Pot holders. Socks. Candles. Soap. Honey.

Clair recalls.

I remember well when we were zooming into the last toll plaza just before Augusta, we pulled out ahead of Gordon's old green-and-white

Chevy truck. The whole caravan was kind of fanning out, going to the two different lines at the booths.

I looked over into the cab of Gordon's truck. Glennice was driving. She's a brown-haired woman with a sort of pug-nosed appearance. Blushy complexion. Trim. She was never one to put on pounds.

Using one hand to drive, she was leaning comfortably against the door. Such a confident-looking way of driving. And those prescrip tion cop-style sunglasses. With the sleeves of her plaid flannel shirt rolled up you couldn't fail to notice that powerful unhurried way she had of shifting.

She had driven since she was a kid, tractors, farm trucks. She enjoyed big machines and outdoor work, though at North Egypt Fundamentalist Baptist Church, where she went every Sunday morning and Wednesday night, she always wore a ladylike dress, girlish shoes, and her best clip-on earrings. And for that she walked pretty, "from the hips."

On the other side of the seat from her was the cargo, Gordon. With his head against the closed window glass, he slept. And wouldn't Glennice see this sleep, that kind of deep loose-limbed sleep, as something only the truly righteous are capable of? Yes, she worshipped him, a step above normal love. Just what TV-land America expected of all of us.

Vancy St. Onge from a future time speaks of Lincoln.

I didn't go. I stayed home to keep checking on Natty and the baby. I needed to rest. Little Natty's launching ten-pound William into the world was enough to tire out five people besides herself. One midwife: me. And four assistants taking turns assisting me.

You asked about Lincoln, though, so I'll say this. It scares me to hear of what went on up there.

Holding William with both hands, all slippery and tasting the air, I am witness to the good fortune of a perfect start in life.

Yes, I am a midwife by training and you may note that a lot of my anecdotes, parables, and jokes involve birthing and the very young.

You ask about Lincoln. This is what my answer is.

There were in another state hikers witnessing a cow moose giving birth right into the snapping jaws and ripping teeth of a waiting pack of wolves. While the mother had labored near the bog, the wolves lounged around waiting for their easy feast there in the tall grass. I despise wolves.

Okay, so there's your answer. Now leave me alone.

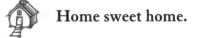

Home sweet home.

The black wall phone's receiver dangles on the end of its long curly cord. Gordon is at one of his desks. All around him loud tropical wallpaper not meant for a kitchen. Apple crate shelves of newsletters, string in jars, tools, duct tape, old empty Christmas cookie tins but no cookies.

The desk before him and the one adjacent to that are slathered with new mail. His phone message spike teeters. The stapler is on its side. The several rotary files look ready as ever to serve.

The window dashes lavender-gold light onto his hands and face from the flare-like radiance of the turning maple tree out back. It's as if it were sunny out there! But the sky itself is bleary with misty rain.

He is rubbing his eyes hard. Then his eyes drop back onto the full-page op-ed in the *Bangor Daily*, dated before the Lincoln project and starring the True Maine Militia. This was sent to him by an old Bangor Theological Seminary friend.

But for its cheery invitation to see the windmill being raised, directions to the Lincoln site included, the piece is similar in form and feel to the *Record Sun* op-ed he had fumed at Bree over. Only Bree's name is not included here. But hasn't her influence taken on a life of its own?

Other envelopes, other clippings or photocopies of clippings or sheets pulled off the Internet. *Brunswick Times Record. Waterville Sentinel. Lewiston Sun. Kennebec Journal.*

Next a fat brown envelope, a page-and-a-half feature with a lot of photos. Lincoln, Maine. So this is what came of it all.

One shows a truck door with a smiling OSHA-yellow not-exactly-round sun. The sun's aura is red, dribbling like an open wound. This paint was *meant* to color up the kiddie-made windmills a few yards away from the real one. But somehow most of it landed on the truck door and on top of one little girl's head. And on that door there's childly lettering: SUNSHINE ARMY. A companion picture, close up, of three painty kids leering into the wide-angle lens, which distorts their faces.

Are the newspaper readers to *fear* these seven-year-olds? Or maybe fear *for* them?

And here are flash-of-pale-hair Samantha Butler and rose-cheeks brown-fluff-haired Margo St. Onge stuffing flyers into disembodied wide-open hands. Samantha's camo BDU* britches show up exquisitely.

And how did it happen that he softened so easily and wholly? Smiled so gamely? At Bree? Then wallowed in the crowd, the ENORMOUS crowd? And then lunged into oration?

He fears himself!

Oh, and here's a photo of that speechifying, his long arms raised prophetlike over that crowd below and around him, the crowd that had been urgently invited by the True Maine Militia op-eds. And with him on the yellow-green hill a few yards beyond his shadow stands the finished windmill, holy to his own eye. But he is amazed they included this shot of the windmill, the real reason for his being there, now lost in the media's lust for fearmongering and other titillations. Such as. Yes, this close-up of himself and Rex, Rex's BDU shirt and Border Mountain Militia patch, oh so central, as with the photos that have captured "his men."

None show Willie Lancaster, so phantomlike at times. Where was ol' Willie lurking in those moments? What was it about him that the TV cameras and newspaper cameras found so uninteresting?

He remembers his wonder, alarm almost, when he first saw the familiar faces in their full-camo and grim-faced soldierly-postured selves among the crowd of strangers, mostly touristy L.L.Bean-pastel-appareled folks. Turns out Rex, etc., had been relatively nearby at the Preparedness Expo in Bangor, which Gordon had neglected to remember. But Rex, no colder a presence than usual, but a *presence*, made it clear he'd forgiven his "brother" for *that*.

---

* Battle dress uniform.

It comes to mind now how the first reporter to accost him had a long brown braid, had been charming in the way that a smart person wouldn't trust, had tried to get Gordon to condense his spiel into a brief quotable quote. He was feeling cursedly agreeable but as we all know, Guillaume St. Onge *can. not. condense*.

Then, with intensifying charm, she asked him for a quotable quote on the True Maine Militia and its goals. There were flyers and Bree's *Recipe* in her free hand.

Again his tongue could not roll out that crisp byte that passes for news in the USA.

But as the gods would have it, a friskiness came into his eye and he remembers hearing the click of several cameras as he, turned into his joshing self, his *let's play* self, raised his fist and roared, "GOD SAVE THE REPUBLIC!" And yet the fierce *feel* behind the words was not joshing. Not play. Something too real had gotten away from him, was born into the jaws of wolves.

Now he slides open the desk's top drawer for a bottle opener with a dangly kid-made tassel, then reaches under an adjacent desk to fetch a long-necked bottle of homemade beer.

Why can't he be like Rex? Cool, controlled, words put in order cautiously before they're allowed to crawl out from between his teeth. Rex need not fear himself.

Gordon considers how his response to the enemy (the corporate-controlled media) was a warm gut response to the human with her pencil standing before him, not to the *thing* that waited wide open to replicate him into millions of Gordon St. Onges and his four words, the rolling presses, the chattering radios and TVs, and the World Wide Web.

Cape Elizabeth.

Janet spreads the paper on the table like the wings of a crucified bird, folded for mailing by an upstate friend. It brings no smiles or whispers from her, just a brittle silence. It is only the low tide pulling farther out that purrs.

Wiscasset.

Marian Depaolo St. Onge with the Brunswick paper on her knee, folded in half as if never opened. The afternoon is too cool for sitting out in the garden, but she can't find her way to standing up from the wicker yard chair. She is sobbing ferociously.

At a Seattle hotel. Duotron Lindsey International's CEO, Bruce Hummer, hangs up the phone in his suite, sits on the edge of the huge bed with the Maine paper he's been carrying around for days opened to such an amazing array of photos. He waits for the glass of milk he just ordered from room service, which will come on a tray "in fifteen minutes." He stares at the closed curtains. He stares. He stares. As if the curtains don't cover a big window but are about to open onto a tragic play. A couple of sharp raps. He stands up from the bed, goes to the next room of the suite, opens the door. Young guy's face. Milk on a tray. Bruce digs for the tip and then speaks in his still intact (when he's tired), soft as silk, slow as dirt Georgia accent.

"Why thank you, sir. Exactly what I wanted."

Cyberspace.

Jip taps out an exuberant e-mail to all in their group listing the Internet news websites she's found so far covering the latest op-eds and the Lincoln event. She adds: *I've e-mailed Brianna Vandermast on this but she's silent. The St. Onge phone is hopeless.*

Olan's e-mail message to all reads: *There were revolutions before convenience was invented.*

Billy's e-mail reads: *We could put a lantern in the Old North Church steeple.*

Olan's next message: *God save the Republic is a joke, right?*

Billy's next: *Must be. I wasn't under the impression that he was on the side of big capital.*

Jip: *He's a complicated man!*

Olan again: *Great shots of his buddies there. So he hasn't ditched his right-wing thing yet. Any comments?*

Blake, who was not among those meeting with Gordon in the West Parlor a few weeks ago, sends an e-mail that reads: *Who says those guys are right-wing?*

Billy: *If it walks like a duck, quacks like a duck, is armed, white, and angry, it's nothing we want to work with. There are no grants available to help fund militias. I personally am not playing the violence card or playing up to it anyway with or without funding. Either Gordon St. Onge drops those loonies or we drop him. We've already been over this.*

Blake: *Patience is a virtue.*

Billy: *That part of the state is crawling with guns and ignorance. And hate. We'll be wasting our time.*

Blake: *Wellll, looks like a lot of work, guys. Guess we'd better eat all our spinach, do an extra set of stretches, put on our smiley faces, and saddle up. Time's a-wasting.*

The Inner Voice of the Bureau.

We seeeee you, Guillaume. We even know how to pronounce your name. We heeear you, funny guy. And this is how it goes, anybody talks this loud in America, your entire profile, from baby goo goos to infinity, will be in our very special air. Yes, air. We don't use so much paper anymore. Some FOIA-minded turd-lovers are always trying to get their paw prints on what's nobody's business. Fortunately, it is effortless for us and our key taps to move our moves to the air of another agency. Ain't that foxy? We have *everything*, brains and bucks. We have *everything* but your pelt nailed to the wall.

Voice of Pirate Radio interrupts.

Our people in debt are today's bonded servants.

And so the St. Onge mail and ringings of the phone multiply to test the infinite.

Yeah, like stars and snowflakes and fleas.

Another weird sickeningly hot Brazilian day in Maine, now dusk, Gordon alone on the porch of the old farmhouse. Glass of hard apple cider clear as vodka held with both hands.

He has again taken the phone off the hook. Otherwise it rings allllll the time. Especially since Lincoln. Even into the night if he leaves the receiver on. The phone message spike on his desk bristles obscenely. Meanwhile, the horses and mule of the mail crew have been more sorely burdened. Included, this a.m., in these flomping weighty bagged heaps of postal miracles, not so incidentally, there was a priority mail cardboard envelope with Bruce Hummer's Central Park West, New York, New York, address. No message inside. Just a key. Looks like a key to an old music box.

Gordon had added it to the bunch on his belt and by persistence alone the telepather has whispered again: *My brother*.

Meanwhile, messages are bubbling over in the box and in the decorated ash can down at the gate. Strangers in cars parked at the gate, asking questions of Settlementers or neighbors who will stop when hailed. All told, there have been hundreds of people most sincerely interested in the stop-corporate-power message of the True Maine Militia. Only *two* asked about wind and solar projects. *All* want to *get in* and meet Gordon St. Onge.

All want to GET IN PAST THAT GATE. Three have had the balls to park and *walk up*!!!. The KEEP OUT sign had no more power than a dried-up leaf to stop them.

Gordon lets the vodkaesque cider pour down his throat. His chair is a rocker but he holds very still. The dusk is the fall kind in that it is settling in early even as the whole world steams.

He is still mulling over how Bree had just stopped by to see him, having "borrowed" her brother Poon's truck. It was only ten minutes ago she sat in the rocker beside him, smoking. She had brought printed-out old and new e-mails from Jip. "They want to meet with you and us of the True Maine. They say it's urgent."

He laughed.

Bree was very very very quiet after that. Just slowly rocked, blew smoke away from him, tapped her ashes into her hand.

Before she left she caught his eye. He stood up from his rocker suddenly. He hugged her hard enough to hurt.

The chair he'd just been sitting in was rocking by itself.

With his bandage gone, the healed but still raw-looking lips of the bite were on full display, the whole finger slightly curvy where it should be straight. She seemed not to notice. Her head was slightly bowed, cheek to his shoulder. He kissed the top of her head.

On leaving, the front wheels of the truck meeting with the tar of Heart's Content Road, she tooted the horn. Her smoke still sagged around the chairs and screening.

A voice jumps the shit out of him . . . a small, *really* small sort of human voice.

"Gusts up to sixty miles per hour. Quarter-sized hail. Drenching rains. Water temperature seventy-five degrees. Continuous cloud-to-ground lightning."

Gordon sees the silhouette of the big bird in the ash tree. Seems to be just talking to himself. Gordon suspects the family has been feeding him from his, Gordon's, own kitchen here. Cookies and coffee cakes that come in the mail from fans.

At breakfast Gordon had directed some youngsters to go down to the gate (a horizontal pole, actually) and nail up another sign. This one reads: ANYONE TRESPASSES WILL BE SHOT. TRY IT. And so it is done.

He drains the glass, lays his head back against the wooden slats on the back of the chair.

From the ash tree the small but well-projected good-lung-power precise voice marvels, "Gordon is God, right?!!! Gordon is God, right?!!! Gordon is God, right?!!!"

History, the Past (1946). George Kennan of the US State Department speaks.

We have about 50 percent of the world's wealth but only 6.3 percent of its population. This disparity is particularly great as between ourselves and the peoples of Asia. In this situation we cannot fail to be the object of envy and resentment. Our real task in the coming period is to devise a pattern of relationships that will permit us to maintain this position of disparity without positive detriment to our national security. To do so we will have to dispense with all sentimentality and daydreaming; and our attention will have to be concentrated everywhere on our immediate national objectives. We should cease to talk about vague and unreal objectives such as human rights, the raising of living standards, and democratization. The day is not far off when we are going to have to deal in straight power concepts. The less we are then hampered by idealistic slogans, the better.

Critical thinker of our time comments on your TV-shaped opinions.

> They are also the logical conclusion of narratives built on what sociologists researching moral panics call "the production of deviance." This refers to the production or manufacture of crises revolving around deviant threats where the characteristically subjective concept of "deviance" is defined as the antithesis of privilege, which is "normal," and imposed on public discourse through, in this case, corporate media domination of mass communication (ideological hegemony). Characteristic of the production of deviance are the high drama and overblown theatrics of ideologically induced hysteria; in the case of the "Terror Scare," deviance production is responsible for turning "terrorist" into an all-consuming identity that defies proactive attempts to understand underlying motivations that, in other circumstances, might be addressed by cooler heads more effectively and with less outrages against international law and human rights. Scaremongering, in seeking to rationalize the scapegoating of a billion Muslims* for the

* For instance.

social, economic, and environmental consequences of neoliberalism as the late capitalist expression of the injustices in irrationality inherent to the system, are in this sense merely the practical fulfillment of the "straight power concepts" Kennan prescribed five to six decades ago.

—Ben Debney, excerpt from *Crises Worthy and Otherwise*

Think tanks on the glories of "otherness."

The conservative population has no sympathy for or amalgamation with (zero, zilch) Muslims, "towel heads," only unease. The (ahem) "liberal" population has no sympathy for or amalgamation with (zero, zilch) American "redneck" men, only unease.

The Apparatus (before redactions).

And so our palette is heavy with all the skin colors and un-colors and, oh, the grays of smoke, the blood-drizzle reds, the piping tints and textures of crises for those televised pageants of hate crimes and of terror, the entrapment sort, yes, and the let 'er rip sort.

Deep State

Yes, we are the thousand-thousandfold labyrinthine other-veil-rustlings that burrow unstalled and unquestioned through the penumbra beneath and above the place you believe is your home.

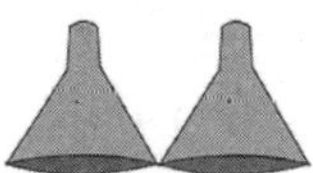

Tin hat conspiracy theorists.

Man, that bunch sure must be up to *something*.

The Apparatus speaks.

Boo!

OCTOBER

Other covert activity.

Bree delivers an e-mail message to the officers of the True Maine Militia from Senator Mary, the go-ahead they've been waiting for. Since they are still at the supper tables finishing the meal with chilled squash pie, secrecy requires whispers, hand signs, special eye winks.

Samantha hisses loud enough to turn a few wrong heads, "This will be our finest hour!"

Several solidarity fists are raised but otherwise there's nothing to give a clue to the ground-trembling escalation of the True Maine Militia's war on the system.

On an early October evening. No frost yet but plenty of geese yelling from the skies. And more messages from Senator Mary quietly delivered.

A cool purply-sweet, field-sweet dusk. Bree is standing, watching Max and Jillian work around their last uncut pumpkin plants. And breaking off what's left of their basil; there's not a lot of time left for herbs. Meanwhile, Swiss chard long gone. Swiss chard is such a big hit with kid farmers because it grows soooo easy, served in vast blobs at meals.

Lee Lynn's baby, Hazel, clings to Bree's neck like a monkey. Bree's head is tilted so that Hazel's cheek and her cheek are wonderfully mooshed together.

Bree *hears* it, a hot rod, one of the classics, then turns and sees it, nice old Nova, burning up the hill past the gardens. She watches it a moment till Hazel pushes her forehead against Bree's temple. "Nob'wy!" the baby commands.

"Oh, yes, let's," replies Bree. Kisses the perfect smart little face, honeyed childly breath, cool cheek.

In this part of the field are mostly "personal gardens." Small. Gardens in shapes. Gardens crowded with scarecrows. One garden has almost no vegetables, but eight mighty fine scarecrows. Scarecrows wearing hats. Scarecrows wearing old dresses.

Bree strolls with the long-legged chatty baby on her hip, stepping among these distinctive "sculptures." Hazel imitates Bree's awed and respectful expression.

Some of these gardens are sequestered with low white picket fences. Bree hops over one of these and Hazel roars with laughter, her voice at times like this seems deeper than her mother Lee Lynn's.

Bree points out some gardens hemmed in by small round rocks the size of grapefruits painted white. Hazel points, too. A young Settlement woman and her visiting teenage sister relax on a stone bench embraced by swells of monstrous yellowing squash leaves. They wave to Bree and Hazel.

Down on the graveled Settlement road below, two solar buggies whir by, steered by two elderly men, trailers loaded with roundwood and bucksawed small limbs for the kitchens. Both guys are nearly bald as stones. Both wave when they see Bree watching them and Hazel's hearty smile.

"See, there's Kirky!" Bree exclaims.

"Kirky," Hazel says perfectly.

Tonight Kirk Martin (the kid with the electronic table town) helps twelve-year-old Dara Ginn stack big, then progressively smaller, rocks for a jazzy-looking upright cairn in her garden. He is turning each rock five or six ways as Dara directs him. Again, Bree's attention is drawn to the deep bluster of the hot rod, now beyond the knoll there, seems to be turning around, heading back out. Bree feels the earthiness and thickening and surge of autumn more than she can bear right now. How swollen and maximum everything is! She stops by one of the more elaborate gardens and breathes deeply of the thick jumble of small and huge sunflowers, their fringes a little browned out. The huge ones, unusually tall, are like trees, some weird super-duper variety, and probably "doctored" in some way. Their faces are the circumference of family-sized pizzas. Ah, Settlement life! Settlement energy! She sighs with gratefulness that HE has forgiven her.

She carries the long-legged adored child back to her mother, Lee Lynn, who is standing there with a little bucket. Lee Lynn St. Onge! Bree stares a moment into the woman's light-colored eyes while the darkening purply October sky bulges out around them all.

Bree settles the baby on her feet now, Hazel still yakking away in mostly baby lingo, pointing at important things, like small grubby gray stones and bent weeds.

"You think Hazel will have a green thumb?" Lee Lynn wonders in that knifelike soprano as she hoists the tyke to a hip.

Bree says, "We could paint it green."

Lee Lynn does NOT have a green thumb. Bree's eyes move over Lee Lynn's flashy fringy peach-colored "prayer" shawl, her gray witchy flyaway hair, shawl and hair swirling. Small tinkly silver bell at the throat, which baby Hazel reaches to feel the clapper of.

True, this is not gardening attire. And all of Lee Lynn's gardens over the years have shown their contempt by putting forth beanless vines, robust weeds, and once, two summers ago, an underground nest of scorching yellow jackets that literally exploded when she came here to whack away with her hoe one day. But Lee Lynn's unquestionable genius with *wild* weeds of woods and meadow which she tirelessly collects and dries and applies for soothing and healing makes up for everything.

"Hazel, don't put that in the dirt," Bree hears Lee Lynn advise, just as she, Bree, turns her head at that engine sound again, but the hot rod isn't passing yet, seems to be content to idle and rev beyond that westerly knoll.

Bree walks a bit, humming. Wanders into the farther gardens, then back again. She kneels to peer under the elephantine leaves of a plant in the very religious Glennice's personal garden and sees a freshly formed pumpkin, waxy and pale and indefensible. Perfectly round but too late in the season to make it.

With her head down, Bree hears Lee Lynn's little bell and high mewly voice speaking a "hello" to someone. Bree can tell from Lee Lynn's voice, and maybe even the quivering bell, that the mystery person is not a Settlementer but is known.

Bree then hears the slow crunch-crackle of grass behind her. She pivots a little, still squatted down, head still down, sees boots and jeans. He squats down beside her, palms on his knees, elbows out, lightly and slightly bouncing. He doesn't say anything. Just smiles and smiles and smiles with his slightly protruding teeth. His pointed beard looks dark in the dusk. His work shirt is short-sleeved, clean, medium gray. His jeans are also clean, faded to gray. His eyes are gray. Eyes that are set in his face with that almost puckery darkening softness around them and a lot of crow's-feet, the way it is for any man who is nearly forty. Like her dear one, Gordon.

Lee Lynn, still standing quite near, is profoundly silent.

Willie Lancaster. The notorious Border Mountain Militia newspaper celebrity who gives some people headaches and others bigger headaches.

Bree giggles.

Willie's eyes move all over the place and all over Bree. But around Bree, too. That aura of fresh light that is around her bright skin and hair. And his eyes move in and among the voluptuous pumpkins and shapely rocks and over the humped backs of youthful gardeners along the nearby hillside. Then, as his and twelve-year-old Kirky Martin's eyes meet, he does a quick salute and Kirky returns the salute and smiles just a little.

Bree knows all about Willie Lancaster. She and Dee Dee St. Onge (Willie's daughter; yes, Willie's daughter who is married to Gordon's cousin) have had some really deep talks. Dee Dee, who like so many here has become even in a short summer's time like a sister to her, and Dee Dee's husband, shy Lou-EE, like a brother. And Dee Dee talks about her dad a lot.

Bree knows everything about Willie, though she can't remember ever seeing him before the day of the Lincoln windmill's completion, he in his camo BDU shirt and militia emblem, and that way he walked around through the crowd. He seemed both heavy and light, reserved and transparent. She has never seen him this close till now, so close she can smell toothpaste and the sweetness of his washed hair and clothes. Regardless. She *knows* Willie Lancaster.

He is still bouncing on his heels and looking around, then looks back to Bree's face and she laughs. Not a giggle but a low velvety laugh.

He says, "I want to talk about somethin'."

She says, "What?"

He looks around. His smile gone, but his eyes still merry.

She glances down at his forearms, a man who for a living climbs trees, swings from tree to tree with a belt and rope, spiked creepers, gripping trees with his thighs while making it look like nothing to lop off hundred-pound limbs with a small-model chain saw, making the chain saw look like a weightless little nothing, juggling everything, including his life, at forty or sixty or seventy or more feet up in a tree that might be punky, might not be a friend. Bree, age fifteen and *committed* to that *other* forty-year-old man, is wild with wanting Willie Lancaster. And yes, in her strange, wide-apart yellowy eyes, he had, in Lincoln, Maine, in the seven seconds their eyes had met, seen this spelled out.

He's smart and he's a problem. Rex York's words once said to Mickey Gammon, the fifteen-year-old militia member, about Willie only a few weeks ago, testimony continuously unchallengable.

Willie says, "I think there might be an eclipse tonight. Or somethin' good in the sky. You know, somethin' good to look at."

She does not lower her freak's face to hide it. Her hair is pinned back so securely these days but she does not hide herself because the feel of Willie's eyes on her face is unquestionably amorous.

She stands up. He stands up. They are the same height. He might even be shorter. An inch shorter, maybe. For she is tall and solid-boned and long-bodied. But like a loaded train shrieking and thundering on the rails, a train with an inflexible schedule, could Willie Lancaster have the kind of stuff to cut you in half? Especially while you are neck deep in the dainty waters of the age of fifteen.

Willie looks around, sees Lee Lynn pretending not to watch, stroking her baby's shoulder. And he studies the little shrieking conflict going on near Glennice's garden, four kids arguing over some crates of spotted gourds. He says to Bree, "Tell the lady you'll be right back."

Bree walks over to Lee Lynn and says, "I'm going home now. See ya tomorrow." Kisses baby Hazel. "See ya tomorrow, Hazel." And Hazel points toward the arguing kids and says, "Bad."

And Lee Lynn's light-colored eyes scan Bree's face. "Everything okay, Bree?"

Bree giggles. Lowers her eyes.

"What's *he* want?" Lee Lynn asks in a whisper.

Bree giggles and puts her arms around Lee Lynn. "I love you, my most excellent sister," she says in a clarion tone, not a whisper. Then releases her, the slim shoulders, the fragrant wild hair and skin, all kooky and particular to Lee Lynn.

"What does he *want*?"

"Nothing." Bree laughs.

Lee Lynn makes a face. Glances over at Willie, cocky, grinning, barely bearable Willie Lancaster. She looks back at Bree, whisper persisting. "You're going *home*?"

Bree says, "Yep."

And now walking with Willie, she doesn't look back at her "sister." She does pause, however, by Glennice's garden again, and she says, "I don't actually live here. I live over on the Shipley-Little Road."

"I know where you live," he says.

Bree stares a long time at Glennice's large Eden-like garden. In fact, Glennice has several large gardens and still makes time to work patiently with all the Settlement kids on their "free verse" gardens.

Glennice's pumpkins are perfect, with skin that seems to blush and breathe.

Bree looks from this holy ground up to Willie Lancaster's eyes. "That was your car, wasn't it? The Nova?"

"My ship," he says. He has a nice voice. Not deep exactly. But not reedy.

Now they walk along by Lessard's experimental grain field with its tall, heavily tasseled blond rye as still as a picture.

And then over into the parking lot they walk, past Bree's brother's pickup, and Willie opens the passenger door of his low-slung old Chevy Nova. "See!" he exclaims as he is about to close the door for her. He points up. There is one white smoldering squirming little star in the otherwise empty darkening sky.

They ride along.

He keeps grinning at her. His car hasn't much of a muffler. The thumping popping rumble bounces back from houses and trees as the car rolls past.

Between the bucket seats is the dark handle of a handgun in a leather holster, with the leather strap wrapped tightly around it.

Willie is pretty quiet for a few minutes.

Bree knows that the test has begun. To sort the unraveling layers. She knows Willie is a bullshitter. Scandalous. Spontaneous. But not compulsive. Compulsion is not part of this. Willie is (Dee Dee and others have said this) cunning. And meticulous. And exasperatingly loyal.

She knows he has an elaborate shortwave set up and an expensive computer. He researches common law and works with a statewide effort to bring back this, "the true law," "the law of the constitution." He does computer e-mail and "snail mail" about the threat of the New World Order. He warns of American and foreign armies training together. He has photos of these combined armies copied from dozens of other Militia Movement–Patriot Movement newsletters from other states, and the computer. He calls Democrats "socialists." He calls Washington "a hotbed of socialism." He keeps thick folders of articles on the evils of democracy and why the United States is a republic and not a democracy, but especially why it should *never* be a democracy. Besides the FEMA conspiracies, the get-all-of-our-guns-away-from-us conspiracies, the FBI-infiltration-of-the-militias conspiracies, the privatizing-of-the-patent-system conspiracy, the unconstitutionality of the IRS and Federal Reserve, and the "homosexualizing of all our kids by the school system" conspiracy, the main thrust of most of the articles is that Republicans (at least some of them) want a republic and Democrats want a democracy, democracy being a synonym for "chaos," while the upper and lower cases of "d" and "r" are bristling hither and yon as you read along about how "Republican" has to do with self-sufficiency and "democratic" and "democracy" or "Democrat" and "Democracy" are about big government, which means HUGE TAXES and "Communism," and, therefore, if not tied in with "Mother Russia," are at least, at the very least, *foreign*.

Dee Dee has shown Bree some of her father's stuff. "His weird crap," Dee Dee called it. And laughed. And Dee Dee had said, "He thinks he's protecting his family. Really truly. He's so like that." And Dee Dee has told of his tenderness. "You have to know him reeal good to know it." And she had made a flustered farts-of-the-lips noise and laughed a little too wickedly. "You can't see it when he's out walking around!"

Bree now sighs deeply, longs for a cigarette.

It is darker as they ride under this canopy of trees, heading out north of Egypt. Willie snaps on the headlights.

Bree glances at Willie, the way he holds the wheel with both hands. His hands are large and the wheel slides loosely inside his fingers and palms. He wears no wedding ring.

As the rumbling car rounds a curve, the headlights swipe over a brown frame house with sheds and one car in the dirt drive, a lot of birch trees. Three-wheeler ATVs. A whirligig of Tweetie Bird on the really tiny lawn. The rest is woods and sand with much willful plantain.

Willie brakes so the rumbling car now moves at a crawl and he leans his head forward with his cheek and chin almost touching the wheel as he tries to see out Bree's open window, something in the yard of these people.

"People you know?" she asks.

"Naw, not exactly. Not really *know*."

Up ahead, he whips the Nova into the ruttiness of a recent logging yard, turns back.

Bree watches the dooryard and house and all the stuff slide back into the headlights. Not a well-lit place. But not dark either.

Willie pulls off onto the shoulder, cuts the lights, leaves the engine thumping and whispering in its baritone monologue of bad exhaust. Bree sits square-shouldered and ladylike, hands in her lap. Her wide-apart eyes are just two hard-to-identify glossy spots in the dark.

Willie tells her, "If somebody besides me comes toward this car, you wriggle over behind the wheel and *go*. Take her a mile down, turn in by that rightaway by the dam. Then wait. But . . . don't worry, sweetie." He gets up into a crouch over the center console and rubs his Jack the Ripper–style beard against her cheek, then kisses her perfect mouth. "I'll be back." Then he hops out, shuts the door easy, and slips off to the left, through the dark.

Bree looks down. Gun is still there.

Bree gets it that Dee Dee St. Onge has no problem with her father's wildness. She's got about a half million Willie stories she gets a kick out of telling, and all of them command a rapt audience. Though none of the stories include messing around on his wife. But stuff like once while having an argument with Dee Dee's mother in front of his mother-in-law, who hates him, Willie, picked up one of the white spotty pug-faced dogs and, calling it by his mother-in-law's name, "Vi," French-kissed it, with his tongue practically down the poor dog's trusting throat, for a long, *long* minute. The dog's legs struggled. But Willie kept moaning, and then disconnecting his tongue from the dog's throat just long enough to gasp, "Vi . . . oh, Vi . . . my gawd, Vi! This *is* you, isn't it?"

Even with the windows open there are no night sounds, no crickets reaching Bree's ears. Just the throaty rumblings of Willie's hot rod. Bree is tempted to whip out her pack of cigarettes. Couldn't be any worse than the exhaust fumes that are probably leaking in. But she knows Willie is not a smoker and she feels something . . . respectfulness? . . . motherliness . . . a kind of sense of preciousness concerning him . . . oddly. Now she feels her face with both hands. The space between her eyes is slightly cleft, just above the bridge of her nose. A wide straining space, at times a little blue-green, as if a normal quite lovely nose were trying to pull her eyes closer together with all its might. Sadly, she sighs.

When the driver's-side door flies open, she jumps a mile. Willie laughs ghoulishly, slips into the seat using one hand to shift, has the car rolling even before his other hand has the door slammed shut, the car backing up fast, down around the curve, Willie's face and shoulder twisted around. Then, by a kind of Willie-radar, a gauging Bree cannot fathom, moving in darkness, blurred and flitting pink of the taillights, shadows and bouncing mirrors, he finds the turnaround and backs in there, ferns crackling hysterically under one rear wheel.

Then they are off again.

Bree is looking hard at Willie.

"Well," he says with a snort. "It was rabbits. Sometimes it's something else . . . turkeys. Raccoons."

Bree takes a slow deep breath.

Giving his navel area a scratching with a finger between his shirt buttons, Willie says, "Nobody should live in a cage."

"You let them all loose?"

He looks at her, not smiling. "Yes, ma'am."

Bree looks down at her hands, smiling. "Where are we going?"

"Look!" He points up at the shaking line of the sky between the trees. "More 'a them damn stars."

"You always take your gun." She does not ask. She speaks this, this truth.

Willie says, "Never go anywhere without your gun and your Bible."

"Where's *your* Bible?" she asks with narrowed eyes.

He reaches across and pats the glove box. In a slow grave way, he confesses, "I had to kill an agent once."

She nods. She knows he wants her to say, "Oh, no!"

He says, "I *had* to. I couldn't tell where he was making his move but I was ready when he came in from the left side of me. If I wasn't wearing my bulletproof, he'd have opened me up here." He grips himself in the rib cage, right side. "He missed, then fired a second time. I had to kill him."

"Wasn't *he* wearing bulletproof stuff, too? That Kevlar? I thought they—"

"I know how to work around that. That's part of what I'm good at."

"You weren't arres—"

"Nooooo." He smiles his sliest cat-that-ate-the-canary smile. "They know better than that."

"But—"

"Hey!" he says so sharply that she looks ahead, expecting something in the road. But it's just more dark winding hilly Egypt road. "Tell me. It's no secret that Gordo is puttin' the meat to all you women. I just wanna know how it all figures. You all sign a pact? You got somethin' that keeps you girls from tearin' each other's eyes out?"

Bree tsks.

He says deeply, "I *heard* you was his special one. I *heard* he loves your mind or something like that. And I says to myself, 'William Daniel, she is pure gold. That Vandermast kid. She is not run-of-the-mill.' Besides, I already knew that back when you were a little twerp when those rumors were goin' around about the Maine Guide scam some of your people were up to in Piscataquis. An' that winter your ol' man and my ol' man with all his arthritis were the winners in the Day Pond derby and we did the whole weekend, about twelve of us sleepin' on the ice and i'twas cold as a witch's tit, nonstop winds. You remember that derby, dear?"

"Sort of. Because—"

"You remember *me*?"

"Well . . . I was kinda young. I remember when that lady was drunk and got burned."

"Fell in the bonfire. That was Maxine Dubois."

Bree says, "Dad doesn't have time to fish anymore."

Willie wags his head. "Tellll me about it. What a bitch."

Bree smiles. "I've probably seen you over the years . . . but lately I guess we don't cross paths much . . . or I'd remember. Up at Lincoln the other day, I *noticed* you."

He looks at her and says almost angrily, "So Gordo gets in your pants."

"So?"

"Don't get your back up with me. I'm just making conversation."

Bree folds and unfolds her hands, looks at the road. She says, "I never saw that lady after that. Did she die?"

"Naw. She wasn't burned *that* bad. Just one hand . . . arm or something. Boy you *were* little, weren't you?"

"I remember the Wests."

"Their kid decided to be a fag."

"Oh, Willie, he didn't *decide* to be."

Willie makes a really wide-eyed stupid face at her and she looks away.

He says in a low voice, "Be careful. Don't let anyone think you're some friggin' liberal."

Again Bree tsks, shakes her head in disgusted amazement. Not real amazement. Just mock amazement.

Willie snarls, "Gordo teach you that liberal shit?"

"No. I was *born* with a brain."

With a huge smile now, his somewhat protruding teeth seeming to squirm around, he says, "I *love* this little fight we're havin'," and jerks the steering wheel back and forth a few times, taking the car all over the road. Then he says in a soft way, "Brianna. I want you to take the time to read Revelations. Then, the next time we get together, we'll talk about it. Okay?"

She looks at him. "Sure."

He asks if she would like to see his brother's hunting camp in Vermont. "It's messy. But it's got a lotta stars."

"Vermont?"

He growls. "Yessssss . . . riding the Kancamagusssssssss!"

She giggles. "Sure . . . if we can stop once so I can smoke."

"No," he says grumpily. "Bad girl."

The road ahead unwinds and unwinds. Gently.

He's not a fast driver (amazingly). He talks about his brother who owns the camp. One of his live brothers. He has five live brothers. And one dead brother. "Gone brother," he says with his big smile. "I mean, he was liquefied or something. Maybe sucked up by a big gook vacuum cleaner. Maybe *worse*!" He bugs out his eyes. Laughs.

There are long stretches driving the Kancamagus Highway where he shuts the Nova's headlights off. The wide black pavement and the lack of other cars and the qualriptillion stars and thin cold-looking piece of moon can be terrifying . . . like being suspended . . . like being lost in emptiness. Bree wants VERY BADLY to fill up with hot tobacco smoke. She wants to lean against Willie. But there is the console, the shift, the gun. She foresees it will be an eternity before it will be possible to be in his arms.

Indeed, it's the wee hours before they arrive.

The camp is not much roomier than a dollhouse. No electricity. No plumbing. No outhouse. A little tin stove. But no wood. The walls are logs. Chinked with caulking and rags. The ceiling is so low that only in the very middle can they stand at full height. But mostly they don't stand. Their clothes are off immediately. Though Willie leaves on his dog tag, which he seems unnaturally attached to, and he and Bree get started so fast they've only managed to get one poorly short-wicked candle lit and the short slanted cabin door hangs wide open, quite forgotten. It's a little cold at first. Breaths are frosty. But somehow the air switches to tropical and clammy after just one of their desperate three-minute kisses.

It it no surprise to Bree that this calculating man makes a rubber appear . . . deftly . . . not fumbling through pockets . . . just kind of a magic trick following her hundred giggles and his antics, his jumping between the two foot-to-foot bunks, pillowcase on his head (everything else on him bare), then pretending to hang himself with a shirtsleeve, sticking his tongue out, crossing his eyes, then talking in "cowboy," "Better cut 'im down now, boys," then leaping Superman style into midair, landing on the floor on all fours so lightly he makes almost no sound and grabbing her from behind as she tries to get another candle started, both his arms around her middle, biting her neck and talking like Dracula. He never grabs her breasts or crotch. He's just an idiot, but also a gentleman. And no erection. Not really.

But then he rubs his face hard, as if to erase something, as if to erase the gentleman, and pushes her into the deep horribly squealing bunk of mouse-pissy wool blankets and gets right to the heart of the matter. And now, yes, he's as hard as a claw hammer. This is when *the foiled rubber* seems to have appeared.

She whispers, "I'm on the pill."

To those words he makes a face like a sarcastic *Ain't you smart*, then continues breaking open the foil. Then back to the business where he comes in less time than it took to unwrap the rubber.

But then, as he rises up on his knees, grinning with his protruding teeth and his damp hair hanging across one eye, he shifts into higher gear and, using both hands to push his hair back across his temples, he screams, "MORE!"

Unlike Gordon (Bree is quick to compare), he has no trouble with seconds. And then lots of energy to get really stupid and start running around again for half the night, hauling Bree off the bunk, tossing blankets to the floor, groaning, "Mothera God . . . Mothera God . . . Mothera God . . ." then fetching his pants to rip open a third rubber and doing it to Bree again on the floor.

Quiet for nearly ten minutes, both of them sprawled like slain victims on the gritty sandy floor, Bree whispers, "What's in Revelations?"

"Read it, then *you* tell *me*."

"Okay."

"All you need to know is in that book."

She laughs.

He grips her arm and speaks in a dangerously ugly voice, "Don't laugh. Or God will spank you," then he powerfully flips her over, which does, yes, scare her, and smacks her bottom twice before she, giggling and shrieking, pushes the blankets over his face, jumps to her feet, breasts waggling around so hard, so fiercely that they hurt, and runs outside. "I gotta peeeee!" she calls back.

But when she returns the short very dark distance, the low wooden door is closed and *locked*.

It is about forty degrees on her side of the door. She says, "Shit," softly to herself. She stands there a huge long minute, refusing to scream or beg. She's not got chattering teeth yet but her goose bumps are big as acorns.

She hugs herself, frowning, listening, disgusted. A lonnnnng unrewarding five minutes pass. She thinks about what's beyond that door. Warm air. Well, *warmish* air. And Willie. And her cigarettes.

She dies ten deaths when a deep snorting and swishing come out of the sky. It's Willie jumping from the low camp roof, falling on her. It hurts because he kind of bashes her shoulder and left arm with his descending weight.

She doesn't giggle.

With both hands, he takes her face sweetly, fingers so light, like mice . . . kisses her. His mouth is sweet. Everything about him is sweet. His beard smells like pine spills and pitch, from the roof, while the cold open outdoors around them is its own confection. With the wavering dismal light that is the dying candle just inside one plastic-covered window, he stops kissing, just looking at her face, his eyes filled with appreciation, almost gratefulness, and his arms go around her and he says quietly, "Don't ever tell my wife. She'd leave me. I don't want that. What I have . . . the home . . . the life . . . it's all I got." And next comes a chuckle. A bitter one. "And besides, sweetheart, you are jailbait. Me and Gordo, your Gordo, your King Shit . . . he . . . he and I could go to *prison* cause of a little girlie like you."

Bree says, "But everyone back at the Settlement saw us leave."

"Sure. Sure. Riding around is okay, ain't it?"

Bree blinks. "But . . . don't any of your *older women* affairs get back to your wife? Judy. Doesn't anything get back to her? Not everyone is as—" She nuzzles his ear. "—as nice and secret as me."

He hugs her harder. She can't fully breathe. Against his chest, one of her breasts feels the sharp cut of his dog tag. He says, "I don't give a frig if you believe this or not . . . but . . . I . . . always have been faithful to Judy. And before Judy, I didn't have no one. I was . . . shy—"

"Shy!" She gives a shriek of a laugh, face against his shoulder.

"In certain ways."

"In certain ways," she repeats.

"I don't care if you believe that," he says hoarsely and, not letting the wee spot of candlelight from the plasticked-over window play on his face, tips his face away.

"Willie, I promise I'll read Revelations."

"You just want ol' Willie to take you out for a nice date again," he says with feigned sulkiness. "You just love Willie. And your promises . . . have . . . what's that they say? . . . hidden agendas."

She giggles and goes for more of his sweet, sweet mouth.

Our epiphany.

So now, what about Bree? What do we know of her desires?

Unlike Gordon St. Onge, whose exhausting sex life is one steeped in duty and borderless, seemingly divine love, might Bree's nature be rooted in just lust? In steamy gobbling boorish feasting?

Had the hurdles that stood between Bree and this feasting been only her face and her shame? And now, something begins? Time-released possibilities unfolding? A parade of men? Wrong men, scary men, married men, men who never smile, men with terrible smiles, reckless men, hazardous men, desperadoes, pirates, men who will die young, die of work or war or mistakes or anger, but dying, always dying, yes, in their prime.

Or could it just be that Willie Lancaster is significant? Ah, *Willie*.

Could it be that Willie Lancaster is, in some singular way, *meant* to happen to her? As it is when you work your telescope pointed up there at random in a night sky and certain unseemly stars and planets come into focus and a comet bashes into somebody else's atmosphere and forever changes everything.

2:14 a.m. of a different night.

Another Lancaster relative's camp. Or a friend of Willie's. Bree can't remember what it was that he said. But this one is much closer than Vermont. One of those Denmark ponds, two towns away. She can never keep those ponds straight. They arrived at dark. They've been together for hours. Neither one eats or drinks. Everything has shut down in their bodies but that electrification of wee wees and tunnels and that inelegance of the tongue and mouth . . . as if the mouth were inside out and the tongue a cold snake. Whose tongue? Can't keep those tongues straight. How many snakes? Thousands. Yes, this is disgusting for *us* to hear about, but for the doers it is not.

Before dawn.

Willie is sitting out on the little stony step, looking off across the water with the splashy reflections of pink security lamps of the many camps on the other side. He is very quiet and somewhat dressed. Pair of work pants. No shirt. No shoes. The dog tag, always the dog tag. Nothing in his hands. Boots and socks on the sill, ready to go.

She does not want to leave. She is not dressed at all, although it is pretty chilly in this musty creosote-smelling camp with too many bad chimneys, plenty of porches, plenty of musty camp beds, plenty of cute knickknacks on the pine panel walls but no stopping of the time.

Time. Please, stop.

She doesn't ever want to put on clothes again.

She steps up behind him, drops quickly to a squat, grabs him by the hair of the head.

"Hey, bitch," he says, beginning to turn toward her.

Bree laughs, not letting go of his hair. "Poor baby. You're gonna be raped," she says.

He doesn't startle easily, not ever, not now, the hair-pulling, all of it. He takes it with a certain ease.

She works his head back so that his bearded chin is up, throat bared. Hair, throat, collarbones, chest, and ribs. Human perfection. It has made Bree forget sunsets, vistas, autumnal country roads. And Gordon.

When she gets Willie down on his back, head "pillowed" on the floor, she lets go of his hair, steps around to stand between his raised knees.

"Don't try to get away," she growls.

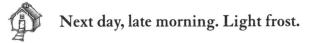

Next day, late morning. Light frost.

Bree comes winding up the dusty Settlement road a little too fast. Her father's hot rod pickup, which used to be a cousin's pickup, WBLM bumper sticker, windshield visor, fender skirts.

Pursuing her, just catching up, is a newish three-quarter-ton sided-up flatbed truck towing a roadwork-sized chipper. Business lettering on the truck's doors. As Bree slips the pickup between other vehicles, the flatbed with chipper swings in behind her, almost broadside. Kicked-up dirt boils up, drifting white-gold across the first bars of cold sun from the mountain.

Bree slips down off the seat of "her" truck. First she hears the ringing hammers of a cedar shingle roofing job on one of the new cottages on the hillside, the one that had been started for Silverbell Rosenthal, though she is still missing. Her not-missing kids believe it is theirs.

Now Bree sees Willie, who appears all at once in a jump, the way Superman always lands in front of you with his chest out (which no bullets can riddle). There is Willie's fearless smile, teeth that don't fully jut out but they do lie more to the outside of his bottom lip than inside, as though he might need them to chew his way through a wall. Or a cage. Willie would never be caged long.

He steps in close to her, away from his tree-biz truck, almost belt buckle to belt buckle, if she were wearing a belt. But he doesn't touch her. No hugs. No stroke of her cheek. His breath is smoking cold.

She raises both hands to her temples to feel for the little ringlets of her carroty hair there, all that's left of those longer side pieces, which only two days ago were snipped off by the beauty crew, not much to hide behind with all that long hair only in back, hiding still being her first inclination. And her breath smokes cold. And Willie and Bree have red noses and wet eyes.

He reaches past her neck and ear to muckle onto a mirror of "her" truck, so now she's happily cornered by him and he says, "Gotcha."

But now her smile wavers. "There're people watching us."

The ringing hammers don't seem to break rhythm.

Willie says, "I'm just being neighborly."

Bree rolls her eyes. "Well, if you're not worried about your wife and my husband, what about the gate you just took down to get in here. You could be shot."

Now Willie rolls *his* eyes.

Bree giggles.

Still with one hand on the mirror, he places the other hand, fingers apart, on his waist up under his short unzipped wool jacket. He is looking hard now at the space between her eyes, the slightly bluish straining bunch where the bridge of her nose should be as if he never noticed it before. "What happened?"

"Birth defect."

"Anybody ever treat you mean about it, I'll kill 'em. I'll kill 'em all."

She giggles a frosty, "Poof!"

He looks at her perfect mouth. Inside the trimmed mustache and beard, his own mouth tightens as one would do before kissing or sucking.

The hammers don't break their rhythm but one of the hammerers would maybe break Willie? Gordon picks more of the ridged roofing nails from his apron, the hammers all around him issuing across the valley and slopes of the St. Onge fields and St. Onge gardens, St. Onge pasturage, sounding like machine-gun fire. He knows that all the men and boys around him also see Willie and Bree down there in the lot beyond the Quonset huts. He flushes a mortified vermilion.

Bold fucker. Comes right up here into the heart of St. Onge territory to do this mating dance. Gordon feels these unspoken words as he smashes another nail down through the shingle.

So.

See all the ways Brianna Vandermast St. Onge, her future big as a lake, with youthful unintendedness and remorselessness, is able to shove Gordon's nose into the fire. But how many of us would call this burning of him, this skewering of him, "justice"?

The cottage for Silverbell (wherever she is) finally has windows and doors. Front door newly painted a heartfelt rose by Bard. Helpful daily advice is available for all from the crow who often stands on the handlebars of parked solar buggies . . . "Change your shirt. You look like a bum. Change your shirt. You look like a bum . . ."

Bree is told that Gordon and Beezer (a woman, but not one of his wives) are doing some wiring on the new cottage. Stepping up onto the temporary cinder block step, she hears four-year-old Rhett St. Onge's dolorous exhortations, sees Gordon standing at a sawhorse in the front room, picking out blue plastic outlet boxes from a plastic bag. No sign of Beezer.

Gordon is wearing his cheapie plastic old-mannish drugstore reading glasses. No billed cap. His head sometime yesterday fell into the hands of the insistent beauty crew and so now his hair is chopped off even shorter than it had been for Morse Weymouth's memorial. Beard *very* short. Mustache still long. He looks down at the blue outlet box that he is turning slowly in his fingers. Another blue box is in Rhett's two-handed grip. And Rhett wears an apron for tools, something clinking and jinkling in the pockets.

He chirps, "See our thing, Meghan. See our thing in here." Rhett still gets her name wrong. She is not around enough, just painting or doing sneaky subversive meetings in the woods. Rhett hustles over to the open studs of the back interior wall pointing out a completed set of outlets, three in a row.

Bree oohs and aahs over these boxes. She asks if he helped.

He nods with his usual melancholy face. She sees so much of his mother Beth in his looks. Not much of her wiseass toughness. And she sees his sweet neck. Sweet fingers. Maybe she, too, could love all these children as her own. Though she sometimes forgets her concerns about the world's overpopulation and imagines one or two of her own blood among the St. Onge tribe. Maybe someday. A day better than this one.

Gordon kneels to begin work on another wall. She watches the hunch of his shoulders, his hand reaching for wire cutters, his twisting jerking wrist as he snips wire and so forth, then works a screw in at the top, one at the bottom. Done.

"Gordon, I need to talk to you about an idea . . . which, of course we wouldn't go ahead with, with . . . without—" Is her voice a little sassy? "Without your permission."

He snorts. "My permission?"

"The phone, your phone bill—"

"In name only, Brianna. It's for the sake of all of us that we're frugal. It's not really Gordon-the-Tightwad. Just Gordon-the-Scapegoat."

She smiles. "Well, anyway, our militia wants to put something extra toward the bill. We made a few militia calls. I do what I can at home . . . it's free on the Internet. But some work had to be done here by . . . the other officers."

He squints. "I'll sit down with the bookkeepers this week and go over it. Don't worry. A few calls to the *Record Sun* and *Bangor Daily* and whatever else you've done to stir up all Creation—" He chuckles. Seems he's green light on this? "As long as it doesn't become a lifelong habit." No, he is not being generous. He's being sarcastic. He turns away now. Picks up another outlet box.

She looks down. "And Gordon, something else. I know you're busy here."

He keeps working, says nothing.

"I know you're busy, but it's about something we decided was best, after all, to get your permission for. For . . . taking the kids to Augusta. We want to take them for a little thing . . . at the statehouse . . . something the kids really want to do. I mean the little kids. It's good to involve them, too. It's good for them. Kids learn what they live, right? They have to *live* democracy to visualize it, not just hear abstractions, right? But it would be *just* kids . . . teens and kids. Me, too. I'm just a kid, remember? You said it yourself." She giggles. "But . . . what I mean is . . . having it be just kids in the public eye is good for uh . . . what we're trying to do. You know what I mean? I . . . I can never say things right." She pinches her lips with her fingers. "Maybe we, you and me, should just start writing letters to each other again.

Like we used to. So much more poetic. I feel . . . really stupid when I try to tell you things. It is important to tell each other things. I think so, anyway. And you . . . you said it . . . about being honest. Remember?" Her large honey-color eyes, so wrongly spaced, show a sheen of frustrated tears, tears caused not by those who pity her but by one who pities himself in this thin and tired hour. "Remember?" she asks again, nudging with the word's three soft syllables.

He says nothing. There's just the tap-tap of wire and plastic bits dropping to the floor and silence for a full minute.

Meanwhile, Rhett is out around the doorstep, picking up roofing nails for his apron pocket.

Bree sighs.

And now a sigh from Gordon, an ugly ornery sigh, and he stands up to his full height, giant six-foot-five height, turns to face her, pulls off his funny glasses. Sneery cold smile. His eyes flit around over her head.

She places one hand at the back of her neck, looking down at a mess of sawdust and shavings and gray wire covering, bent nails, and one cheery Settlement-made pottery coffee mug. She wears a tasseled wool sash that hangs against one thigh of her jeans. It is scarlet. She and Jenny Dove St. Onge made it together, one for Jenny Dove, too. Jenny Dove's dyeing and weaving and stitching. Bree, the embroidery, Oriental-looking gold-and-green boughs. Violet-and-yellow starburst, or is it the sun? A kind of repeated theme, like Gordon's belt buckle of the ancient sun face that he used to wear, like the Settlement's June solstice celebrations and the Settlement's affinity with solar, lunar, seasons, fertility, and *all* things intrinsic? And now Astrid and Misty and Lolly are like a factory, making several more, one for each St. Onge wife, an intertwining of the sisters through the sinuosity of a radiant sash.

Bree wants to tell Gordon that she spends as much time with the women now as she does with the teenagers, that she is at home here, even though she still goes home at night to her little attic room, there on the Shipley-Little Road. And that even though she still works with her beloved father and brothers, here at the Settlement love is, yes, a starburst, a sunburst, power of hands and heartbeats and shared dreams, but what she now instead blurts out is, "You're mad at me about Willie."

When she looks at his face, his eyes are boring right into hers and he makes a low sound in his neck, something like unnnh, maybe meant to be uh-huh, but getting caught in a dry swallow of resistance.

She steps closer to him.

Jinglingly, Rhett comes loping back inside. "When are we going to make the other one?"

Gordon tells Rhett in a low voice that they will soon, and Bree notices that Gordon's dark work shirt is buttoned wrong. She wrings her hands once, then says slowly, "Willie reminds me of you."

Gordon gives her a mildly crazed look, the one eyebrow curved higher than ever over one pale, widened eye. Big mustache kind of ripples on both sides of his mouth and down along the jaws, the jaws clenching, as one might strive against vomiting.

"He reminds me of you *a lot,*" she says.

"You're kidding," says he, in a thin hard fashion.

"He's fun. Like you. You're fun. Sometimes."

He says with steely teeth and tongue, "Words I've heard to describe Mr. Lancaster are things like *trial and tribulation* . . . and *blooming idiot* . . . and *turkey* . . . and *banana*."

"Yuh, and fun," she says, giggling. It is not her seductive giggle. It's a giggle of nervousness as she watches this ugly thing that can't be fixed falling into the air between them, hating the sound of her own voice, betraying Willie's confidence though, of course, Willie's showiness betrays him enough, and she is betraying everyone somehow and sorrowing over the gray look of jealousy on the face of Gordon St. Onge. She has never heard Gordon speak with such revulsion before, not of any human being within the circle of his life. Yes, there are times she has viewed him as holy. As Glennice does? Yes. Like Glennice. Gordon, the superhuman being who grants shelter to all souls. She asks chokingly, "You want me not to come around the Settlement anymore?"

He is turning away, then drops his hand, letting his arm swing, and then turns back to her with an entirely different face, eyes soft.

Rhett is hopping, holding one foot and hopping and chanting, "Now, now, now, now, now . . ." And the jangling of the stuff in his apron pockets is irritating.

Bree sinks to the floor in front of Gordon. To light a candle to the holy one? To cross herself? No, she is drawing with a finger in the sawdust. Drawing little x's. She says, "Duty and Passion." She can't see his face; she sees just his work boots and the legs of his battered jeans sawdusted over as high as the knees, and Rhett hopping around, getting louder and louder, knocking over the pottery mug, which is tough and doesn't break, just rolls once. Bree says, "I came up here to talk with you about Duty. Not Passion."

She hears from him a scouring silence. She stands up, slapping her hands together, and then on the thighs of her jeans. She says, "The True Maine Militia wants to go to the statehouse next week to see the governor. It's important, Gordon. The kids of Maine . . . crushed by the thing . . . the kids of Maine demanding that they grow up to be not pigeons or cattle, but *citizens*."

He watches her moving lips.

She presses on, "It's everything. It would make people out there . . . notice. There would be media. That's the whole point. We've already called a couple of TV channels. And the statehouse has a regular media crew anyway."

He folds his arms across his chest, leans back against the wall of Settlement-milled studs. Now he does one of his usual bear back scratches, his eyes still on her mouth.

She is saying, "We decided we should tell you and not do it sneaky. Because . . . because . . . you are . . ." She smiles oddly. "You're almost everybody's father." She smiles again.

He replies, "And if I say *no*, who vetoes me? Who overrules? Seven- and eight-year-olds? Fifteen-year-olds?"

"No one. We'll do what you say on this."

"Okay," he says quietly. "Then you shall not take those kids up there."

Nervously and terribly, Bree giggles.

He goes to a splotchy new window and looks out, digging his bearded chin viciously.

Rhett is hopping one-legged over to him, chanting "Now! Now! Now! Now! Now!" and Gordon takes the boy's head in both hands and the boy turns sideways and slouch-leans against him. Instead of the view of sheep in a flexing jumble of gray shapes on the hill, what Gordon sees through the spotted glass is Willie Lancaster's hands on Bree. He sees the unfathomable merging of Willie and Bree, hears giggles and grunts. He sees Willie's cat-that-ate-the-canary smile.

Bree says, "I thought you were loosening up. I really did. Everybody said you were. But you're so moody! One minute you're friendly to the whole world, like when we were in Lincoln. The next minute you want us all in a bunker!" She is standing with her boots apart, the way you face an opponent in the dusty street of a Hollywood version of a southwestern frontier town. She rubs her thumbs across her forefingers, her fingers scratchy, not silky like the fingers of most of America's young girls . . . or the fingers of most Americans. She says, "Well, okay, good-bye," and leaves.

Rhett hops around Gordon now, around and around. Hop. Hop. Hop. Hop. Hop. Hop. Hop. Hop.

Duotron Lindsey International's chief executive officer begins each day early, ends late.

Business as usual. The clock tocks, the wristwatch breathes in, out, in, out. Days blink past like guardrail posts as seen from a speeding car. Nothing ever changes about his robust pen strokes, his high-powered mind, his constant realizations that EVERYONE is an enemy of Bruce Hummer. East and west, they all intend to feast on his warm parts, liver, pancreas, spleen, like huge birds with yellow cold eyes, waiting for his one clumsy move. He mails another key. A jokey key as large as a bread cutting board. Plastic. Yellow and pink stars spelling out *Key to the New Century.*

Television and newspapers interview police and witnesses of today's incident outside the Department of Human Services office in Sanford, Maine.

After a few weeks of calm, the hooded men strike again. Three of them. More aggressive than before. Agile. "Like Batman and Robin," one patrolman tells Channel 13, though the Sanford police chief says, "These are terrorists."

It almost seems the men have contacts inside the various offices they hit because they have no hesitation about which person they'll grab coming out that door, which is used by social workers, salesmen, maintenance, postal delivery, and so forth. The hooded men have never grabbed anyone but a *welfare recipient*. It's always a young mother who has just applied or reapplied for family assistance, SSI, or food stamps.*

Concerning the suggestion that caseworkers might be informing the hooded men, a DHS spokesperson snorts, "That's ridiculous."

Today, twenty-two-year-old Ariana Hunter, whose children were in school at the time, stepped from the doors of the building, unwittingly right into the arms of the most aggressive hooded man, the most agile one, the one *without* a black robe, the one who wields the noose. She screamed, witnesses said. She screamed a lot. And she swore at them. She was a fighter. She was told by the noose man that she was about to be hanged for treason and he had no trouble getting the noose around her neck as another man gripped her arms. The third man growled, "Thief" and "Whore of Babylon" and "Pig" from behind his hood. Then, as the noose man and the other man walked her a few yards across the shopping center parking lot, gripping her tightly to keep her from kicking them, as she was trying to do, the third man read about whores from the Old Testament in a low voice.

"It was a chilling thing to see," said video store owner Kevin Gerouix. "It would put you to mind of the KKK."

In past incidents, the trio lets each woman free when she breaks down, sobs uncontrollably, or faints, sometimes after the noose man orders her to "Beg for forgiveness and promise to shape up," in a businesslike voice. And of course, they drop everything if the police arrive. Party's over for sure when the police arrive. Or rather *just before* the police arrive. They have a kind of built-in radar that detects when the police are just around the corner.

Cory St. Onge remembering.

Rex was getting more sour each time we saw his face. None of us Settlement guys and not even ol' Gordo were real members of the Border Mountain Militia. Gordo had invited himself and somehow a bunch of us followed. That seemed to me to be a problem . . . I mean, the problem of all problems was Gordo's spiels about foreign policy,

* We poor people are easily identifiable.

for instance. "The modern pharaohs of organized capital and their spooks! Laws bounce off them! Brutal! Fucking with the everyday people in Central America! South America! The old Soviet states! Africa. The Middle East! You actually believe they have a special place in their hearts for *YOU*?!! Hearts . . . excuse me, I mean the empty, wretched, devil-wretched hole of their missing souls!!" This brand of salvo he was usually not attacking people with, not directly or personally, especially since the Modern Monetary Theory incident that time, which his old blood brother later pitched a (quiet of course) fit over.

But it was just Gordo's generalized bellowing percolating ol' self . . . *heh-heh* . . . that caused stuff like this to bust out. No Settlement supper was without one or two or three or more of his roaring deliveries. But it seemed only a matter of time before Rex would, in his gentlemanly way, *uninvite* us from sitting in on his militia huddles.

So I for one was surprised when the Border Mountain Militia had on their calendars a meeting to take place at Gordo's old farmplace following a tour of Settlement attractions starting with the radio tower setup. There they were, all spilling out of their trucks and cars, most of them having donned full camo or just the BDU shirt with embroidered olive-and-black mountain lion shoulder patch, pistol belts, service pistols in black holsters, black combat boots. A few wore caps and two guys had binoculars. No Willie Lancaster, who it was said had work that day. But there were an even dozen. Made you feel real well-protected. *Heh-heh*.

There were nine of us Settlement guys not tied up elsewhere, all in our day-to-day work apparel.

Our radio tower and its little building structure were up behind two smaller Quonset huts on a grassy rise. Pretty impressive, if I say so myself. Looked like the sheriff's department. *Heh-heh*. Sort of. But it had a long ways to go to be useful. It was Ray Pinette's baby, actually. He'd been a shortwave buff from the age of thirteen up there in the County where he was from.

We all hiked up the rutty road that was cobbled in some places to the top of the bald mountain where all our windmills were. One of Rex's guys, George Durling, was dying of four types of cancer. You wouldn't recognize him from years past. Very thin and full bald again under his brimmed bush hat, but the hair you'd remember him by was thin anyway with some red, some gray round the sides, kind of curly. The chemo has a way of finishing good parts of you off while aiming for the bad thing. Reminds me of how these potentates running our government claim they're targeting some diabolical dictator while they burn and bludgeon and blow to smithereens fourteen cities and ten thousand villages of everyday and every sort of people. Oops. Sorry. Excerpted that from one of Gordo's deliveries. *Heh-heh-heh-heh.*

Anyway, so Butch rode Doug up the mountain on one of the solar buggies. Those things hum like a refrigerator on flat ground but whine like a hydraulic log loader on such a rough ride as that badass road.

Meanwhile, Art, with the sea captain's white beard and jolly way about him, was stout so he got pretty winded but he never asked or hinted for a ride and no one offered, since we were all too thought*less* or thought*ful* to speak up if you know what I mean.

It was a real autumn day and up there on the ledgy junipered height it was b-b-brisk for those with not enough layers. The wind spoke through the trees way down below and through the dozens of sets of vibrating blades on the turbines up above.

The larger-than-life mermaids and ghouls and devils the kids had painted years ago . . . "kids" includes me, *heh-heh* . . . were peeling in some spots . . . there on the one big old European-style windmill's wooden base.

Rex's guys had been pretty much bubble and squeak over the shortwave scene, shortwave being a sort of emblem of the militia/patriot movement. Had that manly war feel to it even though this was the computer age, the age of robots and kick-ass high speeds. But also this was the age of oil company PR. So the windmills did not impress. Just got some polite nods.

Even Rex, who had, back in time, been one of those to get the turbine for the old Netherlands-style critter in place, had little to say in its honor.

But hey, we got fresh air to make us all bright-eyed and bushy-tailed. You can't get more value than that.

Then we all trooped down to the trucks in the Settlement lot so they could drive them down around to Gordo's place for the meeting in the dining room. After a bunch of chitchat about traveling together to meet with some out-of-state and upstate militias that had written to Gordon, yes, US post office handwritten letters, Rex dug out of his camo shirt pockets an olive-and-black embroidered shoulder patch with the mountain lion and Border Mountain Militia lettering, and with a ceremonious arc of that hand, delivered it to Gordo's hand.

Now I was silly with shock. I mean, I guess it would have been more believable if Rex had included with it a roll of duct tape for Gordo's mouth.

Instead, Rex laid out, one by one, patches for all the rest of us Settlement guys who were present.

Rex's fifteen-year-old militia member Mickey Gammon, who always carried a big cloud of moldering stench about him due to the modern inconveniences of living in a tree house, wore an expression like Rex's. Cement-hard and watchful.

Gordo said in a jolly way, "Well, this is it." Probably deep down he knew that Rex's militia wasn't *it*. As far as dying on your feet instead of living on your knees goes, as the revolutionary Emilio Zapata swore he himself would do, Rex's militia's aims were more soft and safe. After all, Gordo was bothered deeply by the big money monster's wicked work on the world, right? That's not a soft, safe target.

At the same time Gordo was not a fighter. He was a mouth. He was a coward. I don't mean to insult my father. My words here are not a jab. They are a rosy posy fact. I will never call Guillaume St. Onge a bad man. He was a good man. But does "good" fix anything?

Next night. Eleven o'clock. Gordon reads two letters with interest.

One is written on stationery with a return address:

From the officer of the Acting Commander Gregory Gleason, Chandler Captain CSDF

Command Headquarters

The rest of this return address is either stubborn or nervous. *Harris, Kentucky State Republic*. No zip.

The sender has used a stamp that depicts the United Nations but a red ballpoint pen has been used to mark over it with a circle and diagonal line, as with NO SMOKING and NO U TURN signs. Red ink is not detectable to post office machinery? Only to believers in the movement?

The computer printout letter inside is brief and to the point. Would Gordon be interested in meeting with this Kentucky militia?

The next letter, this one from western Massachusetts, is gusting with outrage and a hell of a lot of exclamation marks. The letterhead reads: *GOD SAVE AMERICA*. Enclosures decorated with American flags call for impeaching the "socialist president," with map reprints showing where foreign armies are positioned, readying to close in on the United States, and these newsletters and flyers are cooking with biblical expletives telling of God's wrath against "illegal immigrants" and predictions by famous psychics of global chaos caused by God to punish gay men. And the "mud" races. The letter is two typed pages. Spelling errors and typos are in quantity and there is urgency to the signature slashed on with a blue ballpoint. This man's name is Frank Kidd.

Like the first letter, Kidd's letter invites Gordon to attend a meeting of his militia, the Greylock Minutemen. One militia meets on the first Saturday of each month. The other doesn't specify a date. Both explain that Captain Richard York of the Border Mountain Militia suggested that Gordon make his presentation, "which Captain York tells us is interesting." (Rex has said *that*?!)

Gordon writes back to both of them that he would be "honored" to attend their meetings, specifying November to the first man. He explains his need for time to plan for travel and will probably bring some other guys with him. He signs each letter,

Yours in Freedom, Gordie St. Onge.

Then he takes two aspirin and tears open and reads the next twenty-four letters, dutifully answering some but never having time to answer them all. Soon his eyes droop and he falls asleep with his arms folded on his desk, waking at a quarter of one, getting up quickly, still foggy from sleep, slapping on his billed cap, snatching up a wool vest from a shedway hook, knowing his wife Astrid is expecting him, heart pounding in his ears, a weird pressure in his head, and the inaudible whoosh of that which pulls him to whatever it is that waits OUTSIDE the Settlement gate, the shadow figures of so many lefts, rights, overs, and unders who now know his name and want him to step out into the open. And he's ready, right? Camo jacket, Border Mountain Militia patch, and his old blood brother Rex's support. And what else? A belief that everyone has a good side? Well, in the leafy squirrel's nest of Gordon's brain, that belief goes into and out of fashion every few days. So *hurrah!* for the certainties of the *now*.

Busy at the Bureau.

A fellow in a short-sleeved dress shirt of ghostly gray and lighter gray stripes, no tie, gray-haired, experienced. Wedding ring. Lives an ordinary life. Leans forward in his desk chair in the old but well-heated federal building. He mouses and scrolls and scans with thunderbolt yellowy eyes, page after page slowly up over the screen, just scraping along over the facts and the foolishness of the un-Americans in Maine.

The eye is on you, you weird motherfucker Gordie, and your pleasantries with ninety-year-old white supremacists in the far-flung shitholes via the US Postal Service. True, true . . . computers and phones are how we monitor the *full range* of domestic terror and riot-making individuals but when you are the bull's-eye, we'll eventually be drinking coffee with you. And I don't mean just that goofball operative Marty Lees, who goes by another name in your town and the surrounds, the guy who can't seem to chisel his way through Mr. York's unpersonable barrier of paranoia.

But we *love* Mr. York. And we love *you*. You gentlemen are our dream come true. Get that? You are shit. And you are gold.

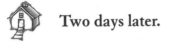

Two days later.

This morning light in autumnal slant crashes through the purply-orange monster maple behind Gordon's old house, then through the spotty kitchen window glass to splay across Gordon's largest desk. Such a torrent of beauty draws Claire's eyes, then she notices two wide-open letters there, and one of Gordon's, half done.

She presses her steamy-from-cold-to-warm glasses to her nose for better viewing, sees that the handy rotary files sport brand-new address cards with the names of strangers. Oklahoma. Texas. Florida. The can of pens is full, ever ready.

The clock chips away a few more minutes.

She finds Gordon in the unheated parlor, where he must have been alone all night. Lumpy couch. Overhead light ablaze, that old-timey frosty glass fixture dangling from a bronze chain, ONE HUNDRED WATTS. ONE HUNDRED WATTS WASTED WHILE HE SLEEPS! He is curled almost into a fetal position, which Claire has never known him to do before. This he has also begun doing, going back to sleep after or during breakfast, a thing he has always called a waste of daylight, especially immaculate cold-weather light such as today's.

She wipes her still steamed-up glasses with a bandanna that is half in, half out of the pocket of her brown wool jacket. Spread over the back of her jacket, her heavy black hair. She smells strongly of the snow-white snow-cold snowless outdoors and that big wind that is tearing scarlet and yellow leaves away, away, away.

She slips her glasses back on and still he doesn't wake, just keeps on with that *sssss-cha, ssss-cha* of his deep weltering sleep.

"Gordon," she says.

His sleeping noises instantly stop.

"Gordon, baby," she says but does not step closer.

She did not bring the letters from the desk. They are carved ruthlessly into her heart. But under her left arm is a basketball-sized hunk of today's mail, letters and cards addressed to him all wrapped up inside the newsletters and ad circulars. A few brown manila envelopes under the other arm.

"Gordon," she says.

He opens his eyes and they struggle a moment but at last find her face and shining parted hair, gray at the ears.

He smiles squintily.

She says, "Shove over."

He unfolds himself and sits up, slides along to make room, eyes still squinting, taking a few deep breaths through his nose, suppressed yawns or something.

She settles in against his side, in that way that she fills a lot of space. "I've been snooping."

He looks down at the mountain of mail in her lap.

She gives a little snort of wonder, then shakes her head.

"Yeah? So what's up?" He rubs one eye with the heel of a hand.

She transfers the hefty blob of mail to his lap, some smaller envelopes slapping to the floor, those special mailers for DVDs and CDs from people who are definitely meowing up the wrong cactus. "The white identity newsletters are disgusting," she says. "Baby, you must see. And I know you don't *skim*-read. You've seen all that crap about Jews and Mexicans and . . . the 'mud' races. Baby, *I* am one of the mud races, right? *And your children*."

His face solidifies, now a mask of what? A vision so naive it smells like mother's milk?

Claire half-cries, half-snarls, "They are awful people!"

He is looking right at her and his stiff not woken-up face stays stiff as he laughs, nervously it seems, and then just shrugs.

Claire alone.

The cottage is cold, the woodstove in the wee kitchen unattended. In the bedroom friend Catherine's flaming purple and orange-crimson tapestry is gone, as gone as friend Catherine's pretty face and sometimes hesitant voice. Well, sometimes hesitant, sometimes snappy. Or flowing as the two women talked into the night, always a light on for Catherine and her little Robert. Catherine Court Downey, everything about her, gone.

Through glass panes, late morning birches with their white and smutched skin can be seen standing stock-still, the wind expired. Cold is cruel but soon comes the season when the trees sleep and feel not.

Hard to recognize a crying Claire. Rarely does she grieve this shudderingly, her glasses tossed onto the sill.

The full-sized bed is handmade and hand carved, significant. His gift.

Yet another critical thinker.

Life is not a spectacle or a feast; it is a predicament.

—George Santayana

Next day. At breakfast head cook Bonnie Loo steps in through one of the two archways to the candlelit Winter Kitchen and slams a big spoon over and over on a kettle lid.

"Announcement!" she bellows.

Most of the breakfasttime chatter and grumbles cease quite suddenly.

"Okaaaaay," Bonnie Loo continues, her orangy brown eyes steamrollering over the faces before her, her big spoon poised like a weapon. "As we all know the fair and reasonable kitchen rules include this: Anyone can take food from the tables or from the kitchen to go out on a job or field trip or to your cottage or to the moon, whatever, but *only* during mealtimes or cleanup crew times. If you have an emergency, leave a note! Not under the cover of darkness are any of you to clomber into the Cook's Kitchen or pantry and haul off the whole shelf of canned cherries and half a chest of deer jerky and seven of the big goat cheeses and then mix some sort of floury mess on the worktables and leave bowls, spoons, and pans out to draw smaller more rodent-type mice! Okay?! Got that?! This is not the first time I've made this announcement! I'm tired of this announcement! This is worse than mice! But thanks a million for not leaving your huge turds in the pans and for not chewing holes in the dishrags! But if you come back for another haul there will be hell to pay, bud!!"

From a future time Penny St. Onge remembering back.

Yes, one thing that was not disputable was our little Jane had to move out of Gordon's house. The swarms the True Maine Militia and Gordon himself had stirred up had caught on that the gray farmhouse close to the tarred Heart's Content Road there on their right-hand side (before they reached the blind curve) was part of the same phenomenon of what came after the blind curve. That which was after the blind curve and just as the tar road shot uphill steeply again was the lazy-looking dirt road, also on the right-hand side, but beautified with horizontal hornbeam pole and sign: ANYONE TRESPASSES WILL BE SHOT. TRY IT.

So strangers' cars began jamming Gordon's welcoming-looking yard, mostly on weekends. I mean whole carloads with cameras and camcorders. And plenty of others just doing drive-by shootings with their Nikons and Canons and Pentaxes poked out of windows.

Weekdays, it was reporters. Less showy, but boldly banging on the porch's screen door. *Hello! Hello!*

When would the social workers, and their police helpers who were all watching this, swarm in to haul Jane away? Which dark night?

Also Gail St. Onge tells how it went.

Our little Jane, while still in residence at Gordon's, always answered phone calls with secretarial flair. "Hello! Gordon St. Onge residence. Jane speaking." She'd do short messages in her boxy print letters on scrap paper from the decorated box then stab them down over the spike. *Sometimes* you could understand what she wrote.

But some frighteningly *sick* phone calls started up.

All our kids were told to hang up on those kinds of calls, then leave the phone off the hook for at least ten minutes.

Most of the real little kids could only reach that wall phone with a chair anyway. Now they were forbidden to answer it . . . period.

I heard that when Jane was told that she was considered a "little kid" and was not to take calls anymore, she gave this advice and the adviser a dark and level stare.

Then she kicked Gordon's little blue supper table so that it skidded into the red painted chimney and everything on it rolled off or flew. Then she held her breath till she fainted. The next day we saw that her eye whites had bled.

As I say, this was last month when she still lived there at Gordon's. I want you to picture one of the reasons we were all at our wit's end, this little girl versus the rest of us.

Beth St. Onge looking back.

Meanwhile, the local talk radio gibber jabber about Gordon as polygamist, as pedophile, as communist, as right-wing militia terrorist, as "he is one of us," as saintly hero and prophet was ballooning. This would inspire people to grab their car keys and head for the Egypt hills? Or to type out a love letter addressed to Heart's Content Road? Or call on our phone to breathe heavy and say sadistic things to six-year-olds?

You want fame or leprosy? Pick one. Pick leprosy. It's curable with antibiotics.

Steph St. Onge remembers.

If you are a TV news watcher or a consumer of any controlled media, you probably would already know in those days that Jane's mother Lisa Meserve was in trouble, at least you would know the official version. She was arrested and held and arraigned for drug trafficking marijuana. Like a hay-truck-sized load or some such. But in the real untelevised world Lisa didn't traffic anything. What she did was introduce two people, a friend who was part of an ambitious deal and a new "friend" Lisa did not realize was a police spy.

Lisa was driving home from her dental assistant job when the cops did their thing. Very hot day. Handcuffed, she screamed that her Scottie dog would die left in the hot car with windows up. She screamed, she wailed. So the extra charge of resisting arrest was added.

The DA wanted Lisa to tell all she knew about the deal and her friend who sold marijuana for a living, things Lisa did not know. These were just your average Maine people getting by. This is a state and a country in a time of fear and secrets, and the drug warriors had a story they wanted Lisa to testify was true because that's how *they* get by.

And since Lisa, quite confused and weary, couldn't understand the game, *off to the dungeon, pretty princess*!

The dog died badly.

And Jane? How to describe it?

Beth again.

I don't give a royal fuck if Lisa actually did a thousand big pot deals single-handedly. You got prohibitions, whatever kind, this is the rot you set into friggin' motion. My brother *did* do a *real* pot deal and it doesn't look any prettier seeing *his* wife and *his* kids and *his* dog and *his* self treated like some medieval street wretches. This is *now*! And this is *here*. Remember? Red? White? And? Blue? Number one and all that.

So don't you girls go on and on about all that doe-eyed innocence of Lisa Meserve.

Secret Agent Jane investigates the language of the Passamaquoddy.

Claire and some kids are here at Gordie's house where I am till Mum comes to get me. One kid is named Weetalo who is practically a baby who sucks her finger even though she's probably four. But also she smiles in a cute chubby way so maybe I don't actually hate her guts, which I would if she were a jerk.

So Claire sets up a game on Gordie's kitchen table.

Montana, you know the giant with the giant braids, has one plain brown eyebrow and one very snobby brown eyebrow. It's always raised up crooked to show you her expression of soo-peer-ree-or-ity. She says to me, "Nah nah this is school" and Claire is pushing her roundish glasses between her eyes better and says explainishly, "No, it's a game."

Montana is looking right into my eyes and makes her lips and teeth perfect in saying "schoooool" again.

This is because I told her my school back in Lewiston has teachers in very pretty clothes and rules and desks and everybody has to hold still, which is okay because it is the law. Up here at the Settlement it is *not school*. I had to go up there six times to make Gordie happy. Dirty Land-kiss-ter* dogs lay on your feet. Cats and chickens climb around on chairs. Sometimes kids are slaves to snap beans and peel stuff. Bonnie Loo has rats to do tricks. A crow flies around and gives you the wrong weather. Old men sing, sometimes in a weird language, and you are supposed to cut their toenails. Old ladies like going to the doctor and you help them walk or push their chair and they kiss you a lot and say *See you later, alligator*. Kids never ask permission to go pee.

Also when I went there Gordie was chasing kids with a horrible growl for being the Swamp Monster. When he grabs you he does juicy

* Lancaster.

fart noises in your neck. Kids go to a place to study plant ginicks.* Another place for karate chops but first you have to bow. Then it was the planit-terrarium† for stars and a big voice telling you stuff.

Gordie is always talking about the world and sometimes munee-soo-pill‡ law.

Once when I was at their buildings for noon meal everyone was screaming like a chant, "Fear art! Fear art! Fear art!" This was hundreds of minutes and when I asked why, they said it was a plit-i-cul stra-tee-gee.§ I had to cover my ears before brain damage. At real school a principal would PUNISH all of this.

There are history skits, big deal, with mostly boys dressed as Romans with helmets of the pepper-mishy¶ and swords and one yells "Vay! Vicky!"** like one of the mothers named Beth always calls Gordie's mother "the Romans" and there are always people playing kazoos or fiddles and piano and a harp or singing while eating. You do not have to stay in a band but do music when you FEEL GOOD. School is not supposed to feel good but to make you learn to do things in neatness and silence *all by yourself*, no cheating!

All in noise and goofing around they are always in the library to look up the stuff of details for making another stupid history skit. Then somebody has to make the old outfits and it takes days for the pepper-mishy "props" to dry all in noise and screaming.

They work on their stupid windmills and solo†† buggies and a purple solo car and find out everything about juice‡‡ and cutting your hair.

They do gardens and fixing roads. They make maps to find their way. They learn Hebrew from Barbara, a lady with a Beatles haircut, all white. They make beer. Yes, *beer*.

---

* Genetics.

† Planetarium.

‡ Municipal law.

§ Political strategy.

¶ Papier-mâché.

** "Vae victis!" meaning "Woe to the vanquished!"

†† Solar.

‡‡ Electricity.

There are apee-arries* where bees live and probably other horridible bugs.

Claire only wears pretty teacher outfits for her job at the college. Mostly here she just wears old work boots or moccasins made by hands and lopsided clothes made by hands. Today she is wearing a baggy red blouse. She is very short and fat. Sometimes she treats Gordie like a little boy which is sooo funny cuz he is as tall as a ceiling almost. Claire never tells jokes or tries to get you to laugh like Beth does.

So now Claire says, "This is going to be fun." Her voice isn't fun. Her voice is like thick meat and her eyes inside her glasses might scare you if you let them. I'm wearing glasses, too, mine with white heart-shapes frames and pink to see through. They give my brain the power to see truth and lies and secrets. When I visit Mum at the jail, she calls them secret agent glasses. Right now they give me the power to look into Montana's eyes and I see the word *bitch*. Nobody should *say* bitch but you can *think* it all you want. Even in regular school nobody can punish your thoughts.

Oops! I can't stop the word from crashing out of my lips right *out loud* into Montana's big fat eyes, not bitch but "blowhard."

Believe it or not she smiles as if I just called her a beautiful movie star.

Claire looks at me mean and says with this game we can only use words in the Passamaquoddy language.

I look at the game board all set up and ready to go. With these glasses I can tell this is a stupid game totally made by hands, not from a store. It has pepper-mishy trees and houses and animals and people and a big turtle. If this gets too boring all I have to do is go upstairs to my room. Wicked convenience. Montana reaches and taps my hand with her gigantic finger and says, "I will win this game. I *always* do."

Claire says in her flat slow voice, "But today there are new words. To level the playing field." She sets out pennies, which we will use to move around the board, and she says, "It's not actually a win-lose game anyway . . . it's for fun. Montana, you're three years older than Jane. You could give her a helping hand in a sisterly spirit."

---

* Apiaries.

Weetalo pulls her finger from her mouth and picks up a penny as if it were a beautiful jewel not the most worthless money in the universe.

Another kid is Ryan. He looks sleepy. He is an actual Passamaquoddy boy and probably knows all the answers even when Claire changes them to trick Montana.

Montana says with giant teeth and lips but no voice right into my eyes, *Schoooooollll* and her weird eyebrow goes biserks like an insane killer.

I am ten million times prettier than Montana. Mum always says I look like a "Gypsy queen." She says my brownish-golden skin and my long neck is "regal." It's true. I keep the "regal" angle to my face and fluff my hair a little extra with my sexy wrist.

Schooooolll, Montana says again without voice, just her opening and closing lips.

In about ten seconds I am going to flip this table over.

Claire says, "Weetalo. What's the date on that penny? You've got better eyes than I do."

Weetalo turns the penny a few times.

Montana leans in. "1991," she says, her big fat pink face so proud.

Claire's voice is hard like rust. "I asked Weetalo."

Montana gives a big rubberish sigh. "Well, we'd have to wait an hour."

Claire says, "We have plenty of time to be sisters."

I look down at my hands folded perfectly on the table. I might have to wait through this whole ordeal for a chance to find out how to say *blowhard* in Passamaquoddy.

St. Onge wife Astrid tells more.

At the same time the DHS "pack of hounds," Gordon's words, were on our trail because they had sniffed their way to Egypt to question us about Jane. Officially Jane was in the care of Granpa Pete after a whole chain of foster folk could not deal with her behavior, which in DHS reports was said to be caused by abuse. Granpa Pete, a quiet-quiet fellow, sat up straight on that one.

"Phooey! She takes after her Great-Aunt Bette," said he.

Meanwhile, Granpa Pete Meserve and Gordon agreed the DHS machine's heart was missing something. Jane needed more attention than a reeeeal quiet-type widowed twelve-hours-a-day-seven-days-a-week garage-owner-and-mechanic all by himself could give but we all know the agency would never approve of the Settlement as a "safe" place. So she was at Pete's only for the days when the DHS visited, the rest of her time she was here.

The big plus for Jane, if there are pluses, is that Gordon's old friend Shawn Phillips, who Gordon said looked like Walt Disney, was the governor's commissioner for the Department of Human Services. Shawn was both sour and good-humored about Gordon's tricks. He was able to slow things down a bit. And we were all humbly grateful.

Nevertheless, some caseworkers were leaving their business cards with whoever was found to be around at Gordon's house, sometimes a card wedged in the porch screen door. *Don't know a Jane Miranda Meserve. But will keep my eyes peeled.* This was what we all said to questioning while Jane hid in a closet or upstairs.

And once, when a DHS worker caught Gordon in his dooryard, he pretended not to speak or understand English. In the patois he knew soooo well, he spoke of beauty and freedom while gazing into the tall no-nonsense woman's bristling eyes.

Vancy St. Onge remembers.

Then we got word that Jane's mother's case had gone federal. This is something you never want to hear concerning your loved one.

So Lisa was moved to Boston. We would have to make the trip into that trafficky mess when we or Granpa Pete brought Jane to visit her mother. And that was not a homey little jail like Androscoggin County's. Okay. Homey, wrong word.

At the same time a cruelly interesting thing. There had been some splashy media moments about the Meserve Scottie's horrible cooked-to-death-in-the-car demise once word of it leaked. And that created an uproar of public indignation. So the drug war publicity press releases on Lisa's case stopped. For what it's worth, the theater piece of Lisa as drug pusher and narcs as heroes came to a close on suppertime TV screens all over the universe.

Leona St. Onge relates to us more of the story.

All along while Jane was living at Gordon's, she was never alone. That was "a pain," a few of us griped, when Jane could have stayed with a Settlement family. But Jane dug her heels in and you can imagine how we hated to upset the poor little dickens with so much loss already. So always when Gordon was out one of us stayed down to Gordon's place, hoping she'd adjust.

But holy moly, she sure did seem to despise most of us.

Glennice remembers.

Then Gordon and a crew of youngsters roped off the whole yard of his place with "ANYONE TRESPASSES WILL BE SHOT. TRY IT." The signs were every six inches apart. These perfectly matched the one at the end of the Settlement road.

From the safe side of the rope, people yelled, "Hello! Hello! Can we come through?" The media. The fans. The whatevers. Calling our bluff?

Gordon said probably anytime now DHS would show up in the night with cops to drag Jane out of his house to "safety." His hotshot DHS administrator friend Shawn Phillips was feeling pressure and might not be able to keep putting holds and waivers on the caseworkers and their supervisors' moves forever. That was probably the beginning of the falling away of all Gordon's influential friends.

Misty St. Onge recalls.

A bunch of us explained all this to Jane, looking straight into her white-frames-pink-heart-shaped-lenses secret agent glasses. We added even all the explicits that an almost-seven-year-old might not be able to juggle but we felt we owed her.

She folded her arms across her chest. Not as in self-defense. But in the way that says an embrace is not invited.

As Claire concluded to the dear little ears our predicament under the weight of so much political villainy, Jane snorted, "That's ridiculous."

"True," Josee said with an almost identical snort. "You got t'at right."

Secret Agent Jane speaks.

It is night, but I woke up. Where I am staying now is in a cute little house with all these little rooms so all us kids have a tiny cute room to ourselves with a bed and bureau thing and closet. Wood walls. Oh-RELL and Jo-SEE are the father and mother. They smooch.

But guess what. No phone! So Mum can't call me. They all say she never calls anyway cuz we always plan it. I say maybe I can call her if I had to. They all say nobody can call people directish to the jail. But I say you can't call anybody *anywhere* without a phone that is *near your ears. Get it!*

Critical thinker gives us these words.

"Prisons do not disappear problems, they disappear human beings."
—Angela Davis, Black Panther, author, inspiration to many

Near midnight.

Here's Gordon coming in onto his porch from his truck. He notes right off that the phone isn't ringing. Oh, well, yes, there are actually fifteen minutes at a time when it isn't. He begins to work some of his shirt buttons. He is scruffed and splattered from toiling on a North Egypt elderly couple's dug well, Settlement guys and town guys all pitching in. To keep on the shrewd and uncostly side but also to the old Yankee ingenuity side, they made the form for the cement well tiles with plywood and jigsaw and they dug down to water level with coffee cans, ropes, and pails.

Now Gordon tugs off his outer shirt, moves through the slurred blue light of his kitchen, squinching his bleary eyes and yawning. He paws through a pile of coats for one of the warm beers underneath a long-necked brown bottle. Walks in a heavy way with the bottle dangling like a dead bird from one hand. The damp shirt drags along from the other.

There are two desks and a long workbench waiting for him, all angling down into the space of what used to be a narrow pantryway, now his tight cluttered office. A thickening of new phone messages are on the spike of the first desk. His yesterday's and before yesterday's mail is slathered everywhere. Today's mail that is also addressed to him is in a banana box on the floor and there's a bundle tied with baling twine on his small blue supper table, which seems to include, yes, more CDs or DVDs, but mostly letters. Some portion will be the militia movement sort, but there are so many sorts and ways to write a letter to a "prophet." He hears it all.

The only light in this room is this depressing low-wattage fluorescent tube across that first desk so he doesn't see her at first. It scares him. Partly sprawled partly fetal-curled body under the wall phone.

Then she moves and sits up, her dark long-lashed eyes on him. Without pink hearts.

"Jane. What the hell?"

It's not one of her usual screamy tantrums. These are silent tears, her cheeks glazed. No voice, just mouthing the word *Mumma* and shaking her head from side to side with utter grief.

He thinks how a phone is only a sort of ghost of the actual person anyway, in this case Lisa Meserve, mother. He steps over to where Jane is now scrambling up into a squat, rocking herself, her mouth opening larger and squarer, gasping. He knows Aurel and Josee are missing her, freaking out maybe.

He squats down next to her, hugs her up to himself. Her wet face nuzzles his warm dark T-shirt. He wants to tell her everything is going to be all right. But she'll know foolishness when she hears it. And she'll see ever-so-close the damp and tired fool that speaks it.

Critical thinker reminds us.

The American Dream: You have to be asleep to believe it.

—George Carlin, 1937–2008

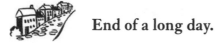

End of a long day.

The gray van eases slowly into the dooryard even though the smiling lightbulb with arms and legs and work cap painted on the van's sides hurries. He never fails to fulfill all your large or small residential or business wiring needs in a timely manner. Arcing over this little frisky fellow is red lettering that reads York Electric, Egypt, Maine.

The face behind the windshield, by contrast, is not known for smiles or frowns. It had, however, shown something slightly elastic as the strange SUV parked in the dooryard with one tire on the grass somewhat came into his sight. And his brown walrus mustache had given a live animal twitch.

Maine plates on the stranger's rig, muddy like those of someone who fancies riding the back roads. Mud on the fender walls, too. Not a lot. But something Rex would notice. He putters a moment with his small clipboard and the day's paperwork, tissuey yellow slips for two customers.

Now as he holds the porch-kitchen door open with one elbow, he tugs off his dark coplike glasses so that his eyes with the softening of age around them, their fiftyness, and that lusty mustache and his whole head with no cap accentuate his voiceless unwelcome of the smiling-away face of the man at the kitchen table.

At the same time Rex sucks in the smell of something oniony. And gingerbread? Or ginger cookies? These are made routinely by his mother Ruth's hand in case of guests. She treats all guests as if they were nine years old, though she never coos. She's so quiet she tends to make you jump when you turn around or back up into her. Meanwhile, she fervidly nibbles her own sweets. Yet she's not stout.

Rex does not greet her or look at her. He doesn't need to greet or look. There is a kinetic-sense-moving-through-space recognition, the feel of one's shoulders, temples, feet penetrating solidly the miracle of home . . . shivers as from the "Star-Spangled Banner," only different . . . "gave truth to the night that our home was still therrrre . . ." Yes, *those* goose bumps; and, yes, Ruth is standing nearby. She is speaking to him in her quick, lopped-off feathery phrases, telling him what a nice talk she and Gary have been having.

The Wizard of Oz movie lion laugh burbles out of the guest.

Rex says nothing. As he approaches the sink to run a glass of water, he smells the aftershave of the guest, its scent crawling around the kitchen, cool, legless, serpentine. So close to his ear, and so hushed, it is like a secret. Ruth tells him that the meat loaf will be another forty-five minutes, to just relax and enjoy his "friend."

"Gary Larch" is wearing his camo BDU shirt-jacket with the ripped-off sleeves over a black T-shirt. He is, yes, as shaved up as a Ken doll and his hair is tended and businesslike. His wide black compass-wristwatch, identical to Rex's, and the broad wrist, to go with the broad-shouldered tall body, that very special watch hovers over the half-emptied mug of milky coffee and the plate with gingerbread crumbs and smear of whipped cream and fork as if it were listening.

Gordon at his desks.

More in-mail. More out-mail. Scribble scribble. *Yours in Freedom, Gordie.*

Around noon of another day.

Phone to his ear, held by one hunched-up shoulder, mail heaped around him like the Great Wall of China, *Record Sun* unopened on the desk between his two spread-out-flat hands, Gordon listens, does not speak.

Seems his mother's voice on the other end of the line must be telling a long story.

Gordon flips the paper to its full front-page size. The above-the-fold headline exclaims: CHILDREN'S MILITIA TERRORIZES GOVERNOR'S OFFICE. He fluffs the paper out over some unopened letters bundled tightly with elastics, the postmistress ever thoughtful as she also is ever law-and-order. The *Record Sun*'s big bright front-page photo shows a face in green greasepaint and several done in white and black to look like skulls, while others sport no paint, just their barefaced recognizability as shouting mouths and blazing eyes enhance their outrage and, as Gordon guesses, their fun. Oh, yes, there's Samantha Butler with a black beret on her flashing cornsilk hair. Camo BDU shirt with pistol belt gathering snugly her slight teenage waist. Crisscrossed cartridge belts of .22 cartridges. They look extremely real. Okay. Real. No gun. But what a mouth, as wide open as the sky.

Another teen, the boy Mickey Gammon of Rex's militia when not St. Onge mountainside tree house resident. Streaky blond hair parted crookedly down the middle in a way that shows there's no mirror in the tree house. Mouth closed, pale with discomfort. His camo jacket must have the Border Mountain Militia patch but he's turned slightly and Samantha is blocking that half of his body from the camera's lens.

Some edges and corners of their homemade placards show but only one is readable. *Fascism is the corporatist creeps' rending of the working class's active solidarity!*

Interior pages of the *Record Sun* display smaller photos. Squirt guns in lime green, orange, and pink in childly hands, held with killer confidence.

And there by God is Gus, who Gordon had led around by a rope and harness to visit and to charm Marian. Surely she recognizes him, the darling little fellow getting his education on the shoulders of his thirteen-year-old half brother Oz. Gus has his mouth open in a rangy blurred way, dark eyes narrowed appropriately for battle, chubby fist raised. It's only a photo with a carefully edited caption so you can't know that he is hooting, "Co-putt! Co-putt!"—baby lingo for *Corporate slut! Corporate slut!*—the words flung at the governor's office door in a chanting of mostly high chirpy voices accompanied by a huge drum, kazoos, recorders, cymbals, flutes, sets of spoons, one set of bagpipes, and a fiddle.

Another sign: *BOMB THE CORPORATE CAMPAIGN FINANCE SCHEME. SPARE THE HUMANS.*

The reporter describes how these were all youths and tykes, no adults. The capitol security assisted them all into quickly and efficiently leaving. Teachers from several Maine schools who were on hand for prizewinning science projects objected to the noise and inappropriate dress of the True Maine Militia and, most of all, the "outrageous and dangerous anticorporate messages." Yes, one teacher's actual words.

Meanwhile, Gordon listens attentively and wincingly to his mother Marian's voice, his deep big-guy baritone un-huhing and groaning his replies. Slowly he sets aside the paper they've been looking at in miles-apart synchronicity, hearing what Marian has learned from her brother, the state rep, what the whole Depaolo family will be buzzing over *till hell gives out ice creams* (Gordon's papa's expression concerning Depaolo grudges, irritations, and hysteria). Now he laughs. "Corporate slut?" Now he doesn't laugh. "Well, Mum, at least they weren't kicked out of the building for *lying*. Maybe it was the doughnuts. I'm sure they weren't leaving any for the tobacco lobbyists and the insurance lobbyists and the nursing home lobbyists. Oh, and the petroleum lob—"

He is interrupted.

He laughs cynically. "Right. You gotta be bewitching to earn one of those public-school-provided doughnuts." He listens. He grunts. "Oh, yeah? Well, natch. So the whole science contest was funded by big business?" He listens. He listens. Then, "Well, I'm sure Senator Joe will think this is funny . . . with Senator Mary involved and all. Mum, you need to just enjoy this. Take pride in such audacity, okay?" A few more minutes of *okays* and *yups*, one *good-bye*, then he smothers the phone receiver holes *smpeeeech!* to deafen Marian's ear properly.

Now he lets the phone receiver spring from his hand and roughly swing on its long curly boingy cord. He leans his face into his hands. He whispers, "Ah, shit."

Same moment.

On the other side of town, Bree is in the back seat of a Chevy Nova with Willie Lancaster.

Janet Weymouth reads every word.

She sees faces, recognizing some who had pleased her splendidly as dangerous chimps. She sees the raised fists, the yawning little maws, tongues, teeth. She reads the schoolteacher's remarks, amazed. She cackles over the theft of corporate-funded sweets. She sees there, in the hand of one tyke who is decked out in hemlock branches, the evidence! One frosted doughnut with a bite missing.

At this moment, at this hour, she was already teetering away from the new Gordon, the one who yells right-wing terrorist slogans such as "God save the republic!!" into the hungry ears of the reporters.

But today his children can still make her smile.

Inner voice of the Bureau while scrolling through news websites and incoming reports.

What in tarnation is this? Oh, ho ho! How gifted. How talented. How precious. But with a little vivacious connecting of the dots you get one of the joys of this job.

So Mr. St. Onge is *not* going to drag us down the usual manly patriot route. No sir, our boy is lurking behind the stage curtains while leading us by the hand to Romper Room, to Daffy Duck, to Mr. Rogers, to Winnie-the-Pooh. Awwww.

Meanwhile, Lewiston, Maine. Department of Human Services. A cold blustery day. Another incident with the hooded men.

The difference? Four photographs. A passerby has hit it lucky with his camera.

Newspaper is happy to buy these pictures from him. Police like these pictures, too.

The front page tonight features one big photo, three others on the inside pages with continued story. There is a toddler this time. Crying, big square crying mouth. Running behind as the hooded men push his mother along among parked cars. The young woman is not a screamer. Nor does she sob. Nor does she beg. She looks stunned and senseless. Big eyes. Her big eyes are the focus of this photo. Rope around her neck. Noose man's fist around the rope.

Two of the hooded figures wear full-length black Grim Reaper robes. But the noose man has just a black hood. Jeans and a work shirt and jacket. Buck knife on his belt. "An arrogant character," Lewiston police chief tells Channel 8. "After he released Ms. Stevens, he bowed to his onlookers."

Down in the bay area of the largest Quonset hut, Bree and some young mothers and two small kids paint two snazzy new electric buggies, one lemon yellow, one red. Yes, with *brushes*, the Settlement way. One buggy they call the "girl buggy" because Beezer and Cyndy Harmon made it. Over by the red buggy, little Anna steps in a tray of paint and there's confusion there.

Gordon comes in with two Settlement guys and a town guy. Gordon veers away while the other guys go over to the workbenches and, fumbling around on some sort of search, they talk back and forth. Gordon carries a newspaper under one arm while he devours a fat blackberry muffin and drinks cold coffee and smiles strangely at Bree as she works her thick paintbrush over a rear fender of the buggy.

"Hi, Gorgy," murmurs a little tow-haired girl, child of Ben and Willa Wentworth, a Settlement couple. Nothing this moment in this universe more beautiful than that paint-splattered smiling face.

Gordon squats down and sets his coffee mug and newspaper on the floor and mashes the last of the muffin into his mouth, puts his arms around the little girl. The older girl keeps painting earnestly, long yellow strokes. And Bree is quiet. Keeps her head down, painting with exaggerated care. But now in her vision, Gordon's feet appear as he squats down next to her. He lays the paper down. By her foot. The front page. He swallows most of what's in his mouth. He asks, "Know this man?"

Bree looks. The terrified face of a young woman. Big dark round eyes. And hooded figures. One hooded guy is quite blurry. Another is back-to. But there is one she *sees*. Jacket, short gray dark wool with fine crisscrossing lines of red. Zippered pocket. The jacket is open. Work shirt buttoned. There is one hand in focus. It's the one around the noose. And there, both eyes in the eyeholes of the black hood. In focus. The pictures are color. The shirt and eyes are gray. The unwrinkled shirt, so smart-looking across the chest, just as she remembers, easy to remember, for she sees him every day now, sometimes only for five minutes, as they stop their trucks whenever they meet on the road, stop to talk, to tease, to flirt. The look of that shirt and those two square pockets is marked in her head like a favorite recipe, like a map of the world, like a psalm, like an inculpable fog that softly lays itself over the dog tag, dog tag of his dead brother. Dead in Vietnam.

Gordon says, "They describe the mysterious hangman as agile, leaping over hedges and car hoods or something like that. And . . . arrogant. I myself would go on to say monster." He opens the paper to show her the other photos. "Brianna, it's not just your jealous husband doing some wild guessing. It's coming through others, too. Militia gossip. Rex's guys are like the proverbial old hens. Eight of their phone messages on my desk." His eyes sparkle. "Doc can't keep his mouth shut and the other lovable Christian, Tim, who I forbid you ever to meet . . . see . . . they don't show up well in these pictures . . . but, trust me. It's them." But the star here is . . . is . . . your amour. He outshines them all." He sighs.

Bree says absolutely nothing. Just giggles like a teenage girl, which, of course, she is. The small blond girl looks over toward Bree's happy giggle and smiles and wiggles her painty brush in the air.

Gordon picks up his coffee, swallows some, washing down the last bit of his muffin.

"Can I have a sip?" Bree asks.

He places the mug in her fingers.

She sips a little, eyes cast down.

He can tell this little bit of newsy news hasn't hurt Willie Lancaster's chances of getting hold of Bree again and again and again, not one bit.

What would it take?

Same day. Rex York stops at Bean's Variety.

The guy behind the counter is on the phone. Rex places his roll of paper towels and bag of walnuts on the counter and waits, hands laced behind his back, chin raised a bit, eyes on things, eyes sliding over bright packages, display signs, shiny magazines, stuff. Newspaper rack. *Record Sun*. Front page. Rex's eyes widen. He steps to the rack and lifts the paper. He stares at the paper. *Continued on page 14A,* it says. He flops the paper onto the counter next to the paper towels and walnuts.

Nearly midnight.

Dee Dee St. Onge is in bed in the tall, five-story funny little pink rocket-shaped* house beyond her parents' mobile home. She feels like a turtle. Hard to turn over when you're nearly nine months pregnant. As she turns, she grunts.

Her husband, Lou-EE, is on the floor with a pallet of blankets and quilts and his Scottie, Cannonball. Cannonball needs him right now. Fresh from surgery, the removal of a small benign growth on top of her head, eight stitches. The vet suggested Cannonball wear a plastic "Elizabethan collar" to keep her from bothering the stitches. In other words, a big plastic funnel around her head. Lou-EE is a quiet gentle young man, devoid of exclamations. To the vet's suggestion, he answered with a soft, "I guess not."

So to keep her still it will be ten nights of sleeping bags on the floor with Cannonball, her round solid shape resting trustingly under Lou-EE's long-fingered work-thickened hand.

Cannonball is really *not* Lou-EE's dog. She in the legal sense still belongs to the people Willie Lancaster stole her from, though Willie sees it not as stealing but as one of his highly moral "freedom missions." The true owners of Cannonball (or whatever her name was then) had her tied twenty-four hours a day to a vinyl igloo-shaped doghouse. Maybe now Cannonball herself feels ownerless, but committed to Lou-EE, her mate. Cannonball may notice that both man and dog (herself) are bearded and stoic.

Dee Dee hears her father's hot rod Nova pull into the yard. Headlights go off.

She groans to her feet, steps over Lou-EE and Cannonball, carefully descends the four shaky ladders of her towerlike house.

When she walks in through the door of the mobile home, her father is already at the table slathering peanut butter on toast. The smell of peanut butter and warm toast is nice. The place is quiet. No TV. No kids. Her mother gone to bed an hour or so ago.

* Willie Lancaster calls it "pecker-shaped."

Willie smiles, "Want one?"

She says, "Okay."

Even now, Dee Dee St. Onge looks too young to be a wife. Brown hair. Cut cute. Little wry secrety smile most of the time. Childly wrists. The gold wedding ring has a leafy design. An orange-sherbet-color nightshirt is filled massively with her pregnancy. You rarely see her angry. She's one person who brings the Settlement its harmony when she's there.

Her father pops another slice of bread into the toaster.

Dee Dee pulls out a chair, rubs her bare legs. Her feet are bare, too. The floors are freezing. It is not a warm evening. "Did you get the note?"

"Uh-huh."

"He was here three times."

"Zat right?"

"He's coming back." She is looking at him hard. "Tonight." She has no trace of her secrety smile.

He settles back in his seat across the table from her. His smile. His cat-that-ate-the-canary smile, his gray eyes on her.

"I want to talk to you, Daddy."

He keeps grinning.

"About welfare."

He puts up a hand. "But first! Let me talk to you about work." He tells her what she already knows, about how he works ALL THE TIME. Dangerous work. Twelve to fourteen hours a day in the summer in trees and narrow situations around people's property, edgy people, nasty-tempered people, hard-to-please spoiled people. And bugs. And sun. And "fucking heat." Then in the winter with O.B.* working in the woods, which is "pure picnic." And then ice storms and so forth, all that kind of cleanup "where you got two hundred people all wanting to be first." And he offers to show her his scarred ankle again and his horribly twisted toe. But he doesn't. He just keeps talking. About *work*. "All the skin peeled off that time," he adds.

The toaster pops up. He is out of his seat as beautifully as a cat.

---

* O.B. is Willie's neighbor who appears in other books of the four-o-jilly.

She sees on the table a gun. Always a gun. She sees his guns so much it's like seeing the peanut butter knife or *TV Guide*. He has probably just brought this gun in from his car. Wrapped in a shoulder holster. He is not sloppy with guns. He is good with guns. He is a dramatic person. But not stupid. And seldom is he foolishly angry. So this, which everybody suspects of him, the rumors, this hooded terrorist thing, has really shaken her.

He fixes her toast on a nice little plate and presents it with a flourish and he reaches to pat her hand. He sits in front of his own stack of toast and looks into her face, smiling again. His eyes are haggard. Willie Lancaster. Never grows old. Just a raw tiredness at the end of every day.

"Dad?"

He says quickly, "I work my ass off and they lay around on the dole and my taxes are fucking breaking me!" The end of his sentence is shouted. Then he adds, "Fucking socialism! What's next?" He leans forward on his palms. "They're diggin' my grave! They're diggin' *your* grave!"

"Dad," she says quietly.

He covers his ears.

"Dad."

He drops his hands.

With her secrety smile again on her lips, she says, "Being a mother to kids isn't lying around, unless you are a rich person and can afford governesses."

"Fucking welfare queens are rich," he snarls.

"Do you want facts?"

"I know the facts."

"No . . . I mean . . . the *real* facts."

His smile softens. It's a tender fatherly smile. "Eat your toast. Want me to make you another one? I don't want no thin pitiful pale grandchild."

"Food stamps and the federal portion of aid is . . . federal . . . so it's in the modern monetary system . . . *not taxes*. It's not like the states that have to *raise* revenue."

"I don't care."

"Your IRS money is erased. Up at the Settlement we did a research project on the Modern Monetary Theory. Federal expenditures are from *thin air*. A tap tap tap of the keys. Your taxes to IRS are just erased from circulation to regulate the economy. The two so-called piles of money are unrelated . . . totally. This is *not* what we are told right out cuz they love it when we all fight and they don't want us to ask for anything back but just keep on blaming other little people for taxes! *They*, the bad guys, love . . . it . . . that . . . we . . . are . . . fighting among ourselves." Yes, sly Dee Dee is playing this for all it's worth. And yes, like Art, his fellow militiaman, the nobility has a snuggly place in Willie's heart. The poor and near-poor are punching bags. So Dee Dee edits out DEBT. Meanwhile, in midair the treasures of many a Settlement salon consensus wish list skulk into perfect shadow: progressive global tax on capital, international financial transparency, prohibition on usury, cautions with inflation, kaput to austerity and gonzo to privatization of the commons. All these and more turn like the dots, dots, and dots of light of a faraway city in Dee Dee's gray eyes.

Willie snickers. Gives the underneath of his pointy Jack the Ripper beard a little evil stroke.

"You don't believe me?"

"I just don't want those whores to have *any* percent of *any* money."

"Whores?"

"Yuh, whores."

"Why, that makes you sound like a dumb parrot!" She pushes herself up, leans with one hand open on the table. "Especially since you don't mind so much of your *state* taxes going straight as an arrow to corporate subsidies and other corporate goodies and sweetheart deals and shit! And the fact that rich people don't pay the painful percent for tax that you do out of your basic life needs! No, you don't mind *that*. Those guys are the ones who are costing us so much at all government levels but . . . if one of them asked you to bend over for them, why you would just bend over! Tell me now, Daddy, *who* is the whore?!!!"

He lowers his eyes. Says gravely, "You're getting twisted in the head by all that liberal horseshit you're exposed to down there." He jerks his head toward the direction of the Settlement.

"If I got the dictionary out right now, will the definition of the word *fact* be 'liberal horseshit'? How much money do you want to put on it, O righteous father?"

He grins his bucktoothed happy grin.

She asks, "What if something happened to Lou-EE and here I was with a new baby and no income? If I go get welfare, does that make me a whore? How much you wanna bet on that one? The definition of the word *whore* . . . it means—"

"I know what it means."

"It means go out and pick up men and fuck them and take money for it."

"Stop, my little daughter. Don't use the F-word."

"Daddy, I've *never* seen you be mean, really mean, before." Her voice shakes. She looks toward the quiet dim living room a step up from the kitchen area. She waits till the trembling of her chin stops.

He is silent, just looking at his toast pile.

She walks pregnantly over to the sink, finds a glass. "So, what if something happened to Lou-EE and—"

He says quickly, "Lou-EE don't make no money now and he's *alive*."

"He makes *some*."

"Whatever," he says dismissively.

"Well, so, let's say he dies and I . . . don't have anything to do with the Settlement . . . they move away or something. But there'd be no job for me anyplace else where they'd let me bring the baby with me."

He looks at her incredulously. "Sweetheart, I would take care of you! I'm not about to let you and a little baby starve."

"Certain little babies. You wouldn't mind *some* little babies starving."

"They won't starve. Their mothers will be up and at 'em . . . out *worrrrkinnng*."

"So many excess workers, the wages will flatten out to pennies, and all these people carrying their babies on their backs?"

"Sure. It's—"

"At McDonald's?"

"Sure."

"Okay. Never mind." She is blinking back tears. "What if you fell out of a tree? This whole family would need to go work at McDonald's—"

"Delores." He calls her by her real name and he is snickering. "You just got to argue, argue, argue. It's all about that damn German blood of your mother's."

She runs water into her glass and says, "Lately, I'm scared."

He turns to face her. "You oughta be scared. The gover'ment—"

"No!" she hollers. "Not just the government. I'm scared of *everybody*. The way people are getting." Headlights flash over the wall, over Dee Dee's face. A white pug-faced curl-tailed dog comes out from under the table, others drop down from living-room chairs. Another scratches the inside of a bedroom door. All of them coming to life to check out the arriving guest. Truck door slams.

Willie says, "Willie's persecutors are coming out of the woodwork tonight." He gets to his feet.

When Rex comes in, his own tired eyes stare into Willie's tired eyes. Rex's eyes do not blink but his neck muscles jerk. Maybe Willie's latest bad PR thing makes Rex's whole body hurt.

Tonight Willie will carry on, sport around, give Rex a headache, and cause Dee Dee to lie awake in her bed all night crying silently. But in the end, what has been said here tonight *does* matter to Willie Lancaster. Dee Dee matters. Rex matters. Maybe the world sucks, but these "familiars"— buddies and blood—they matter.

In a future time, all will look back and remember—

. . . that no one ever saw the hooded men around the DHS offices ever again.

America invaded.

While the squeaky wagon loaded with cartons of eggs rolls along across the parking lot and bricked Quadrangle paths through the unnaturally-hot-for-October late morning, one tyke about age five says to another among this rangy group, "In Mexico was Pancho Vee-ya. He invaded America *first*."

Nine-year-old Montana is along to supervise this shipment of eggs from the nests in the smallest Quonset hut in its journey toward the hulking dark-brown-stained horseshoe of shops. Her supervising capabilities seem substantiated by the utilitarian ship-cable-like yellow braids thumping around her. "The first invaders were guys like Columbus. You're too young to remember the Columbus skit. It had everything.

Murder and nudity almost." She flips her braids to her back and squares her shoulders for oration. "You guys are onto when the Industrial Revolution made so much become different everywhere, less feudal. Bigger populations. More inventions. People began living farther away from water sources. Wage slaves instead of chained-up slaves. Expansionism and imperialism. Fancypants US was ah-gree-gious to Mexico."

Little four-year-old girl says, "Pancho Vee-ya. On his horse. He rode in, then rode out."

"Was he *with* the man Columbus?" wonders a wee small girl with Passamaquoddy hair and her eyebrows as delicate as vapors. She carries a small decorated box half full of rocks. Some mica in there keeps catching the high sun.

Montana rolls her eyes, fluffing herself up for more voluminous oration, but a wee red-haired white-eyelashed boy with Band-Aids on both knees crows, "Col-wumbis was in a boat!!"

A small girl with four Band-Aids on one knee and a ripped sundress offers, "Monarchs use wings to invay Mex'co."

Montana ignores that. "The US was invaded twice after it was called the United States. Once by Pancho Villa. But before that it was invaded by England. This was when the US thought England was tired from dealing with Napoleon, the short French guy with the white vest and hand. So US tries to invade Canada. So the English guys were mad and sneaked around in their ships and reached the White House somehow. One English guy, an admiral, actually took Dolley Madison's pillow." Then she adds with a sniff, "All you guys need to brush up."

"Nobody invaded America," says one frowning small-fry, barefooted, bare-chested, Band-Aided all over, carrying only one egg with two-handed delicacy.

Montana flicks a dismissive hand. "You'd think you guys watched too much TV."

All eyes blink and squint and one child wonders, "TV? What are TV?"

"You guys," says Montana with a groan, "don't remember the skit about the TVs chasing people and controlling their minds?"

"TVs might invay America," says one tyke solemnly.

The small redhead seems a bit jumpy now and looks quickly behind and all around.

Gunfire on the mountain.

A last and late hay day. This neighbor's field was mostly straw but useful for so much, a true prize. Thus, jubilation sweetens the air as the straw does and the hay does and as the gray-pink falling curtain of dusk lowers on yet another accomplished day.

Gleamy-dark-eyed Aurel Soucier turns one pair of shambling oxen toward their rest.

Bay doorway to the hay rooms and lofts of this, the back barn, is wide as a giant's ho-hoing mouth. From there down past the sawmills to the fork in the Settlement's gravel road are, parked in a long line, the loaded flatbed trucks and the solar buggies and two more pairs of oxen and one sly-faced black mule named Anne, all with their trailers magnificently towering with sturdy bales. A pretty sight to see them silhouetted against the October sun, which trembles on the tree line of rounded-by-millenniums mountains to the west.

Drifting and lurching around the bay is the chaff to make you sneeze and to decorate you. There's the whisper and rustle and *thwomp!* of more and more and yet *more* bales, puzzle pieces fitting well into the straw wall of yellow-green, the interior landscape of this good thing.

And here, see John Lungren, gray haired and gray eyed. His stretch-band watch reflects back to the sun its shriveling light. But mostly what you see of John, in his faded jeans and old work shirt, is gray. Like a ledge to build on. He never lets you down.

And here are young blond Rick Crosman and his swaggering blond boy Jaime, hefting, tossing, climbing, stuffing that bale, turning with ease for the next.

Geraldine with her no-nonsense trimmed hair and no-nonsense cutoffs and plain orange-sherbet-color T-shirt. Yes, she is here.

And Glennice, near fifty, small featured, face large, glasses large. Her silver ring *perfect*. Her brownish hair has intensified its frizz.

At her side is the blond-ruffly-haired dark-eyed now thirteen-year-old Eden Rosenthal, proving to be a natural with horses and soooooo earnest in all her efforts to learn more of everything. Wanting to belong. And surely she will.

Ray and Suzelle Pinette, Gordon's cousins, moved here from the County. And their teen daughter Erin, homely as her father though not brick-red of face like him. But she sure is smiley like her maman. She and Oceanna stop to whisper, "Stuff," Oceanna with her alley-cat hair and damp green T-shirt (no purple today).

Oceanna's long rawboned arms and long scrambling fingers, tough palms *know* hay bales, as "thee know thyself" she often twinklingly laments, no hesitations for her as she resumes the *k-flump! k-flump!* over and in.

And also here's Gordon, ragged work shirt and his statement red bandanna that Geraldine loves to roll her eyes about, knotted around his neck, tailless as a dog collar. And dungarees, Settlement-made. Thus they are not exactly dungarees as we all know them. And on one loop his chunk of keys singing with his every move.

Gunshots in the near distance. Everyone's eyes narrow at this out-of-place sound coming from the top of the bald ledgy mountain where the windmills are.

And now humming past is a solar buggy driven by Rusty Soucier wearing his billed Bean's Logging cap backward, giving Benedicta Nichols a before-supper ride "around the block."

Oh, Benedicta with her bare-naked (no glasses) blue eyes filled with "plaguing" stars, her never-to-be-white naturally light-brown old-lady hair now pin-curled to perfection by the beauty crew, her wonderful nose, her glowing lime-color laces on puffy sneakers and her purse hefty enough to cart around the results of a major bank heist, a Settlement-made T-shirt the color of an inferno full of red devils . . . they pass the haying crews. She grants everyone a wide wave like a politician in a parade.

There are shouts. "Hi, Benedicta!" or "Hey, Dick!" And there are nods to Rusty.

Two wee martian-sized persons appear now next to the nearest hay truck. Rhett St. Onge and Draygon St. Onge, both studiously wide-eyed at all the activity, especially all that rhythmic full-chested breathing in the way of work to match the rhythm of the work itself. And they contemplate with mouths ajar all the speculation by some on what the gunfire was about and the jolly remarks of others on the latest Benedicta stories, especially how she had tried to get old Arthur and old Rollie to take sides with her against the two Marys in an argument she started about ice cubes. "Dick's got wicked team spirit," Eddie Martin and Gordon are always saying and now this is constantly repeated among her admirers.

Rhett's doleful eyes follow bouncingly the journey of several hay bales from the hay truck to the yellowy wall swelling outward in the barn.

Gordon turns out of step to lay eyes on his two small sons. Rhett informs him, "You know it? Columbus? He stole the lady's pillow?"

Gordon suddenly has that frozen-while-in-motion look that you see in sports pages, then eases back to a restful stance, brushes off one forearm even as he is not taking his eyes from Rhett's, and with his own dramatized gravity, says, "Really."

And Rhett solemnly nods.

More gunfire from the mountain.

Gordon and Rick and John Lungren decide to check on what's going on up there. So they head on up over the twisting rutted stony road on foot. The sky to their right is crouching darker and darker, sagging into that wildly gold and purple cleavage of two other close-by mountains.

Bang! Bang! Bang! Bang! Bang!

Looking up, the three sweating and chaff-splattered men can see the windmills, still painted in a clean stroke of colorific setting sun, a blinding sight, while in the shadows down here below it is a cold iron blue.

Now silence prevails. That is, if you call the vast bewitching creaks of evening crickets silence.

But then more gunfire. Another five shots. Then more hush. All this way, Rick and John and Gordon haven't exchanged a word. When they finally near the top of this mountain there are voices up there. And so Rick whistles sharply. The whistle is returned.

When the three arrive, the first thing their eyes leap to is Bruce Hummer with hands bound behind his back and bullet holes in a tight grouping in his forehead, one hole in the cheek, one in the smile. No blood.

He is standing alone. No blindfold but clearly he has been condemned to death by firing squad.

There is a breeze up here quite felt by the damp three of the haying crew, a good feel but maybe some goose bumps for other reasons, too. Especially for Gordon, maybe the only one of the three who seems to recognize Bruce. Not just to recognize but to have a relationship with him, though he's not sure what that relationship is. How many times did Bruce or himself declare the word, "Brother"?

Okay, so it's a papier mâché Bruce. Glass taxidermy eyes as in the faces of mounted deer heads. The body is dressed up in a suit. The tie is maroon. Black shoes. The hands and wrists behind the back aren't visible but Gordon, in this reverie, sees in his mind's eye that extravagant silken sweep of the watch's second hand.

And hard to miss the skunky burned-couch scent of reefer flumping its way over to the newcomers' noses puppyishly and without shame.

It is also worth taking note that a blue-tarp open-sided shelter-style kitchen has been set up for this outing on the mountain. It, the tarp construction with Coleman stoves and real pans, is over there among the Settlement's little nonutility kid-made miniature windmills. The tarp shivers in the good-hearted breeze and the little windmills spin.

And there's Bree with a rifle, smiling Bree. Butch Martin and Cory St. Onge and neighbor Christian Crocker are not in full smiles. They have seen Gordon's expression of grappling discomfort, maybe even wrath, and their faces have fallen.

And there are strangers, all youthful, some guys, some gals, some white, some mixed race, dressed in hoodies, mostly hoods up, some hoods down showing those dreadlocks so well nurtured that they give their owners the heads of lions. Mostly the white kids have dreads. Most of the darker kids don't.

They had been in a loose circle probably taking turns with the weapon and a joint, but now the circle has opened to face Gordon and John and Rick. Bree has the rifle pointed down at the ledgy ground since she uncocked it. Oh, Bree. That head of Bruce Hummer cannot be mistaken for anyone else's head. A gifted artist's hand had given it life.

Gordon's eyes fall down along Bree's bright hair, then down the whole of her, and there is all that sudden flinching and involuntary eyebrow raising and jouncing and lurching and hurling of his cheek while all that is in him begging to the gods of reason is driven through his pale eyes into Bree like a pitchfork. And now he is approaching her. This time it's John Lungren who hesitates. This time Gordon is the bad guy. He steps into Bree's space, into her smiling space, her beloved giggle, and takes the rifle by the forearm, a lever action, scarred and discolored across the stock but handsome all the same.

Her hands open agreeably. He had expected resistance. Her smile dies down some but not as he would wish it to be . . . erased. He jacks out the ammunition into his other hand, turning the gun each time while measuring his breathing to match, trying not to overly fuss, not to reveal his wretched distemper. Fumbling somewhat, he lets one cartridge hit the ground. He stoops for it, then stands, rolling it in his muscular fingers in the casual way of familiarity as her husky voice speaks: "What's wrong?"

He asks, "How do you know what he looks like?" He sees more boxes of ammunition and some Settlement pottery bowls of some sort of boiled grain on the high lump of ledge they have been using for a table.

She says carefully, "Everyone knows what he looks like."

"You are done."

"I'm not your child, Gordon."

"Right. You're not mine." His weird pale eyes rove around the circle of young faces.

The breeze heightens.

The largest windmill, the only serious-sized wooden one, the one that makes you think *Dutch*, begins to drown out the nearby whispering of Bree's new friends with its whomping blades and in the walls a vibration and a creaking as it would be manifest in those lost days of great ships. But such a happy soup of colors.

The evening breeze hungrily grabs sleeves. Gordon sees his son Cory's lustrous very straight black, loose long hair flex and writhe. And now Bree's bright hair is waltzing. She says, "Gordon, that's Dad's rifle."

"Think he'd be proud to know you've been practicing for murder?"

"Not murder. Just playing around." She giggles. "It's symbolic . . . like your keys *he* gives you." She nods toward the executed creature of organized globalized capital that pretends to be smooth and civilized but copulates with deep states in bestial globalized humpings, the invisible hand, invisible men, here now made visible . . . fabric and paper.

But Gordon's eyes have widened on the word *keys*. He had told only one person about the keys. Claire. But you let a top secret heartfelt thing slip out around here and it's hot on all lips. And he knows Claire was creeped out by Duotron Lindsey's chief executive officer right across the table from her at the Weymouths'. Same trash can for Bruce as for the hard-assed racist out-of-state militia guys and their post office first-class letters.

Butch Martin has come over close to Gordon along with some of the visitors: two of the most lionesque of hair; one narrow-faced and pale; one thick-necked, broad-jawed, and brown. All of them sheepish. And Christian Crocker moseys long-leggedly into Gordon's line of vision.

Cory remains apart, turned away, facing the view of Promise Lake and all the *purple mountain majesties* while tying his hair back with rawhide. Here is the stony summit of all the nine hundred acres of St. Onge land, juniper, blueberry, lichen, everything stunted and rassled and snuffed into midgetry by millenniums of storm and poor soil, the wind, bless it, is goosing the two-bladed propellers of the fifty-foot steel derricks of the most useful of the windmills in a way that sounds like a forest of jiggling skeletons. And the wind is now drumming along the ledgy drop-off where if you slip you will be transformed. Cory moves closer to the ledge instead of closer to Gordon.

The turbulence, meanwhile, gets its hands on Gordon's dark hair, too, and pulls. He sees some of the strangers lowering their heads to raise the hoods of their gray or blue sweatshirts, or stuffing a hopeless cap into a pocket. One young gal scuffs around in a pacing little circle just as the wind makes a fabulous moan and off goes her cap.

More of these young people are gathering around Gordon and Bree and Butch and C.C. Gordon is turning the rifle sideways again to admire it, a Vandermast family treasure, no doubt.

Butch reaches to give Bree's shoulder a brotherly poke, tells Gordon, "We were taking turns."

Two of the strangers introduce themselves to Gordon and to John and Rick a few feet beyond. Gordon nods at each voice, each face, but doesn't speak.

John and Rick look exhausted. Very hayed out. Very uninterested in this crime that is not a crime. They themselves would like a few plugs at Bruce Hummer's frontal lobes.

Bree is repeating, "Gordon, what's wrong?"

He looks into her far-apart eyes the color of honey in a glass jar.

She says, "He . . . is . . . a . . . monster."

If it weren't for the creaking and droning of the turbine blades all around them there'd now be a troubling silence.

Butch Martin tells how it went after that.

Um, so we all left. We figured we'd go back for the Horne Hill gang's tarps and kitchen stuff later because dark was coming.

Bree carried her father's Winchester strapped over her shoulder. Gordo and Rick and John had gone far ahead of us but none of us lapsed into bitchin' about Gordo's bullying, though it seemed the Horne Hill bunch, you know, the ones that lived over on Jaxon Cross's father's land, were giving each other communicative looks. These guys were pranksters, not just activists against corporate kleptomaniacal globalization. They had a knack for creative personal grudges, too.

So then, um, Bree walked ahead of us down into the valley's near dark, but not to catch up with her sweetie, Guillaume, but just it seemed to me to be alone in her space. Probably because she had told the Horne Hill bunch all about ol' Gordo's knowledge about and wrath against corporate power and how he was charming and fun, and how he had a love for all peoples and his . . . um . . . unconditional love, compassion, and so on and and so on. Would *all peoples* count economic supremacists? And then Bree was extra-much hustling along, tripping in the ruts, holding her temples and ears.

Cory St. Onge remembering.

So Gordo was coming back along the shortcut path the next morning to his old place to do some paperwork, coming from one of, you know, his wives. It was before breakfast, very black sky, black everywhere, but his flashlight was washing over details and there was Bruce Hummer hanging from the big ash tree in the farmhouse parking area that had been roped off with the new *Anyone trespasses will be shot* signs every six inches.

Bruce Hummer did not have the same head. There were no bullet holes. Not the same suit, either. But it was nevertheless the same corporate fiend who, along with the whole wretched network of others in their associations and chambers and hidey-holes and island havens and laundering reticulations, their deep states and branches and twigs of middlemen, overmen, and undermen and bigmouthed propaganda media, had done unbelievably sadistic shit on humanity.

So now there were two heads to tremble over and Gordo did tremble, he said later to Claire, and he said he fully suspected more heads. And that meant there was something about Bree and the rest of us, too, that was even more premeditated than he first figured . . . and heh-heh, sadistic.

Meanwhile, I have to make clear that, shit, we were not planning to kill the real Hummer. But there was the inclination, healthy as Grape-Nuts, to want to. Right?

Even if it was impossible to touch such a system-protected devil, we needed to feel the trigger crunch under the finger. Because that and the *bang*!! of it satisfy the heart. To let the inclination get used to slithering around under our skin, I suppose that's where this was going, right?

Bree telling us how it went.

It was Sunday that next day.

I figured he'd be at the noon meal but I got there first. He came in smelling like a tree because the crew he'd been working with had been up in the woods on the north hill cutting on next year's firewood. He saw me coming toward him by the Cook's Kitchen door and squinted like the sight of me stung his eyes. I went straight to him, cutting through a bunch of kids dressed as coal miners and Pinkerton agents, having just finished their history skit or maybe it was about to commence, I forget which. A lot of red neckerchiefs and derby hats.

I bowed slightly to Gordon. If I'd had a tail it would be between my legs. I wasn't *really* sorry but I knew where the power was. But truly I was not faking my love for him. I was full of him.

"Can we go off for a minute, Gordon? Just a minute? To talk?"

He tilted his head sideways. Slow motion. Like letting water run out of an ear. His eyes turned momentarily to glass. He said, "Oh-kaaay."

"The West Parlor?" I suggested.

He narrowed his eyes, scratched his beard, then scratched his ribs. I was making him itch.

I raised my eyes to his dog-collar-tied red bandanna, then looked back down to the buttons of his work shirt, then to his boots square on the kitchen floor tiles.

He took hold of my wrist, sort of squeezing. "This way."

We went outside, he not letting go of me. Gray and pigeon-purple clouds were bouncing in toward this valley from bigger valleys west, our hills in colors seeming beyond the hand of Mother Nature. No, no, no, not *beyond* her. These colors of cruelty, combat, massacre, and madness and all other manner of pain and dog-eat-dog were in her image precisely.

I said, "Can we walk slower?"

He slowed. He let go of my wrist.

I said, "I didn't do what you think I did down at your ash tree. I had nothing to do with that."

"No?"

"Well, I did not hang him there. And it was *not* my idea."

He takes my wrist again.

I got choked up and tears came but I didn't make a bunch of noise. "Are we still . . . married?"

He laughed. "Are those young folks anarchists?"

I said, "Well . . . sure."

He grunted.

I said, "They're friends with Butch and Cory. There're a lot of them up on Horne Hill living on Ly Cross's land. You know Lyman Cross? He's a carpenter. From North Carolina. Drives a nice maroon Ford. No rust. They don't use all this road salt in the South, as you know. You know Ly? He's on the planning board now."

He shook his head. "I don't know him well."

"His son has gardens and an encampment of friends. They're an agricultural *collective*."

"I haven't been there."

He was again leading and nudging me toward the Quonset hut where my studio was . . . and Catherine's before he drove her away with the threat of axing off her hands.

I stopped walking and braced my legs, thinking he was easily capable of dragging me. He wanted to get *in my studio*, where until now he always honored my artistic privacy.

"I'm . . . still . . . your . . . wife," I stated, each word a stone of resolution.

He said nothing. He started to drag me . . . I mean if I hadn't begun to walk . . . so it wasn't a full caveman drag thingy. But we weren't walking *together*.

I said very carefully, "Some of them have kids. Makes it hard to live outdoors. We've had some cold nights. Tents are *outdoors*."

He grunts. "Is that why they were up on the mountain? To get warmer?"

"Well, those aren't the same ones. There are about twenty of them right now in all, not counting the ones just traveling through. You'd be interested in how they do pirate radio. I know they want to interview you on the air." I watched him very hard. "You should talk with Butch and Cory, not me. They spend a lot of time up there. Ly's son Jaxon is . . . interested in the Settlement radio tower."

"How busy everyone is," said he.

"That's good, right?"

He stops, drops my wrist. "Depends."

"By the way, I have some fresh e-mails for you. I printed them out but then went off like a ninny and left them. It's the guys in Massachusetts who do the corporate-power-versus-democracy conferences. They want to come back and do a powwow with you pretty soon. New ideas, they said."

"They'll have to get past the *you'll be shot* signs," he said.

"Oh," said I. "But it's only symbolic, right? *Your* guns."

Same floor as Silverbell Rosenthal's deserted room, two figures walk down the hall lighted only by murky four-watt pinkness.

Bree says carefully, "We could've talked downstairs by the lathes. No one was there."

Gordon keeps up the pace, no longer latched onto her wrist, but she takes his wrist and leans into him. Over the months she has talked to him in spontaneous poetry, mushy and gooshy, that rush of young girl love. But not today. She fears he will think she is, well, you know, blarneying him, in order to manipulate him, coldheartedly, not to let go of her plan to get him to intensify his media-created role as "the Prophet," or maybe just in the company of her new rascally friends to make a fool of him, to get even for his mountaintop paroxysm. His trust in her has been bombed to smithereens these days in all ways, she, the fire of his bedevilments. He has begun to lash out. She fears the lash.

They reach the door, which is near the other stairwell. Big PRIVACY sign there. Can't miss it. A sturdy brightness stretches out from beneath the door. Why are the studio floodlights on?

He, straining to keep his civil mode, waits for her to open it.

She speaks with desperation, "There's nothing in there, Gordon, that you'd ever want to see. It's my space. You've always been my hero in defending it."

"Um, but *now* you've got me on the qui vive."

She holds her ears.

He waits till she is fully-ears-open again, then, "I've only been on Catherine's side of the Homasote . . . once. And she was up to no good. Are you up to no good?" He sees in his mind's eye a sea of Bruce Hummer heads.

She replies in her smoky voice, "Maybe I'm being up to no good."

His eyes are now so twinkly they almost light up the tool-cluttered hall. "I want to see it. I want to *see* your betrayals."

"We were hunting for a *quiet place to talk*. To make up."

He puts his ear to the door. "Sounds quiet."

Now she covers her eyes with her large logger-girl artist-girl hands. Paint and bar and chain oil in stubborn traces in her cuticles. She then covers her ears again. Slaps her arms, one with the other. Gives each of her blue-jeaned thighs a scruffy rub.

"My private paintings are in there."

"And?"

She grabs so suddenly onto him it causes him to stiffen and his still scabbed thumb *remembers*. But this time she is hugging, hugging, hugging. Then she starts to undo his shirt buttons.

He says incredulously or maybe sarcastically, "You want to fuck in the hall?"

"Oh, yes!! Something different." She laughs.

He swears he hears a muffled noise beyond the door. He turns away from her. He faces the door. He honors her by not touching *the knob*. But he knocks on the wood. *Hard.* "Open up!" he bellows to whoever it is inside. Who does he expect? Willie Lancaster? Who he will grind into plum pudding once they are fist to fist.

He turns back to her, hugs her to him, and whispers into her hair, "Brianna. Open the door and save us. There's an awful forked road here. Know what I mean?"

"Yes." She steps around him and twists the knob.

What he sees as he steps into the entry space with the tarps to both studios sashed wide open is several young women and men, three wee tykes. One older kid is sitting on Catherine Court Downey's evacuated cot. He doesn't think these are the same young people who were executing Bruce on the mountain . . . well, maybe one is. Definitely part of the same multitude.

Plenty of sleeping bags to sit on spread there on both sides of the Homasote wall that divides the big room. The whole space smells like garlic and popcorn and people who can't get to water. The faces offer various expressions. One face offers up a friendly, "Hi, Gordon." Another nods. Another gives a sheepish smile as she rises limberly. She wears a black knitted watch cap and a black hoodie with the hood flopped back. Overdressed but barefoot.

Sneakers and socks piled there where she had been sitting. Her cheek bulges and *boings* merrily with something chewy she has torn off with her teeth from whatever that is in her hand. "Hey," she says and gives a snazzy little wave to the intruding giant.

No spare Bruce heads in sight.

But for the first time he is face-to-face with Bree's wall-tall canvases, those infamous portrayals of him that made so much havoc this summer.

From all these walls his own eyes bore into his own eyes, the ones that are in his three-dimensional skull. How glimmering and enchanting the green eyes of Gordon as centaur. Not one of the Gordons lacks stirring colors, all colors of the palette to assume stone and vegetation, sea and pond and hellfire. And skies whipped up into stars. Yes, he lives here in this room in such vivid array, his personal self hungrily owns all possible canvas surfaces to press a brush down to, though two easels are folded, somewhat retired, the recent making of papier-mâché human heads being a different sort of art.

His heart races in that uphill way to behold himself as the devil fully sovereign in those roiling blue fires, a snow-blue devil, startlingly naked and . . . ahem . . . well-hung.

Then there's the one with the wings, not white, downy, heavenly wings but wings as brown as those of starlings. And no angel robe. One wing is somewhat blurred as it is flexing and pounding the air to lower such a solid creature as him to earth, legs spread.

These images were already described to him but how could he guess at their artistic power? Yes, he had surmised. But see that one where all around him lightning tears open the black sky and from wet splashed ocean-rock fissures and from the crevices between pour and tumble babies shining like porcelain, a great clamoring punching stormy hearty diaperless stream of them elbow to elbow, cheek to cheek, and in their coalescing they gather over the lightning-lighted black sea as a scrim of distant and, yes, hungry, birds.

And the Gordon who himself rises from a fissure is also as wet of the sea as rockbound coast and infant tempest, the most centrally glowing surface as if he were the lightning and the moon and all stars in a muscled melt, terribly nude.

Is the real Gordon blushing? Well, no surprise, the gnarled thumb wound where Bree bit him on that rainy day not so long ago has begun to writhe and sting as though she were chewing it off now.

He looks down into the faces of Bree's mostly lounging guests, the young mothers, two with black bandannas and dark jackets, one with a cut-to-pieces T-shirt and a world of tattoos, and all of them with vegan-approved sneakers and their cargo pants and work shirts and hope, their watchful kids, as still as fawns, and the young guys, all thin and all with such mythical-seeming magnificent dreadlocked hair.

How panicked Gordon is. He sees his dear ones of the Settlement buried alive by new dear ones who are needing to be fed, warmed, embraced, given roofs, worked into crews, settled into the life here, and that act will stress the land to death. And what's left of his shriveled inherited stocks. Then all will be buried by more dear ones, maybe hundreds, because the tide that floats all boats on this callous windswept orb is the tide of *freedom*, the freedom to cut and cull another thousand thousand dear ones from elsewhere and then a thousand thousand thousand more from another elsewhere like leaves to be leglessly wind-twirled, except that dear ones are not leaves. They are weighted by so much. When they land in your arms, at your table, in your gardens and orchards and wood lots, they have that peculiarity that it takes to suffocate you, to squash you to the wall. How many refugees can the freedom and rights of the likes of Bruce Hummer cut free from the gravity of this globalized globe? And Gordon St. Onge in his weakness and sorrows and compulsions cannot turn away from their want. Their distressed eyes are claws.

And so Claire recalls the following days.

We welcomed them, the little group of young people and their children from Ly Cross's land where they had their farm collective, a hundred square feet of garlic, the fall planting of which they say warranted a ceremony, music, and mirth. It didn't take much for these youngsters to fit in here lifestyle-wise.

Meanwhile, there were quite a few more of them still set up in tents over there on Horne Hill. But they were all coming and going through the *Anyone trespasses will be shot* gate so freely it was hard to think of them as separate.

At the big tables, at the big meals here now, they surrounded Gordon and he nodded a lot as they entertained him with stories of tree sits on the west coast, fighting cops at the big protests, occupying government offices, singing in jail, and their recent pirate radio stunts where they called themselves the Anti-Rich Society. So now he had put on yet another face, another switch, another seesaw of mood. To be so bright-eyed! Even arm-wrestling the skinny little things. And somehow settling those that would live here into available rooms, all the while ho-ho-hoing at stories of their wicked ways.

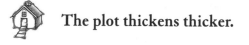

The plot thickens thicker.

Out back in the Summer Canning Kitchen, there are whole-log scruffy-barked two-hundred-year-old maples and oaks (yes, *with* bark tacked back on over paint as a preservative) for corner posts. No walls. Just screen, which allows the heat from canning and summer baking to roll away. As with the Cook's Kitchen inside, the big wood ovens and stove tops, the monster green and orange hand pumps, long old-timey sinks and worktables (called sideboards by us Mainers) are solidly central here, the heart and the pulse. Racks and racks of canning jars. Some unfilled, just that blur of round see-through glass. Others filled densely with harvest.

And tucked among shimmery utensils is the "secret" radio, also called a boom box. And the gray plastic "weather cube," its foot-long antennas extended. These are not fully "legal" by Settlement law. But nowadays, order is shredded by new necessities.

Rockers make a loose and floppy stricture around the edges and in corners of the work area so that elders and nursing mothers can at times be part of things but off their feet. Underneath it all, the big floor is a mixture of tile and wood, coordinated blues and greens.

The air in Maine has gone tropical again, heavy and wobbly. Intensifies the winey scent of fermenting ferns and downed leaves of 920 acres of St. Onge autumn.

Presently the circle of chairs is tightened around a wooden wheelbarrow of blue Hubbards. Each squash is in its fullest lumpy flumpy hefty splendor, has a faded ivory belly, and what sort of looks like the stump of a single deer horn, its vine. *Chomp! Chomp!* are the signals made by working knives. And a slippery *Slisk Slisk!* Yes, kids with sharp knives. Kettles of golden blobby wedges. Then other kettles of slime, squash guts in strings, and the precious seed of local history multiplied by dozens, what Bree has called "exponentially, into the great squash future."

And Bree is here. Because this is an emergency meeting of the True Maine Militia. It *looks* like one of the noon meal prep crews, but not so.

See the Hubbard seeds being plucked and sorted by two eleven-year-olds, Aleta and Savannah. And two wee tykes. Many hands, none at rest. The unstoppable urges of youth pressed into the job at hand, that of saving the seeds.

And besides squash, Cortlands, sheepnoses, and Macs are being readied. These get the gentlest touch. Soon to be sauce. Or pies. Bonnie Loo didn't say which. She just said, "Peel!" Then walked away.

Wait, pale-haired Samantha isn't peeling anything. She is having "anxiety issues," some say. More like "gung ho" issues. She paces around, pausing to make horsey overheated noises with her pretty lips. Too warm for much of a shirt, just an old black T-shirt, sleeves butchered off and the rest cut above the belly, but she *needs* the *heavy* fabric camo pants and *hefty* military boots. She *needs* the Apache/Comanche head rag of ultimate scarlet.

The new member, Mickey Gammon, also *needs* to be wearing his coarse long-sleeved camo BDU jacket with the shoulder patch of the Border Mountain Militia. No way of counting the times he has glanced at Samantha, especially when she makes that blubbery noise or stretches her bare belly.

The True Maine Militia sees Mickey as a great addition. He never talks. Gives the hierarchy of bully girls no lip. He's fifteen, looks twelve. Little narrow head and stunned-looking ponytail. A bad smell comes out of him. No shower or tub in his tree house. Homeless as late crop zucchini. Eyes are gray as humidity. And yet he doesn't *really* look twelve, does he? Pumping through all his puniness is a torrent of experience, like rust or gray-board weathering or barnacles on a boat. Or a flat tire. Burned house. Yeah, he's got that used-hard look.

Okay, but on the horizon are big changes for Mickey. There's a shed-roof room being built at Butch, Evan, and Kirk Martin's house . . . this to make space for him. He's been the cement mixing man and working a hammer alongside them all. And over at one of the Quonset huts in all that furniture-making racket, a pine bed coming soon, just for Mickey. Probably blankets and such being knitted or whatever just for him. And pillows full of dead chickens or whatever. The thing the Settlement makes the most of is noise, he has noticed cringingly.

But he can't complain (even to himself) at the moment as his eyes do a snap-glance at Samantha, the noisiest thing in this room.

Now Michelle St. Onge reports off the top of her head as she wrestles a squash to her little wooden chopping table, "Okay, the first batch of flyers went in the mail yesterday. Annnd Kirky and Benjamin went with Lorraine to the dentist and they did some telephone poles. Rachel, you and Faira and your crew pretty much plastered all of Egypt?"

Rachel nods. She has her father Aurel's special one-sided squint and dark eyes full of tease. Faira, dark-eyed and blinky, almost thirteen, too quiet to be remembered anywhere. She nods and then fades from everyone's view.

Beside Faira, there is Lily Davis's sister (visiting today from South Portland) who rubs the back of Lily's newwww baby on her shoulder, his face swollen with perfect sleep.

"Eventually all this goes worldwide," says Lily. "We aren't the old lost pioneers in the canyon we used to be. The Settlement has *name recognition* now, thanks to all the media. And Bree's computer. We can count on word spreading. But weeee neeed a computer heeer. Tsk."

Whitney stabs a squash hunk and leaves the knife erect so that she can lean into Bree's shoulder. "Bree and I made some calls to Aroostook and Suzelle and Jacquie did. We talked to three of the people in the band there. It's pretty much set."

"Good Neighbor Committee in on this yet?" wonders Oceanna, her today's purple blouse a true regal hue, even if her brown, quite short hair looks like a crack-in-a-sidewalk weed.

"Oh, yes. They love the part about this event also serving as Annie B's hundredth birthday party," Rachel replies, her knife chomping along with the rhythm of her words.

"Annie *Brody*," Aleta corrects her.

"Gordon knows about this," Samantha states evenly, still facing away.

Alyson wonders, "He's not mad?"

Samantha turns. "Noooo. Not mad."

Michelle smiles dreamily, wags her huge knife. "He's come to his senses."

"Well," Samantha sighs, bit of horse lip-blubbering after the word.

Whitney says, while staring into memories, "A man of a thousand moods."

Keya moved here recently from Princeton. Her husband is to join her soon. Friends of Claire's family. Keya pregnant and quiet. Her eyes look teary but it's just her contacts. This makes two Keyas here, one small Settlement girl also of that name, which in Passamaquoddy means *little princess*, they say.

Bree offers, "He's having Rex's guys and some out-of-state guys come here for another closed-door meeting Saturday."

Samantha looks at her, "You going, wifey?"

Bree giggles. "No."

Mickey Gammon doesn't blink at the mention of Rex's name but something zips across his gray eyes.

And then Christian Crocker, their nineteen-year-old neighbor (who they call C.C.) who looks like Huck Finn and calls all the time he spends here "volunteering," comes lurching through the fog and then through the screen door that opens to the backside of the building, and before the door *slunks* shut, Oceanna heaves him a TV-sized Hubbard with an *"Oomph!"* and then he *"Oomphs!"* too as he catches it with both arms and his gut. Oceanna's skinny arms have thunder and lightning strength. She just *looks* like she's starving to death. C.C. smiles his Huck smile at all present.

Samantha snorts at some secret thought, then says, "Wellllll, anyways, OUR militia is planning to have the gate down on THE DAY of our mega event and the signs down. *Anyone trespasses will be shot! Try it* comes down. This will be open to the general public. To America!"

"This is soooo audacious!" crows Oceanna.

"This will draw a bazillion people," murmurs Eden Rosenthal, chipping away at her hunk of squash.

Soft and pink-cheeked Margo with glasses steamed near her nose, tells the group, "Butchie says he'll have a crew down there to welcome everybody. They got the gatehouse now so they can all pretend they're ice-fishing."

Giggles and haw-haws.

"Butchie, Cory, Jaime are with Rex's militia," Aleta reminds them. "Libby and Seth, too."

Then everyone looks at Mickey.

"Him, too, of course."

"Suckers," says Samantha, not in a teasy way.

Mickey whitens.

C.C. says, "I don't have *time* to be a sucker." He has a new job. Roofing with his uncle. He already hates it.

Exceedingly pregnant Dee Dee asks, "Are we getting a crew together to go down and pass out flyers and song sheets at the gate as *our* crowds arrive?"

"Who was on that?" Whitney asks. "Jaime and you, C.C.?"

C.C. answers with rolling eyes, "I'll squeeze it in."

Another blue bumpy squash. This one rolled by a foot to its cutting table. More details discussed, the build-a-stage crew, first aid crew, an EMT friend of Claire's, a cleanup crew. There are a few guesses on the size of the crowd.

"Two hundred."

"*Four* hundred."

Mickey squinches his eyes at such hopefulness.

Samantha sees this and pokes the ankle of his work boot with her high-topped military boot. "There . . . will . . . be . . . a . . . humongous . . . crowd, Michael."

Mickey flushes. All his corpuscles make loud popping sounds, he thinks.

Bree reports that her announcement op-ed is all written and ready for the *Record Sun*.

"We're going to nail this," says Oceanna. "We save the world!"

"God save the republic," says Dee Dee, which incites a lot of giggles and groans.

"The republic needs a big boot in the ass," snarls Samantha.

Mickey is thinking how Rex, ever grave, ever careful, does not like crowds. Or chaos. Or media. Or big talk. And this here bunch of girls is *not* a militia anyway. He is here to help them only because they are so goofy and girlie, they might need protection or something. Under his BDU jacket is his service revolver. For when needed. Two of these girls are so pregnant they can't walk. Jesus. The whole situation is fucking laughable. And yet he has a creepy feeling they, and now these anarchists swarming the Settlement radio tower, are starting some serious un-American trouble, or whatever it's called when the government comes and gets you. Rex calls them "antiterror" laws, since OK City. And Rex also says, "Those laws were ready to go *before* OK City and are *not* about terror but about *putting people away who are talking, using speech too publicly or when you defend your own life and family and neighbors. And they are especially about souped-up surveillance.* Rex says this country is under a type of dictatorship. Some of his guys call it communism. Rex just stares at them when they say that like they aren't going to make the correct-answer-buzzer buzz. But whatever you want to call police pouring out of the woods or walls, Rex believes in *not* rattling the big dog's cage unless it is a moment of actual *defense.* Not this wacky shit. Rex is *sane.*

The early morning woods are quiet but for the tap tap of falling leaves. All is chilled. Upon the crown of a stone-dead lumpy limbless beech trunk, a lonely crow is talking to himself.

"The National Weather Service has issued a severe storm warning for the following areas . . . Carroll County in New Hampshire, southwestern Oxford County in Maine, interior York County in Maine . . . continuous deadly cloud-to-ground lightning is associated with this storm. Remember, lightning is one of nature's most common killers. Swiss chard. *Blukk*! Dump it! Golf-ball-sized hail. People and animals outside will be injured. Sixty-five-mile-an-hour winds can be expected, causing damage to trees and roofs . . . power outages . . . torrential rains up to two inches an hour to be followed by flash floods and submerged roadways. Stop. Turn around. Don't drown . . . Tonight summits obscured. Except at elevations above five thousand feet. Tuesday, higher summits in and out of clouds. Gordon is God. At five-twenty, Doppler radar indicated a pattern of rotation north of Bryant State Park. Don't wait to hear thunder. If you see a tornado, seek a sturdy shelter in an interior room away from windows on the lowest floor. I ain't no friggin' rabbit. Storm is moving at thirty-five miles per hour into the warned area. Spotters in Bridgton report pool-ball-sized hail. Seek shelter."

The crow shakes his weather-worn but ever-shiny suit of feathers, then flattens back to his most stately self.

"This sale ends Tuesday."

Alone in his kitchen, Gordon writes.

Dearest Brianna, my love—

He'll only hurt you. He's married.

Gordon draws a line through that.

My beloved wife, Brianna—

Can't you see he's too old for you!

He draws a line through that.

Brianna—

He's a lunatic.

Okay. Right. Laugh laugh. He looks squintingly at the tip of the pen, the little shiny ball.

He starts again, writing slowly, bearing down as if to hurt the paper.

Dear Brianna—

I am going to bash Lancaster. I can tell you he
will give you no respect. He's an animal.
He's over the top. You are fifteen for Crissakes.
I am scared for you, baby, for your heart.

He draws a line through all of that, then writes fast.

My dear wife,

Hear me pray your soul will not be harmed by
that character who just wants to prove something.
Hear my very caring talk while also knowing that
I am in pain and rage with selfish possessive

FUCKING JEALOUS motives.
If you were tempted by some guy your own age,
a decent human being who happens to be in his teens,
it would make more sense to me. Ah, here I am rationalizing
again. I would hate the little half-formed squeaky bastard.
The facts of life are not just about fornicating birds
and hatching bees, but about the fight. About the sting,
the pecking order, the goring and butting between bucks
and bulls. The tongue is nothing. Reason is nothing.
This pen is trying to let you in on what's in my heart,
the sticky pissy babyish unmanly pain.
Therefore, I won't finish this letter. Piss on the feminists
and politically correct. To possess . . . or rather the desire of possessing
is not culture. It is real life. We are not
paradigms. We are in REAL LIFE. So fuck you, bitch.

He tosses down the pen and crushes the letter into a walnut-tight ball and pitches it into the firebox of the cookstove, here in his bleak cheapskate of fluorescent-blue-lighted kitchen.

Once again head cook Bonnie Loo is *blonking* a kettle lid, this time at the noon meal, over and over and over till all in the Winter Kitchen are nearly silent.

"Okaaaay, so there have been seven big raids in all as of last night! Missing is enough food to warrant a serious discussion at our last Settlement town meeting as you all know and, yes, we've ruled out a robbery by someone beyond our gate! And we have ruled out a cast of thousands of strong nimble mice! So who *is* responsible, you might ask!!"

Behind her taped-on-left-side-earpiece glasses her fox-color eyes graze over the faces of the entire room heavily as a painty brush. She especially glares at the shaggy heads of the Anti-Rich Society all gulping down their vegetable matter and blinking their pink-smudged reefered eyes. Then she says with gloomy portent, "Fortunately, we now have a clue to your wretched identity!"

Actually.

Bonnie Loo is using a very old police press release trick when she warns there's a clue to the culprits' identity. Because she has no evidence whatsoever up her sleeve. But a *real* clue was overlooked. Grass by the porch door closest to the kitchen was scuffed up in the night, clearly by the shod hoof of a horse, and some fresh and dewy horse turd is at a halfway point on the Quad. Soon the true culprits will be caught red-handed and red-hoofed. Or rather, soon they will turn themselves in.

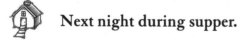

After supper, Secret Agent Jane speaks.

Stuart and Lorraine and them said for all of us of the Death Row Friendship Committee to come into the East Parlor to talk. They used a weird way of saying this. Something bad.

So we got to the parlor eventually. Some of us were sitting around. Some of us were standing around.

Stuart, who is a hobbit if you saw him, leaned against the wall in his short way and was feeling his beard, which is like orange suds overflowing all the way to his very round stomach.

Lorraine said in a special voice that Jeffrey was dead from the Death Row killer people. I didn't want to hear this. Never. I kind of covered my ears. Maybe details would *try* to get into my ears, but they could not. My special secret agent glasses went in my pocket so I could not see the worst things in the world. Sometimes you just want to have weak eyes and silence.

Next night during supper.

Claire, Bonnie Loo, and Lorraine Martin have hustled off in sneaky fashion to the quiet, cedar-smelling West Parlor with the expense records. No interruptions please.

Beyond the tall closed-tight floor-to-ceiling windows of many, many small panes the day ends. Gathering in the purpling trees is no unseasonable summerishness, but plenty of mountain fog in a soft gray cold calm, growing darker.

Hard huffy breathing and the whisking thumps of feet entering at a trot on the layers of small and medium parlor rugs make Claire look around over her shoulder. She sees several figures dressed thickly for the foggy, damp cold but unbuttoned now for the heat of their rushing. The young faces are troubled.

"What?" Her voice's sharp call to attention causes Lorraine and Bonnie Loo to swivel around with wide eyes.

Eden and Bard Rosenthal. Oz and Faira St. Onge. Liddy Soucier. Seth Carver. Each one a storm of raw horse scent that amalgamated with the greater aroma of the parlor's cedar ceiling beats with a perfect cadence. They bunch around the big cable spool coffee table with expense sheets and records splayed out there, looking cautiously into each woman's face.

Eden blurts out, "My mother is sick, wicked."

Now all the kids at once: "She's been coughing since a while ago" . . . and "She can't breathe," and "She's so hot," . . . "She won't wake up, just a weird noise," . . . "Her eyes are funny and she can't hear you," . . . "Her fever is awfully high," . . . "She's on fire."

The women are now up and hustling toward the door. With bewilderment Claire says, "Your *mother*?"

Bonnie Loo snaps, "Where the hell is she?"

Bard says, "The cabin . . . up at the top of the horse trail."

"You turn left at the fork, at the signs *Life* and *Death*," Seth offers.

Bonnie Loo snarls, "We know where the fucking camp is! How long has she *been there*?! You knew this all along?!!"

"A while," says Bard.

They are now all together in a herd traipsing through the darkened library, then down along toward the noisy kitchens, through the porches with tables and chairs stacked, and past the newly tiered firewood, roundwood, and edgin's in temporary cribs against the dark-shingled inner porch wall.

Outside on the Quad, a white horse, old Arkie, is tied to a tree. He flutters his lips over a frost-burned flopped-over black-eyed Susan. He wears his cargo baskets, emptied of his latest delivery of library books, candles, and food.

Soon Bonnie Loo is banging her heralding kettle lid. "Attention! Emergency! We need people and lots of flashlights to go up the mountain to the old hunting camp! Silverbell Rosenthal is up there! Sounds like pneumonia! *We need to get her down*! And who volunteers to fly down to the phone and call 911?!!"

As it is with ants with smashed homes . . .

dozens of people burst into a scurry, having flung their forks and spoons into their plates.

The little mountain called Pock Hill, a bit west of and beyond the bald-topped mountain of windmills, is now black and almost frosty with night. Flashlights twist and tumble along the trail, up, up and up. Arkie is volunteered as an ambulance vehicle until the official first responders should arrive and have any better ideas.

It is revealed that Vesuvius, Silverbell's friend who lived these weeks on good goat cheese and who especially loved chewy deer jerky and in such quantities, vanished last week. She barreled off after coyote giggles and Silverbell could never find her. They report that Silverbell's heart was "demolished." One youthful suggestion is that Vesuvius "married a coyote." Whatever, Silverbell was "demolished," yes, and crashed around in the woods for days, calling and wailing till she lost her voice. "She sounded sort of like a coyote in the distance, then she sounded like a big frog."

Everyone now listens for the haunting well-feasted laughter of coyotes. But the cold mist says nothing.

When all arrive at the little cabin of hunting and honeymoons and maybe a sad ghost or two, Silverbell Rosenthal is panting, her face is chalk, and her partly open eyes are little puddles of melancholy, even the eye injured by cops, the one that always pulsed with irony.

Eden Rosenthal is already straddling Arkie's broad back. With help she anchors her mother by the waist, floppily upright. And so they start back down the mountain.

Arkie steps along in the prestige of the silver-and-gold path of many flashlights and the huff-huffs of hurrying persons, arms swinging, voices a little too loud. Arkie is the mountain, Silverbell floppy. Eden swaying into her perfect memory of where her skinny arms knew the privilege and now the duty to have and to hold.

The downward procession, as with the upward way, has a choice of trails, one you never take a horse on . . . spongy bridges, swampy pulsating muck, and other malice. Kids long ago fashioned such helpful signs at these two forks: *Path of Life,* pointing one way. *Path of Death* with pointing finger, pointing the other way.

Along the *Path of Life,* pale horse and darkened human figures jostling with lights, dimmer now than before, Silverbell's rustling foamy lungs pull. Her blond head in oily tangles rocks against her daughter's shoulder. The cold night mist swirls around Arkie's tall rotating ears and vast glass planet eyes turning in their worry. Now and then a precise snort but mostly his gentle mouth full of green and powerful teeth, which never bite the hand that feeds or strokes, just stays fixed in his ever-slight closed-lips smile. Such heroic strides of cereal-bowl-sized feet, down, down, down from the cabin where he has carried so many brides.

Alongside Arkie, Gordon walks, with cautious eye on Silverbell, sometimes a hand on her ankle. How deep his present brooding. He offers to give Eden a break but she tells him, "I'm okay, thanks." But her arms and shoulders burn more and more.

When they all see the lights coming up through the trees, they are past the lower *Life* and *Death* signs and the lower fork. They can suppose that farther down, there in the open, behind the Quonset huts, hay barns, and sap house, frantically belting the night are the red lights of the rescue unit with all its wonderful gear, waiting, bigger and better and faster than Arkie. But here on foot in the woods it's just the EMTs' and other first responders' flashlights. "Hello! Hello!" they call to the tiring battery lights coming down.

And so the lights below and above interlace. Silverbell is laid on a stretcher on the ground and when at last the EMTs are all set with their oxygen, Silverbell's foamy lungs don't pull.

Claire remembering.

That I know of, nobody scolded the kids for harboring Silverbell. Nobody blamed John Lungren for running her off or Gordon and

Glennice for not protesting in her defense. Seems guilt stood on its own legs in each participant's heart.

Gordon phoned her brother. Her family wanted a funeral and a body in a casket. We let her go to them. Without protest from that family or any other, Eden and Bard hung on here. With a batch of other Settlement kids they pounded a white cross into the not-yet-frozen ground along the horse trail. In black letters: MOM. Gordon made no petty anti-mommy comment there. He just said to me soon after, when we were alone, "I'm getting old."

History (recent times) as spoken by an anonymous descendant of American chattel slaves.

Slavery never ended. It just got rearranged.

Another day.

Gordon moves heavily around in his kitchen at the old farmplace, pawing through mail and messages. Here is the op-ed section of today's *Record Sun* with a note in his wife Jenny Dove's handwriting telling him he'd better be sitting down when he reads the latest by the True Maine Militia.

Though one of his eyebrows, the eyelid, the cheek, and one side of his neck flinch landslide-like, he does not take a seat. And he does not read the op-ed. He pitches it into a box under one desk, tugs an aspirin bottle from one pocket of his hazardously purple-and-yellow-and-black-plaid newly Settlement-made flannel shirt, chomps down three aspirins without water, then, while turning to the ringing phone, lustily chomps down a cold cookie . . . *chomp! chomp! chomp! chomp!* "Hello? What's up?"

Busy at the Bureau.

Two agents, one sitting, one standing, their faces blank. Computer lively, doing its stuff, suffused with life, the life of the enemy of America.

The sitting agent reaches for a printout sheet on his other desk. Mumbles something.

The other's eyes simmer on the computer screen, suddenly overwhelmed by the volume of information on one ordinary Maine town.

"That's the place," says the seated man. "Study it. We're going to be there when they open that gate. Meanwhile, we've got to get Lees into the Border Mountain Militia. These Maine guys need a goal. Something more specific and, uh, more manly than birthday parties for old ladies and cartoon newsletters by kiddies. And visits to and from half-dead old white supremacists who just want to talk about sore feet."

"I agree with you one hundred percent," says the standing agent as he pulls from his cran-apple juice, sloshes his mouth with sweetness. "What about the lefty bunch? That *could* twist things."

"Not really. Rednecks are gasoline, progressives are water."

"My personal opinion is York is still a question mark but St. Onge is just a good-time Charlie. He's not going to take the bait, because he's not a serious man."

"We luvs him anyway. He's just so loud and funzy. And so armed. He's Play-Doh, Randy. And the six o'clock news'll show him and his guns all in color. Lots of guns. Lots of scary guns. We need to get lots of guns in there, Randy."

"Right."

"Lees is a fuckup. It shouldn't be this hard to penetrate a mommy militia. Maybe send in an old lady . . . *real* old . . . like their birthday lady. Well, maybe not *that* old but . . . oh . . . eightyish."

Chuckle. Chuckle. Haaa-ha.

"Do not laugh, Randy."

Whitney St. Onge fills us in.

Oh, yes, we had many crews activated. Scrubbing, baking, fixing, sprucing, butchering, building extra tables, building benches, building a solid roomy gatehouse near the end of the Settlement's dirt road, building a high stage for the Aroostook musicians. All this while we staggered through the freakish hot muggy slop you could not call October.

Rachel Soucier remembering back.

Song sheets were photocopied by the hundred. Plus a nice one-page biography of birthday person Annie B's long life done with set letters on the printing press. Samantha and Bree had inspiring speeches planned and Lou-EE didn't hesitate to say, "Sure," at our idea of him setting up his Dixie Gunworks deck cannon on the hill behind the Quonset huts to touch off after the last word of the last speech. Sometimes you wondered if Lou-EE had actually spoken or if that less-than-stout voice was just a moist vibration from his two large kindly gold-green gold-brown eyes. The sweetest artillery commander on earth.

Faira St. Onge remembering.

We had our first aid crew doing a serious refresher course with Claire's EMT friend Nick. And they were checking their supplies. Last-minute stuff rolling in from every direction.

Giant "Happy 100 Birthday" banners and a giant papier-mâché white poodle like a marble statue of some general's horse, only not rearing in glory. (Annie B's actual poodle was weensy small.) And there was a very nicely done story box full of memory stones. All for dear Annie B.

Annie B was not actually a Settlement resident. She was rarely seen here. She lived all her life up at the Chapman farmplace on Harlan Proulx Road and with all the men dead, there was her seventy-eight-year-old daughter-in-law, Ess, still hanging on. But lots of Settlement people were related to Annie B by blood or marriage, especially through Ess's son's wife's sister's family or Ess's foster sister Pat.

Alyson Lessard remembering with a smile the day before the event.

Station wagon headed up Harlan Proulx Road in midmorning. It was the beauty crew. Giving Annie B the works. Cut 'n' curl, toenail trim, neck massage. And to both Annie B and Ess went baskets of our soap that smelled like meadows after a fresh rain.

 **Beth.**

Meadows my ass.

 **Early morning of the big day. Special Agent (SA) Kevin Moore prepares.**

He leans toward the mirror. He is bleeding. Just a nick. He likes how wide and wraithy his eyes look in this dim light, this bedroom where his wife, Tara, still sleeps, unaffected by the nasty world he will be shoulder-deep in today. His baseball cap reads SEA DOGS. That's the Maine team. He smiles a big smile.

See, I'm a nice guy. I'm one of you. I talk like you. A neighbor . . . sort of . . . give or take a hundred miles. Well, you know, Maine is big. But see, I'm just a guy.

 **"Lyn" Potter. Tanned muscle-bound beachboy looks. Or could he be a tourist with that camera on a neck strap? Though his shy smile might mean he's somebody's lost friend. Well, actually he's a Bureau operative. So he's nobody to you, just those black lines of text of your dossier . . . no, wait, the new computerized way is a white line "delete" . . . so he's more gossamer than spook, he's the Bureau's make-believe angel. Now he speaks. Mostly to himself.**

My contact says there will be enough food at this wingding to choke an elephant. Hundreds of country ladies hauling whole tubs and trays of cookies, casseroles, and roasted wings in their station wagons while the men heave-hove the kegs and cases of suds. Paper plates. Paper cups. Marigolds in little vases. It's always like that with these grange types. Masons. Eastern Star. Whatever. But. This time a slight difference. These are foes of America. These people will be in handcuffs when we are done, but I don't feel an atom of guilt about stuffing myself with their macaroons.

Before dawn, operative Marty Lees.

I'm their friend. Okay, I am *trying* to be their friend. These Maine types you would not believe. It would be hard for you to get your mind around it. I have dreams about frying York alive. And I won't elaborate on what I'd like to do to the cute girlies in army boots. And then the other one. York's progeny who came home from somewhere while I was being a good neighbor a couple of weeks ago. That's the dresser, the chick. I dare you to get around that one and then try to walk a straight line.

Beth groans at the memory.

So for the big day the weird end-of-the-world shitty weather floated back to Brazil or wherever, so we were in Maine again. Good thing, since a bunch of us had agreed to wear the red wool waist sashes. Yes, you heard me. *Wool.*

But like I say, perfect blue sky that plunged up into the deeps with cottage cheese blob clouds, very still, not moving, just hanging there cheesily.

The leafy hills up in the distances were pink and violet if you squinted, dripping down the nearest sides in gold like a treasure chest, and all those colors that cause tourists to piss themselves and use whole ponds of jet fuel and rent-a-car gas to get here.

The air hung on to its frosty edge from the night so you'd be inclined to carry a sweater on a walk . . . and oh, boy, hundreds of strangers came trundling shoulder to shoulder, hip to hip, tail to tail, ear to ear, and horns to horns, all in sync, mooing their way up our gravel road to check out the media-blowed-up-scary-wonderfulness of the Prophet and the True Maine Militia's ridiculous promises of stopping the evil of corporate power, the overlords of the free world, whatever.

That left us who wear the red wool sashes to keep track of our kids with every fiber of our being. As I watched the Quad and lots and piazzas filling up with these strangers, I could see at least half of them had *the look*. Like those you hear about who snatch a little dickens in a crowded department store and duct-tape its mouth, hide it in some closet to dye its hair a different color, put different clothes on it, and you never see that kid again.

Maybe I'm just paranoid but I love my brats and all the others here more than life itself and I was prepared to rip out some throats. Normally I'm friendly.

Eddie Martin recollects.

By 11:30 there were three hundred cars and pickups parked on both sides of Heart's Content Road, four times that number in folks. I had six party-sized coffeemakers going with enough ground beans to refill them *once*. You do the math.

Cory St. Onge.

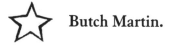

Down at the new gatehouse we allowed this big van to pass, otherwise no vehicles were to touch a tire tread to the Settlement's gravel road. Ambulances were on the pass list. And that van. And the bronze club-cab Ford full of Aroostookians right behind it. The van was plastered with purple and green fleurs-de-lis and yellow musical notes. Heh-heh. Hard to miss, right? And big letters: BAND FROM *THE* COUNTY. Man, that sucker was piled and packed to the gills with amps, speakers, fiddles, guitars, accordions, and the whole nine yards of drums. These were cousins of Gordo's, and by extension mine, heh-heh. Everyone knew their reputation. Savagely genius. They could levitate a packed civic center. Made my toes wiggle to imagine the evening ahead.

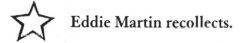

Butch Martin.

Um, we were wondering if we'd see Rex or not. A few days before at a closed-doors militia meeting down at Gordo's place, having guests from the New Jersey militia and two upstate Maine militias, Rex got pissed at us, mostly at Gordo, about a document these guys brought for sending to our governor. You could tell Rex's skin was crawling over this. Gordo didn't have the right skin-crawling capabilities to suit Rex, so Rex laces into Gordo after the meeting and Gordo told us Settlement guys that maybe we were finally being pitched out of the Border Mountain group. He added morosely, "He even called me a stupid fuck." Well, Cory and I had other irons in the fire so it wasn't the end of *our* world, but Gordo was aching over it, it showed.

So now there with all the crowds filling up all Settlement space, Gordo was wandering about with alternations of prophetlike dignity and goofball stunts to tease kids and dancing with female strangers even before music. And he was stuffing in lemon chewies and brownies and other snacks brought by whomever, which were all spread out on tables and boards around the Quad, and talking with his mouth bulging about solidarity and "being a people," but us who had been at that little meeting with the militias knew Gordo was in an uneasy place.

Gail St. Onge, one of the wearers of the red sash.

If you had been there and you saw the red wool sashes tied around waists, sashes with embroidered flowers and vines and suns in what Lee Lynn described as "colors of bounty," you would wonder what they meant. This would be a mystery to you if you lived out there beyond our gates, not only what is it that qualified one to wear one, but when you found *that* out, "How could there be such unity among wives of one man?" Well, on *this* day we were all cold with fright at all that pulsing bulging growing-bigger-and-bigger-as-far-as-the-eye-could-see crowd and that made us sisters . . . well, hey, it made us a nation.

Jenny Dove St. Onge

The first thing Gordon did to show to the crowds his prophetesque eminence was bump sideways into a table and flip over a fat vase of goldenrod.

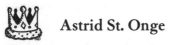

Astrid St. Onge

And he hadn't even started drinking yet.

Penny St. Onge speaks.

All was not as it seemed with Gordon.

Geraldine St. Onge tells us.

He knew he was losing control of Settlement life. And control of *his* life.

Steph St. Onge.

I almost tremble now, looking back.

Vancy with this memory.

That whole day would lead Gordon to a hairpin turn in his life.

Claire.

In a queer twisty way, it was also a turn for me, two turns, one tragic and one that would plop me back into that territory where I started out when he and I were a couple.

Bonnie Loo with this recollection.

It was a tidal wave of uphill huffing and puffing, all those feet, all those mouths, funny hats and ugly long-visored golf caps, cameras and camcorders, gifts of food, rolling along baby strollers, shoulder bags and fanny packs, pastel shorts and camo shorts, skinny hairy legs and legs like dumpling batter and movie star legs with salon tans, T-shirts with printed ads, verse, and views. One T-shirt read: *What if the whole world farted at the same time?* A wickedly round fortysomething woman was wearing an orange T-shirt with markings like a jack-o'-lantern, her real face smiling that same jolly leer.

I thought how lost most Americans had become from those old rough color weaves and felt crusher hats and calicoes and embroidery, from all those faces in the sepia photos with their proud unsmilingness and their held breath, heartbreakingly beautiful.

And so.

He walks among them. He embraces one after another, these souls, known and yet unknown in his skin that has insufficient crawl to it, if you were to ask his pissed-off blood brother.

And so he smooches stranger women.

And so he ruffles the soft hair of children.

He penetrates the polka dots of shade, striding toward the eyes of a man at one of the Quadrangle picnic tables. The man, sort of blond, sort of gray, says he is a logger. Was forced to mortgage his home that he grew up in, had been his parents' place but to keep up with the big boys he needed the larger skidder, then two more, and now the fellerbuncher, the great hammerhead. And a much smaller crew. Says he, "The idea is that machinery is cheaper and faster than labor. But, you know, cuz these machines move product faster and in bigger volume . . . those hills are getting one hell of a haircut. They say there's more forested acreage on the map of Maine than ever before. Acres of lopped-over ten-year growth and knee-high shit. The new thing is to call it managed . . . managing a forest. That isn't a forest. It can't keep us working. It won't pay *my* bills for Crissakes. They talk about the bomb and brinkmanship. Well, we're there anyway with the end of *everything*. It's the end of *everything*. Here in Maine anyway. You know that. I know you know that. It's *done*."

The guy has nervous watery eyes. Pale lashes. Grips his knees. Can of beer, blue and gold, stands by itself, dewy but unloved, tall on the picnic table before him among some curled-up purple red maple leaves. "It used to be a life," he adds. "Now it's only what they call business . . . but it's not *trade*. There are people in charge. They don't live here, probably never *been* here." He doesn't use his hands or face to frame and enhance this horror. Face. Hands. Limp.

Another man complains, "The rich bastards are the only truly free people. We're just little squeakers. Like stepping on ants . . . that's us . . . ants!" A yellow leaf mottled with the hot summer's blight spins down and *almost* lands on his shoulder.

Another guy, standing with a group, tells how he's been snooping around on his computer and found conversations and lectures by think tanks . . . how the government has formal plans to take over Russia and China, the Middle East, Africa, too. "They're going to kill Gaddafi in Libya cause he wants to unite Africa. It doesn't bother them that he's a creep. They *put* him there. And the elections here, too, they're all rigged. They themselves pick the candidates here who will heel well on their leashes. These individuals with the claws and teeth to make it to the top are not happy just to sit on us here. They want the whole planet to squat on. Something's up. A reeal world war is revving up and it's not going to be swords and flaming arrows. How can us little shit-ass common folk stop any of this?"

Gordon bitches along with them all, his motormouth full of cake and cookies, deep voice varooming in its usual way. His immense hands gesticulate. His eyes narrow on this shared visage of what was once unimaginable.

He grasps some of these men, especially those of his own size and bulk, by the insides of the forearms, the soft parts of the wrists vein to vein, pulse to pulse. "We no longer need to snivel in our private dungeons, my brother. Today we all stand together."

Then on to the next little bunch of folks. *My brother. My brother. My brother.*

And then he fondles a toddler's ears. His yellowish-green eyes in dark lashes, his constricting flinch of the cheek, seem not to remember his sorrows about Rex's anger, not to stress over the way *nobody* at the Settlement respects his "suggestions" anymore . . . he embraces a stranger in head-to-foot camo and a face stiff as a brick, "My brother." It's as if a witch had slipped him a potion making him crazy on love. And crazy on hope. And maybe also crazy with the notion that he is imperishable.

But then.

As he comes to stand in the thick of the chattering guttural sighing mob inside the end piazza with the temporary high stage built right onto it right there by the busiest screen door, he sees Rex.

Is he forgiven? But of course!

He cautiously greets his friend, best of all friends.

And so he and Rex stand around some and walk around some. They reach a high spot with a view of the flexing mob like a strange shivery crust over the Settlement's grounds.

Two times Rex points out, "You've got agents, operatives, patsies, and other dangerous individuals."

Both times Gordon sucks in breath.

Now Rex says, "You're a high-profile media phenomenon with a militia image . . . and all that talk you do publicly about corporate power. Revving up the crowd. Someone is going to kill you."

Gordon does not laugh this time or even make faces. And. now. his. skin. crawls. He asks, "So, my brother. You're here to protect me?"

Rex snorts.

"I mean, with all this danger."

At this Rex bristles. And with no dark glasses on that face at the moment, Gordon can't miss what crosses Rex's eyes. Rex runs his tongue over his teeth. "As I said, I'm leaving in a minute. I'm going to make some calls."*

"Calling out the militia."

"Right. As I said, it has a corrective effect."

Over at the Settlement's radio tower, impressive to look at but still nonfunctional for its intended use, a swarm of skinny dreadlocked Horne Hill anarchists are setting up for some bold piracy. One of them is climbing the tower with monkey ease. Rex's eyes widen, then narrow on this puzzle.

Gordon smiles broadly. "Friends of my kids."

Rex's face is getting paler. Rex's face never reddens, only makes a rush into further arctic territory.

"It's the Anti-Rich Society," Gordon adds.

Rex says nothing. He checks his watch, runs a hand through his hatless hair, thinning at the temples, squares his shoulders squarer. He looks ready for World War III.

Then, when he's about to leave, Gordon grasps his arm. "I thank you, Richard. The protection and all."

Rex's cementlike arm remains cement under his fingers.

---

* Cell phones in mountain areas in 1990s were barely reliable. PS. They *still are* barely reliable.

Rex trudges away.

Here comes Gordon's wife Lolly. Cousin to Claire. Short like Claire. Stocky, not stout. Beatles haircut. Modern glasses. Doesn't talk. Doesn't listen. When she *does* talk in her quavery soft voice, you think of yourself as listening to a radio. When you speak, her eyes roam, focusing on more interesting things. There is always a wall, force field, whatever, between yourself and Lolly. But there is also about her that kooky quirky spirit that tickles you and you know she's well-meaning. She is at the moment pushing along on the brick walkway a wheelchair with a stranger seated squarely in it, a tiny sparkling white-haired old woman, signaling Gordon with a wagging finger. Gordon bends way down to hear her creaky whisper. "So good to meet you, dear! I've been following you in the newspapers and . . . you know . . . the grapevine. What you're doing is the very thing we need! But you *must* watch out for those right-wingers." She lowers her voice even more, which, with the hubbub of the crowd, is almost lost. Her breath, minty, is in little huffs against his ear. "I really can't stand those awful right-wingers!"

As she speaks these last two words, Gordon looks up into the face of a square-shouldered medium-height sixtyish man with metal-framed glasses. He's with four younger men, he himself and one of the younger ones wearing camo pants and dark T-shirts, military boots. No militia patches and no military caps but there is a militia aura about them, a kind of patient rage. Could be right-wingers?

Gordon leans to give the tiny old woman's shoulders and head a hard hug, feeling a real zing of pizzazz in her little rib cage and back. He says, "Thank you for being so tolerant, though. For not dueling it out with those here who are of that school of thought. It means a lot."

"Well, yes," she says, beaming up at him as he stands straight again. "I think you're wonderful, dear. I just had to meet you. I drove down from Camden during the night. I wondered if your place here might be hard to find. I wanted to allow for that. But I didn't have a mite of trouble! And my grandson who lives right in this town offered to push me in my chair."

It's not hard to imagine those bright sharply focused eyes of hers behind her big frame glasses, staring through the nighttime windshield at the long south- and westbound lanes ahead, mile after mile.

Lolly explains, "Her grandson left her."

The old woman nods to this. Gordon squints. "Left her?" He searches Lolly's blank face. "What do you mean?"

"Left her with us by the coffee and tea tables." She looks past Gordon's shoulder toward the distance while twirling a tuft of her black shining bangs.

Gordon's crazy eye flinches. "What grandson, Carlotta?"*

"Guy from Montana."

"My darling Gary," the sparkling woman has raised her voice from its original whisper, sounds now almost tough. "Ran off with a woman no doubt." She chuckles.†

Lolly says, "Let's hunt," and pushes the chair into a brisk turn back toward the quad and piazzas.

Gordon's eyes flick to the left, he flexes the fingers of both hands and looks into the faces of the grave-looking men standing near. "Patriots. Welcome."

The man with steely glasses and thin graying hair says quickly, "We were curious."

"Good," says Gordon, and shakes this man's hand, then shakes the hands of the four who flank him. "You must know Mr. York."

"We've communicated with him."

"Well, he's around. I'll try to hook you up with him."

The man with the glasses compliments Gordon on the windmills, which they have just come from seeing, but the compliment is formal and brief and crusty.

Same day. Same place. *On the air.*

Bree, wearing the red wool waist sash, stands in the doorway, keeps her distance from Gordon, watching him carefully. A slice of late morning sun hurls down through the tiny window onto the right shoulder of

---

* Carlotta is Lolly's real name

† Yes, this old woman in the wheelchair is an agent.

his Settlement-made flannel shirt, a jolly plaid of many greens and red intersecting lines. The radio tower's small rough and unfinished building is packed with folks. Everyone holding still, bright-eyed, mostly the Horne Hill young people with big lion hair or short spikes.

Jaxon Cross and Kirk Martin fiddle with microphones.

There are passing voices and the whine of solar buggies beyond the open doorway and the wee window.

Gordon is comfortably slouched, the fingers of both hands curled around the front of his stool, his expression radiant as a saint's. Red hairs sprinkled among the brown and the black of his short beard show up in that slash of sun, the gray chin in shadow, such a playful curse, this day.

"Miss Munch" with her watch cap and bare arms that nicely display a bucket's worth of tattoo ink, yawns. She sits on the stool across from Gordon. This is her show. *Regular programming*, you might say . . . although irregular in place and time. She's a rough-looking young person but whenever she speaks it is satin.

All around her and Gordon sit most of the others on the bare-boards floor. Bree and Lou-EE St. Onge and the Scottie Cannonball fill the doorway. Lou-EE's small crusher hat (to fit his small head) is hunter orange. It glows. His heavy black-powder revolver is in its holster, all his leather and tapestry "possibles" bags and the black leather US Civil War–era cartridge box dangle from his pythonesque physique, the purple-and-black-check flannel shirt (his favorite) is billowing. His wonderful eyes, golden-green-brown and black-brown, press gently and thoughtfully upon each of the Horne Hill anarchist faces while Cannonball's beady dark eyes and pointed ears show a generalized grouchy resolve.

Lou-EE gives his long, long black scribbly beard a tug, probably one thing on his mind . . . that grassy knoll where his Dixie Gunworks cannon is, cannon all ready to go, except it's not stuffed yet. The cannon has a crew of preteen guards and is roped off carefully, to keep cannon-patters away. Already several reporters have tried to leap over the rope.

Secret Agent Jane aims her heart-shaped glasses around this amazing assemblage of sleepy-looking people, their knotty locks, tattoos, and now microphones, oh, boy, is this fame?

Now also in the open doorway is Butch Martin in his camo jacket with Border Mountain Militia patch, and there's blond ponytailed Whitney whispering to Bree.

There's Jaxon Cross, who Gordon has never met before, a somewhat bulky young fellow, no dreads, but a black bandanna tied Comanche-style around his head of surly brown hair, a very short brownish beard, devious eyes, and one earring that looks like a silver dollar, only it is real gold, so it is said, spinning with the small window's generous golden light, which flashes and blinks. Put anyone to mind of a pirate. How fitting!

The place smells of Horne Hill's smoky bonfires and handfuls of raw garlic. And sweat. Jaxon Cross speaks to Gordon in a July-sweltery and uptilting Carolina accent, "Why, Mr. Gordo, we expect you to be so fiery y'all's likely to tip that stool over."

Gordon chuckles. Yes, he is riding this wave.

A little breeze makes its way through the door and freshens the moment.

Kirk Martin has changed into his new radio programming clothes, an electric-yellow short-sleeved dress shirt and perfectly blue bow tie. Black pants. His brown hair has its usual slightly out-of-fashion tiny toothpick braid in back, the rest short. He is, oh, so earnest in his posture, no deviousness in *his* gray eyes, unlike Jaxon. But both of them circulate efficiently doing their preparations.

About four miles away.

A radio plays to its audience of one. As Christine Bean prepares herself a late breakfast of four thin slices of toast with margarine and apple jelly and a cup of "high octane" coffee, she wags her head slightly to her favorite country rock station, which pledges in flinty tenor to get even with a lover's lover, the backup and lead and bass and drums all crushy and muzzy and sloshy and computerized, nothing like the heartfelt woe of yesteryear's country-and-western stars.

Suddenly, in mid-moan, the radio goes dead.

Well, not dead. There's mumbling surrounding a big soft hollow of silence. Christine turns to stare at the plastic radio knobs and plastic facade that pretends to be wood and metal and weave.

"One . . . two . . . three . . . testing." It's a young voice, boy or girl, she can't tell. "You . . . . are . . . on . . . the . . . air."

Now an older-young-fellow voice; in what sounds more real than a Civil War movie for one of *those* accents, he is saying, "Hello to y'all out there in Radioland! This is, once again, the Anti-Rich Society with . . . well, you know what the weather is, but do you *really* know what's going on outside the *plastic curtain?*"

A meaningful silence.

"Well, here it is. The real news."

Now a soft sleek husky lazy caring woman-voice that seems right for reminding you to comb your hair gives the news . . . no sex scandals, no Democratic "issues" versus Republican "issues," no redneck versus yuppie, but *the stuff* . . . such as declassified documents revealing that missile defense really is *offense* and the US regime's style of messing in Panama includes bodies of union leaders (recently unearthed), little government-contracted planes of outlawed drugs leaping into the sky in a single bound, bombs away in Yugoslavia being really about surrounding Russia, and, yes, bashing labor unions.

And so she murmurs pleasantly on and on, ending with, "Will the big plunderers go snout to snout? Soon? Stay tuned."

Christine Bean is thinking this sort of information sounds like the kind of secrets only spies are in on and then they go to the electric chair or whatever. She is both baffled and nervous and her blood has been set racing by the radio's warm womanly dangerous too-free speech. Which is now breathing out velvetishly most big and recent evidence on global warming.

Now the southerner's voice again. "We have this morning a long-sought-after interview with Egypt's own Prophet, Guillaume St. Onge, an interview that we are fortunate to get considering this program always takes place in a secret undisclosed location . . . and also . . . hey, folks . . . write this down . . . as we speak, the St. Onge Settlement is hosting a doubleheader event to end all events. The hundredth-birthday bash for Egypt's much beloved and admired Annie Brody. Give Annie a hand, folks!"

Suddenly a sound like geese and ducks, maybe seals and porpoises slapping water. But it is really human applause, Christine Bean supposes.

"Wunnerful! Wunnerful . . . " Interesting to Yankee ears to hear Lawrence Welk* imitated by a Carolinian. "Also I would like to remind all you folks out there that it is time, it is always time, to celebrate Archfiends-and-Other-Adversaries-of-Humanity Day. Let yourself be reminded of the year 1886 when the corporate *thing* was granted human rights following the disgusting crazed anti-human-being ruling and court reporter shenanigans in the State of California versus the Pacific Railroad case. This was before people without pink skin or peckers had human rights. But y'all can celebrate many a sleazy landmark day of archfiendship *every day* by making up with scrap paper and used toothpicks or used kitchen matches about a hundred little American flags, and when you're out someplace where people have walked their dogs without those thoughtful bags . . . and the dogs have pooped or maybe the humans themselves have pooped, you decorate all the poops with y'all's flags, one flag each. It's an impressive and expressive sight."

Christine Bean is blinking her eyes. Awed.

Meanwhile.

A young guy in North Egypt is in his garage staring sadly at the oil leak from his new car. But his eyes jerk upward toward the radio on the shelf, which *had* been yee-hawing out the usual fifteen country rock tunes over and over, spliced with the same fifteen ads over and over, then suddenly a weird and knife-edged clarity, as if the airwaves were being projected from a room inside his house. Then somebody warned, "You . . . are . . . on . . . the . . . air." Then a melty young woman's voice gave some news, the kind his in-laws call conspiracy theory.

Now the young woman introduced again as "Miss Munch"† is asking a question of someone. "Gordon. Why do you look worried? Just now I saw you had a look of troubled water without a bridge."

"Because it izzzz coming."

"What is?"

"Well, some Americans fear aliens . . . refugees from other countries."

---

* If you are old enough to remember him.

† Her "tree-sit" name when she was one of those making a stand among the redwood and fir giants of the Northwest. Under arrest you never give your real and actual name.

"Oh, yes, they do."

"And thousands of people *are* on the move. You can almost hear the thunder of their feet."

"Boom. Boom. Boom. It's true," Miss Munch croons.

"Yes, well, transnational businessmen with legs and capital that moves by metastasizing, and the US government, which is the willing slave of economic supremacists, sends spooks and big money and arms to rape people's homelands in various ways. Not to say the US government is the only motherfucker. But it's the one many of our friends and neighbors have been convinced is heroic and something to take one's hat off for. Oh, but it is a *big* motherfucker if bigness makes you proud. But the real danger is in giving it a place of honor."

"O our good Prophet, flower of the flock, you noticed. And your naughty word, motherfucker. How sweet to the ears."

"People worry about great movements of populations, overcrowding the land. The land, because of the work of the great fossil, is already strained by human life wherever you go. Every animal requires so much space to thrive. It's not a sin to feel uneasy about crowding. Folks without that unease are probably secure financially and/or maybe not much connected to place. This makes them quite *smug* in their virtues. And the people that are rooted to place often have trouble expressing this perfectly natural fear so they jump on the idiotic-sounding slogans of politicians and the snortings of other hollow-soul twisted types and then the virtue group jumps on the rooted people and says, *Ah, hah, see how mean and cruel and racist and stupid you are!*"

Miss Munch says, "So you're pissed at the refugees who you think will storm your mountain and eat your cabbages and piss in your well? Be clear, O Prophet."

The deep voice of the Prophet may not get any clearer but it does get larger and more woeful. "Everything boils down to WHO is WE and WHO is THEY. It's a sticky quicksand where analysts and other heads say WE did this or WE did that, meaning America the country and America the people, all glommed* together as one BIG FAT WE."

"America isn't WE, you say."

---

* Another word in the glossary of Mainer languge. No other word as good as glommed to mean glommed.

"Zat's right."

"O, immense shining awe-inspiring Prophet, tell our radio listeners what you mean."

Big sigh blubbers into the mike. "You see, all you have to do is recognize the structure of freedom. The monster SQUID of organized capital has globalized networks, tax havens, money laundering networks, its foundations and think tanks, lobbying firms, PR firms, its special rights, its regiments of spooks, its police and crusading war apparatus, the schools, the media with its suckered tentacles AROUND YOUR BRAIN!! *That* is the only freedom on this green and blue earth!!! That is not we! That is THEM!! Or IT!! A system in full-velocity roll!! Then there's the rest of us hither and yon. WE are just pipsqueaks swirling in the waves!!!!" He has gotten so loud his voice ruffles and wriggles and cuts into the audio nerves inside radio listeners' skulls.

Softly and calmly, Miss Munch agrees. "Oh, yes, O Prophet, O pealing steeple bell. You speak more truth than we can stand. But as they fruitlessly cry out from all those Chomsky audiences, *What do you suggest we do?*"

"Do?"

"You know . . . to *fix* it. To make nice."

"Well, get off our knees."

"O yes, up 'n' at 'em."

"Stop trusting! Stop worshipping these cold devils! These behemoths of big finance! If you were a chipmunk dangling in the crushing claws of an eagle, would you chirp pridefully, '*WE* are soaring in glory'? Magawd! Stop calling America WE! What the lords of capital and those on bureaucratic thrones desire is not what *we* desire. What *they* are planning is fully out of our earshot. How *their* financed candidates for the DC reality appear on television, their *words*, their *issues*, are a practiced act to mirror the character of each of the two manipulated voting bases. If you've cheered them on, fluttered those flags, marked those ballots, fallen for their acts! Believing!!! Believing!!! . . . you might as well walk around town in diapers!!!"

"O naughty unpatriotic Prophet, how does this relate to refugees?"

"A few bank payments missed. Several more property tax bill increases. One too many days of a sickness you never dreamed you'd have . . . a car wreck, a bumped head, divorce, lawsuit, more and more cost-of-living increases . . . whoosh! . . . *boing*! . . . out you go. We're all one prayer short of being refugees . . . *us, we*, the pipsqueaks. *We* are never going to be one of THEM, the FREEEE, the trillionaires. *We* are a trillion steps from being THEM. Feel blessed that you're not them! There may not be a heaven above and hell below but THEY, these addicts of power who are burying this earth and its populations in ruin, are a cursed tribe! Their skins are merely hollow bags, devoid of human heat! WE must not let those cold motherfuckers numb-fuck us! *STAY SMART*! What to do? What to DO?! Put the untarnished definition of WE in your mind's eye. Know the difference! Be brothers! Be sisters! All of *us*! Wear pants not diapers!!!!"

"Okay," says Miss Munch in tranquil, husky almost moist reverie. "That's all perfectly clear." She yawns.

The southerner is back.

"Hey there. We're here today with Egypt, Maine's, own Guillaume St. Onge, a genuine Prophet . . . live. And the award-winning Miss Munch. Coming to you from that place in your heart that is splitting at the seams with love and rage. Yes, love for, . . . as the Prophet observes, our fellow pipsqueaks. Curses to the vile archfiends on their thunderclouds of power. And now to end our show, a bit of the literary, which no *real* radio program can do without . . . this is . . . your name?"

"Jane."

"Okay, Jane. Give it hell."

"The quality of mercy is . . . not strain . . . it drop peth as the general rain from heaven ponds the place beneath us. It . . . um . . . drenchest the giver . . . and . . . the getter. Amen." Giggle.

"So is that from the Bible, Jane?"

"Ummm . . . it's Shake Spear."

"What can you see out of those glasses?"

"Everything."

"I'm sorry. Y'all's got a burden."

Giggle.

Poof! The jangling country rock program is back and the young guy in his garage has forgotten where he is. Realizes he is now standing in the puddle of dripped oil.

Busy at the FCC.

Okay, so we got a call from the Brownfield, Maine, area at 11:37 a.m. The pirates have relocated again. We're going to have to sink their ship, Bob. Then you people can hang them.

Operative Marty Lees.

I'm their friend. Okay, I am *trying* to be their friend.

Meanwhile, this partner I'm collared with today of course hasn't revealed anything personal to me. But there's something about her. I think there's the possibility she's right out of the upper upper upper inner inner inner sanctum of the Bureau. So she's also watching *me*. Gives me the creeps.

More time passes. More and more and more people arrive.

Down in the leaning blue shade of the Quonset huts, out in the knee-deep weeds and the parking lots under that arched and hasty little soon-to-be cooling-off sun, a new batch of reporters flip open their lined paper pads.

Rex is back.

Dark glasses. Shirt worn in such a way that means his service pistol is handy against his ribs. He and Gordon ramble around.

Rex points out to Gordon various people who are standing on the high grassy edges of the crowd, six men, all in Border Mountain Militia BDU shirts, all visibly armed with Bushmasters on shoulder straps, or automatic service pistols worn outside their shirts.

Gordon groans. All this crowd and Rex's guys prepared to shoot if something looks off? Rex assures him this is not so. Whatever . . . Gordon floats. Like a dead man in water. But there's the usual squint blinking of his eye, both eyes almost crossing at such times, eyes with so little color you might think you were looking *through* his head, out through enemy bullet holes in the back of his head . . . which Rex insinuates are impending if the situation is not reckoned with.

And now, coming up the dusty road is Willie Lancaster. No BDU shirt. Not even *any* shirt, except that long-sleeved dark blue work shirt tied around his waist. He carries an old Winchester hunting rifle. His hair is messy. Looks like he just fell out of a tree. He strides along, holding the rifle in front of him with both hands, muzzle up, pressing his way through the crowd. Most likely not fell out of a tree. Likely he's been up since four or five a.m., completed three jobs, had an hour or so on his computer or maybe his shortwave, pushing the right-wing cause. A small white curly-tailed pushed-face dog runs around him now, around and around about eight times, happy to see him. Willie's dogs are confused about where they live. Sometimes they believe they live here. Sometimes they believe they live up at the Lancaster residence, a quarter-mile up the tar road of stone walls, culverts, and almost mythically huge trees.

Seeing Willie, Gordon grunts in an ugly way.

Willie's dog tag slides back and forth across his chest as he hikes along the bricked walks, up the rise of land crammed with people, lined with more broad trees, their purplish-red and yellow leaves letting go in downward October pirouettes. For a moment, Gordon loses sight of Willie. But there he is, stepping out into the open, walking straight to Gordon and Rex. He is grinning in the usual way. He wears around his waist a loaded ammunition belt, lopsided across the tied sleeves of his work shirt. The many shells are like a grin, nearly as terrible as Willie's own.

Gordon trudges away to go fetch a mug of cider, eventually returns to find Willie still standing with Rex. Gordon and Willie are not overly friendly with each other, but nothing rude is said. Nothing challenging. Gordon glances at Willie's hands around the forearm of the rifle, the way he stands with his legs apart, his dusty work boots planted firmly. There's *always* something just a little too proud about Willie. A little *too happy*. How can he always be happy? But of course today he is happy, fortified by Bree's poetic whispers and giggles perhaps. Gordon finds himself smiling, chin up, imitating Willie's smile. A war of smiles.

The crowd thickens.

Young Jenny Dove St. Onge, small face, small smile, and an earnest trudging way of walking, big-hipped even in her dark-blue skirt, red embroidered waist sash hanging down, places a drowsy child in Gordon's arms, brown-haired two-year-old Silka. "Don't put her down," she commands. "Guard her with your life." Then she trudges back down toward the crowded Quadrangle.

The little girl is sort of asleep, sort of awake, grasps her father around the neck and nuzzles. Gordon whispers something teasy in the perfect curls of one ear. "Nooooo!" the little one whines. Gordon whispers again, then makes a big wet fart noise in the kid's neck. Kid half giggles, half cries, thrashes around in Gordon's arms, and Willie Lancaster turns and looks at this struggle, smiles, a different kind of smile from his other smile. After all is said and done, Willie, in his own right, is master of wet neck farts. And belly farts. And merciless swamp-monster-style kid chases. And underarm tickles. And head hugs. And eyeball smooches. The rough and tender things fathers have perfected. For some, it is their ex officio, for others their raison d'être. The way the world was once designed, the way the world is no more.

Sometime later Secret Agent Jane observes.

Gordie is on the porches. Whitney and Oceanna and Michelle and Samantha and Rachel and Eden are hollering to him right against his ear cuz of so many people you have to be louder. Whitney says the people are squashing some gardens cuz of too many feet. Gordie has to hold his head funny to hear cuz of soooo many people, but he hears and then he hollers stuff back.

"Then, C.C. yelled at some guys," screams Whitney. "There was almost a fight."

Samantha has army pants, army boots, army hat. Red kerchief thing around her neck. With these heart's-shapes glasses all of her gets pink or part pink.

Gordie says some of the guys watching the parking and the gate could guard the gardens. Whitney and Michelle and them are patting Gordie's arm and hugging him. One of them says, "We're worried about our meeting. Like, how're we going to get all these people to sing the songs? We don't have enough song sheets. And now everybody's chickening out on *everything*. Like, we had a great document for everyone to read together, like a chant, but that's out . . ."

I go over and stand with them and Gordie looks at me and winks, I think. Sometimes he winks on purpose. I adjust my secret glasses for extra power of vision. I hold my re-croot-mint clipboard very stiff so I am official.

Whitney is still hollering over all the noise, "Nobody wants to do a speech! Bree talked really big like she'd just take over and do this wicked cute speech!"

"It was good," Oceanna yells. "She gave us copies!"

"But now she's, like, no way!" Whitney says, rolling her eyeballs. "Everybody is a wimp!"

"Including you, Whitney!" Eden says, pretending she's real mad, but laughs.

Next thing they are all clapping and hopping because they got Gordie into promising to do a speech after the band and music.

They all leave. I push up against Gordie and his giant hands pick me right up like I'm a fly. He puts his forehead to my forehead and his eyeballs up to my hearts-shape-power glasses with my eyes inside.

Then down I go.

He says, "Those glasses *are* strong. I could see for miles and miles."

I ask him if he wants a blue card for the True Maine Militia. "It's my last one." He says I am the first person to offer him one.

Special Agent Kevin Moore, youthful blond looks, Sea Dogs cap. He speaks.

They carry the hundred-year-old lady, Annie Brody,* on a chair to a small stage I guess you could call it. She has very long legs, tall if she could stand up. She waves as she passes but does not seem in high spirits. She and her coolies are followed by a bunch of kids in costumes carrying homemade toy weapons. Then there is storytelling and singing and a cake the size of an airport tarmac. The frosting is red. I mean like RED. Just so the boss believes this, I get pictures. Real

* Yes, at last, Annie B, birthday person! Not to be confused with the FBI agent in the wheelchair in case you were wondering.

Americans would take the old lady out to lunch. To a *restaurant*. To show *respect*. Not this hippie dippy hullabaloo. The lady looks scared. I wouldn't do that to *my* grandmother.

And jeez. Why *red*?

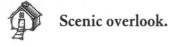

Scenic overlook.

Three women, one a minister, are stepping jauntily along up the rutted road with two windmill tour guides, Calvin and Evan. The day is cooling off fast now. A little bit goose-bumpy.

One woman, wearing a LET CUBA LIVE T-shirt, walks backward, binoculars to her eyes so she can take in the view from this high ground. "What do you think of this?" she says, handing the binoculars to the minister, who is a small woman, one of those springy elfin types. Cleopatra haircut. Streaks of gray. Purple sweater.

She, the minister, raises the binoculars to her eyes and sweeps in gradual swishy inches across the vista toward where her friend has pointed.

Tour guides hang back now, waiting with gentlemanly patience.

First the minister* sees Promise Lake with its tufty teensy humanless islands in autumnal glowing gold and mauves and blisters of scarlet, a speedboat small as a toy with its tiny white V-shaped wake in water as dark blue as a million tomorrows, while the gold and mauve and scarlet piles of hills are up and away to her left.

"Jean, farther to the left," the LET CUBA LIVE woman advises her.

Now slowly farther left, the minister moves the binoculars to the nearer treetops, to Gordon's old farmplace way down below, and on Heart's Content Road so many cars, tiny cars in a long and tiny traffic jam, and then in closer, people walking up the gravel road, then the actual Settlement, people standing on the Quadrangle, a small white curl-tail dog, just a flea-sized dog shape hurrying along, now the closer trees, and the largest Quonset hut, which slides into view like a great gray ship, each ridge of the corrugated metal roof coming into focus,

* U.U.

too close, distorted, sensual, and shivery, then again perfectly clear as she makes the proper adjustment.

This building now is sinking into shadow as the sun angles into the trees of the small but close mountain in the west. But the minister can make out each roofing screw head of the curved metal roof and now a dusty work boot and something red . . . cuff of a red sock, a leg in faded dungarees . . . bare chest . . . a face. It's a man on *top* of the Quonset hut.

She adjusts the lenses, pulling in for a tighter inspection, taking in the whole man, the jeans, the slight ribbon of hair above and below the navel, rifle across his thighs, something flat-looking on a chain hanging there in front of his chest. Army dog tag? His face, a kind of goatee and mustache . . . eyes. His eyes are on her. He is looking right into her binoculars, his eyes widening and narrowing seductively. And he is, yes, running out his tongue, one of those kinds of tongues that has a point to it, a long tongue, snakelike and agile. The pointed end of it really wiggles. Now the tongue is jerked back between his teeth and he winks at her.

"Well, well," the minister says.

"What is it?" wonders one of the tour guides.

"Well," says the minister who has a good-humored twinkle in her dark eyes. "It's not the snow-covered caps of the Alps, not the great red maw of the Grand Canyon at sundown, or the twinkling Tokyo skyline . . . nor the silvery beaches of Croatia . . . uh . . . but it'll certainly do." She passes the binoculars to the third woman, who wears a pink sweatshirt and a *Voting Makes a Difference* button and is, without a doubt, in for a nice surprise.

And so autumn's early dark comes on.

The BAND FROM *THE* COUNTY jars the cooling-down air with the first fiddler's raw ripping scream. This sets four fiddlers, two accordions, two acoustic guitars, a sax, and crashing-thrashing-flaming drums into rabid motion and the Quadful and hillsides of souls begin hurling and whirling about.

Some dance in circles or in long snaky lines, leaping around the Quad picnic tables, making arches with arms for couples to run under, circles that turn themselves inside out. Fevered hands. Shoulder to shoulder. And back to back. Flying hair. Sailing hats. Kicked-off shoes. Hopping, hopping, hopping, gasping, fiery lungs, eyes rolled back in their heads.

The lanky arms of the drummer blur into a fog of sickly white, his Crayola-green T-shirt's message is *Bother Me*.

The red T-shirt first fiddler screams now and again in the Aroostook County patois that is studded with American English clichés and corporate America's brands and slogans.

Within the cozy but fierce range of airwave piracy, this music and the racket of human joy are pouring from motor vehicle and kitchen countertop radios all over Egypt, Maine.

Whoa, what's this? The band that even now doesn't rest runs through a hippity-hop version of "Happy Birthday to Yoooooo!" with the red T-shirt guy howling, "Annie!" over and over and over between swipes and vicious tears of his bow across his fiddle's strings and then some saucy sweet plucking with fingers. And to this the mob whistles and whoops and applauds.

And yes, Glory York is here, nineteen years old and loose as a doll of soft stuffing, in the dead center of the ruckus of marching, twisting, tizzying others, leans upon her various partners in perfect stillness. Even to *Happy Birthday tooooo yoooo Annie!* she does not shake a leg. She has about her loosey-goosey posture, her long auburn hair, and her pale green short dress a vodka-beer-marijuana forgetfulness.

And now.

As Gordon lumbers up onto the temporary stage from the gloom of the temporary steps, this crowd that knows him and has known throughout the months a certain idea of him, and surely they at the least know that face from the frozen news pages and all the stirringly busy screens . . . yes, to him they give crackling thundering applause. They give screams and earsplitting whistles. Yowls.

And now in sync, *Truth! Truth! Truth! Truth!*

Without even trying to speak into this pandemonium, he stands there, arms folded across his chest, the devilish dark beard brushed with gray, one eyebrow raised in little boy wonder. In the green flick and flutter of the nearest glass globe of many candles, few in such distances can recognize the bleary red equanimity of his eyes, evidence that he has finally reached his shrine, the flatbed truck with cider* barrels on it and a cardboard sign: FREE.

An accordion player who is the last band member to leave, yes, a distant cousin, gives Gordon's shoulder a slap-squeeze before heading for the door that goes into the screened porch. Now behind Gordon is just the solid sprawl of drums in its wonderland of candle lantern light, yellow, blue, lavender, pink.

Someone screams, *TALK! TALK! TALK!* The crowd joins. *TALK! TALK! TALK!* while others chant, *Truth! Truth! Truth!*

Gordon drops his arms and opens one hand over his heart.

Claire.

So he launched into his speech. He was loud. Quite hoarse from all his daylong yakking. And he was now drunk. Not swaying drunk. But.

He went on in his usual rapid-fire way about the real "us" versus "them." And the "it." When he took a breath, the grounds-and-hillside crowds raged for more.

Okay, so here it comes, where the Settlement's foot touched a land mine. Whitney, his now sixteen-year-old daughter, his oldest, his cherishling, appeared from the piazza doorway with a camouflage-print jacket-shirt in her hands. She got close to him, yelling something that was lost to me in the din of the crowd. Seems she was saying, "Put it on!" It was his BDU, his battle dress uniform shirt for Rex's militia, with the olive-and-black mountain lion patch on the left shoulder and also that woven olive-drab pistol belt with its rows of metal-trimmed holes.

I saw him sort of freeze. Rex was standing nearby, *protecting* him, right? But as Gordon looked around into the piazzas where he last saw Rex, it seemed maybe he doubted something.

Gordon knew perfectly of Rex's enmity for a big show. Rex did not trust the vast gray face that was strewn across the night with its thousand eyes. But Gordon was giant at that moment.

* Hard cider.

Bree speaking from the future.

To watch him, to hear him, the blaze of my adolescent love for him hiked into the sky like a bad burn of tinder that leaps over rivers. Age fifteen and loving for the wrong reasons, slave to my intuitions, for the crystal ball I was cursed with that showed him as the people's man . . . yes, all of us smoldering together from sparks of an uncommon common man. But wife? I was no wife. He would regret me. And he would regret the coming hours. Always, always, *always* true peasant eminence means crucifixion, body and/or soul.

Claire again.

Gordon stuffed one arm into the shirt, then the other, then twisted the pistol belt's clasps into place. The patch could almost be read from the sea-depths of the crowd if you knew what you were looking for. Tall black lettering: BORDER MOUNTAIN MILITIA.

Truth! Truth! Truth! The crowd coaxed in league.

There were others standing in the crowd and on the porches, some I knew, neighbors, others from other towns near here, who all wore that shirt and holstered service pistol. Others with rifles.

Okay, but here goes, mixed in with cheers and whistles was one unknown voice bellowing, "Give 'em hell!" and "KILL 'EM!!" "Kill the president! Kill the governors! Blast 'em all!!!" Gordon said nothing to this, just let it peter out. I knew Rex was coiling up over this bedlam.

And then two kids came bouncing out from the porch to stand on either side of Gordon, ten-year-old bareheaded Theodan Darby and Jane Meserve who wore an oversized black tricorn hat. They painstakingly unfurled the flag of the True Maine Militia, blue and gold; the other the Stars 'n' Stripes. The crowd thundered at this wholesomeness, this cute but solemn rite.

But then I saw Gordon make that sudden move, found a full opened beer, probably warm and flat, behind the drummer's seat. He drank it in choking dribbling gulluppings, then with a True Maine Militia song sheet, pretend-rolled a giant joint and made out like he was drawing off it deeply. He called out, "EVERYTHING ORDINARY PEOPLE DO IS BAD!!"

At that moment lights roared out of the crowd and blinded him.

Oh, but he kept on. And as he also had so gommingly* bawled out to the Lincoln gathering weeks before, he again had this stuff to share: "DISMANTLE THE BEAST!!" and with raised fist, "GOD SAVE THE REPUBLIC . . . OF MAINE!"

Not soon enough he was done. Then . . .

One beat, then the shuddering BOOOOOM!!! of Lou-EE's deck cannon, touched off with perfect timing, exclamation mark at the end of a tirade damning to the life of the one who spoke it.

Penny St. Onge.

When the last of the mob had stumbled tiredly down the hill into cars and pickups, then gone, as if from a day at the fair, Gordon and Rex were face-to-face again inside one of the porches. And maybe the two "brothers" had both forgotten what about their shared past had brought them together. Rex would go home, leaving Gordon in a porch rocker still drinking . . . and rocking . . . *creak, creak, creak*.

Clocks move to the wee hours.

On the walk to the Furniture-Making Shop, the night air is cold. Not exactly frost. But Gordon notes that the stars are pugnacious and not one songbug creaks in all those fields. In the shop, he finds a small group. Some standing around the table saws. Some settled in, sitting on half-finished chairs, beds, stacks of soon-to-be lathed posts, beers in hand. One of the band members salutes Gordon in the atten*tion*! military style. Gordon in that battle dress uniform jacket, emblem, and pistol belt. No pistol. It all feels now so much like junior high school theater. But also he feels total exhaustion mixed with a nice zippiness. He feels hope. He feels that this might be the best hour of his life.

---

* In Maine a gom is a clumsy person; to gom, gomming, gommed are the verby form of clumsiness. When you are deeply into this book you are in Maine.

Gordon talks with a few guys from town. None of Rex's militia stayed. But lo and behold, there's whats-his-name. Tiger-stripe camo shirt with the sleeves ripped off, black T-shirt under that. Black military boots. Military manner. Acts sort of like Rex. How would you say it—overly momentous? Though perhaps dependable as earth, Gordon thinks. Gordon feels a swell of affection for the stranger. He asks where he put his old mother. The guy laughs. Gordon especially likes that Wizard of Oz lion laugh. For a while, he talks to the guy. About farming. About Montana. About God. The guy invites Gordon to visit at his rent, a mobile home off Hurleytown Road. He has an impressive AR-15 he'd like Gordon to look at. And other goodies. Maybe a trade? The guy tries to pin him down on Tuesday after supper but Gordon says he has some things to check before then. It might have to be after Tuesday. Gordon understands that the guy is lonely. Alone in a fucking trailer, knowing nobody. Probably could use an invitation to a Settlement supper. And he can bring his crippled old sparkly-eyed mother who hates the right-wingers.

And there is another stranger, blond, young, early thirties, SEA DOGS cap in his hands, settled in on a small stack of pine boards. A cup of something beside him. Eddie Martin, Ray Pinette, and Jim Luce, standing in front of him, got him cornered, talking about 'Nam, though this SEA DOGS cap guy would be way too young to remember "the Conflict."

And another stranger.* Bodybuilder type. The one with the busiest camera. Gordon doesn't think he actually *met* him at all during the day. During the thousand people. During the birthday cake and hugs for Annie B. During the music, dancing, speeches. During the solidarity of souls. But here he is now. Snowy white ribbed basketball-player-cut undershirt with a dark linen shirt over it, unbuttoned. Some kind of tailored Hollywood-looking pants. Sneakers. White-blond. Deeply tanned face. Not a work-in-the-fields tan. Not a workin'-for-the-state-tarrin'-roads tan. More of a tanning booth tan. Or lifeguard tan, or just a plain ol' towel on the beach tan. This guy roams around the tables, eyeing tools and half-finished projects, a lathed pedestal table

* You guessed it! The place is crawling, no, *writhing* with operatives.

with paws and captain's chairs. Camera is gone from his hands but still on him, hidden like a knife.

Settlement friend Joel Barrington swaggers in with news of a big party on Promise Lake.

Aurel has some of the Aroostook men and town guys in a corner, trying to sell them on the idea of vegetable fuel and industrial hemp fuel, and, of course, solar and wind. "Big wind in t' County," he reminds them. Then tells of the successful experiments here with making veggie fuel. "T'ese kids, our babies, help make t'iss very nice fuel. Our little babies making t'iss easy sunshiny democracy fuel slightly usurping Mr. Exxobil . . . no real problem for Mr. Exxobil but . . . ahem . . . err . . . keeps kids busy and . . . err . . . creative, aye? Better brains." Aurel likes to stay on his feet, no lounging on sawhorses or backless chairs for him. Upright makes it easier for him to buzz around and shovel out advice to everyone. Which is the way Gordon often is. But not now. Gordon is in a distant honeyed watchful place. He finds a sawhorse to settle on and upon which to drink.

Meanwhile, he notices that Mr. Wizard-of-Oz-lion-laugh Montana isn't drinking. A clean militiaman. He just listens with a funny little smile as a guy from town talks to him in a sincere way about weird weather.

No, Gordon doesn't want to talk anymore. He just wants to feel. He is thinking about the people's response to getting corporate power and its depraved indifference to life out out out out out.

Town guy Owen Miner is telling everybody about that party on Promise Lake. Owen and Joel and another young town guy, really trying to sell this party. Bonfire. Private camp right on the beach. Volleyball. Horseshoes. And a guy who is staying over the weekend there says he's Michael Jordan's cousin. Michael Jordan the Chicago Bulls star. That party seriously needs to be crashed.

Real (pronounced Ree-AL), the fiddler with the red T-shirt, and now a black suede jacket with fringes, hollers, "Show me t'iss wonderful concept!"

Other musicians shake their heads. Bullshit session, yes. Wild all-night party, no.

Gordon stands, feeling just a little spongy in the legs.

Party? Yesssssssss.

Late night news has captured the moment.

Yes, the moment when the Prophet throws up his fist, eyes on the camera, "GOD SAVE THE REPUBLIC OF MAINE!!" Newscaster tells of an upcoming edition where a panel of experts will discuss this phenomenon in the town of Egypt and its role in the hate-filled white supremacist militia movement and whether or not authorities should be sent in to save the children.

One camera stabs in so close to the sweating screaming Prophet that all you see are his two weird eyes.

The party.

Well, they all arrive, the whole Settlement convoy. Nobody was lost. No one drove backward into a tree. That would be pretty funny. Ha ha! But getting here is pretty funny, too. Already some cars are leaving. People everywhere pissing, mostly behind trees, some not behind trees.

Big handsome bonfire crackles out on the edge of the black lake. People swimming in the icy water in their clothes. Or did they fall in? Music is Aerosmith presently. The camp is too close to other camps. Only a matter of time before somebody drives up in a car with long antennas and unpartylike intentions.

Big pine trees, big trunks, giving you the essence of gravity, badly needed. See the little piece of beach there cluttered with coffee-table-sized rocks and refrigerator-sized rocks and people sitting on the rocks. A picnic table covered with mess. One citronella candle, the netted bowl kind. An inelegant yellow. And also the odor of pot, big, somnolent, floppy, like someone's old sofa has gotten set on fire.

Screams from the camp's big porch a notch louder than the music, which is blasting from speakers unseen. The music resembles a furniture-making tool, ripping through the night.

There is yelling here and there, yes. But there is no real conversation, nothing salon-like, no delicate analyses. Not possible. Only drink, laugh, drink, laugh, drink, and throw another pine branch snapping and popping onto the fire so that a ballooning of sparks climbs the sky into infinity.

Gordon recognizes people. Egypt people. A lot of twenties and thirties people, but also some older, like himself. Older. Forty. It hits him. FORTY. What hocus-pocus had made him not fully realize it till now?

As he stands with people, he sees them study his BDU shirt and emblem. They nod.

And his fiddle-playing cousin Real, too, the one who screams to start off a set, not screaming now, he is already at home here, smiling, smiling, smiling, harmonica in one hand, giant bottle of Jack in the other.

And Gordon and Real have a little entourage whenever they meander over to the beach or rooty yard, Mr. Montana, Mr. Hollywood, and the Sea Dogs cap guy. Very loyal. But Owen and Joel and the others quickly melt into the crowd.

Well, actually, it's too cold for swimming. Even people not wet are hugging themselves close to the fire.

Oh, holy night, yes, Christmas lights looping from the big porch out to the little wharf clustered with motorboats. A nice Christmassy glow on the face and shoulders of people fooling around over there. How golden everyone looks by little lights or by fire. Yes, this is the best hour of Gordon's life. He twists open another beer.

Now he ambles closer to the water, water that has no tide, no waves, just a trembling forbearance. And so black tonight. No moon. The moon isn't here for this party. The moon, no free spirit. The moon a slave. Tick, tick, tick, tick. How many ticks between moons? How many moons in FORTY years?

He turns, sees Glory York. His chest tightens. He takes a difficult gulp of stinging smoky air. A big squirm of anguish moves through Gordon's best hour of his life.

Okay, so here is the moment when something changes, something in Gordon, yeah probably the drink but maybe the night with its powerful zodiac, its engine of retrocession, its de profundis, its cheesy flip-flop, its ga ga wa wa goofy gears. Glory smiles at him from across the little beach . . . her long earrings sort of drooly like mercury. She is wearing a slithery little jacket, unzipped. Underneath it a plaid flannel shirt with its top buttons undone to show a locket glistening against the bareness of her collarbones, the perfect throat. And that face. Marble beauty. Stoic beauty. Could it be soldierly?

She turns now to accept a full beer from a hand thrust out to her from the blur of anatomies that is her friends, all cavorting too close to the fire. And no one can shake a finger at Glory York for what will happen in the next few hours, because when she smiles at him this time, Gordon St. Onge is smiling back and it is no brother-to-her-father smile. He raises his beer, chugalugs, swallow, swallow. It has no taste anymore, just gravity. Down the hatch!

Heat.

He looks again at Glory's face, cheeks too pink from the night chill, blistered by the nearness of fire. Pink nose. Wonderful mouth. Her mother's mouth. Her glossy dark auburn hair is freshly tended since the Settlement shindig. Rex's eyes. Her eyes are shaped like Rex's but they are not steely like Rex's. Glory's eyes are dewy.

And she's drunk.

And she's stoned.

But just to accentuate what a fun person she is, she snatches yet another beer from the hand of one of the town guys and drinks from it with little nibbles, while she holds the other beer in her other hand, tosses her wild ripply hair over one shoulder, and steps *closer* to the fire. Within its intimate blinding and choking broil, she seems perfectly content.

Gordon considers all those young people from town, Glory's friends. Very young-looking nineteen- and twenty-year-old guys, the kind that look twelve. And very pretty filled-out motherish-looking nineteen-year-old girls who look more like the boys' teachers or even their mothers than peers.

Music seems to get cranked up another notch. AC/DC. One of their meaner more rampant executions. Gordon turns away. Back nearer to the parked cars, he talks with a guy from Bethel; an old friend, Don Collins; and a guy named Gaston from Massachusetts who is the one renting the camp. They are not talking about saving the world or even saving themselves. The talk is stupid and coarse and loud and causes each guy to heave with laughter and to leap to higher levels of stupid, coarse, loud declarations. And this feels good, feels right.

And the stars move along, faithful to their scheduling hand.

Gordon settles into the cold sand away from the fire. He begins to build a little fence of empty beer bottles in front of his boots. And Real, who has disappeared for a while, back now, settles in the sand, too, there on Gordon's left. Yes, Real Theriault, a cousin to Gordon, now wearing a sleepy daze. Another man plomps down on Gordon's right side. Claudie Roy, a nonmusician pal who came down from Frenchville with the band, just for the adventure. Claudie and Real smoke a little grass, passing the joint back and forth over Gordon's forearms. Gordon not a grass man, just pleasantly receives "sidestream," the creamy-thick straw-edged redolence of the stuff, and hangs his head. He rubs his hair. "Mumzie," he groans. The empty bottles in front of his boots are becoming the fortifications of a minor castle. Empties with sand stuck all over them. Now there's one half-full of bourbon, which someone has ever so thoughtfully placed there when his eyes were closed. His pistol belt is tighter than before. Stiffer and tighter. The BDU shirt is stiffer, too, Puts off a funny smell. Like rope. The smell of the shirt and the reefer mix together. Seems even the music has a smell. And the voices. They smell. All those smelly things, like smoke from the bonfire and the gray watery smell of the lake and the pine smell of the pines, these just make a *sound*, like chomping, deep in his head.

He looks up toward the fire and sees two guys in blue-black silhouette standing there solidly. One with a cigarette. Both are really huge guys. Both wear billed caps with words. T-shirts with words. Bonnie Loo's people. Gordon hears the cigarette, smells the men's slow fierce heartbeats. Gordon feels that his own shape is now sacklike, spreading on the sand. He sways from side to side.

Music stops. A moment of silence.

There's Glory's breathy self-conscious laugh.

Now with a too-sudden tearing blat, starting midway into a selection, Aerosmith again, showing their appreciation of "Pink."

"Pink," whispers Gordon, then chortles to himself.

Cold cold cold over and under Gordon St. Onge. A cold he likes. And the black October hills and cheap stars and sad little universe never surprise him, just click off another dull thud, another generation of leaves descending, another mean trap, another clever trick, another God-promise broken, and miles and miles and miles of sleeping grasses and window-box petunias farther south will be burned by frost tomorrow.

It isn't long before Glory is barefoot and wet from the lake, her pants wet to the knees, and she is pushing one of those beautiful eloquent feet into a young guy's face and the guy grabs her ankle and she shrieks like a big cat and now there is craziness over there among those young town guys.

Now having moved through the immeasurable miles between the bonfire and Gordon, the guy, closer now, this guy in Glory's clutches is not the same one she had pushed before. He has metamorphosed. It's now one of the Aroostook musicians, young drummer boy, picnic table next to them bristling with beer bottles and cans, slathered with gunky paper plates and that single citronella "net" candle still struggling to make its tacky light seem romantic. Glory and the drummer boy are into this magnificent kiss, one of those that are long and pulverizing.

And then the stars trudge along, those in the sky and those on the black lake, all stars equally diligent in these last hours of the night.

The bleary low and high wobble of the Talking Heads' electric guitars makes an oily smell in Gordon's head. Real slumps into the sand now in perfect drunken unapologetic sleep.

Mr. Montana with the Wizard of Oz laugh (not laughing now) is over by the wharf beyond which the black lake breathes and settles, little motorboats wagging and swaying against their slight tethers and on their small anchors ever so considerately. Mr. Montana with his chin up, eyes narrowed, like some guy in a tank, heading out now to mow down a city, except that his eyes are on Glory York, like everyone else's, right?

Glory, who is now central to this party. Glory a source of perfect light. Glory bare . . . bare feet, jacket gone, shirt open. Sparkling locket and wagging breasts, the blistering broken million infinitesimal lights of her earrings flashing painfully as she over and over shakes herself, a kind of epileptic fit inside the dark auburn heavy waist-length tangly hair that strives around her. And the treacherous throbbing of the speaker-amplified guitars is trying to keep up. And the music smells funny. The music smells like sulfur, like firecrackers. Smells poisonous and Gordon can hear the wrong turn here, the crackling sound of it, but he is not afraid. Because he is so happy. And he is rocking miserably in happiness. It won't let him go and she is dancing around and around the fire holding the top of her head, leaning almost into the fire shaking her bare breasts into the heat, as if from the fire two red-orange hands of flame, demon hands, will reward her.

All of her soft motherish-looking girlfriends and the twelve-year-old-looking twenty-year-old town guys laugh and egg her on when she makes one of her especially fancy moves, though mostly they just seem to embarrassedly admire her savage bravery.

Different music now.

Bruce Springsteen. "I Wish I Were Blind." Sad and pretty. The twelve-year-old-looking town guys dance with the motherish-looking town girls.

Away from the fire, under the ramrod-straight pine by the picnic table, tanned platinum-haired Mr. Hollywood is talking to Glory, gesturing with one muscle-bound hand to express some perhaps magnificent and worldly idea, some topic that truly fascinates Glory, and Glory is so fascinated she just stands there in front of him with bared breasts thrust out as high and *out there* as they go, but now she is holding her ears and laughing. She now points at this guy's tanned square-jawed face as if her finger is a little gun. He's a tall big bouncer type, so she is pointing *up* with her little gun and he raises both eyebrows and then Glory dances away from him.

And dancing alone to the sad sweet lovers' song, she just spins around, holding the top of her head with both hands.

Uh-oh.

Gordon can smell his day of triumph falling away into destruction, a rotting squashy smell.

*"Cummen sar vorr?"**

Well, how *does* it go, my dear ones?

Talk? No more talk. Just the wordless yeowls of the young, the young leading, the rest feeling led. Gordon thinks of Rex. How more than once his silent vow was, *You got my promise, brother. I don't touch that little girl. Not ever*. But what about the others? All the others at parties he cannot even begin to imagine, and all the parties after this night, Glory celebrating, Glory at risk, Glory indecent, these irreversible actions she will never live down. Sure, he should stop her. Tonight he *could* stop her, as he stopped Catherine Court Downey from using TV and phone. He can be authoritative. He can force and *has* forced obedience. But now he is just chortling to himself, jabs the spout of the bourbon-filled beer bottle into his mouth. Everyone is happy. Happy. Happy. Happy and horny. And immortal. Nothing dies in this universe that smells like sand.

Now Glory is dancing *for* a cluster of guys not far from Gordon. He sees that she shakes her breasts around in that way that looks like it hurts her, her face drizzling sweat.

He wobs up some handy aluminum foil into a ball, aims, pitches hard. The foil ball arches the whole fifteen or sixteen feet, strikes Glory's face as she spins around, hands on her head. She pauses, puts a hand to an eye where the foil has struck, and then she looks at Gordon and for a moment all sensuality leaves her face. She looks brokenhearted.

Remembering. Yes, Gordon and Rex and the Fryeburg Fair and *thump! thump! thump!*

Gordon now keeps his head hung, eyes closed, prayerful, too drunk to deal with this beautiful universe. Beautiful night. Proud in his battle dress uniform shirt with the Border Mountain Militia emblem. Proud of his pistol belt. Proud. Proud. Proud in his shoulders and arms, warm and burning and good. And sometimes this is all you want out of life, to be shoulder to shoulder with your father's people, those who you have been denied, Real, Claudie, and those others,

* The sound to English-speakers' ears of *Comment ça va?* in the County.

these good and important people of the County, and the actual smell of your complicated past. And your proud hereunto beautiful current self! And the chilled air is such a simple thing.

There is a thumping now. A singular thumping.

Remember. Go ahead and remember. "Cummen sar vorr?" Here they come, the ghosts from his papa's side, settling lightly on his shoulders, they touch his sleeves. Six hours northeast, the icy bossy St. John River, valley of potatoes, nothing *but*. This is one of the fountainheads of Gordon's chemistry, the way it is that you and your people grow out of your geography, from what bodies do with leaf and tuber and wild things, chewing, digesting these shared ingredients, becoming nourished, your tribe. And that tumbles back and forth from town to town and over the ice-choked St. John into those other blue and black winter-spring hills and yellow wallpapered rooms of Canada, it is his genesis. *How does it go? Nice day.*

And he lets his head and shoulders sway and he smiles.

But it is still there. The thumping of bare feet in the sand.

And now, not genesis, but . . . yeah, the past. Déjà vu or synchronicity? A rerun? Replay maybe. Regression. A taste swims through his mouth. He remembers how his jaws had ached at that fair. The sound of the stripper's bare feet thumping on the hollow plywood stage, louder and louder, both Gordon and Rex young, Gordon very young, both at the rail, feasting deeper and deeper into that surprisingly small cunt, like reverse birth. The stripper's thighs were like hands gripping their heads, holding, supporting. The cradle of knowledge. *I will teach you something about yourselves*. He remembers how the music had stopped and then that musicless hollow thumping of the young stripper's feet. Would he only in death be more submissive? And Rex, too, compliant, forced to wait and take his turn with her.

And Rex's only child hadn't been conceived yet, but she, even then, may already have seen the geometrical designs of power.

Rex?

"Rex" York never wanted power. He only fears chaos. It is order that he demands. But Glory? Gordon gets it.

Glory, go home.
Go the fuck home.

How does it go? Comment ça va?

Thumping. The feet thump twice, then stop, thump twice, then stop.

He sees now, three yards away, Glory up on a picnic table, still dancing with her hands over her head, shirt wide open, flying behind her, and now, too, the black pants she was wearing and whatever was worn under them are gone. Her motions are no longer epileptic because for this haunting underwater music, she accommodates, swirling almost on tiptoe. Gordon likes this. He stares. He says to himself, Fine, okay, fine. Fine. Yes, come near me and you will be just fine. How does it go, you? Come close.

Yes.

You got my promise, brother. I don't touch that little girl. Not ever.

But.

Glory dancing in the sand again, churning closer to Gordon, though stopping in front of a seated young man, another one of the Aroostook musicians, who has turned up late, and she spins around, to make her shirt flip and fly, her bare bottom and hips blurring with the rest, and when she stops, facing the guy, he lays a hand on one of her thighs almost apologetically, but then she laughs, throws back her head, and leaps away, spinning again toward Gordon.

Next to Gordon, at his right, Claudie Roy is wide awake now, smoking a Pall Mall fast, fast, fast.

Glory churns closer.

Glory's breasts, Glory's locket, Glory's flying shirt, Glory's sweet almost bony hips whip through the sphere of darkness opposite the bonfire, then back to the light, then dark again, then light, and Gordon braces for what he knows is his, gripping his knees as if to keep down the whole beach, the rising weight of sand and thirty-five or so male individuals being engorged, yes horny, which is fused to his own arousal, old and necessary, not a lot different from one's regard for one's ancestry . . . it is a thing between brothers.

Though it is *not* about sharing.

And he has forgotten the actual Rex, how Rex fits into this. Rex's fatherly concerns lost in some leaden place. Though Rex's eyes come closer now in *her* face, her beautiful flushy face and heavy hair. She arrives. She places one bare foot to each side of him to nearly stand over him, claiming this prize as hers. And so his empty beer bottles go everywhere.

Close up, her eyes aren't so pretty, but smeary with drunkenness, and his eyes, too, are smeary with drunkenness. What do looks matter now? Now it is only about relief from the pressure of arousal. He is sweating in the scratchy BDU shirt, and she, still standing motionless over him, is dripping, glassy. And now, slowly as an opening flower or setting sun, she raises her arms, arches her back, long hair heavy, waves her hands at the black sky, throat to the black sky, knees bent, presenting to him the purply swollen entrance of her vagina. He makes a sound. A neck-sound. Mouth closed in a swallow. He clambers forward on the sand, gripping one of her calves for balance, and works the fingers of his right hand between her legs, meaning to be tender, meaning to do something that he has already forgotten . . . he moves his tongue, blood in his mouth from biting his tongue in the struggle to climb up to her, his brain swims away . . . she is sinking heavily. He is still working his hand, as into a glove that is too tight. She howls or cries something. Everything is clear again, a face, Claudie Roy's face, as Claudie gets to his feet and moves away.

But now, all this clutter, struggle, too drunk to unzip right, too drunk to remember how to get from this business of Glory out to the colder edge of the night and the weeds where he needs to piss. Hunched like a bear, he is pissing here and everybody is laughing and Glory wants him to remember what he started with, Glory is helping him, Glory is strong. She is opening her mouth. Baby words come out against his ear. "My pretty Mr. Militia so hammy handsome all done pee pee. All so perfect in yoo booeyful army shirt. Where is your gun, Mr. Militia?" And he knows what gun she means for she has it in her hand. And he loves her. And gravity pulls them both to the sand, and somehow between her knees and the troubled sand and a crush of stars, he is eventually to find relief and saying, "You are perfect. You do it perfect, baby . . . sweet fuck." And there are feet around him, enough feet to make a centipede, all moving away and maybe there are voices telling him to stop . . . but maybe that was the new music, a tangle of guitars and drums . . . *stop! stop! stop!* But he doesn't stop. It goes on and on and on, this business. Seems like an hour. Dry humping. But she does not complain. Her legs are wrapped around his waist like welcoming arms that have missed him. He will always remember that, and his own deep satiated growl, he will remember that forever . . . well, not forever, just for as long as he lives, right? . . . although he doesn't know that his death of a certain kind is homing in nearer like a clean cold night star brought in close by a telescope. A telescope? Ack! Just another one of those haughty foolish man-made playthings that have never done a thing to make what matters matter more. Because birth, procreation, and death can't be perfected. They have always been perfect.

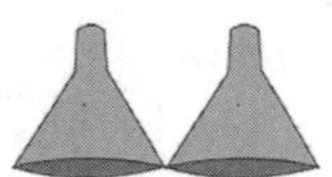

Think tanks and the Apparatus both speak of phantoms, wiles, and gentle mists.

Not even a vibration, nor anything you all can detect with nostrils, palms, or wits. More like heat rising off a car hood, more like the silken path of the farthest star, like closed oak doors, these whispers, unheard by your fully committed trust, we give you things such as "opinion management" with "psyops" to grease our moves.

Everything we do is to see to it that your left eye only stares at your right eye, that the hot little furnace of your heart is constipated with spite and revenge for *the other*.

No matter how politically correct you are, we shall arrange for you an *other*. At our fingertips is power that you have not the depth of a consummate bedlamite to imagine.

What about the screen?

Concerning a discussion of the aforementioned, the screen seems to be blank.

Tin hat conspiracy theorists.

Uh-oh.

BOOK FOUR:

Some Days Are Diamonds♫ ♪Some Days Are Stones[*]

* As sung by John Denver.

York residence.

The truck with the red firefighter's light on the dash, the van with the lightbulb cartoon, and Ruth York's little beige car are in the dooryard under behemoth maples of orange and wine purple whose leaves sift down, spin, caress fenders, layer onto hoods.

A stranger's late-model pickup slows, then eases to a stop behind the van. Such a California-beachboy-Hollywood-looking individual stepping out, even though his plates read: MAINE.

Ruth York welcomes this muscle-bound square-jawed gold-tanned "Andy" into the kitchen, leads him through warm breakfast smells to the livingroom to wait for "Ricky," Ruth's name for Rex, who is "out back."

When Rex appears, Andy already has a brick of snapshots thrust out, which fit perfectly into Rex's hand. A brick. And yet Rex looks at only the top one, barely the second. His eyes become frayed, soft, almost grassy, and daydreamy, a rather magical gift for a man who is facing such a world of reavers.

In the parking lot of Denise's Diner.

Even before the action starts, the eyes of both men are baggy, blistered by too much daylight, stupid about direction. Which is north? Which is south?

So first they tussle, a foolish dance of shoves, til Rex's fist crunches into Gordon's face. Then again. More. More. This makes fissures. The eyes drool blood. Now a baseball-sized rock. A torrent of grunts. Some of Gordon's teeth are falling like half-chewed nuts. The rock grinds one ear into the skull. More fissures break open the secrets of Gordon's head. Blood beats out as if the face, ears, temples were Gordon's jumbo living heart excised. A ring of diner customers are bellowing, "Stop!" and "Hey! Hey!" Gordon has gone down on his knees into the sand and Rex is kicking him. Then more rock. Gordon tender, seedy, runny, pulped. Rex kicks him. Kicks him. Kicks him.

Janet Weymouth at home.

The phone spills into her ear phrases, syllables, in the crickety, brisk voice of her friend Cynthia, news of the beating, the coma, the brain, the eye, the nose, the ears, the teeth, tongue, the ribs, the hand.

She tries Marian's number right away, out of good manners and true grief. Nothing but the "male" robot telling her, *Can't come to the phone right now. Leave a message after the beep*.

She dials the Settlement phone, busy or off the hook, which? Those rude farts of those rural phone exchanges, more animal than high-tech.

The hospital tells her nothing except that he's been admitted. She acknowledges that this must mean he hasn't died.

Late night television news shows three sheriff's deputies leading a man into the Oxford County jail a short cramped distance from an open cruiser door. The three newcasters brightly relate that according to witnesses, Richard York, a self-employed electrician, brutally attacked Guillaume St. Onge with a rock. St. Onge is the leader of the Settlement, a separatist compound, where he allegedly has twenty wives and many children and an arsenal of assault rifles. The news team, in its usual emergency run-on words, adds that the arrested man is the head of "an armed right-wing militia that St. Onge is a member of."

Janet cannot see the attacker's face. She can't imagine it. Nor can she imagine Gordon's new noseless, earless, eyeless face. Life is becoming an escalating series of metamorphoses and malicious realignments and erasures. She chokes. Like a sob but more throaty than nasal. She presses fingers to her lips, though no one is in this room but herself. Now she fidgets with her wedding rings, making them spin on her finger. She has commenced some old lady twiddling these days. The ghost of her old sense of humor stands like a soldier in the corner.

What was Gordon to her? A sturdy quirky child grown into a mountain. In some ways she liked to take credit for his pranks and those theatrics of his kids. For his miracle work, raising a village, embracing the poor, the vile, the untouchables. Oh, his solid, solid self!

But it feels now that he is drawing abomination to himself . . . drawing it into this world from another world. He has at last gone too far. She fears the Jonah.

Inner voice of the Bureau.

Well, okaaaay, this storm is sending our ship awry. Today. But there's still tomorrow. If only York had killed St. Onge, or *if only* St. Onge weren't Jesus Christ or something, all that live-and-let-live-forgive-and-drop-the-charges hogwash. Then York would have been *ours*.

Wouldn't you yourself with gun charges and aggravated assault and attempted murder charges piled to the rocky moon, agree merrily to be a spy? In every state and beyond, we've got webbed-up flies screaming in their tiny buzzy voices for a step backward into freedom. Yes, indeed, ma'am, sir, *you would be a fly-turned-spy*, an operative, to work on any entrapment project we so desire of you.

But nope, York's big buddy hasn't got the divine revenge instinct. The force of the stars in the heavens, in this instance, has swung the wrong way for America.

BOOK FIVE:
*Cui Bono?**

* Who benefits?

The voice of Mammon speaks.

Growth! Growth! Growth! Growth! Growth! Growth! GROWTH! GROWTH! War! War! War! War! War! War! WAR! WAR! When I want what I want I just call it "war." All those Americans out there will just bend over and let me ream 'em all, for the W-word, war of whatever kind.

Keep the fear factor up on high scorching red purple. Keep people's minds full of NOISE and nagging. Shake the jar, get those neighbors to fight, fellow workers to take offense, the teeth-gnashing "isms" need stoking, the countries beyond our borders and shores crawl with menace.

The universe has plenty of room for financial growth, baby. After all, who was it that discovered the universe, not some praying fool noodling around in the Bible or other such holy moly scripts and scrolls. Not some hippie farmer on a green bicycle. Not Gandhi in a diaper. Not some redneck ass in Egypt, Maine, who wants everyone to be his brother or another wife. Now *that* is abnormal. The proletarian rebellion among this gullible citizenry? I fear it not.

Critical thinker in recent time.

Man is rated the highest animal, at least among all animals that returned the questionnaire.

—Robert Brault

BOOK SIX:

Brianne, tu sais, la vie est dure. (Brianna, you know, life is hard.)

NOVEMBER

Here we are in Room 422. No longer in the intensive care unit. He will soon be moved to rehab or home. Depending.

Four strangers enter the room. They find him on his side napping on top of the freshly made hospital bed. Green work pants, a johnny opening at his back, big bare feet. Pillow has fallen to the floor. He is using his arm for a pillow.

The four people nod at the man in the other bed who is drinking from a cup of juice and looking up at the wall-mounted TV as if it were on, but it is off, just a gray-green screen of motionless reflections.

Gordon's bed is past this man's bed. The plate-glass window beyond Gordon's night table is steamed over. And beyond the window, the day is filled with a hard windy rain.

For a moment, the four people just stand, studying the sleeping Gordon, making faces at each other. Then they arrange themselves, one in the deep vinyl chair, another against the heater by the window, another squats on his haunches. Another admires all of Gordon's cards, flowers, and cute plants. There are also a few stacks of letters, a lot unopened, leaning against the plants and flower vases.

When he stirs and opens one eye, Gordon doesn't seem to recognize these people. He looks at them intently. This one good eye has no white, but a vivid red fireball and an uncooperative lid that hangs swollenly and lazily below the four scarlet lightning bolt scars and the shaved eyebrow. His other eye is still bandaged mummyesquely. He looks hardest at the person standing nearest to him, a guy who is in his twenties, okay, maybe twenty-nine, a very brown guy (much browner than Secret Agent Jane), striped white dress shirt, vest sweater, jeans, no whiskers, just a look of inquisitiveness in his tired *slightly* reddened black, black eyes. His short hair is rain-wetted.

Gordon's eye moves to the other faces. He does not find any one of these to be familiar.

He sits up, swings his legs down, facing the visitors and the window, rubs the back of his neck with his unbandaged hand, wiggles his toes. The hair on his head and face is starting to grow back dark as ever, but scarred areas have a shine as rivers through a forest do when seen from a high-altitude jet.

The small blond white woman, angular and boyish in mannerisms, with steel-rimmed glasses on her straight unbreakable-looking nose, gives the windowsill of flowers and plants a sharp look, then she turns to Gordon, her eyes twinkling. "We almost brought you a nice plant."

"Sorry about your trouble, Gordon," says a dark-eyed, very bald on top, intense-looking, wet white guy whose watch starts to buzz and he cuffs at it as if to tame it. It stops buzzing.

"We were worried about you," says the woman. Her short curly dark yellow hair is damp, her khaki jacket heavily rain spotted.

Who in hell *are* these people? *They* know *him* but *he* knows *them* not. His heart clobbers around in his big bruised chest.

There's a guy with a short beard. Long neck. Hands deep in the pockets of his "Eskimo" jacket that was the fashion thirty years ago. A jacket too heavy for just a rainy late fall day, one would think, even though he wears it with the fur-trimmed hood down.

Gordon shows his torrent of confusion, staring now at one knee of his work pants. He raises his face now, says brightly, "I'm going there . . . heart." He blinks. "*Home*. Tomorrow. Once you are conscious, they throw you there . . . throw out."

"For some, they don't even wait for consciousness," says the black guy. He steps forward and puts out his hand for Gordon's good hand. "Blake Richardson. Great to meet you. Frank couldn't make it."

Gordon murmurs, "Good we meet." The roommate is only in his sixties or thereabouts, but frail and, like Gordon, has had most of his head shaved. He is still transfixed by the blank TV.

Blake settles into a molded plastic chair next to Gordon's crank-up eating table, which has on it, along with Gordon's new pair of plastic reading glasses, a newspaper opened to the editorials page, chock-full of all the latest ever-continuing debate on whether or not the True Maine Militia is "the product of neglect" or is displaying "refreshing activism." "In the tradition of guerrilla theater!" one letter writer exclaims. "Like a bunch of Bolsheviks" gripes another, "especially with armed men behind it all," and lots of revelations about the morals of "these people" considering "the murder attempt on St. Onge."

The curly-haired woman says, "Olan and I were at your big party there a couple of weeks ago but couldn't get near you to bring greetings."

Gordon smiles, his broken and missing teeth making a very dark hole on one side of his mouth.

The visitors each have taken in the details of Gordon's stitched-up, colorific face: purple and yellow. His nose not the same shape as before. One ear is just a small lumpy purple knob. Doctors have said that much of Gordon's scar areas can be fixed with plastic surgery. Some of those teeth that are missing can be replaced with implants. And bridges. But he has shown no interest in all these repairs. Or maybe everyone, especially every doctor, talks too fast, while Gordon's brain is now oh-so-slow.

"It was wild," Olan explains. "We came late and you were up onstage giving the TV channels everything they wanted."

Gordon hesitates, then: "Yeah, it was . . . out of step . . . out . . . not control . . . the family tells me. Out of the thing there . . ." He trails off.

The visitors glance at each other, and the dark-eyed bald white guy says, "And remember, not only can we give your parties more form, we can help you take them out of Maine, spread out a little, spread the word."

"Yes, yes," says Gordon softly, looks down at his hands. He squints his one eye. "Who are you guys?"

They introduce or, rather, reintroduce themselves. All but Blake had spent that great evening with Gordon in the Settlement's West

Parlor. Organizers. Leftists. Including "Frank." The ones Bree was so hot to bring around. Bree. Bree. Bree.

Gordon sighs. "I'm . . . wa . . . s . . . sorry. We'll have to . . . do it over." He laughs. And so they laugh.

He grins. So many missing teeth. "And I don't remember the . . . big crowd . . . thing . . . the event. They *say* I was there."

Next day.

He is sitting on his bed waiting, his nice new work boots on his feet, his dark green work shirt buttoned to the throat, green like the pants. And hooked to one belt loop, the huge chunk of keys, keys to a dozen trucks, machines, padlocks, and door locks; keys to innumerable jobs and responsibilities. All of them weighted with forgotten names. Like lists of insects in Latin. And all these keys have been carefully cleaned by someone, blood gone.

He and a brand-new older man talk. This guy is a lot more chatty than the last guy, while Gordon speaks with lulls, rills, hollows. This new guy and Gordon recall the shortest river in Maine, the Chute River . . . pronounced with a hard "ch" like "church," then the man tells all he knows of the Songo Locks, then on to dams. "Used to be the Oriental Powder Mill in Windham . . . on the Presumpscot. I heard they used to supply both the North and the South in the Civil War. It's near where that inn used to stand on Gag Corner. Know that area?"

Gordon says, "No. The main drag. Goes into . . . all that. Route . . . 25."

"This is off 237," the man says.

Gordon is expecting either Butch Martin or Aurel to come fetch him.

His own plan was for one of them at the Settlement to bring and leave his truck so he could drive back one-handed and one-eyed. But that intent got blown to smithereens by his antiseizure drugs and swollen brain. His "forgettery."

Now he hears Bree's voice in the corridor, a "Hi!" to a nurse, her voice low and smoky. Settlement people and the nurses and aides and housekeeping people of two floors here have all gotten pretty chummy.

He sees her now. Newly sixteen. But still not a legal driver. His cherished outlaw in her old wool work jacket and a long forest green skirt. Work boots. High-topped, laced tightly. A necklace of painted acorns, most likely child-made. The way she looks makes his shoulder muscles thicken.

He gets off the bed. She leans into him and his long arms go around her stoutly. Then she hands him his billed cap, the one with *Bean's Logging and Pulp* printed on front and a little image of a yellow skidder. "To keep your sort-of crew cut warm," she tells him. Before fitting the cap on, he rubs his velvety new hair. To remember it. Cap on makes him look even taller than he is and he seems very tall in this small packed hospital room.

With a thumb Bree presses his eyebrow too near those lightning bolt scars over his unbandaged eye.

In a bloom of queer blurs and fogs he feels retroactive botheration concerning Bree. Something or some things she has done to him before his memory was blitzed. But if he can't remember it, is he newborn under her touch?

Now he left-handedly shakes the hand of the man in the bed and him good luck. The man laughs, wishes him good luck, too.

The wheelchair is waiting at the door beside a nurse*like* person. Hard to tell these days with no white caps. She has a name tag on her blouse and abbreviations but everyone moves too fast even as everyone is slow, explaining he needs to be in the chair all the way to the vehicle parked by the door. Bree hefts five satchel bags of the stuff he's bringing home. There is one for his lap.

The elevator doors close and the three of them are whooshing down, down, and Gordon sees Bree's callused sometimes painty hands gripping the bag handles. He reaches, grabs a thickness of her forest green skirt, and bowing his head whispers slowly, trying to get it right, "Brianne, tu sais, la vie est dure. Moié p'is toié, on est souvent durs, I'un avec l'autre. Mais j'garde mon coeur ouvert moi'e, et p'is toié, tu peux entrer dans mon coeur comme un p'tit papillon doré, pour boire mon âme, ma vie."* This said with many pauses and more stammers than words. And maybe he didn't quite

* Maine-Acadian patios.

say those words, just thought he did. He ends with a hard swallow. He looks down at his boots.

"Know what I said just then?"

Bree is very quiet. Nurselike person very very *very* quiet. Elevator dings. Bree explodes in a symphony of giggles.

English translation of Gordon's words to Bree (at least as he *thinks* he said them).

Brianna, you know, life is hard. You and me, we're often hard, one with the other. But I keep my heart open, me, and you, you can enter my heart like a little golden butterfly, to drink my soul, my life.

Lee Lynn tells us of those first days after Gordon came home.

At times he was too still, a wax museum specimen. Throughout the long days, all eyes were on him sitting square in one of the big rockers in the warmest part of the Cook's Kitchen. His cousins from Aroostook returned, making that six-hour drive to help "celebrate" that he was alive. Fiddle, guitar, concertina. Sweet and indoorsy old waltzes and cloggy stuff.

I made him little cups of healing teas. He looked into my eyes as if to remember my name but looked at the tea as if I had given him the world.

I can't bear it. Such ruin. My beautiful husband so torn and bruised. One eye still having to stay covered from the light. The other that you'd look into when you spoke to him had a lid quite fat and houndy and hanging, lots and lots of tiny stitch marks like cartoon train tracks. His ears looked the most painful. One cheek had been ripped completely from his mouth to his eye. His nose was not *his* nose. All this in my heart, no relief, crushed memorial to the madness of men.

The kids didn't get it. Sure, they stared. Sure, the questions came and came and came. Some brushed his head of new spiky hairs and little Anza said, "This is very nice." Like cats the smallest kids took turns in his lap or hugged his ankles with sleepy smiles. But Michel and Kedron stood before him with pine swords hanging from their belts. They said, "Wanna fight?" giving him menacing sneers and lunging at him, "Arrr!!" as if to startle him from his stillness. They were impressed by his new warrior countenance, the rips and tears. Out of their little boy bodies, their own blood understood glory and nothing more.

No, they didn't get it, that Gordon won no war.

He'd haltingly ask questions of some of the old ones among whom he sat, that huddle of ninety-year-olds, some with, some without full sense. He asked about the old tools, the old ways, and their replies gave him an expression most penetrating. Nothing else seemed to get him that alert. And he'd give his chair a lunge now and then, remembering it was a rocker, remembering that for the time being, maybe longer, he, too, was just a whisper of the past.

**Meanwhile, in another place,
Bruce Hummer dreams.**

Through this strange blue of hallway, a terrible thing. Or is it the right thing? *Wrong! Right! Wrong! Right! Left! Right!* Boots marching. A marching army of hundreds of uncommon men, not common men, these the gifted, the finely tuned executive stuff, as he himself is in some distant drone of retrogression. He sees their identical suit jackets, dark gray of a costly combed fiber, tailored to fit. Shirts blue. Ties all black. Maybe. His dream eye feels more than it sees.

Maybe he can't see the boots, either. But the sound of them is black, all in step. GROWTH! GROWTH! GROWTH! GROWTH! they thunder. But also they sound like rain. GROWTH! GROWTH! GROWTH! GROWTH! they patter from lipless skull faces. Upper left sleeve of each suit jacket has an embroidered patch in contentious yellow-gold and blue, black and white, MORTMAIN MILITIA. The dead hand.

He writhes. No, he *tries* to writhe. And he tries to feel their intentions, to read them, but they emanate nothing. Though clearly these are the countless powerful enemies he has made. Or *friends*, because that's what you always call them, right? That network of handshakes and luncheons where daggers are sheathed and snarls resemble smiles.

Seems these militiamen have no guns. Guns would be better. As the leader had kicked open the door to his office, it was plain to see that worse than guns is just the redness of their live tongues in those white skull faces, the plump liquid look of their unwavering live eyes set in the skulls' stone dead eyeholes.

He alas rises up from his immense desk. In his neck he cries because his mouth is hardened.

Along with the chanting of the deep voices are drums. *Boom! March, march boom! March, march boom!*

But now it all stops. Now just whispers of costly sleeves and chests breathing, altogether resembling furnace fans.

The leader just stares. The weird lubricous eyes most frightening. Human eyes. What is more ruthless than human eyes? Seems the eyes speak. Do they spell out: *Growth is dead?* To some a fear worse than personal death? On and on the skull face stares, teeth slanting in gluey foundations, though this, too, is blurred and more of a feeling.

Now the leader steps toward him and raises the skeleton hand, the dead hand. The fingers open with ease. The attacker peels Bruce's face off.

He wakes. There *is* a hard rain trouncing his window. There *is* the furnace running, the fan whining. He feels his face. He flips over onto his side to squint at the red digitals of the bedside clock.

Follow-up appointment with surgeon. Again Bree drives, that halo of risk around her fiery hair.

He had settled himself into the truck. His truck. Not a Settlement vehicle. His will was strong on the matter. But now as they ride along, he sleeps, his shorn-short and scarred head against the glass, hands loose in his lap. His new darkening beard is still short enough to look brisk and steely. His cane, which they say he may need forever, stretches horizontally across the red plastic gun racks.

Bree keeps looking over at him, his great size and yet his vulnerability so apparent. His face lumpy with scarring. And what of the brain? The brain a mystery. Like the unseeable illimitable blackness of outer space.

Once she marveled regularly at the miracle of this man's strange pride at standing beside her that rainy noontime to say the "vows," he so striking, she the freak. Now side by side behind this windshield with the dried-up ash leaves under the wipers, two visages equally ill-favored.

Nearing the city, she is startled when he speaks for he makes no waking-up sounds before she hears him. And his one useful eye, pale-green dragonlike, is staring at her intently. He is saying, "Remember things. Re-*mem*-bering things. I've been coming . . . back . . . to it."

Bree swallows sadness. She says motherishly, "You see. You'll be as good as new. Soon."

He grins his new gap-toothed grin to tease her. "I'll be good." He growls. "Not new." He laughs.

Now with his left hand he fusses through pockets. The bad hand is no longer fully bandaged but has two stiffly taped fingers. Something materializes in the palm of the untaped hand. A ring. An impossible ring. Too thickly studded with stuff, pearls mostly. There are fine blue-green-pink leaves, like the color of case hardened receivers of some rifles. There are flecks of what must be garnets. And flecks of pink you can see if you narrow your eyes like suspicion.

"I . . . forgot . . . how I got this but it was pretty time . . . time . . . uhhh . . . late . . . *recently*." He studies the old ring now in the cup of his hand, the broken fingers not useful for gripping. He frowns.

Bree takes her eyes off the road for glimpses of his anguished facial gymnastics with memory and vocalization.

The truck nudges along through a congested business area, the cab creaking and whiffing in its frame and mounts, as the tires rise over manhole covers or patching tar. Gordon is very, very quiet. Then, "You want this ring?"

"I have one." She wiggles her wedding ring hand at him, the humble little hiccup of silver right there where he put it.

"I *want* you to have *this* . . . one." He leans toward her, pushes his mouth into her blaze of hair. Like a baby sucking, she thinks.

She giggles while keeping her eyes on the brake lights of the car ahead. In her peripheral vision there's a tombstone-shaped sign with lists of businesses whose entrances are set back beyond a continent of tar and parked cars. The littering of humanity is such well-meant ruination.

He says deeply and hoarsely, his voice never again to be the *rich* deep voice of before, but a bray? "Brianna, pull this . . . truck . . . over. . .

high . . . ahead here by that car water . . . car water . . . car *wash* . . . so I can . . . get . . . push . . . this ring on your finger . . . and give you a . . . kiss."

She is sickened at herself that she is now sickened by him. His new elderliness! The prominently missing eyetooth in his grin. The floppy eyelid. The Prophet is gone!!! The Prophet that *she* created. Her will versus his will. The lion king had bowed down for her. She coaxed out of him his greatness! And then he had straddled her. And then . . . back then . . . it was all splendor!

She flicks the directional and cuts into the car wash lot, stops, keeps the truck running while he fumbles his grandmother's ring onto the only finger it fits, her right-hand pinkie.

He kisses her mouth.

Midafternoon. No sun. These November hills are muffin brown but not muffin warm. The utterness of outdoors glints in its hard frost and assorted little crusty rugs of shade snow. In their sleep, trees wag and wave and whine. See the swing and sway of frozen laundry on the lines of the many cottages, while downhill the "Anyone Trespasses Will Be Shot" gate is opened for a car full of out-of-state visitors.

Gordon is ready for the planned arrival of the organizers, waiting in the Cook's Kitchen in his big rocker with its carved bear heads. He is dressed in a work shirt buttoned to the throat and natty dark sweater vest. His beard thickens more every day, the wisdomy gray on the chin sadly deceiving for, as you can see, his head is hanging in sleep and there is drool.

There has been a cot set up for him on the other side of the stoves so that he can "be spoiled 24/7." His cane is always handy. But dearly he loves that chair by the hot cookstoves near the half dozen other rockers where usually sit or slouch several old, old men and women. Presently there are two, one being Benedicta Nichols looking ready for fun. Her fluorescent lime sneaker lacings seem to vibrate. Her huge bulging pocketbook between her feet looks as mysterious as ever.

The kitchen is too hot. Two youngsters of one of the firewood crews are dumping armloads of roundwood and biscuit wood into the boxes, the boxes never, never empty.

The last of the cleanup crew has hustled away while soon the supper-making crew will coalesce around Bonnie Loo who, like the tree-tall goddess of steam and grease and hot bubblings, straddles this territory from dawn to dusk.*

The two sets of French doors (rarely open), on either side of the solid door between the porches and this room, allow in only a slow gray woolly light in which lie two of Willie Lancaster's free-roaming ever-roaming homely white squashed-faced curly-tailed short-haired swamp-smelling dogs with their chins on their paws and eyes on Bonnie Loo, whose rule is no chickens allowed and only dogs who resemble a bowl of fruit . . . actually she said "still life."

When the organizers chatteringly step in from the cold porches, Gordon raises his head, opening his eyes. Today, the first time since surgery on that close-to-being-blinded right eye, the bandage is off. Used to look like a hot coal, that eye, whenever it was unveiled. Now just its normal wild-man weirdness.

Claire is standing nearby. Her job, when she's not at the university these days, is to never leave his side when he is having "an audience."

Bonnie Loo, lining up quart jars of canned shell beans with bacon, believes the big kitchen has suddenly taken in a high tide of foreign air, the smell of the awfulness of oily cement and garbage-scented brick . . . the city.

But due to her pregnancy, all smells are revolting and many-dimensional with threat.

Willie's dogs seem to share Bonnie Loo's opinion because their noses almost suck the socks off the new arrivals until Rusty Soucier of the firewood crew ushers the two outlaw curs out.

Benedicta lowers her chin and smiles her deceptively sweet smile. She glances at old Reggie Lessard in the chair to her left to be sure one of her gang is here to witness whatever happens next.

---

* This is poetic license. Like everyone at the Settlement she has oodles of free time and rest. ☺

No doubt these visitors, when they showed up to see Gordon at the hospital, were disappointed by his scudding cloudlets of speech. Now each one takes in the details of his face, more key lime now than Concord grape.

Last week Marian Depaolo St. Onge had (first time ever) visited this kitchen with reminders that she will pay for her son to have implants for the raw empty side of his mouth . . . her gift, she had insisted. She knows the significant stocks she transferred to him almost twenty years ago are nearly all sold off, with his oft-repeated declaration, "A dollar doesn't work! People do! Capitalism does well because most people make piss-poor money for their labors. For us to own stocks is to own slaves!!"*

But this time when she visited him Gordon stuttered out only the cloudlets of speech, so she didn't have to hear any of those tirades that always used to wreck her day. But, oh, she remains upset! A tirade in his lost voice, his velvety deep big-guy voice, would be, alas, to her ears, a symphony. And anyway, he seemed almost offended by the idea of having the dental work done, let alone the necessary plastic surgery to smooth out all that scarring. And what about his new prizefighter nose?

Now he smiles his partially empty smile at his leftist visitors. Surely *they* would appreciate his wisecrack about owning stock. But he only nods once at each face. And he jerks a hand of stiff taped fingers toward Claire. "My official . . . my officially assigned bodyguard."

Claire shakes each of the outstretched hands. She is dressed all in browns, knits and weaves, her stance one of certainty, her hair a braided crown. Her smile seems so indifferent but, as we know, Claire is no grinner, no salesman, no *ha-ha*. It's nothing personal.

Organizer Jip with the dirty-blond lamb curls and beige dress shirt, which, combined, give her the complexion of someone who has been on a lo*nnn*g sentence of bread and water, tells Gordon, "Frank sends his regards. He is attending a working-class studies conference in Ohio . . . Youngstown . . . home of the famous Jeannette blast furnace."

* Or, nowadays, robots and intelligent computers, which is yet another awful kettle of worms.

Gordon has forgotten Frank. But he nods and raises his left hand with a little heigh-ho wave as if he could see Frank in Ohio.

Lorraine Martin bustles through to the pantry hall, her usual half dozen clothespinned-on notes flapping from the button placket and pockets of her mint green jersey. She gives Claire a significant look timed so none of the guests catch it. Some Settlementers feel Gordon's bulging river of almost daily visitors is a hindrance to his healing.

However, a skinny chirpy old woman and a teenage boy named Ricardo (Eric really), who bows like a waiter, insist everyone sit for fish chowder and robust slices of buttered oatmeal bread almost too hot to handle.

Claire has claimed the orange-painted pine rocker with seat pillow of roses, there at Gordon's left. She glances toward the tall small-paned windows on the outside wall, with trees rocking, trees striving, tasseled frost-burned grasses bouncing, one pithy burst of sun, one crow eye on her, or *seems* to be on her, her philosophical crow friend riding the swaying dead top of a pine near the compost bins.

Now there is coffee in the air.

The visitors waste no time suggesting Gordon go with them on the road, Gordon and the True Maine Militia. Lots of red-letter days on their organization's scheduling calendar.

Claire nudges her spectacles.

Organizer Billy, who still hasn't pulled off his Eskimo jacket, regardless of the woodstove swelter, says eagerly, "As we said at the hospital, Gordon, the True Maine Militia statehouse rally was a masterstroke! The children speak! And then in the papers folks get to see all these cute kids, the children of Maine, being tossed out of the people's house, exiled from experiencing the democratic process by a gorilla cop."

"Security," Claire corrects him with one rogue eye-twinkle.

"Whatever," Billy sort of giggles. Billy's light-color beard is very short, like Gordon's dark one but short by choice, not scraped away from its jellied face by a hospital barber then spottily returning as do roadside weeds. "Law enforcement is to protect the ruling class of people," he adds.

Claire nods gravely.

Beth, her boingy blond ringlets tied up with a piece of faded bandanna in Bonnie Loo's style, comes from the porches lugging a couple of covered baskets. She seems furious about something, pink of cheeks from cold and hopping heart. "Jeezuhss!" She kicks the door shut behind her. "Life is nothing you'd sign up for if you were asked first." She says this in a general way, her eyes sweeping the room.

The lean teen boy Ricardo over by the big sinks snickers. "And what pray tell do you have there? Can I wager that it has value?"

"One is the head of the king and one is the head of the queen," replies Beth.

The short, broad-chested, balding organizer, Olan, almost sprays both knees with chowder from his mouth, his laugh having sneaked up on him. One would wonder if this performance was prerehearsed, *pray tell*, and all that.

Gordon's eyelids are starting to droop.

Beth crosses the big kitchen and around to the worktables beyond, still muttering, and Ricardo springs ballet-style out of her way.

Claire's imposing dark-eyed glower turns on Billy. "About our kids at the statehouse, they were seen as delinquents by most."

Organizer Jip, a fortyish gal with a law degree, labor history degree, and other stuff, nods sagely, then says, "As every *adult* practicing real democracy is also seen."

Claire's bespectacled eyes are squared right between Jip's bespectacled eyes. "There has been a lot of discussion about whether—"

"Yessssss!" Jip nods fast. "Puts it out there for the public in a way that other working-class small-town people can identify with. An indisputably brilliant move. The True Maine Militia."

Claire says evenly, "What I was saying was there has been a lot of discussion about whether the DHS should take our children away. Talk radio. Op-eds. And Gordon's friend who heads the DHS has let some cats out of the bag when we called. It's getting a lot of push. Ever since the kids did their thing, more so since Gordon was . . . injured. And of course his inflammatory speech on three TV networks and so forth."

Gordon's eyes open again, his knees working his chair into two contented rocks. "Nothing . . . under . . . nothing about . . . *to do* with me," he says. "The statehouse . . . them only."

Blake, late twenties, is quiet through all this, eating quietly, smiling a closed mouth lukewarm smile. Even his chair has no creaks because he doesn't rock it. He is after all the youngest in his group. Feeling deferential? Maybe. Or is it intense strategizing?

Billy, fortysomething, looks like an explorer with all that fur of his hood around his face, the beard, the bracing of his narrow shoulders. He says, "Gordon, everything you touch bubbles up and revolts. You raised those kids. They are the future as it ought to be . . . curiosity, creativity, group confidence, big questions, a hard-to-ignore bunch." He sneezes onto the sleeve of his jacket.

Gordon has no chowder or bread, just empty hands, one on each chair arm. "I . . . did not up . . . I did not *raise* Bree."

"Who we still have not met with face-to-face," smiles Jip. "Where is she today? Our teenage Wonder Woman."

"Brianna Bunyan," says Beth, coming to stand behind Gordon's rocker, one hand on each carved bear head. "She works in the woods with her family." Beth now gives Gordon's chair a playful jarring, leans over his shoulder, her upside-down face close to his. "Peekaboo!"

One of his eyes flinches in the old way.

Jip remarks, "We are so fond of Bree . . . her sagacity, her imaginative—"

Benedicta interrupts, saying to Jip in particular, "You ate a lot. Don't you have decent food in your state?"

The intensity of Olan's dark eyes turns toward his own chowder mug. "Everyone in Cambridge is skin and bones," says he.

Benedicta raises her chin proudly. "A shame."

Gordon's mouth has been shuddering on unsaid words, muddled thoughts of Bree, damming up his brain more thickly than a billion beavers. *Trying* to remember something. A Bree treachery, deeper than the rest. And something else. *These people*. Something about . . . uh . . .

Olan leans forward, elbows on chair arms, his spoon sliding around in his empty chowder mug. "These kids are up and at 'em. For the people here in Maine, the first shot has been fired. With squirt guns." He snickers. "The revolution is heating up!"

Gordon's eyes have been moving from one face to another sluggishly. "I . . . remember . . . you guys."

Nobody makes a reply to this.

"It's coming back," says Gordon.

Benedicta is admiring her fingernails, which are not long or painted but she wiggles them as such.

Gordon's eyes, the slightly pinkish newly unveiled one and the clear one, both get a wry luster. "Maybe, I got you . . . mixed with . . . mixed *up* with somebody else." He looks directly at Olan. "I thought . . . you guys . . . only wanted . . . only . . . seminars."

Blake stands up from his very-quiet-in-sound but loud-in-color popsicle-green rocker next to Gordon's, carries his mug and empty bread plate to the row of sinks, whispers something to Bonnie Loo and she whispers back, pointing out a glassed cabinet of pottery bowls as big as tires, which he admires.

Billy, still in his Eskimo jacket, is beginning to sound badly stuffed-up. "Well, organizing a movement has to start where the people *are* and go from there. And where your youngsters are is guerrilla theatrics. Of course the war and guns are symbolic. That's evident. Believe you me we've hashed this out with Frank and the others. The squirt guns *should* be eliminated. And the word *militia* is unfortunate, *I* believe. The costumes and youthful zeal, however, are grabbing the media. *Corporate slut* would have to go but we can come up with something . . ." He chuckles. "Something more circumspect. We'll hash this all out before we hit the road."

A small group of preteens, tots on their shoulders, and two young mothers with toddlers on hips, clamor through the Cook's Kitchen from the porches to the pantry hall heading for the door of the screened-in summer-canning kitchen, a shortcut to outdoor chores. A few nods. A few whispers. Some of the overwhelming cookstove heat rushes out both doors.

Young Blake has pulled a snow-white handkerchief from his dressy sweater vest pocket, cleans his fingers of the buttery lunch, shirtsleeves rolled up. Casual? Or ready to take on the good fight? His arms are dark, dark brown, knottily muscled. Slender wrists. His sweater and Gordon's both navy blue, both cable stitched.

Gordon covers his bad eye with a palm. Claire watches him. She's heard him call his new souped-up headaches "railroad spikes."

Blake has stopped just inside one of the archways in the wall of cubbies and studies the Winter Kitchen beyond, the long tables wiped clean. Mismatched chairs. A lot of highchairs for tykes. A small raised stage next to a piano. Papier-mâché fish spinning as slowly as the world turns, or seems to. All these floors of small hand-painted tiles, heated by pipes below, the clutter, the order, the mingled resonance of indoors and outdoors.

Beth is back to work filling deep drawers with fresh folded dish towels from the big baskets.

Jip's voice is speaking almost by rote, "The question is, *Which comes first, organizing or education?* Those of us working on this project have come to an agreement that both at once is quite effective. Solidarity is *not* just a roundtable *idea* . . . it is the fight. Shoulder to shoulder."

Claire nudges the nosepiece of her specs.

Benedicta is watching Blake as he has returned to this room to stand at the exterior wall of windows beyond which the mostly naked trees dance. And he sees the crow.

Benedicta now crosses her legs ladylike, her new dungarees a deep blue. Her turtleneck top is a print of little pandas. How huggable she looks. She still watches Blake when he has come back to his chair next to Gordon's. He takes Gordon's broad wrist into his long dark fingers. Squeezes. Benedicta says brightly, "This is very interesting."

Blake speaks to Gordon's colorific profile, "Man, this place, these rooms with their own natural laws, I can see where you'd feel it's worth defending."

Billy snorts, "What the fuck are you talking about?"

Olan says huskily, "Sounds martial."

Blake says, "I'm musing. I'm trying to, as you say, start where the people are." Huge smile, teeth brilliant, none crooked, gums and tongue the pink of a young person who uses care on himself and those around him.

"Fine," says Jip. "Musing is good, but what Gordon is referring to is when we visited here in September with Frank we discussed objections to the very *real* paramilitary feature of the patriot movement."

Billy almost hisses, "Guns, violence, crazy, racist, right-wing fringe wackos. Real-war guns. Not hunting rifles. Not squirt guns. Not guerilla theater. And we know that Gordon's publicized ties with the patriot movement could be detrimental to our project. We need to get clear of that tie."

Gordon's voice seems disembodied. "Tie is broken."

Billy insists, "But reputations stick like glue. Frankly, I've been cautious about this whole project."

Claire is thinking how Gordon has had, since the beating, visitors from upstate Maine militias, Vermont militias, Connecticut militias, Kentucky militias, militias from Texas, Virginia, and the Carolinas, dozens of men come to sit in these same chairs, have lunch, talk to that one unbandaged green eye . . . all men of the patriot movement, Gordon now a perfect symbol of suffering, and of their fears. They say the government must have been behind what happened to him. The fact that he makes few replies gives him great power. Like the way the sky never answers when you pray to it. Claire says nothing about this to these guests. And Gordon does not mention it. Fine.

Billy says, "So it seems you had a hard lesson, Gordon, about the nature of the beast."

"B . . . beast?" Gordon tips his head like a dog making sense of a squeak or squeal.

"That individual who attacked you . . . racist, sexist, angry, white . . . right?" Now Billy's nose seems VERY stuffy.

Blake clears his throat. "I've communicated with many who have, like myself, come to the conclusion *finally* that it has been a mistake to declare anyone of the working class our enemy. To *focus* on the isms of conservative working-class people is polarizing . . . a detour and a distraction. *Polarizing*. It's *polarizing*, man. A hand grenade into the wrong bunker. That's not the bunch *I'm* declaring war on. I declare war on the tyrants and their systems. *Those* beasts love it when all of us in the sandbox clobber each other with our little shovels."

Billy snickers cynically. "Well, some groups are quite dangerous. Fascism is taking root."

Jip says, her voice like pink lotion, "*But* we are *here*. This is where we are. With Gordon and his people because they could be a better inspiration to *some* conservatives. The word *militia* might actually be a positive thing, kind of wavering between theatrics and rural Mainers' identity. *We* have *not* been grabbing the ears of the rural New England working class. We've been over this, Billy. We are not holding their attention. We are not pulling them in." She snorts boyishly. "And the political correctness when it is in attack mode has been ruinous. Justice is one thing, but . . . yeah, the nagging, the zooming in on a wrong word. So . . . then . . . nobody shows up. I'm *with* you, Billy . . . but this work isn't so precise as weeding around the marigolds. But think a minute. There is *justified* hate."

"Like we don't love the wild and free-market savaging of democracy," says Olan mildly.

Jip gives a thumbs-up. "Right. And there is *identity*, normal as hair on the head. All these identities hating each other. Our job is to give a breadcrumbs trail to the place where hate *belongs*. And to pull together in solidarity around *that beautiful hate*."

"We'll be beheading people before you know it," Billy sighs.

Jip laughs. "There do seem to be repeated patterns in history, in human nature. But we can't stop being hopeful."

Young Blake's rich low voice declares, "We can't *control* the whole thing. We can kick-start. We can inspire. But you can't herd thousands of people. Only indoctrinated people are herdable. And we aren't in *that* business."

Gordon says, "Thomas Merton . . . you know of him?"

Nods.

"Forgive me if . . . I fuck this . . . up. *Do not . . . depend on . . . the hope or results. When* . . . uh . . . *you are doing the sort of work you have take* . . . uh . . . *taken on, you may have to face* . . . uh . . . *the fact that your work will be apparently worthless and* . . ." While his new broken-nosed voice had tumbled on, Claire had stared at him; now her eyes are shining when he gets stuck a long moment, then, "*and even achieve no worth at all, if not, perhaps, results opposite to what you respect* . . . uh *expect. As you get used to this idea you will start more and more to* . . . *con* . . . *concentrate not on the results, but on the* . . . *value, the rightness, the truth of the work itself.*"

Claire is *really* staring at Gordon now. Then she says to the group. "He was in the Bangor Theological Seminary for a year. He has his heroes."

"Merton?" says Olan, disbelieving. "In Bangor?"

"No. Gordon was," says Claire. "One year."

"Pretty liberal," Jip remarks. "A connection there to the liberation theology folks in Central and South Americas."

Gordon says, "I had . . . friends . . . there in Bangor. I up . . . I *go* where my friends are." He winks both eyes happily.

Claire now studies one of her knees, seeing those days of their youth all gone as if washed down a sewer grate.

Billy sneezes into a tissue from his jacket pocket.

And then.

Olan jumps in, "By the way, no need to say the obvious but if we Americans were to rebel with arms as the Zapatistas have, it would bring horrors unspeakable here."

Blake speaks in a marveling way, "While carrying on and on nonviolently, we know there's yet a slow rising tide of horrors unspeakable. Horrors if we do. Horrors if we don't."

Jip sits up straighter in her rocker, speaks to Blake in a mournful murmur. "I hear you, friend."

"He's a provocateur," Olan jokes.

Blake snorts. "I find it unsurprising that the country we fear most is ours."

Silence.

He adds, "Sometimes even just to talk too freely can get you the dungeon, if an entrapment cop is in your midst with a recorder."

There are groans and tsks from his Massachusetts buddies.

Then he further adds, "There is pain here in the United States, body pain and grief to millions, moral pain to the rest." He grimaces. "I have a quote, too. This is by Robert Wedderburn, a born-into-slavery abolitionist. He said, 'It is degrading to human nature to petition your oppressors.'"

Jip frowns. "Fortunately we are not here to petition the oppressors. We're doing the work of teaching the hidden history."

Benedicta sniffs loudly. "When I was in school we had to do a lot of history."

Jip smiles at Benedicta's proud profile.

Billy glances wistfully around the room. "Not to harp, but to show how serious I am . . . this has to be understood. I am committed to nonviolence. Period. If starting where the people are means . . . if your concept of solidarity means holding hands with a bunch of trigger-happy extreme right-wing loonies, then I'm out of this project." He pushes himself out of his rocker. Then as he turns his head again, his eyes widen on an enormous-in-height-and-shoulders long-haired Indian-looking kid in a camo BDU jacket standing behind Gordon's chair. Is he seventeen? Eighteen? Twenty? How did he materialize without even a rustle? So light of step, even in his heavy work boots and brawny six-foot-three self. And how long has he been there behind the crescent of occupied chairs all facing the stoves?

All the organizers shift in their chairs to better behold him.

One of the boy's hands opens on Gordon's shoulder and gives it a soothing rub.

To this person Gordon murmurs, "You didn't go."

"Nope. We had two more moose just come in, plus the Wainwrights have five bucks and we're still on Andy Larravee's doe. Brandy Land hit a deer and they're coming up in an hour. Aurel got down on his knees . . . heh-heh . . . and begged me to stay. Heh-heh. I felt wanted. Heh-heh."

He draws back his hand to fondle one of the chair's carved bear heads. Then squeezes between chairs to squat in front of Gordon, looking up at the riddled face and then away. "I'm here to go frig some more with the sign-up sheets for Saturday an' figure out how to be in three places at the same time . . . heh-heh." He looks at his watch, similar to Rex's but not black. It's spotted in camo greens, tans, and brown like his jacket. "Bree signed up for Aurel's crew for Saturday. She's skinning. She's been helping do her brother's skipper this week."

Gordon works his mouth oddly. Then speaks to the circle of faces above the circle of rocking chairs, "This . . . Cory . . . my . . . son." And to Cory, "Bread and Roses . . . school . . . *Folk* School . . . people."

Some of the seated guests rise to shake the tall boy's hand. There's only the slightest rumple in the weave of the camo jacket's left shoulder where the Border Mountain Militia patch used to be. Sadly his Hostile Indian patch is on an old BDU shirt that doesn't fit him anymore.

Billy pushes the hood of his jacket back, gives Cory a nod. Returning to his rocker, he doesn't sit yet, just stretches a bit, then says, "As we have mentioned, we hoped on this trip to do a roundtable orientation chat with the True Maine Militia." He smiles at Cory. "Are you one of them?"

"No . . . heh-heh." Cory pats the chest of his camo jacket with both palms. "You can never tell by looks who is one. They're like the Vietcong."

Claire explains, "You'll meet them at supper tonight. And Bree plans to come by afterward. She does supper with her family."

Cory studies the visitors' faces boldly with those midnight eyes of his that ooze over a whole person, just as a suspicious cop's hands would frisk you, but also with the lightness of a little kid's shy play-pokes. After all, Cory has just turned sixteen. He says, "Most of the True Maine members squeal a lot and hop around like cheerleaders . . . *heh-heh*." Then Cory's eyes narrow. "I was with an armed militia and that sort of ended but I keep up my aim with my friends and family . . . I'd help the True Maine out in a pinch, their theatrics and all, cuz I think diversity of tactics is the right thing . . . because it's how you surround the bastards."

"Anarchist, eh?" Young Blake smiles.

Cory looks at Blake. "You could say that . . . heh-heh."

Billy unzips his Eskimo jacket finally. Seems to be heating up. "You say you keep your *aim* up. So actually the tie is *not* broken with the extreme right wing."

Cory cocks his head, bewildered.

Claire watches as both Billy and Olan sort of writhe. She says, "I wouldn't even have called the Border Mountain Militia extreme right wing. Republican mostly. Some of the Settlementers are Republican, especially some of the elderly, except those from the County who are Catholic Democrats. Maine historically has been a Republican state . . . you know, Republican the industrial North, Democrat the plantation South. Most people keep the party they grew up with, don't you notice? They hardly know what it's all about . . . the average person, that is."

"But the violence," Olan almost groans. "The gunzzz."

Cory says, "Violence was never part of where Rex was going with the group. Preparedness was their thing. I don't see anything wrong with preparedness."

"For what! Preparedneses . . . for . . . what?" Billy cries out. "That's just paranoia! Nobody's going to invade a bunch of rural New Englanders!"

Cory shrugs his big shoulders. "I read a lot of history. I'm not into believing America has evolved into some special supercivilized floating island where humans behave wicked sweet. Like buttercups. There's no evidence that such love and peace exist in humongous societies . . . not past . . . not present. Or ever will. You guys probably believe in the great transformation, where rainbows are stairways to paradise."

"You can't fight the US government with guns!" Billy shrills. He glances at Blake but Blake's eyes are on the ceiling again. Blake is grinning.

Cory's black irises grow blacker as he focuses on Billy. "Then go play with your rubber duck. It's like abortion. If you don't want one, fine. Leave other people alone."

"It's not the same thing as abortion," Olan says, leaning forward in his rocker.

Cory swings an arm to the side and does an agitated half pivot on one foot, just as his father had been known to do *before*. "You afraid some tyrants will get hurt?"

"Don't be silly," Jip says. "You can't touch them."

Cory sighs. "Well, anyway, I didn't say *attack them*. I said be prepared to *deter* . . . *deflect*. If everyone were armed then just that alone would deflect." He has said this *slowly*, as if to persons of low low low IQ.

Brat! both Billy and Olan are thinking.

Blake glances at Gordon's profile in the next chair. Gordon seems to be sucking on his tongue.

Olan says, "In the cities, children are dying of gun violence. Blood is running in the streets."

Cory almost growls, "And what are those streets? Miles and miles where the only reasonable job opportunity is dealing. Black market. Whatever's in the black market. Drugs. Guns. And stolen stuff. And so the business model is the gang. And everyone's squeezed together in projects. People get hurt. It's economics, not *objects*! It's America's musical-chairs economics!"

"True," says Jip. "But—"

Cory is getting a bit loud. "In ghettos everyone's essentially fenced in. No respect, man. No money, no respect. No respect, you're treated like a wild dog by the larger society and the system. So you turn into a fuckin' soldier. Sounds like there's already a war in America, huh? Only it's all fenced-in inside these urban drug-doused hellholes and the soldiers fight each other! And there's . . . what's the word the lady in DC said? Collateral damage!!! Turf wars, man! You know . . . like *big* US business . . . they're always in some turf war . . . like in Nicaragua, Honduras, Yugoslavia, Ukraine, whatever! They send out armies to crush their competition! Little businessmen in their little ghetto companies, they have war, too! It's in the business model. Only it's not out of sight, out of mind like the CIA has the privilege of. Fuck! *Think* it out! These little gangs probably working for the big drug dealers, all tied in with your favorite politicians, law enforcement, and all that cuz that's the nature of prohibitions! And folks like you want to start a nice new big fat fuckin' prohibition! It's crazy!!!" His face has started to shine, his several furies equal to a ten-mile run.

"But Cory," Jip says softly. "You can't *attack* the ruling class."

"But why eliminate that option before you get to the day when things look wicked different!! Why eliminate your own options?!!! Makes no sense!" He bares his teeth as if to bite.

Meanwhile, young Blake's grin is as big as the moon. White as the stars.

Cory thrusts a hand through his hair so hard that it stretches his eyes up comically. He squints at Jip, who is squinting at Blake as if his starry teeth blind her.

Cory says, "Lotta people like you . . . I hear them all the time and I read their shit . . . they want a ban on handguns or on what they call assault weapons. Some want a total ban or a federal gun registry. But . . . heh-heh . . . there're more guns than toothbrushes. And anybody could *make* a gun. The technology is centuries old. Prisons don't make guns go away! They just pop people out of view! From life. From being a revolution. That's the greatest fear of the folks in power . . . being outnumbered by hostiles! Prohibitions are for cleaning up the hostiles!"

"Yes, Cory, you said that," coos Jip. "And Blake says it." She giggles. "Two peas in a pod."

Cory looks at Blake, blinks, then glares back at Olan: "Blood in the streets, huh? The streets will get squeaky clean . . . washed of thousands more . . . maybe millions more poor and working class. So if they lose in the game of musical chairs? Stick 'em in the dungeon. Whose fucking side are you on? The moneybags crowd, right? So fuck you!"

"Cory . . ."

He has moved away from his father's chair. "Then with black market and government corruption, there'll be MORE guns . . . heh-heh. Don't you get it??!! They gotta keep the numbers down on the hostiles! Or at least major control. Like when the Panthers were getting up steam, and the Black Power thing in general, along comes Nancy Reagan, the pumping up of the drug war on black ghettos, oh, boy. The justice system is as good as leg irons! So you have prohibitions on abortions, drugs, guns, undocumented workers, and that makes it so you have millions of illegal aliens *and* millions of illegal *citizens*. Cuz, see, if the hostiles weren't so cut down in numbers by being crammed behind bars, or crawling and super edgy and under the probation thumb but somehow got their asses organized and got their rage focused on these fuckin' lordies and ladies of Mammon, our true and total enemy, and we all had weapons, I wouldn't say for *absolute certain* that those billions of hostiles couldn't *deter* an attack *orrrrrr* if need be, attack them. And *overcome* them. But you types want that option erased. You say, oh, dear me, the government's army has the bomb. But it's not the sophistication of weapons that wins wars, it's numbers, the *unity,* and not being caught off guard. It's better if we—"

"They have high-tech surveillance and spies," Olan cuts in. "Provocateurs and the media with the eyes of the public soaking up the establishment's version of what the *troublemakers* are about."

Cory nods fast, his eyes beginning to bulge. It is clear he is freaking out. "Oh, yes, and by the way lady and gents I wear my tin hat proudly. Government has laws against *us* having conspiracies. But folks, you types especially, say, oh, no no no, the *government* and *Pentagon* and *chiefs of staff* and *think tanks* don't have conspiracies. Jesus H. Christ, what's the matter with you types!? Don't you know you have to expect the worst out of those goddamn evil cocksuckers. But you want more hostiles swept away so you can clap your little hands for the sweet smell of clean streets and for your election of the lesser of the two evils, one hundred percent evil versus one hundred and one percent evil and—"

"Cory," Jip cuts in. "We're off track. We just want to do some educating . . . like you say, to get people to understand who the real enemy is . . . so we're on the same page in that respect, and—"

Cory cuts in. "You say you love history. But it's in the historical record, the lordly and deserving always got a big grab for property and resources and slaves of one sort or another. So they want what they want and they *don't want any fighting back*. The trick is to get the buffer class, that's you guys, to beg for what the lordly class needs. Okay? So then there's some weirded-up right-wing people in this country. I've met some of them, okay? Oh, the holy founders . . . la la la. Where did all that weird belief come from? Ed . . . u . . . ca . . . tion! All that weird public school shit. The way schools are set up. Prussian military-industrial model. And the liberals want to give more money to that. Beef up the horseshit! Make more right-wingers!"

Jip says, "By education, we mean little seminars and maybe skits and rallies and radio programs all over the country straightening out that misinformation. And the True Maine Militia's style is just what we're interested in working with," she adds in as kindly a way as possible. Blake's blinding smile is soooo lodged in there in her peripheral vision. She tries not to glance at him, because that smile is contagious.

Cory steps close to give his father's shoulder another squeeze and turns away, heads for the cubby wall where sign-up sheets are dangling importantly on the other side.

Beth has returned to partially fill the spot where the giant Cory had stood, places a hand on the back of Gordon's big pine rocker. "You all have a funny idea about Rex's militia. But if you want the reeeal picture of the Pink Panthers, I can tell you *plenty* anytime." She rolls her eyes.

Blake's head swivels, eyes on Beth. "*Pink* Panthers?"

"That's right."

Again Blake smiles large, stands up again, his chair rocking without him. He leans to his right and offers Beth his hand. "Sorry. We didn't introduce ourselves. I'm Blake Richardson." Then he shakes hands officially with Bonnie Loo, who is bent over a worktable chopping and dicing, then he shakes with old Claudia and teenage Ricardo, who are wiping down other worktables.

"This is a business meeting?" Benedicta asks. "Making deals?"

"Making friends," Jip says warmly, leaving her chair, slipping around to Benedicta's and Reggie's chairs, shakes their hands. Reggie's hand is cool. Benedicta's is not.

In another minute you might notice that Blake and Cory are both beyond the Winter Kitchen talking low.

Eventually Jip sidles over, her Hush Puppies even quieter than Cory's boots. So now the three are murmuring. Cory's black, black eyes stab Jip's light browns as he hisses, "I hate to break this news to you but Bree is a wicked fuckin' good shot with that thirty-two special she totes around mighty often." He looks over at the back of Gordon's head, the cropped dark hair, the creepy silence there, and he gets tears in his eyes. "My father . . . before he got the shit beat out of him . . . he was . . . a squirrely son of a bitch . . . moody, you know? He'd go around and 'round all over a thing and . . . and he'd say so many times that whenever the classes try to take something from each other, make some law to *take*, the only people to benefit . . . it's the overlords, the regimes."

He pushes a palm against one teary eye and cheek. Then he says, "Rex's militia was a chance to be a pack. To be a pack, as Gordo always says, is a normal human condition. It's how you stay alive. How you feel strong, not weak. Prevents depression, right? But you types probably would like to force each and every pissed-off working-class person to go *one by one* in front of a fucking psychiatrist, some superior personage of the system, get practically naked, drug 'em with the fuzzy-wuzzy pills. Break 'em. Piss on 'em some more." His lips are tight, his teeth welded into a bitter clench.

Jip says, "I apologize, Cory." She bows her head slightly. Then, "You're right that it's big. To learn the truth about corporate power and all its effects. And how to build economics that make sense. A good friend of mine, now deceased, once said it's like going into the woods where soon you're lost because there's so much . . . it's so complex, the tentacles are around everything. We sure have a lot of work to do, not just teaching but learning. You and our org *are* really on the same page. Truly."

Cory makes no reply, neither agreeable nor sulky. When he finally goes to leave, Benedicta calls out, "See ya later, alligator!"

Cory turns and beams boyishly. "After a while, crocodile!"

Benedicta waggles her head. "See ya later, hot tomata!"

Cory just laughs.

Gordon has nodded off, both the green eye and the slightly pink eye closed loosely.

The thin old woman, Claudia, gray hair short and bristly, who has been fussing with things by the sinks and tall green hand pumps, calls out, "Coffee?" She bustles over toward the stoves and rockers with a large painted tray of pottery mugs. She has a dowager's hump; her T-shirt, blaze orange, reads *Big Bucks Club*. Her dungarees are old, almost white. She wears a thick leather belt with a large knife in its black leather case. She pours coffee for everybody except napping Gordon.

A quart-sized canning jar of cream goes around.

Gordon groans in his dream.

Blake frowns.

Claire says, "He can't stay awake. It's his antiseizure medicine."

"Is he going to be all right?" Jip wonders softly.

Claire says, "He was to be sent to a rehab facility, you know, a nursing home, but we believe we can care for him here."

The organizers are looking at the coffee mugs in their hands, flushed of face from the stove heat and from the snags in an otherwise perfect project.

Claire says flatly, "The doctors all say Gordon should get his normal speech back . . . or at least improvement."

"I call him Rocky," Benedicta tells everyone brightly, her bare-of-eyeglasses teasy eyes so blue and glowing they seem like special effects.

Everyone is quiet for a long wrenching moment, some coffee sipping, an oven door woinking open. The wind beyond the handsome windows rattles, croons, and clomps.

Jip says, "I'm so sorry. We don't mean to seem like vultures."

From a future time, Cory St. Onge tells us this.

That night, late, I went to the kitchens to see him . . . I mean, to watch him sleep. To just watch what was left of him, right? You know, they had him pretty knocked out by bedtime every night since what happened happened to him.

Came into the first kitchen, closed the door behind me easy-soft, feeling like an outlaw. This was the Cook's Kitchen, warm, just some dim light through the cubby-wall archways and my flashlight spot sporting around over the solar-heated floor tiles of clovers, clouds, cows, Christmas trees, hearts, pumpkins, bees, and best of all, monsters, painted by kids, Butch Martin, for instance, just before I was born. And I could see the orange flush of coals through the partly open dials of one stove.

I could hear Cindy Butler, Vancy, and Penny murmuring in the Winter Kitchen.

Gordo, he'd never been a snorer before, just maybe a little chuffing like a toy train. But with his nose sort of mashed you could count this new sound as a snore.

I went to the nearest archway and waved a hand at the night shift. Only one of them would be the designated night watch for Gordo, the others keeping them company. They had an electric lamp in a low-watt glow on their table, a paper shade of flowers. Made me think of Gypsy fortune-tellers, their big pupils, Cindy's yellow head scarf, and their all-wise expressions . . . heh-heh.

I said, "I'm going to sit with him a minute."

Vancy, who was pregnant at the time, real soon to hatch out another one of my littermates (my bad joke, but basically true . . . heh-heh), was sitting squarelike in a captain's chair. She said, "He's going for his tests in the morning. Last time they said they might take him off the antiseizure stuff any day now. He's been doing real good, don't you think?"

I grunted or something.

Cindy Butler was rearranging the pins to her yellow bandanna. There was a trace of that gleamy wiseass look in her eye, she being Samantha Butler's mum. Though Sammy's wiseassness was higher voltage, both of them were hyperactive, both huffy, both sky-white blondes. And no, they were not wife and child of Gordo.

Penny said, "He *thinks* soon he's going to go back down to the farmplace, be there by himself." She shook her head.

"I don't like that," Vancy groaned.

I guess I shrugged, not knowing what to say. Gordo's willpower used to be something you couldn't move with a 410 excavator.

"Where were you at supper, Mr. C?" Penny asked kind of cautiously.

"Had to work," said I.

All three of them squinted at me.

"Why'd you ask if you already know the answer?" I tried to keep my shoulders straight, eyes dead on. On Penny's face. I knew Beth's and Eric's . . . Ricardo if you knew him by *that* self-proclaimed name . . . their hinges had probably been flapping nonstop, passing along the fine details of the whole intense spectacle of Gordon's Harvardly guests.

"Just a way of saying we missed you," Penny said, crinkling her eyes. She was a great lady. I regretted being snippy.

"I'll eat twice as much at breakfast," I warned her.

"Uh-oh," Cindy kind of snorted.

Penny said, "We'll be looking for you."

As I trudged along back into the darkness, I splayed the spot of my flashlight all over the little painted floor tiles till I got around the stoves and sinks and worktables to his cot. He was on his stomach, a much bigger son of a bitch than the cot was made for. I took up a stool and got settled. The snoring stopped. He sounded dead. Or listening.

I zigzagged my light spot on the deep drawers where I knew speckled kettles and roasters and pie plates were stashed. I zoomed light over all the big windows as if to wash them, and then the walls. Bonnie Loo's rules, *framed*. Helpful cooking hints on index cards. Photos. One showing Misty's brother with a pickerel the size of a nuclear submarine.

A hand closed up around my ankle.

I said, "I liked it better when you used to do mosta the talking. You'd've hung those yuppie assholes by the ears."

He said, "They're good bits . . . good . . . *people*." He let go of my ankle.

"You said that about Rex."

Silence.

"Don't you remember it yet? When he was hammering your face and crucifying your brains?"

He, this gray shape in the dark, rolled up onto his side to look at me (*my* gray shape) in the dark. "*I* don't remember it but my . . . my face does." He laughed.

"So, about those guys. They talk you into trying to get the average redneck Mainer to identify with their message?" Now I was aiming the flashlight up under my chin the way kids do to scare each other.

"To-break-the-corporate-monster's-ass . . . message? That's us . . . *our* message, too . . . right?" he said deeply.

"They got *other* agendas," I hissed.

"When Bree and Whitney and . . ."

In his pause, I cut in. "Yeah, Gordon St. Onge and the True Maine Militia. Sounds like a 1950s rock and roll band," I sneered.

"*You*'re a fan of . . . diversity of tactics. You're also pretty darn . . . tight . . . with . . . Jaxon Cross and the Horne Hill anarchists . . . another 1950s band."

I tried not to laugh.

He said, "They're taking over . . . your mind."

I laughed.

He said, "I'm smarter than I see . . . than I *look*. And *talk*." He laughed. "The Cambridge folks are smarter than *they* look. And talk."

"They're weaselly."

"Good to have *some* of the world's weasels . . . on *our* side," he said.

For a full minute, I felt it in my chest, what seemed like the right heat of a wisdom new to him, a foretaste of a rigorous test that in fairy tales would be just this way, spoken of so simmeringly in the dark.

The yard of the meat-cutting shed.

There are pickups. As well as one old fiberglass-repair-jobbed Bronco with duct tape and see-through plastic for a passenger window. And a fairly new Chevy Blazer. Two Explorers. All these parked close to the open doorway of the shed. The Settlement keeps its books happy in November. Nice little money in November. Almost nobody these days cuts up his own deer or moose or bear.

Inside the door, it is clean. And it is cold. Cold as you can stand. You wish for cold in November. Warm November days are the ones that make so much worry.

It is not the congealed blood or the stripped muscle or fat or bone that is of itself eerie. Maybe not even a deer's head and its collapsed-looking face in that cardboard box. It is the fluorescent light on stainless steel and on the calm movement of human fingers, on the faces that don't shriek at what they see in this chilled laboratory of death. If you are the Dead, you won't quiver even the smallest muscle to fight the skinning knife or the saw. This is the highest form of submission. And always the question that no one asks. Such a god who made all this! How can anyone be redeemed?

Bree Vandermast St. Onge does the work she's known since she was nine years old. It comes easy to her, though each deer is subtly different. She works a ground-down boning knife around the slim wrists and ankles of the enormous buck who is sprawled on the floor. Bree not listening to the men's words around her, just riding on the rhythm of their voices, just feeling that sound in her scalp and on the fine red-blond hairs of her arms. She works the skin off the old buck's front legs, always working inside up, so as not to sever hairs, pulling the skin back like sleeves.

At the back of the deer, Butch Martin works the spreader through the back tendons. He is not part of the conversation either, though alert to it. His jacket isn't bloody, but Bree's shapeless old blue sweatshirt is bloody, the blood of the doe she just finished and the five small bucks before that. She is squatted down on the cement floor with her head down, her weirdly far-apart yellow-brown eyes not seen by anyone in the room; just the high hard orange knot of her hair is visible. Now when she murmurs a word, someone works the chain fall with slow tight pulls, either Butch or Gordon, she's not sure which. She doesn't look. She is focused on this, the steady, almost considerate pressure needed to pull the skin away.

When Aurel turns from the counter and says, "Cape t'at one, Bree," she almost doesn't hear him, not with her ears, but her hands register it and will begin the process of caping.

In a moment she will stop, wag her head to give herself a little circulation to the brain, and flex her back; and as she does, she sees Gordon next to her and knows it is he who has worked the chain fall. It is this difference, the miracle of the seizure medicine's dosage now cut to a trace. Hallelujah!

Near the door, two young men, Passamaquoddies from Princeton, down for a few days, both quiet, shy to the point where they won't really look you in the eye much.

Occasionally peering in from the open doorway are some rowdy teenagers. Owen Miner and C.C. and Caleb Barrington, Jaime and Evan and even Bard Rosenthal and Seth Carver. They are all listening to Arnold Turnbull's far-fetched hunting stories. He is seventy, toothless, chain-smoking, eyes blue and filled with the joy of lying, of perhaps believing himself. The young people listen with one ear, enough to remember some of what he tells them, remember it *someday*, though *now* Arnold seems more like just part of the clean gray weather.

Back inside the shed, a few feet away from Bree, Butch is leaning with one hand on the counter, scratching his ear. Butch and Cory, not *real* brothers but like brothers these days, so inseparable, but not today. Cory is out hunting up back on what they call "the rocks" on the far side of Pock Hill.

Now Bree works at the back of the deer. Gordon, like Bree, is deft at skinning, a lotta years at this ritual, a lotta stories that go with the ricketiness of overlapping decades. This is one of the ways in which Gordon was an A-plus student of Guillaume St. Onge, his papa, who was one of that long line of Aroostook life's teachers. Gordon wears another black sleeveless dress sweater over a raggedy blue-white chambray work shirt and dark blue work pants. He looks almost natty again today. Except for the blood.

A bunch of men from town have arrived, joining those in the doorway, more oldish guys and a young Bean and his wife, relations of Bonnie Loo . . . all out there laughingly listening to Arnold's fibs, drinking hot coffee, dressed heavy, each with at least one item of blaze orange, their breathing frosty and pluming. One of the old guys leans into his truck cab to pull an Australian-made Enfield from the rack . . . World War II vintage . . . bolt action . . . stripy-looking wood, heavy. He powerfully flings open the bolt, almost one-handed, and simultaneously tapping the ash of his short cigarette, passes the empty rifle around for all to admire. None of these people from town are meat-cutting customers. This is just a hunting season social call.

Aurel and Paul Lessard are murmuring and chortling gossip to each other in French as they finish up with the doe. Labeled white packages, purply bones, hooves, the skin, the doe's head in a box, and a bill on a peg on the wall are all that is left of that doe.

Bree waits quietly while Gordon works the chain fall and the spread-out rear legs of the buck lift and sway till the rear end is raised enough for Bree to continue work. Then Gordon goes to wipe down the counters and to help Paul lug the coolers of meat (the doe) out to the side room to await pickup, a copy of the bill taped to the top. Without his cane, Gordon walks with a teetery limp.

A truck engine starts outside as someone leaves, two other trucks arriving.

A chicken steps into the doorway and looks in, eyes blinking around the legs of the two Passamaquoddy guys. Her head bobs. She's a young white part-Leghorn chicken, legs long, spurred, and gray-yellow.

Butch slashes an X next to the name Sanborn on a list on the wall. Near his head, on a windowsill arranged like an alter of holy tokens, are objects such as hefty flared hunting arrows with only an inch or two of shaft left, snapped off by various deer who carried the arrowhead in a muscle or jaw for days or weeks or years after rubbing the shaft off on a tree, deer who were finally killed by bullets of a second hunter. Also on the sill is a pile of bird shot (all dug out of one moose). All these objects go on this sill as objects having once belonged to what Aurel calls "Members of t'Asshole Hunting Club" or "t'Ping Pong Brains."

Now there's a commotion outside, guys squawking. Makes the chicken nervous so she backs up and trots long-leggedly away down toward the Quad.

Then he's standing there in the doorway, hands behind his back, thumbs in the back of his belt, heavy wool jacket unzipped, eyes sweeping around the shed, big pleased grin. Willie Lancaster, who else?

"Hey, Willie," murmurs Butch in a low, manly, chuckly way.

The Passamaquoddy guys study Willie quietly.

Paul Lessard returns from the side room, raises his blaze orange fuzzy earflaps cap enough to smooth his hair out, and looks at Willie with no change of expression. Gordon is stepping around Paul, closes the side room door behind himself. And Gordon nods, eyes on Willie's face a moment, then looks down at the deer, whose front half still sprawls on the cement, waist twisted.

"Nice rack," says Willie.

"Bobby. Prescott . . . Horne Hill," Gordon says in his new choppy fashion.

"Got many coming down from upstate?"

Aurel snorts with disgust. "Five. And dey wass all blowed to hell, dem. Lead sandwiches of the t'Ping Pong Brain Club." Aurel speaks this without turning around. He keeps churning water down the sink, mopping around the edges, leans his weight more on one foot, using only the heel of his right work boot to move his body to and fro.

Willie sneaks glances at the maelstrom of scars and remolding of Gordon's face.

Willie's son, Danny, steps in around his father against the elbow of one Passamaquoddy guy, the one wearing a billed cap that reads CAT on it, and golden-framed glasses. The glasses turn and the dark eyes move up and down Danny. Danny looks down at the deer that Bree, now using Gordon's old field dressing knife, has worked much of the hide from, the raspy taffy-like strings of fascia snow white in every purple cleft of muscle. Danny, not light on his feet like Willie, stands quite solidly in his big squashy sneakers. Danny is round in girth, round in the arms. Has an extra chin. And under his new orange felt crusher hat, chubby cheeks with a two-day beard. Danny wears no *official* blaze orange. Nor does Willie. Neither one a hunter.

Butch asks Danny, "You workin' with ol' Willie Nilly all the time now?"

"Yep," Danny replies. Without beer he's not an animated person, not even much facial expression, didn't seem to inherit the Willie-Lancaster-cat-that-ate-the-canary smile. But in Danny's gray eyes is a gentle humor. He sniffs a bit. Seems to have himself a little flushy fluey cold.

Willie cackles to himself, then informs everyone, "Dan doesn't work. He just holds the box of Band-Aids in case I fall."

A few snorts of laughter around the shed and from a couple of eavesdroppers just outside the door.

Danny's eyes twinkle good-naturedly.

Aurel warns Danny, "Not sneeze around t'meat, you."

Danny salutes Aurel.

Willie says, "National Weather Service says four to eight inches after midnight tomorrow."

"Good," says Butchie. "That'll bring 'em in."

Aurel again pipes up, "In t'County t'ey had fifteen inches in October, firs' part. Iss not melt and t'en more on it and t'ere wind t'ere push it all in t'roads overrr and overrr. Plow t'same snow over five times, t'ere." Aurel turns from the counter and his dark eyes burn fiercely around the shed, from face to face to face. He wipes his hands slowly on a striped rag. The plume of his breath is long and twisty and elegant.

Bree, not looking up, murmurs, "Raise 'im."

And Gordon cranks the animal up a few more links.

"Shit, what's that boy weigh, anyway?" Willie wonders.

"Two-eleven when he came in," Paul Lessard tells him, one hand on his hip, eyes on the spread hind legs of the buck.

Bree leans toward the buck, gets a no-nonsense grip on the hide, and pulls with all her weight. The hide slips downward and the great purply corpse and Bree swing together as the hide lets go a few more stubborn inches at a time.

Willie Lancaster's eyes pulse over the purple strata of meat and satiny white fascia swaths. Then his eyes press onto Bree's hands, the hands that have infused themselves with every deep stratum of his own live person, every twist and turn of live nerve. And he sees Bree's ornate ring, chunky and pearly and bloody. His eyes widen at the ring. He understands something about this ring though he has never laid eyes on it before.

Willie hears his son sniffing miserably and germily. He sees the blue wrinkly bandanna tugged from the young man's jacket pocket. He sees the brittle fluorescent light that speaks so well the language of death. He sees the little chalkboard with familiar names in blue and pink chalk. Now he sees Bree's knot of red hair and loose squiggles of hair on the back of her neck. Yeah, he sees the ring. He understands.

A young Settlement kid comes humming up to the doorway on a big-wheeled solar buggy. Another kid running after him, huffing and gasping. Both kids push in around Willie. "Is it time yet?!!" one asks breathlessly. Both are dressed in blaze vests. One has a blaze-orange knit cap on his long dark hair.

"No!" replies Aurel grumpily, tosses the striped rag into a box.

Gordon works the chain fall and at last the deer's black muzzle and antlers and front hooves swing free. Deer spins slowly around. Bree looks into Willie's eyes, her back to Gordon.

Willie has not stopped smiling his utmost cat-that-ate-the-canary smile since he got here and so now nothing needs change about his face.

He says, "What's a pretty girl like you doin' in a place like this?" This could sound like a stupid wrong thing for a person to say, considering Bree's deformity. But those who suspect what's between Willie and Bree know what these words actually mean. Passion is blind.

"You never guess what we juss found on Sanborn's doe," Paul Lessard says with a shake of his head. "Fucking wood tick. Blowed right up and pleased with t'e whole world. Thinks it's the month of May, him."

"Shit," says Willie. "They're gettin' tougher every year."

Bree goes back to work. She leans into the swaying deer and muckles onto the hide again, rises right off her feet with all her weight, the deer and Bree swinging together. The skin with its glue of fascia crackles. And with finishing touches of the knife, the last whole shapely floppy piece of skin pulls free and she hands it to Gordon.

And the two Settlement boys shout, "Now!" and "Time!"

And Aurel says in a pissy dark way, "Change t'tone of your voice to respect, you! Not fun! T'iss not t'circus. Maybe you be transform' to a new prayer committee, get your lessons on what t'iss is really all about." And he turns his fierce dark eyes on each boy's flushing smoky-cold-breath face.

They force solemn expressions to pacify him. Then lunge, one to each of the deer's swaying shoulders and gripping, one to each foreleg of bare naked bone and hoof, snap them cleanly off.

Snap!

Snap!

After supper.

The clouds are torn to shreds by a slow quiet cold front, so as Gordon, cane in hand, stands alone out under the trees on the Quad, he stares straight up into an exquisite black, black sky loaded richly with stars. But he isn't thinking of God as maker now. He is thinking of God, the helping hand, knowing he, Gordon, a mere flawed human with bashed knee and mashed face, is no longer the gem of Brianna's honey-color eyes. With his lost memory heaving back into view he is wondering miserably if he will ever have the big fat and goodly feat of strength to stop wishing death on Willie Lancaster.

Eden Rosenthal tells us how it went.

I remember how Geraldine had just had a hair trim, wore kid-made earrings of hemlock cones painted gold. Her red peasant blouse was loaded with yellow embroidered wee houses and stars. She had been teaching me to ride Prometheus, who was scary, a head tosser and a dancer. So Geraldine and I had become buddies that summer and fall and my head was far more full of horses and most excellent shivers of my newfound heroism, *not* the organizers' educational-style politics. But I was also crisply aware of how Geraldine dressed up for this, how she could go from T-shirt, raggedy jacket, riding boots, jeans, and strong-arming monster horses to being almost inflammably lovely and dainty, that tiny waist! And oh so poised and oh so smart. Ready for the visit from the Massachusetts organizers. La-di-da.

Off his barbiturates or whatever, Gordon was no longer napping in the middle of sentences. His motormouth hadn't been reinstalled but he didn't trail off as much. Still, he had no interest in our after-the-Sunday-noon-meal walk with our VIP guests . . . lawyers, professors, whatever.

Everyone got bundled up and off we went, my twin brother Bard in the lead, encircled by his worthy friends, a mix and match pack of dogs, two of the squashed-faced Lancaster mutts included. Somehow those two little guys never ran out of pee.

Mostly we referred to the organizers as "the Mass people" unless they were present, then it was by name. Beth called them "the Harvardtonians." They were in high spirits, having gotten Gordon and Bree and Whitney and the rest of us to agree to interviews and/or guest appearances on six mainstream and local radio shows starting after Christmas, and they planned to put out the word that we'd be available for more. Cory was noticeably missing all day and at supper. All fluffed up with disgust and botheration, he had said more than once we were being used, that that class of people saw us only as jokes. He and Butch and C.C. and Jaime were over at Jaxon Cross's father's land *a lot*, the anarchist cooperative "farm" around three barely heated sheds, everybody eating seeds and garlic and rice and getting stoned and talking about a future society without hierarchies. Even the half dozen anarchist mothers and their kids who were technically still living at the Settlement would rather be there with the seeds and garlic and shivery cold than "be organized" by the degreed class.

But also they would congregate in Bree's studio, which was warm, or the radio tower shed. Loosely, spontaneously, lolling imperiously in their well-understood covenant of no compromise.

I was just really into this walk. Fall and winter have always been my favorites.

As we reached the woods there were crunchy streaks and stretches of snow, most of our November storms getting melted back into earth like Gogolian ghosts, but the quiet air smelled as if there was more snow on the way very soon. And although we strutted along in a veil of quietness, waaay up in the sky there were many sleigh-clouds and their white horses skimming along at emergency speed.

Our group got more and more chatty as we huffed up the mountain; fast hearts make you have more zip and gaiety but Geraldine hugged me to her, watching out for me as usual, cradling my broken heart, cause we were about to come upon Mama's cross.

All the dogs of many sizes and shapes were zigzagging over the path, sucking up bright and dark scents into their noses, leaving the prints of their paws in the snow like fossilized flowers. Shadowed by the low-armed hemlocks and the pines and spruce and balsam, the snow, as we got higher and higher on this hill, was still as blanket-dense as when it had landed days ago.

The Massachusetts guy Billy, with his Eskimo jacket and funny city boots, kept stopping to fling his hands all around to illustrate his spirited, almost frenzied tales of his old hiking days, then hauling out a big yellow-gold paisley bandanna to wipe his nose while Olan was waiting for Bonnie Loo's little Jetta to pick up more hemlock cones that lay on the crusty snow. These were for Olan's pockets, she said. So this was a slow walk.

Olan didn't wear a hat even though he was a bald person. He kept reminding us, "I'm Scandinavian." Did I mention yet that Olan was a political science professor on sabbatical, working on a book? He said research is fun. Looking back, I think we were part of his fun research. And, ha ha, he was part of ours.

Jip was wearing gray leather-palmed gloves on this outing but I remember how whenever we were indoors for one of their "critiques" or a Settlement meal, her fingers were cool if she placed them on your arm. She was a funny little lady, about forty like Olan and Billy, and also Gordon as a matter of fact. Age forty resembled a hundred and ten to me then.

Jip said she was a lawyer of labor law. Seth Carver piped up, "You mean like the Thirteenth Amendment means only the government can own slaves?"

Jip nodded. "And then all the ingenious laws our corporate-controlled government finagled to slip various elements of slavery back under the guise of *the rights of the people*, as if it were our privilege and honor to be slaves of the overlords. They do a lot under the banner of bringing America back. Seeing that the original America was built on the torments and humiliations of millions of captive and displaced people, the idea of bringing America back ought to make the hair stand up on the backs of our necks. Hard-won labor laws meant to halt those torments are now being dismantled in a bipartisan orgy of bringing America back. The word America is where the Word Wizard does some of his finest hocus-pocus."

Seth might have had a crush on Jip after that. His many blushes gave him away.

When Jip visited us she always dressed in men's button-down-collar pastel shirts. Her face was furrow-browed, metal-rimmed glasses focused on some sprawling maze of laws, historical and current, but she also knew *sixteen* hilarious how-to-change-a-lightbulb jokes and said her dream was to dye her hair green.

It really caught my attention when at one of our philosophy salons that she sat in on she described how when she was still in college and working in Central America one summer, some of her friends who were union leaders there were murdered by US-funded paramilitary under US-supported regimes. When she said their names, her voice shook.

Jip taught law, but I never heard about a sabbatical. She was just a person who could, against the laws of physics, fill more than one space at the same time.

Blake was the youngest so the most frisky. He made snowballs fast and stockpiled them in the big pockets of his leather car coat. Blake was a published novelist (one book), an editor of radical "zines," and a freelance journalist of mainstream stuff.

Geraldine and Claire told Blake the story of my mother Silverbell and how we were about to come upon her cross.

Bree was mostly walking alone smoking. A lot of us bitched about how the smoke, even without air currents, was lunging for all our cardiopulmonary centers. She stayed waaaay behind. But she didn't lose track of any conversations, kept calling out questions and remarks. Unlike Cory and cohorts, she loved these organizers. They were huge rainbow trout she had personally snagged and reeled in and if anyone was being used, our devious victorious Bree would say Cory had it backward.

As others added to the Silverbell story, it seemed to be getting farfetched and otherworldly. The faces of the Mass people were hard to read but the anguish of Silverbell could not be exaggerated.

How many times had we in our Settlement philosophy salons, facilitated by our "peace man" Nathan Knapp, discussed for a deep two hours the question of suffering, how it's considered by our culture to be a contest. Suffering by the agonies of war versus apartheid versus the agony of a tiger's teeth and claws. Dying in a watery squeeze and suffocation and terror as the *Edmund Fitzgerald* goes down versus dying slow by the mental crucifixion of depression that leads to suicide. Dying in a concentration camp versus cancer ward versus prison cell versus nursing facility versus burning house versus flaming car wreck versus serial killer's strangling hands versus lonely, drugged, and drunk on a couch with the tinny sound of the bedeviling TV. Versus! Versus! Versus! Who wins the contest of suffering!!!?

Our conclusion always winds up being that suffering is supreme with each person alone in his or her temple of pain, whether you die of it or not.

It matters not your skin color, whether the ordeal is "just" or "unjust," your temple walls keep out true sympathy, your brisance is total and to all other hearts silent.

I only know that my mother is now serene.

So we all stood around the kid-made white cross and I felt only Mama's quietness. *Gone*. GONE. What is better than gone?

The dogs didn't sniff the cross or, horrors, wet on it. There was nothing there to interest them.

Geraldine kept playing with my fingers and squeezed them and patted them. My brother Bard went to the cross and from the pocket of his wool pants dug out a little ceramic sailboat from a tea box in the Cook's Kitchen; this he'd brought to add to all the other little boats and fairies and pretty stones he'd brought before.

Then I heard above the aureole of quietness around the cross, Billy's voice. "Some of you here must remember this," he said in a teacherly way. And he sang in a burly alto, "Bridge over Troubled Water." His voice, despite all his allergies and snot and red eyes, was like the air with its coming snow, rising whiffy and soft and pure.

And when he was done, Olan said prayerfully, "Simon and Garfunkel. We had a blessed youth in *some* ways, eh?"

Rusty Soucier said brightly, "Lee Lynn and Jenny Dove said we could have a séance to go with the winter solstice events. We can bring people back here to earth to communicate. Like Silverbell!"

"No! Never!" I practically choked. Then inexplicably I kicked snow onto the bodyless grave.

Everyone's eyes widened at me.

Olan stepped close and hugged me very hard.

Bree was smoking a hundred miles an hour.

Blake tossed his gloves on the ground, pulled all the snowballs from his pockets, and smooshed them together with his bare hands, dark on white. Then he rolled the one fat blob over the sticky snowy ground to get it even bigger and then worked it till a woodchuck-sized snowman now stood sentry beside the cross. Then Blake made hair with sticks. Looked like arrows but you could tell he meant hair. And then breasts. A snow *woman*. Then he gave her wings.

While others honor Silverbell's "grave," Gordon arrives at the old farmplace for a nap.

He has walked the whole way, using the shortcut through the spectral yet friendly tree giants, then clomping over the dark-stained elvish bridge that spans the chattering icy brook. His cane gives him precious aid over acorn, root, and icy stone. It jumps him as he reaches the open yards to see a hooded figure in a rocker down at the farther end of the long, narrow, screened porch. The garment droops in black folds all the way to the floor.

He walks faster to face this thing square on, his limping gait causing his fob of keys to jangle-flop tunefully.

He yanks the screen door open and strides the length of the porch, his cane tonking the floor, his eyes on the sinister figure that is no mirage.

She raises her freckled face.

"How drom . . . m . . . dramatic you are," says he. "Always. Dramatic."

"You don't remember me. He erased your memory of me."

"I remember you . . . you, Glory." His old eye-flinching comes to life. "I just don't row there . . . row . . . ruh . . . *remember* the party, nor the deed."

"I don't, either." She speaks this in a quirky simpering and yet blushing way. "I mean, I don't remember it well . . . just a haze, you know?"

There is now a single braided-together *mmmmm* sound, their two stifled laughs. He can tell she is nervous. With no buckets of alcohol and no gang of friends, she is once again the tenderhearted, in some ways babyish, introvert he had watched grow up.

Her gray Rex-like eyes scrape the narrow gray-painted pine boards of the floor. She says, "I decided to come here all covered . . . my new identity. Like a Muslim person." She raises her eyes.

"You look more like the . . . Grim Reaper to me. But probably that's because . . . hit . . . *he* has been on my mok . . . my *mind*." He eases his tired bulk into the rocker opposite hers.

She says, "I didn't go *up there* looking for you. I don't want anyone *up there* to see me. But Suzelle and Lorraine were just here looking at your shed. They want to make it an Internet shop." She shrugs. "So Suzelle said you come down here around two-thirty for a nap. Wah! Wah!" She wags her head. "Nappy for the tired boy," she teases.

"I have a teddy bat . . . *bear* with a zipper. A hot water . . . b . . . bottle can go inside."

"Oh, stop!" she scolds and giggles.

"No, *really*," he insists, his eyes warm.

"You were an hour late but I waited. Brrrrr!" She hugs herself. No coat under her costume. She does not study the mended rips, the new maplike terrain of his face, his slightly flatter nose, but now again brushes his pale dark-lashed eyes with her own, then glances away. "I heard you couldn't talk." She hugs herself tighter. Without the hood, her nose is getting pink.

He says, "Where's your cart . . . c . . . *car*?"

She smiles beautifully. "On the road, behind those trees. I guess I wanted to shock you."

His laugh is more like a cough. He shakes his head.

But now nervousness is back in her eyes. Does his fear, worse than his nervousness, show in *his* eyes?

She says, "I brought you a present from Gram. She made me come. I never thought I'd get up the nerve . . . but I used positive thinking." She snickers. "Gram left you a letter in your message box by your *I'll Kill You* signs." She snickers again. "You never answered her. So she's having a bird. Worried you'd become a vegetable. I don't live there anymore but I keep stopping to see Gram . . . she's my best friend, right? So it's sneaky-schneaky while Daddy's at his jobs. Gram never stops talking about how you dropped the charges. She wants to repay you forever with presents and love letters." Glory laughs girlishly.

"Is my present something to eat?"

"Of course," she laughs, almost a hoot. She reaches for her huge corduroy satchel in the chair beside her for the foil-covered pie plate.

His spine jerks. Here it is, richer and more rooted than passion, these bracings of two souls crouch-cringing from the possibility of peril. What peril? Bigger than Rex, yes. After all, Rex has only *two* fists.

Now she rises. To hand him the pie. And her thick glossy auburn braid, so bewitching to admirers, slithers free of the hood like a live python.

She covers her mouth, such a sudden hiccuppy laugh.

He holds the pie treasuresquely on his lap.

"I couldn't stay there anymore. At Gram's. He scares me." She sighs. "There's a murderer deep inside him." She is still standing near Gordon, still hugging herself, her black robe brushes his knee. "I'm so sorry about the beach . . . only how it made Daddy crazy . . . I . . . never dreamed it would go there. But you never know what little things set people off. Daddy's a funny person. He's easy. I mean, he's really wicked sweet. But . . . my Bumpa Lovey Bear, my Pooh Bear Daddy is transformable, you know? I'm out of there. I can't live in that house. The whole house scares me now." She spreads her right hand to smooth the black folds of her garment.

Gordon sets the pie on the white birch stump table beside his chair and pats it. "All mine," he says good-naturedly.

At last she allows her eyes to stroke his ruined face, particularly the scar that ripples from his somewhat sagging lower eyelid to the corner of his mouth through the forest of his dark beard. Her nearer dangling hand flexes as if it is thinking of touching him.

The cane between his knees shivers. Easy-careful so as not to startle her, he presses his face with its brushy beard against her hand, and her fingers stir willingly upon the nerves of that face. She is the first woman to caress him since he has come home. Maybe the others fear his ripe scars are still painful. They don't want to hurt him, right? Or is it that they are all repelled? Whatever, he lies no more with any wife.

"I will never forgive myself," Glory moans. She raises her other hand slowly, considerately, *she* not wanting to startle *him*. His whole face is now inside her cool hands. She turns his head as an archaeologist might examine a fine find, pottery or bone. She sighs. "You are *not* hideous if that's what you've been thinking. You still look good. You look . . . *intrepid*." She means to say this playfully but it unfolds silkily. With fingertips she caresses his lips that are braced against his teeth. Then she withdraws her hands and steps back.

He is so stricken with longing that his knees loosen and the cane clatters to the floor. He bends to fetch it.

She makes a little cry deep in her neck. "Why is it that when a person gets really sloshed your brain blows a fuse and you can't remember things?"

"S . . . sun . . . seb . . . *science*," he replies.

She isn't looking at him when she says, "I wish I could remember the beach . . . you know . . . that part. Otherwise, I *sort* of wonder if it's true." She again flushes. She turns toward the big corduroy bag again and tugs out a resisting envelope, her fingers shaking. "To read when you're alone. It's another letter from Gram like the one she left you when you were first home. Just more of her heart pouring out."

He opens his hand for the envelope, his hand shaking not from the cold nor from the tension. His hand is afire.

She says, "I feel guilty that I still love him. That's the worst part now. I shouldn't love him."

Gordon makes little nods. "I'm okay with it."

When she kisses the top of his head, his dark hair beginning to spurt again with all its defiant cowlicks, his terror returns to prickle him. Oh, the possible consequences of her touch, should it be known.

She slings the big bag over a shoulder, her hood all the way back, her beautiful-beautiful-beautiful face saying, "Thank you." She pulls open the screen door, gives him one of her playful little-girl waves. He gives her the shadowlike nod of a deity.

Voice of Pirate Radio interrupts.

Dear ones, our precious people, neighbors, pals, blood, we need a plan, we need to draw a picture in the sand to see what our heart's content looks like. Hurry. Lean into the covenant, march into the *munch! munch! munch!* of our giant steps because this is no light matter. The second most common death in Maine is suicide.

Secret Agent Jane tells on sexist women.

Today I helped make ginger men but guess what? These are not for sugar. They are mostly salt! And flour and color stuff. Yuck! But really cute little cookies. They are small. You actually bake them. Then we add eyes with brushes or markers. These tiny men and ladies go on some of the wreaths we are making to sell. I mean these are really adorable little men (you can tell by the hat), little men the size of my pinkie almost, and little ladies (you can tell by the skirt).

Beth and Bonnie Loo both kept laughing out of their minds over the men, saying this was the perfect size for men. ALL men. Astrid said they wouldn't be able to get into so much trouble that way. Beth said she'd keep her tiny husband in a jar with holes.

Claire looking back.

And so the leftists, in their persistence and faith in the goodness of humanity, eased into our family's routine for several days at a time, crowding into our evening philosophy salons or rolling up their sleeves to help with this or that chore like cooking, feeding livestock, milking, snow shoveling, even lugging the toilet buckets to the compost bins.

Blake had a habit of striding along in his bouncy boyish way as if to pass you by, a distracted look in his eyes, then hook you with his arm and hug you, press his shaved velvety cheek firmly to yours, and while still staring straight ahead, go on where he was headed, his arm slipping away in a kind of underwater swirly-swirl.

Jip helped herself to our sinfully abundant maple leaf candies kept cool in canisters in the pantry hall, but fretted, "I'll lose my teeth and gain fifty pounds before we're done with this project."

One day, they helped us load a truck with pine tables and rockers, headed to Portland to a friend of Gordon's named Tony Corsetti, this furniture traded for many ten-pound trays of mackerel, sole, flounder, bluefish, and halibut, which we were picking up in season through the year. Afterward, Blake and Olan had stood there in the cold open bay of the furniture shop, staring out at the way the loaded truck rolled down the grade nice and easy in low gear, and the November day was gray and frigid and yet delicate. No breezes. Blake murmured to Olan, "Anarcho-mutualism."

Olan nodded.

Geraldine and I glanced at each other.

Then Jip said gravely, "The IRS has another word for it."

Olan looked at me, then back at Blake. "I believe our Settlement friends take many chances . . . like Gordon told us a while back . . . a lot of little broken laws."

"Exactly," said Jip. "The Settlement exists *entirely* in the spirit of revolt."

Geraldine was walking away to meet a crew in the parking lot. But I tarried.

Olan said, "Every damn agency probably has *the Settlement* written in lipstick on the wall. We *heart* the Settlement." And he shoved his chilled hands into his pockets, Scandinavian that he was.

I saw animal-lover Billy watching a yellow-and-white collie mix slumping into a corner of the Quonset hut with something chewable.

The next morning after I cleared one of the window shelves of new snow and poured my crow friend his cracked corn brunch, he burst onto the scene with a gift for me, a lug nut sans rust. I thanked him with a deep bow and added it to his other gifts displayed on my bookshelf. A brass-colored button with anchor. Clothespin spring. One golden eyeglasses bow. Snowshoe buckle (I think). Two earrings, not matching.

Of course these weren't *gifts*. They were *trades*. As I tossed an extra handful of corn, I told him, "You're a most notable anarcho-mutualist."

With one of his satiny black wing-shrugs of fury, he reminded me, "What! Salad again! I ain't no friggin' rabbit!!"

Then that next night after the organizers had gone back to Mass for a few days, a bunch of us were setting up the East Parlor for a guest lecturer from the Historical Society. Beth was saying, "I sent a bunch of those maple leaves home with Jip. And Lee Lynn loaded her up with remedies for migraines and Billy loved those leaf-print hankies Tante Lucienne gave him." She gave her ripply hair a two-handed fluffing. "It's like we've adopted them. These homeless yuppies."

Glennice was thoughtfully arranging the many small pottery trays painted so gorgeous of leaf and flower and bees you hated to smother them with hors'd'oeuvres. She dropped both hands to her sides and said, "I feel like I've known them all my life."

Days later three Settlement trucks in a small caravan . . .

are headed down Heart's Content Road, braking against the steepness and prankishness of what some call the Tenorman curve, others call Suicide Hill. The three trucks, all flatbeds, two with boarded sides, are loaded high with tarpaulin-covered Christmas wreaths, another item that keeps the Settlement books in the black even into the winter and spring.

A lot of people in Lewiston, Brunswick, Portland, and Westbrook, and a whole slew of coastal shops and garden centers, will tell you a St. Onge wreath is the best around. All double balsam. All fresh. Thick. And they come in three sizes. Huge, regular, and a sweet fat little dinner plate size for smaller decorating needs, like a cupboard door or small window.

Along the shoulders of Heart's Content Road, the first four little snowfalls and now this last ten inches are pushed back by the town plows clear to the culvert. Behind the snowbanks the stone walls loom. Part snow. Part rock. Tangles of evergreen and snarly baby beeches with tenacious blond leaves. Crunched-up fern. A few indications of old, old barbed wire and fallen limbs.

Seems there is enough room for Willie Lancaster, who is coming *up*hill, to ease his dump truck and chipper off into the first step of banked snow, the deep tread of his tires crunching down, rolling along easy as the lead flatbed truck of wreaths coming toward him passes. And through the windshield of that lead truck he sees his Bree.

She tips her head and watches in her side mirror, sees that Willie has stopped. Close behind Willie is another truck, a pickup with raised snowplow, its driver Willie's son, Danny. Danny eases to the road's edge behind Willie.

With Bree in the cab are Lee Lynn and little Hazel. Though Hazel has a translatable vocabulary these days, she is now singing wordless, toneless, "Daaaaaaaaaah-naaaaah-daaaaaaaaaahyaaa daaaaaaaaaah" and thwomping her boot on the footrest of the torn and stained child seat.

Bree says, "I got to pull over here a minute."

Lee Lynn's high, almost flute-like voice says, "Sure." But nothing more. She just strokes Hazel's fingers and stares ahead at the steep downhill curve, blue shadowy crosshatchings of winter-bare limbs and pale frozen sun between.

The other two trucks of wreaths ease to a stop, too, close behind, salty mud flaps hanging, engines rumbling, tailpipes thumping contentedly.

Bree drops to the salt-streaked pavement, whacks the door shut, and runs past all the stopped trucks back to Willie, who is walking down the high crown of the road toward her, swaggering. He kind of hops. Like a blue jay. Like a crow . . . smart-ass-type birds known for their energy and insatiableness. His brown beard is less pointy now, getting long for winter, as she had noticed when she got that quickie glance at him in the meat shed a week ago. He wears a black knitted cap today. He is smiling.

Each of them makes a thrusting-along blue-black shadow across the road.

Close now, Bree says, "Hi."

He just keeps smiling, his spaced and slightly protruding top teeth hooked into his bottom lip. He has one hand in his jacket pocket in a kind of funny way.

She says, "I miss you."

He says, "I been too busy to even shit." He begins to pull his hand from his pocket. He says, "Open your hands and close your eyes."

"It's not something alive or gooey, is it?"

His eyes move over her thick hair, fixed with a red-and-green plaid bow, fixed lovely for town and city. He sees her perfect mouth, perfect ears. Perfect throat. And eyes perfect, each eye, perfect unto itself, if only the in-between had accommodated. Her white frozen breath climbing up into this perfect winter day . . . perfect. He says, "I ain't got time for Twenty Questions, baby."

She opens her hands but kinda peeks between her closed eyelids. Willie Lancaster is, after all, capable of tricks.

He fills her hands with two cold hard clams.

Her whole frame jumps a little and she opens her eyes wide fast.

Hard cold chalky creamy-gray clamshells. Whole. Still hinged together.

"Open 'em up," he commands.

She picks one open. Inside, the bottom shell is neatly lined with flowery fabric and a little fabric pillow with a pearl the size of a knocker marble, artificial pearl . . . it would *have* to be. The mother-of-pearl shell's interior has a smiling face drawn on it with black felt-tip marker.

"That's the clam's face," he tells her.

She opens the second clam. Same thing, only the fabric is tiny red stars on a yellow background. "*You* made these?" she wonders incredulously.

"I did," says he.

Pearls. The correlation is all too clear. Pearls *much* larger than the ones in her ornate old Profenno-Depaolo* ring.

One of the smiling clams, the girl one, has a little mistake with its eyelashes. A little slip. Bree hasn't the heart to say that valuable pearls don't come in clams, they come in oysters. But she wouldn't put it past Willie to play dumb, a kind of mischievous dumbness of the kind that sweetens certain things.

Bree can hear the restless squeals of some of the Settlement kids in the nearest truck. She sighs. Then looks at Willie's face, those slightly protruding teeth, his million splendorously exasperating and disturbing flaws, and the way there seems now not to be any frozen visible breath coming from his nose and mouth, the way he is *holding* his breath.

"Willie," she says, her weirdly spaced eyes fixed boldly on his eyes. "I love you." And she hugs his neck, quickly of course, not wanting to ever make trouble, the wife trouble, or maybe even prison, these things he fears so much. Home versus *the cage*.

Then for the rest of the day she is different. Fuller. Her adolescent monster awe for Gordon St. Onge is an even colder corpse. Small ordinary raggedy prickly outlaw Willie-love fills her one hundred percent now.

* She has no idea at this time of the Profenno-Depaolo connection.

BOOK SEVEN:
Bread and Roses

DECEMBER

Bruce Hummer considers growth.

Death played with him last summer. Desolation mattered too much. He'd count the rattling hailstorm of accumulating pills in his desk drawer. But that impulse passed, easily enough that he was delivered cleanly into another day by the sheer force of his work.

Oh, but he playfully imagined his martyr's death by a lone gunman, an old obsession, but in teasing St. Onge with his fun, there came something to his blood, too warm, like tasty steam pinwheeling from hot pie. And so he took his eyes off death.

Now the unbidden giantess is veritable while he, Bruce, is shrinking. He has refused the most recent treatments. He has come to Maine in the silence of December not to wrestle with the giantess but to feel her grow.

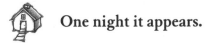

One night it appears.

A white van known to no one, dark tinted glass, Maine plates. In the morning there it is in the snowy lot, nearest the furniture-making Quonset hut, as quiet as though empty but to look at it, it does not *feel* empty. Knocking on the dark glass while yelling, "Hey!" brings no return "Hey!" Trying the doors, you find they are locked. It is a jack-in-the-box, a leghold trap, a Pandora's temptation.

For three days, there it sits, an unsettling spirit. An hour of light snow on Tuesday hangs about it, a veil of creepy wonder.

Word now has it that it is Gordon's wife Tambrah whom no one has seen in four years.

Tambrah with the no-joke scar across her throat like a guillotined princess. Tambrah with the scarred wrists. Always something bitten off her or broken, maybe a toe, maybe a finger. Not a skydiver. No Evil Knievel. Tambrah who once said she wanted to die "when my time comes" by hugging a bundle of lighted dynamite "so I can splatter all of you with my shit and goo!" She, of course, would have wailed this, keened it, or laughed it in trills of lunacy.

Tambrah whose golden brown eyes are wide and white-edged all around, even while calm. Tambrah who has been diagnosed, before and after days and/or nights in jail, as manic-depressive, bipolar and/or schizophrenic, and with all the alphabet disorders. Tambrah who claims people in a room look at her too much, can't be trusted, have been fondled by the devil. Tambrah, when at her most normal, laughs like a goat. But then Tambrah screams bloodcurdlingly in the middle of quiet conversation where you forget for a bit that you don't always get a warning before she jumps the daylights out of you.

Tambrah, a wide-faced lovely young woman; you'd say gorgeous if you didn't know her. If you didn't fear her smashing your stuff, throwing water on your cat, throwing large objects at closed windows.

They say she has now turned up here in Egypt with her boyfriend, the one she left Gordon for . . . no . . . they are saying his name is Mike, *like* the other one but he's not the same Mike she left Gordon for. She is not a close relative of Claire, Geraldine, and Leona, but was a near neighbor at the reservation when they were all young. She's now a late-thirties gal like Geraldine. In the old days, teen years they were friends, before Tambrah was "over the top" and as the old saying goes, *Stick with me and we'll both be in handcuffs*.

The only person who *seemed* not to be made jumpy by Tambrah in those days was Gordon. Like keeping your head during a cyclone while your ship is taking on water, your crew being washed over, the captain keeps his cool and understands that for the time being the ship is alone in the universe.

Then she was gone. *Not* back to Princeton, not anywhere, just *some*where.

So now this white van has just sat parked and mysterious for three days and three nights. It was today that there had finally been someone who saw Tambrah and now everyone knows how Geraldine got a visit. The child is not with her here, Gordon's son, Justin, one of Gordon's heartbreaks, the tyke being carried off in the arms of madness. At least no one has seen hide nor hair of him in these three days.

No one has seen the new Mike, either. He stays in the van, it is supposed. The rumor here is that he is a fugitive from the law, that there is a warrant out for his arrest. For something worse than Tambrah's crimes, such as her refusing to take orders from an officer who had been called when she was turning all the televisions up full blast at Sears.

The rumor has it that New Mike might be a heroin dealer or might be connected to the discovery of a grave of bones, hair, and empty wallet near the reservation.

How in tarnation do such rumors tunnel into the Settlement so thick and furious?

It is said that as Tambrah was making her way up the path to Geraldine's cottage, she, Tambrah, was decked out in Goth attire . . . her brown hair cut very short and spiked and dyed flat cast-iron black. Her part Passamaquoddy, part Euro golden-pink face was made up in stark white.

Geraldine has not been sighted since then, not even here at supper tonight, so how can these details be confirmed or denied?

Yes, the world is here!

Special adults-only meeting in the library a few nights ago. Gordon sat straight backed, his hands in a prayerlike pile on the big table, one hand scarred so pathetically by the rage of his "brother" that it looked in the pinkish light of dim lamps and candles to be constructed from the fingers and sinews of several men.

Behind him the filing cabinets made of pine and painted in storybook colors. So much that is the makeup of the Settlement is soooooo solid, rhinoceros-wide, hulking, enduring.

Above the cabinets on fibrous beige Settlement-mixed-and-mashed-and-dried paper is a drawing made by a child back when the Settlement was born. See the trees that look like green beach balls on sticks, little houses with chimneys puffing happy smoke, chubby-faced sun, the rest of the sky bobbing with purply-red hearts instead of clouds. Wiggly cursive along the bottom reads: CHEZ NOUS (our home).

The Settlementers are explaining that although they've been against the Internet all along they are starting to see it in a better light. Oh, yes, the kids have nagged for months about the wonders of unlimited info. "In-fo," breathed in two golden syllables.

Now the only obstacle to this miracle of the turning century is Gordon. But obviously they see him now as more pliable, more of a door than a wall.

Oh, yes, the computer would have to be hooked up in the little shed-way off Gordon's kitchen, where the only phone line is. And no need to buy the computer itself. Rick Crosman's brother has a new one and wants a home for the old one, just needs some tinkering.

Gordon's tongue cannot grasp words; his brain is all blue light as though shattered to smithereens by a bigger fist than Rex's. His eyes are chilly upon all those faces he loves.

Deep State (if you could hear it).

Joy! Joy! Joy!

Claire reminds us.

Before we go on, I want to talk about Gordon's personal policy of never seriously fondling any one wife in front of others. If it could be said that our life here knew whole swatches of peace, it was because of this wisdom on his part. I've seen some close calls but the loaded ship always swerved around that damning iceberg just in time.

Outdoors is blustery and dark. Indoors the big kitchens are hot and rosy. Welcome!

Gordon's latest guests arrive. He meets them wearing his camo BDU shirt and olive pistol belt. Yes, this is the same shirt that once had the shoulder patch of the Border Mountain Militia, because these visitors are of that mind. With his cane tonking along the brightly tiled solar-heated floors, he leads them to a long table that stretches across the December-dark windows of the big Winter Kitchen, the table making bouncy fluttery blue-and-pink light on the ceiling, so many candles and lamps, so much warmth, and Gordon's even warmer grin of depleted teeth.

It is said that the big guy, Mark Hurley, and his little rosy-faced buddy Roland Sturgeon are both game wardens but this could be another Settlement rumor that has gone winding out of control.

Secret Agent Jane reports.

Some people call the beauty crew the end-door-feen therapy crew. And the Beauty Shop they call it the End-door-feen Therapy Shop. I like the part where I get to cut hair. Washing hair is not so much fun. Old people come to have feet soaks and Vancy, who is homely and pregnant, cuts their toenails. Some people come to just have shoulder rubs, hair brushed, and maybe braids and some little kids just pat you. This sounds sooooo goofy. But it's *science* because of end-door-feens. They squirt out of your brain when people pat you and fool around with your hair. Also, just in case you want to know science, if you sing or dance to fiddles, play them, or bang drums, you get end-door-feens. Really, this is actual science. End-door-feens stop pain and sadness.

This morning I did Glennice's hair in two braids. Short, puny ones. But she said I saved her day for what I did to her brain.

Now it's supper. Paul Lessard says Glennice is "the Vermont maple syrup girl."* She said, "Thank you very much."

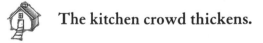

The kitchen crowd thickens.

Claire arrives with her little research group, two hours in the library planning their up-and-coming skit on the Haitian slave revolt of the late 1700s–early 1800s. Saint Domingue it was then. The kids

---

* Such a girl was on a maple syrup label.

are bonkers over the mind-altering war-drumming and the voodoo medicine, the invincibility of a pissed-off people churning in sync, the hot steam of outrage, the mighty waterfall and turbine of bare feet running toward freedom, okay no such thing as freedom in this world but at least to its imagined likeness. To solve an argument, there are *three* Toussaint Louvertures. To solve the argument over which Toussaint Louverture wears the one available fringed general's hat, everybody wears a red or yellow bandanna tied slave-style with the ends in back. Plenty of cardboard swords. Sadly, no one knows the Haitian patois; the kids know only the Maine version, but, oh, well, unlike Broadway's, the Settlement mealtime audience is never overly vigilant of minutiae.

Claire now slides her hand into the cubby that is hers among all those cubbies and sign-up sheets, which create the room-dividing archways between the Cook's Kitchen and the Winter Kitchen. Yes, cubbies for incoming mail, messages, returned books, work gloves, flashlights, pads of paper, pens, whatever fits.

Claire's hand seems stalled, stuck, though nothing in her cubby has disturbing significance. Her dark eyes rip into the eyes of one person, the man who has rescued so many from desolation, then gored them with buck antler thrusts of heckling risk and an embrace no one person can ever fill. His eyes and her eyes come together across the whole sweep of tables loaded with overbearing ceaseless food. The air kind of screels like train wheels on rails. The head honchos of the Greenville Militia or Moosehead Lake Militia, she can't recall which, are arranged there at the long table that is also lined with certain Settlement men who had once been so full of zeal over Rex's militia, all now talking low and secretively and as formally and as self-aggrandizingly as the chamber of commerce. Cory is there looking like a peacock, and strapping Butch Martin with his bushy-to-the-jaws Rex York mustache. John Lungren. Rick Crosman. Jay Harmon. Ben Wentworth.

One woman guest, a Disney Captain Hook look-alike hairwise, cardboard-looking dark curls. Jeans. Cowboy boots.

And the two guys rumored to be game wardens. How can this be? One is the same height as Gordon but an extra hundred and fifty pounds of belly and spare chins and a weighty wide black beard poofing over the bib of his overalls. He is red and hot and his camo T-shirt fits tight over his colossal bare arms that are scaly with eczema or something. Hair short and churchy.

The other guy, a little fellow, *could* pass as a warden, his black-and-red wool jacket hanging over his chair, his eyebrows black and brushy and commanding.

How much more robust Gordon seems with this group than with the Massachusetts organizers, and yet with the organizers he continues to accommodate. *Accommodate.* A kind of falseness? She watches him lean in toward these "Mainer" folks. She knows his heart is scrambling with a hot fit of loyalty, if for no other reason.

Approaching this table straight on now are Samantha Butler and Erin Pinette, Samantha especially prancy in her red jersey and deerskin tunic showing under her unzipped jacket and such tight jeans. Logging boots. Pale hair all aswirl with the static of a just-pulled-off knit cap. Then little square-faced Erin. Both have ear-to-ear smiles. Both smell of the long walk in the dark, that scent that is simultaneously snow-cold and warm-throated.

"Goorrrdonnn," Samantha sings out. "We have our first e-mail. And it's for *you*! Pretty ironical, isn't it?" She spreads a printout of the communiqué over his bare, yet-to-be-loaded plate.

Gordon digs unhurriedly for his old-man reading glasses.

The printout essentially reads backward and the lines are cut off in funny ways. There are three reports from Jip. She says they had put out the idea that the "youthful True Maine Militia and the charmingly infamous Gordon St. Onge" are available for radio interviews, television guest appearances, and college seminars on the dilemma of corporate power overwhelming and contravening democracy. They expected interest but *the resulting response is so voluminous it is melting our hard drive. Ha ha.*

Gordon looks up at the two girls, Samantha bouncing on the heels of her logging boots. He says clearly and coldly with no stammer, "You want me to dance a jig?"

Samantha screws up her nose and, before turning away with Erin in tow, leans close to Gordon's more mangled ear as if to nuzzle, but hisses, "What a big baby."

Secret Agent Jane speaks.

I found a place at the first table. Right there like a beautiful dream is a jar soooo tall with strawberry preserves, seeds so pretty.

I look everywheres. No one is looking. Some kids are singing "Dancing Bear."

I very oozishly slide my hand toward the very big jar. "Uh-uh, Jane dear. Not yet." This is Glennice with coffeepot for people who want it, coffee to pour and pour down their mouths and nobody says stop. But for me, I have to suffer. She pats and smoodgies my arm and the back of my neck. Then off she goes to another table.

Beside me is Misty, who is pretty and has mean cats in her cottage. Very quiet person, till I put my fingers next to the jar.

"No, Jane. You can't pig out on sugar. Your teeth will rot. Think about your pancreas."

I don't even look at her.

Gail who has too much tattoo around her neck is going by. "Move that jar," she tells Misty.

I stick my tongue out at Gail but then I wave with my fingers and smile cuz on the end-door-feens crew, you try to *keep the nice vibes flowing like beautiful waves*, which is Lee Lynn's words she says over and over to make us memorize.

Misty doesn't move the jar much. Just a touch.

I put my fingers back near it and she says, "Cut it out."

I scream with laughing.

Across the table is Jacquie, who has a long ponytail same yellow-streak color as my Mum's hair but longer. We are looking eyes into eyes. Jacquie has gross squash on her plate. And meat pie.

Misty says to her like I'm not there, "Food disorder."

Jacquie's eyes are still in my eyes, then she looks to Misty and says, "Sugar addiction, more like it."

"I'm right here," I say, and I touch the jar.

I like the part in "Dancing Bear" where they sing about the food stuff the queen gives the cabin boy. CANDY, for instance.

Some of the kids sing real high while others go low. Ricardo's guitar is flumming and strumming. The bear is lifting his big foot.

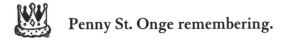

Penny St. Onge remembering.

When the thunder punched the ground and sky about ten chimpanzees* away, most talking, dish clunking, and rustling stopped. After all, thunder had been normal in Maine only in June, July, and August, when normal had been normal, each year now lopping off another stratum of the familiar. But this night our home shivered a long moment, as if being ceremoniously accursed.

Yes, accursed.

Between the tables a figure in Goth attire is walking in such a floaty way you know it is drugs. She hugs herself because in her hurry to leave for here she has abandoned her jacket, so it seems. This is Tambrah, who this morning looked like a chalk-faced beautiful hyped-up impulsive and compulsive mid-thirties female Dracula when she arrived on Geraldine's cottage doorstep for raspberry-and-goat-cheese-filled pastries, coffee, and catching up. But now both eyes are glued shut, vermilion and purple, the bottom lip split, still dribbling blood, transformative work of a fist. New Mike's fist, right? Something has been bothering him?

Tambrah walks and walks the miles from the cubby archways straight to where Gordon sits at a table, an almost abyss of bewitching light, fat candles, and stained-glass candle lamps, dreamy faces and a maelstrom of foods. When he looks up from his prodding fork, he sees her, her seemingly baseball-sized swollen eyes. She stops short of his elbow at the corner of the table, palm to mouth as if to block a wail or weird croak or even one of her big *baa-aaa-ahh* laughs. She lowers her hand and through her eye slits she marvels at Gordon's punched and punched and punched and punched face, his face one of sympathy for hers, like none other.

* Speaking the word "chimpanzee" takes one second. One second equals a mile apart for lightning and lightning's noise when you hear it.

And then.

Bonnie Loo hides both of her large hands in her jumper pockets as if this place and these exhaustingly steamy kitchens were suddenly arctic. This wonderful jumper! She has been trying to find time all summer to spend in the Clothesmaking Shop, just to finish hemming it. It is now done! Roomy enough to be filled by the last months of her pregnancy. Corduroy. Perfect seams. A violet that *varoooms*. Embroidered with small black perky snails gliding across the neck and wide shoulder straps. Her hair rag and jersey are black. She is ever majestic. No one of higher rank here, *if* rank were a spoken-aloud matter. And indeed she almost grows another few inches as she watches Gordon stand up from his chair. Her hidden hands contract into fists.

Secret Agent Jane tells us about the last straw.

One thing Bonnie Loo is good for is bread and right perfectly in front of me near the strawberry stuff is a plate of what's left of a loaf, the nice white kind. Not the stupid beige kind. Even without my pink secret agent glasses tonight I can see the truth about the bread . . . white, chewy.

Kids are singing all the parts of the "Dancing Bear" song, the chimney guy, the ship, the Gypsy, the perfect bear. I know all the parts but I am busy.

I am blobbing the strawberry preserves on a very small piece of the bread, actually still warm. I have soooo much preserves all seedy and red. You can't actually see the bread, which is waaay under. This is scientific, I think, cuz probably sugar makes end-door-feens cuz I feel more zoomy and happy than usual just getting it ready. I do it sooo fast cuz Misty and Jacquie are turned talking to some of the snow-shoveling crew that just clombered in here late.

I look up cuz of a weird noise. It's some weird lady with blood-popped eyes but a very sexy black outfit with tops of titties kind of showing and Gordie has his arms all around her. She is making a sheep noise and he looks sad about it. So then he rubs his whiskers on her ear.

You guessed it. Hands of mothers from every direction grab my plate.

"No sugar now," says one mean voice, Lorraine.

I hug the whole tall jar of strawberry preserves still perfect and beautiful. But somebody grabs me by my sweater sleeves and my arms. The whole jar makes a sound of dynamite on the floor. Noise is everywhere. Strawberry stuff is in the air and some jumps on legs and shirts. Glass with picks. Singing stops.

Well, this is a mighty last straw.

All by itself, my foot whams the table leg so more food and dishes explode like bombs and people yell. Lorraine says, "Ow!" I am so mad. My foot kicks again. And again. Stuff is practically floating, juicy stuff, forks, candles with fire.

"Owwww!" That's me because someone has my hair and my arm.

People screaming, "Bonnie!" cuz it's Bonnie Loo who is dragging me, then smashing me, sort of, against the cubbies.

"Owwwwww!" I am crying and laughing, too.

Bonnie Loo is so strong. Like twenty guys. I *almost* faint cuz of how mean her face is. Her eyes behind her glasses do not love me, never did. But now there's a sound like a cat, "Meeeeee-ow!" It's Bonnie Loo. Crying. So I escape while I'm still alive.

Then somehow, the lady who was over there with Gordie having pats and snuggles, she's over here, standing in the busted mess, goop, and glass! She and Bonnie Loo are eyeballs to eyeballs, Bonnie Loo with murder eyes, the lady with horrible puffed-out eyes but *laughing*. Really, honest, this is true.

And the lady has it in her fingers, one tiny pea, while everyone else is running around screaming, "Watch out for those shards of glass!" and "Watch out for the broken bowl!" and "Watch out!" and "Watch out!"

And then the weird lady says, "Ooooooo food fight!!!" and throws the pea at Bonnie Loo and laughs hideously. I didn't make this up.

Whitney remembers.

I remember Bonnie Loo's face. Wide-mouth grief. We were all trying to help. My mother, Penny, was trying to pull them apart because then Bonnie Loo had a death grip on Tambrah. Tambrah was yowling and wailing *and* laughing and spitting and kicking but Bonnie Loo was just burning through all that, herself panting like a dog, both hands around Tambrah's shoulders and slammed her into the cubbies, gloves, flashlights, papers floating.

My mother Penny whimpered, "Pleeease, Bonnie!" and pulled, and others, me, too, pulled to pry them apart for they were welded by a specter, some convergence of evil outside us all, a god-sized ticktock controlling this awful day. I couldn't recognize even myself, slapping and squeezing Bonnie Loo. My own gulping of air sounded to me as if it was coming from someone else.

Gordon was pushing into the melee now. No cane. His eyes were on Bonnie Loo. In seconds, Bonnie Loo melted away, but it was too confusing to tell where she zigzagged off to. Little Jane had melted, too, backing away into elbows and concerned faces and emergency postures, paralyzed postures.

And then Tambrah, too, melted away.

And my father, Guillaume St. Onge, as in a photograph standing with arched back, dressed as a soldier, chin up with the gray on that chin of his beard pronounced, purely terrestrial, the earth growling with lightning again, its perfect retaliation, its witchery rolling up all around him, you might see in him a kind of torque as the planet itself has the power to integrate souls. That was the legend I grew up with. But on closer look you suspect that legends are concocted by storytellers, not the result of frank witness.

Late at night. Secret Agent Jane considers.

My beautiful Mum. Can you hear me through the air and the miles? Probably not. You never banged my head or hit or pushed or grabbed. You were my beautiful perfect person. Now you are so foggy and so far I can't always picture your eyes anymore, the way they were beautiful blue jewels. And Cherish, my beautiful Scottie, cooked by cops. All my real life is far away. A hundred people and dogs here to be alone in.

Every year the night before the winter solstice day, the festivities begin in a fiery furor.

And so the bonfire on the snowy Quad has been fed truckloads and cartloads and armloads of pine and hemlock branches, rotted boards, and livestock bedding but still it roars for more. *Feeeed meeee*! Take note that this year's solstice fire is circled by not only the usual Settlement-made yard chairs but almost twenty wheelchairs with Horne Hill anarchists sitting in them. Two are playing guitars. Many are with legs out straight, crossed at the ankles while they are just staring hypnotized into the fire.

"What happened to all those crippled people?" wonders Benedicta standing on the cold piazza, the fire lighting her face yellow-orange. And besides that, she is pink-cheeked and plenty warm in her spiffy new deerskin vest over a red sweater over some shirts. Wonderful mauve knitted cap with tassel. Jeans. Sneakers. In spite of the weighty anchor of her big purse she looks hoppity as a bunny. And as usual, her eyes are filled more with jokey stars than sympathy. It's in her voice that there is a soft shading of concern for the faces and figures obscured by distance, smudged by shadows, and bleached by firelight.

Rotund Mary Bean, with walker, standing at Benedicta's side, replies in her quavery way, "That's those hippies. They got the wheelchairs at the dump. They have no pride. They're like seagulls."

Benedicta bangs on the near screening post. "Hey, you! Seagulls!!"

But she cannot be heard over the ruckus and rumpus of celebrants and the snapping popping sizzling voice of the great fire.

Youngsters, teenage and younger, in pagan costume are bunching up to begin their march, not up the mountain as with the early morning Summer Solstice Welcome the Sun parade, but around and around this woody smoke and blinding contorting light of flames.

Wow, there are cloth masks sewn very nicely.

Papier-mâché heads startling and gruesome, mythical and demonic, some with real horns of a cow or goat or buck deer.

Face paint, the skull look being the favorite.

Voices of men in practiced chant behind female voices soaring in high melody or wailing like winter winds.

Pans and kettle covers *bang-bonk!*

Drums build in a crescendo to bring on passion of the blood. One mammoth drum: BARRROOOOMMM!!

Spoons *kuchinka-chink-chink*!

Haunting flutes.

Kazoos *zhip-zhip-zhipping*.

Two small figures riding ponies, riders and ridden all dolled up in deer hides and paint while even tinier figures, the toddling kind, ride older kids' shoulders.

An old man with no eyes gets a solar buggy ride, the cold night stroking his face.

Horne Hill Anarchists push Settlement kids FAST in the wheelchairs, a tooth-jarring ride over the ashy icy "avenue" around the blaze. The kids shriek. Joy! Joy!

More older people join, some quit, groaning, "Enough!" or "Aren't you dizzy?"

It is noted that the white van is gone from the parking area. Tambrah's New Mike never was seen. Ghost man. While Tambrah left the blood of her lip and nose on Gordon's neck and BDU shirt. Also blood on the cubbies and on Bonnie Loo's violet corduroy jumper. So Tambrah was no ghost but now she is once again ghostily gone.

And Bonnie Loo's pink cottage is empty. All her stuff gone. Kids gone. Pet rats gone. Bonnie Loo gone, gone, gone. Free of the convulsions of indecision. Free of Gordon's tender and lofty love which might be worse than New Mike's fist. Free!!! Finally.

More important e-mails.

The organizers are beside themselves with news of *phenomenal public interest* and they are raring to go.

The venerable veteran of the civil rights and anti–Vietnam War movement,s organizer Lenny Britt is joining us on our next drive up. He has had decades of experience and we can all heed his directives.

Gordon never sets foot in the Internet Shop, which has its own outside door with two panes of glass at the top and a cozy pink floral curtain and valance. And also, as we speak, the chattering solar crew is shoveling the snow out of the shedway roof valleys to prepare for one of the boxy passive solar collectors made with tinted glass and roadside soda and beer cans painted black. It's our "Yankee ingenuity style" as some call it, others call it "the Flintstone model." Perfectly matches the larger one on the main part of Gordon's house that heats (sometimes) the dining room.

Meanwhile, Gordon is never never never tempted to reply to any of his now *hundreds* of incoming e-mails, printed out and thrust into his face, many of which begin: *To the Prophet St. Onge.* But also concerning e-mails from his organizer friends, he has no compulsion to rush to the keyboard.

When these messages arrive from Jip or Blake, a True Maine Militia officer (all are officers) will paraphrase Gordon's remarks and press the "send" button.

Tiny kids poking all the buttons at once lose *a lot* of incoming messages and have half a dozen times jammed up the works. They are down there eight or nine at a time, crushed shoulder to shoulder in the wee shed, playing with and poking the wondrous device. They are warned not to get water on it.

WILM Talk Radio

This is a live show. Gordon has refused to do any radio that is taped, super-paranoid creature that he now is when it comes to media. Blake and Jip and Bree are with him at the roundtable of microphones. And the interviewer, Sheila Pratt. Sitting or standing on the other side of the glass partition is Claire, stone-faced as a good bodyguard should be, her hair in a bun held in place by a Tyrolean patterned band, purples and greens. Also there behind the glass are Samantha Butler and Oceanna, both in their best True Maine Militia camo getups. Whitney, ordinary, wheaten sweater and jeans, ponytail and all. Erin Pinette with her winsome smile. Billy. Olan. And the revered Lenny Britt, gruff-voiced, famous within the world of social movements. Note the short-visored flat-tweed early-1900s porkpie cap that never leaves his head. From the table of mikes Jip feigns a big alligator smile at Lenny and he narrows an eye and points at her. The wordless teasing of friends.

At the table, Blake looks at walls, bulletins, gadgets of the radio broadcasting universe, not that he is a stranger to it. Gordon sits in front of his fuzzy mike, his legs apart, but wrapped around the wheeled chair, giving his lengthening dark mustache a few deep thought strokes. In this fluorescent lighting, his brutally scarred face is still Kool-Aid-colored and neither of his ears looks especially human. One bottom eyelid still doesn't hold right. The engineer has just stepped in to adjust all the mikes, explain the earphones, and then further adjust the mike of the interviewer. Sheila fusses overmuch with her collar and her "root-permed" blond hair. As if radio listeners could see her.

Sheila has agreed to let Bree read part of *The Recipe* on the air, before the calls come in. On the table in front of Gordon are his new plastic reading glasses, of an unbecoming style similar to the ones that got crushed in his pocket during the "fight."

Also on the table before him a cup of water. No ice. No ice allowed. Ice rattles. And here's his copy of *The Recipe*, its cover page blaze orange. There is also a copy in front of Sheila. She has underlined and marked up a lot of it.

The engineer leaves quietly and it seems only a moment before he is on the other side of the glass again, jerking a finger up and down, a little like pulling a train whistle.

In his earphones Gordon hears tweetly music and Sheila's trained, almost robot voice welcoming the listeners and then telling them that she has here with her this evening Jeannette Greenberg* and Blake Richardson from the Bread and Roses Folk School plus a founding member of the youthful True Maine Militia, Brianna Vandermast. "Also with us is very special guest, Gordon St. Onge, who some call the Prophet, some call a problem."

The switchboard lights up, all three lines a hot orange simultaneously.

Sheila ignores these lights. For several minutes she prompts the organizers to discuss their mission.

Jip explains that the corporate charter, a piece of paper, has acquired over the years rights equal to flesh-and-blood humans but has so much more power than any human, not only because of many *special rights* granted it, but because it does not possess natural human limitations, like a conscience, fear, or death. Years ago a charter could be revoked by a state legislature and often was, "but now these pieces of paper are immortal."

Sheila pops in with, "But isn't a corporation made up of people?"

Blake says, "It's a piece of paper. It's a fiction. And yet it's usurped the rights of flesh-and-blood citizens *because* it has, in the cases of corporate giants, incredible resources and therefore access to all levels of government that few of us mortals have, thus it influences and, in

---

* Jip.

fact, puts its figurative hand, through the *real* hands of its representatives, to the writing of laws and policy to the detriment of the lives of real people and all life on this planet."

Jip says, "There is absolutely no social responsibility in the design of a corporation's duties. Only to make more profit in the next quarter, more in the next, more in the next, more in the next, ad infinitum, for its stockholders. No matter what, it must grow. Once the growth stops, the whole thing collapses. Growth is its only purpose. There is no moral center to this paradigm. It is as ethical as a leprosy bacterium."

"Give me an example," Sheila sort of croons.

Examples begin to float and flap off the lips of both Jip and Blake, like clouds of seagulls off a herring haul. Sheila interrupts for ads.

Yes, Sheila has creamy blond looks. No chapped lips. No split ends. She could effortlessly alternate between radio and TV. Whenever she speaks into the mike, all true warmth evaporates from her. During the series of bouncy ads paid for by mostly large corporations, her face and voice and gestures regain evidence of a human soul. Then back on the air, she silkily invites Gordon to reveal what he feels should be done about what many people are coming to fear is a growing crisis in America, deplorable acts of racism and sexism and all the issues of gender.

Gordon feels each of her words coming from the earphones as though from over many miles. He is thinking how on the way here, Blake had said, "Sheila is a friend of the democratic cause."

Gordon stares across the table at her. A long moment. He seems confused. His damaged eye widens. His mouth and mustache quiver for the memory of speech. Another few seconds and now he is smiling at her. Mostly with his eyes. No great display of missing teeth.

Sheila's face warms. She smiles. Looks down at her glowing copy of *The Recipe*.

Gordon fondles the reading glasses in his pocket and begins to speak in that deeply soft hoarseness that has melted many hearts. "Good to be hee . . . here. Nice place you got here." He blinks both eyes playfully at Sheila.

She laughs. "Well, it's not exactly my place." Then she prods him to open up a little about "Settlement life." She omits Gordon's Border

Mountain Militia ties as the organizers requested, though Gordon considers this silly. How short a memory does the public have?!!

Suddenly Gordon looks faint. Presses the fingers of his right hand to a spot between his eyebrows, says in a bleary way, "My wife has written a beautiful piece." This is a slip. This is a fucking uh-oh slip.

Sheila quite keenly looks from his face to the sixteen-year-old Bree. Now everyone is studying the *husband* and the *wife* in a state of frozen marvel. But then without stumbling Sheila says, "Before we take calls, Brianna, you have something to read, something you and a member of your group put together as a sort of poetic guide to democracy."

Bree giggles. "Well, Gordon's not a member of the True Maine Militia. He and I did this last summer. I guess I wrote it but he helped me tune it up."

Sheila says quickly, "Well? Let's hear it. This is Brianna Vandermast reading an excerpt from *The Recipe*."

Bree's freaky face cannot be seen by listeners but her smoky voice swirls and circles like the calligraphy that lays out *The Recipe* ingredients. She has no haltings as she reads along about the malignancy of *the* Thing. The Thing is central.

". . . *Our minds are left in tangled dingle dangles straining to simplify, hungry for the slogans, ohhhh, the Thing's management of our airwaves and printing presses and schools, our art! It has penetrated all of us intravenously. No one is spared, but all are transmogrified into numbered appliances for its use. Nothing can be realized until we get it out of our musculature and arteries and glands, even as it dictates from a cloud of power through all its organizations, media, shut doors, sticky webs, and systems, both private and governmental. Our technology has evolved faster than we have. We are dumbfounded primates. The race is on.*"

She looks up into Gordon's eyes. Of all in these rooms he seems the most bewitched by her genius . . . or is it just precociousness? *My wife*, he had said, hadn't he? But he is swept under her voice, her pen marks, by utter awe that never pales. Her eyes move away.

She reads on: "*We are the outside, the wee flecks, the creaturely. But we, compounding our voices, if we could, are a single HURRAH!! We are the mothers, fathers, welders, builders, growers, cooks, soldiers, teachers, young and hoppity, old with the remembering, nobody must be left behind. We must rise like a hot mountain of red ants, and then our size will be known.*

The Thing MUST fear us. THE THING MUST FEAR USSSS! Which comes first, learning who we really are and tearing up the myths? Or does our rising come first? BOTH!!!! Or The Thing won't fear us. LET US BEGIN. THEN ALL WILL BE KNOWN. Pick up the drum."

Bree finishes with an intake of breath just as Sheila introduces a blatting string of corporate ads.

Then back on the air as Sheila turns to the guests. Prods them for concrete solutions.

Jip and Blake suggest some ways to get people organized and educated to "political self-confidence," then various steps for breaking up the power of corporations. Blake says many people have suggested a statewide referendum in Maine, for instance, to change the constitution to specify that human rights do not mean corporations. Corporate personhood would be a crime. "It would be challenged in court but it would keep the pot stirred."

"This is certainly going to get a conversation going," Sheila says, eyes on the mike. Then she glances at the giant, Gordon St. Onge.

He leans back a bit, shrugs his shoulders, flexes his neck, leans forward again, mouth to the mike. "The situation . . . it is life and death. It seems . . . unba . . . un . . . un*bearable* at times, for me personally . . . that we are limited to making it a *conversation*. We're dealing with a poo . . . poot . . . *plutocratic* empire . . . but without an emperor. We can't beha . . . *behead* the emperor. We can't appeal to his conscience. It is a mindless, heartless, flash . . . fl . . . *fleshless* system run by power addicts and supported by the average Jane and Joe, who haven't a clue. It's feeding off the lives and human dignity of two hemispheres. And turning planet earth into a fur ball of carbon." He has been talking into Sheila's eyes. She keeps looking away, then back again, at his eyes, one with its ghastly rip that zigzags into his dark beard, ends at the corner of his mouth. His eyes. Both eyes are frighteningly *sane*.

He pauses now, but before she can cut in, he says, "Protest demonstrations and all these activities are important for us, to drum up the ol' revolutionary spirit . . . but in all of hris . . . horis . . . *history*, peaceful protest has n . . . *never* changed anything . . . and don't tell me about Gandhi . . . his millions of human sicerfs . . . sic . . . *sacrifices* were backed up by a mutiny in the British-controlled Indian army."

Sheila opens her mouth, "But—"

Gordon is talking again. "We're dealing with the coldest, most feelingless . . . puh . . . power this planet has ever known. You can't fight a dragon with a powder puff. Political correctness is . . . soom . . . sum . . . something that is safely institutionalized. Institutions in this American system won't bless something that *really* threatens to change that system. Thi . . . thi . . . the New Deal, for instance, is always held up as an act of human decency by FDR. But it was fear of many armed re . . . re . . . re*volts* and masses of militant labor union actions under way that gave that rich sucker a bit of a nudge. Not to mention that brown guys and gals weren't eligible for most of those New Deal goodies. Obviously, until the Black Power movement, brown people weren't *feared* enough."

Sheila raises a finger. "Let's take our first call." She explains again to the listeners who it is she has with her in the studio and includes the words "challenging corporate power" and "political self-confidence," which it is clear she rather likes as opposed to "armed revolt" and "gave that rich sucker a bit of a nudge" and militant brown people being feared. "Hello. You're on the air," says she.

Gordon doesn't look toward any of the organizers. He knows they are pissed at him.

Bree's far-apart honey-color eyes slither over his big shoulders and the buttons down the chest. His more scarred hand is spread wide over *The Recipe*, almost perfectly centered over: *Pick up the drum*.

And Cory? Cory isn't here. But Cory *is* here? Because all along hasn't Gordon's accommodation to the "Harvardtonians" been a symptom of his temporarily swollen brain? He seems taller each day. Straighter. His workingman's logic is awakening, taking Cory's face. Maybe now Gordon is really an enemy among the Harvardtonians.

Phone caller's voice now coming into Gordon's earphones is deep and deliberate. "Hello, Mr. St. Onge," it says. Then dead silence.

Gordon says, "Here."

More dead silence.

Gordon and Sheila look into each other's eyes and Sheila glances toward the glass room. "Hello," she repeats. "You're on the air."

"Mr. St. Onge," the deep voice also repeats, but in an odd, disconnected way.

"Yes, hello," Gordon replies, in his own deep voice, perhaps a bit too soft. But nobody signals him to speak louder.

The caller's voice: "It's true, isn't it, Mr. St. Onge, that you and your people are heavily armed, have been a bit obsessive with the Armageddon as prophesied in the Bible? Sources tell me that you people have stockpiles of weapons that are illegal, stockpiled food, bunkers. One source said you're slyly dealing banned assault weapons to the cities along with your milled lumber, produce, Christmas trees, and wreaths . . . paying nothing to the IRS. This is baiting several agencies at once to a showdown, am I right? Sources tell me that the Department of Education and the Department of Human Services have both had problems with you, Mr. St. Onge. Children forced to work, kept from learning basic reading and math, children dirty, naked, underfed, sexually abused, primarily by yourself . . . in fact, that name mentioned a few moments ago . . . Brianna . . . that is Brianna Vandermast, only fifteen years old . . . you called her *your wife*. I'm told that people of your Settlement, when *outside*, seem dazed by who knows what? Some would testify against you, but are afraid. Could you comment on these allegations, please, Mr. St. Onge?"

Gordon fingers his more mutilated ear. For it has started to squirm mightily. He picks up the cup of iceless water, his mouth still close to the mike, and presses the rim of the cup to his lips, drinks. Noisily. Like bathtub water gurgling down the drain.

In the elevator leaving the studios, Jip wastes no time asking Gordon in a low whisper,

"Bree is your *wife*?"

He says, "Yes."

Jip looks away from him, up at the changing elevator numbers, which are digital and red, as on a microwave oven. Then, "I had assumed most of the untoward accusations I'd heard before I met you were horseshit."

"She's not fifteen," he says.

Bree and Claire standing nearest him wince. Then Bree giggles. "I'm a Libra."

"You mean you're sixteen," Jip hisses.

Lenny Britt, just beyond Claire, and not a lot taller than Claire, says, "We need to talk. We need to work through some damage control. This whole project is getting wobbly legs."

In the following days.

The mail increaseth. The messages at the gate increase. The phone calls increase. The e-mails on both the Vandermast and the Settlement computers are in vivacious spilling-over mode. Some callers want to be part of things. Some callers want to see Gordon arrested. Some callers just grunt.

Claire's memory of then.

There were more radio shows over the next couple of days. Three in southern Maine, one in New Hampshire, three in Boston. The rides were long. I stuck close to him and feared for him. The organizers were torn up over the revelation about teenage Bree. And of course Gordon's verbal spotlight on what they called "armed confrontations."

But they couldn't let go of "the Prophet," this juicy carrot that was a draw to the public's eye and ear, heart and mind, where it would also be immersed in a hidden history and a hidden *present*, and the question: How can the people challenge the corporate "it"?

Gordon was scolded.

Gordon was flailed.

Gordon was prepped. In all those critique sessions, sometimes only twenty minutes, their juicy carrot got boiled. And so for the next few radio shows he acquiesced. Meanwhile, there were the usual devious and conspiratorial secret musters of the True Maine Militia officers. You get the picture.

Secret Agent Jane at Christmastime. Another good-bye. She speaks.

It is wicked late. But nobody says, "Time for bed." People are here from other places, even South Portland and Canada. Some guys are around the stoves even though people in charge let all the stoves go out. But lots of pies. Cherry and pudding kinds are my type. Some are round. Some are made in big trays.

More people come in. I get another piece fast before it gets wiped out. Nobody says, "Don't, Jane." Probably because all the mothers, including Josee (who is where I live now), are nowheres here. They all go to the East Parlor, which has the best piano for singing and showing off for the other people from South Portland and Canada. East Parlor is waaaay across the Quad thing.

So nobody here in the Cook's Kitchen looks at what I eat or what time it is. These guys are laughing and stuffing whole gobs of pie into themselves like dogs, no plates, no forks. Just grab and pull. So I get another piece of the cherry kind and nobody cares.

All these guys are wearing hats and they are in their jackets and boots cuz the whole place is like outdoors, freezing.

They are all laughing, laughing, laughing. They lap their goopy hands. Some are drinking beers and weird stuff. Like I say, these are all guys. Except Cannonball who just barked to come in from the piazza which is even more *freezing*. Now she is sniffing some legs.

You know for a minute when my eyes saw Cannonball my brain thought she was Cherish, *my* Scottie dog who I still love, who is dead because of cops.

Nobody even looks at me, they all just laugh laugh laugh at all their stupid stories about hunting. One's about a fish. Fine. I'm the only one on the planet that knows the kitchen izzz *cold*. I don't have my coat on. It would cover my outfit, which is all white like an angel and very Christmassy. I decide to secretly drop a little blob of pie to Cannonball.

She is poking one guy, Danny Lancaster, with her rubbery nose.

I look the pies over and the mincemeat one has real meat in it . . . gross . . . but a good choice for dogs.

I secretly drop a blob. Her nails go click click click over to me and the blob goes down the hatch. Her eyes look me up and down, up and down and her tail quivers like a rattlesnake.

Danny Lancaster, whose hat is orange, is looking at me and then at Cannonball, and says, "No pie for her. No sugar."

Jerk.

Door opens. In come more guys. Also a brown dog with flap ears. Cannonball races over and becomes nose to rear with the brown dog and brown dog nose to rear with her and they go around and around. Cannonball lifts her lips and her giant teeth are white. Grrrrrrr.

Danny Lancaster pushes his beer bottle onto one of the cold stoves and swipes Cannonball up in his arms, then holds her high over the brown dog. Cannonball goes totally berserk. Garlgakgalgakag!

Someone pushes the brown dog out the door with his foot. "This could save your life, Clovis," the guy with the foot says laughing.

Everyone's laughing. Danny Lancaster is smiling a very nice smile. He is a mess. Holes in his jeans so you can see his long underwear. And some smoodges on his jacket. You can tell he doesn't care about Christmas. Not like you're supposed to. His work boots and cuffs are wet from snow and also ratty. It's a shame. But he smiles even after everyone isn't. It makes me happy inside because his smile has happiness and love, sort of.

He says, "Watch this." He still has Cannonball in the air so her jaws are still snapping in the direction of where the brown dog went out and her stubby thick bear legs are pedaling away.

Lou-EE looks sad. He's not Cannonball's owner but he is her friend. He doesn't like her to be a fool. I keep seeing my Cherish in flashes, like a frosty ghost all over Cannonball. I'm not kidding you.

Danny Lancaster announces, "This you all are about to see pertains to climate change! You may not believe in climate change, but this dog *believes*!" Danny's eyes go around on all the drinking, chewing, slurping, smiling faces and then stop on me. He smiles bigger. And more lovish. "Wanna see?" he asks me in a really nice voice.

I nod very fast. I feel fast all over.

Slow, slow, slow the Danny guy lowers Cannonball to the floor, and then holds her so she can't move. Her eyes are looking forward to her trick, whatever it is.

Danny says, "Ready? Ready for a climate change disaster?"

I nod fast. His smile has a little space in his top teeth. He is so nice to me now, looking in my eyes, and then everyone is yelling "Ready!" and so do I.

So now Danny screams this out: "Ride! Theee! Tornado!!!"

Cannonball's hind feet squeeze together and she spins. Once. Twice. Three times. Each time, between spins, she does a spiffy thing . . . for one second she stops. Then she does three more spins. And a stop. Then three more spins. Then done. Not dizzy.

Everybody cheers.

Cannonball's tail is stiff and quivery, her eyes swiping over all the clapping hands.

Then everyone forgets and they go back to talking about shooting deer in the head.

But I am thinking about how Cannonball is like an angel to me. I watch Danny who isn't looking and I hold out a secret piece of meat from the pie Cannonball likes. She comes closer on the blue and green and orange floor, click!click!click! of her dog nails, her eyes on my hand and there it goes. She even laps my fingers, her tongue squishy and lovish. With my other hand I reach fast to pat her and you won't believe but her head inside my fingers turned into iceberg teeth and she bit me. GRHGGRRRAR-RAKK! RAKK!

"Don't!" Danny screams at me. "She don't like kids!!"

I hold very still. I hold my hand. She didn't actually bite me bad. But sort of burning.

I say meanish, "Don't worry about it!" and turn around so no one will see my dorky tears. Do you think Cannonball *is* Cherish's actual ghost, very mean now? Cuz everything about the world is very very very wicked mean.

Meanwhile.

More e-mails. More e-mails. More. More. More. More. Not to say the phone in Gordon's kitchen doesn't ring. Oh, that, too. Yes, and the weighty billows of US mail. So add an extra horse to be towed along behind Eden's mare. Or Oz's. And the message barrels down by the gate. Can't even squash their lids down all the way. So add another barrel. And those cars that drivers park along the tarred (and heavily salted) Heart's Content Road, waiting to snap a picture or smilingly accost someone. Lots more this week than last. One got stuck in a snowbank trying to make a U-turn.

JANUARY

Claire recollects.

After New Year's Day we started doing the seminars at colleges. We brought some of the Settlement tots with us for the "adorable effect." For instance, Minky. Silka. Rhett. Leo. Michel Soucier. Gus. So we had a rangy convoy of vans and cars, some with the Mass plates, some Maine.

"There," said Gordon one night. Awe was in his low voice. We were taking that unpaved road out of New Hampshire working our way back to Route 160 when up ahead there was manifested before us a jumbo TV satellite dish ablaze in hundreds of red, white, and blue Christmas lights, hundreds. I mean HUNDREDS.

This road was thick of forest. Not many homes. No vistas. Just the woods and this big bewildering fantastical *thing*. As we came alongside it there were, several yards into the woods, dim window-glimmers of an eensy house. The dish was bigger than the house.

Gordon clamped one huge hand over his eyes. He was laughing. "America," he purred. "It's such a wicked weird place."

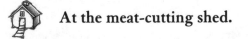

At the meat-cutting shed.

Bree has signed up to be one of Aurel's crew where they will be "doing" three lambs. She arrives early. Dane St. Onge and Evan Martin, both younger than Bree by a year, are standing in heavy jackets, Dane leaning on a snow shovel, Evan leaning on the jamb of one of the shed's open doors. Morning sun angles in. The roof eaves drip.

Gotta wait for Aurel and Rusty with the truck of lambs. No sheep-dogging it here yet at the Settlement.

Bree smiles and nods as the two boys plot and stew and bitch and joke. Evan's face has more cruel pimples today than yesterday but his tawny eyes have such directness that it's clear he knows his worth.

Finally, when the truck arrives and things begin to happen, Bree removes Marian St. Onge's mother's thick pearly ring, as its complex engravings tend to collect blood. "Don't let me forget it's here," she tells Evan as she slips it down over the calendarless calendar nail in the inside center of the open door.

From the the ice white and punky gray dead top of a spruce at the foot of the trail that takes you up to Pock Hill where the hunting camp is, honeymoon camp, Silverbell's last home, whichever your association is with that, Claire's philosophical wiseacre crow friend watches Bree's hand retreat into the shadows beyond that open door. He gives his midnight feathers a shrug of cunning judiciousness.

He listens to the silence of humans, the baaing of Shropshires.

A swan-shaped cloud glides by overhead.

The woods are achingly silent.

When there's a decisive crow-wings *thwomp! thwomp!* behind them and two of the humans turn to see Marian's ring being filched, Dane laughs and Bree's mouth makes a perfectly round "O." Then she says with a soft fatalistic gulp, "There goes my special ring. Into the sky."

FEBRUARY

Critical thinker of the present era.

The earth was small, light blue, and so touchingly alone, our home that must be defended like a holy relic. The earth was absolutely round. I believe I never knew what the word round meant until I saw earth from space.

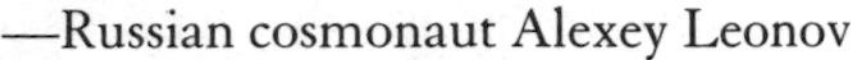

—Russian cosmonaut Alexey Leonov

The screen is charged up over the following crisis news.

The surgery on the polyp on the left side of the president's tongue went well today. At ten a.m., medical spokespersons confirmed that the president was sitting up in his bed drinking a nutrient drink through a straw. It is not known yet when he will be able to drink orange juice, which is high in acid. We'll turn you over to Frank now, who is speaking with Dr. Theo Langer of Harvard University, expert in surgeries similar to what the president underwent. Frank? . . .

See here. Somewhere out there in America.

This loose thing hanging from a few feet of his mother's clothesline rope tied to the garden hose hook in the cellar stairwell. This weighty object had been a boy, age fourteen, twenty minutes ago. Thin. Long-armed. Yes, his parents loved him. But do not believe the Beatles. That *"All you need is love"* business is a sad and foolish myth.

Well, well.

On this matter, the screen seems to be blank.

And so.

The world turns. More swollen. More noisy. More desolate. More hollow.

Secret Agent Jane gets serious.

Believe me. Hearts are for babies. My new spy glasses aren't pink, either. Kirky says these give a look of a killer robot. Now I'm going *on the road* with everybody, I need to be serious. Astrid, one of the mothers, who loves to sew, made it . . . my spy "trench coat," which is for when you are serious. I can carry *ten* spy books and all my pens and stuff in the pockets. Also it is black for when I do night. I have done night, yes.

I ride with Gordie and Blake and Claire sometimes and my job is to help Claire with the atlas. This is to go and do our "panels" and Q and A with college people who want to get democracy for America. What I want is to do REAL SPY JOBS, not just fooling around with Q and A. I want to sneak into the president's house. I will stand outside doors and draw in my books all the awful stuff he says. We are called CITIZENS. I learned this. And our big job is CITIZENSHIP if you know what it is yet. Bree and Whitney and Geraldine said at supper once it is insulting when we are called CONSUMERS. Butchie says, "Whoa, that's like being called a garbage disposal," a grinding thing in some people's sinks.

We are CITIZENS. If I can actually catch the president and governor calling us CONSUMERS I will write it bearing down hard and make their faces, too, and they will be exposed.

For now . . . you guessed it . . . I have to ride in the same van most times with Montana to go do Q and A and you know patience is a virtue, which I learned is actually true.

Bree has this to tell us about the last one of their first batch of seminars with the Bread and Roses Folk School.

We showed up real early to do a panel discussion in a big seminar room at Dartmouth. Up front there were two long tables where the organizers and a few of us founding members of the militia dropped smilingly into seats. There were rows of folding chairs facing us. Sammy preferred to stand and do little stretches. Graysha Carver, not a Settlementite, but one of our Egypt town-person militia officers, she drove her own car with our convoy of seven cars and two vans. She and Liddy Soucier and Alyson very efficiently reached for some chairs still folded against the wall and set them up for all the younger kids like Jane Meserve. The *real* small-fry like Gus sat on laps. Gus's face was tear-streaked from protesting what he could plainly see was another boring hour or more in a brick building. Gordon held him and rubbed his ears.

I sat next to Gordon but Claire didn't take the chair on his other side. She stood behind him. Her plaid flannel dress accentuated her roundness and her shortness. Her huge plaid breasts were *out front* like the noses of two plaid Delta airliners. And her old-timey specs accentuated her dark glare. *Everything* on her was silently accentuated.

When someone from the school saw that Gordon had quickly drunk all his water, the guy filled the glass and set it on the table and Gordon nodded thanks. The guy said in a low but sort of happily hysterical way, "A *lot* of people asking where this is taking place! Professor Stengel wishes now he'd reserved thc auditorium."

Gordon snatched up and drank the second glass of water just as fast as the first like chugalugging beer, then burped, not softly. Gus picked up the empty glass with two hands and copied the burp, his dark eyes fiercely proud.

I could see in Gordon's expression something like a mix of sorrow and defiance, which actually radiated from all over him like steam off a cold pond. Was he wondering why we were here? Yes, it felt a little bitty bit like the thirty-two governors' wives all over again. By "juicy carrot" did the organizers really mean sideshow?

Oh, yes, all of us Settlementers had been soooo saintly at these seminars and panel discussions so far. A halo over each and every head. Even Montana the Mouth and her little brother, doleful Rhett. Even me! It was suspenseful. It was eerie. Like when would the cork pop off?

So here we were, the last stop on our itinerary, the room filling fast with spectators and our militia's exchanges of wicked glances.

Claire rested a hand on one shoulder of Gordon's sweater vest. His flannel shirt was all in greens from a favorite bolt of the Settlement's Clothesmaking Shop crew. His green eyes were keen on some thought as though through rifle sights on the heart of a charging bear.

I looked down very often at my naked finger, missing what the crow stole. I'm sure Gordon noticed it gone sometime since the crime was committed but I didn't tell and he didn't remark.

It was still early but there were a lot of people wending their way through the crowded doors, more than there were folding chairs. Quite a few people now stood or leaned. Or sat on the hardwood floor. The big room was packed. Another student came to explain to us that this turnout was a complete surprise considering there had been only an interdepartmental bulletin and flyers for the hallway boards. Honoring fire codes was going to be an issue.

Gus gave his Italian loverboy smile to all the persons in the front row. Some smiled back. More and more people came squeezing in sort of sideways, then the doorways looked perfectly clogged.

So then it was time and we did our thing. Halos were shimmering. Angel wings folded primly.

Except Sammy. She paced in her tight corner. She pulled off her Comanche head rag, stuffed it into a pocket of her BDU jacket, puffed up her cheeks, blew out. Indeed, it was getting warm. Sammy's white-blond hair had more swish to it now. She was accelerating.

The organizers told a little history, made some fine points about charter revocation and getting courts to roll back decisions that had given corporations human rights "even before women and people of color had those rights." They elaborated on the Supreme Court's ability to change the constitution . . . that these nine justices are appointed, not answerable to the people. "Aren't WE the people supposed to be the authority?" asked Blake. "So the myth goes."

"Quo warranto," asked Olan gravely.

Billy remarked how what are *called* liberal Supreme Court justices are liberal only on the people-dividing social issues. "But all of them are *neo*liberal on economics, meaning, as we all know, *let the great beast run wild*. Presidents of both parties are appointing ever more neoliberal justices."

Jip pointed out that even when the people vote, big money schemes misinformation, so even the so-called right to vote is disabled.

Meanwhile, Gordon was taking in each face of this audience and, with his own banged-up face, smilingly acknowledging each. Those standing at the edges of the crowd kept jostling slightly, trying to get a better view.

Gus leaned back into his father's chest and began to suck his thumb. Dreamily. Wagged one small moccasined foot.

There was a college newspaper reporter and two mainstream newspaper reporters all taking notes. And there were audiotape recorders set up on our table and one video camera on a tripod in a back corner of the room, sometimes blocked by the heads and shoulders of those people standing. At one point Gordon picked up a pen and gave one recorder a push toward the table's opposite edge, then winked at me mischievously. But otherwise he was being a lamb of accommodation.

When our panel began with the Q and A, an unbreakable-looking dark-haired woman said with great feeling, "What you're saying is that the big protest demonstrations we're hearing about such as the IMF protest in New York, the WTO protest in Seattle, and so on are not enough, and calling for this or that injustice to be rectified or a few laws to be changed . . . this is not enough . . . that we need to make *big* adjustments . . . for instance, the contracts clause, or that Supreme Court ruling in 1886, giving corporations human rights, or maybe even the way the Supreme Court has the authority to make such a ruling. And how justices are chosen? In other words, we need to throw out the *design* of our government?"

So the organizers got into some heat while all our cute tots and us of the True Maine Militia and Gordon just twiddled our thumbs so to speak and Claire flexed the fingers of her hand deeply into the weave of Gordon's sweatered shoulder as if she and he were arguing through the pulsations of body heat.

A small late-seventies woman in a dark pantsuit, a cap of straight white hair, glasses in hand, smiled indulgently. She spoke in a husky almost male voice, "I was in the Battle of Seattle and the IMF-World Bank demonstrations and Quebec City and . . ." She raised her chin. "A few . . . " She looked so *serene*! "others."

People sitting close to her smiled and sighed appreciatively. She resumed, "There were, indeed, many people at these demonstrations who challenged the whole paradigm of corporate personhood."

Jip responded, saying she knew that and "that's important, but in addition to protest demonstrations, we need to educate all people on everything from labor history and corporate history to foreign policy and how these all knit together, and to do this in ways that work for all these people such as plays, music, movies, picnics, and so on. We need to especially reach people who don't cotton to words like 'hegemony.' "

Chuckles.

Billy spoke through a stuffy nose, "To cut the corporate jugular, there has to be a force of millions decidedly but *peacefully* standing on the toes of leaders who work to maintain the status quo."

Olan cut in, "The world can't survive if the population remains in childlike darkness as to the transgressions and usurpations of globalized out-of-our-control corporate power."

Just two gleaming eyes under that very squashed-down porkpie cap and Lenny Britt's snarl: "The corporate charter . . . *free* trade, *free* market, freedom to *hide* their money . . . *their* freedom means *our* slavery. And there is no status quo, by the way. Unchallenged, this thing is going to balloon out to every inch of this world. And permeate to the bone. It'll make lives like ours obsolete. By the present system what will be done with the redundant people? We already know the answer to that. Check out your local privatized prison. And recall . . . when they came for the poor and the lawbreakers, I did not speak up and so then they came for me and no one was left to speak up for my well-behaved risk-free ass."

Applause.

"*The Recipe*," said the old deep-voiced gal with another long, slow smile of perfect off-white teeth, "is magnificent. But it is . . . not written for the common man or woman. It is not heavy with jargon. But it is literary. Lots of subtleties."

To this Olan said, "There is another version but we thought you all here would dig this one."

Jip said, "The True Maine Militia's young people have placed several op-eds, written in a way to rouse a lot of souls. Hundreds have rallied around them and their message. I myself congratulate them."

From the seated and standing True Maine brass came a burst of cheering, hooting, and self-congratulatory sharp whistling.

Finally, an English actress-looking person spoke in the very voice you would imagine, throaty and . . . well, not English . . . but la-di-da, sort of, "What can we do? I want to get started ahf-ter lunch."

Sympathetic and appreciative laughter all around the room.

Oceanna waved an arm and Jip gave her an encouraging nod.

"Whatever your style," Oceanna advised. "There's no right or wrong thing, really. It takes lots of ways. I think corporate power is only part of the problem. So it'll take all kinds of rearrangements . . . to . . . make it . . . uh . . . a cozy homey life for everybody."

Then our sassy Samantha exhaled with vast impatience and called out how the turn-of-the-century anarchist organizer Lucy Parsons had suggested to a poor bum who was about to commit suicide that he do it by tying a stick of dynamite around himself and "taking a few rich people with him."

Billy quite audibly tsked.

Some in the rows of chairs groaned.

"That's murder!" trilled a youngish woman with a button on her sweater that read: MAKE A DIFFERENCE.

A fortyish guy in a golf shirt and backward ball cap narrowed his eyes on Gordon, not Samantha, and nearly bellowed, "The use of violence is *never* acceptable!"

Sammy gave her silky white-blond hair a swish. "I was just clueing you in on some history. You must be part of the crowd that likes to burn books?"

Graysha Carver cut in, her brown topknot looking exploded due to static, maybe *internal* static and fury. "Maybe, sir, you're saying that *remembering* violence is not okay. Maybe you want to pretend humans are not subject to human nature. That we're all just Tolkien hobbits."

"Impossibly incorruptible," Whitney twittered.

"The thing is a thing," I offered. "The system. It won't *feel* dynamite. But *we* earthlings sure are feeling *its* cruelties."

"Cruel drool!" crowed Termite and Rusty in boyish goofiness.

"And there is no face to the system," Whitney added. "*No face*. So we blame each other."

The golf shirt guy again glared at Gordon, not us girls, as if Gordon pulled our strings, eh? Ha!

Gordon just smiled at the guy with closed lips like a smiley-face button. Then he looked down across his little son's chubby knee to his empty water glass.

Bree remembers more.

Claire touched the nosepiece of her specs. Claire never spoke at any of these affairs, though her gestures were thunder. Her eyes. Said. It. All.

When Gordon finally opened his mouth, I was jarred into remembering how kaboomingly I had fallen in love with him that early summer, how, yes, he could be loud but when he soft-talked, it wrapped around you as if his voice were his broad green woodsy acres of land minus the *Anyone trespasses will be shot* signs. "There are people out there . . ." He jerked a thumb toward the tall windows, "whose lives are agonizingly s . . . sti . . . stee . . . *strained*."

Silence. Just creaking radiators.

He made a soft puff-puff sound, looking down into his toddler son's drowsy eyes. He looked up, "Self-defense being seen *by citizens* as immoral has been a dangerous turn. It has been a product of political treachery for the benefit of the lordly . . . and by intense media mind-fucks . . . and mostly foundations that have turned valid peace movements into self-castrations . . . and turned . . . schow . . . *scholarship* into booster clubs for the paralysis of a once rebellious nation that made labor equal to the boss."

Gordon's halo clanked to the floor, which was already littered with the fallen halos of all us adolescent girls.

About four . . . or five . . . hands had already shot up, now a couple more, but Gordon ignored them, looked down at his water glass, and spoke to it: "Things look different at the other end of the lop . . . lok . . . *lost* home when home is our soul . . ." He closed his eyes, the only closed eyes in the big room.

More people shot up their hands, thinking he was done.

"And all that's left to you," said he softly, softly, "is exhausting servitude or drug dealing and you're told that exhausting servitude is the more honorable . . . and when you are a mini-Atlas with the weight of the world ski . . . skar . . . *square* on your chest . . . yes, on your chest!, on your heart muscle! . . . the full fucking weight of the world . . . millions of little Atlases, each a firmament unto his or her self . . . no relief in sight. And when what little dom . . . di . . . i . . . *dignity* you had is taken away . . . sometimes your children whom the experts say you don't love, are run off with in the night by good-doers. Drugs! Oh, drink! Those devil soothers and the community of fellow drugged persons who, down to the bricks with you, don't look *down* on you as the correct people look down on you." His eyes swept the room.

Oh, that silent room.

"And so the sickened culture grows," Gordon softly went on. "Some with homes, some without. And by the way, why are people driven from their home by war in Central America or Yugoslavia or Iraq considered victims of human rights violations whii . . . whe . . . *while* here in our exceptional America, when you get driven out by bad luck via tax men and land*lords* and banks and these complex *civilized* pressures, you're considered an object of trash. Oh, yes, an object of *trash* . . . unless you're of dark skin . . . then that becomes a race issue, which is a red herring only it's a f . . . *fucking* red WHALE because then no one has to talk about the big vacuum cleaner in the sky, the thing that has no *unified* population to challenge it. It becomes an entirely different conversation." He squeezes his eyes shut, then opens them again, smiling so broadly, that his missing teeth are no secret here.

"But I like to imagine a unified population cutting the hose and nozzle to that system that the fiends and archfiends of capital are sucking the bejeezus out of our society with." Gordon sighs. "But how is that done? H . . . hal . . . howl . . . *how* can it be done so that the great fiends of capital don't respond violently? Because there . . . is . . . no . . . other . . . way . . . but to cut that hose. You can write to your senator. You can by . . . bck . . . boycott stuff. But that has to be paired with force. We're warned that we'll get hurt if we use force. NO FUCKING SHIT."

"Nosh its!!" Gus laughs heartily around his wet thumb.

Gordon narrows his eyes, still ignoring the raised hands. "Pet dogs don't usually bite. But there are a lot of people of all races here in this exceptional him . . . hi . . . *home*land who, whether we like it or not, aren't petted as much as the rest of us pets by the big hand and are justifiably on hair trigger. They want to fight *some*body. Politicians and talk radio and public radio and so forth suggest we all fight *each other*, the identity wars. Don't look *up*!! Look *across*!! That, my friends, is fascism. *Break the force of people*. That's what fascism is. Mobilize the millions into a whirlpool of mean-assed and self-virtuous stupidity."

His green gaze chopped up with flinches and blinks of that rogue eye sweeps over the shoulder-to-shoulder standing and sitting people.

The audiotapes and tripod video camera rolled on. The room was still full of raised hands. And frowns. Two pairs of people shouldered their way out.

Gus wiped his wet thumb on Gordon's sweater vest.

I caught sight of the organizers looking at each other darkly.

Then I saw Samantha over there standing arrow straight with raised fist. Then Whitney and Oceanna and the others around the table all went fist up. I raised my fist then.

I could see a guy, like in his thirties, standing by the tall, stout, old, many-paned windows, the guy in a professional's light tan shirt, little stripes, blond hair cut expensively. He was for some reason pointing at me. He called out, "How unfortunate, if all you need is just a little working-class identity, that you use the word militia. Why not call it a team? By using the word militia, you're encouraging this kind of thinking, encouraging others, particularly the young and foolish or the insane . . . to settle problems this way with—"

"Direct action?" This was our Egypt village neighbor Graysha.

"No," the guy said thinly. "Terrorism."

"This isn't about sports," Oceanna called out. "Team is a high school word."

"Exactly," the guy lamented. "You're all too young to understand the realities of war. Mr. St. Onge is old enough to imagine . . . but perhaps it's a code of honor for the conservative right-wing mind-set that I'm sure he's steeped in."

Another man said, "With Oklahoma City . . . with the bombing . . . and the Columbine school shooting, 'militia' just isn't the name you should pick."

Gordon said thickly, "You see, the intelligence agencies dislike union organizers, protest demonstration organizers, the American Indian Movement, the Black Panthers, and back in the day, they went after Martin Luther King Jr., and now high school kids against military recruiters in schools are termed a *credible threat*, animal rights activists, Earth First! and Patriot Movement . . . fi . . . fk . . . folks all on the same list . . . enemies of the state all the above. Sir, we in this room did not create the militia movement. It was already there. Sometimes . . . mal . . . maf . . . manifesting itself horribly . . . as we already noted, the manipulated wrath aimed at other American folks or refugees rather than the overlords. So if there's something about the mis . . . mish . . . *militia* movement you d . . . din . . . don't lof . . . *like*, all that right-wingness lathered up by political leaders and well-funded talk radio and so forth, do you think it wise to turn your back on it? Or to antagonize it? Get involved. Get inside. Infiltrate. Be a goodwill operative. Bring your too . . . to . . . *tolerance* and education into it. Get intimate with these people. Know these people directly . . . not filtered through those who benefit from an ununited people and psyops expertise."

He rubbed one eye tiredly.

People waving their hands side-to-side like some sort of suboceanic grasses were still trying to catch his eye.

He smiled at them like a benevolent prophet, then went on. "I am . . . not . . . nah . . . *not* promoting a US citizenry attack on the government. I feel . . . at times . . . like a martian . . . watching sadly . . . these facts of life . . . helpless. Helpless, yes. Like our Samantha here . . ." His eyes pressed Sammy's profile. "Like Samantha, I like to think this college is where we put on our thinking caps. It's serious, right? It's naw . . . nack . . . *not* a little swim in a dish of sugar."

He winked at Sammy.

She wagged her head.

He went on. "*Think* about this, for instance. We fear the oligarchy's violence, its immeasurable force, so we allow whatever it wishes . . . like smooching with the Guatemalan dictator, smooching some and installing others such as in Iran . . . the history is ugly. But, oh, we are so damn *peaceful* . . . and we do what the oligarchs command. Better do it . . . or else!" He sighs. "But since *they* don't fear *us*, they make no sacrifices for us. These are facts of life. It's not *my* pleasure that this is so. But I'm not on some *Brave New World* soma."

A voice from the rows of faces hollered, "Violence is not the nature of life! It's cultural!"

Gordon rubbed Gus's chubby ankle, Gus to be a Cory-sized teenager someday but now still a wee suckling without outrage. Time would stretch us all bigger and time would strain both facts and fictions right before our eyes. And Gus would be someone to be reckoned with. Gordon pressed the table with a finger. "Militia is a natural human reaction to oppression. And violence, natural as the sky. And by the way, even those *you'd* call right-wing are regular people. I'm not right-wing or even Republican. But I am militia and it suits me. You see *my* idea of a strong citizenry is millions of us, each with an AK-47 paired with a kind and cautious heart in the chest. Deterrence and vision. We would work to make thousands of economically humane little communities . . . it was Gandhi who championed millions of little villages, right? Our primary focus should be on humane economics . . . atta . . . attic . . . at least I believe so."

Bree with more.

Then Jip flicked a hand toward the center of the audience where a woman with short spiky hair, puffy sweater, and bracelet of silver shells spoke thus: "Are you asking us to *care* about armed right-wing white men who boo-hoo themselves to sleep now that they've have lost their great jobs and homes after all the horrors they've brought down on people of color or the wrong gender for many generations? I'm sorry but I have not one iota of sympathy for that element of society. To have them even brought into this conversation causes many of us to be nauseated."

Bree again.

A guy with shining eyes said thinly and triumphantly, "So, Mr. St. Onge. It's curious. You're proud to be one of *them*, the wonderful militia movement, but have obviously been *mutilated* by one of them." His eyes shone ever more so like glass . . . no, I mean like diamonds.

From a future time, Oceanna remembers the "critique session" that took place in the lace and Jacobean East Parlor a few days later.

Well, of course we weren't going to escape a flogging. Even this tall stout guy, Frank Parenti, was at this one. Most of us had never met him before. He seemed to be of some elevated stature in Harvardtonia, even had the kind of glasses with thick black frames and a perpetual deep-thought squint that you associate with the interpretation of law or physics.

Billy had quit. No surprise there.

His replacement was Meggie Marsh, a remarkable six-foot-threeish strong-looking gal in a gorgeous blue-green Japanese kimono top, short black skirt, black leggings, and blue-green fake alligator boots. Her hair was like a white-blond lion's mane. She had dangling gold dragon earrings. Her nose was classic. Very blue close-together watchful eyes. Her hands were ringless. And *large. Very large*. She bragged that she was not afraid of height, speed, tight places, snakes, rodents, or sick jokes. She called herself a VIB, "very important bitch." You'd expect her handshake to be like having your hand run over by a tractor but it was as gentle as a warm breeze over your fingers. She sighed a lot during quiet moments and preferred to tell you asides while others were lashing out over the destruction of their program by Gordon's and our "off-putting blunders."

The fact that our e-mail, US mail, phone calls, and outside-the-gate lurkers had intensified over the last few days didn't seem to impress Frank Parenti. He said in his deep irrefragable way, "We all need to stick to the script or we've created a whole different program for which grants will dry up. So even if stampedes of eager beavers are following you all around, all gaga over your new direction, your armed militia crap, it won't charm the folks with the dough."

Whitney said quite firmly, "*We* have not taken a new direction."

Silence, into which Meggie Marsh sighed. Then Meggie recrossed her legs and her alligator boots made a slippery noise, then she shook her head of leonine hair. "How did Nelson Mandela and the African National Congress get money?" she asked.

"That," said Frank Parenti, both ironly and moltenly, "is not the right question."

Meggie flushed, shrugged her broad shoulders, sighed. "I was curious." Then she uncrossed her legs, feet flat, and her voice took on a startlingly deep and nasty edge to it. "I'll get my trusty search engine popping tonight. There are no wrong questions in cyberspace."

Blake seemed to be napping, if you didn't notice his fingers drumming on the knee of his new-looking jeans.

MARCH

As Gordon still can't legally drive, Aurel takes him up Seavey Road and onto the little dirt road where Bonnie Loo and her children are staying with her mother and stepfather.

Gordon leaves his cane in the truck. Limps to the cement block step of the porch.

No one seems to be home, not even the stepfather, Reuben, who Bonnie Loo had said all summer was pretty sick. Maybe he's in there not answering the door. Probably not at the doctor's office, Gordon realizes. The Beans have very little money but "too much land," some separate parcels other than what this building is on, all woodlots. This makes the Beans ineligible for modern medicine. But there's "MaineCare," the program where they eventually grab your home and woodlots in their "estate recovery" clause. This leaves your kids nothing of a legacy, just the usual ground zero in the fashionably hearty war on the poor, pushing, pushing, pushing the common man closer to the trigger, where Reuben Bean in his lustier years, his pre-prison years, would not have needed *too* much pushing, Gordon guesses. But presently there's this silence, this surrender.

These facts of life always leave Gordon cold in the chest, especially when he is teetering on this hillside reality of Bonnie Loo's people.

He gives up on banging the door, decides on a note. Sits on the passenger's side of his truck with the door hanging open, scribbling away in his handwriting like bloated barbed wire, while Aurel keeps interrupting with cheery observations of the scene, all the great stuff the Beans have around, some still snowed under, some shoveled out, some with snow melted off; for instance, the doorless Dodge Coronet, the wheelless Dodge Ram pickup, and that old legend the International with flat log bed, clam loader, and seat, mostly abandoned during "Rubie's" prison years so a load that was left on by the family during a breakdown went fuzzy with moss. This is the log load Bonnie Loo's father stood on, going berserk, and so state police ripped him up with seventy-two bullets.

Aurel is especially intrigued by the *newer* logging truck with its rusted frame and cab mounts that leans into a tower of rusty window screening, torn-up aluminum culvert, steel roofing (brand-new), and pig iron. Aurel sighs over some skidder tires still on the wheel. His gleamy black eyes glide across clotheslines zigzagging around the yard. Clothespins on them but no clothes. A grave. Just a grayed stick in the snow with the word in black marker: BIRD, and a 💔 (broken heart). Gray, blue, and white industrial pails. One with ice in it. Some on their sides. A Samoyed way out back there, tied to a doghouse. Doesn't bark. Just watches the visitors' truck in eerie silence. Big sedate leafless maple tree with block and tackle drooping from a limb that is as thick around as a human waist. A big-box store flyer there on the wood-ashed ice path. Spent twenty-two shells in the driveway. A small bank of beach-like sand, all bared by the swelling March suns, with a plywood target board and a two-by-four shelf of shattered bottles, twisted milk jugs, and splintery clusters of bullet holes in the plywood. Spots of oil. Spots of antifreeze.

Meanwhile, the air is made both sweet and sour by fallen leaves having slept under the months of snow, now mixed with sawdust of green firewood being recently worked up for next year beside a shed whose roof is covered with a blue tarp, the old wisdom of orderly orderlessness. Old Yankee thrift is never a lawned vista.

Gordon's letter reads thus:

Of course I wanted to chase you over here hours after you left, but that was the last thing you needed. Nevertheless there is unfinished "business," to use a word too ugly for the stuff of both our hearts' content . . . yes, in the ways of the heart, dear Bonnie Lucretia, I do want to see my children, including Gabe. I call him mine.

If you want to have Rubie or your brother drop them off each morning, they can still do the crews and committees and such. I know how you feel about our life at the Settlement for the kids. I know you know that that arrangement would be best.

Also tell your folks that Loren and Mary and Tanja are welcome to come for the day. This might be a good time to start doing that. Screw public school.

Let me know if it would be easier for you to have someone from the Settlement come over and get the kids, if the transportation part turns out to be a problem. Especially for Reuben.

Please tell your Mum and Reuben how really sorry I am that things have turned out this way.

Maybe I shouldn't have come back over here today and made matters worse, but you deserve a communication.

So here it is. I'm not here to beg you back. I'm here to congratulate you.

With love and respect.
Guillaume

APRIL

Patriots' Day* in Portland.

In the Egypt hills, the skunk cabbage is standing tall green in among the old glazed patches of snow, while some hillsides still know three feet of snow and the brooks are thunderous with hurrying melt-off, frothing, spinning, bursting over rocks.

But in Portland, cement is cement. Brick is brick. Tar is tar. And the big digital clock over the fourteen-story bank building flashes the next recorded minute of time and the temperature drops to make colder cement, colder tar, and brick all around the square.

Traffic on Congress Street, Spring Street, and Cumberland Avenue is at a standstill. Almost from one promenade to the other, the sidewalks spill over with people. And all kinds of improper parking, blocking of driveways and hydrants, filling of spaces for the handicapped and "private parking only." People in doorways. People in windows. On roofs.

Set back almost against the base of the monument is a really small wooden temporary stage, bristling with shrimpy windless American flags. Nobody is on the stage, but a crowd of people are crammed around it, necks stretching now and then, to see better over the rest of the crowd.

Snow had been predicted in the mountains and foothills today. And by tonight, the County will be buried. But in oceanic Portland,

---

* An old New England holiday also called Paul Revere Day.

the cold front is, thus far, only this gray, steely, bone-aching funny air, air on the verge.

Portland Police gave a permit for this rally but this is not a rally. This is a mob. For the Fourth of July, yes. For the Sidewalk Art shows, sure. But for politics? Well, sure . . . if you got Lyndon Johnson riding through town, remember that? Or some other such royal mucky-muck. But for just a buncha dipshit speakers, leftover hippies from the sixties, still not "with it," still whining over "the system," forget it. "John Lennon is dead!" a taxi driver screams from the window of his cab lodged in the frozen river of cars and trucks.

There's chanting of "Prophet! Prophet! Prophet!"

Between the groups of chanters are just people who are curious, bright-eyed, soaking it up. People who hear there will be "a crowd." Hands in the pockets. Or a child in a stroller. A lot of teenagers, what some call "the loser types," the ones who aren't home studying, the types "you have to watch." This, a crowd that seems at first glance thoroughly working class . . . the Fourth-of-July-loving people, those very ones the Harvardtonians have yearned to "reach out" to.

Behind cop glasses, cop eyes watch. Radios on belts hiss cautions. Cop cruisers edging down side streets. Outer intersections now thickening. How will emergency vehicles ever penetrate? Up near the monument, it's a big problem. The way the crowd has gotten so tight. And alert. And breathy.

The monument reads: FOR PORTLAND'S SONS WHO DIED FOR THE UNION. Monument is as tall as the older brick buildings that used to stand around her without contest. Stone laurel wraps her stone hair. She bears a stone sword and shield. Her robe, though it is stone, cascades.

Below her, around the small stage, several people are dressed for speechifying and Gordon St. Onge is dressed for the woods. Gordon is thinking how those people gathered closest to the monument are the only ones who will hear the presentations, even with the small speaker on the pole, but Olan, standing near, chomping breath mints, his eyes sliding over the crowd, hollers to Gordon, "This is good! This is very good!" And winks.

And there is the new guy, the veteran organizer, Lenny Britt, salmon-colored sweater showing in the V of his open jacket. He adjusts his porkpie cap, watches a cop a few yards away talking from the side of his mouth at some young people with skateboards.

At Gordon's side is little stoic Claire, lots of wools, her hair today in one long glossy braid. Eyes behind the spectacles are almost wooden with worry.

On his other side, his other "bodyguard," Meggie Marsh, not dressed for the cold. Now and then she hugs herself. Today the boots are yellow patent leather, worn with black leggings and a very short skirt of red-and-yellow zigzags. A jacket of something silkesque. Wraparound sunglasses. The volcanic white-blond hair. As impressive as the monument woman, but differently so.

Gordon now sees the True Maine Militia teens shouldering their way through the mob, Samantha in the lead, black beret, jacket, jeans, and military boots. She walks straight to him and opens her arms and he embraces her. And then Whitney and the rest hug him from all sides. The embrace of the crowd-noise is even squeezier.

Lenny is pulling himself up onto the stepless little stage. At the podium, he raises his arms and the nearest two hundred yards of the crowd makes a different sound, more of a rustle, more like alertness. But not yet a listener's silence. Lenny feels the mike, causes the big speakers to thump and scrape. The crowd doesn't wait for him to open his mouth to introduce the first speaker but like a long wave starting at the center, spreading east and west along Congress Street and down along every side street into the hollows of the parking garages, there is stomping and clapping and the many-voiced demand: "Pro-*phet*! Pro-*phet!* Pro-*phet*! Pro-*phet!* Pro-*phet*! Pro-*phet!* Pro-*phet*! . . ."

Lenny glances toward the cluster of scheduled speakers at his left. He rubs the mike again. Raises his arms again. "Hello!" he speaks into the mike. "HELLO!" he *screams* into the mike.

"Pro-*phet*! Pro-*phet!* Pro-*phet*!" the crowd demands.

Television crews and radio and newspaper reporters are jostling themselves into closer positions, while the whole crowd tightens.

"Pro-*phet*! Pro-*phet!* Pro-*phet*! Pro-*phet!* Pro-*phet*! . . ." The crowd gets louder, sharper, deeper, less playful, more muscular. "Pro-*phet*! Pro-*phet!* Pro-*phet*! Pro-*phet!* Pro-*phet*!"

"Prophet for president!!!" a not very far-off voice shrills.

And so.

The crowd watches the scarred bearded guy with the billed baseball cap and wool jacket step up among the flags and now beside him an early-teens boy who unfurls a dark blue flag that has the State of Maine seal and the two figures, farmer and sailor, and between them the moose and the tree that signifies the forest, and above and below is the crescent of yellow-gold lettering: THE TRUE MAINE MILITIA. And this young boy wears a camo jacket and military boots and he is unfurling that ol' flag very slowly, with intended drama, and the crowd, like the billowy fires of a guided missile, produces a garbled roar.

Lenny still on the stage nods to Bard who braces the blue flag high. Down below, Samantha is helping Rusty Soucier with a boost up onto the stage, then passes the furled American flag up to him.

Gordon's eyes widen on the faces of his sons Cory, Dane, and Oz and the two older Martin boys. Cory nods manfully. And there, faces, shoulders, and black bandannas at throats or around hair, the Horne Hill anarchists including Jaxon Cross with his broad villainous smile. And the venerable Miss Munch.

Gordon now effortlessly twists the mike, small-looking in his hand, a few inches higher to accommodate his tallness. Lately he uses his cane for only rough terrain. Maybe this day is a certain kind of rough terrain, but caneless he is.

Again the deep garbled human engine revs up, laughter, groans, cheers, yells, whistles, and applause moving westward along Congress Street in stuttering ripples.

Gordon stuffs his hands into the pockets of his jacket, stands sideways a minute, eyes closed, head down, visor of his *Bean's Logging and Pulp* cap hiding his expression. He is *trying* to be good. He is *trying* to stick to the script, right? He is *not* Nelson Mandela. No, militia is not *allowed*. No, it will not be funded.

The gray furry animallike head of a TV audio boom slips out of the crowd and hovers near Gordon's elbow. And now another at his other elbow, a little behind him. And there a glassy TV camera eye, oh, so intimate with his knee. He turns and looks at it. His scars, though fading some, are still scars. His mutilated ears, moist, wrinkled, obscene. The last few months his short beard has more of that devilish gray through the dark. The mouth shows darkness on one side where certain teeth are only a memory. Eyes ever so pale in the dusky face. How perfect for the hungers of TV news makers, the look of utter depravity cast upon the crowd as it continues to cheer and stomp and clap-clap and many hundred mouths smoke with the growing damp chill of the day.

Gordon's deep big-guy voice now pushes through the mike and speakers, "Come listen, my children. And you shall heear. Of the midnight ride. Of Paul Reveeeeere. One if by land. Two if by sea. And three if by statehouse and Capitol Hill lobbies! Blink!" He turns and throws up a hand toward the top of the fourteen-story old bank building, the one that on its rooftop displays digitally the time and temperature for miles, where one can now imagine the three Colonial-era lanterns signifying the nature of the enemy's advance. "Blink!" Pause. "Blink!" Three blinks in all.

The crowd chuckles happily, getting into it. "The English are coming!" a woman's voice hollers. And another. "Tell it like it izzzzz!" And then frenetic applause.

Gordon crosses his arms over his chest as he waits, looks down at Butch Martin who stands protectively in front of the young Settlement teens, his arms crossed over his chest, too. He wears his old Border Mountain Militia shirt minus patch. But there's the woven olive drab pistol belt, black knitted watch cap, and outdoorsy black-faced wristwatch. So remarkably like Rex, that dark mustache that crawls to the jaws. And Bree beside Butch, wedged in there with Jip and Jaxon Cross on her other side, the crowd pressing tighter. When the noise settles, Gordon says, "Our forefathers, such as they were, wrote a good thing into most constitutions . . . like for instance the New Hampshire constitution, that if you find you have an alien government one day, you have the right . . . the *right* to go *put 'em out*! But maybe it was written to represent only the rich, not all flesh-and-blood people. Tough shit! We're going to *take* that right! If you and I all go up to our statehouse here in the Pine Tree State and then off to Washington Deeee Seeee and put every corporate lobbyist out, no one has the right, by *our* definition of the constitution, we the people's definition, to stop us. I'm not saying they won't mess with us, maul us, haul us off. I'm only referring to what is *right*! I mean, after all, we'll do it *nice*. We won't rough them up. We'll just point to the door. The constitutions do not specify *nice*. But we're decent people, so we do it decent. But, my friends and neighbors, mothers, fathers, sisters, brothers, children! We MUST do it!!!!"

Applause rolls forth and roars of agreement, and now three or four screams, and now a cackle.

A few more fuzzy TV boom beasts are pushed forward and several more big round eyes of the local news bore in on Gordon's face, which is now displaying his most madman expression, one eyebrow raised, eye wide, other eye squinted. "Revolution," he whispers into the mike. And pushes at the bill of his cap, his cap now far back on his head.

The response to this word is deafening.

"Revolution is our right. Revolution is our *obligation*!" he bellows but hardly a soul hears this, the mob noise grinds and groans like the earth's plates in a quake. This is *not* the same as Dartmouth.

Pulls his cap's visor low, folds his arms over his chest. Waits. And waits. And waits.

Crowd settles.

"My friends and neighbors," he tells them, now jerking his cap off, forcing it into a jacket pocket, "this little problem we are having . . . needs clarifying . . . uh . . . uh . . . uh . . . what exactly are we revolting *against*?!!"

Various yelled answers crackle and squeak from the near and far faces. Some answers seem not to be connected to the *subject* at all.

On both sides of him, the flags are held with such unshakable duty that the stone lady statue above them couldn't do better.

He again lowers his voice, mouth close to the mike so that the crowd kind of leans toward him, and his mouth is so close to the mike that the "p" of the word "planet" pops when he says, "I never believed in the devil until I met the Market God as he strode over planet earth."

Tight civil applause and one or two whistles.

Gordon takes a few steps, reaches for Lenny Britt's sleeve, then tugs him close, big good buddy hug. "My brother Lenny," Gordon says, dropping his head sideways to the mike. "He said it all in a nutshell the other day. He said *free* trade . . . *free* market . . . its freedom means our slavery."

Crowd cheers.

Lenny smiles grimly. Which means he's satisfied.

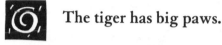

The tiger has big paws.

Back behind the mike, Gordon rears back and screams, "CORPORATE PERSONHOOD!! WEEE ARE COMING TO KICK YOUR BUTT!!!"

Crowd roars. It seems some people hear him and there are those who watch him, without moving, just their eyes taking him in. He is thinking how most will never divine the meaning of this corporation-versus-democracy concept. But they do feel his growls in their blood, a shared fury about being ripped off by whatever the hell it is.

Almost suddenly there are about fifteen more fuzzy or padded TV mikes and cameras pointed at him and he wonders how these guys will carve out from all his words something harmless and cute for tonight's news. Or harmless and *scary*. Harmless to the *system*. Scary to the *people*.

He turns to the crowd grinning and wagging his head. "First of all, does every one of you know what a corporation is? Some tell us it has all the feelings of a mother. All the instincts and responsibilities of . . . a loving parent. This is not true. Because a corporate charter . . . is . . . not . . . a . . . mammal! It . . . is . . . a . . . legal . . . fiction! A friggin' *baaad* cartoon!"

Then he says deeply, "If you heard that your government gave human rights . . . constitutional rights to a cancer tumor, would your jaw drop?"

A few moans. Some hisses.

Gordon laughs. "So if you had a big tumor in your brain or lung, it would be against the law to bother it. Even when you know it'll *kill you*!"

The near crowd growls. The farther crowd applauds, oblivious.

Gordon shakes his head, looks into Jip's eyes. She nods. "Then, too, the cancer," he explains into the mike, "would have the rights to free speech and privacy and due process of the law. And in all manner of speaking, the right to petition the government, which is the worst of them all."

The crowd makes some subdued noises. Some are talking to each other. Laughing. Enjoying. The gray dank sky sags and bags more deeply among the brick shoulders of the old city.

"FUCK THIS SHIT!!" Gordon screams, and faces are once again riveted on him. "It gets worse! Add to this tumor's constitutional rights, limited liability. Add in its tendency toward unlimited property, unlimited capital. Now the tumor has more rights than you! Now give your tumor the best lawyers money can buy, lobbyists galore with a well-greased revolving door, give it special and secret meetings with judges, senators, ownership of the airwaves, ownership of the entire United States telecommunications system, and *all* the big newspapers, control over our higher education, our prisons, control over energy! And food! And genetic engineering. Very special scientists who swear the planet hasn't got an end-times carbon problem in the sky. And there's the devotion of the police. Has its tentacles in the Pentagon! The right to declare war! Give it the nod to use pretty palm-tree havens with no global monitoring or tax. Give it the best public relations setup money can buy . . . that is, MIND CONTROL . . . BRAINWASHING!" The near crowd boos and howls. In the distance, car horns blow.

He leans back, strokes one side of his mustache, eyes on some thought. *Am I making the organizers happy?* He grips the mike. "Now give your tumor NAFTA, the WTO, FTAA, GATS, the IMF, the World Bank, and such, the most powerful rights a tumor can buy, having sovereignty over local, state, and national government. Give your tumor cozy closed-door clubs, think tanks, foundations. And a seat of honor in the United Nations where it can show *who's boss*. Give your cancer high regard." He sucks in his breath through his nose, his mouth tight.

Applause begins but peters out as he cuts in with a screamed word, "Give!" Shakes the mike angrily like a throat he intends to crush. "*Give* it our kids!!! Set up all our schools so that our kids learn deeply how it is you compete for favors from the cancerous tumor!! That if you march to its drums, maybe the tumor will eat your brother instead, or eat only part of you! Like maybe just your nuts!"

The crowd howls horribly.

The crowd again tightens.

Gordon reaches inside his jacket to a chest pocket of his work shirt. Unfolds a piece of paper. He flaps the paper loosely, now holds it limp at the ends of his fingers like a dirty Kleenex. "A piece of paper." Pause. "A charter for a corporation." Pause. "That has so many dangerous possibilities." Pause. He is breathing hard. But no longer is his tongue lost to him.

He looks at the piece of paper a long moment. "To have given this *thing* the right to be mightier than the people, the right to LIVE! . . . has been a crime against all flesh-and-blood people everywhere! And here, in America, it has been a case of TREASON!" Suddenly and violently, he mashes up the paper with both hands, screaming, "DEATH! DEATH to the thing that has no business being ALIVE! OUT with this criminal corporate-infested government!"

Claire's fingers close around his left forearm.

Meggie grips his shoulder.

He throws up a fist, in effect thrusting both their hands off. "DIE DEVIL, DIE!!"

The little stage under Gordon's feet trembles, hands and knees and hips of the crowd almost embracing it. Mouths howling, many mouths, one howl. *DEATH! DEATH! DEATH! DEATH! DEATH! DEATH! DEATH!*

The two boys get better grips on their flags and unconsciously move closer to Gordon, even as Claire and Meggie do the same, nearly squashing him between themselves.

And then Gordon bellows, "LIFE! LIFE! LIFE! LIFE! for we the people!!!" And the crowd calls back, "LIFE! LIFE! LIFE!"

Now soft as velvet he speaks into the hardworking mike, "Welcome to the no-wing militia movement, brothers and sisters! Welcome to the FRINGE!"

Graffiti on an overpass on I-95.

So what if the hokey pokey really *is* what it's all about?

Back in Monument Square.

Now Gordon hears a whomping. Helicopter beating its way over the buildings. Olive green, big white star on each side. Not bearing down on the crowd. It can't. It can't even observe much. But it can, yes, oh, yes, terrorize. Gordon watches it a moment as it swerves around to the northwest, toward where he knows the park is, then churns its way back again, leans in as the crowd, engorged and lusty, is pressed hard against the little stage. Bard draws the True Maine Militia flag back sharply as hands reach to feel it or snatch it, he can't be sure which. Crowd is making noise and a rigid pressure like an epileptic's muscles in grand mal.

Chopper hovers. Such noise!

Claire and Meggie and Blake all lay hands on Gordon, shouting lost syllables. Probably they are telling him to *be done*. But then he feels something on his work boots, sees that some people are on the stage belly down, reaching to touch him. Now a tug on the cuff of his work pants. Not unpredictably, the crowd's chemistry has changed, its voice broken apart now, sparkly and disjointed.

Another hand on him, on his jacket, as a young guy in a ski jacket is now poking at Gordon's shoulder, calling through the uproar, "GOOD JOB! HEY! WILL YOU—" Gordon grasps this young guy's hand, which is cold, fingers icy, and slaps his shoulder in camaraderie. But the guy wants more than a friendly hand. He wants to talk. He wants to press something on Gordon that is urgent to him, a thing that has distressed him, a pain that might be erased by listening ears and observing eyes of a caring prophet. It is all around, the urgency, help me, help me, help me.

All on the stage are about to be swallowed. The organizers are bellowing to each other.

The helicopter at last veers away.

Gordon speaks deeply and softly into the mike, as to his own cattle, sheep, and hogs. "Be easy. Be easy." But no one hears this for the crowd's voice is still deafening. He wags his head from side to side twice, playfully, squinting out across the hundreds of close and tiny far-off faces.

"HEY! HEY!" the young guy at his side has not given up tugging at the sleeve of Gordon's wool jacket. And now another guy and a wild-eyed woman are there beside him. The little stage seems to totter. The crowd is witless, stouter, guttural, and spilling over . . . another stranger hoists himself up onto the stage. Now another. Blake and Lenny and Meggie grab Gordon from behind, pushing him and Claire, Bard and Gabe, flags and all, to the back edge of the stage as the streets of Portland wax naughty and self-conceited. A lot of minor vandalisms are happening, which will total a few thousand dollars; one or two detainments of juveniles will come of this, shouting matches and official outcry.

Then as Gordon is pushed by the organizers through the crowd along the street, he takes a hand here and there, hands that are thrust at him. He smiles, he tries to speak, but the noise is too much. The organizers ram him onward, rough as cops. A fortyish woman in a fake-fur-edged purple coat pushes her face into Gordon's left hand like a dog.

Critical thinker of our times.

"When a well-packaged web of lies has been sold gradually to the masses over generations, the truth will seem utterly preposterous and its speaker a raving lunatic."

—Dresden James

Marian St. Onge.

She watches the television news with her shoulders pressed back into the softly firm sofa. On every channel she flicks to, Gordon is screaming, "DIE, DEVIL, DIE!!" with raised fist and those little arteries standing out on his scarred temples. Like Hitler. Well, no. He doesn't look like Hitler. But could there be people who would see that shadow of resemblance? And how embarrassed she is about his teeth, the whole top right side of his mouth . . . the ones he *could* have implants for . . . and then the camera flashes to an interview with that horrid right-wing-sounding militia guy from somewhere in the crowd, snarling about "Democrats" and "sodomy" . . . would he be a friend of Gordon's? She can't tell, the news is so fast, so choppy, flits now to a young man kicking in the taillight of a Mercedes and a young woman screaming words that Marian can't make out, but then in a hollow interior there is the chief of police with his curly hair and deep concern. A need for more crowd control. More "backup" when needed. Next, on the national networks, it starts all over again, as a "riot" in Maine, the news personalities' voices in their usual celebratory tenors. When did they start calling her son "the *mad* Prophet?" More of that stupid militia guy, more stupid vandals, more of Gordon's fist, face, scars, screams, terrible screams. Her throat clenches. Her eyes fill with tears. She wonders why he keeps this going? Rex led him into all this and she thought it was all over with him and Rex. "Rex," she says, hard with venom, soft with sorrow.

In time, there is just the colorful inoffensive rollicking of a situation comedy and ads for insurance and new cars. She wipes her nose. She stares into the purple, pink, and red spectacle of this gala of small harmless lives, of crisp entrances and exits, of the gentle plenteousness of the way your life can be if you choose it.

Janet Weymouth at a luncheon in New York.

From the corner of her eye she sees gray and a little splash of red. Someone has hustled from the doorway to the temporarily vacated seat beside her. A friend, Justine Clegg, who murmurs to her about the big stir in Portland, Maine, caused by "your friend."

Janet says she has been out of touch with him for a long while.

Justine sighs, moves a little piece of flatware to one side. "After his brain injury I was under the impression he was bedridden and had a severe speech disability. Obviously not bedridden, but anger problems often present themselves with the brain-damaged. Unfortunate when it's allowed to disturb the peace. Riots, they said."

"Peace, yes. Peace is best," Janet replies softly, almost defeatedly. She pats the warm hand of her friend. "But as we get older we all find the wisdom to make amends with the gods."

Worn out?

Two a.m. She has the storm window raised, the inside window ready to be raised the moment he appears there. She never hears his truck stopping a hundred yards downhill, so she knows her father and brothers, who are in their beds, haven't heard it, either, tonight or any of those other times. Her gown is long with a ruffled hem, a print of big and little roses on cream. Big wool work socks on her feet. The only light is a yellowy dingy glow from her Minnie Mouse night-light down low between her two bureaus, a light she has always known.

He is, as promised, silent and shadowless and agile beyond belief, balancing on the short edge of the roof that meets the dormer, part shingle, part aluminum flashing. Then, as she raises the window, he is slipping in, smelling of the cold fresh-snow April night and of something like scorched pork chops on his beard.

Neither he nor she speaks, not even a whisper, just kissing and kissing, and breathing and biting and humping and humping. Then, with his clothes on and boots back on, even his jacket and knitted cap, this Willie Lancaster sits very straight-shouldered on the bed beside her in this hot attic room, holding her hand. Twenty minutes or more, no words, a big grip on her hand; they are like teenagers visiting bedrooms to listen to favorite music. Everything he does has such a funny little twist of propriety. That sweetness within the sting that drives Bree bonkers.

But then one night he tells her he needs to stop for "a vacation from this situation," explaining apologetically that he's too old to live like "a hot cat."

But really ol' Willie just didn't have the heart and guts to tell her that "the thrill is gone."

But doesn't Bree now have a sweet crush on one of the Horne Hill anarchists? This, the season of Bree's and Willie's steamy safaris, comes to a gentle close. *Peace be with you.*

Out in the world.

Professor Catherine Court Downey squeezes her new remote-control car door lock, drops it into her small beige leather shoulder bag, and strides toward the building where many thousands of people (in a manner of speaking) wait for her.

Marian Depaolo St. Onge watches prime-time TV.

Her nephew, the architect, who stays with her for a few days at a time now, has scolded her for continuing to torment herself with the TV news when her son is "the star." And now this "special," a network "special" . . . advertised for more than a week.

It begins with these words: *The following program contains material that may not be suitable for certain audiences. Viewer discretion is advised.*

It is a personal and soft-spoken interview with the art professor Catherine Court Downey, a woman who "escaped" the St. Onge Settlement.

Catherine is an attractive youngish woman with thick dark quirky eyebrows and an educated accent. A tan suit jacket with a little silver pin on the lapel. A sweater top of brilliant violet. The interviewer, the well-known Deb Howland, is a blonde, crisp, with a nondescript TV-personality-type attractiveness. Her suit jacket is gray. Blouse, red. Both faces are made up perfectly for the camera. The set is made to look cozy. For telling secrets.

There are a few moments of warm-up when footage is run of a crazed-looking but unscarred pre-assaulted Gordon St. Onge, fist thrust above his head, screaming hoarsely, "GOD SAVE THE REPUBLIC OF MAINE!!"

And then there is a close-up of the Settlement gate and gatehouse, the hand-painted signs that read: ANYBODY TRESPASSES WILL BE SHOT. TRY IT. And then a long shot showing a few state police gathered along the shoulders of the paved Heart's Content Road (during the Annie B birthday event). The police look restless.

And then a state police lieutenant speaking with a churning of green and yellow behind him. Breezy boughs. "We could have a problem," but declining further comment for "security reasons".

Then we go to a series of emergencyish insurance ads, new car ads, some new cars seeming to fly, others that murmur quietly of tangible success, then back to the studio with Catherine revealing how she wound up at the Settlement, her weakened condition at the time due to illness, and Deb, looking almost touched, asks in a careful manner, "Catherine, can you describe what it was like living at the St. Onge Settlement?"

"It was an incredible shock to me. I had gone there not understanding the nature of their *arrangement*, or the remoteness of the place . . . or anything . . . and so at first I kept thinking I must be wrong, that what was actually so obvious was something that could be explained in normal terms eventually. But then as time went on, I stepped out of denial and faced it . . . Gordon St. Onge was a dictator. What he said was *law*. And these people were in a subservient state of mind . . . uh . . . as in masochism, to be blunt. The worse they were treated, the more they adored him. It was painful to see."

"Can you give examples?"

"Well, it was everything. From whether or not you were allowed to have a television to what was acceptable food . . . to what people were allowed to *think*."

"We've all been hearing that the St. Onge followers are forced to live without indoor plumbing, no electricity, no modern conveniences, no computers, no outside news, things most Americans take for granted."

"Well, there was a definite paranoia about utility companies and to cut himself off from this, Gordon and some of the others, mostly men, had created this whole very complicated, very *in*efficient system for power and heat. So electricity had to be excessively conserved, which was a hardship for the women, especially since they were relegated to all of the cleaning, cooking, and drudgery . . . it all fell on them. The bathroom facilities were actually—" She simpers. "—composting devices. Compost for gardens!" She simpers again. A simper of disdain but also of nervousness, of injury, of a memory she needs to tread lightly on.

Deb Howland nods, her mouth showing amusement but her eyes blank. "One of the most amazing things we're all hearing is that Gordon St. Onge has something like twenty wives. Echoes of David Koresh? Is it true? Does Gordon St. Onge have twenty or more wives?

"It's true."

"Were you expected to be a wife to him?"

Catherine misses about eight beats. "I think he knew I would refuse. I was not as impressed with him as everyone else seemed to be. I made it clear in conversations with the women there. Everything you say in that place would get back to him. He had a frightening power over everyone. To try and hide something from him was not a good idea."

"How young are his youngest wives?"

"Well, I knew one very well who was fifteen. She came from a home where her father and brothers sexually abused her and went right into Gordon's bed from there."

"Did Gordon St. Onge or any of the other men at the Settlement sexually abuse young children, others besides this unfortunate girl?"

"Yes. There was a young girl from outside the Settlement. Actually she was older than the other girl, but not much. I wasn't clear on her age. She was the daughter of a friend of Gordon's, so perhaps arrangements had been made. I had already left the Settlement by then but I still have connections *inside*. This particular episode happened late one night. Outside the Settlement, actually. Down on the nearby lake. It was after the big public party and rally they had last fall, the one covered by so much media. There were about thirty men present at this special lakeside ritual. You can call it demonic . . . whatever . . . but it was absolutely unforgivable. She was made to strip in front of all of them but with the idea that she would give herself to him . . . Gordon. While she stood in front of him, he thrust his hand up her vagina . . . to the wrist. And then raped her."

"This is dreadful. How often did this sort of rituals take place?"

"It wasn't clear. Many things were not made fully clear to me, probably because they were seeing I wasn't sympathetic. But every day was a new surprise!" Catherine relinquishes a tight little laugh.

A series of commercials jerks the viewer into the peppy positive musical world of driving a wonderful new car, one of the same ads shown earlier, and then the wholesome warm family thing of a cell telephone talk with the faraway big brother you are never with any more, but now manage to be virtually with hour to hour, place to place to place. And then the broad white pristine beach with a darling baby turtle, the whoosh of benevolent cold blue water rolling in under a celebration of salty white foam. And the message. *Nuclear power. Clean.*

Back to a distortingly close shot of Catherine's face, two eyeballs, two nostrils, the tender mouth remembering pain, while Deb Howland's voice condenses for us the astonishing and titillating interview that took place before the ads.

And now Deb's face, at a less intimate distance. "Are children abused in other ways there? Punished physically? Or . . . ?"

"Oh, yes. The children, particularly the boys, are worked like animals, building roads, sawing down trees, stacking firewood, fixing machinery, working all night long in the sawmills. Farmwork. And furniture-making involving dangerous tools. There was one real young girl working on a band saw! And kids were weeding and haying when it was over ninety degrees! One pitiful child was not allowed to eat for weeks. She told me this herself. It was during a time in which she was apparently kept in isolation down at Gordon's old house, which is not inside the Settlement but quite some distance away. I was never clear on what this child did to make them feel she deserved this kind of punishment. But she was a black child and my guess is they resented her. These people are primarily right-wing."

"What about drugs? Did you ever see any drugs in use?"

"Well . . . some. It wasn't central. But I'd say alcohol most certainly was. Very often I saw babies getting up on the tables and freely helping themselves to hard cider. Or beer. There was heavy drinking with some adults, especially Gordon, who is, by the way, an unabashed alcoholic. And I knew of two children* who smoked tobacco in front

* Mickey and Bree.

of the adults. It wasn't some secret thing. The adults just watched this and made no attempt to stop it."

"Guns?"

"These men are heavily armed. The whole militia element was one of the most frightening aspects of my time there."

"Was there any evidence that they had plans of aggression on the government? It's known that they are antigovernment. Gordon St. Onge's speeches are riddled with antigovernment sentiment and what some would call inciting others to violence."

"Absolutely. The Settlement men in particular are violently opposed to the United States government. They seem to want a lawless world. And Gordon forced children to attend actual militia meetings to 'educate' them . . . which affected them strongly. It was no time before these children had formed a militia of their own, which was highly publicized as harmless. But it was not uncommon for children to handle firearms there, more often than they handled toys. More often than schoolbooks, essay writing, and tests. Excellence was not in the picture. War was. War was their . . . motif!"

"What is Gordon St. Onge like as a person?"

"Dictator." She seems hard pressed to leave this.

"And?"

Catherine's shoulders hunch up and shrug hard in remembered terror. "A big scary man."

The interviewer pauses. And there is more footage now of "the mad Prophet" (before the scars) standing in front of a mike with an attractive child to each side of him, one golden, one white, one kid wearing a tricorn hat, the other an oversized camo shirt, each bearing a large flag, and "the Prophet" has upended a longneck beer and all but pours it down his own throat. Here he is screaming, "THE END OF THE FUCKING WORLD!!!" The word "fucking" blurred slightly by editors who live and breathe in the shadow of the FCC.

Now back to the warm lights of the studio, the rustle of a sleeve, and the precise professional voice of Deb Howland. "Catherine, can you tell us how many children Gordon St. Onge has fathered?"

"Don't ask."

The interviewer smiles, mouth smiling, eyes forever blank. "More than thirty?"

"More than thirty."

"More than thirty-five?"

"More than thirty-five."

Marian St. Onge opens and closes her hands on her lap.

Hew nephew, Mark, standing nearby with a tinkly glass of bourbon and Coke, almost speaks, but can't. He just turns and quietly goes back into the kitchen.

Brother law.

The parking area near the Quonset huts is strewn with cars and pickups, some still with snowplows. And there are dilapidated farm rigs. And there is Blake's car. "Borrowed," he explains. "Mine shit the bed."

Stuffing gloves into his pockets, he takes from the trunk a partially disassembled Bushmaster. "Maine-made," he adds with a full-latitude grin. And then with a sigh, "Illegal in Beantown." His voice, as always, is deep and sometimes sleepy but his youth is always ready and astir. He is snapping the rifle together. A lot of unimposing plastic sounds.

Gordon says, "You crossed two state lines with that?"

Grin still in place. "It's not mine. You'll meet Richard Fowler sometime. Lives in Auburn* for the minute. He was going to come along but his schedule had no room. Statehouse business today. Nothing as impressive as what your kids did. But Rich and his outfit have the gift of making public hearings less short and slippery than the reps and their corporate acquaintances have their hearts set on."

"I thought you and Meggie were both coming today."

"She couldn't move a doctor appointment."

"I see." Gordon squints. "You know she said she was in the military. Well, she kind of *bragged* it." He chuckles.

"Yeah, coast guard."

"*Coast guard*?" Gordon squints again. Harder.

"Yeah. Then commercial fishing. Then cab driving. Moved on to ambulance driving while she was at school. Presently she's an EMT

* Auburn, Maine.

and part-time manager in an independent bookstore. She's going for her MSW."* Blake's eyes twinkle. "She's well-rounded."

Gordon nods. "I think she's a character myself. I mean it as a compliment."

Blake's hugest grin blossoms. "Well, she certainly works at it."

It had been arranged at the breakfast meal that after their morning work crews had finished up, Cory and Oz and Butch and others were to meet at the East Field, which is partially walled up with logs skidded down from Pock Hill. Beyond that the area is nicely bermed, some majestic-looking ledge.

Everyone wants to try the Bushmaster. The Settlement is heavy only on the side of Winchesters and other old sturdy family guns.

So Gordon and Blake head up the still-mucky-in-some-spots roadway, ice-and-thaw runnels squirming hither, some washouts. Gordon's bad leg still has no spring so his cane remains handy for such a traipse as this. But note that these days his work-gloved hands grasp it with less rigor, more flair, like a country gent's walking stick. With the end of it he pokes at some tracks of boots, of which lots and lots more show up, boots of large persons trekking both ways quite recently.

Blake carries the Bushmaster in a case with his right hand, left arm around Gordon's back and shoulders as they yuk it up, funny stories about their mothers.

Blake's jacket is really a sort of car coat, rust-color leather, belted. It squeaks as he goes along. Bareheaded, as usual. His black, otherwise blustery hair is always trimmed in a professional man's cut. His dark brown face is, as ever, shaved so nothing hides the pleased dimples and faint smile lines.

Gordon wears his red-and-black plaid (reversible to blaze orange) wool hunter's vest unzipped and is looking uncomfortably warm though today the mountains are foggy and cool. Mountains way off, foothills near; all these giants and semi-giants are bunched around the Settlement like heads and shoulders around a high-stakes card game. Through holes in the fog you can plainly see their gray and twiggy

* Master of social work.

steep nearer sides, while on the north sides, snow in wide bands and crescents like quarter moons are still in the skidways of the latest forest-tearing-up superific monster machines, used by the guys who need to "get big or get out."

As they approach the road's crest and then go on to where the yard opens wide, Blake says, "Oh, ho! What's this?"

Gordon scowls.

The boot tracks that they'd been seeing end. But nobody is here. Except yet another real-as-life Bruce Hummer tied to a stake, ready for execution. Hands behind. Same nice suit, it seems, but a new tie of plaid flannel from that popular Settlement bolt that has made a galaxy of smocks, tunics, nightgowns, dresses, aprons, baby bibs, quilts, and even one of Gordon's own damn shirts.

Gordon has been thinking how easy it was for young Blake, the youngest of the Bread and Roses Folk School organizers, to have been in several cahoots-type huddles with Cory and Butch and Jaxon Cross these past couple of weeks—the very reason Cory has thawed a bit toward the folk school project?

Once they find the flat spot facing the ledge where the Bruce dummy stands with glassy brown-green eyes watching them, Blake picks open a box of cartridges. Gordon watches not Blake's hands but the side of Blake's head and his eager profile.

Blake looks up from his fingers working the shells into several clips, pauses. Gordon's eyes are wide and contrary, Gordon breathing slowly or maybe not at all.

Blake asks, "What's on your mind, man?"

"D'joo already know about this?" He nods toward the Bruce.

"Vaguely . . . and . . . um . . . I heard something about which genocidal piece of shit this represents."

"Yeah?"

"They said you were heard once at a formal dinner at a seaside mansion to call him your brother."

Gordon sees from the corner of his eye the sun pressing through one of the cool threadbare holes in the clouds.

Blake is thinking how this effort of the sun feels good, the way it touches him, handles him, not hot but friendlyish.

Youthful voices are heard down beyond the crest of the hill, drawing near.

Gordon squirms the fingers of both work-gloved hands on his cane, which by the way is a carved masterpiece, a gift from the Settlementer they call "Beezer," who carves art and tools and big bowls in her spare time. There are carved flames on the cane from the ground up, so finely etched, while the whole thing ends in the head of a phoenix, eyes stained crimson to match what's in the crevices of flames, while most of the surface is in brooding Jacobean.

Blake is frowning. "You called *me* your brother. You call John Lungren your brother. I heard you call Olan and Billy and Lenny your brothers."

Gordon studies Blake's wristwatch. White gold and professorial. Time that may or may not be an illusion, as Albert Einstein expounded, a theory especially fondled and strangled by participants in a few Settlement parlor philosophy salons.

Blake snaps one of the clips into place; the dull black plastic finish of the Bushmaster seems too cheesy, too airy-light to have a voice. "I believe before we're done with the folk school project, we'll be true brothers. Bound by the cause, the frustrations, the victories. In especially risky civil disobedience, people are nearly wed . . . like any war . . . you never forget your comrades in arms, even if there's not one weapon between you, that fear is in the air, because you know the willingness and capabilities of the apparatus to make you hurt, to want to bury you. So when you've got groups whose strategies are to lock down, to block streets . . . people getting rubber bullets in the knees, bullets that are *not* rubbery but like the stuff of bowling balls . . . and you've got the tear gas and the pepper spray and the nightsticks across the back and kidneys, faces ripped across pavement, handcuffs that are just these big bread bag bands designed to *cut* . . . and you're stuffed together into hot buses for hours, no way to piss or shit except *on* somebody . . . that's true bonding. That's a class-two struggle, man. Not the full beating. Not the lynching. Not the mowing down by full auto. Not the burning of your village. But a kind of nice struggle, a sweet pain. And there's no love without pain. There's most definitely no story to tell without pain." His black eyes graze over Gordon's towering form. He says, "Yeahh. It's more than team spirit. The worse the apparatus kicks your ass, the more love there is. It's probably why some get so addicted to street activism. It's where we become one mighty hand on the pitchfork and scythe outside the castle walls . . . even if it makes not one iota of change."

The voices approaching come closer. Some footfalls crunch.

Blake cocks his head. "You guys here . . . your setup . . . it feels right to me. They say it was your idea . . . it's your baby . . . a man like you, rara avis."

Gordon turns to glance toward where the kids will be arriving in a matter of moments. He says, "It takes a lot of hands and backs. And then, you know, a lust for learning."

Blake says, "I've been told that half the residents here were destitute." He shakes his head. "That's not just vision. That's opening the arms to expose a naked heart. Kind of weird . . . on the surface of the thing . . . but good. But why the fuck this brother shit with Hummer? You're over the top there."

Gordon's torn and scarred-over cheek twitches, the pale, pale dark-lashed eyes settle on his accuser.

Blake has the rifle in both hands across his belted jacket, muzzle up at the clouds. He says, "One of your kids said in one of their philosophy salons I attended that he figured out how class works in the US. You heard them on this?"

Gordon squares his shoulders, cane now up under one arm. "Well, they've had forty million discussions on class. They run one subject into the ground."

"Well," Blake muses. "They . . . he . . . it was a boy . . . he said there are two social classes. He said most of the population are in one class, the commoners. I like that. The commoners. Then the second category, smaller, it's the gods. Or devils, depending on your life's view. But they have the power of gods, these topmost creatures."

Gordon snorts. "That was probably Kirk Martin. I don't know what gets into these kids. They eat too much leaf spinach."

Blake chuckles deep and satisfied. "I think it *was* Kirk. And *thennnnnn* he broke the commoner class into layers. He said the professionals are one layer. They get a certain amount of token honor from the edifice. But they're driven hard. By fear of loss of status and those comforts . . . those extras that come to be necessary. It's called the velvet whip. Then there's the layer that has always had to toil toil toil and to fight to get and keep home and hearth."

The sun opens a bigger hole and it's as if Gordon and Blake had a spotlight on them.

Blake gives the Bushmaster's receiver a little pat. Frowns. "Then, according to Kirk, there's that layer the Bible speaks to, the New Testament. Does Kirk study the Bible?"

"Sometimes they discuss and read up on religions. But Kirk, he's an electronics man. Inventor. He made a city run on solar batteries. And loves to throw a monkey wrench into the salon discussions. He doesn't attend many of them."

"Well, ha! Great kid. He said society in the US treats the poor as a profit opportunity. Or for ugly social experiments. They're not considered useless but not considered human. They're all but measured by the pound."

Gordon looks down at the grass, blinking.

Blake says, "He was wearing a turquoise bow tie with red stars."

Gordon's dark beard splits into a grin, the gloom of his missing teeth substantial.

Blake smiles in a considerate, closed-lips way. "You must be amazed by these kids. These thirteen- and fourteen- and fifteen- and sixteen-year-olds." He shakes his head. "All of them."

The young voices are almost now where they are soon to appear at the top of the road. One voice is clearly Cory's. Another is Bree's. Another has the rolling warm music of the South, Jaxon Cross. Pirate. Gordon rubs his eyes wearily. "They're a pain in the ass."

Blake giggles.

Gordon winces. "Nobody should have kids. Just adopt four-leggeds. Then when times get rough you can eat 'em."

Blake inhales the now coldly warm day, the almost-smell of the sun. The frustrated sun that can't seem to find a big enough hole in the clouds. All this flutter of light and the warmth of words between two friends.

Gordon makes a happy noise in his throat. "My wife Beth. She says there are three classes . . . the aliens, who live on another planet . . . she means the billionaires. Then there's the yuppie-virtue-our-shit-don't-stink group. And then the bitchin' group."

Blake's eyes crinkle with appreciation.

Gordon switches his cane from hand to hand.

Blake says, "Well, it's time to accept the facts of life, Gordon. You know people can transcend the artificial divisions of race to become brothers. But they can't transcend the fires between the human-being class and the . . . uh . . . *god* class to be brothers." Even as the last five words are sort of snarled, he is swinging deftly to his left, raising the rifle against his shoulder, lifting off the safety, even as he seems not to be aiming but the rifle itself is aiming. Though of course it is *he*, Blake, who is aiming, all in a heartbeat, no stranger to this star object of so much American divisiveness, all in concert, this aiming, the trigger finger and his spread legs and his one wide eye at the scope, the weightless weight of that eye pushing into the next moment: *Koorack! Koorack! Rack!-Rack!-Rack!-Rack!-Rack!-Rack!-Rack!* . . .

The hits dig in back and forth across the papier-mâché throat, Bruce Hummer staring, not flinching, not afraid to die, and so this face of familiar brown-green eyes, this head begins to teeter as one would do when listening hard to a promise: *Rack!-Rack!-Rack!-Rack!*

And then like a heavy overripe fruit . . . no, like a *real head*, it flumps onto rock and ice and flat, gray, surrendered grasses, rolls almost a couple of yards before stopping, its unchanged eyes staring up at the meridian of the sky where the smiling sun would be if it were summer.

Critical thinker of the present time.

If you force people's faces into the mud, they'll start throwing it at you.

—Investigative journalist Lance Tapley, in correspondence with the author

The hardworking Bread and Roses organizers are now *really* ready to roll.

A moderately attended rally in rainy Albany, New York, then on to the Midwest. Most of these rallies are pretty enthusiastic but not rowdy, not dangerous. When and if the media covers these rallies, it's only in varying degrees of brevity, and/or "Ho-hum-just-another-little-special-interest-group-making-a-little-fuss."

Then it's hanging out one weekend in the country outside College Park, Pennsylvania, where Olan has some friends and an ex-wife who is still a friend. Then they start in again, small rallies and get-togethers, more rallies in the works. Autoworkers, steelworkers, blast furnace guys,* all suspecting more shutdowns in the near future, "no work, no life"; most of these being black guys, one telling how "Gimp'd give you a tour of the place but your shoes'll melt." Then he laughed like hell.

But now each rally gets more intense. They are beginning to know of "the mad Prophet," depicted on the tube as a bad sort. But being a bad sort is starting to feel like being the right sort. Good is bad and bad is good, eh?

At most rallies, two kids bearing flags stand on either side of Gordon, different rallies, different kids. Usually one boy, one girl, maybe a teen, maybe a "fry." Samantha is picturesque with her beret, camo BDU shirt, cartridge belt, red or black neckerchief, and that new homemade fluorescent orange button on her chest that reads: FRINGE AND PROUD OF IT. And Jane, who for some reason insists on her trench coat, even though it's quite warm. And boy, does Jane love travel. She has become a pro with maps and directions. With *some* assistance, of course. Seven and a half years old, she rides in the front of the van, calling out, "Next exit!" and "Don't get excited. Youngstown isn't for a long ways." Slaps the atlas shut crisply. And now she has a wristwatch that she checks obsessively. All her trench coat pockets are bulging with notebooks and pens.

But the rallies get more and more ominous. People grabbing at Gordon. Samantha's beret gets made off with. The stars and stripes get torn. Gordon lets people touch him. And *he* fondles *them*. Shoulders, hands, ears. A few he has embraced. The organizers scold him. "Don't encourage them. Just tip your cap or something. Keep your hands to yourself." But Gordon, impulsive as ever, leans right into their embraces, kissed a bunch of women widget makers on their noses. Kissed an old derelict on the head, then gave the old guy his

* Poetic license here as the Jeanette blast furnace imploded in 1997, about three years before this scene.

Bean's Logginga and Pulp cap. One man pointed a gun at Gordon. Within twenty feet. He was young and blond and fresh-faced and wore a gray sweatshirt with US NAVY on the chest and a painter's white cap with a little mirror button pinned to it. Wasn't even trying to be discreet. The sun flashed from cleaved purple clouds above as a bunch of laid-off autoworkers, fifty- and sixty-year-old black guys, none under six-foot-two, jumped the attacker. Gun did not go off. But one of these autoworkers, after the brawl, had a heart attack an hour later in an open parking lot and died among his friends.

Lawmen took the attacker off in cuffs.

But seems there wasn't enough evidence to bother him with. Everyone who calls is told this by a city police spokesperson.

Again.

Only for a weekend this time. And *no kids*. The organizers have arranged plane tickets for this one. They warn Gordon that this rally might get out of hand. "And need I remind you, stick to our folk school message," Lenny gruffly commands. "The reversing of all corporate-personhood Supreme Court rulings and rejection of any corporate personhood language in any law. Just talk charter revocation. Free speech. Labor rights. Cool it on the aggressive stuff, okay?"

Up at the mikes, the Prophet, hatless, black T-shirt, jeans, a haze of badass heat in this Midwest city, the electricity of the crowd even hotter so that the spooky group nervous system and the place and the history of it all, its two-hundred-year wail, bind to him and swell within his guts and the sound of his mother Marian's voice once lecturing him, *You love everybody. Your love is cheap,* and Claire draws something on his arm lightly with one finger, maybe a Valentine heart, maybe a smiling face, as if to remind him that he is the light of her life, to not handle dynamite too roughly.

And also Meggie is near.

The two women "bodyguards" in their contrasting sizes could be something to joke about in a less sinister scene. Not to speak of differences in style. Claire with her braided bun and navy blue T-shirt and dungarees. Meggie flowing in pale apricot, which she has bragged is the same color as her "cherry Camaro" . . . obviously not "cherry" as in color. Her earrings are big gold hornets. Her shoes glittering clogs. Her apricot gown with mandarin collar seems more fit for a ball. Perhaps to her, who fears nothing, this *is* a ball.

Gordon runs a broad hand over his chest. His face glistens and he hasn't even started to hold forth.

To this hazy midwestern mob, including a multitude of farmers, the many-generations kind, the conservative kind, the newly landless kind, the butchered men, butchered families, relegated now to boxy ranch house suburbs and the "housing" in cities, "service jobs," betrayed by the patriotic promise; to these, he starts with a kind of squashy calm, mouth close to the largest mike, sweat trickling into his eyes. He works in Lenny's sentiments, the reason he is here, right?

The crowd barely rustles. Eyes on Gordon, the bad mad Prophet, who is now wiping his face with a red bandanna, then a look comes into his eye and he ties the thing around his neck and says firmly, almost imperiously, "Redneck."

The crowd makes a reply so deeply felt that Gordon's rib cage vibrates.

Eventually a subsiding.

Gordon speaks softly, "The word redneck comes from the days of organizing coal miners who made up an army of *thousands*, wearing red bandannas. Companies stole *their* farms with funky mineral-rights leases, worked them cruelly in mines. Gotta fight a thing like that. It isn't dignifying to beg. Do not believe the twisted lie that redneck means sunburned neck. No sun in the *mines*. The *TRUTH* . . ." he screams, "is always dangerous!" More crowd thunder. Then he begins again in a kind of hoarse mode going back to charter revocation and free speech. Words. These being just sounds soon to fizzle and disappear. But there *is* a low buzzing groan out there. Gordon waits, listening. It is there, added to the rustling.

What is it?

He stares at the mikes a few seconds. "In our capitols, ordinary people, people capable of kindness, are committing unforgivable acts. Acts against all of humanity. Their minds are twisted with the religion of investment and corporate purity, of . . . of . . . primacy. They are within the well-meant pus-filled tumor that izzzz *growing* . . . GROWING! The tumor *must* grow by the next quarter. That's how it works. *Every* quarter. Forevermore. And to do that, my brothers, my sisters, YOU must be . . . MUST be . . . tossed overboard. They cannot afford wages anymore, they say. Mechanization is cheaper, they say. But it's true! Cuz the tumor's gotta *grow*. In the next quarter! And the next! They cannot afford to spend, only to *take*!!!"

Groans. Growls. And squirming pain-filled shrieks of a crucifixion a hundred times a hundred.

Gordon's eyes drag over and across the crowd, then the sudden wincing of his Tourette's-like eye and cheek . . . and all his scars never cease to blister him in his increasing understanding of how worthless every human being is when the rug gets pulled. How flesh tears. How flesh corrupts. Melts to stink and dust. And worst of all how man eats man, minus fork, spoon, and knife.

In the foreground, the faces of this crowd are nodding, a wavelike purling of their concurrence with what they perceive as his rage, a lotta people with arms across their chests, some with hands in pockets . . . while in the peripheries, there's disturbance, something, hard to tell what . . . screams, motion.

Gordon continues softly, mouth close to one mike, heavy mustache scratching at the mike, words with p's popping, s's striking the open spaces like sparks. "A few years ago, in a city in New York State, a nice well-meaning lion got loose from the zoo and mauled a little boy and his grandfather to death. *One* grandfather. *One* boy. The lion was, yes, well-meaning, just being a lion. Nothing untoward. When something is created to grow big and maul you, it SHALL!!!!"

He leans back, crosses his arms, squints up to his left at a fantastically tall building, then back to the closest faces, many with sunglasses, so he cannot see their eyes. He stares at the closer regions of the crowd, while there is still, in the distance, something bubbling. He leans to the mikes. "What next?" Pause. "WHAT NEXT?!!!"

The crowd makes an uneven grating howl, shouts . . . a lot of deep voices, mostly men, mostly middle-aged and older, mostly in some stage of grief. A lot of militia element here, he has been advised. Men ready to tear something apart, those who haven't taken up heavy-duty "white identity" church and gone winging up into the wrong sky.

Gordon throws up a fist. "WAR!" And the crowd howls again. More keenly. More in sync. "WAR! That's what's next!" Gordon doesn't glance at the organizers behind him here on the stage. He does not look at Claire or Meggie, his guardian angels, though again Claire's reasoning fingertips knead his left biceps and on the other side Meggie's dense six-foot-three shadow holds back the sun. He rubs his face violently with both hands, and from his reddened face asks, "Oh, you say you want peace? Well then . . ." He throws up a fist. "PEACE!!!!" He laughs a deep weird laugh. "Peace is . . . *great*." He nods while the crowd grumbles and makes a wrinkling sound, like burning plastic, like something made cheap thrown into the fire. He calls to them, "But you see, peace ain't peace if it's in a cage, brother! Or under the eyes of the overseer! Or when you're despised by your brother. Submission to that peace is peace only for those archfiends of capital!!"

The crowd crackles and swells, squeezes closer, tighter.

Now the Prophet shakes his head in sorrow, leans to the mikes, "Oh, my brothers and sisters, can't you smellllll it? Can't you smell the big-money men and the government in a sweaty humpa bumpa embrace? Centralized power! Faceless power! Full spectrum dominance! Gonna take over the world. Gonna take over outer space! Gonna corral all that fossil stuff and street drugs and gold and water . . . gonna corral *all* stuff! Fooood! Food, *they*'ve said, is a weapon, the arrogant bastardly sonsabitches! Oh, my brothers and sisters, see their shiny tools: Money laundering! Tax havens! Subsidies that pour from the Fed via computer keys and debt into their wide-open maw! Stock manipulations. Teams of lawyers bigger than football teams! Media! *Their* media. PR think tanks! Foundations! Lobbyists. Rigged campaigns! Laughable elections!" He laughs. He is holding his head as if it hurts, ruffling his hair thisaway and thataway and he is laughing. "It is bee-yoo-tee-full, brother . . . from where they stand!!"

In sync the crowd sort of laughs, talks back, grieves. Crowd is concordant. Crowd is wide open, mouths twisted, hands spanking, work boots and sneakers stomping.

Gordon smashes his fist against his own breastbone. "*I* am nice! *I* want to give them time! *End* human rights to corporations, limit their sizes . . . whatever . . . whatever it takes. Rip it up! Rip up all their fucking goddamn tricks! Tear them to confetti! No more! Whatever time they need to do this shredding . . . ah . . . one year! Plentya time. They can request an extra week for real good shredding. But no subterfuge! No sneaky-sneaky! We want to see tiny . . . VERY tiny pieces of these documents in piles . . . tiny *tiny* pieces . . . or they better hide . . . man . . . cause man, oh, man, *we.are. coming*!"

Whistles split the air. Bellows. Growls of agreement.

"But!" shouts the Prophet, crossing his arms over his chest as so many others here are doing. "We've got a major problem with our ranks. Our ranks are weak. Yes, *weeeeak*."

Buncha boos rise as ugly vapors through the heat.

Prophet frowns. "See? This is the clincher." Prophet sadly shakes his head. "An army of suckers."

More boos.

Prophet snorts. "Boo. Yes. Boo. Cuz races hating each other and all that bashing of gays and bashing poor people has gotta go. Cuz while thousands who do this got their eyeballs tied in knots *horizontally*, the CORPORATE BEAST WALKS!!!! While our weakened army of suckers wets its pants over *each other's* minor differences, the BEAST WALKS!!!"

He unfolds his arms, looking lost and especially sloped-shouldered, all those years of heavy lifting and he is breathing a bit hard.

There have been a few more shadowy boos from those he shall never win over.

Prophet smiles quirkily, face drizzling rivers through his short dark and gray beard. Big-guy neck swallows hard. "Okay, hear this fact, this solid law of nature. No weakened shit-ass army can ever cut that big demon fucker down!!!"

A roar of mixed applause, shouts, boos, and restless shifting of sneakered and booted feet. So many herd-type sounds.

The Prophet clutches his T-shirt directly over the pounding muscle of his heart. He studies faces, some giving a single nod, some bewildered. From the several speakers the Prophet's voice now stretches to further distances. "We gotta take the evil eye off our brothers! Otherwise, methinks some of us don't have the balls to face the one *true* Satan! He's up there making deals! Deals on our jobs!

Deals on our homes! Our farmland! Our food! Our water! On our kids! On our old age! Deals for new prisons and more laws to put us there! Deals to enslave *you* . . ." He points a finger into the crowd, yet not singling out a face. "Satan will lynch *you* because thousands and thousands of suckerrrs for *generations* gave their permission to . . ." He covers one eye. ". . . to crush potential threat toooo THE BEAST!!!" He is gasping out the rest. Is this a heart attack? "For instance, the Apache threat! The Nez Percé threat! The Cherokee threat! African slave threat! The pissed-off Irish and Italian and Russian Jew immigrant factory worker threat!!! The freed slave threat!!! The pissed-off miners threat!!! The pissed-off all-races poor people threat! The pissed-off women threat! The pissed-off farmers threat!! And each threat . . . that was beaten back from bothering Satan . . . occurred . . . because thousands of us were goddamn suckers!!!"

He has bowed his head, not to be in silent prayer but still raving breathlessly into the mikes, "There is not much time left!! No time!! No time to get our army ready!! Because *their* army is united! *THEIR* side is always united. Cuz SATAN IS NOT A SUCKER!"

Into the brick-thick sky and furious gargling noise of the crowd, the Prophet raises a fist and his oiled-looking face screams. Maybe it was a word but it sounds like just a plain agonized scream.

Someone is yanking on his arm. Not Claire. The other arm. Someone who has a mighty rough touch. Trying to shut him up. He can see in a glance Meggie's huge ringless hand.

Now the men closest to him are jamming against the platform as another portion of the crowd behind them, just so naturally and gracefully, has begun tipping over a police car, which Gordon did not know was there until he saw its wheels from the underside . . . and the yellowy steam of this nervous, heated-up place begins to smell ripely of gasoline.

Then.

The crowd is said to be thinning out but as Gordon and his friends are taking the steps at the rear, somehow an arm of the many-armed crowd is scalding Gordon's face, this because Gordon was twisting sideways to shake the hand of an intense-looking little black woman, so the small knife that was intending to fuck with his heart or maybe a lung, opened up his face from cheek to the corner of his mouth . . . that which was still scarred from before. He almost doesn't see a human being to go with the hand that draws the knife back for another try but then the image flicks into his mind's eye, a wiry guy, young eyes, wearing a black bandanna to cover his face from his nose down, just those eyes . . . but then the eyes and face sail away . . . as though into the humid sky as Meggie Marsh (lunging against Claire) directs her cantaloupe-sized fist in a perfect right hook to the jaw of the "lone" knife man who is mewling now even as Claire shrieked and Meggie had bellowed like a sumo wrestler, so there was all this noise including Gordon's whining unmanly moan as crimson is splashing in teacupfuls over his boots because, yes, the head and face do bleed exceptionally well. The knife sort of trickles to the asphalt and the attacker, with something of his jaw probably in shards under the black bandanna, returns to the outer veil of reality where he came from.

At the hospital.

While he is getting his stitches, Jip tells him the local media mentioned the attack "but they of course gave top billing to the police car and the cop's concussion. They say you were inciting a riot, exactly what we've feared. Very serious. They briefly mentioned the attack on you, but that the disappeared masked person was said by *witnesses* to be a jealous husband of a militia element, most likely someone close to the mad Prophet."

"He was very close," says Gordon in a muffled swollen way. "Right here," he holds his spread fingers over his chest.

Jip sniffs indignantly.

Gordon laughs deep in his throat.

The physician's assistant doing the repair job says, "I'm going to have to ask you to hold very still."

Meggie speaks with a not very girlish snort, "Without our wonderful TV and excellent mainstream newspapers Americans would all be twisted up in the dark on what's happening . . . like in those awful other countries."

Blake, standing at the edge of the examining room's private curtains, snickers.

Claire is nearer to the gurney than Gordon realizes; mostly just the highly focused physician assistant's face fills his present narrow firmament.

From beyond his shoulder Claire's small golden dimpled hand dribbles down his bare arm to his thumb, muckles on tightly.

Now Meggie rustles orangely in the corner of Gordon's eye. "I," says she huskily, "expect some sort of special thank-you for my quick thinking and accuracy in poking the little creep. Without me, you'd not be in this cute little curtained cubicle with the pretty pouch of nice fresh blood going into you there through your arm. Instead, you'd be in a refrigerated drawer downstairs. And you're not the first person who I've saved. My rescuing reputation goes way back. And each and every person was grateful. Two words are all I ask. *Thank you.* But you, big boy, act like what I did is your due." She tosses her magnificent white-blond lion's mane before hip-swingingly walking out.

Cory remembering.

Well, heh-heh, you see, Gordo was not really owned by the organizers. He was a . . . sort of traitor, you might say, meeting with the right wing at the Settlement or a few of us driving to their location.

So we got into the belly of an April sleet storm, in Paul Lessard's old patched-up Chevy club cab, the Settlement station wagon, and Ray Pinette's Explorer, like three ice-plastered snails inching along down the long open middle of the County, Aroostook County, yes, and Bree was with us, her drawing pad on her knees, her knees curled up, she in one of the back seats, in our company, seven Settlement men, including me and Butch.

Gordo was not always in the same rig with Bree. He might be in one of the others ahead or behind her, then switching when we pulled off to carve some more ice off our windshields and mirrors, wind giving the bits of sleet the qualities of bullets. So Bree and Gordo weren't exactly the old sweethearts they used to be, but Gordo was always a part of what was going on inside *me*. I wanted to *be* him, but first I had to figure him. Was being two-faced good or bad?

Butch thinking back.

Um . . . Claire had classes at the university that were critical to finals, she said. So on this trip she wasn't Gordo's bodyguard. He hadn't had any of those seizures we were warned about anyway. And now he had his license back. Except for his limp and funny ears and flatter nose and old and new dents, crags, and mutilations, he seemed his old great self. Once in a while he'd say something queer like "cloud" for "wax" or some stuttering. Once in a while.

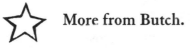

Bree looking back.

I did sketches of the people and their homes that we visited. We did seven residences on that trip but three stand out.

More from Butch.

Um . . . you couldn't miss the expressions of some as we stepped from our vehicles or crowded inside their kitchen doors. Gordo's height and Mr. Maine–type shoulders in his BDU jacket making a room seem to shrink, and the ripped-open and scarred-over face they'd already seen in miniature on their screens and in newspapers . . . again and again and again and again. He would reach out as if to shake hands with our host but would lock his fingers around the guy's forearm, wrist to wrist, pulse to pulse for a moment, eyes into eyes, pouring himself into the other's brain, a wicked trespass but then the goofy smile. He would say real solemn-like, "Great to be here."

I noticed how mostly . . . um . . . they usually didn't look at Bree at all, at first. Of course they *saw* her. Her freak face. Not the result of violence. No fist. No rock. No heroic bearing up. Just a face out of sci-fi. But, you know, people get used to anything. It's just a matter of the brain processing possible danger, a dangerous difference versus a harmless fluke.

Bree again.

Yeah, I was kind of being digested. I understood. It hurt a little.

Butch again.

There was this old place we showed up at outside Houlton, Maine. There were only three guys and they were real quiet. They had the TV on, staring at the screen, didn't even offer coffee. Um . . . okay . . . it seemed like they were mad at us. The guy who was captain of this militia, whose house this was, had a framed picture of Eisenhower on the wall and a bunch of bowling trophies that I studied for a long time. Then it seemed like maybe they were mad at *each other*. One guy was about late twenties, two were late sixties. The captain was one of those in their sixties.

After a VERY long, very weird, very endless hour of this, it was mentioned that their militia of eighteen active members had just that morning split off into two groups, fifteen members with the new captain, two guys with the old captain. So these three guys here around the TV were now the whole old Aroostook County Militia.

The new captain of the other militia . . . um . . . the *new* militia, was a guy by the name of Douglas Cash, whose full name was used and pronounced distinctly, like most of us pronounce the word *snake*. Then another name was spoken with curled lip, Barry Winters, who was also now part of the new *other* group and all that new other group were basically "thieves," "control freaks," and "suspicious." Suspicious might have meant "agent," but suspicious of course also probably meant *ex-friend*.

We couldn't be sure of the real details. These guys seemed rendered practically stone by the trauma of the experience.

The Millinocket Minutemen. Cory speaks.

Heading back down across Maine from wee town to wee town and through broad valleys, we were in our search mode for the Millinocket Minutemen, nine of us in three rigs. Many "sore-ass miles," Butch Martin called it . . . heh heh.

Finally, where we showed up had just *one* guy, though he had invited us to come meet his "whole militia." He was young, thin, nervous, shy. Wearing jeans, sneakers, and sweatshirt. Pale eyebrows and lashes. Mustache pretty faint. A *white* white guy. He made us sandwiches and passed a bag of Oreos around while, yes, the TV droned. Eventually, he explained he was waiting for his father-in-law to get back from taking "Millie to work," whoever Millie was. Turns out his father-in-law was the other half of the whole two-man militia. A militia that had *never* been more than two, never less. When the father-in-law turned up, the young guy, whose name was Darrell, came to life. Even the TV went off.

The father-in-law was a life-of-the-party type. And you could tell these two were wicked pals. They told too many hunting stories to count, and tarring road stories. The father-in-law had a paving and seal-coating outfit until last year. Went under. "Bubble bubble." *His* words.

And they told quite a few stories about some guy named "Ed," some character, a neighbor it seemed, because whenever they said "Ed," they'd jerk their head to the left or roll their eyes left, like this meant *next door*.

At one point, the young guy proudly showed us a snapshot of himself as "militiaman." Head-to-foot camo, the "Swiss camo" with a lot of bright red mixed into the green "foliage." Dark cop glasses. He braced a Springfield M-16, butt-down, against the side of his right foot. I wouldn't have known it was him. He didn't look shy and stoop-shouldered as in real life. He looked like a defender.

Yep. Dignity. If you ain't got it, you are gonna *get* it.

Bree speaks.

I did all my sketches from memory after we were riding away. I never brought a sketch pad into any of their homes. I have only one sketch of that third visit, a visit that truly spooked me. Twelve militia guys, a big supper table, bare but for coffees, hats, an ashtray, newspaper, a demolished half of a maple frosting birthday cake, and some sort of receipts.

See, in my drawing is our host's old grandmother in her glider chair, not gliding, by the window with its blue glass dreamcatcher dangling above. Her hair, thin. Not bald but you can see the shape of her head. Glasses. Her dentures didn't seem to be fixed to her gums but more like a really big and very whole sandwich she was trying to chew up. She looked really clean and fresh and cared for, pink floral blouse, dungarees, and sneakers. Wedding ring, fingers old and veiny but not swollen.

Suddenly her eyes widened on Gordon as he limpingly crossed the room for more coffee which was near her chair. No BDU jacket that day for Gordon but a T-shirt and work shirt and his favorite red neckerchief tied dog-collar style. The old woman spoke to him in a dry deep voice with an edge of panic, "Devil's food!" And her popped-wide eyes swept over his legs, arms, and middle.

In a softly low apology, our host Greg Day said, "She's got old-timers' disease."

Gordon said, "I understand."

The old woman kept ogling Gordon's body with such alarm that she began to breathe fast and then kind of swooned. She never looked at anybody in the room but Gordon, her eyes following him precisely as he returned to his chair.

"Devil's food," she said again and raised her hand in clawlike fashion as if to dig at him.

"Gram." Greg so gently spoke to her as if she were the size and power of a horse who if spooked could trample us. "We got your doughnuts. Is that what you want?" He ambled to the bread box. Rustled through crinkling bags but his "Gram" now leaned *waay* back, hand on heart, still breathing fast, eyes now really bulging on Gordon, but at last found his face, his face upon which so much past wrath and then the recent calculation of the knife had trampled and rent.

"Devil!" she rasped.

Greg Day had swung around empty-handed. "You okay, Gram? You aren't having chest pains are you?" He chuckled nervously.

His wife Lora tried to fit a doughnut into the poor old creature's hand.

Greg Day said, "She's not really with us." And he repeated. "Old-timers."

The doughnut tumbled unwanted into the old woman's lap. Now she pointed with an almost fisted hand and one curling finger at Gordon's work boots, then up up up and down again all over him and her puckery dentures-packed mouth smiled seductively, now both hands and all fingers raking through the air slowly, firmly, as if to comb him all over.

Greg Day flushed red. "She didn't use to talk like that."

"Of course not," said Gordon. "That condition does that." But he went pale when she nodded fast and with that one finger trying to pull him toward her chest, she commanded, "Come." And again the seductive smile.

The others had ceased even the thinnest trickles of conversation. They watched, some straight-on, some with sneaking glances, the wonder of this.

Then the old woman cocked her head and barked, too loud and clear for us to mishear or misremember, "The devil hath the power to assume a pleasing shape!"

Greg's militia buddies shifted in their chairs or where they stood as if to reset their bearings, for they were obviously just a little bit creeped out.

Back in Egypt. A few days later. Gordon and Eddie Martin in Gordon's old green-and-white Chevy pickup truck. Black night. Only one cool fuzzy star off there in the southwest. Close to midnight.

They are driving home from Gordon's mother's place in Wiscasset. She has been having some reporters hanging around and some weird calls. Her nephew, a cousin of Gordon's, "the architect," who has visited a lot, is going to move in with her for a while. He, Mark, can work right there at her house in one of the big upstairs rooms. This way, he can keep an eye on things.

So Gordon and Eddie have helped him move his stuff up from Concord, Mass. Took only one load, but all of the day. Now, in the black of night, the only things riding in back are a box of books Mark wanted to get rid of and a carefully made up Tupperware tray of homemade éclairs from Marian.

At the turnoff onto Heart's Content Road, the nighttime darkness suddenly fills with foreboding liquidy blue light in front of them and behind them.

Eddie snorts an *Isn't life interesting*? kind of snort.

Gordon inquires, "Got your seat belt fastened, Edward? We don't wanna be breaking any laws."

Eddie repeats the snort.

Gordon grabs his wallet before his truck has come to a full stop. Cranks down the window.

Two faces immediately appear, not faces, just eyeholes, the ski mask variety, 9-mms drawn, aimed at Gordon's face and Eddie's face. And out there on the edge of the blinding blue swerving wash of light, four figures, maybe six, dressed in black, full-auto-looking rifles aimed at the windshield. These cops are the door-kicking kind.

And there's slight movement in the lesser blue distances, more of these black bulletproofed figures.

And now a man in a denim jacket and jeans, dark shirt, comes up to Gordon's window. No gun in his hand. Just a flashlight. And another plainclothes type, wearing a dressier jacket, kind of L.L.Bean, appears at Eddie's window with a flashlight.

Eddie is having a little trouble with the window crank on his side. It's been screwy for years.

Oh, by the way, in case we have forgotten, this is Eddie Martin, father of Kirky, Evan, and Butch, owner of a studded bejeweled jazzy belt that he wears a lot and a salesman-like smile that he also wears a lot, but neither of which he wears tonight.

Denim-jacket guy says to Gordon, "License, registration, and insurance card."

Gordon's hand is right there with the three items.

The denim-jacket guy's eyes move over Gordon's face in vigorous little circles.

Gordon now looks straight ahead to the several ski-masked figures with rifles, wondering if he made a fast move now, mightn't all these people shoot *each other*. He looks back at the black-masked guy next to the denim-jacket guy. Black-masked guy with a black 9-mm pistol aimed at Gordon's face and throat.

Cop on Eddie's side swipes his flashlight over Eddie's waist and knees, the floor, the dash, the empty gun racks. Tells Eddie he wants to see some ID.

The denim-jacket guy carries Gordon's license and registration off, but another guy, one Gordon hasn't seen before now, guy in a sweatshirt and no mask, works his blinding flashlight beam over Gordon.

In the back of the truck, many flashlights at work and the truck shivers and rocks as cops climb in and out.

Gordon sees at least a dozen figures now moving around on a dirty low bank of leftover snow. All with rifles.

"Damn it," Gordon whispers to Eddie. "I knew I shoulda fixed that hole in the header. New sticker wouldn'ta been *that* hard to get."

Eddie doesn't laugh.

L.L.Bean-dressed cop next to Eddie's door asks, "What's that you say, Mr. St. Onge?"

Gordon smiles politely, "Hope everything's all right."

Man in denim jacket returns, does not give Gordon his IDs back, just says, "Mr. St. Onge. We need to have a look inside this truck. Could you step out, please."

Eddie is told the same. Also, his IDs seem to have disappeared.

Gordon asks, "Do you have a warrant?" And one of his eyebrows rises, the eye widening, the other eye squinting, his crazed look, his criminal element look. His bestial scarred mad-Prophet-pumping-up-the-masses look.

Denim-jacket guy says, "Eat shit." And Gordon remembers how in addition to the Rosenthals' nightmare, a cop put a boot on Lisa Meserve's face, after they had her handcuffed and down on her back. And then her Scottie dog was cooked to death. If they could do that to women, children, and dogs—

He hears a voice saying from Eddie's window, "Mr. Martin, you baby fuckers ain't seen nuthin' yet."

And so it happens.

They tear up the truck. They literally pry and rip all the fenders off. They force both men to strip, bend over, then stand, arms over heads. They ask questions. They ask them slow. They ask these questions while insisting Gordon and Eddie keep their arms over their heads, knowing how the circulation of blood works, how it hurts. Gordon and Eddie are separated at first, then positioned face-to-face with a few feet between them, as if this might add to their humiliation, and each man is aglow as if onstage, dozens of lights trained on their faces and bodies, even their feet. Steady white and dizzying blue. The questions are really far-fetched. Some have to do with drugs. But some have real weirdness, no possible answers. Questions to leave a person confused and haunted.

Gordon catches sight of two cops eating éclairs.

The books are left as only blasted-out squashed and confetti-ized shadows of their former selves.

There were things under the truck seat Gordon never dreamed were there, each thing pointed out to him under the sunny white lights. More questions. "What is this, Mr. St. Onge?" A baby's pacifier, a Polaroid of a decorated Christmas tree, a chicken feather, a mitten, five mismatched plastic barrettes, a toothbrush, a 3/8 wrench, a boogery handkerchief, a business card of an art gallery Gordon has never heard of, a couple of Kleenexes, pens, a *lotta* pens, a copy of *The Recipe*, a hunting laws booklet for 1976, a clothespin, an *old* apple (maybe a pear), a grocery list in Bonnie Loo's huge rolling script, a flashlight battery, a mouse nest long evacuated, ash leaves, a *lotta* ash leaves, an empty aspirin bottle.

But no drugs.

Gordon expects to be framed. For *something*. But he is not. Not tonight.

He thinks about the warrant. There is probably a warrant, at least a funny warrant, a funny drug warrant, one of those funny things provided by the new funny laws and Bill of Rights mutilations passed by the funny Congress. But then maybe there isn't a warrant. Like maybe there are no such things as leprechauns and gnomes.

Now the plainclothes cops, agents, whatever they are, just walk around and stand around and they smile a little. The ones who have faces. They don't *seem* disappointed that they have found nothing incriminating. They watch Gordon and Eddie getting dressed. They watch with their flashlights still trained on them, on their genitals. When cars pass on the road, the flashlights go off. Then on again after the car taillights are gone around the curve. Then the cops hoot and howl and whistle like fans at a basketball game or prizefight. All their eyes back on Gordon and Eddie, Eddie dressing fast, Gordon dressing slow, stubborn, pissed . . . but, yuh, afraid. Afraid of the next moment.

When these "lawmen" finally let Gordon and Eddie go, it is almost four-thirty in the morning.

But the truck is in pieces and won't start and the two Settlement men have to walk the rest of the way home, Gordon keeping one eye squinted tight, wishing there had been aspirin in that bottle under the truck seat.

When he finally reaches his house.

He leans against the frame of the closed kitchen door, trembling. Little childly sobs in the big neck. Eyes wide open in the awful dark. He prays, "God in the heavens, protect all of us in this world . . . from the humans." He closes his eyes, thoughts zinging, out of focus. He now grips his face with one hand to hide even from himself his wretched cries.

MAY

One night around eleven or so.

Glennice and Beth are driving back from visiting some of Glennice's church friends, using one of the Settlement station wagons. Glennice drives one-handed, drives manfully. She has always loved driving. There is nothing she can't drive—tractors, trucks up to first class, and, of course, now and then the church bus.

Beth is griping about how her parents want to come live at the Settlement. Sometimes when Beth gripes about a thing it means she's all for it.

Less than a mile from the Settlement road, big curve, the night explodes in dizzying churning blue light. Fore and aft. Both Glennice and Beth have heard the worst details of what happened to Gordon and Eddie, so here we are. Beth covers her mouth with both hands as Glennice brakes easy, not a full stop yet. Beth begins to cry, her cry high peeps like a box of new chicks. Not a sound you would think Beth's throat and tongue could make. And then Beth is crying out words, "Oh my God, no no no no no no."

And Glennice wails, "I don't get it!"

And then.

A few days later, Rick Crosman gets stopped. Alone. It's always the same. After dark. Late. Always the ski masks, guns, keeping the IDs, the invisible warrants, the strip searches, taunting, weird questions, threats, staving up the vehicle, leaving it fenderless and missing a coil wire or tire. With Beth, before they ordered her to strip, she was shown pictures of dead bodies . . . dead women . . . mutilated, eyes gouged, hands cut off, one was scalped. Glennice yelled, "Who are you?" to her tormenters. And this was, yes, the paramount question. Who were these guys? What agency? What did they want?

A few nights later, they will get Stuart, who is, as the women have been, visibly shaken for days. "They aren't really looking for anything," he says huskily, he and Eddie alone in the West Parlor one morning while the noisy breakfast goes on in the kitchens a few doors down. "Just trying to drive us nuts. Trying to get us to fight back."

Meanwhile, out in the kitchens, Astrid is feeding three Settlement babies in three high chairs, all three mouths slurping away on the spoonfuls of eggy rice. She says, "I'm getting a gun tomorrow."

Glennice says, "To do what with? Those guys will have about fourteen full auto rifles pointed at you."

Astrid says, "Thirteen."

Glennice says softly, so that no one else in the crowded kitchen can hear her, "Gordon wants us not to leave here after dark. No coming. No going. Nobody on those roads after dark. He told me. He's going to have a talk with everyone. Make it clear. Nobody is to be *out there* in the dark. No more trips to the planetarium in Portland for the whole day. Or pipe organ concerts at City Hall there. No field trips to the Boston dinosaur museums."

Jenny Dove says, "Great. Looks like a siege to me. Welcome to Waco."

And Glennice hugs her, presses a cheek hard to Jenny Dove's. "Don't hate me anymore. I know you've always hated me!"

Jenny Dove hugs her in return. "I have *never* hated you."

Glennice hugs harder, now sobbing, but laughing, too. "God bless you."

Jenny Dove hugs harder, too, eyes closed tight. Yes, the zealous Christian thing has always bugged her, but next to the cop thing, it's just fairy dust now. Does it say anything in the Bible about being in the same boat?

The three babies, cheeks fat with food, lips like small red bows, eyes solemn, watch the two women.

Lee Lynn recalls.

No more going in or out after dark. Nobody was to be on the roads except in full daylight. This was now Settlement law. Gordon's law. Not a group decision. But who was to argue?

Days pass.

It is mid-May. Pale new leaves filling in the foothills, all of Egypt the color of lettuce plaited through the dark evergreen. Longer days, purply-red sunsets, purply-red trilliums in bunches around rocks and along paths. May, sweet sweet sweet May. A new stage of terrorizing begins.

Helicopters.

After midnight. Floodlights sweep over the little dark houses of the Settlement, those clustered in the open field, while those houses clinging to the rocky hillside in the woods get somewhat spared. The big lights sweep from side to side. The sound is horrible, like something breaking to bits in a tornado, a gigantic god-sized cat kicking cat litter, over and over and over, around and around.

Gordon calls Senator Mary Wright but she is not to be reached. He calls his old friend Senator Joe. Joe says he'll look into it. "It might be the DEA or FBI or . . . ah, both. Or the BATF.* Or . . . let's see. The Department of Education . . . or . . . when have you last upset the Department of Agriculture?"

Gordon laughs. Yes, Joe is funny.

Joe asks, "Can't you just call them yourself? Reach a supervisor? Ask what's up. I bet if you talk civilized to them, they'll explain."

Gordon understands that Joe is starting to back off from him. Disassociate, chill.

**At the home of Aurel and Josee Soucier.
Something new.**

Aurel walks to the open bedroom door, his shoulders slouched, like shame. With no hat or cap, even with his thick French-Indian hair,

* Bureau of Alcohol, Tobacco, and Firearms.

his head looks small and vulnerable. Hair flattened from so much hat wearing. Paul Lessard is with him, close behind. Aurel draws back the flowery closet curtain to reveal what he once never dreamed would be here. Behind hanging shirts, dresses, and jackets, two unbayoneted Kalashnikovs, rigged back to full automatic. Without the needed permits, these are about as illegal as it gets. He hefts one, places it in Paul's hands. Paul is click-clattering open the breech . . . even when new, slick as a new baby in grease, he is one to check. Loaded? No.

For Aurel back in time there were thousands of Kalashnikovs, the black-burning hardworking steel, red-gold wooden forearms in the enemy's red-gold dawn, and the definition of silence was the jungle's ten million fear-thrill smells, while the definition of the Kalashnikov was those black-garbed running legs, *millions of them*, their phantom agility, their ace in the game nobody wins.

Aurel steps back. "Take it, you. I spread t'em out. Two in one place t'ey are too cozy." He laughs.

Paul slips into French. To him guns have always been fun. Now they are unspeakably primary. And words. Once words were about work and life. He has never wanted more than that.

Aurel laughs again, though nothing funny has been said. He is just going a little bit crazy.

Settlement sixteen-year-old Mickey Gammon speaks.

In the night, who can sleep? Helicopters makin' the walls shake, knocking the tree limbs against the house. And big lights so they can trap you like a bug down here walking around. But so what? I go out. I ain't slept all night for nearly two years anyway. With homelessness you can't cut many z's. So what's another few nights?

In the day, the FBI fuckers, or whatever they are, vanish like cockroaches.

Today after dinnertime, I decide to mosey up to my old home sweet home. The tree house. Pretty stupid really. Lots littler than I remembered. I had to laugh at myself. I lived in this thing all last summer.

So now I climbed up. Sat there a minute. Well, the thing was still solid. If your roof don't leak, it'll go forever. Imagine someday I'm this older guy and I'll look at this thing and really crack up.

Hmmmm. Actually, it's kinda neat here. Real quiet. Except for the bugs. If you had to, you could hide here and blow away anyone coming up that path . . . or flying around overhead in the sky. I don't keep this service pistol on me all the time now and loaded for nuthin'.

Helicopters.

Every night is nearly the same. Like a cuckoo bird at midnight, thrust out of the clock, the whomping aircraft comes from the sky.

Gordon's calls to Senator Mary Wright's home find only an answering machine and Mary's recorded voice saying, *Leave a message*. He calls Janet Weymouth but a housekeeper explains Janet is in Ireland with friends, won't be home till late this month. She offers no number in Ireland. Even when Gordon reminds her that he is Janet's very good friend.

He tries the attorney general, yeah, now desperate enough to try the ridiculous.

He even calls the FBI. Gets a "menu." Then a human, a female human so hurried that she seems to be using a phone out on the sidewalk. She transfers him to the voice mail of a supervisor. He hangs up.

He calls all sorts of official phone numbers. But no officials ever call him back. He tries Senator Joe again. Senator Joe seems even more weirdly distracted and hurried than those agency operators who don't even take the two extra seconds to say "Bye now" when hanging up. Gordon calls various lawyer friends and law types at their homes. Real voices never answer, there are only the hi-tech replies. Rarely reaching live office receptionists, he finds it's always the same. Leave your name and number so "they" can call back. None do. So much for phones. So he writes to them. Gets no replies from most. Scribbled notes from three of them, saying they *wish* they could help.

Militia visitors intensify. Some from Texas and Colorado and California, places that seem almost off the edge of the planet earth to a Mainer. Other time zones, for sure. These men are all bright-eyed into the wee hours of the night. Talking about the looseness of society. The "liberals" who are "evil." These guys resent the "New World Order." But they WANT order. They WANT law. But a kind of nervous God's law, law that will BRING BACK something. What?

Gordon understands that what they might be straining to "reshape" is the movie and school textbook versions of simplicity. The black and white hats. The Ten Commandments. The world of hard work, polite love, a loaded table, guiltless sleep . . . and for those who scoff at these laws, the noose. Or something worse.

His expression is almost loving, almost drugged-looking, as he studies them across the table, out on the summer porches, listening to their complaints, their eating sounds. He understands that the ultimately terrible possibility in their minds and hearts is: CHAOS. And yet the ultimately cherished thing is: FREEDOM, that strangely elusive construct. Maybe because freedom and chaos are the same damn thing.

Once in a while he murmurs the stuff of corporate personhood, rebuilding unions, the wickedness of endless growth. But mostly he now just says, "I hear you, brother."

And a young Settlement teen or oldster asks, "More coffee? More pie?"

And the sweet late spring air mixes with the smells of food and overly warm skin . . . *abundance*, which "we" have always believed is our "right," here in America.

Yes, Gordon welcomes them. Invites more, welcomes another batch, invites more. But always with the warning that they must never arrive at or leave these premises after dark. Most hear him and accommodate. But some are challenged. They defiantly come driving up the mountain in darkness, hoping for confrontation, their weapons loaded. And what happens is the unexpected. None of these men are stopped, though some say they saw what looked like government cars and vans parked along the road.

Meanwhile, no more young teens are given guard duty down at the gatehouse. Not without a pair of men with walkie-talkies. Friendly to visitors, yes, but armed and edgy. And really fussy now about who gets by.

Although the whole guardhouse business is really a joke, isn't it? Anybody can get in on foot who wants to traipse up through the woods and open fields, the several miles of boundary that shape the St. Onge acreage, north, east, south, and west.

Dee Dee St. Onge, whose husband is Gordon's cousin (Lou-EE St. Onge, in case we've forgotten), tells Gordon that her father (Willie

Lancaster, in case we've forgotten) told her to be sure to tell him that one out of every five militia people could be an FBI agent. "They get in a group and try to get you to do a stupid thing. It's called entrapment. You think you won't do a stupid thing, but the stupid thing might be just that you *say* something stupid, just feeling relaxed, just joking. You don't have to actually *do* a stupid thing. Just talk big. These operatives have little tape recorders and cameras and they get it all down. Then they do their sting thing."

Gordon kind of laughs. Says to Dee Dee, "I've already said a lotta stupid things. Before crowds of hundreds."

Next, Willie sends, via Dee Dee, some articles from mainstream newspapers backing up his warning, all except the "one out of five" figure. The articles just mention "increased use of these agents."

Gordon tells Dee Dee to tell her father thank you, that he appreciates his advice. That he respects his advice.

The caress.

The engine is out, its submissiveness to the will of men almost warm to the touch, though as heavy as a small mountain under its chain fall. It is figuratively the still-beating heart of the Settlement's two-ton flatbed truck, that greasy ward of Butch Martin's genius. Between Butch and the fifteen-year-old scrawny bird-butt Mickey Gammon there are few words, indeed no discussions, philosophies, theories, just the screaks of wrench twists and crisp bangs where there is corrosion. Fingers flick away a furrow of rust. The dear truck will live on and slave on, due to these hours of rough and tender touch.

Then Cory St. Onge's huge triangular shadow is upon them. He is only months older than Mickey but Settlement-born, Settlement-flavored. To Mickey *anyplace* is just empty sky under an untrustworthy parachute. But today is a good day and the sort of dungeon smell of the engine and the rest of the big Chevy's open mouth is sending him a big nice smooch of appreciation, for when it comes to the work on motor vehicles, Mickey, too, is no slouch.

Cory has not come to remind them that food is on the tables across the Quad, although that is the case. He wears a red-and-black plaid flannel shirt and an eye-sting orange hunting vest with spent 32 Special shells in both pockets, left from his early mountaintop target practice with Jaxon Cross. He says he was reading more on spies last night. Willie Lancaster's warning had struck a chord.

Butch gives him a weary look, standing up fully straight to unstiffen his back.

Mickey's gray eyes are not direct. They never shoot *into* anyone else's eyes but skitter around. Today he wears a Settlement-made shirt and he also wears that zingy Settlement smell, dandelionish. No, he is no longer a tree house orphan.

Cory squints one eye, palm to his other eye, "I've decided not to let this eat me."

Butch grunts, "What?" His one word in this cement place makes a cool watery echo.

Says Cory, "Spies. It's even worse now than the eighties and nineties . . . no surprise . . . but . . . well, you could say in America there are more spies than UPS drivers."

Butch rolls his eyes to the white low-hung evening sun in one of the small windows of this Quonset hut. Butch is the older, twenty-one. Butch in his occasional moment of eminence in the company of teens.

Cory whines, "It's like a can of spinach is really a pink flamingo."

Mickey, who rarely smiles, releases a dainty tsk-snort and fingers his cigs pack square there in one pocket.

Butch snatches up a rag and presses it between his fingers.

Says Cory, "And a friend is really the devil's asshole."

Butch says offhandedly, "There's no coming home from Pickett's charge."

Cory sniffs. "Yeah, that's the intended aim . . . like Fred Hampton, the Panther . . . for one example. Shot him ten million times through his bedroom door. First one of his friendzzz gives him a mickey. Turns out *all* his friends thereabouts were FBI . . . COINTELPRO deluxe."

Mickey looks more alert at the moment than he ever did at any of Rex's meetings. In fact, he has taken two very deep chest-expanding breaths.

Cory is pacing, puts you in mind of his father, Gordon, when *he's* worked up and puts you in mind of a sturgeon trapped in a bathtub. He is going on, ". . . interested parties. So they used the FOIA and they wait and wait and finally a little bit of stuff is spit out and they see most of the names on the documents who were Fred's friendzzz . . . were blacked out! Same with Mumia Abu Jamal. And those people leafleting in England about fast food . . . almost *all* the people in their group were spies. And Bree dug up all these articles on the militias . . . I've looked at only a couple so far, there's a lot. The fucking agents push these guys into doing things. Jail for life for *you* for what an *agent* does or does with you, pushing you while you're depressed and fucked up. This vilifies a movement that has potential and makes the FBI and so-called America look . . ." His word "heroic" melts into a vicious snarl.

Mickey says, "Figures."

Butch's mouth under his lengthening mustache is coiled and curled into a most fantastic grimace. "Well, this is just how it is. *They* got it all. Bombs, cops, spooks, armies, courts, TV, teachers, Congress, Madison Avenue, Brinks trucks, computer networks, drug dogs, spies. And public support. Public *fear*."

Cory half turns away, swinging a long arm out loosely. "But whatever . . . this is not the point . . . see . . . it's not what I'm getting at. Okay, so I mean like paper companies, real estate investment guys, shampoo research labs where they torture the shit out of mice, rabbits, pigs, goats, dogs, monkeys, these buncha companies send out *their* spies and so you've got them *and* agents and operatives from the FBI and you got cop spies—"

"Russian spies?" asks Butch, winking an eye.

Mickey actually laughs. "Boris and Natasha," he murmurs, then reaches for his only jacket, his camo BDU jacket minus the Border Mountain Militia patch. Cigarettes in those pockets, too. All his cigs seem to hug him. Like a grammy would. Especially in moments like this.

Cory says, "So my *point* is something else, okay? My *point* is . . . think about it . . . your friends aren't friends but spies . . . guys who want to see you *fry*. Your friends are . . . you know . . . its like your head is inside out . . . your *brain*, it's just floating . . . cuz you don't know what the fuck to believe! It's a kind of psychosis. It makes you crazy!"

Butch murmurs, "You can still believe in your own . . . uh—"

"Integrity?"

"Yeah."

Cory looks from face to face, his black eyes swimming with not tears exactly but a dry bulging grief, then he looks at the truck's engine hanging from chains like the trophy head of a foe and smiles in a way not natural to him. "Man, to informers and entrappers it's only showbiz. An award-winning act. But—" Maybe real tears in Cory's black-black eyes now, no, just more homely lamentation, that glaze. "—I always thought of friends as, you know, sacred. Not to be corny, but you know, a friend is one of the laws of nature . . . like how we function . . . how survival works . . . almost like the laws of physics, gravity, parity. You don't fuck with that or humanity will . . . not . . . survive. To be a spy they gotta be some kind of freak of nature. And to defend yourself against this shit, to sort out spies from non-spies, you have to become a freak of nature yourself! Like Agent Orange, it'll alter the way people will be in the future. Our genes will change! Trust will be gone! Buried! Like arrowheads and buffaloes! And the people of Pompeii!"

Mickey is squinting, possibly a little lost in such tangles of logic, but his skin senses the logic's heat.

Butch tosses the rag. "This is nothing new, Cory. You read this stuff nonstop, then work yourself up."

"*My* problem, huh? Well, then that's some excuse to stay dumb!" Cory barks.

And this causes Butch to get a look, like someone whose face has just been slapped. His right hand contracts. A fist. If he snapped now, there would be soreness and maybe the breaking of small bones. *If* he snapped. But his own eyes track Cory's eyes as they, those midnight black swimmy eyes, swing back again to the motor.

And Cory says in a velvety way, "So you guys *did* it. Record time. The old girl izzz immortal. Everyone says it." He, yes, struts, his more-abundant-today-than-yesterday black tail of hair lashing across the back of his jacket, and he reaches with a bare hand to give the truck's dingy red fender a caress.

The sacred.

Behind the largest Quonset hut, Edward "Butch" Martin might be the only one not at the Settlement's lively noon meal. A crow settles on the truncated poplar behind the building, poking at something between his toes. And maybe he remarks in his thin zingy crow voice,

"This ending is lousy." Butch watches and wonders. Then he stares into the nearer mountains, for they are trilling with springtime hopes, weirdly supple and swelled up as feeling beings do when desiring to be touched. Then he gazes into the sky, also a rounded body.

No, Butch is not a reader. Nor much of a talker. Ideas are there but as with thick schools of recently hatched brown trout, their way is to remain below that which divides two worlds, the two kinds of breathers, nose breathers and gill breathers. So words aren't his forte but his mind's eye is robust, more perhaps than all the world's smartypants and their books put together and as he stays motionless on the Quonset hut doorsill regarding the soft violet shadows of this confused day, his mind's eye holds, as a hand would, Jaxon Cross, and Blake Richardson, as well as various militiamen he has come to care about.

Jaxon Cross, for instance, rocking to and fro, his voice, his knowledge coming at you like poetry, like a lilt, like spring blooms so that you are not the same person that you *were* when you were fallow, now you are sown, now you are Eden's apple; knowledge! And that courtly melt-everything-for-miles Carolina speech. That way he looks at you like he doesn't see you yet, like you are too far away, but coming closer and closer and closer. The gold doubloon earring, as with stolen treasure, spins . . . sometimes seeming more like a hot coal, injurious if touched, but always only inches above the thick shoulder, the gesturing arm.

Yes, all things as mountain-rock-dear as Jaxon and Blake can turn to jelly, Butch knows, now that he has tasted the world. Beyond the sweet Settlement walls anything goes.

Jaxon himself has bitched about the fact of infiltrators in the overall anticorporate movement. And the patsies set up to take the rap for government-schemed assassinations and false flag events. "Our government is a cudgel. It's a cudgel in the hands of those who stand on that small sharp point of the big pyramid called accumulated capital. The stakes are high, boys. It's called full spectrum dominance. World dominion. *Whatever it takes* is their motto. Why, I have to laugh when I hear people say the American government wouldn't be "*that* bad" to murder those nursery school tykes in Oklahoma City." His smile is all razor and luster.

Now here on the Quonset hut doorsill, in the late-day May dankness, the dankness test . . . like how long can you endure a cement-damped ass? Butch sighs.

Could such a thing as friendship be faked, strategized at corporate headquarters or some FBI-Mafia hangout café to enhance Jaxon's authenticity in the eyes of the collective, so that his many cargo pockets full of "bugs" would never be imagined? And Blake's car coat pockets, sweater vest folds? A hot mist is settling and Butch on the Quonset hut doorsill feels the mightiness of it. He hears Jaxon's voice like a choir, something said one day on top of what was said on another. *Fuck, man, people actually had to sign loyalty oaths in the 1950s. To America. What is America? Let's start with the dictionary definition of patriotism. It says to love, support, and defend your country. Okay, so the word here to squint over is "country." And then consider the word "your." Jeez Louise. I love, honor, and defend my umbrageous spirit murk, my shrinking opaque vapors, and all my rigors of relentless gas filler and cloy and bugfug.* He presented his widest throat slitter smile. *I am only the loyal and loving defender of my friendzzz. And my family. And other various concrete flesh-and-blood people and life-forms of my choosing.*

The voice of the mountain across the field from where Butch sits crackles. It is not an angry biblical God, but just a tree letting go. Yeah, there are always misunderstandings when you badly enough want to believe a thing. GOD SPEAKETH. Although a talking crow could jar your faith in cold hard pragmatism. "Oh nooo! My floors!" the small tinny voice wails from the headless poplar.

Butch hunches. Stomach growls but his mind's eye still fumbles with its pictures. Jaxon says, *Don't kid yourselves, boys. There is no government that can give you freedom,* quoting one of his buddies' dozen bumper stickers. *America is not the demon among angels. But due to absolute chain-em-up slavery, easily movable nations of previous American residents and seemingly endless resources, the US izzzz a vehicle for empire . . . and boys, it prances.* And he spoke ever so honeyed, as he rocked in that way he does, foot-to-foot like a little girl who needs to pee, but also there was his cruel smile and his lawyer's phone number tattoo showcased there on the palm of his hand as he thrust out spread fingers to indicate the absolute and utter prospect of Egypt, Maine, foothills and waaay beyond in his definition of preciousness. Then he stuffed his mouth with seeds, the primary food these days of the "collective" and of rats.

Butch swears he sees the near mountain breathe but maybe he's just tired. Tired of the farce of life, as they say. Today he has remembered to wear his new shirt made by Mickey's widowed sister-in-law just for him in three clownish colors, warm and whispery to touch, hot and noisy to look at. He hears how so many today think of honor as meaning good grades in school, college degrees, promotions, money, the meritocracy. But it used to mean that you would be a mountain for your people. Temptations to be otherwise would wash off your granite shoulders like mere freshets. He hears Jaxon's voice, the courtly *ma'am* and *sir*, the sugar of it all, the lissomness of it, the prayer, but sometimes the deep throat-to-rectum truth-fury . . . the sorrow. Can that come out of the jaws of a spy? Can *that* be faked so well?

Yes? No? Check one. Only one.

And which is worse, to trust a spy as a friend? Or to doubt your friend? Butch fingers the bottom button of his shirt. Mickey's sister-in-law, yes, widowed, not a lot older than Butch. A soft person. He would like to think about her, to submit to that order of things. But strip searches and helicopters. What the fuck is happening here? This war on the people of this country, and this world, pure stealth, a war by ghosts on the real and the alive.

"No sugar, thanks." A reedy somewhat haughty crow voice speaks from the roof overhang and Butch doesn't bother to look this time. "Church is at ten." The tone of the thin scratchy voice is less haughty now, more informational and helpful. Butch closes his eyes.

Deep State (if you could hear it).

The . . . best . . . spy . . . is . . . in . . . the . . . shed.*

---

* Computer shed attached to Gordon's house. Remember?

JUNE

Ah, yes, graduation days out there in the real world of real school.

In upstate New York, high school principal Larry Fields has a great new system. He has the honor students step up first to fetch their diplomas, then those students with lesser scores receive theirs in order of their descending scores. The last student now steps up for the last diploma. He is a tall thin young man with a shock of electrifying straight black hair, combed to one side, and a look in his eyes that nobody can read, or cares to.

Claire remembers.

The Settlement adults started up a buddy system. Especially women alone at night in their little houses. Or women who had just children for emotional support. Some were wives of Gordon. Some not. Few of us women alone were getting to sleep very well. Though often we did stay together at night anyway, before this. Just for the company. But you know, being alone was nice, too. A kind of refreshment from the day of swarming humanity. But now, it was different. The buddy system was not a choice.

Being together helped soften the terror of that big wash of the searchlight, monstrous whomping of the thing itself bearing down on the roofs of those places built in the open field. Those guys would come down so close it seemed they were going to misjudge and crash.

Some nights, they used a loudspeaker, which pushed a tinny voice through our open windows, though none of us could make out the words.

A heifer had struggled and hung herself in the livestock Quonset hut. Sheep were losing their minds. And horses had grown wings. Some men and older boys signed up to go sleep in the livestock Quonset hut to try and calm the crazed animals there.

And here was something. Now with all this extra-careful scheduling about where each woman was at night, buddied up and safe, we knew where Gordon was spending his nights. Before, you didn't always know for absolute certain, except during those months of his recovery from the head injuries. Now we knew. And we found that he was sleeping with Toto (her nickname). Toto, who had showed up last winter barefoot in her tiny Toyota. She had ducked out on her husband, who had promised to take her face off with an ax after doing a demonstration of the concept on her beloved spaniel Murphy. She didn't have to come far. Only from Brownfield. You can picture her little car screeching around all those curlicued roads. We were glad to give her this sanctuary, glad, glad, glad. But it didn't take us long to figure out that Toto was not a person to bathe a lot. Rarely changed her clothes, all those Settlement-made outfits we heaped on her! She was obviously depressed but she was so nonverbal none of us could get close enough to help her, you know post-traumatic stress disorder when you see it. Her brown hair was in thick noodly tangles. And here now, Gordon was going to her little temporary shed-cottage (mess that it was) to be with her in bed! We were all totally disgusted with him. And confused. Because she wasn't wearing *the silver ring*. He was just being . . . a rabbit. Thank heavens Bonnie Loo was no longer among us, for wouldn't this be the last straw? A big fat shiny kitchen knife to his balls?? A frying pan over the head? Poison in his cupcakes?

It gave us something to fuss over besides our apparent impending doom. You know, some blessings just come heavily disguised.

The delivery at midnight.

A warm spooky fog. Like the breath of a sleeping dragon. To those manning the gatehouse, time and fog coalesce thickly. Suddenly headlights, headlights queerly close together, becoming as big and perfectly round as two suns behind the mist. One of the men waiting in the gatehouse, John Lungren, says with a relieved grin, "It's Scott. Open the gate."

The other man closer to the open door rushes for the new white-washed wooden gate and in a moment of scuffing feet, creaks, and clanks, the gate is opened wide. Old rattly Jeep passes. Once inside, Jeep brakes again.

The two gatekeepers arrive at the plastic windows of the Jeep, which are now being unzipped and folded down. The driver is wild-eyed, not smiling yet. There is the smell of his cigarettes and nervousness. "Everything went wrong," he says. His voice is high and husky. He is fixing another cigarette in the corner of his mouth, stuffs the cigarette pack into his shirt pocket.

"We got lost," says the passenger. Big smile. Shakes head.

"Very lost," breathes the driver. No smile yet. Just flame, then smoke.

"Did you get stopped?" John asks, then realizes what a stupid question that was.

"If we had been stopped, we wouldn't be here now," the driver says with pained seriousness. "Or ever."

Right.

Inside the Jeep, the smoke. Outside the Jeep, the fog. And frogs. The ancientness of frogs, their continuing, is the flower of their legions. Translated into English, their chirps in the ditches say, "Survived! Survived!"

Also inside the Jeep, in the small rear seatless area, under a small plastic tarp, about thirty loosely wrapped Chinese-made SKS's. Rigged back to full auto, never used. No special paperwork. No law-abiding goody-ness. Just the guns. And several plastic ammunition boxes, chock-full of what's needed to make these guns crack.

The guardhouse man outside the passenger's window is young Jay Harmon. His eyes graze over the rear plastic window, rather dewy from the fog, then he says with a snort, "Welcome!" He points up to the narrow winding gravel road, unseen there in the foggy trees. "Go up there until you come out in the open, veer to the right, park inside the first Quonset hut bay. The bay is open. Stuart and Ray and Aurel

Soucier are all there waiting for ya. Stuart an' Ray. You'll know them when you see 'em. Maybe you know Aurel."

"Yep," says the driver, shifting. "I know 'em all." The Jeep jerks forward, whines up the hill, up, up, and up, then fades, as if into the sky.

From a future time Rachel Soucier recalls.

On top of everything else, the mothers had been worked up about some letters "Secret Agent Jane" was sending out with the mail crew, so one morning when Alyson Lessard and I were coming into the library and we spied Jane alone with what sure looked like another letter, we cheerfully offered to be editors.

Jane said in a teeth-gritting way, "Don't make noise."

So we sat one on either side of her with the shadowy light plumping and pulsing from the big windows behind us onto our shoulders, her hands, and the deadly-looking letter.

All those hushy rugs, carved wooden zebra (zebra-sized with saddle), walls of books and journals, soft lazy chairs, two big tables, a room for learning and deepest pleasure. And because the sun wasn't around that way until evening, we were as cool as cucumbers. A break from the tropical heat outside, heat that older people said was "not right" for Maine. In fact, Mary Bean announced shrilly, "This used to be Maine!"

I peeked between Jane's fingers, could make out enough to tell that her printing had gotten awfully good. But also bigger. Like shouts. Alyson and I glanced at each other and smiled. So far, so cute.

"Don't you want some help with spelling?" Alyson asked her.

"No."

"Maybe after you're done," I suggested.

"Maybe."

"Who's the letter to?" Alyson wondered.

"Shhhh!" Jane said. She carved out each giant letter with white knuckles, lips also tightened. On and on. Then she blew air from her cheeks like a sigh of exhaustion, pushed the letter away, and collapsed her face on her arms on the table.

Alyson got up and stood at my shoulder and we read it in leaden silence.

Dear stupid govimint.
As soon as I find a bom you are gong to be sorry. (Picture of bomb.)
Let Lisa Meserve out now. (Picture of Jane's mother. Blue eyes. Long eyelashes. Yellow hair. Black dress. Orange-and-red shoulder bag. Some sort of black shoes, clogs maybe, too hurried and messy to tell for sure. Red hearts poured out from one side of Lisa Meserve's head.)
Or you will be in flames. (Picture of flames same color as shoulder bag.)
You also need to take your hellcopers away and all the ~~spoots~~ spoocs who tak peeples close off.

There was a picture of what looked like a flower with a fat stem with stick men inside it. Followed by people with no buttons or belts or bows, their bare bodies like sticks of chewing gum. But the bare feet were impressively detailed. Spooks had big eyes and snarling teeth and buttons and hats. The words continued:

Also when you killed Jeffrey in his jaile you made a big mistak.
You suck.
Kerky says you are Natsees. That is a word you wont like.
Sinserly Jane Miranda
Meserve

Alyson right beside me sighed as she finished staring at Jane's creation. She looked deep into my eyes, one eyebrow arched.

I said, "Jane, you have to use charm to get the government to do stuff."

Alyson snorts, "Try oodles of money and some revolving-door crap. That's—"

I poke Alyson. "Let's try charm. It's all we've got."

Jane covers her eyes with her hands. "Okaaaay."

Jane's next try reads:

Dear preshos govimint, a very pretty bom is coming your way.
(Picture of pink and yellow and green striped bomb)

Love, your fan
(Picture of Jane's face and poofy black-brown hair. Smiling.)
Jane Miranda Meserve

Alyson and I are very quiet a minute. Actually, both letters were fine. Why is that? They felt awfully healthy and good for the soul. Like, bombs away! Fuck you, you fucking fuckers.

But her letters might really get mailed. So Alyson and I both praised with gooey *Oh, boys* and *Excellents* how much her printing had improved. And her spelling. And how she hadn't broken any crayons lately. And then we suggested doing a third try . . . ah . . . without the bomb.

Little purple plaid bow in her topknot of wavy dark hair, the bow that she herself made in the Clothesmaking Shop using the treadle machine. Adorable orange sundress with ruffle hem and the clashing blue-and-pink plaid T-shirt thingy underneath. Golden angel locket her Granpa Pete gave her. Very skinny little kid. I can't begin to tell you how you could fall into the black oceans of her eyes, the imploring deeps, and all you never wanted to know about grief.

She made no reply to our suggestion of a third version of her freedom of speech. But those eyes showed reflections, tiny versions of our own faces, our flubbery insincerity. My silent question: How many letters like these had Jane already slipped into the outgoing mail bags. Those Mount Vesuvius–like human powers she might be irritating OUT THERE made my neck, head, and teeth hurt. And I realized, too, that if I feared the government then I would have to also fear Jane.

Claire St. Onge remembers.

There was something new. They were out there in the daytime now. Not the helicopters. Those were the night-shift terrorists. And not the black ski masks and blue lights. But what looked like the National Guard. Or the US Army. Or BATF? You know, trucks with canvas backs, Jeeps, and such, all painted camo. No registration plates. They were parked a hundred yards down the tar road past the driveway of Gordon's house (the old farmplace). This was no attack. It was just these bunches of guys standing around drinking coffee. And sometimes maybe one or two guys and a whole line of empty trucks.

We suspected they were ramming around on Settlement land, scoping us out, though when we passed them, going to do our errands in town or whatever, they seemed to ignore us, find us uninteresting.

Gordon and I were in his pickup, yes, reassembled, coming along down the mountain that first time they appeared. He braked the truck hard, stopping alongside an officerish-looking guy. I'm not knowledgeable on identifying rank. Gordon had his thick forearm along the open window. Cop-looking sunglasses. About fifty new gray hairs in his beard every week, the kind you get when you see your own ghost too often. And he had an exhausted, unfriendly expression. But I heard his voice come out quite friendly, "Hey there. What's up?"

From where he stood at the rear of the tarped truck, the guy turned to look at us. He didn't move closer. His eyes, which were brown, were cool. I have always thought of brown eyes as warm. He said, "All set." And just waved us on, the way cops do if you slow your car at the scene of a wreck.

And Gordon said, still with his foot on the brake and his eyes on this soldier, "What's your business?"

And the guy just made that same *Move on* gesture and turned away. Another guy, sitting on the stone wall beyond the culvert, which was St. Onge land, stared at us. He was *very* young with a small face, pointy chin. He had a rifle across his knees.

I said, "Gordon. Let's go."

He stared at the young guy on the rock.

I said, "Gordon. You going to get out and give them a little fatherly shaking?" I laughed. Then my chin was trembling. Next would be a big ugly sob. But he lifted his foot off the brake.

Maybe it sounds like nothing to you out in the world in your "normal" lives. Just a bunch of National Guard guys doing some maneuvers, right? You see it all the time. Sounds like nothing. But for us, one thing was following the other. This was war on only us. And it felt terribly lonely.

Gordon turned the pickup and went back, driving slowly past the long line of trucks, then into the yard of the farmplace where he got on the phone and called Jim Rafuse, who lived in Bridgton but owned the land across the road from where the Guard (or Army) trucks were stopped. No answer.

Before supper, he tried again. Got Jim's wife, Karen. She said that they had sold the land last fall to LBS Investments. Gordon said, "I never saw any *For Sale* signs."

She said there hadn't been one. That they had had a good offer. I could tell he was sensitive about how the Rafuses hadn't checked with him first. Given him first refusal, he an abutter. A neighborly custom. I know on top of everything else, he was feeling betrayed. On top of everything else.

And the days passed and the camo trucks kept reappearing. No questions answered. No sign of the missing men. Which side of the road had they skulked off to? You couldn't know unless we sat out there before dawn and waited to see them arrive. So we planned that. Five Settlement men who had been walking the boundaries these past weeks now waited in the trees as the dawn swelled over the road and the military trucks grunted up Heart's Content Road single file.

Our guys saw that some of the guardsmen walked uphill out of sight. Some walked downhill. Some went into the trees of the old Rafuse land.

One night at supper, back inside the Winter Kitchen because the day had been so damp and chill, Gordon spoke out, "If you have never *really* prayed before, pray now." He folded his hands on the table. "Dear God. Help us. This is really happening."

And we all, having folded our hands on the table or in our laps, bowed our heads, repeating his prayer, and some of us then held hands. And Glennice whispered to me, "Claire, did you feel it! That heat passing between our hands and fingers! Did you feel it, the God heat?"

I said I did feel something. But it wasn't her loving humane God.

A sweet June night, frogs making a jangly racket in the ponds.

He walks. He walks the porches. He walks the mosquitoey Quad, stands in each of the Quonset huts, including the new machine shop, the expanded greenhouses, what he calls the "hothouses," where tomatoes and such get their early start and where he finds one of Willie Lancaster's scrappy little dogs asleep beside a chewed-to-smithereens moccasin.

The moon is close to full. Out by one of the hog fences, he stands and stares, smacks away at the mosquitoes pricking his ears and neck. The sky has that total haze. June skies are never black. Moon looks as dull and dimpled as a soggy pilot cracker. So the moon, it's not such a great moon, but the grassy night air, wet as the pond but cool, is the best that money can buy. Yeah, that's right, you *buy* it. No money, no land. You *must* pay. It isn't free. Nothing in this hour on this harnessed planet is not priced. He does not feel privileged, however.

He finds himself cocking his head. A certain sound. Might it be a helicopter? No? Well, then, what *was* it? A US marine? A Navy SEAL? A masked spook? An organized crime hit man? His whole body is sore with every nerve ending employed as radar to detect their assaults. He feels sorry for himself. A sob moves into his neck.

He has not forgotten Lee Lynn, who is expecting him in her sturdy little house of many windows and sparse furnishings, like an old-style Japanese home.

Before opening her front door, he lays his face against it, forehead to painted wood. The sob is still in his neck. He has succeeded in trapping it there. It is alive. Feels as if it has legs. A backbone. Fangs.

Although it is after midnight, she is still up. Weak light exudes from a weird exotic lamp.

His child Hazel lies sprawled long-leggedly in the white crib by the east window, where the morning sun will kiss her awake. Windows all open, screened. Mosquitoes wishing to get in. Some do get in, haloing Gordon's head as he had slipped in the door. The house is cool. It's not really a hot night. But what he sees first of Lee Lynn is her navel. Perfect. She has always had an amazing hard belly, hip bones, long torso. Her crotch only softly, delicately haired. She is wearing just a little shirt, unbuttoned. Everything else bare. Even feet. She is working with a knife at the table, cutting out something . . . herbed chews . . . or something. He doesn't look.

He looks only at the open window now, past his little daughter's crib. He cocks his head. Thinks again he has heard the whomping.

He kneels by the short-legged crib, lays a hand on the child's back. Hazel is dark-haired. Sweet. Clean. A few nicks from earnest play, doctored up with some sort of grease. Lee Lynn has always been the queen of concoctions for healing the body, and the "inner spirit" and all that, as we all know.

Lee Lynn's voice. Her accent is Chicago, a word like "dragon" pronounced "dray-gon." She tells Gordon she is not doing a garden this year, in case he hadn't noticed. She has been putting more time into other things.

When she is done with her work at the table, she snaps off the light.

Her bed isn't a bed. It's a mattress on the floor here in the one big room. No curtains on the windows. Now with the lights out, it is all moon and tree trunks and heavy boughs. In one window hangs a single brass thing . . . it has some sort of power, she once told him. Maybe it does. There is always power here in this cottage.

He undresses. Takes his time. Now settling down on one corner at the foot of the mattress, upright, reluctant to lie down.

He watches her shift around cross-legged in the moony dark on her side of the "bed." Her hair streaked with early gray. Early wisdom, she had insisted once, with a laugh. Though some suspect she uses bleach to make the white hairs, she always calls herself a crone. Her voice is high. Too high. On the verge of annoying but for Gordon it is a kind of chafing that turns him on. She is brushing her hair. She is probing his penis with her foot. She is, in so many ways, an abstraction. A supreme being. Unself-conscious. Without weight.

And yet now she is very much in the flesh, wanting.

"Gordon?" She prods him again, foot to his genitals.

He looks at her face, the darker recesses that are her eyes, then at the small shoulders, the unbuttoned little blouse, then back at her face.

This is not one of his failed memory spells from the brain injury where what is familiar becomes strange and unreliable. He knows very much who Lee Lynn is, what she is, where she is, and what she wants.

"Gordon?"

"Yeah, baby." He looks down into the dark obscurity of the blanket under his bare legs and bare feet.

"We're okay," she says. She lowers the brush. She places the brush somewhere. "I have had so many visions lately of this horrible time evaporating and a transformative life unfolding for us all . . . all our hard work will not be in vain. You know that, don't you? We shouldn't shut down. We shouldn't stop blossoming."

His eyes are now closed. Squeezed shut. He is familiar with this. So many of his wives hungry for him, owning only that one night a month on which he is theirs, and he knows what is demanded of him, that he must be everything there is to be in those short hours, he must compensate, he must please, he must strive.

She doesn't remove her blouse, just walks to him on her knees. Her long arms so thin. They tangle around his neck. Her voice, her breath, her mouth against his face, cheek, ear, "No one is out there, baby," says she.

He grunts disbelief.

"Love me, Gordon."

He moves to accommodate, crawling forward as she slips backward and settles down on her back. Loose-bodied, knees up, feet flat, and while he powerfully positions himself over her, her little chafing voice circulates, multiplies, coming to him like a choir. And she is one of those that beg for a baby. Every time! She always cries this out, about a baby, and in his desperation to please, he always actually tries to make this so, concentrating on summing up whatever multitudes of microscopic tadpole-like whip-tailed critters he harbors. But tonight, seeing her silvery face, silver-streaked hair, and all that spotty moonlight over the pillow, the soulful shapes of leaves, he sees with horror a picture of all his existing children, their deep intelligent eyes, their hands, their shining hair flashed upon by light, then flames, cut across horizontally now by the sound of helicopters whomping, loudspeakers howling and laughing, sputtering arrogance from above. And maybe worst of all, the black-ski-mask spooks who ask cryptic questions. Could there be behind the masks only gray plastic computerized faces? Could it be humanity is gone to dross?

His arousal is flaking away like ash. His fears and distractions make everything smell like salt.

He pulls *out*, gets to his feet, trembling in the legs, tilts his head. But there is no helicopter. There are no blue lights. Just frogs. Just mosquitoes. And one low *murrrr* of a cow calling to others downhill.

The brass piece in the window is spinning weirdly. There is no wind. He can't tell what has set it off.

Lee Lynn's skinny voice, "Gordon?"

He is breathing hard. His mouth fills with saliva. He is going to throw up.

Lee Lynn, standing beside him. Lee Lynn's voice, "What's wrong?"

He heads for the sink, then the door. But Lee Lynn is there beside him again, touching his arm. "Gordon, what is it?"

He thinks now he is not going to throw up. But he is thinking, too, that more than anything else in the world right now, he would like a good drink. But this is out of the question. Never again, drink. Again, the hard feel of a sob in his throat. It stretches its spiny body, it bites. But sobbing, too, is out of the question.

We are cornered! he hears his own voice scream inside his head.

Lee Lynn spreads a warm hand on his cold bare back. She rubs him.

What catches his eye now is the complete motionlessness of two-year-old Hazel in her crib across the room. He is upon her in an instant, jerking her from her sprawl. Hazel shrieks in alarm.

He bellers "You! Should not have been born! You should not . . . be!" He shakes this shrieking little thing. A baby rabbit clamped in the jaws of a fox sounds the same. "No more!" he groans into her shrieking, then upon his back come mother claws, Lee Lynn's, attenuated, not especially robust but ripping out of his back its warm blood.

He is backing away from the crib, the toddler's legs dangling but also struggling against her father's naked waist and hips.

"Get out!!" screams Lee Lynn. She pulls at Hazel's middle and Gordon opens his arms, Hazel in convulsions of weeping. Lee Lynn in fury, smacks his shoulder with the small finger side of her bony fist. She sees in the puny silver light his eyes, as he turns. All in three or four moments her dreams and her ardor have turned to repugnance.

Jenny Dove tells how it went.

He once again stopped "visiting" us wives at night. It was easy for us to figure this out, due to the clearly mapped buddy system.

Bree remembers.

The next week would be the solstice. The kids were all revved up, as usual, costumes, papier-mâché heads and swords, flags. Bells. Drums.

The box of "musical" spoons was located. And new kazoos were in the works, the fine art of kazoo-making, a Settlement specialty.

This would be my first summer solstice thing, or "soiree," as Gordon and his Aroostook people called it. I knew that everything, yeah, e-v-e-r-y-thing was celebrated at the Settlement but these solstices . . . the crystalline New Light Winter Solstice and this, the longest day of the year, the Old Light, were the biggest celebrations of all.

But this time, we had to break it to the kids that we might not be having as big a crowd, not as many neighbors. To most of the kids, this wouldn't have been a disappointment but they were hearing fear in our voices. And of course, they knew it had something to do with the helicopters. And *other things*.

One pre-solstice morning I drove over to the Settlement real slow, smoking, tapping the ash into the tuna can that I kept on the seat, playing one of Poon's old Bruce Springsteen tapes. I was still living at my father's house. I would spend most weekend days at the Settlement, hurrying back home to beat the dark. Like everyone, I was a nervous wreck when I was out alone under an increasingly dusky sky.

But that morning, as I slammed the truck door, the mountains around the Settlement were alive with birds singing fancy, and the kitchen and porches were alive with banging pans and whooshing water and fussing babies and grumbling murmuring women. But also I heard tiny bells, these from the direction of Pock Hill, as if the birds had arranged the accompaniment of fairies. Tiny, tiny silvery bells, tiny as mere twinkles, but defyingly rhythmic and brave.

Once I arrived I found men who seemed painfully watchful, but still gave welcomes and smiles or stoic nods. The tables were all set up for breakfast on the piazzas, though maybe it was a little too cool to be doing breakfast out there. Everyone was kind of hunched and dressed heavy. Beth snorted that this was like an old European TB clinic minus the coughs.

I hugged a few kids who came up to me, the little ones, with cheeks made fatty for pushing kisses upon and red noses and runaway giggles. I was wearing a jacket, still had the truck keys in my hand, twirling them, as I was talking with Whitney, who had Ben and Willa Wentworth's heavily dressed new baby Olivia on her knees, swaying her knees from side to side to make a glider for her. Olivia clutched

Whitney's thumbs and gurgled, unaware of anything past our adoring faces.

Still there were the bewildering distant tiny bells. "What's with the bells, Whitney?"

She said with furrowed brow, "Silverbell Rosenthal's birthday today. They're marching to her cross."

I cocked my head to listen some more. "Sounds like dozens."

"Yeah, I think about twenty went up. Old and young." She sighed. "Hard to put the thing into words."

"Bells are best."

Then there, in the Cook's Kitchen, I caught sight of Jip and Blake getting coffee, and Blake stepped out of that door and over one of the Lancaster dogs and headed toward me for one of his cheek-to-cheek hugs. And Jip gave me that nose-twitching smile of hers, pushing at the nosepiece of her glasses as if to correct her nose of that mischievous twitch, and Meggie was in head-to-toe dusty rose, her signature mandarin collar and a black shawl, her hair its usual white-blond maelstrom, more so than my red storm of hair ever dreamed of being. BIG hug for Meggie, and oh, I loved them dearly but—

Olan was roaming around behind Jay Harmon and Bob Cross, looking for empty seats near the center of the porch. Wore his *Honor Labor* button, his dark eyes wide. His eyes, always too wide open. You'd think he'd never seen this place before. And I loved him, too, but—

But I was scared now. Scared of them. Not that these organizers were responsible for the evil that was upon us but, for a while, I kinda just wanted to enjoy the pretty babies, including Dee Dee's baby, who was now going past me under the arm of his father, Lou-EE, gripped like a football with arms and legs. Cannonball waddling behind daring anyone to pat her. All I wanted was to melt in with all the little kids, in their scheming wicked joy over the solstice march. Wanted to be, yuh, a little bit kiddie-like, free of the terrible Duty. And one of Willie's naughty dogs I was especially attached to, Marybelle, I yearned to teach her cute tricks. Yuh, dog tricks. Give me your paw! Give me five! High five! High five! Just a small simple thing, a silly pleasure, mere, and not at all earth-shattering.

But peace would have to come later. Peace is not a gift. You must give up everything for it, right? Forevermore.

I could see Gordon coming across the Quad, that limp still with him. And shirtless for some reason. An odd sight on this cold morning. Work pants were wet to the knees. Around his waist, an ammunition belt, olive drab. The kind with a row of snappable fat pockets. AK-47 strapped over his back and shoulder, barrel up. I know that some of the men, and a couple of women, here had been walking the boundaries all night, a futile activity, if I may say so. Why bother? If the government wanted them, it would take them. Its genius! Its manpower! Its resources! And all public opinion was on the government's side, sort of . . . certainly *would* be, given time. The Settlementers' efforts to defend themselves would be seen as those of "crazy paranoid fanatics."

But, yeah, the Settlementers had been *a* people too long, nourishing the modern world's tiny vestiges of human synchrony for learning and living and autonomy. And besides, *who could they call for help?* I heard Gordon had been making calls but, as with Major Tom lost in space, there was outside our gate only space.

Bev and Barbara were two women who lived in a yellow house in town, short grass, no dust, swimming pool of warm blue-green-looking water, who still had time almost every day to drive up Heart's Content Road and be part of things here. Presently they joined Gordon on the path, and now a bunch of small kids asking questions. Bev and Barbara not much taller than the kids. Just stouter. Stout in body and heart.

The moment Gordon came up onto the porch, the moment he entered this space, everything about us changed. A kind of kinetic flip-flop. He wasted no time in lifting a wildly giggling three-year-old from his chair, tipped him upside-down, put squashy kisses in the little boy's ears, on both eyes. Next, he was wrestling with old Walt, not an all-out wrestle, more like a waltz. Also pokes and play punches. Teasing. His batch of keys sang on their belt loop. He was faking this good mood, I can tell you that much. About the rifle, the organizers shared a whirling silence. And no one *seemed* to mind the smell of him, which was almost sickening, one of Lee Lynn's special bug dope concoctions, his dusky skin oily with it and streaked from all the pollenish grime of the woods. And he *looked* so happy to see the organizers, kisses for Jip and Meggie, and from one of his work pants pockets two small yellowy-pink fieldstones, smooth, almost fleshy. Warm from being against his body for hours. His idea of jewels for the girls. And for Blake and Olan, his sheepish grin. He asked about Lenny. Was told Lenny would be around next week. Got caught up for a few days in the dull business of grant writing.

Next thing we knew, we're all at a table on the next porch, listening to their plans. Plans for a big statehouse "siege." With gesturing hands and almost white-lipped intensity, Olan told us, "We're hearing from dozens of serious organizers all over the United States, all committed to making a showing here in Maine with their respective groups, hundreds of people given major notice . . . if you want to do this, Gordon. It might be the biggest rally this state has ever known. It's a pure people versus corporate power moment."

Jip leaned on her slim pointy elbows. "The word is, we can expect a peaceful event. Not as volatile as the midwestern farmers. These would be your basic rivers and forests bunch, God bless them. And some campaign finance reform people. And Greens. Anti-MTBE gas groups. Antinukers. And best of all, labor union folks! You could speak easily to their concerns . . . but with your added ability to invigorate. The old recidivists get a little sleepy. So shake a fist, hoot, rage . . . they need it." Then she batted her eyes. "I've changed my mind about rabble-rousing . . . I think."

Olan gave a grunt and his usual just-don't-go-overboard look. "It's working out all right."

Gordon continued to stand there, both hands on the back of an empty chair, rifle over his shoulder on its sling.

Whitney reported that there were now over a thousand members on the True Maine Militia computer file.

Olan looked at Jip, and Jip said, "We've wanted to talk with you about that. Frank Parenti suggests we all combine our lists."

I watched Gordon rub his face and eyes. He hadn't said much through all this, just gave pleasant little nods. But now he said deeply, "Well, you know, we've had a little trouble here."

Jip sighed. "I know. I got Bree's and Whitney's e-mails. I had hoped it wouldn't last."

"The helicopters," said Oceanna with a shiver, "are real creepy."

"Strip searches," said Glennice rather icily, arms folded under her breasts. She stood behind Gordon, as if he would merely, by his body mass, protect her from them, these leftist troublemakers. And Bev wasn't far away, hanging near, eavesdropping.

Gordon focused his dark-lashed, dark-ringed, very tired eyes on Jip and said, "I fear for my family."

"Yes," said Jip.

I looked at Blake. He was staring out through the screen at something, maybe at how breathlessly green everything was, clouds bunching thicker and thicker in the open sky over the Quonsets. You could smell the rain coming. He slowly turned his face to the table and then upward, met Gordon's eyes.

Whitney said, "Those. Cops. Are. The. Lowest. Life-forms. Below. Maggots." She spanked the table with the palm of a hand. "We haven't done anything wrong. It's so weird."

Blake patted Whitney's hand, then folded his hands there on the table, as if for a grace, and said, "When we declare war, we get war. Even if we declare our end of the war to really be about peace. It's still war. And they'll play war their way. And historically they do a pretty good job of making their wars look like peace to the greater population."

"Their biggest weapon," Olan said, "is PR. They plan to get those thousands of people who are *our* weapon against *them* turned against us . . . against *you* in particular, Gordon . . . I'm sorry."

Meggie had just come back from the toilet off the pantry hall and sat sideways on a stool, spine straight, in all her dusty-pink-and-black-shawl splendor. She glanced quickly and hard at the center of Gordon's chest.

Samantha arrived, hugging herself, teeth chattering, goose-bumpy. Shorts and a T-shirt. Her pale hair, her Comanche head rag, hurriedly composed. Even raw from sleep, she was beautiful. As often happened, my face felt suddenly hot, as though neon was lighting up my deformity from the inside out.

Then Cory and Oz were pulling up chairs. Cory's hair had dusty cobwebs in it. Chicken house or cellar or something. Yuh, probably night duty with the cattle, which the helicopters were driving crazy, even as they swung in here a little less often, the impendingness, the cow-sheep-and-horse PTSD, was real.

"The statehouse siege, or let's call it the People's Lobby, can take place in October. We'll demand that they represent the population, not organized money. The sooner the better. A mere gesture, true. But a grand gesture it will be," Jip said quietly.

Gordon, still standing, said darkly, "In the beginning . . ." Pause, his eyes squeezing shut, headache time. "You folks said you wanted help stirring up interest for just seminars. With healthy snacks."

Jip was unconsciously drawing circles on the table with her finger.

Olan reported, "A hundred and twenty *scheduled* seminars. And more. More than we can schedule. Thanks to you. And remember, it was *your* style that gave us a somewhat new direction."

Jip smiled. "And during all your rallies, Gordon, I noticed the Food Not Bombs guys out there with their table. Rice and beans."*

Gordon, scowling miserably, missed the joke.

Glennice said, "When we pick up our mail now, it's been opened."

"Torn open," Oceanna corrected her with a sniff. "Some is taped closed again. But most of it's all squashed and bunched up."

Gordon at last pulled out that chair, his ammo belt clunking against the dowels as he sat down hard. He laid the AK across the table in front of himself, right where a cup of coffee would go if he had one, the short barrel gently tunking against Olan's coffee cup at his left. Mistake? Or on purpose?

And he is thinking about a certain piece of mail.

It arrived yesterday on his kitchen table, one of the few not opened or mutilated. A cardboard Priority envelope, red, white, and blue. Inside there was no letter, no note, just a key. He hadn't received a key from Bruce Hummer in ages. This key, a skeleton key, what did it mean?

Some sort of devil promise? Threat? Whatever.

After all, Bruce is one of the turbo engines of the edifice and its apparatus. One can't fail to recognize the master key to Gordon's fate when one sees it. And the sneer of betrayal that goes with it.

---

* Healthy snacks, right?

But these Bread and Roses guys, the *good guys*, here at his table now, the love he feels for them prowls into and out of his grasp, while the fear holds perfectly still.

Claire remembers how it went.

When I came up onto the porches I saw the Bread and Roses organizers, but first I saw Gordon. I doubt there was a single Settlement adult who hadn't heard how Gordon had turned violent at Lee Lynn's cottage a couple of weeks before. Some were sure it was from his brain injury. But since a lot of us were having breakdowns, in various ways, from the government harassment, why not Gordon? He certainly wasn't puncture-proof. He wasn't God! But I heard from many mothers they'd never trust him alone with their tykes anymore.

And now here on the porch I saw he was squinting both eyes, hands in a loose grip on a rifle . . . AK I think . . . actually, I didn't study it. The organizers and youngsters were wrestling with details for a future rally, something bigger than we'd known so far. But my eyes slid back to Gordon whose body language would put you in mind of an animal treed by hounds.

I then saw that Blake saw what I saw and Cory and Butch and Bree, too, eyes flashing toward Gordon, whose brain now seemed strangely fixed on a brass-and-glass candle lamp nearby. No flame inside the lamp. No lovely light. It was, after all, not night. But somehow the lamp spoke to him of emergency purpose. I missed seeing his right hand rise up off the rifle forearm and grasp the lamp, but I did see motion and then heard the *clatter-thump!* and everyone was hollering because he was crashing the thing against his own skull and forehead, the ridge over one eye, a temple, and his other hand was just barefistedly socking the other temple. The dreadful cracking sounds were the stained glass and brass frame falling to pieces but my heart thought it was hearing his head breaking apart.

Two open hands as large as his own enfolded his and slammed them down onto the table, the remains of the lamp skidding away.

Tears were running down into Gordon's beard but he made no sounds. He did, though, bow his head, maybe eyeing the huge hands that still weighed down his own.

I didn't rush to him. Nobody did, except the giant rescuer who remained in place. Gordon's strength and his intensifying madness . . . oh, how he frightened me now.

But he did not scare Meggie. Meggie who bragged of having no fear of speed or of heights, and there you go, now, too, no fear of the mad Prophet. Her black lacy shawl dangled off one shoulder all the way to the floor, her pink dress front and small breasts underneath driven against his bare back.

People who had been eating on the adjacent porch had stopped chewing and swallowing, several filling the divider doorway. *What happened?* was whispered.

Then Meggie released Gordon's hands, straightened herself and her shawl. She swung ever-gracefully around and strode to the long wall of screen that looked out onto the Quad. She said huskily, "And Gordon, honey, when you finally cool down, I expect a thank-you."

Penny remembering.

We talked him into going into the First Aid Shop where there was a cot. The room was almost cold. He sat trembling on the cot quietly while Cory built a little kindling-and-stick fire.

Claire knew where his seizure pills were so she went for those. Even though he'd been done with them we wanted him to numb down. Also she was fetching him a shirt, but in the meantime I slung a flannel blanket over his bloody shoulders. Then I washed his face from which the blood was crawling. He continued to be docile. Maybe it was shame.

Leona knocked softly, then joined us. You know, Leona, Cory's mother. She talked to Gordon tenderly about how the blessed rain had started and it would be sweeping like a caress over all our fields and gardens, so badly needed.

I had checked his eyes to be sure that neither one was dilated oddly. I asked Leona for a second opinion. She leaned close to pull his head back. She squinted. "Such eyes," said she. "A lot can be blamed on those eyes."

He closed his eyes with a good-humored-seeming snort.

Leona and I looked at each other with matching headshakes and she winked.

I applied gauze to his worst laceration there over one eye and pressed it with my thumbs but it bled through the gauze so I tried again. When the adhesive made a zippy-rippy sound pulling away from his skin, he chuckled.

After Cory set the draft dials on the little stove, he sat on the cot next to his father and put an arm around him. He said, "Meggie's sulking out there. You need to thank her."

Gordon looked bewildered.

"She's touchy," Cory said.

Gordon nodded.

"But she *did* save you. *Heh-heh*." Cory squeezes the tightened muscles of one of Gordon's shoulders. "That's one of the perks of having a friend who is trans."

Gordon's one twitching demon eye went into its thing. But no verbal response to this "trans" news. News to *him*.

Claire remembers more.

We set up another cot in the First Aid Shop so Cory could keep watch through the night on his zonked-out father and to be sure he got a second dose of *the stuff* on time.

There were no helicopters that night. We hoped there *would* be one so that the organizers who were staying over could *appreciate* our predicament. We thought they were way too blasé about it.

We set up breakfast inside in the Winter Kitchen due to the super blukky damp of the rain.

Kids put on a special history skit of the Triangle Shirtwaist fire and the labor organizing of the era. For some reason there were three Clara Lemlichs and only two firemen. *Lots* of girls jumping to their deaths. The firemen were not *supposed* to laugh. But the Triangle owners were perfectly snooty and heartless. At the appropriate times our visiting organizers sighed and gasped, cheered and whistled, booed and hissed and then applauded most enthusiastically with a long, long, standing ovation.

Gordon wasn't there. But by the noon meal he and Cory trudged in and Gordon (whose face was crosshatched with Band-Aids) wrapped his arms around Meggie, who was in a new, quite slithery gown of pale sea-mist blue-green and her black shawl. He said "Thank you," then, "Forgive me for the delay."

She said, "Maybe," and twitched her nose.

So then—

At one table there was more brainstorming and information-sharing concerning the very important Augusta rally. Still a bit drugged, Gordon quickly nodded off. And snored.

Mothers.

Late Sunday afternoon, after discussing with the True Maine Militia officers more strategies for the Augusta rally and some damage control concerning Professor Catherine Court Downey's big network broadcast and lefty assurances that the government's terrorism against the Settlement "will lighten up once these agencies fail to get shot at," the organizers headed back to Cambridge. All but young Blake. So here he is at supper, surrounded by the lively True Maine Militia officers including Samantha Butler who has confided to her co-militiapersons her crush on him. And Margo who has not confided hers, being smaller of ego than Sammy.

And there is Cory in blue denim shirt with sleeves hacked off, black-black hair longer today than yesterday, it seems, and tied back with rawhide. Settlement work has tanned his powerful arms to be nearly as dark as Blake's, though Blake wears a stripy short-sleeved businessman-type shirt and spends so much more time than he likes inside motor vehicles in front of stoplights and at tollbooths and then more hours in fluorescent-lit rooms.

Also Butch Martin is nearby. His red T-shirt keeps catching eyes in spite of his usual silence.

And there is Gordon across the table, three squares of gauze taped to his forehead, eyebrow, temple. And two Band-Aids almost between his eyes.

How nearly obscene these acre-sized platters of chicken and smoked fish, potatoes drowned in goat cheese and herbs, bowls of moose stew, wild cranberry preserve, home-canned veggies plain and pickled. Biscuits. Raw milk of goat and cow. A big fat ol' feast. Everyone sluggish and oversated like lordships and ladyships. Musical instruments are being tuned. A guitar. A fiddle. Real drums and inverted plastic bucket drums. Kids digging into a wooden apple box filled with newly made kazoos. Two preteen girls shrieking as they hurry in from the porches, slamming the door, both wrapping their bare arms around themselves, one crying, "Horripilation! Horripilation!" And then the other crying out the same. The rain has ceased. The air has been washed clean and blessed. Now a perfect heavenly dry chill plunging among these green green hills.

Most of the True Maine troops have now roamed toward the cubby wall, whispering, including Sammy who has left the table sucking on a dried apple slice.

Butch digs into more smoked bluefish.

Cory squints into the lowering sun there at the windows, that after-supper June angle that makes even a sixteen-year-old like himself ache with panoramic hopes.

With the heel of his hand, Gordon rubs an eye, the one without the newly gauzed swollen-purple eyebrow. He yawns.

Blake murmurs, "Those stories a while back . . . about our mothers. It's got me thinking."

Gordon looks up, eyes twinkling. Pushes his plate away.

Cory lifts his fork and laps it. Lays it back in his plate easy-careful.

Blake gazes out at the shadowy twilit trees as he often does, leaning on an elbow, chair turned a bit sideways. Then he looks into Gordon's eyes and says, "There are *other* organizers I'm doing a newsletter with. The New Millennium Abolitionists. Somewhat militant. Some are from Philly. Some from Alton, Illinois, my hometown." He picks at a clean soft rag given him as a napkin. "They've collected a few funds. For land. They want to meet you. I mentioned them before, but we've been too busy to get into it."

Gordon says, "You mentioned militia."

"Well, yes. They are that in that way of being pro–Second Amendment." He smiles at Cory. "They, too, get riled at all this talk of disarming citizens, particularly people of color. They say gun control is racist. Another excuse for tossing blacks into the dungeon. You've said as much yourself, Cory. You all have. Those who've declared hostility toward their oppressors are the obvious target of such laws. There'll be loopholes for the privileged. Deep state dwells on this in a global way. It's like physics. Political *science*." He sneeringly chuckles.

Cory is looking exceedingly alert.

Blake taps a finger on the table, one tap in the direction of each face. "And like you guys, my friends out there have dreams. Concrete dreams. Goals. And a willingness to work for them." He draws his hand back, close to his chest. "But first, they plan to teach awareness through their zines, their books, essays, documentaries, and panel discussions. As we all agree, education is part of organizing."

Music starts up, guitar and kazoos. Sounds like church hymn tunes, but with a different twist. Blake watches some old people quietly turning the pages of *Your Weekly Shopping Guide*. The obituaries of fellow Egyptians hold their eyes the longest.

Gordon glances over at the faces of the kazooists, cheeks poofing in and out, bouncing shoulders and tapping toes keeping rhythm. Kazoos make church music sound like a cathedral full of elves. It pleases him how it isn't just the kids who love to play kazoos. A lot of adults are apt to join in. He gets a hard swollen feeling in his throat. Sweetness that is like sorrow. And terror. Yes, the intended result of spooks, choppers, and skulking soldiers. And the thing that has cracked open that big rotten egg is the rallies schemed by the Bread and Roses Folk School. He fears them, yes. He wonders where Blake is going with his present confidences. He looks back and sees Blake is watching his face, watching his thoughts.

"I feel protective of my family, like you do yours," Blake says now into Gordon's pale eyes. "I love them and I want to be with them more than whatever else there is to love and be with and it's . . . hard. My wife and I are divorced. She has the kids. Two. Two girls. Nine and ten. We were married young. Meanwhile, I have a sister who is about the age of—" Turns in his seat and points to Samantha Butler, who is standing back-to, arm and arm with other teens, swaying to the buzzy churchy tune. He looks back at Gordon. "My wife . . . I mean my ex . . . lives off and on with a guy eight years younger than her, a nightclub manager, Mr. Body. She's on welfare to supplement her crappy job. He's an okay guy. But . . . you know, it's the American dream. Appliances, new car, credit. No drugs. Just Mary Jane. But the best Mary Jane and, well, he likes it in the clouds when he isn't driving fast and spending money. Because what else is there to dream? Seems nobody in America can remember the depths of real belonging. Not the new generations. My mother's name is Pauline. She's beautiful. I mean, like a movie star. And funny. She calls waitressing 'performance' and herself 'an entertainer.' Well, *that* she is. She's quicker than a fly. She says *all* Geminis are comedians. My parents both love cats. But where they live now, no cats allowed. My dad was a union man. I don't know if he understood what a union meant . . . until . . . it was gone. For all the racism and crap that was always taking bites out of me as a kid, I was privileged to be the son of a man with a union job. And a mother who could make me laugh." He snickers, eyes shining, but then, "All you have to do is look at the difference between my mother's job and my father's for a lesson in the difference between nonunion and union."

Gordon makes an affirmative grunt.

"I have two living grandmothers. Mimi and Granma Lot. And cousins, cousins, cousins, uncles, aunts. I'm related to a lot of Alton. And I . . . love . . . them . . . all." He picks some more at the hand-wiping rag by his plate, the zippy kazoos and rocking guitar filling his pause. And now the blood-stirring power of drums.

Gordon still *seems* sluggish, just nodding, his hands folded on the table. He looks foolish with all those gauze squares sticking to his face.

Cory fiddles with a bone in the bowl near his plate.

Butch has the expression of an engorged cat, stroking over and over his dark Rex York mustache.

Blake gently smiles. "I want *this* for them." Puts out both hands to indicate the whole Settlement. "But when I asked my mother what she would think of living in a place such as this, she made a face like she was seeing a house afire, cried out, *Blake! You went to Cornell just to be an ol' Amish?!* I expected her to say hippie."

"I thought you were Harvard." Gordon blinks as though the light had changed.

Blake grins. "The ivy intertwines."

Gordon gets one of his wild-man expressions. "Well, don't feel bad about your ma's wisecrack. My mother likened this place to Cuba and said I was Castro."

Blake laughs.

Gordon stares a few seconds at Blake's laughing mouth and eyes, then adds solemnly, "She even said I *look* like Castro."

"No matter how hard I try, I don't see it. Not enough eyebrow." Blake is still laughing, his words unruffled but sputtery. "Could it be that mothers are primarily analogists?"

Gordon says grumpily, "At every opportunity."

Blake gets over his laugh, resumes his confidential solemnity. Stares a long moment at two women by the cubbies and sign-up sheets, coat hooks, layers of life. One woman is saying, "When I heard it walking by I thought it was a mouse. Its feet made a tap-tap-tapping sound. But mice are silent. I should've known. When I looked, it was a spider as big as my hand!"

Blake smiles again at Gordon and at Cory and at Butch, but a smile of anguish. "I want for all of Alton, Illinois' towers residents to have this. But would they *want this*?" He uses a single finger this time to indicate the Settlement, then shakes his head to answer himself. Now he glances bleakly around, at hippie-looking Del in his wheelchair cutting into a pie at the far end of this table, plopping huge pieces onto a small stack of Settlement-made pottery plates. Blake rubs the back of his head, his short crinkly hair. As if to comfort himself. Then he digs into the aching muscles at the side of his neck, the way the neck gets when you hold all you want to say to the world in the hollow of your cheek. "They're proud of their city," says he.

Butch stretches to fetch a dried apple slice from a loaded bowl, opens his mouth, pops it in.

Blake watches this. "My New Millennium Abolitionist friends have had this idea about economically viable communities *within* the cities. They'd be centered on tiny schools, libraries, coffee shops, little stores and small tradesmen outfits such as machining, and larger network cooperatives and medium-sized worker-owned manufacturing. This was a long time before we heard of you . . . but *you*—" He looks away from Gordon's gauze-patched, scarred face to the big guy's hands on the table. "You have it perfected. That's why I suggested they come up here and meet you."

"It's not perfected here," Gordon says flatly.

"Well . . . but it's pretty good. In the right direction. Especially the way all of you have connected with others around the state . . . selling and trading. The cooperatives such as furniture made from local trees, the Community Supported Agriculture. All that. To me when we speak of reparations for American blacks, I'm on the same page as you when you say there should be *big* federal funding . . . via a tax on those who have extra . . . to create and nurture those beautiful seven words into reality: *thousands of small economically viable humane communities*."

Gordon nods, fingers one of his squares of gauze. "Yeah, well my notion has been that racism gets beefy only when the targeted race is poor, helpless, for long enough to associate the skin with the wallet. Like you're saying, reparations can be directed into building the America we've been *told* we have instead of this bullshit America we actually have. But there needs to be *a lot* of vibrant communities for *all* the colors. After all, how would reparations categorize the *deserving* black person . . . by *shades* of brown? And . . ." He closes his eyes. "Beware of the intensifying of racism, of divisiveness in the struggling classes, which black-specific funding would cause. And Christ Almighty, are you going to segregate these communities . . . blacks only? Lots to consider."

Blake says, "A ridiculous charge that I'm pushing segregation." His eyes smolder at Gordon's.

Gordon sighs.

Blake says evenly, "People have got to know what dignity, self-esteem, self-governance, solidarity, and useful skills look like. Nobody can aspire to something unimagined. All people know of is a world institutionalized, corporatized, syntheticized, consumerized, and standardized, impersonal and restless, within the limits of classism and racism. When we say, 'Let's get rid of corporate power, corporate myth, corporate values,' and consumerism, people imagine a vacuum. Or covered wagons . . . or spears and loincloths." He turns, sees Samantha Butler settling in the chair next to him on the right. She has a piece of pie. She pulls her chair close. Lays her head on his shoulder. "I don't wait on men," she says when she sees him eyeing the pie. "Go get your own. You too, Gordo." She makes a snarly face at Cory and Butch.

Across the table, Gordon's eyes scintillate on her sassy pretty pink mouth, which has spoken these words, her stuffing a forkful of pie into that mouth, her eyes scintillating back at him.

Blake reaches around now and takes hold of the back of her chair, resting his hand there. "Apple is my favorite."

Samantha says, "I have a heart of ice."

Gordon's eyes twinkle ever more fiercely.

Blake pats the girl's shoulder, her shoulder on the farther side.

She says, "Do not try to melt my heart. See, my heart is melting now and I'm still not getting out of this chair. Men have legs, too."

Gordon's pale eyes blink. "Those who don't serve at the tables usually change flat tires, shovel manure, and fall trees. *Annd* kill chickens *or* work on the roads . . . like stumping . . . the shovel and the pickax."

Samantha makes loud smacking noises around her spoon. "Fine."

Kazoos are unrelenting. Zzzzzzzoooozooozoozeeee . . .

Samantha whispers to Blake, "I'm signed up for three days of painting swan boats." She holds out her free hand with a color of lemon sherbet in the creases.

"Ah-ha," says he, and winks as if this were a mighty grand secret.

A brown dog tail passes between the tables.

Blake leans forward now, hands under the table, between his knees, looking into his coffee cup, looking for words. Looks now at Gordon. "I want my family cut off from the crap. To be *free*. I'm pissed at shackle slavery. I'm pissed at sneaky mind-control slavery. I'm pissed at what you get to be when you don't even get to be a slave of the new kind. Imagine! You don't even get to be a new-style slave. You get to be just . . . just litter. I want my loved ones out of that *idea*. See?"

Gordon starts to commiserate.

Blake cuts him off, flinging an open-fingered hand between his own face and Gordon's face.

Blake doesn't want Gordon to talk. It's like when whites talk of the situation blacks are in, they are trying to own it. He just wants Gordon to listen. To hear. To feel . . . feel *what*? To feel guilty?

There have been a hell of a lot of times when Blake's blood flares to hear whites speak of the blacks' situation. Almost anything whites say about it feels like *Oh, here is my sympathy. Aren't I nice*? Or worse, it feels like a sneer. Whether it was or wasn't either of these, their voices, thin and reedy, come from a place of privilege.

Okay, suffering is not a contest. He knows this. But his militant New Millennium Abolitionists friends, they are different. Very different. A guy like Gordon, they'd love to tackle, make him bleed. No, not with bullets or blows. But with words. Word-bullets. Word-blows. Word-kicks to take his feet out from under him. Make him *lose*. At last. Get *even*. Make him blanch or flush but surely apologize. On his goddam knees . . . figuratively.

Blake says to Gordon, "Some of my family is white by marriage and we got the Indian factor. But we're labeled 'black.' And we're labeled 'inner city,' which is like being labeled 'toilet.' This didn't happen overnight. It's the setup. I want to see my family having a break from that setup of the forefathers who had a particular idea of how a New World should be designed. That design has shaped the psyches of all of us. How we see ourselves. It isn't just the names people call you, it's a lotta generations of names that you start to believe because you don't visualize anything else."

Samantha is *really* quiet now.

Cory and Samantha, both natural yakkers, tongues invisibly squirming behind closed teeth. Butch just munches on his remaining smoked fish and more dried apples.

Gordon says to Blake, "I hear you."

Blake doesn't smile. He looks down at his own two hands angrily. "I'm a poor man . . . by Cornell standards. Hell, by University of Maine standards! But Cornell . . . you leave there and . . ." He sighs. "If you got organizing, social work, people-work . . . well, you know, the rent and the car payments are bigger than the pay of people-work. I had a passel of significant scholarships for that rocketship to Ivy Leagueville. But not enough. I got debt. So getting a setup like what you have here would be impossible for me . . . alone. But my friends. They have ways. They're good at getting money together." He looks very hard into Gordon's eyes. "They beg from foundations." He keeps staring into Gordon's eyes. "They won't borrow. We've made an agreement on that. No debt. Ever."

Gordon chortles. "There's always stealing."

For a moment, Blake is silent again. *Beg. Borrow. And steal*. Right. He considers how Gordon must assume these friends are all African-Americans, which they *are*, though he has never stated it. He sees in his mind's eye how his friends would take that remark about stealing as a slur against their race. And when he imagines his friends verbally battering Gordon with their gift for debate, he feels protective toward Gordon. His silence stretches on and on.

Gordon says, "Bring your friends around sometime. You don't have to push buttons too hard here if you want to talk about community."

"Yes! Make them come!" Samantha urges, erasing the last of the pie crumbs on her plate with her tongue. Lowers the plate. Blake brings his arm around her, hugs her to him a moment, does the quickie cheek-pressed-to-cheek thing he is famous here for. He has a knack for winning Settlement hearts. And vice versa. Though in Samantha's case he has also won her deepest essence. It makes him a bit edgy that fifteen- and sixteen-year-olds in this place think they are women, not unlike all of working-class America, that very hardy garden he, too, flowered in.

Gordon says, "It's cropping up everywhere, people saying no more corporate grid. Fuck the big fuckers. Ha! Imagine it just shriveling from nonuse." He digs in his beard. "Hey, maybe we could—"

"My friends aren't as anticorporate as you and I, Gordon. Or anti-big the way you are. Well, *that* and *that*, but also . . . for them it's mostly something else. One *big* thing . . . they are antiwhite. They want to abolish white."

Gordon's eyes narrow. Then the wild cheek flinching leaps into action.

Blake continues. "They want to abolish white privilege. They are not against people with white skin, but against 'whiteness.' That's where they are primarily. And I know you are against the thing *they* call 'whiteness,' but they want to hear *you* call it 'whiteness.'"

Gordon is as silenced as though entering a country where no English is spoken.

"That's what the word *abolition* means to them," Blake says deeply.

Samantha looks with *extra* interest at Blake's profile, this conversation ripped from the heart. "How 'bout we abolish privilege," says she. "Any type."

Cory snorts. "Nice, Sammy. Very anarchistic." Then Cory says to Blake, "There are a lot of anarchist zines on this white privilege idea. They use that term . . . *a lot*."

Gordon smiles thinly. "Well . . . if they want to come here and see what we're doing, meet the folks at some of the exchanges, share ideas back and forth, they are welcomed."

Blake nods.

A fiddle screels as kazoos and drums trail off and now people are clapping along.

Blake smiles a small warning smile. "My friends will . . . want to make their position known. They're confrontational. They'll want to be sure you know this place of yours exists only because of white privilege."

Again Gordon narrows his eyes. "Like hard-assed mean motherfucking feminists." He speaks these words with the f's made nearly into *hard* consonants.

"Like lawyers," adds Samantha wagging her head playfully.

Gordon's voice grows crusty. "I would not in ten million moons deny that whites have had, *as a whole*, societal privilege. And many more have had a special place above the law and into beastiality when it comes to the treatment of one's fellow human beings. But I have a big fat problem with how so many academics . . . I, too, have read their stuff . . . they sound like a stuck record on that phrase 'white privilege.' Do they want everyone to believe white persons who *fail* in the musical chairs game of this rigged system are deserving of their struggle because they all made bad choices? They had white privilege and didn't use it? *Choices!* That's fucking yuppie lingo, man! I thought you were working-class, my brother."

Blake says, "There's some question of whether *you* are."

Gordon freezes, face, body, and soul.

Cory says to Samantha, "You guys did a salon on this white privilege subject, didn't you?"

Blake considers the word *salon*. Comes from privilege, right? Something in him is suddenly boiling bitterly all around this one little word. *Salon*. Okay, so he erases the rage. It sparkles. He erases. It glimmers. He erases again. The dizzying waltz between heart and reason never stops.

And so he misses part of what the two youngsters have to say, but then Samantha's voice is breaking through: "And so there is white privilege. And there is extrovert privilege. And you get resistance-to-depression privilege. You get born with that just like you do skin—"

Blake quietly cuts in, "Black is not a disability."

Gordon says, "In a society that thrives on cold-blooded enhanced competition, there are a hell of a lot of disabilities. In the very old days if you were different, you'd not get to be called disabled . . . you were devil possessed . . . offensive to God. It's always something that can be pinned on the loser . . . humans are mean and nasty creatures, it's beyond talk of industrialism and market capitalism. It's primatology."

Samantha, head wagging again: "That's what we came up with at the salon. Being human is not a bragging point. And remember our skit for the governors' wives that—"

Gordon cuts in again, "Back to privilege. I'd like to add to the list the absence-of-anxiety privilege. Some people are very anxious personalities. *A lot* of very white people can't make it cuz society trashes them, too, for who *they* are. Nazis murdered and/or worked to death Jews, gays, Poles, retarded people, mentally ill people. Andrew Jackson signed into law that *every Indian should be put to death*. Because it was against the law to *be* who they were. Now full-out extermination, that's illegal. Chain slavery and lynching are mostly illegal. But society remains a silhouette of its former self worldwide. You're illegal if you're not a success, a certain definition of it. But the most criminal *to me* thing about these academic elites . . ."

Blake scowls.

Gordon keeps rattling on, "and all their antiwhiteness haranguing is this . . . all those soapboxes . . . all that lather . . . it could be used to build *solidarity*! Think of the Taft-Hartley Act, for instance. Why aren't they jostling to rid us of *that*? The other name for it when it was passed in 1947, *as you know*, Blake, was the Slave Labor Act!

I'm wanting with all my being to see people-power mighty enough to wrestle with the corporate power beast. Vibrant worker-owned businesses and real safety nets can't *ever* happen without mammoth support from an organized working-class people. But the motherfucking foundations keep giving prizes and grants to academics who write and speak all this divisive redundant rat shit!" He is simultaneously trembling and crushing something in his hand, the seedy juice sliding through his fingers. A hunk of tomato?

Samantha and Butch and Cory exchange looks.

Gordon's voice is near blubbering. "Let's suppose in 1947 along with the Taft-Hartley thing, blacks were given triple privilege. Triple black privilege . . . the TBP Act. While pale people got lynched, redlined, ghettoized. To this day, you'd still not see all blacks become so-called success stories no more than all whites have. Because the rat race isn't designed for all people to thrive in it. I guarantee that just as many dark-skin people as light have severe dyslexias, anxiety, shyness, personalities meant to show their giftedness in a more gentle, less competitive world. The old biblical meek come in all colors, my brother! The all-is-equal society is a lie! Preparing everyone for the big race is demonic! That setup makes mincemeat of the proverbial meek."

Samantha looks pained. She would *like* to interject, cut in, add her two cents. For instance, the need for a global progressive tax on capital with an international agency to monitor all wealth, to sniff around in those tax havens. This could slap some of that vast boodle back into circulation. *Maybe* help all people flourish in a way that, ahem, still honors capitalism, for many a questionable goal. In a proper salon, all ideas are worthy. But she sees no way of cutting in on Gordon's fire. He just goes on and on.

". . . All these precious good-hearted liberals are so proud of their female CEOs and black senators and actually believe that a *good education* will make everyone into the professional class. They don't really support or honor the working class. Meanwhile, there's no safety net, only a . . . goddamn . . . di . . . di . . . dragnet!" The mess in his hand, the ex-tomato, is spreading over the table. "I don't want those shithead friends of yours here," Gordon snarls, his teeth and non-teeth sort of bared.

Blake is noticeably bristling. He is thinking, *We've hit a wall.* He says in a gravelly way, "You aren't much for apologies, are you? Just like your problem with thank-yous. Those humilities stick in your throat."

Gordon smiles his broken-toothed edge-of-wickedness smile, identical to his snarl. "Should all Americans, every single one, whatever color, get on our hands and knees and apologize to the people of the world who've had their heads exploded, homes squashed, loved ones tortured per order of DC's prominent figures and supported by the nastiest and stupidest sons-a-bitches among us? Yes, I'm for reparations. No, I'm not for academics who want to tangle us all up in foundation-supported funhouse mirrors. FUCK ACADEMICS! FUCK their souls!!" A hand settles on Gordon's shoulder. Claire's small dimpled hand, the left one with the silver ring.

Gordon inhales big, exhales big. Then he cleans his fingers with his own rag napkin, tosses it down. He speaks in a quelled fashion. "What are these guys? Agents? Big monkey wrench for our silly little solidarity efforts. But it hurts, man, it hurts. Cuz I *was* getting a kick out of the image of those DC senators and so forth shitting in their pants and skirts turds the size of basketballs if the left *and* the right, the black *and* the white, and *all of us* walked into their castle shoulder to shoulder, brother and sister. See, I want my family to like people. All races. There's so few varieties in Maine. When we're lucky enough to meet different sorts of people, it ought to be a good thing. But nobody can get heartthrobs over a buncha assholes who want to win something. Racism is ugly. This way or thataway. Nobody should win any trophies in its honor. Call me paranoid, but what your friends are up to just creeps the hair on the back of my neck! There's something behind this."

Blake says gloomily, "My friends involved in this would accuse you of avoiding dealing with your racism."

Gordon throws up his hands, pale eyes blistering. "I'm guilty of anything they want me to be guilty of. These kinds of people put themselves in positions of being supreme judges. Their college degrees raise them to clouds over our heads. Fuck 'em. I do not want to deal with *them*, absolutely true."

Yeah, a wall. *Smack*! Blake is aware that this very argument of Gordon's is one he himself has so comfortably argued with his New Abolitionist friends. But with Gordon, his fire-breathing bursts and rivers of preaching, the big bellowing voice that *sits on you*, are not about debate. And then there is something else that Blake can't put his finger on. Something way inside himself also bellowing. And old. The cooling off of good-brother feeling shows in Blake's face as if under a spotlight.

Gordon reads that face. He stands up. All six-feet-five and two-hundred-plus pounds, all stiffened up for redneck-style battle, the scarred face and gimpy leg testimony to his acquaintance with brawls. Brawls even with himself.

Claire inches away, dark eyes huge behind her specs. "Don't, Gordon," she whispers.

Gordon steps around the table and Blake is rising, too. Samantha watches them with the knuckles of one hand digging into her cheek. Cory pushes his chair back. Butch also.

Others in the big room are noticing, kazoos fading, fiddle drags.

Gordon grabs Blake by both shoulders, Blake resisting, his face terrible, one hand fisted, drawing back.

Gordon hollers, "Fuck, man! We been through some shit together out there—" Jerks his head toward the door. "And we've been *dealing* with it just fine! It is a *privilege* to work with you!" He gives Blake a two-armed brutish backbreaking hug. Smooches his ear.

Blake laughs, "You're so crazy."

Gordon stands back, a sneer on his face. "I hate your friends. I love your mother, your funny mother. And your union brother father. I hate your very unbrotherly friends."

Claire fetches some empty plates and vanishes.

Blake shakes his head. He is disappointed in Gordon. Gordon St. Onge, prophet. No, *not* a prophet but flips his cookie like . . . like a regular redneck, the twisted definition of the word. While his New Millennium Abolitionist friends are movers and shakers. Yes, masters and doctorates. Quick on the draw. Classy but tough.

And thennnn—

Before he met Gordon he had heard somewhere that "the Prophet" preyed on desperate impoverished American Indian women. Okay, that's debatable. But he also heard that the guy is this incredibly hypocritical fake, *not working class*, not not not not. Nine hundred acres of inherited land. And stocks!

But then what kind of brother is Blake, who, along with all the Bread and Roses Folk School organizers understands that Gordon is now being inadvertently and with oh-so-good-intentions set up to be wide open sacrificed to the jaws of the behemoth?

He watches Gordon swing limpingly away now, slipping sideways between elbows and shoulders of the family, which has resumed singing and clapping. The fiddle soars, chops, creaks duskily. The drums thump.

Samantha stands up. Rolls her eyes. Tossing her pale hair over a shoulder. "I know where he's going. He's gettin' a pie. He'll be back. He'll have a whole pie for himself. You watch. He's a bottomless pit."

And yep, here he comes. Whole pie on one open palm. In the other hand, big knife.

Samantha leaves in disgust.

Cory gives Blake a playful punch to the shoulder. "See you at breakfast."

Butch salutes Blake before turning to follow Cory.

Gordon now straddles his seat, though not really *seated*, more of a crouch, and saws the pie into two equal halves, sliding half the pie onto Blake's greasy used plate.

Blake settles back into his own chair, watching Gordon.

Gordon says, "Seriously, about your family, if your plans for a better city life don't jell but your folks think they'd like to visit here and see what we're about here and—" He plops the other half of the pie onto his own plate. "And you know they're welcome to stay, if moving all the way up here appeals to them."

Blake is in a wash of whole and wrenching silence. He is now mulling the rumor of Gordon shaking the baby, how *next time*, he might shake one to death. Then all witnessed him smashing his face and head with the lamp. How some Settlementers say they have come to fear the inside of their home as much as they fear the outside. And now here's Gordon's refusal to face those layers of logic in the race quagmire; racism, that old, old, oh so ancient crime against humanity. Those big hands of his. Just shoveling bigger and bigger forkfuls of apple pie into his mouth, even before he gets down onto his chair, straddling it like a horse.

Blake picks up his own fork, studies it coldly. Then he looks at Gordon who is munching away with horrible sloshy noises, one bearded cheek enormous.

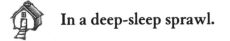

In a deep-sleep sprawl.

On the old sofa of the farmhouse parlor, Gordon wakes with a groaning cry. Opening one eye to the dark room, he sees the dream is not yet dissolved. There is Blake, a tiny figure walking far ahead, indistinguishable from anyone else in the dream's greenish spiraling haze, but he *knows* it's Blake and that's what counts. Blake, yes, his brother, stepping onto a side path that cuts into ancient dusty woods.

And in this dream this path leads away from Gordon so utterly, it is as death.

JULY

Marian watches the noontime news while she embroiders a baby bunting for one of her brothers' grandchildren, due in the fall.

Today a news team has gone to East Egypt Village and interviewed townspeople to find out how they feel about having the "separatist" St. Onge Settlement right in their own "backyard."

First a fiftyish woman with a young, very darling child in her arms standing outside the post office. "Oh, it's terrible. It's the drugs, you see. Everyone knows they're into that quite heavily."

Now a woman whose graying hair is cut with bangs and a bit of a youthful flip to it. Professional class, out-of-state city accent. A two-fisted grip on a big wob of mail. "I heard that some of those people want to get out. But can't. We're afraid for them."

The interviewer asks, "Do you know anyone who has been inside the Settlement since the gate and signs went up a while back?"

"No, I don't. We heard that no one can get in . . . for instance, relatives of those living there . . . and social workers, school department, people trying to get in to help. People fear being shot. And some have seen militiamen in and out of there. I never knew we had militias in Maine! It's pathetic about those children. We hope the authorities can get in there pretty soon and help these poor people. To save the children. People have been hearing helicopters up there regularly. I just don't understand what gets into people. I just hope the authorities can get those children out before something happens."

A man standing by his car, white short-sleeved shirt and tie, a bundle of outgoing bulk mail under each arm. His reply is, "The mass suicide possibility. It would be too bad."

A woman with upswept hair: "Nobody can sleep at night, just wondering when the whole place will just go up . . . you know . . . set themselves on fire or something . . . like all those others . . . Waco and those others . . . it happens. You can hear the helicopters up there on the mountain at night. What if one of those insane men shoots at the helicopters?"

Two young women in T-shirts with messages and cartoons on the front. One's chest huge and straining, sleeves huge and straining. The other's, less strain. Bony neck. Bony arms. Both faces are pretty. Little ski-jump noses. Eyes with makeup just right. Both are brown-haired. The rounder gal reveals that she has known Bonnie Loo Bean for years. "We went to school together, same grade. She's up there with them. Been one of them for a few years. She's one'a them that's had kids by the leader." She flutters her eyes. "He used to be cute as hell."

The other young woman laughs. "IGA guy says he, like, gets eggs and veggies from them, like, for the store. You ought to talk with him. I bet *he* knows some stuff." She gets the visible creepy shivers. "Brrrrrrrif."

The first young woman: "There was a big party up there last summer. You could hear the music for miles. Lotta people went up. We heard there was some pretty wild sex. I wouldn't call that especially religious, would you?"

The second young woman frowns. "They tried to kill the leader, I heard. Bashed him with a rock. I heard he died. But then we saw him driving around last week and we say, like, oh, my God, it's him alive. He musta rose from the dead!" She laughs.

The first gal says excitedly, "But it scarred 'im. He has a big scar here." She opens her hand over her right eye and temple, jaw, and cheek.

Most of the interview with these two is edited out due to time limitations but the visible creepy shiver and "Brrrrrrrif" are artfully retained.

Hardware store owner Jim Mertie: "I always liked Gordie. Those people don't bother anybody. It's none of my business about what they do up there."

"Owner-in-the-store" IGA man, Carl Marchant, smiles. "Gordie? He's a real nice man. I like all of them up there. Nice people. Friendly. And the kids come down here a lot with their flyers about this and that. Great kids. I always let them set their history flyers over there by that *Sportsman's Guide* rack. Some people get a kick out of reading them."

And now a small, sly-looking old man in work clothes on the little open porch of Denise's Diner. "Well, Mr. York Electric tried to kill St. Onge right here last summer. Something to do with a drug deal or a gun deal. Some saw the gun before it was confiscated for evidence. York . . . they call him Rex . . . he's into the militias deep. It's all to do with that now." He raises his chin authoritatively, eyes half lidded, as authority often makes one look serene. "Looks like St. Onge is lying low now. 'Cept for that stir in Portland. Big incident there. He goes in there, in Portland, to make riots." Shakes head, eyes still sleepy with knowledge. "Awful lot of people getting into the militias these days. Guess they better outlaw *that* in a hurry."

Camera zooms in on one young guy in a blue-and-green plaid shirt.

Interviewer leads him: "You've been inside the compound since the gate went up?"

"Compound?"

"Yes. Their gated-up place. You've been inside, right?"

"Yep."

"For?"

"They did my steer."

"Your steer?"

"Yep."

"Do you find that Gordon St. Onge is tightening things down pretty much? Think he's getting ready to attempt a siege like many others have suggested?"

"Nope."

"Did you see Gordon St. Onge while you were inside?"

The guy nods.

"Did he seem strange, like maybe you weren't as welcome as you used to be?"

"Nope."

"What *did* he seem like to you? Can you describe him?"

The guy shrugs. "He just looked hisself."

Actually this interview is edited out completely. In fact, most of the above interviews Marian does not see, because they were edited to a few mouthfuls, because the speaker either said too little or said too much. All Marian sees as she watches, breath held, is what seems to be an eyewitness account of an armed siege about to break out. Or . . . mass suicide. Or both. And perhaps she believes it.

AUGUST

And so now.

The hills creak and cheep with songbugs. Every weed tassel, every creature feeling its bright hormones and burping enzymes shifting into the mode of very late summer.

Under the sinks in the Cook's Kitchen, one cricket. Creaking mightily. A sign of good luck.

SEPTEMBER

Claire remembers.

Day after day, night after night, but never at the same hour, the "law" did its work on us.

I worried about everything. Even things unrelated to our assailants. Maybe everyone's mouth was running with the water of nausea like mine. Then John Lungren's mother started showing signs of a heart attack, but that passed. To the idea of a doctor's visit, she said, "Nah!"

Nowadays, Gordon would say a beautiful grace. Every meal. A grace of thanks for our family; the wind; the sun; the season of winter, which was on the way, winter being his favorite, we all knew. And this would make us smile because most of us hated winter. We knew he was teasing us. Playful in spite of it all.

But one night, in the middle of grace, Willa Wentworth burst into tears. First she wept, but then she was making a sound like madness . . . bleats and howls. Some of the men stood up from their seats even as her husband Ben was already holding her. And Settlement women converged to take her into our dozens of comforting arms, while most of the men standing or sitting were as still as stones. Some children shrieked. Some were flushed and big-eyed. All the different ways that by watching us, children learn their world is in danger.

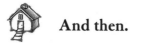

And then.

The cricket creaks under the sink. Its sweet abrasive ancient song. That promise of good luck? Well, crickets have been known to fib.

OCTOBER

Critical thinkers of the past.

Once the game is over, the king and the pawn go back into the same box.

—Italian proverb

Into the box.

He knifes open a multiply-postmarked manila envelope that now lies flat on his desk in his kitchen of sad blue light. Inside the big envelope, a brief note in shaky elderly hand. David Kord. Old friend of Gordon's and Claire's from her college days. "The gang." David was Simmie Green's boyfriend. He wasn't one of the *real* regulars, getting wasted and waxing philosophical and blathering on about the poets who rebelled against form. No, he wasn't even at PoGo U.* He was MIT. But there's no forgetting him. He was ambitious and crisp. His warmth seemed more of practiced utility than part of his nature. Even then, a kid really (none of them more than twenty-five), he was on a ladder. No dillydally for him. He was not going to be subject to much gravity or centrifugal force or romanticism.

David Kord. Gordon heard he had wound up as a hotshot chemical engineer in some hotshot corporate lab, or so Gordon thought. But then he heard that David was actually something vaguely military.

* University of Maine, Portland-Gorham campuses.

At first, he thought US military, of course. But then he heard it was the Brits. But how could that be?

But after all, DC and Wall Street aren't really the United States, so London probably isn't Britain. There's that island in the sky where all the ladders go, remember? And so David would have found it. The planet of power. Supranational as the sun and moon.

But now on the little notepaper, David has written, oh, so shiveringly that he has recently retired at age forty-seven and has *four* kinds of cancer. And he wants "a private audience" with "the Prophet," which "our mutual Maine friends are calling you." Notice the word private is underlined.

Since Gordon recalls David as a young twentysomething guy, this elderly touch of the pen creeps him out. David Kord used to snap to and jump on you, stop you in mid-word if something you were saying smelled of bullshit. So he's not seeking the frivolous *now*. Not a sightseer in the carnival of Gordon's politics and personal miseries.

About this out-of-the-blue impending visit, Gordon feels dread. No, he feels dreads.

For David Kord's privacy, the old "parlor" of the St. Onge farmplace fits the bill.

This is not the David Kord Gordon remembers, even altered by age and savage illness. This is not David Kord. Even as the person Gordon knows he actually is, he is nearly unrecognizable.

As Gordon stands back flat to the door while his guest toddles into the room, sliding forth on an aluminum walker, Gordon's eyes dart elsewhere around the old parlor. Uncozy, sticky, coffee-splattered couch. Cold brass-shaded single bulb hanging in the room's center, as planet earth was once thought to be the center of all existence. And the old windows, wobbly glass, no curtains. The purply gold October light stumbles in onto the old rug, old ladyish blue-and-gray wallpaper, boarded-up fireplace, a constellation of straight-back wooden chairs mostly piled with papers and books and books and books.

The visitor has not replied to Gordon's, "How did you get in past the guards out there?" though to Gordon's offered hand, the guest did reach but then the bony hand tumbled away too soon. His head and face are bald and yellow. No eyebrows. No eyelashes. He is moving one creeping footstep at a time, three steps counting the walker, but purposefully. It's as though another Bruce Hummer, the brown-haired and brown-mustached one, has already found a seat, crossed his legs, and begun to explain something while this shadow drags along to catch up, the tinny thonk of the walker keeping poor rhythm. Yes, this is Bruce. He replies at last, each halting word still an unfaded flower of Alabama: "Oh . . . there . . . are these . . . tunnels . . . steamy tunnels . . . everywhere in . . . the ground . . . that lead to the . . . boil and brimstone suites of my realm. One opened up . . . right outside . . . your door."

Gordon squints. "You told them you were David Kord. I left word with them out there to let David pass. How did you know I knew David?"

"Brother. I know . . . everything about . . . you."

Gordon still stands like a soldier, back against the open parlor door, trying to give a full smile of welcome.

Bruce gargles haltingly: "I and you. One is . . . ghoul . . . in the eye of them . . . while the other . . . is ghoul to . . . the eye of these. Very plain. One plus one . . . equals zero . . . soon."

Gordon still stands like a soldier, his pale blue clean chambray shirt flat against his breathing body. His visitor's revised appearance includes a skull for a face, little dull brown enamel eyes in the eyeholes. Otherwise, he has not spared the trouble to look his best. Navy blue cardigan, a custom size to fit his withered shoulders and swollen belly though his beige dress trousers are loose in the legs, just two flappy flags. Deck shoes like right out of the box, none of the mileage scuffed into them by the man who *"moved up"* in business so fast he was as a contrail in the blue skies.

Now Gordon closes the door, a damp swollen still-summery *ERNK*!

The definition of brother.

There is this which Gordon does not want *them*, the family out *there*, to be touched by *in here*. No, it's not the four kinds of cancer. Not the frightening-to-look-at forty-seven-year-old yellow wax and ash walking dead man, but the indecipherable, unimaginable universe-sized chess game of Bruce's associations and counterparts, that other planet, cold orb of power. More than ever, Gordon realizes its destruction. Gordon doesn't want to hear the family's voice now, nor their melodic steps coming his way calling his name, which to his ears is blessed milk in their mouths. This visit is already vile and his guest hasn't even really spoken.

And yet a sorcerer's hand crawls down Gordon's throat and swells. Sorrow for his brother. What is it in Gordon's floppy nature that gives all green lights to such wrong turns? What is the justification for this twisted love? How did Gordon cross the bridge to this defiled definition of brother? Queer circumstance brought them face-to-face once, in a manner not properly hecklish: *Hello!* to Fate's face.

The guest's face was always lightly swarthy in a keen urbane way, now brown-yellow, as grasses are when chemically ruined.

In the meantime, Gordon's face has gone pussy willow gray. His beard and eyebrows look too lush. The room is cold. Not hospitable. There are cookies on the coffee table as if left from a long-ago evening, maybe back as far as when his mother Marian used to live here with his father "Gary" in their brimming ordinariness, welcoming chirpy guests.

But Gordon doesn't now feel the damp unlived-in cold of this room, so he can't apologize. Bruce specified a private place, didn't he?

The car tarrying in the light and shadows of the hulking ash tree has been driven here by a woman who talked at Bruce Hummer as if he were deaf or three years old. And there's a back-seat passenger who had leaped out first to assist Bruce in getting his feet under him, offering an Atlas sort of arm, and Bruce had gratefully grabbed on.

Woman was introduced to Gordon as "Jess." Rugged young fellow was "Keith." The plan was for them to wait in the car during Bruce's visit. They were all smiles. Now inside the parlor, Bruce's profile seems serene. There he is on one end of the awful couch, a folder on his lap. No longer going "*up in the world*." No more of the world by the tail. He has a belly now, swollen strangely like a box, but his head you could almost balance on one hand. No cheeks, no pudge around the eyes, no jowl. His tongue is licking and digging around inside his large teeth.

But Gordon has known and loved stinky sick people, eyeless people, burn-scarred people. This—that we are only garbage on legs kept fresh just by being perfectly tuned; one slip and our cheapness is verified, the rotting commences—this fact of life is not why Gordon now has a single shiver. Hot refrigerated sweat has begun to let go, creeping through his dark beard. Yes, he is *always* startled by Bruce Hummer because Bruce has a way of materializing unnaturally like a black swan, then whooshes back into the watery netherworld . . . except to pop up in the form of jokey keys. But that most recent key, the skeleton key, not jokey. Gordon gets its meaning now.

Meanwhile, what of all the Bruces who have died here at the Settlement, been jitterbugged by bullets, hanged, even one tossed onto the winter solstice fire . . . that one Gordon never witnessed . . . but all these papier-mâché Bruce ghosts sulk around this very room now in their enduring agonies.

So that is really it, isn't it? What he most fears in the coming together of his family with this celebrity is not Bruce's contamination of *them*, but *their* malice, that which Bruce Hummer's very name brings into their faces, into their smirky deeds. He lowers his eyes.

The coffee table here at Gordon's home is actually a wooden crate of filed papers with a board on top, which Gordon shoved over there with his foot when he was getting ready for this get-together. The cookies were made by the hands of a "crew" and delivered an hour ago by two kids on the Settlement's new donkey, the donkey all done up in embroidered cloth bridle and blankets and a Haitian straw saddle. Ta-da!

Gordon's dreams are in that wooden crate. Journals, reports. And from researchers Gordon has come to think of as friends, letters or notes adhesived to newsletters. The subject matter? Better cover crops. And crossbreeding grains such as wheat to make deep-rooted perennials, a crop you never plow or harrow for. Your soil, your treasure, *locked* in. But for now, not enough funding for this grand project, they say. Not enough political guts anywhere in the clean halls of power.

Some of these guys of the new agriculture mind-set may be offering the Settlement a "micro-sized" cross-pollination project "down the road." So in that box, under the cookies by the knee of the guest, might be the rising sun for the world's grandchildren versus starvation. If you can set aside for a moment the reality of carbon skies. All Gordon wants is those yet-to-exist seeds in his hands. Not this brush with supra-international militarized capitalist power and Bruce Hummer's small, dry-as-biscuits but once very warm and humorous, no, *shrewd* eyes on him, pulling him out of this room, off this mountain, into the embrace of the damned.

Bruce peels open the folder on his lap. His skull smiles, the wee eyes, the huge teeth. "I . . . like . . . these." The voice is bony, too. He rests a hand, skeletal knuckly fingers spread there on the long and short versions of Bree's *Recipe*. The orange cover giggles under his hand. His eyes seem to have lost Gordon's location but widen on him when he is found. There is something drunk about the visitor. Painkillers? Roaring mess of toxic stuff rushing the brain, toxins which a dead liver can no longer sieve out?

Hospitality.

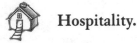

Gordon settles onto an empty straight-backed wooden chair painted a semigloss brick red. He has turned it so he can straddle it and rest his forearms across the back. With only the file box and cookies between him and Bruce, he gets quite close. He marvels, "You actually did read it? Nobody does." Vexation now marches from him to Bree's red-haired and honeyed image, her kitty-cat face. He is blaming this visit on Bree.

Bruce's trundling along dry laugh precedes the march of his words, overly thought out and with not with much push to them. Does the man have only one lung? "It . . . is . . . the . . . eth . . . ical . . . glow . . . of it . . . that . . . im . . . presses." Now he rests. Gasps softly.

Gordon nods.

Bruce: "Com . . . bined . . . with . . . your . . . Bor . . . der . . . Mountain . . . Militia . . . mem . . . ber . . . ship." He stops. Rests. Then, "I've . . . googled . . . all . . . articles . . . on . . . your . . . angry . . . white . . . men . . . associa . . . tions." He stares into Gordon's eyes. The look doesn't match the words. The tiny dark (dull until now) eyes in the skull's holes seem to be calling Gordon up on something.

Gordon's eyes drop. "My neighbors. It's a neighbor thing."

Bruce's huge teeth hiss, "I'm . . . over . . . joyed." He rests. Gasps. Runs his tongue around in one cheek. "And the . . . socialist gang . . .

stirred . . . up . . . all . . . the . . . hornets." He raises a finger to point upward, makes it circle around.

Gordon looks up, smiling his bad-doggie goofy smile. "I'm glad you are glad." Then, "Hey, Bruce. Do you hear much from Janet these days?"

Bruce's small but now dull iron eyes stay on Gordon's. "I'm . . . sorry . . . who . . . is . . . Janet?" He rests. Sighs. Clears his throat harshly.

Gordon swallows.

Bruce's bony bruised-by-IVs hand strokes the *Recipe*'s cover and his deepening eyes gaze into the orange as into a bunch of spirits in their forms of "majestic" not known yet to Guillaume St. Onge's big and yet miniature life. So Bruce becomes the most appreciative reader of the *Recipe for Revolution*!

Gordon is awfully quiet for Gordon.

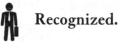

Recognized.

Irritation at or fear of how another day is vanishing brings Bruce's bony shoulders up into a series of hunchy shrugs. The sparse sandy voice proceeds, "My . . . memory . . ." He gasps. Works his tongue again privately behind his teeth. He seems about to faint or fall asleep. He rests, silently huffing. He searches for something inside his little yellow head.

Gordon jumps up. "You want some water? I'm a terrible host. Tea?"

Bruce raises and swishes a hand to erase the offer. Swallows stiffly. "My . . . memory . . . is . . . some . . . where . . . else . . . For . . . give . . . me. Yes, Janet. I . . . miss . . . her."

Gordon closes his eyes in sympathy.

Bruce's eyes roll. Is he dying now? Or snoozing?

Gordon is squinting mightily, bracing his legs to leap up again if the man falls to the floor.

Thumping and door-shutting racket out in the kitchen. Voices. Voices widening, getting close. "Hey! It's us!" Cory's voice that no longer cracks as it used to but melts and goes crushy-soft-warm, then back to barrel-deep, that voice comes plowing up to the closed parlor door. Door *ernks* open; in storms Gordon-sized Cory and those keen dark eyes. Over his shoulder a phantom-black Bushmaster on a green woven strap. Butch behind him, holstered revolver and camo pants worn with the cuffs tucked into tall black military boots. Belt buckle is, of all things, the cartoon Yosemite Sam.

Now pushing in around the others, Evan, one of Butch's younger brothers, the one with pimples as bad as the pox, who wears in its leather case a nearly sword-sized knife.

Last, swaggering into view, that cocky anarchist from Dixie, the one that plies everyone with zines and books with previously unimaginable ideas and footnotes, now carrying two-handedly and familiarly one of the yellowy harsh-grained SKSs that oozed into this situation one foggy night. Jaxon Cross.

"We heard there were cookies," says Cory ever so brightly.

Gordon is realizing that Bruce Hummer, lord of death-and-destruction-products-and-policy, is not too withered to be recognized after all, not by those who have declared his death sentence in new and more fascinating ways by proxy. Their passion clarifies. Bruce's presence is surely known all over the Settlement by now, burning from ear to ear from the moment the farmhouse dooryard crew waved him and his caregivers on.

Gordon speaks. "So you guys've been walking the boundaries."

"Yep," says Cory, tromping more deeply into the cool room.

"Who's out there now?"

"Rick and Jay. And John's crew."

Now the others edge in.

Besides the rifle, Jaxon has what looks like a radio on his belt. EMT on call. No doubloon earring today. No golden flash. He's all in black. His smile, ever large, seems to be egging on some cruel mischief, not the look of a citizen trained to save lives.

"See any military vehicles along Heart's Content?" Gordon wonders.

Evan says, "We were doing the back side of Pock. We saw a duck."

All four young men gloat over this reply.

Gordon notices that Bruce is studying not the new arrivals but the torn-by-rock-and-fists, slit-by-knife, bashed-by-once-lovely-candle-lamp planes of his, Gordon's, face. Indeed, both Bruce and Gordon seem on the road to erasure.

All the young guys grab books and papers off the chairs, arrange the chairs in a semicircle around Bruce and Gordon and the crate coffee table.

They delve into the mountain of cookies, mashing them starvedly into their mouths, while their eyes drill Bruce's little yellowed head and face like wolves around a lamed-up calf.

The cookie-eating noises are exaggerated. The cookie mountain of white-frosting-on-white cookie and colorific jimmies and those that are raspberry-filled begins to erode. Evan has three in each hand. Nobody politely asks the guest how his trip here went, did he get lost. Or would he like the solar-heat flap raised to warm up a bit. None of that, just beaverish chopping noises, bleating swallowings, and those direct stares.

But a beatific smile of the skull's tall bare teeth spreads in a tawny way to fill the room. "Oh, boy . . . a party," Bruce cackles.

Gordon sighs.

But the party is over once the cookie platter is glaring like pond ice, not even much for crumbs, the boys and their guns and knives gathered up, boys nod at Bruce, leave.

Gordon stands, reaches over to the highboy where yet more cookies are, somewhat blocked from view by a robust tower of journals. These cookies are made to look like pumpkins, light orange frosting with yellow smiles and eyes, green stems. He transfers the plate to the "coffee table" with a flourish. He winks. "Help yourself."

Bruce swallows as if to dislodge a splinter. "I had . . . made up my mind to . . . have . . . no . . . treat . . . ments . . . no surgeries. But my . . . will weakened to . . . the . . . promise . . . of . . . relief. But . . . about . . . relief . . . they . . . lied."

Gordon says, "I didn't know anything about this. It sucks, my brother. I'm in shock."

Bruce's voice scrapes along, "Forgive me . . . I . . . only . . . ask . . . of . . . you . . . one . . . big thing. And . . . to . . . give . . . you . . . fair . . . warning."

 **One big thing.**

Gordon's greenish eyes widen in botheration on this yet-to-be-divulged request. And warning.

Bruce braids his fingers together as if to crack his knuckles. Whatever it is he has come here for wants to rip out through the back of his head because it isn't breaking through that mouth, but stiffening his mouth like that of one of the smiling cookies.

Gordon looks down at his own hands. He can never handle with grace long silences between himself and another human being.

Bruce's lips move at last, "I ask you . . . I ask *only you*, the King of Hearts . . . to . . . help . . . me . . . fly."

Gordon sees the blue-and-gray-papered room wobble. Is Bruce once again suggesting Gordon shoot him? Motion catches his eye at one of the front windows, two Settlement girls coming out of the woodsy path on solar buggies, doing a slow-motion turn in his sandy parking area, like a silent movie to his sight but he knows by heart the homey refrigerator hum of the motors. They will park close to the shed doorways, one of which is the Computer Shop, doing one of their obsessive e-mail checks. E-mails being gazed at even more heartily by agencies certainly than those bulging post office bags and boxes.

Bruce gurgles, solid and clay-gray sounding. "As . . . with . . . the . . . Man . . . hatten . . . Pro . . . ject . . . persons . . . expert . . . in . . . their . . . field's . . . work . . . with—" He rests, breathing like a straining bellows, then: "Only . . . a . . . piece . . . of . . . the . . . program . . . And . . . so . . . it—" He rests. Then, "made . . . its . . . way." He holds up a hand to mark his place while heaving with agitation. Then, "But . . . this . . . now . . . on . . . the . . . burners . . . has . . . a . . . wider . . . scope . . . Techniques . . . . and . . . tech . . . nolo . . . gies . . . are . . . making . . . Full . . . Spect . . . rum . . . Dom . . . inance . . . more . . . pos . . . sible . . . as . . . well . . . as . . . a . . . sophis . . . ti . . . cated . . . bulgingly . . . financed . . . inter . . . national . . . psy-ops . . . network."

Gordon jiggles his foot.

Bruce huffs, "There . . . is . . . artis . . . try . . . in . . . this." He alludes to alliances, a vast branchy twiggy tree of conspiracies in constantly shifting state as, yes, a great oak would wave and wag in unexpected breezes. He grimaces.

Gordon asks, "What can I do? Sure you don't want water?"

Bruce waves away the idea of *that* sort of help, his expression one of intensified irritation. "Every . . . de . . . tail . . . of . . . the . . .

lives . . . of . . . the . . . world's . . . common . . . per . . . son . . . is . . . under . . . the . . . micro . . . scope . . . and . . . mani . . . pul . . . a . . . tion . . . by . . . expert . . . tech . . . niques . . . of . . . the . . . First . . . World's . . . best . . . minds." His eyes widen, focusing keenly on Gordon's. "*Your* . . . minds . . . slipping . . . in . . . to . . . new . . . realiz . . . a . . . tions . . . in . . . some . . . cases . . . due . . . to . . . impoverish . . . ment . . . of . . . the . . . once . . . proud . . . *must* . . . be . . . de . . . toured . . . So . . . these . . . events . . . must . . . be . . . engineered . . . with . . . care . . . with . . . you . . . could . . . say . . . preciousness."

"Events?" Gordon's foot goes from wagging to thonking.

"Ter . . . ror . . . events."

Gordon, "Here? In the United—"

"Because . . . empire's . . . nature . . . is . . . thus . . . And . . . full . . . de . . . regula . . . tion . . . and . . . privati . . . zation . . . of . . . the . . . whole . . . world . . . is . . . a . . . must . . . Govern . . . ment . . . merged . . . with . . . and . . . controlled . . . by . . . certain . . . organ . . . ized . . . com . . . munities . . . of . . . wealth . . . is . . . already . . . in . . . effect . . . as . . . you . . . yourself . . . have . . . been . . . preaching . . . to . . . the . . . hordes . . . Police . . . and . . . war . . . Police . . . and . . . war . . . War for all time . . . The . . . major . . . empires . . . are . . . fixed . . . bayonets . . . Ready . . . teddie . . . The . . . stakes . . . are . . . high . . . Re . . . source . . . de . . . pletion . . . must . . . be . . . made . . . pro . . . fitable . . . Climate . . . change . . . profitable . . . Starvation. Profitable . . . Thirst . . . profitable . . . The . . . common . . . per . . . sons . . . world . . . wide . . . will . . . writhe . . . In . . . the . . . US . . . there . . . has . . . been . . . a . . . certain . . . illu . . . sion . . . use . . . ful . . . to . . . main . . . tain . . . order . . . for . . . ages . . . Now . . . the . . . illu . . . sion . . . is . . . losing . . . power . . . The . . . US . . . pop . . . u . . . lation . . . must . . . be . . . steered . . . into . . . more . . . and . . . more . . . confusing . . . terri . . . tory . . . while—" He again holds up a hand to mark his place, to keep Gordon still. "I'm . . . repeating . . . myself."

Gordon is rocking his chair backward. It's not a chair with rockers. Its wooden pegs whimper.

Bruce has covered his lower face with a handkerchief, spits.

Gordon again leans his chair back on two legs and it whinnies.

Bruce says, "Efforts . . . are . . . being . . . made . . . to . . . mainstream . . . what . . . you . . . once . . . called . . . the . . . 'ugly . . . prayer.' Full . . . blown . . . re . . . action . . . aryism . . . In . . . all . . . the . . . First . . . World . . . Normal . . . ize . . . it . . . Make . . . it . . . seem . . . ordin . . . ary . . . While . . . the . . . liber . . . al . . . folk . . . just . . . become . . . obsessed . . . with . . . their . . . own . . . health . . . Their . . . gray . . . ing . . . hair . . . and . . . thinning . . . lips . . . Veggies . . . Mindfulness . . . and . . . correct . . . speech . . . And their . . . issues . . . of . . . course . . . Tightly . . . focused . . . Issues . . . that . . . pooh-pooh . . . others . . . and . . . generally give . . . themselves honor . . . The class-defined new Aryans . . . Thus . . . they . . . too are reactionary . . . Fascism . . . in . . . motion."

Gordon digs at one of his mutilated ears.

Bruce licks his wooden lips with wooden tongue. "This . . . gives . . . conspirators unrestrained . . . power . . . and . . . with . . . in . . . certain . . . chambers . . . no . . . oversight . . . The . . . stakes . . . are . . . high, yes. There is nothing . . . too . . . unscrupulous . . . They . . . will . . . do . . . anything . . . Power . . . can . . . never . . . be . . . quenched . . . It . . . won't . . . cease . . . till . . . it . . . reaches . . . the . . . farthest . . . wall . . . of . . . the . . . reachable . . . universe . . . and . . . even . . . then . . . it . . . always . . . will . . . be . . . panting . . . for more."

No surprise to Gordon, any of this. So why is he sickened?

Bruce now murmurs as if the secret is sweet and close to the ear. "I . . . warn . . . you . . . if . . . they . . . are . . . willing . . . to . . . cause . . . thousands . . . of . . . people . . . in . . . an . . . American . . . city . . . to . . . die . . . *horribly* . . . then . . . what . . . they . . . are . . . doing . . . to . . . you . . . and . . . what . . . they . . . *will* . . . do . . . *after* . . . *this* . . . is . . . nothing to them."

Gordon braces himself, "What do you know of their beef with me . . . their intentions?"

Bruce shakes his head. "Nothing . . . It . . . simply . . . follows."

Gordon nods. "Right."

"We . . . are . . . at . . . the . . . dawn . . . of . . . the . . . final . . . war . . . on . . . all . . . of . . . creation . . . progress . . . versus . . . life."

Both sides of Gordon's face flinch.

Bruce's face vibrates in a yellowy bony dither. "My . . . brother, technology . . . in . . . the . . . sky . . . Holding . . . the . . . world's . . . people . . . in . . . place . . . intelligence . . . Hellfire . . . missiles . . . remote . . . control . . . Everywhere . . . above . . . the . . . earth."

Gordon covers one eye. "Motherfuck."

Both of Bruce's eyes are watering. Gee, he's going to miss the big war, Gordon marvels.

Then he almost bleats, "Remote control?"

Here it comes. Gordon sees it. Bruce's eyes turn sharply onto him and lock.

Gordon's blood zings.

"Their . . . Recipes . . . are . . . on . . . hair trigger . . . I . . . cannot . . . tell . . . you . . . every . . . detail . . . because . . . as . . . I . . . said . . . each . . . player . . . knows . . . some . . . but . . . not . . . all . . . Because . . . nobody . . . can . . . be . . . trusted . . . to . . . know . . . all . . . For . . . instance . . . the . . . cancers . . . that . . . eat . . . a . . . person . . . slowly . . . are . . . the . . . great . . . oiler . . . of . . . hinges . . . and . . . tongues . . . I . . . am . . . here . . . I . . . can . . . no . . . longer . . . be . . . trusted . . . because . . . they . . . know . . . I . . . can't . . . die . . . stuffed . . . with . . . such . . . knowledge . . . I . . . can't . . . let . . . my . . . portions . . . of . . . the . . . intelligence . . . die . . . with . . . me, you understand?" His eyes move toward the curtained window suddenly. Eyes widen. What has he seen?

Gordon shifts to look. Nothing out there. Just beauty. And weather.

But several small white ceramic cherubs are on the bookcase, left from when Gordon's mother Marian had a ceramic-making frenzy. Ordinary life. *Was* that ordinary? Beauty outside? Frumpy inside? Is life as he knows it soon lost forever?

Bruce's hand comes up and strokes his dead skull of sheer yellow bone. Again he smiles. His shrunken eyes creep up and across the wallpaper in strokes like a metal detector searching for lost coins and rings. He says, "Their . . . *Recipe* . . . is . . . breath . . . taking . . . ly . . . funded . . . Unaccountable . . . accounting . . . Foreign . . . banks . . . Much . . . laundering—"

Gordon opens his mouth to speak but Bruce's voice splutters on. The world-heavy weight of cognizance pains Gordon more and more as little shriveled Bruce, by the moment, weighs less and less and his tongue makes lewd flickers involuntarily. His throat braids its strands. One word, one secret, one gasp, making more lucid the tale he has borne to Gordon's home, no, not tale, he said "intelligence." He, yes, unloads the wondrous unspeakable now spoken details, international deals, international players, intelligence agencies on full boil, bribes, lobbying, blackmail, theft, funnyish news. The American and other western populations will be made to fear and revile the Muslim world. For starters. It will be the first big ball rolling. This is what the richest and best-organized of the human species have ripped into shape. It is a rogue government above all governments, tidying up its rough edges. Throttling any unified revolt against it. No news to Gordon and yet these halting oh-so-genuine *details* are new and dearly sting, those grinning specterish details that dribble-spit from the specter's mouth.

Gordon finally observes wearily, "It's big, yeah." So this is what it feels like to be taken aboard a spacecraft and you can never tell anyone. He sighs. A railroad spike suddenly crashes into his left eye and temple. He feels pockets for aspirin.

Bruce stares into the air, breathing noisily, hot and doggy, desperate panting. Then the slow painful trudge of his words on and on and on and on, Gordon holding his breath wondering what favor Bruce wants of him. Is he, Gordon, to blow the whistle? Gather arms? Attack? None of that makes sense. Little fly and his little fly comrades bouncing off the chest of the gods of Mammon. The Settlement's efforts to defend itself are already comically senseless. Jesus. Jesus.

His last drink, his last *drunk*, was almost perfectly a year ago! But now, if only he had a gallon jug of hard cider to crawl inside of.

As he watches, Bruce's two bony hands caress his pottery-smooth skull, then drop. Big smile. Some gold crowns show. "The . . . principles . . . the . . . principle . . . figures . . . in . . . this . . . can't . . . kill . . . me . . . I'm . . . dead." He chortles. Then frowns. "Mean . . . while . . . even . . . the . . . most . . . important . . . players . . . can't . . . stop . . . this . . . scheme . . . even . . . if . . . that . . . were . . . their . . . pleasure." He dabs one eye with a handkerchief, the eye having again begun to leak something, then flicks the hand of that wrist that once wore the elegant watch with that languid sweep of time. "Nobody . . . among . . . the . . . mil . . . li . . . ons . . . of . . . or . . . din . . . ary . . .

people . . . can . . . ima . . . gine . . . the . . . fear . . . and . . . noise . . . and . . . knee . . . jerk . . . nationalism . . . that . . . will . . . be . . . blasted . . . into . . . the . . . Western . . . world . . . *soon*."

Gordon groans.

Bruce flicks his shrunken head sideways upon his little stick of a neck. Looks at his purpled IV-riddled hands, which he probably can't recognize as his own. "It . . . is . . . ne . . . ces . . . sary . . . to . . . mas-ter . . . mind . . . consent . . . of . . . the . . . Western . . . pop . . . u . . . ation . . . to . . . allow . . . itself . . . to . . . be . . . ordered . . . per . . . fect . . . ly . . . You . . . see? To . . . be . . . mobilized . . . For . . . end-less . . . war."

Gordon wags his head boyishly.

Bruce folds his handkerchief formally as if to end the conversa-tion. Then suddenly, again, his sunken dull eyes widen on the win-dows. Gordon turns but sees nothing at the window, no Peeping Toms, no agency spies. And Bruce is still talking, huffing, pausing. "I . . . know . . . enough . . . of . . . the . . . past . . . successes . . . of . . . these . . . power . . . ful . . . men . . . and . . . a . . . lot . . . of . . . their . . . smaller . . . mani . . . fold . . . agendas . . . and . . . the . . . thing . . . it-self . . . the . . . new . . . order! . . . And . . . the . . . newer . . . order . . . to . . . come!!! . . . And . . . I . . . have . . . been . . . its . . . servant . . . its . . . slave!" His eyes grow perfectly round. "Highly . . . paid . . . to . . . be . . . a . . . gree . . . able . . . To . . . be . . . unable . . . to . . . turn . . . from . . . it . . . all . . . com . . . pen . . . sated . . . ex . . . quisitely . . . to . . . be . . . *weak*! . . . Yes . . . I . . . know . . . a . . . few . . . of . . . the . . . conse . . . quen . . . tial . . . brains . . . behind . . . this . . . ma-jestic . . . intrigue . . . Conspi . . . racy . . . theorists . . . are . . . said . . . to . . . be . . . nuts . . ." He leans forward suddenly. "But . . . conspir-acy . . . *plotters* . . . are . . . nuts."

Gordon raises his eyes again to Bruce's, which are in wild-horse fashion rolling. All his noises, bubbling and percolating in throat and chest and middle. All these are his voices, his confessions. But where is the request?

Gordon points at the cookies. "Help yourself, Bruce."

The guest nods. "Thank you." But the skeleton hands stay in the lap with the folded handkerchief, folder, and twinkling orange *Recipe*. He tells Gordon of plans for changes in international law, more and more government-subsidized privatizations, total deregulation for transnational corporations, China and Russia bristling against the West's obscene hip-thrusts, and vice versa. Reconfigurations for a new feudalism. Disappearances. Funny courts. Prisons. Torture centers. And detention centers. "For . . . those . . . who . . . fight . . . this . . . And . . . refugees . . . Call . . . them 'shelters' . . . Call . . . them . . . 'havens.' Words are magic." And as Bruce speaks he is now looking toward the window as if Gordon were beyond the glass. Gordon does not turn this time to look. He knows he is in his chair! Not outdoors! But not everything is right with this world. *Out there* in THE *WORLD* cherished deities are being transmogrified. Coming for his dear ones. Crushing all who are small and dear to *someone*.

All that he and Rex or he and Bree or he and Blake have turned over and over, sometimes in argument, sometimes in sweet sync, here it is out of the dying horse's mouth. Armageddon.

And now Bruce is looking out the window again, this time raises a hand. He waves.

Gordon flashes around to look. Nobody there. Jesus Christ!!

Bruce looks back to Gordon, clearing his throat as if on a podium at some ordinary symposium on the subject of selling rug cleaners. There is a smile, tender, unchanged. Charmed. "I . . . came . . . here . . . because . . . I . . . have . . . been . . . watching . . . you . . . Gordon . . . And . . . yes . . . the . . . media . . . can . . . make . . . a . . . plain . . . person . . . into . . . a . . . giant." He smiles wider. "And . . . they . . . are . . . doing . . . that . . . They . . . are . . . giving . . . you . . . power . . . But . . . you . . . see . . . It's . . . different . . . for . . . you . . . than . . . some . . . Be . . . cause . . . you . . . *are* . . . the . . . King . . . of . . . Hearts." Bruce goes rather suddenly silent, taken with a beatific smile.

Gordon looks hard at the cookies, the cookies touched by the hands of the family.

Bruce, the stick man, Bruce the shrunken head, Bruce on the threshold to the enviable mystery, whispers sandily, "The . . . King . . . of . . . Hearts . . . you . . . are . . . *that*."

Gordon squeezes his eyes shut, embarrassed.

Now the guest is again panting. His one lung, or tiny lung, or no lungs cannot puff out the most important part of his request.

What izzz Gordon good for? Human sacrifice? Gordon has lately understood this to be so. That he will probably be killed by *the foe*, but not in effigy. Because he is *not* a winner of *all* hearts. And there is *nobody* who is truly his brother.

Gordon looks back at the cookies, their round pumpkin faces smiling.

Bruce places his handkerchief over his wet eye. He is smiling. Hand and handkerchief drop to his lap. Other hand falls to the stained couch that is wavy and rough and smells mousy. Bruce strokes its surface. "Homey."

Gordon laughs nervously.

Bruce blinks his eyes, brown irises, yellow whites. "The . . . poison . . . in . . . my . . . brain . . . has . . . made . . . me . . . senti . . . men . . . tal."

Gordon asks, "Did your family have a faith when you were growing up, my brother?"

Bruce chuckles. "No . . . Only . . . in . . . the . . . certain . . . ty . . . of . . . our . . . small . . . ness . . .But . . . I . . . was . . . not . . . satisfied . . . with . . . small."

Gordon, "So good and evil are not an issue. Big and small are?"

Bruce, "The . . . only . . . thing . . . I . . . am . . . *sure* . . . of . . . *now* . . . is . . . men . . . live . . . by . . . design . . . they . . . are . . . not . . . gods . . . They . . . are . . . adaptive . . . organ . . . isms . . . I . . . say . . . *they* . . . when . . . I . . . speak . . . of . . . men . . . not . . . *we* . . . not . . . to . . . put . . . myself . . . above . . . them . . . It's . . . just . . . it's . . . that . . . a . . . man . . . I . . . am . . . no . . . longer . . . One . . . of . . . the . . . cures . . . for . . . one . . . of . . . my . . . cancers . . . has . . . been . . . a . . . busy . . . knife."

Startled by his honesty, Gordon flushes but speaks flatly, "That's not what makes a man. According to my all-wise Uncle Joey, 'Boys fuck. Men weep.' I was too young then when he was alive to figure out what he meant. Time gives—"

"Why . . . did . . . I . . . come . . . here?" Bruce interrupts with a grunt, leans forward again suddenly.

Gordon pushes himself up. "You are in pain, brother."

Bruce leans back, eyes closed. "Well . . . I . . . have . . . morphine . . . but . . . I . . . have . . . chemo . . . brain . . . I . . . have . . . bilirubin . . . I . . . have . . . people . . . to . . . feed . . . me . . . and . . . to . . . dress . . .

me . . . I . . . am . . . at . . . the . . . delightful . . . edge . . . of . . . it . . . all." Then with his Alabama accent pitching about warmly, he says, "The . . . favor . . . I . . . came . . . here . . . to . . . ask . . . you . . ." He bows his head. "I . . . cannot . . . fly . . . with . . . this . . . boulder . . . on . . . my . . . back . . . my . . . brother."

Gordon's two hands squeeze the back of the chair that he straddles.

Bruce cocks his head. "So . . . you . . . have . . . no . . . more . . . to . . . do . . . to . . . help . . . ol' Bruce . . . It . . . is . . . done . . . What . . . I . . . have . . . told . . . you . . . it's . . . all . . . yours . . . now."

Bruce stands with no warning. Teetering. One little deck shoe accidentally strikes the file box coffee table. He almost goes down. The handkerchief and manila folder remain in his bony grip.

Gordon's left work boot accidentally stabs the "coffee table" making the untouched cookies do a square dance on their pottery plate.

Gordon has grabbed onto one of his guest's, no his *brother*'s stick arms. And also the walker. Both tinny and mere. Now he sees that Bruce is riveted by the widows again. Gordon turns. Standing on something to get high enough, yes, what? A bucket? Secret Agent Jane in her new coplike dark glasses and her trench coat, her face dropping out of view again . . . Gordon tsks. "Sorry about that, Bruce. One of our kids." He still has Bruce by the arm but Bruce has the walker, the folder, the handkerchief, and sweeping presence of mind. And Bruce is now in a twisted-neck position of looking up at Gordon the giant's face, robust, farm-fed, farmworked, failed fruit of the excellent Depaolo genes, no degrees, no ambition, just too much fucking, *Boys fuck, men weep*, the words still inflicting themselves upon the dank, mousy-scented, blue-and-gray-wallpapered room. And what are those wallpaper figures? Clipper ships. And some sort of stains. Gordon smells a little mousy himself? Or is it Settlement soap? Yes, *this* is the creature upon whom Bruce Hummer has placed his last wish.

When they get out to the dooryard.

The car Bruce came in is now in the sun, the shade of the ash having crawled away, the woman at the wheel, the brawny young guy already crossing the grass to assist. The car is a Lexus, silver-gray like some weapons are. Gordon suspects these are a pair of nurses.

Secret Agent Jane is now at the corner of the far end of the long narrow porch, squatted down, bending back a page of her small secret-agent notebook, scribbling evidence. News of his very special guest could not by any law of nature be contained.

No good-bye hugs between Gordon and Bruce. Not even a handshake. Bruce's whole person is concentrated into getting those last steps to the velvety back seat of his ride. He is airy now, vague, indecipherable, refreshed. Gordon is heavier. Like a loaded garbage truck with six flat tires.

Secret Agent Jane Meserve on the rules of engagement.

I used to hate night. Now that I'm almost eight it's not that bad. Kind of friendlyish actually. Even with the helicopters. No big deal. Everybody acts like it's a big deal but it's not. You just go into a porch or scooch under a tree. At first the helicopters seem huge and mean. But nothing ever happens. They come. They go.

It's like when I was little. I was afraid of nature. And stuff. Like gardens. Big shapes under the leaves. Bugs on legs. Bugs of no legs. But now woopie big deal.

Tonight I am just walking around and around very nice night, naturish and nightish. I had no problem getting out because Oh-RELL was asleep with his gun. He tries to be a guard all night waiting for scary men but his chair is probably too soft. He's always just hanging his head cutting some z's.

I am thinking about Gordie's old guy who visited. Very sad. I have only one picture in my spy book because you would be too sad to draw even one picture of a skeleton walking and everyone holding him up. Maybe Gordie's uncle. Also I saw Cory and them eat all his cookies. Even I wouldn't do that!

I am hoping now to run into Mickey. He is sixteen. Almost older than that. He likes the night, too, and sometimes we stand around and talk. He is starting to treat me like I am somebody. He talks. I talk. He talks. I talk. We have to do it real whisperish, though, because of the new rules. Once we sat here, this little seat. A wooden bench thing. He lights some of his cigarettes and smokes fast and slow.

If I sit here now I can remember everything we said before, which was almost love-ish if you look at it a certain way. This is a bench one of them built near the gardens on one of the highest parts of the earth. You can see everywheres but also the nearest garden, which is a garden of just flowers and mossy stuff and things they call urbs and a tree . . . I think it's for cherries.

Mickey isn't here. Maybe he will be soon. Maybe if he and I are sitting here and a helicopter comes it will be love-ish because maybe he'll put his arm around me and to be nice, kiss my neck while the helicopter makes the dead animal noises and music that upsets everyone.

Helicopters are really cops. Maybe army. Big deal. I used to be afraid of cops but now it feels okay because *everybody* hates cops. It is the feeling of EVERYBODY that makes you strong.

Maybe Mickey is sleeping okay tonight and will never come out.

It is quite possible that Mickey is getting a crush on me. Sometimes he looks at me funny, a moosh look in his eyes. Or something. I have my hopes up.

I dig my heel around in the grass stuff. The moon has a face like "Oh!" Very adorable. Chubby cheeks and everything. Total pudge. The grass has twinkles. You call it doo. The moon isn't exactly round, though. Kind of baggy. This is all very good for spying and keeping records. Nobody can see me but I can see for miles. I yawn. My eyes trickle wicked.

What's that? Oh, it's just a bump of some kind. It could have been Mickey but it's not.

Uh-oh. Guess what. It is it. Yes. Way off. Helicopter. It might be coming here to make the noises and scare everyone.

Yep. It's coming. I'm getting one small twingy of fear. And I got pringly arms and hoppity heart.

It is coming fast, right here to the Settlement and mountains on all sides. It is right over now and on come wicked big lights.

I stand up. I stare right up into its horrible mean light and its horrible huge noise and wind that wiggles the air. I make a mean deadly look and STARE.

The searching lights sweepy-swish from side to side over the shops and hillsides of little houses where Oh-RELL is waiting with his gun and the fields and the Quonsets and sheds and fences. All the old trucks and tractors. A cat squeezes under a wagon. The noise is wicked whompish. Sticks and sand smash around at the windows of houses as usual. The helicopter is huge like a bus and is so close like a bus. Only it is *up* instead of *beside*. Now it goes way off sideways then swings back to make everything crazy again with wind and whomps and lights.

I am still standing there so I turn slowly around keeping my face right on it. I am turning, turning slow to follow it as it goes around over me but really mostly around me, blowing mean wind. My expression is so disgusted. That light . . . it is really pushing down on me now . . . it is like noontime of a very scary world. The vibrashins and thunderishness is so total. Oh my gawd, I almost lose my thoughts. The gardens of millions of doo drops smash around and everything is wagging and cold. Stuff smashes my pantlegs and neck.

And you will not believe this. It is the thing they keep doing, very weird these guys are so crazy. It is a loudspeaker that speaks with voices like coyotes and tortured animals. And it swipes me some more with the light like it is trying to knock me over with light. But woopie doo. I turn around and around in the wicked brightness and wind and the screams of tortured animals.

Another October day. Less red-purple, more gold.

Cardboard box of Gordon's personal mail. Much of it preopened by agents as usual. Bottom of the pile is an envelope from the Weymouths' daughter Selene addressed to Gordon and Claire. No note, not even a Post-it hello. Just folded clippings from the *Wall Street Journal*, *Washington Post*, and *New York Times*. Article-style obits. All trumpeting Bruce Hummer's "hard-work" ascendancy to the "defense" industry's stratosphere. And wow wow wow his magic hands that built Duotron-Lindsey International into a weapons manufacturing and chemical engineering empire. Listed are his business school degrees. And early on, Bowdoin. Liberal arts, of all things. A mention of two ex-wives and three children. And "predeceased by his parents."

Though of course each article admits Bruce Hummer was born, it doesn't say where. Not even a whisper of Alabama, the cradle of his veiled humanity. None say that he "died at home surrounded by family" and "will be sadly missed by several nieces and nephews," "best friend" such 'n' such, and "faithful dog" such 'n' such, as it would include in *Your Weekly Shopping Guide.* No community stuff like "gave so much of his time to driving for Meals on Wheels," no "won the ice-fishing derby on Mine Pond," no photo of him with a dead bear as there would be in *Your Weekly Shopping Guide*, or maybe a photo showing him with a sated grin, squashed down into his La-Z-Boy under a pile of giggling little kids with birthday cone hats, as often is showcased in *Your Weekly Shopping Guide*.

And naturally, not a peep of the dread covenant of the club of those whose idea of fun and duty and brotherhood and pledging one's honor and one's stuff in that grand chessboard with little black and white and tan *alive* men, women, and children of the globe under the boom and squeal and crumble of war that will not end in anybody's lifetime, all to commence stridently once Part A of the plan sweeps aside the curtain and the horrorific pieced-together Godzilla terror events tromp some cities, viewed repeatedly from the comfort of ten zillion homes on ten zillion TVs, which these days are big as mattresses.

And no mention of the deceased's "courageous battle with cancer" because he didn't battle it but danced with it. Well, naturally, these lofty publications had no way or manner of fact-checking such things. Though, hey, they would have saved so much space if they'd just said: *Ghost dies*.

Brunswick, Maine, eclipsed by sheets of cold rain.

Marian had resisted the suggestion at first but Janet insisted because Janet has always been a woman of adventure, fun, and discovery, even though this meeting for lunch at one of those clam chowder sorts of diners is based on wailings of the heart, their common loss. Odd to grieve for what didn't leave you precisely but what you yourself have jettisoned. Yes, we are all living in days of fear, even the well-heeled ladies in their lacy forts with their sighs of lost patience for their child transmongrified.

Both women have had to park far from the front door because of all the vans and trucks with boomed buckets and tool boxes, this that portends the counter stools and booths will be beset by a crush of workmen.

Simultaneously each woman steps out into the rain, Marian fumbling for her umbrella off the passenger seat of her sporty red car, Janet no umbrella, just a wonderful wide-brimmed brown canvas hat. "Marian, you look wonderful," she breathes silkily into the iron rain.

The apology.

Hundreds of orphaned white kittens skitter weightlessly through the loveless October blue above, while far below on the tractor road from the Pock Hill logging landing an ox-pulled wagon of split oak firewood heavily moseys. Bunch of young guys and preteens including Oceanna are sprawled upon this load, all eating dried apple chewy bars. The older folks walking along ahead, sweaters and outer shirts tied around the waist. Gordon way ahead, jogging in his bad-leg way, his bunch of keys singing, reaches Claire's front yard, calls her in a muffled way, one cheek bulging with half a chewy bar.

"Here!" Her voice from behind her cottage.

Coming around back, he sees only her feet and shins, sheets making flowery walls that stir because the air is so nervous.

He has, for some reason, stopped in his tracks. He sees her hand reach down for a sock in the basket. Dried in the seams and around the nails of that hand of pudgy fingers is a blushing coral like the freshly painted rocking chair in the West Parlor, her early a.m. project.

He swallows the last of the chewy bar. "We have your green oak coming," says he.

"Good," says she.

He parts the two rows of sheets, sees her dark bespectacled eyes lift to him. She doesn't smile. But he thinks she's glad to see him. It has always been that he's had to use guesswork on that.

What happens next is not something he has planned. It comes from a place of dark, of unease. Perhaps it is that welling of wrongs climbing the throat, that regret Blake demands of him, that is a forsaken and brutalized people's right . . . but different . . . because this is like that pillar of moon's blaze white that breaks down through the boughs this time of year and spotlights one small oval of holy ground.

To move the basket he uses his booted foot, which has a splat and a splotch of lilac paint on the lacings left from his work last week helping the swan boat crew . . . those sturdy pastel fleets that help keep Settlement books in the black.

"Claire?"

"What?"

He slides down to the ground, on, yes, his knees, arms around her legs, forehead thrust into her squishy middle. "Claire?"

"What?"

"Forgive me . . ."

Silence.

He groans miserably. "You know . . . for *all of it*," he adds, just in case she's not clear on that.

Claire.

I promised to be your guide, to tell you our story, so here's what happened next. One night at supper a helicopter swung in as usual but this time *two* of them from polar directions. Just as it seemed our heads would pop with the pressure of the whomping rotors mere yards above us, there came a KAR-BOOO-HROOMMMM!!! and KAR-BOOO-HROOMMMM!!! that shook the walls and floors and punched our chests. They were bombing us! Of course there were gagging screams and sobs and cowering and running and every manner of freaking out.

There were six of these thundering-shaking explosions, glasses falling out of cabinets, babies wailing, dogs disappearing under tables, a crinkling here, a bang . . . a screen door slam? . . . all sounds amplified as though even whispers of "My gawd" were bombs themselves.

After the cowardly men turned their monster craft away, crews and straggly groups of us went out to check the damage. No sign of damage. No bombed buildings. No craters in the earth. It had been only sound. It had been only their frosty total-power blood playing with our prostrate blood.

Beautiful October afternoon.

The old Ford station wagon crammed with people bumps along the narrow tar road, passing a short series of new homes, fanciful glass, dormers, elegant porches, shrubberies, and three-car garages.

Old Ford keeps going. Old Ford turns into the rutted dirt lane. Old Ford arrives. At the home of the Beans. Bonnie Loo's people.

Small cluttery front porch. Three mismatched additions with small crank windows at the back. Stuff around the dooryard. Quiet Samoyed chained out back. His eyes stare from his deathly still, white face. On the steps of that front porch two pumpkins. One crisp and green with an important smile. The other, carved too long ago, has an old man's caved-in mouth and fruit flies going into and out of the squinted eyes.

The Settlement women stand around the yard. Smiling. One holds a big tray of apple crisp. The sky is the blue of endless joy. The tall-grass bugs sing. The weeds are tasseled yellow but appear russet across the distances, seeding, bending. No hard frost yet. Everything still buzzing. The one huge tree in the yard here that is alive is a maple. Brightly colored now. It is one of those two-hundred-year-old gnarly brutes so it has seen a lot.

The visiting women all wear red sashes. This is noticeable. What does it mean?

Someone comes from the house onto the porch. Not Bonnie Loo. It is a woman in her mid-forties, long light-brown hair tied back, yellow-blond once. Those Settlement women who remember her younger still see her hair as yellow-blond. She wears jeans and a green blouse. Sneakers. A small woman. Not what you'd expect for Bonnie Loo's mother but this is Bonnie Loo's mother. She has one arm across her middle as she would do if both arms were folded there, or if she held a sweater together, but there's no sweater and her other arm is down.

Penny St. Onge steps up onto the porch. She smells something apple in the air, but she presents her own apple dish anyway.

"Where's B.L.?" Beth St. Onge demands, glaring around with qualmless coplike eyes.

Bonnie Loo's mother's name is Earlene. She laughs. "She's out back. She just got home. Come on in."

"Where're the kids?" wonders Geraldine St. Onge, giving Earlene a hello hug.

"My sister-in-law took them to the hatcheries in Gray. 'Cept Gabe. He's in school."

All the Settlement women narrow their eyes on this terrible word, then one at a time they hug Earlene. It's the first time they have come to visit since Bonnie Loo's leaving the Settlement months ago and this visit feels like a focused mission. When Beth St. Onge finishes with her hug, she snarls, "Like hugging a fly."

Earlene gives her a playful slap on the arm.

Bree has never been here before. Not till now.

Nor has Misty, even thinner and more cautious than Earlene. The same habit of hugging herself with one or both arms.

In the kitchen, Earlene apologizes for running out of coffee. "And there's only three very old tea bags." But there is plenty of apple dessert, both the Settlement-made one and what's coming out of the oven now with two darkened pot holders.

Earlene says, "Your sashes are beautiful." She tosses the pot holders into a basket, turns back toward her guests, who are all sitting at the table or standing, Bree looking perfectly comfortable in her manly squat. They show Earlene how each sash is different but all of them are red. And all intricately embroidered with green, purple, orange, yellow, blue, and wedding ring gold. Sun faces, hex signs, leaves, stars, fairies, and snails. They mention that last they knew, Bonnie Loo had one, too.

Earlene seems not to know this fact, squints bewilderedly, then says, "Well, they're all gorgeous." Then she fusses around in the cupboards and drainer to collect saucers and bowls for the apple desserts.

There's a hard cough from beyond a doorway. A strangling cough. A man. None of the Settlement women remark. And Earlene makes no explanation.

"How are Bonnie Loo and the baby doing?" Claire asks.

Earlene smiles sadly. Raises her chin a bit. "Bonnie's lost too much weight."

Claire says, "We miss her. We've tried to honor her wishes and not pester her, but . . . she was a sister to us."

"She ain't started job hunting yet. She feels anxious about that. She knows what's out there. There's not much out there that pays a living."

"We heard she had a girl," young Natty says.

Earlene smiles. "Her name is Grace Earlene."

"Where's her rats?" Beth asks, making a face.

Earlene laughs. "Rats are all set up over to Dale's apartment in town. He ain't afraida rats. I am." She laughs again.

"Bonnie loves her rats," says Beth.

"*I* like her rats," says Gail.

Bree says, "I've never seen them. I was never at her place."

"One of them rats wears a real cute blue hat," says Gail.

Earlene shakes her head, smiling. But she is thinking the terrible thoughts, the visions of the dangers of Settlement life under attack. She prays daily for their safety and gives thanks that Bonnie Loo and her kids *are not there*!

Again the deep strangling cough. But now from the doorway of that room appears a small child in a flowery shirt and little jeans. Barefoot. Dark hair. Funny little face. Bleary eyes. Sleepy.

Earlene squats down to feel the child's pants. The kid has a vague resemblance to Bonnie Loo, being both half sister to Bonnie Loo and distant cousin to Bonnie Loo's dead father.

Lee Lynn says, "Earlene, none of us would do a thing to hurt Bonnie. We've spent a long time working up the nerve to come here. She can't possibly hate us."

Beth says, "She should get her ass back to her cute cottage before Toto* moves into it. I heard it's coming up at our next meeting. B.L. designed it. It's empty and waiting."

Geraldine says, "I pumped Gordon to see if he's spoken with Bonnie but all he said was let Bonnie Lucretia decide for herself."

Glancing at Geraldine, Earlene is smiling a thin, quirky, knowing smile.

Leona says, "She doesn't have to come back to Gordon . . . just come back."

"He's not been himself," Beth moans. "He doesn't visit anyone anymore . . . if you get my meaning."

Earlene fetches from one of the linoleumed workbenches a pocket watch. She puts it in the two-year-old's fingers. "Tanja, take this to

* Toto is the new person who arrived barefoot from Brownfield.

Daddy. He's been looking for it." Little Tanja pads away through the open bedroom door.

Bowls of apple crisp are served. The orangy late day sun slashes across one of the workbenches strewn with red tomatoes and warty gourds, a box of macaroni, a child's cup, a box of Saran Wrap. Each Settlement woman glances at the sliding away triangle of sun with a look of consternation.

And Earlene stands now with one arm folded across her middle, that habit. And Lee Lynn asks if Bonnie Loo knows they have come.

"Yes, she knows you're here," Earlene says with her thin sad smile, a smile that *knows*. For she, in the way of heart-to-heart talks, is Bonnie Loo's mother and true sister.

And then a man's voice, raspy, deep, speaks beyond that open door, "Stop, Tanja."

And Earlene calls out, "Tanja, come for apple stuff. Get out of his hair."

And again the strangling cough.

And Earlene speaks low and softly to the visitors. "It doesn't look good. It's in his lungs."

The child pads out to the kitchen. And then another door is heard closing beyond a narrow hallway of jackets and tools. Bonnie Loo. And yes, she looks different. Her face, thinner. Her glasses in her hand. Green bandanna knotted in her brassy hair. No eight-month-old baby. No Grace Earlene. Somewhere sleeping? Not available for show-and-tell.

All the St. Onge women rise from their chairs. Bree from her squat. Bonnie Loo lowers her eyes a moment. Sees the sashes. Their moccasins, shoes, sandals, and boots. Skirts and jeans. Their hips. A whole collection of his beloved mares, their easiness together, which she cannot fathom. How it pains her, the dread force of their bellies and cunts (Bonnie Loo's word). Now she raises her eyes. See there, their faces.

Geraldine recalls.

And so a few nights later, in Bonnie Loo's little pink Settlement cottage with the dark green trim there was a soft light.

BOOK EIGHT:
Here to Protect

Critical thinker of the past.

"Community is a response to the prolonged emergency of being alive."
—Gary Greenberg

It has come to this.

No skits. No singing. Voices so low they seem beyond doorways to be only mooing and clucking. The kitchen crew has insisted: no electric lights. For now. Only a few candles are to be set out, those turning out to be a real blaze of about sixty Settlement-made candles in all shapes and weedy odors. And there are the candle lamps as usual. The mixed "perfumes" are heady.

Penny and Astrid and Paul Lessard open a few windows, as the two cookstoves and one simmering airtight have made the two adjoined kitchens swelter. Blooms of light flutter and bounce on the shiplap ceilings. Geraldine makes big eyes and remarks, "Perfect for ghost stories."

"War stories," Ray Pinette sullenly corrects her. There is a hole in his family now since his wife Suzelle and teen daughter Erin are among the eleven people so far to leave the Settlement, worn down by the government's sorties.

"Do ghosts!!" several kid voices yeowl.

"Nooo," moans little Delaney St. Onge, covering her ears.

Glennice suggests the silence of prayer "in these times." Often she has a silly flash that all people of the world are holding very still in cellars and dark rooms, muscle-tightened by the floor-shaking *KAR-BOOO-HROOOMMMM*s of these proudly cruel foes of humanity, a comfort really, to think your people are not being singled out.

Old Jim Feeny has somberly begun his whole repertoire of horror stories.

Many True Maine Militia teens are murmuring about whether or not doing the big Augusta rally in two weeks will twist the government's meanness screw further.

Del at the third row of tables has rolled his wheelchair in closer and is talking with Dracula's accent perfected, softly, which makes it twice as horrible. The red stained-glass candle lantern near his left cheek makes evil pulses over his profile and hands. Plates of Bonnie Loo's best Popeye casserole look purple in this light but are, of course, really green.

With this mood, they all stiffen in their seats as they hear someone walking slowly down the long connected porches to the two kitchens' French doors, which open into the Cook's Kitchen. All food swallowing stops. Forks freeze. Around them, the walls shake with the rosy candlelight, some candles hissing and sputtering. Jim and Del have stopped telling stories. John Lungren slides his hand under his overshirt to draw out his revolver and rises with bent knees. Everyone in the Cook's Kitchen watches the vague shapes beyond the small-paned French doors, doorknob turning. And in the Winter Kitchen beyond the two archways, some stretch their necks, some stand. It seems the knob turns as slowly as a stalactite is made. Like millenniums of tiny drips.

This is not a late-for-supper Settlement person's hand on the knob. You can tell. There's a difference. A creepy difference.

Door opens.

Rex.

Dozens of flushed, overly heated faces stare at Rex, this man who attacked Gordon so ruthlessly, caused things to be different here, obtrusively different. Terribly different.

Then they all look at Gordon, who does not look even a teeny-weeny bit shocked. Then they all look back at Rex as he tugs off his soft visored military cap and lays it on top of the pie chest. And then four other familiar men gather behind him, full camo, rifles, the Border Mountain Militia patch. Rex, no rifle, but a holstered service pistol on the woven pistol belt around his shirt under his dark unzipped jacket. His pale eyes slide over everyone. His mustache and jaws move rhythmically and some can smell on him the cold night and his spearmint gum.

"Take off your jacket, Rex," says the new thin Bonnie Loo, stepping from the stoves. "I'll get you a plate. All you guys."

"Just a little bread and butter," Rex tells her.

The other men just nod to coffee.

Bonnie Loo knows Rex doesn't mean corn bread, which is already on the tables and sideboards. She knows the kind of bread he likes.

Rex nods to two ancient women and even the hairless, toothless, eyeless old guy, Fred, the nearest of the elders to the porch doorway. There are so many. Most of them keep to the deep armchairs or rockers over there within a few steps of the simmering woodstoves that distinguish the Cook's Kitchen from the Winter Kitchen as, dear reader, you surely know by now.

Now he flops his dark jacket over a free hook in that row of hooks by the cubby wall and watches Bonnie Loo's still broad-shouldered back as she takes a serrated knife from a heaped drawer. She always has a pretty mean look, but now also squinty from trying to see in this romantic but useless candlelight. Still in this first kitchen, Rex runs a hand through his thinning hair and he gives a sign to his four men. Just as on his jacket there is high on the left shoulder of his long-sleeved gray workshirt the black-and-olive patch of his militia.

As he steps through one of the archways in the wall of cubbies three of his men remain by the porch door, rifles on their slings, chins up, like guards. One guy follows him. How many remain outside, on the porches, on the Quad?

As Rex moves along between the tables John Lungren, who is back in his seat, revolver back under his shirt, is turned to face him, nods. Noncommittally. And Eddie Martin also facing him now gives him a look, a room-temperature nonverbal *hello*.

Meanwhile, a few voices regather soft momentum around the rooms, and the utensils clank.

Forever the strategist, Rex turns now, and in a moment's glance sees an empty seat beyond Eddie Martin and John Lungren. Another pause. He sees there are no strangers. None that worry him. He checks eyes and the set of every mouth. He observes hands, oddly thick pockets. He can't help noticing that with an especially frisky candle in a green-and-blue glass globe lamp before him, Eddie Martin's close-shaved bony jaws and chin really shine. And though it is hardly a time for celebration there is his belt with coins, studs, and fake jewels. But then Eddie always has had a light heart.

The man who had been following him hangs back against the wall of cubbies, waiting for his coffee?

Rex steps around a couple of roaming kids and over a huge black Lab mix stretched out there and he settles down in the empty chair. Gordon directly across the table from him, a long pan of meat loaf between them, meat loaf that smells like a goat, and a pottery bowl with one green bean left in it. Nobody can sit straighter at a table than Rex.

There are *many* unfriendly looks cast his way now from every direction of the room.

Eddie swirls the gravy in his plate with corn bread. He looks over at his son Butch a few seats down.

Gordon smiles strangely at the half-eaten gob of spinach on his plate, butter stiffening around it. Rex's presence seems to hold him in place with a ton of bricks. And yet some here, such as Claire, suspect that Gordon and Rex have agreed on this visit . . . perhaps a couple of scrawled covert notes via Mickey Gammon, the "tree house orphan" who has been reunited with Rex for months.

Cory St. Onge, looking more Passamaquoddy as he has gotten older and less like Gordon's Italian-Irish-French-Indian mutt mix, leans around Eddie, digs out another big scoop of Popeye casserole.

Montana St. Onge, blond braids, glasses, chubby, magisterial of expression, sinks into somebody's vacated chair, looks down at an unfinished piece of meat pie, wrinkles her nose. Then she leans forward and stares at Rex's profile, five profiles away. And now Paul Lessard and Raymond Pinette pull up chairs and Eddie thrusts his chair back to make room.

Mickey Gammon comes over from another table to slouch against the wall nearest Butch. He has a crisp new pack of Luckies in the fingers of one hand. Seems he may have been wanting to get outside for a smoke, to get out there undetected, not that there's a rule against smoking, but THE NEW RULE, heavily stressed: *nobody outside alone* at night. The rules are starting to feel oppressive. And yet Mickey the Tree House Orphan is here. Here is Mickey.

Bonnie Loo places a plate of warm white bread slices in front of Rex while Aurel, hatless and wet-haired and looking eager for talk and who has the seat at Gordon's right, pushes the dish of orangey farm butter toward Rex from behind the pan of meat loaf.

Rex's thank-yous include the words *ma'am* and *sir*, the manners that always used to cause Gordon's mother Marian to flush with high regard for Richard York. Until the militia. And especially not after the fight. Naturally.

Now Rex is looking around and around. What to do with the gum? Napkins in the Settlement are all cloth rags. He wraps the gum in his own handkerchief, stuffs it into his pants pocket.

Officious Montana St. Onge watches this procedure closely but without remark.

Aurel wonders of Rex, "Out on t'road dere, see any black ski masks or guard, you?"

"No, sir."

"T'at wass what we figur'. T'ey gott nobody to . . . err . . . pester anymore, dem. We doan get much company in t'evening t'ese days. People doan like dere clothes off and dere fenders laid in t'high grass."

Rex says, "Actually, we didn't come in on Swett's Pond Road. We came from over by Supernik's on that tractor path."

Aurel narrows his eyes. "You not come in by truck! T'at hole dere is twelve feet deep. Rocks t'size of t'poost office."

Rex's eyes hold a bit of gleam. "I'm aware."

"Still got a tailpipe?" Ray Pinette asks.

Rex says, "Last I looked."

Oven doors squeal. The hand pumps at the sinks *gronk*.

Rex listens to Gordon's noisy eyes on him. The bread has none of Bonnie Loo's experimental herb combos, no tricks. Just coarse and chewy and yeasty and nice. Rex says, "I know a few who want to come in here and help you hold these monkeys off. But . . ." He looks around at faces. "I wouldn't open my gates too easy . . . not without a checkup on them." Again, his cold unchanging eyes sweep around the table. "One out of every five militiamen could be an agent. Besides that you want to avoid giving the big dog any reason to get off his porch."

John Lungren snorts. "He's *on* our porch."

Rex says, "Figuratively speaking, he's still on his porch. Do not engage. And maybe he'll—"

"We're doing that. We're holding on."

Rex says, "Make sure everyone understands that." He tears another piece of bread into smaller pieces, bite-sized, says, "Keep your animals under cover. Especially dogs. They love to blow away pet dogs . . . to press your buttons."

"We're aware of that," says Ray Pinette.

Using both hands, Rex wipes his mustache on his table rag in a gentlemanly way. He looks up into Gordon's face, the pinkish white satin-like lightning bolt scars radiating out of the right eye, the nose that is somewhat different, the beard that is not as thick on one side, but now stripy with scars. The twisted little hump of a right ear. The other ear, a sort of seashell. And the frisky colorful light of candles squirming all over this visage. Gordon isn't saying anything, just looks steadily back at Rex with an unreadable expression. So far he has not nodded any hellos.

Toddlers stagger past. A thick yellow dog tail slides along beyond the farther table. A curled short-haired black tail passes. Looks like a gigantic scorpion.

The rooms are still way too hot, but with little drafts of the fresh outdoors breathing in from the open windows.

A baby babbles.

Claire St. Onge and one of her cousins now stand back-to, watching Del drawing Dracula on scrap paper. His version shows Dracula to be a bit chubby like himself. Claire's and her cousin's hair both in long single braids down their backs, straight as falling water, black as no compromise, black as unimagined beginnings: tomorrow's and next year's. Or black as *the end*. What is the Settlement's fate?

Young girls, teen and preteen, are bunched around the cubby wall now, whispering. As usual.

Josee Soucier comes to stand behind her husband, Aurel, and places her hands on his shoulders, studies Rex frowningly. Aurel takes thirds on the meat pie and some dark fruit sauce, mooshes them together.

Lee Lynn kind of floats along one side of this table, collecting plates. Something sliskish and soft-sounding worn on her feet. "Who wants coffee? Or tea? I'm filling the coffeemaker now. We have four kinds of mint for tea."

"Tea!" hollers Beth. "Black's all I want. Nothing funny, Lee Lynn."

"Coffee!" calls Nova.

Meanwhile, Jenny Dove St. Onge is lighting more candles.

Misty St. Onge is refilling water pitchers and not looking at all at Rex.

All five of these women wear the red sash tonight. And yes, Bonnie Loo is wearing hers.

A few hands have gone up for coffee, remaining long enough to be counted. There are three hushy requests for mint tea.

Beth, standing over Rex now, studies him close up, fingers of candlelight rippling across his right arm, and she says, "You guys have solid gray shirts now? What's that all about?"

With a straight face, Rex replies, "This is our city camo." For a moment, he looks down at his now empty bread plate. "You know, all these big city riots all you people seem to be having to do lately. *Chaos gray*, it's called. We want to blend in."

Beth does a double take at the side of his face, trying to read him.

Gordon leans forward on his forearms and asks deeply, "Chaos gray?"

"He's just joking," Butch Martin tells Beth. And then looks down the table at Gordon's profile. Gordon, who knows it's a joke but was not *expecting* the joke. *Not from Rex's mouth*. Gordon now leaning back on two legs of his chair, stretching his arms above, now fingers lacing behind his head, a big gap-toothed smile.

Rex fusses some more with the table rag, getting butter off his fingers.

Montana St. Onge leans forward giving her new glasses a significant adjustment and calls out to Rex, "You ever hear of this? It's Shakespeare. *And so from hour to hour we ripe and ripe and then from hour to hour we rot and rot and thereby hangs a tale*."

Rex puts his steely eyes on this child and replies, "I never heard of that. No."

Paul Lessard says, "I see no purpose in that Shakespeare stuff, me."

Montana says to Rex, ignoring Paul, "I know the whole thing practically. I memorized it. It's called *As You Like It*."

Jay Harmon is pulling up a chair now and also young Tim Ridlon steps up with his new baby over his shoulder. Baby has tiny sneakers dangling there. Baby asleep in that deep part of sleep that is like death, only warm.

Montana announces that in the days of Shakespeare, there were no TVs or movies. "No *novels*!" She shakes her head. "Novels were after that." She is telling only Rex this. He nods politely.

Montana, on a roll now, carefully explains that before the printing press, "Architecture was an *expression* for politics."

All the men at this table are very quiet, some fiddling with their utensils. Some motionless. Mickey is staring off at a more interesting part of the room. Beyond the cubby partitions, a cat is in one of the big sinks. Licking the hand pump spout.

Montana gazes at Rex's black-faced watch a moment, his hand with the wedding band. "You ever been to Paris?" she asks.

All the men laugh heartily.

"Paris, Maine!" Jay Harmon almost chokes, caught in an outright belly laugh.

Rex says, "No, I haven't been to France," Politely. His reply is directed at Montana.

Aurel says with a bit of an edge. "Montana hasn't been t'Paris, e'dr. But she's about t'visit one of 'tos o'tr nice tables, right, Montana? This is t' *men's* table t'night."

Montana squints. "Josee is not a man."

"I'm leaving," says Josee. And laughs as she heads back to the other part of the room where Del is now making dozens of paper Dracula and Frankenstein masks by the red bloody candlelight. And on the way, she catches sight through an archway of the cat in one of the Cook's Kitchen sinks and does a detour dash to go drive him out.

Montana doesn't move.

Aurel says, "You mind me, Mademoiselle." He is pointing at her and he pretends to stand, bracing his legs.

Montana stands up straight. "Burn in hell," she says and prances away.

Aurel says gratingly, "I put t'at little person over my knee, but I saffe it for emergency situation. Too much spank not good. Juss emergencies." He speaks this into Rex's eyes, though Rex himself was never even a part-time disciplinarian with *his* own kid. And Aurel never used to be. These days, things feel so terribly strained. He looks around at all the adults sitting at or standing around the four rows of tables, all looking immeasurably bright-eyed . . . all those flickering green, gold, rose, and blue candles . . . and that dark into-eternity look of the many small-paned windows along the back walls.

To no one's surprise, the spaced *whomp-whomps* approach, louder, deeper, heavier, seeming not limited to sky but as if out of the granite and red and gray shale below. So many *whomps* overlaid and braided, the choppers tonight could be in the dozens.

Rex's always-marble face strangely flexes. Hueys in all quadrants of the sky swinging down to take away the dead? To bring in fresh faces? More supplies, whatever, to deliver more burn to the already fantastic heat of miles of jungle, miles of motionless watery reeking rice?

But now is now. Different air. Different age. Different scars.

KAR-BOOO-HROOM!!! Windows rattle. Floor hops under his boots. And there is Gordon's shredded and riven face, the pale eyes, staring into his own. Then, overwhelmed, Gordon's eyes close.

KAR-BOOO-HROOMMMM!!!

Rex rises to a crouch, palms flat on the dancing table of shivering water glasses, lurching candles. He's no longer straight in his back. Puts you in mind of the old movies, *Screaming woman leaping onto table finds safety from a mouse*. But he doesn't do that. Just lets the chattery table talk to his palms.

One toddler *is* screaming.

One enormous dog crawls under the table near Rex's leg.

Mostly the rooms of people are desperately quiet. Waiting it out. Someone calms the toddler.

But three infants are now squalling.

Rex notes his second in command Big John still standing by the arched doorway, also a vet of "the conflict," also perhaps feeling his neck and shoulder muscles bunch up with smoldering memory.

Gordon raises his chin.

And yes, Rex is writhing inside, though he now has his chin up, too, throat bared, posture erect, the superhero stance, like he means to be a protector, here to guard the Prophet from—

Kar-booo-hrooommmm!!!

Papier-mâché fish over the tiny skit stage jerk from side to side. How flimsy this valley, these foothills, this world.

Then the enemy is moving away, swinging off to the south and to the east, it seems, fading, fading, nearly gone, just a dry smug trail of *whomps* and from out of the breathing, rustling silence of the big room of flickering fairy colors and corner-dark and of worried hearts and of maimed hopes, an old woman's voice directed at the fading threat, the smart-alecky wiseacre pain-in-the-ass Benedicta Nichols loud and clear: "See ya later alligator!"

Over by the tall windows, a young guy: "Heh heh!"

Now a titter from that other direction. Now the entire room is gagging and gasping with deep whole-gut laughter.

Rex works his tongue around a bit, his almost smiling eyes on a thought as he eases back into his Settlement-made straight-backed chair whose cushion in better light would reveal itself to be a polka dot print of moonbeam blue.

THE END

PS

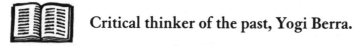

Critical thinker of the past, Yogi Berra.

"If you come to a fork in the road, take it."

Yes, Another PS

Days later.

Coming home after a lonnnng day at the university and the lonnng drive there and back with the station wagon full of her Settlement teen assistants, Claire felt her guts ache when she realized the dark would crush down on them before she reached the Settlement gatehouse.

However, no blue lights or hooded figures stopped them. All of Heart's Content Road was elegantly empty. *This time.*

As she reaches the door of her cottage, there's pressure in her temples, so maybe she's extra smarting in the presence of any light, especially that which sparkles at her, like what is there just beyond the closed bedroom window. Darkness outside now but for that odd thing. Okay, so it's not so much sparkle as a manifold glow, like an eerie eye that recognizes her.

She tugs the window up. Of course all the crow's cracked corn is gone and she wasn't here today to hear his awful weather reports, his cocky advice, or his panicky complaints. But there on this particular feeding shelf is another of his gifts. She folds her fingers around the cold thing. Holding it under the bedside lamp she is amazed by the case-hardened silver, those swirls of delicate color. And loads of tiny pearls! Garnets, blood turned to gems, so wee she wonders if she imagines them. Oh, but the pearls melt her heart most; she envisions them being "birthed" patiently by the humble majesty of such helpless funny-looking creatures as oysters pinned into place by the cruel but blessed power of the sea.

The human craftsmanship of the ring itself is also patient because it is so obviously an old ring and in the past there was a thing called human patience.

It is, yes, overly ornate, loud, in fact. It looks familiar. She decides to try it on.

Stay tuned.

The Official and Complete and Final ☺ Gratefulness Page

There are SO many people to thank for this and that, the list would fill a book, so I have put all the names "in a hat" (a box actually) and with each book finished in this *School on Heart's Content Road* series, I draw a portion of them out. There are a few repeats. For this book, the huge feet-kissing thank-yous go as follows (no particular order): Littie Elise Rau, Ellen Wilbur, Don Hall (in heaven), my old friend Jacquie Gaisson Fuller (who made possible all the Maine Acadian French spoken in these pages), Jane Gelfman (world's best agent), Lisa Gardner (television personality ☺ and adviser), Stephanie Johnson (Dragon of the West), Katie Raissian (internationally most awesome editor), Sara DeRoche (computer genius), Caroline Trefler (copy editor extraordinaire), Ollie DeRoche (mini-muse), BPCP (world's best accountants), the MacDowell Colony, Ana Rothschild and James Ketcham and Michael Rothschild, Don and Nichole and Layla and the not-so-young-anymore gentlemen, Aric Knuth and all NELP'ers, Guy Gosselin, Tyler Mudgett, Bendella and David and Spoticus, Nick and Eunice and the Scottish contingent at Morgan's house, Carol and Michael, Hillary and Victor, ALL my family on all sides and in all directions, Lance and Peggy Tapley, Susan James, David Diamond, Julia Berner-Tobin, Jo Eldridge Morrissey, Maureen DeKaser, John Siesweda, "Miss Cathy" Gleason (world's best everything), Meadow Welch, Cork Smith (world's best editor, in heaven) and Sheila Smith who still keeps one of the earliest drafts of this book in a golden chest by the fireplace. Fire-place? Also a jillion thanks to W. D. Kubiak and Rita Kubiak and Cathy Kubiak, to Beek of Beektown and all who creep and sneak through the streets of Beektown, and a jillion more thanks to Ellen Weeks, Thurman and Fern Mills, Cynthia Riley, Gil Harris, Marsha Michelin, Mary Emerson, Cyndy Poirier, Sandy Hamlin, Carlton and Christine, Tita, Paul, Donna, Sue, Cathy, and Andy; also the Parsonfield Planning Board (where there is always an exciting evening out without paying anything at the door or bringing a casserole). Gratefulness also to Ken Rosen (poet, teacher, and friend), Rebekah Yonan and Pete Kellman (Pete, our working-class hero, teacher, and friend . . . and you guessed it, political organizer), Tom and Alison Whitney, Chris Kukka, Jim Chiros, Thomas Naylor (in heaven), Sub Steve Kelley (philosopher), the Jersey girls and Architects and Engineers for 9/11 Truth, Andy Fard, Tony Ford (in Livingston, Texas☹), Ellen Wilbur, John Kozyra, and Tyler Mudgett. Also thank you! Thank you! Thank you! to Balenda Ganem (for all the *real* details of the Mt. Carmel Massacre from personal experience), Bob Monks, Sheila Bernard (remember when we narrowly escaped those dozens of governors' wives?), and Cullen Stuart (our superhero! in heaven), Hal and Mark Miller (in heaven) and George and Janet Webb (in heaven), Susan Moody, Les Robertson, Mary Garland, Mary Carswell (in heaven), Robyn Rosser, Tina Gilbert, Laura Childs, Will Neils, Isabelle Troadec, Sarah Crow and the whole Crow gang. Also Richard Grossman (in heaven), Jason Trask, Lieutenant Colonel Robert Bowman Ret. (our Scottie dogs want you to stop by again), Rubin Pfeffer, Roger Leisner, Gary and Beth and Margaret at the Gulf of Maine, Audrey Marra, Julian Holmes (in heaven), Sub Steve Kelley (philosopher), Susan Gamer, Steve Burke (in heaven), Sally Brotherton (in heaven), George Caffentzis (philosopher), Dana Hamlin (in heaven: he who inspired much of what is in early drafts of this work), Leo Kimball (in heaven), John Muldoon, Ruth Webber and Russell Webber (in heaven), Blake Tewkesbury, Maryel and Deb and Rita, Mark Hanley, Peggy and Ray Fisher, HOME of Orland and Sister Lucy; also to Catalina, wherever you are. Meanwhile, anywhere and anytime a hundred or more revolutionaries come together, may they do so as wisely and humanely as the 2nd Maine Militia. You are all the best!!!

Character List

The Prophet

Guillaume (Ge-yome *hard* G like golly!) St. Onge. Also Gordon or Gordo or Gordie. Age thirty-nine until the first September of our story. A head taller than most, six-foot-fivish. Darkish beard with a splutter of new gray on chin. Brown hair, cowlicky. Dark lashes around pale creepy (to some people) yellow-green eyes. An almost Tourette's flinch to one side of the face. Crowded bottom teeth. Work, work, work, though not without talk, talk, talk, and then bitch, bitch, bitch on the world's injustices, LOUDLY. His mother had once sobbed, "You love *everybody*! Your love is cheap."

Place

In the town of **Egypt**, a little dot on the map of **Maine**, is Heart's Content Road, which used to be called Swett's Pond Road back in the day. As you head windingly up that road, up, up, up into significant foothills (small close mountains), you eventually see on your right Gordon St. Onge's home, a gray farmhouse, long porch, and ell, and connected sheds. Barn gone, burned once upon a time. Huge ash tree.

Hidden in the hills behind this visible farmplace is the **Settlement**, a sort of village of gardens and orchards and cottages and several utility-ish buildings and a big horseshoe building with screened porches (some call them piazzas) encircling a Quad of trees. About nine hundred acres of land spread out beyond. All this has one deed with one name: Guillaume St. Onge.

Factions of Revolt in Alphabetical Order

Border Mountain Militia. Yes, this is a bunch of rural white Republicans (at first). **Richard "Rex" York** is captain and founder. About age forty-nine or so. Brown walrussy mustache but thinning hair of the head. Humorless eyes, gray, some would say cold. Medium height. Fairly fit. Almost never eats sugar, even his mother's hard-to-resist cookies. Yes, he lives with his mother **Ruth** and nineteen-year-old daughter **Glory**. Rex is an electrician. Not a yakker. Uneasy with chaos. His wife divorced him a while back but he still wears his wedding ring. Back in the 1960s, as thousands were, he was drafted into the Vietnam horrors.

Other Members of the Border Mountain Militia: Art Mitchell, "Big John," Mickey Gammon, George Durling, and Willie Lancaster. George Durling is dying of many cancers. **Willie Lancaster** is too alive.

Bread and Roses Folk School. These **organizers visiting the Settlement** are leftists all presently living in Massachusetts. They are hell-bent on educating Americans on the dangers of corporate power. Here they are in alphabetical order:

Billy Watson. Struggles with allergies, age fortysomething, narrow shoulders, usually heavily dressed and snivelly. Sneezes a lot. Pale. Short, even, light-color beard. Brings "nonviolence" into most discussions. Can sing impressively. Normally his organizing work has been environmental stuff. He has a lot of uneasiness about this Settlement bunch.

Blake Richardson is youngest in the group, has one published novel, is an editor of radical "zines," and is a freelance journalist. Does some residency teaching at various colleges. Dresses conservatively. Hair short. Clean shaven. Very dark; African heritage. Quietly outgoing and often playful as the young frequently are. Grew up in a stressed neighborhood in Illinois. Very family-oriented. Another layer of his political work is that he belongs to one of the "race traitor" teaching coalitions, one quite militant. Yet he is more expansive in his dreams than that group; he pines for less corporate control of the world, less neo-feudalism. Like Gordon, he aims to see a more humane economy for everyone. He becomes a favorite among the Settlement youngsters.

Frank Parenti. A serious, somctimes sour head honcho of the folk school. Doesn't show up often in this story. His main purpose seems to be grant-writing, grant-getting, and not alienating grant-givers.

Lenny Britt. Older (sixties) and experienced: civil rights and anti-war Vietnam War–era protest veteran, and antinuke movement. He's been to jail *often*. ("For the cause.") Short. Broad, terrier build. Gray, of course. Watchful but not as sour as Frank. Fond of old raggedy sweaters. Porkpie hat has grown onto his head.

Jeannette (Jip) Greenberg. Tight, short, dark blond curls. Sweaters. Corduroys. Hush Puppies. She's fortyish. A lawyer of labor law who teaches at Harvard. Has a way of calming flared tempers. Always focused but never sour. Collects lightbulb jokes. Has sorrowful memories of Central America and corporate power's reprehensible treatment of its people.

Meggie Marsh. Not shy. Not pushed around. She's about thirty years old, about six-foot-three. Dresses in satiny outfits; mandarin collars are her favorites. Colors! The colors are not for the faint of heart. Dressy boots. Hair as white and full-blown as a lightning storm. Studying for a master's in social work. Quick to act in emergencies. Brags a lot.

Olan Engstrom. Balding but doesn't wear a hat in cold weather; cheerfully boasts he's Scandinavian. Short. Stocky. Sometimes you can see the gold crowns on both sides behind his eyeteeth. His front teeth are tall. Short brown beard some of the time, other times clean-shaved. Seems a patient sort of person, works well with the group. A political science professor on sabbatical, he has mentioned a book he's working on but gives no details except that he loves the research part.

FYI: Bread and Roses Folk School was named for the largest labor strike in the United States, the 1912 Lawrence, Massachusetts, textile strike. Striking mill girls carried picket signs: WE WANT BREAD AND ROSES, TOO. The wealthy mill owners and the government apparatus responded in war mode and many strikers suffered dearly while fighting for the right to be paid better than slave-wage and against a slave's work hours. Bread, molasses, and beans were usually the only food most mill workers could afford, if that. Thus "Bread and Roses!" remains to this day organized labor's battle cry, especially of those who know this mostly censored history.

Horne Hill Anarchists (also known as the Anti-Rich Society). Two or three dozen young people and a few tykes. Started as a cooperative on Jaxon Cross's father's land on Horne Hill in the town of Egypt, with tents, sheds, gardens. As the weather chills, there is a migration to the Settlement. **Jaxon Cross** (and his younger siblings and his father **Lyman Cross**, who we never meet in *this* book) recently moved up from the North Carolina Piedmont's Panther Branch Township. Jaxon is in his twenties, brown hair not short or long, often wrapped around Apache-style by a black bandanna. One dangling doubloon-like earring. Famous for his rather cruel-looking smile. Bordering on hefty. Often wears a radio on his belt, he being a trained and employed emergency medical technician, as a few of the other Horne Hill anarchists also are. He does a restless rocking-to-and-fro on his feet but can spend hours reading and researching history and radical "zines," then "sharing." He is one of those especially involved in pirate radio, along with "**Miss Munch**." That's her "tree sit" name from her days of trying, with others, to save old-growth forests. You always want a phony name in case of arrest. And you write a public defender's phone number on the inside of your forearm. But Jaxon went all the way, the phone number on his *palm*, a *real* tattoo. And Miss Munch is not short on tattoos. She has wonderful, almost blindingly bright tattoos all over the place.

True Maine Militia. Settlement teenagers (mostly girls) and neighbor Brianna (Bree) Vandermast think Rex's rather covert militia is not going anywhere. Even before the leftists appear actively on the scene, the True Maine Militia has schemed up a lot of publicity and public participation. And chaos. They have a grudge against corporatism (the merging of government with big biz).

Secret Agents

Names sometimes mentioned, sometimes not, sometimes aliases, sometimes real. Some are special agents, some operatives. These folks appear in many scenes, scheming and plotting for "America." There are times when the Settlement is crawling with them. You can't even trust a sparkly old lady in a wheelchair not to be an agent.

Secret Agent Jane Meserve, almost age seven when the story begins. A gorgeous graceful golden girl, tall for her age, she is trying always for glamour even as she wears white plastic-framed sunglasses with heart-shaped pink lenses, which allow her to see and hear and know everything about the predicaments of life. Her mother is the newsworthy **Lisa Meserve** in jail due to America's "drug war." Her father is the famous rap star **Damon Gorely**, whom her mother met once at a concert.

Some Who Live at the Settlement and Wear the Red Sash

Claire is about ten years older than Gordon and is as short as he is tall. And quite stout. She teaches adjunct archaeology and history stuff at the University of Southern Maine and gets a little dressy for that, her long shining hair in a bun or a braid. Her old-time round frame specs and grim midnight-black eyes can give you an edgy feeling.

One of her cousins whom she grew up with on the reservation and who was in on the Settlement's planning is **Leona**. Like Claire, Leona has long hair. She loves metalwork barrettes and a well-brushed "tail" of hair down her back. She has many kids. One is **Cory**, who is six-foot-two and still growing. Age fifteen. He, too, keeps a "tail" of long hair, as black as his ma's. He is somewhat vain about his good looks and his powerful build. He is *not* quiet. He can talk himself hoarse when he gets on what some Settlementers call his "complain train." He's an all-around man when it comes to Settlement jobs. Younger brother **Oz** (**real name Jason**, age thirteen), has a special gift with horses and other animals. He can be rather sulky and aloof. Some of Leona's other kids are **Andrea, Faira, Draygon, Shanna, Katy and Karma (twins), and little Bianca**, age two.

Claire's other cousin here is **Geraldine**, who has skipped having kids. She prefers spirited horses. And being busy busy on many Settlement crews. Her first name is really **Wendy** but in high school there were three other Wendys so she switched to her middle name, which came from a great-aunt she never knew. Her hair is a no-nonsense cut.

Also from the reservation is **Lolly (really Carlotta)**. Her kids include **Weetalo**, age four; and **Gus (real name Miles)**, age one and a half or so.

Beth. About age thirty-five. An Egypt, Maine native. Squirmy ringlets of blond hair to the shoulders. Cusses like a sailor. A daughter **Montana**, age ninish, is "quite the ticket," some say. Or "quite the rig," always trying for sophistication. Beth's **Rhett**, four-year-old, is doleful.

Bonnie Loo (Lucretia) is the head cook of the Settlement. Her face is often gloomy, like her thoughts. Her dark hair has some orange streaks (from bleaching) and is worn in a loose "cavewoman" topknot. Her amber eyes glitter dangerously when she wears her contacts. Her regular glasses have a taped bow. Her kids are **Gabriel, Jetta,** and **Zack** and she is pregnant again. She is trying to give up her cigs. She made a swanky apartment house for her rats but they get bored inside it and bust out.

Lee Lynn. Tallish. *Very* thin. She dresses in gossamer fabrics that would set a whole colony of Puritans to collecting brush and firewood for the stake. Her voice is high and sirenlike. She has one child, a toddler, **Hazel**. She is an avid wild-crafter and maker of soaps, candles, tinctures, salves, and teas. Her hair is early gray and witchy. She's mid-thirties.

Penny. A blonde and pleasant, lovely as a movie starlet. Some say prettier than her only child, fifteen-year-old **Whitney**. Whitney's ponytail is always dancing since she is always bouncing around with enthusiasm. Whitney has much interest in architecture and pop physics and democracy and the hell-raising it takes to make democracy live and breathe.

Glennice. Knows her agriculture stuff. She has won piles of blue ribbons at the Fryeburg Fair for her pumpkins, gourds, cukes, and so forth. She attends the North Egypt Baptist Church regularly in one of her dressy dresses. She wears glasses. Brown hair. Has a confident way with machinery. Her young son is named **Benjamin**. Everyone calls him "a nice boy."

Gail. Ex-biker and ex-alcoholic. Tattoo of flowers across her collarbone, wreathed all the way around her neck. Short brown braid. Face lined from smoking and sun. Forty-five. Husky voice. Eyes dark and close together, as if always remembering. Quiet person. Her daughter is **Michelle**, who is fourteen.

Steph (Stephanie) is also quiet and shy. Early forties. Pink-cheeked round face. Short brown hair. Her daughters, **Margo** and **Oceanna** (pronounced O-shee-AH-na) are fifteen-year-old twins. Margo took after Steph in her looks and wallflower ways. Oceanna looks like a hungry long feral cat. Wears a lot of purple.

Misty can be added to the shy, quiet list. Short dark hair. No kids of her own but does a lot of art and library projects with Settlement tykes. She has plenty of snobby cats in her cozy cottage.

And let's not forget **Jenny Dove**, who seems always to have that little smile on her freckly face, a smile that could mean contentment or sarcasm. Hard to tell. It's her only expression. She is rather wide in the hips. Not tall. Looks huggable. She has a toddler named **Silka** who likes to crawl up on things and jump off.

Astrid. About age forty. Dresses like a lawyer. Haircut like a lawyer's. Thinks like a lawyer. Brisk, confrontational, but polished. Her sons are **Dane**, age twelve; and **Okley**, who doesn't appear in *this* book (nicknamed **Oak**). He is twenty.

Vancy. Skilled midwife and quite nurturing to the elderly. A Settlement jewel, therefore. She is fairly young, twenty-fourish, pregnant, a plain boxy-shaped person with brown hair that is clean but not fussed over. She is partial to plain white button-up shirts.

Natasha (Natty). Not a starring role in *this* book but part of the crowd. Pregnant at beginning of story.

Ellen. Often thought to be "a little slow" but she's possibly just schemy. You might say *cunning*. She's not a beauty but not a horror either. When she speaks, her voice is loud and flat. You might say, too, that she is rarely diplomatic. She objects to broken rules that the rest of the world ignores. She has no sense of humor. Meanwhile, if you need help, she's there in a flash to save the day if the solution is within her power. She does not like kids, however, and pretends they aren't there when they are there.

Others Who Live at the Settlement

Soucier Family. Aurel (pronounced Oh-RELL) and **Josee** from Aroostook ("the County"). Aurel is short, wiry. Dark short beard and hair, gleamy-eyed. *Very* chatty. Wears khaki Dickies a lot and a narrow-brimmed Vietnam War bush hat. Josee wears fashionable glasses and is a blonde like her twin sister Jacquie (from the blonde-creating stuff the beauty crew uses). Josee, like Aurel, is a lively, cheery, yakky person. They speak the patois from the St. John Valley at the top of Aroostook (Canada is across the river). Their English purrs with many r's. Aurel is first cousin to Gordon and also has the Tourette's-like flinch but his eyes are black, not pale. Aurel and Josee have a bazillion kids including but not limited to **Rachel** (age seventeen, blond Dutch-girl haircut, a beauty crew specialty), **Lydia** (**Liddy**, age sixteen), **Rusty, Tamya, Michel**, and so on.

Jacquie (Josee's twin) and **Paul Lessard**, also from the County. Their one child is gentle, dark-haired, unpretentious, earthbound, steady **Alyson**, age fourteen. Her pet hen is the estimable **Pooky**.

Edward (Eddie) and Lorraine Martin. Lorraine is from the County. Eddie is not. Lorraine, a cousin of Gordon's. Lorraine, not a rememberable person to look at except for all the reminders she has pinned all over her sweater vests and jumpers. She's one of those "in-charge" people. Eddie, on the other hand, has some flashy clothes, some satin cowboy shirts in painful colors, and the belt he is famous for, plastered with studs, coins, fake jewels. He's one who shaves his face to a shine, longish in the jaws. Works in the sawmill and Furniture-Making Shop among other things. Martin kids are **Edward, Jr. (Butch)**, about twenty. Dark-haired like his mother. Walnut-color eyes. Grows a Rex-like mustache once he gets involved in the militia stuff. The weapon he carries at *all* times is a kazoo, which he can hypnotize everybody with when necessary. Has some dyslexias. Not a reader or a big talker but he is A-plus at keeping the Settlement motor vehicles on the road. Also at driving the lumber deliveries and making other such voyages "out into the world." **Evan** is about fifteen, dark-haired, struggles with acne. Twelve-year-old **Kirk (Kirky)** is an inventor and scribbler. Not into physical work. Loves flashy clothes, especially his vast collection of bow ties, mostly Settlement-made. He wears his light brown hair in a yarn-diameter short pigtail with the rest of his hair cut short, this look being fashionable in the late 1980s, early 1990s. So he's a wee bit out of fashion in the way of mass "culture."

Stuart Congdon. Head sawyer of the sawmill crews and active on various committees and salons. *Very* short, about five feet, blazing red hair, and bushy beard. Bit of a belly. Looks like a "troll doll." *Very blue* blue eyes.

Ray and Suzelle (Gordon's cousin) **Pinette.** From "the County." Their teenage daughter is **Erin**, homely like her father but nobody notices due to her many smiles and pleasant agreeable ways. And besides, the pug nose looks better on her than on Ray. Suzelle keeps her dark hair short and curled. A quiet person but hither-and-yon as an ant on many crews.

John Lungren. About age sixty. High hairline, gray. Face shaved. Light eyes. Jeans, work boots. Looks good in a T-shirt. Billed caps. Eyeglasses slightly out of fashion. Goldish stretch-band watch. A finish carpenter. One you can depend on, a rock. Divorced once. Widowed once. Shares his cottage with his elderly ma.

Cindy Butler. Wears a bandanna on her dark blond hair peasant-style. Been at the Settlement only a couple of years. Son teenage **Chris** has a love of piano and group discussions and skits. A severe skin affliction, covered in sores *all the time*. Daughter **Samantha (Sammy)** is a bold and beautiful girl, about fifteen, wears head rags Apache-style around her straight white-blond hair.

Bev and Barbara. They actually live in a yellow modern house in town with a swimming pool but arrive every day to tutor kids and be on various crews and committees. Bev has a coastal Maine accent, Barbara a New York City accent. Both are short and square and ruddy.

Del Schumann. Grew up in East Egypt. A ponytail. Very very blond. Uses a wheelchair, the you-get-brawny-arms kind. Involved in most committees and salons. Heads one of the furniture-making crews, specializing in the pedal-power swan boats that the Settlement sells at fairs and that he designed. He also designed the mini Viking ship that runs by pedal power but there is only one of those so far. Del is late thirties, has a girlfriend in Brownfield named **Cathy** who visits. They often drive to Boston to see museums and other stuff you get only "where the *bright lights* are."

Catherine Court Downey. Comes to live at the Settlement from Portland. USM art teacher and interim chair. Rather beautiful. Green-brown eyes, Frida Kahlo eyebrows. Dark hair. Her son is **Robert**, age four, an earnest gentlemanly sort, half Vietnamese, shining black hair.

Michael (Mickey) Gammon. Fifteen years old. Scrawny. Longish streaked blond hair. Often wears his camo jacket with green-and-black Border Mountain Militia patch on left shoulder. His brother, under much stress, kicked him out. After a tree house residency, Mickey comes to live with the Martins at the Settlement.

Sarah ("Silverbell") Rosenthal. Arrives at Gordon's house in the night with Gordon's old friend **Jack Holmes**, a lawyer and advocate for the poor. Silverbell's adopted twins are **Eden** and **Bard**, almost thirteen. They are survivors of the horrors of the "drug war." Their young father **Aaron** died violently in prison.

Benedicta Nichols. About late seventies or so. Mysteriously arrives in the driveway of Gordon's house one chilly night. Becomes a Settlement citizen effortlessly. Has had her eyes lasered so doesn't need glasses. Her brown hair is only a tweak grayed, worn shortish with barrettes. Blue teasy eyes. Plagues and taunts everyone. Tries to get things started: little contests, little fights. Yet she has many fans.

Willa and Ben Wentworth and their baby **Olivia** are shadowy figures in many scenes, as are **Jay and Ginny Harmon**. Also **Rick Crosman** and his teenage son **Jaime**. And many many others.

FYI: Settlementers of mid-adolescent age on up are paid a percentage of the profits in sales of wreaths and Christmas trees, honey and produce, meat or meat-cutting, sawmill services, swan boats, furniture, etc.

Egypt Neighbors

Besides Rex and his family who live on Vaughan Hill Road and Jaxon Cross's people on Horne Hill, there are the **Vandermasts** on Seavey Road. This is where **Brianna (Bree) Vandermast** lives with her father and brothers. Bree's hair is a thick long red turmoil, such gorgeous hair and there is her shapely fifteen-year-old self. But her face did not turn out right while forming in utero. Eyes too far apart. Her hands are often smoodgy with artists' oils. She is usually dressed for the woods, where she works logging with her family. She has the silly belief in liberty and justice for all.

Lancasters. They live uphill from the Settlement's dirt road entrance and Gordon's driveway. **Willie D. Lancaster**, who is with

Rex's militia, has a tree work and landscaping biz; a wife, **Judy**; several kids; and many small homely dogs. Willie makes a lot of people jumpy with his spontaneous antics. He has a dear side and a dark and cruel side. As Rex has often said, "He's smart and he's a problem." One of Willie's daughters is **Delores (Dee Dee)**, beloved at the Settlement, although she and her husband **Louis (Lou-EE) St. Onge** (yes, a cousin of Gordon's) live in a little building next to the Lancaster mobile home. Willie's son **Danny** works with him in the tree-work biz.

Beans live nearby. Bonnie Loo's people. Her ma is **Earlene Bean** and her stepfather **Reuben (Rubie) Bean**. Several half siblings. Meanwhile, in town lives grown-up **Dale Bean**, Bonnie Loo's brother, rescuer of pet rats.

Scottish terriers. Cannonball. Covertly rescued from a doghouse in a distant neighbor's yard by Willie Lancaster, who is *always* rescuing caged or tied creatures. Cannonball, a grumpy girl, is mostly fond of Dee Dee's husband Lou-EE. As everyone knows, you cannot TELL a Scottie dog to do stuff but Cannonball thinks up many tricks to earn applause and cheers (when she's not biting people or big dogs). Her legs are stout and short. Wide muscular chest and neck. Big head. Enormous teeth. Beard, mustache, eyebrows. Dark beady eyes. Voice raspy and managerial. In too many ways Cannonball is the dog version of the Settlement nine-year-old, Montana.

Cherish. Lisa and Jane Meserve's Scottie dog until the drug warriors arrested Lisa and left Cherish in the hot car with windows up. The tow guy found the dead dog under a seat.

From Aroostook ("the County") comes the Band from the County ♪♫. Pretty much the star of their performances is the lead fiddler **Real** (pronounced Ree-AL) **Theriault.** There are several fiddles going during a set but Real is the wildest, does most of the vocals, interspersed with wonderful yells, whoops, and growls. **Claude** (nicknamed **Claudie**, pronounced Clodie). **Roy** is a friend of the band, goes along sometimes to help set up.

Lou-EE (Louis) St. Onge. As we mentioned before, he is married to Dee Dee. He is tall and pythonesque in shape, not much for shoulders. Wears a brown felt mountain hat. Loves black powder guns, especially all the patch boxes, cartridge boxes, and "possibles bags." His favorite is his Dixie Gunworks deck cannon, makes a very nice KABOOOMMM that rolls over the mountains for nearly a full minute.

Those who live on the coast.

Gordon's mother, Marian (actually it is Mary Grace) Depaolo St. Onge. She lives in coastal Wiscasset, Maine. Eventually her nephew **Mark**, an architect, moves his stuff up from Concord, Massachusetts, to keep an eye on her when the public starts to figure out she is "the Prophet's" mother. Her family are *the* Depaolos, construction business people who have accumulated $MONEY$ and political influence for at least three generations.

The Weymouths. In their sixties, these are friends of the Depaolo family, have been for years. **Morse Weymouth** has headed an environmental lobby for his beliefs (he doesn't need to labor for money, unless one sees volunteer lobbying as a type of labor). **Janet Weymouth** has been on many, many committees. Both are passionate about stockholder activism. Gray-haired Morse, until his strokes, was stocky, direct, a kind of bulldozer. Janet is a recovering shy person. Even in crowds she likes to get you in a corner and hold your wrist so she can pretend she and you are alone. For a shy person she has taken on a lot of dragons over the years. Reserved and respectable on the outside, rebel on the inside! She has short streaky blond hair. Sort of tall. A lovely person.

The Weymouths' daughter is **Selene**. Their son is **Richard**. Grandkids are **Gretel** and **Henry**.

Argot is the big gray standard poodle, perfectly groomed with "human eyes," who welcomes guests to the Weymouth residence in various ways.

Elected person.

Senator Mary Wright. About forty-five. Small in stature. Italian heritage. From an old working-class Munjoy Hill (Portland) family. Long-time friend of Weymouths and Depaolos. Shining cap of black hair. Always dressy. Always on the go.

The Devil

Bruce Hummer. Medium height. Mid-forties. Somewhat introverted but gets his job done well. Warm green-brown eyes. Brown mustache and hair. CEO of Duotron-Lindsey, a bunch of corporations within corporations with lots of silent banking activity in the Cayman Islands, Switzerland, and France. Duotron-Lindsey is a leading maker of cluster bombs, artillery shells, dainty war widgets, napalm, bioweapons, and lawn poisons. It used to hire a lot of American people but big layoffs come almost every day. *Plenty* of automation. Bruce Hummer is one of the biggest parts of what makes the world burn (if we don't count *all* of humanity's spontaneous role in propping up the eternal pyramid As our old friend Yuri Karageorge always used to say, "Ack! Humans! Such dummies!").